THE ODESSA LEGACY

A NOVEL

DR. RICHARD BEND JR.

HM3 (SS) USN

outskirts
press

Dedicated to Veterans

I wrote this book because I am a veteran. It was the experience of being an active duty member of the United States Navy that provided me the ideas that I eventually turned into a novel.

Writing this book also caused me to revisit the introspection that is often forced on those serving our nations armed forces. Serving is at the very least a crucible for your soul. You will get to know who 'you' are if nothing else; whether or not that is a good thing is entirely up to you.

For me, I feel, it was a good thing. I found out just how strong a person I truly am inside. That discovery however required I go through an arduous journey of self-awakening which, at times, was heart breaking. My self-esteem was, for the longest time, lower than whale shit.

Boot camp cured me of that self-defeating exercise as did going to sea and actually encountering the Soviet Fleet up close and personal in a Fast Attack Submarine off of the coast of Russia. How many people can say they have done 'that'? I cannot tell you what happened; it's classified... if I told you I'd have to kill you...and that is not good for book sales.

Anyway, it gave me a boost of self-confidence that allowed me to 'attempt' to get the attention of the hottest babe in St. Clair Michigan. J.A. is all I will use so not to embarrass her publically as I was, at that time, not the smoothest character. Exlax had nothing on me. The flame that came off my tail surfaces was impressive. I at least gave it a shot whereas before the military I wouldn't have even tried. Yes, I crashed and burned…magnificently, but *I tried* and 'that' is what makes the difference.

My military service was transformative, as was holding my first born in my hands for the first time. Each of these experiences solidified something inside me, allowing me to grow as a man. I am equally proud of my status as a father as I am a veteran of the United States Navy as achieving such status requires that you become more than you were before. Does it make life any easier? No. It does make you stronger so you can bare the heavy loads that life has in store for you. I am the man I am today because of my experience.

This book is dedicated to every veteran who has ever served our nation in peace and war to honor the sacrifices you suffered for the good of our nation. This goes especially for our friends who have paid the ultimate price for their service and are now on Eternal Patrol.

God Bless You.

Thank you for your service.

Synopsis

A world weary man finds his career and personal life in shambles. To make matters worse his wife has engaged in a rather heated affair with an attorney. A fact he discovers when his wife accidentally calls home and gives him a ringside seat to just 'how' heated things are. Broke, disenchanted and numb Rick takes a vacation he cannot afford to sort out his life, if possible. Vacationing in a run-down resort on a shark infested island in the Caribbean he goes exploring against the advice of a local preacher who isn't really a preacher at all but a former British deep cover agent with secrets to keep. What he discovers, quite by accident, is a secret that will change his life, a secret that spans a century beginning in a darkened palace chamber of the Kaiser to a dank bunker in war torn Berlin, ending in a musty church where the Odessa Legacy is reawakened.

Ego and War

Eastern Prussia, Kaiser Wilhelms Summer Palace 1905

The Kaiser stood silently arms crossed behind his back his head bent low in thought. A solitary electric light from his desk lamp gave his face an ominous appearance as he looked upon the gardens of his summer palace. It was the only light in use. There was no need to light an entire room when he only needed one. A brooding man he preferred the dark. It gave him a sense of solitude and freedom to think about affairs of state without the annoying input of his advisors and cousins who happened to be most of the Royal heads of Europe.

He was brooding over a slight he'd received from his cousin King George V of Britain. A remark made while playing cards on the deck of Britain's latest Battleship 'Dreadnaught', which wouldn't be officially commissioned for several years. King George boasted of the British Navy being the largest and most advanced navy in the world. It wasn't meant as a slight but rather a statement of fact made under the influence of wine. However, as Wilhelm suffered an inferiority complex he was easily insulted.

The meeting was between Kaiser Wilhelm of Germany, King George

V of Great Britain and Czar Nicholas II of Russia seeking to address recent changes in Europe, changes threatening their respective monarchies. The Ottoman Empire was struggling with a Turkish Nationalist movement which threatened to destabilize it. Being that the Ottoman Empire was the oldest single family Monarchy to exist the fear was that if it collapsed European Monarchies would soon follow.

Growing unrest and a general dissatisfaction with monarchies was not a new problem, but it was a persistent one. An age-old threat that ebbed and flowed with time, the mood of the church, the harvest and the people the harvest was meant to feed and too often did not. Extravagant displays by a King or Queen in such times often fed the anger of people starving in the streets. Such anger was easily exploited with powerful words and gestures of solidarity with the common man, thus the seeds of revolution are sown. This meeting was meant to address the growing communist movement in Russia, what they all feared was an off shoot movement of the Turkish Nationalist Movement. What they could not know is that the communist movement would one day see Czar Nicholas and his entire family executed and the Romanov Dynasty end and the Soviet Union rise.

Great Britain being the most politically stable nation participating in the conference played host in order for the conference to be held in relative safety. To enhance that safety the meeting was held on a ship in Scapa Flow the British Fleets home anchorage in the Orkney Islands. To further enhance security they were surrounded by 40 of the Royal Navy's most advanced ships of the line as well as countless patrol craft, each bristling with deck guns, torpedoes and a new type of gun called the heavy machine gun. If so much as a canoe approached within a mile of the meeting it would be turned to splinters.

That evening following the conference the Kaiser strolled out onto the fantail of his ship anchored a half-mile from the Dreadnaught, which King George had lit up like a Christmas tree. The ship itself, the Dreadnaught, was merely a shell, which the Kaiser already knew through his intelligence agency. The guns protruding from her faux plywood turrets were empty barrels. She didn't even have operational boilers yet. Having been pulled from the yards she had a plywood superstructure built and painted. It was meant to look impressive for the purpose of intimidation, a show of pre-emptive force specifically directed at the Kaiser. Of course as impressive as the faux superstructure was it was nothing compared to the reality that was to follow, a deliberate understatement. The king knew to keep his cards breasted with regard to the Kaiser. In reality the guns would be much bigger and the armor plating stronger than anything known.

Once commissioned the Dreadnaught would be the most advanced ship on the high seas, not to mention the deadliest. King George wanted the Kaiser to see it to let him know that if he ever quarreled with Britain this would be waiting for him with hundreds more just like it. The Kaiser knew immediately who the message was for and he took it the way King George intended, only it did not deter him, but drove him to act more aggressively, spurring him on to dangerous and provocative actions, actions that would eventually lead the world to war.

Her massive guns and sleek, fast hull would be a dominant force on the high seas. Two Dreadnaught battleships could stand off entire fleets sinking them at will long before they came under fire themselves, if they ran out of ammunition could outrun any ship afloat. No other battleship could match the firepower of the Dreadnaught class. In fact they were the first of their type to exist and would be the standard from which all future battleships were designed.

The sheer firepower of hundreds of these ships would make Britain all the more powerful. A nation that controlled the sea-lanes controlled commerce and a nation that controlled commerce controlled the world and a fleet of Dreadnaughts would guarantee Britain's dominance of the sea for decades to come.

Barely twelve years into his reign, Kaiser Wilhelm wanted to make his mark on history and to make Germany a major player on the world stage and he was insanely jealous of his British cousin, King George. It was said that "The sun never set on the British Empire', in 1905 this was, in fact, true. Being a truly global empire a large, powerful and sophisticated navy was a logistical necessity. The purpose of such a naval force was to protect and promote commerce on the sea-lanes not to satisfy the ego of the King, a fact that made all the difference. That and Britain, with its global empire, had the means and wherewithal to support and maintain her fleet.

Germany had never needed a navy as large or as powerful as Britain's because the German Empire was far less extensive. With three land locked colonies on the African continent and a few islands in the Solomon Archipelago there was little need for a navy as expansive as Great Britain, much less the revenue necessary to build, house and maintain such a fleet. Nevertheless the Kaiser sought to build his own Navy into one that would rival Great Britain, an act that would create tension and lead the world into a global war, all to satisfy his ego.

However when he wasn't consumed with petty jealousies and egotistic pursuits the Kaiser was a thoughtful and conscientious man and realized that matching British sea power would be a monumental task if not impossible without straining Germany's economy, a thought he would keep to himself. If he couldn't match the British ship for ship, he would out maneuver them and change how wars were fought at sea.

His plan for the German High Seas Fleet was to keep it in home waters and send it out only when necessary. His recent thoughts had turned to commerce raiding. Ships disguised as merchant vessels armed with naval rifles, torpedoes and cannon to attack and sink enemy supply convoys from within. Such ships would require a home base, preferably near enemy shores where they could strike from and hide while repairing damage and reloading. These forward bases were to supply and support his raiders that would hopefully wreak havoc on the sea-lanes and disrupt commerce sufficiently to allow him an edge in the event of war.

Another idea, still in its infancy, was a new type of ship what Germany would call U-Boat or undersea boat. A radical new technology but an idea that dated back to the American Revolution and Civil War with the 'Turtle; and the 'CSS Hunley' respectively demonstrating crude yet imaginative concepts which were limited by the technology of their time, limitations that proved fatal for the crew of the 'Hunley', though they did succeed in sinking one Union Blockade ship, proving the tactical concept albeit with tragic consequences. The idea however, did not die with them.

Germany built their first U-boat in 1895 and had already worked out most of the bugs. In fact they were initiating plans to build them for international sale as well as to build up their own fleet. The Americans had just acquired their first submarine the USS Holland as an experimental ship. With the Hunley a dubious reminder the US was suspicious of the technology. But where the Americans were reluctant Germany eagerly embraced and sought to develop undersea warfare.

Where Germany couldn't afford to build a fleet as large as the British they could build ten U-boats for a fraction of the cost of one battleship. Eventually other navies would seek to develop this technology but not until Germany had mastered it giving them the technological advantage.

Kaiser Wilhelm had visions of hundreds of U-boats sinking enemy ships without risking his own more expensive fleet. Of course he was thinking also of using them as commerce raiders. By placing hundreds of submarines in the shipping lanes and off enemy ports Germany could disrupt the flow of material to the front, theoretically. Reality however has a bad habit of poking holes in even the soundest theory, often with devastating consequences.

Germany would eventually excel in this endeavor but it would be its unrestricted use of this advanced weapon that would ultimately cost them the war. When the passenger liner Lusitania was sunk and several hundred American citizens killed America entered WWI and tipped the balance of power in favor of the allies. There simply weren't enough submarines to counter America's unchallenged industrial might; a fact that would overwhelm Germany with a wave of men and material that would eventually flood the Western front with weapons, men and food forcing the Kaiser into exile and Germany to surrender. With one torpedo Germany had lost itself the war.

However, in 1900 such events had yet to come to pass and the Kaiser remained in control of Germany's destiny. It was close to midnight when his naval architect arrived. He had with him plans for a secret naval base. Commander Johan Weiss had been assigned the task of building a forward base for the purpose of housing commerce raiders. "Your Majesty, it is an honor to finally meet you" he said saluting crisply. 'As ordered I have completed the designs for a forward base as requested."

Kaiser postured slightly "Show them to me"

Johan swallowed to hide his nervousness. "Yes, your majesty'. He laid out his plans on the Kaisers desk and spread them out flat. 'At first we considered using an island that was already in existence as a starting point, but the jurisdiction of who claimed authority over the island posed a problem. Then we considered buying the island only that would automatically draw unwanted attention of hostile nations rendering the secret base useless. So we believe that the most viable solution to creating a forward base is to build an island around it." He paused for the Kaisers reaction.

The Kaiser had been looking out the window listening with his back to the Commander. With a start he whipped his body around "Build an island? Are you serious?" Leaning into his desk he looked down at the blue prints and began to scrutinize them more closely. "It's one thing to finance a base but it is quite another to build an island. I hope you have figured that aspect into your design costs" he said in a soft, imperious tone.

The commander swallowed and nodded his head eager to explain. "Y, yes your majesty. The concept of island building is not as far-fetched as you may think. The Dutch have been reclaiming lands from the ocean using dykes and dams for centuries. The design is not much different, except the materials we shall be using will be concrete and stone which are resistant to erosion and degradation and will last for centuries, though in Holland many of the dykes are earthen and have also lasted centuries.

The location I've chosen for this project is off of the French South American colony of Guyana in international waters. There is a broad reef there that is an ideal location for what I have in mind, with direct access to the Atlantic, Caribbean and within easy reach of the Gulf of Mexico. The water is too shallow for large ships to approach closer than a mile and the shallow depth makes the water too rough for small craft to approach without damage or being turned over' he said. It is an ideal location for such a base because it is miles from the nearest commercial shipping port and close to international shipping lanes."

Waiving his hand impatiently the Kaiser spoke in even tones "That doesn't tell me how you propose to finance this endeavor. We are wealthy nation commander but such expenditure will draw unwanted attention. It would be best if we could keep this project quiet and off the official book keeping record."

"Yes, your majesty I understand. The island itself will be a landfill. We've already created a company based out of Columbia. I have taken the local name of Juan Dominges from Cartagena, Columbia. The companies name is established as an industrial waste disposal firm, "Cartagena Industrial Disposal." We have already applied for permits to remove waste from construction sites and demolition sites from Columbia, Venezuela, French Guyana, Mexico and three states along the American Gulf Coast. We will obtain building materials by removing debris from construction sites along the South American coastline, as well as along the American gulf coast. The best part is that they will pay us to remove the debris, which should cover the bulk, if not all of our costs.

The plan calls for us to use huge shallow draft barges to carry the waste material to the site and dispose of it. Here' he pointed his pencil at the map of the area and traced the line he'd already drawn for the purpose of showing the Kaiser 'We will build a containment wall with hydraulic concrete from a prepared foundation in the coral reef itself. Under the coral is a solid mass of granite a perfect foundation for our plan, the trench will be dug into the granite and the concrete blocks laid into the trench.

We plan to build the wall 30 feet wide at the base and ten feet at the peak, which will be 20 feet above the water line when we are finished. The block wall will then be encased in another layer of concrete several feet thick in order to reinforce the block structure, the independent mass of which should be sufficient to address the intended task, only I want to ensure the survivability of the structure with an added layer of support which will then be covered with tons of sand and stone to give it even more support.

The plan is to create a system where the main lagoon is a huge lock where we can pump the basin dry and pull ships into a covered facility then fill the lagoon up again. The projected construction time is roughly ten years providing we have the material necessary to fill in the island mass, which we can acquire by dredging if we must. We plan to build a large tower at the southern end of the island that will house the garrison and commanding officers quarters, as well as provide protection from bombardment in the event that we are discovered and attacked"

Wilhelm looked over the blue print and at the map. "Can it be done?"

"Yes your majesty. Once the barrier walls are in place and reinforced against storm surges from hurricanes that frequent the region, we plan to blast into the granite basin to a depth of 150 feet. Our deep-sea divers will then carve out the basin using dynamite. We plan to use a dredge to remove the waste rock from this effort and incorporate it into the concrete mountain"

The Kaiser nodded but said nothing.

Swallowing hard Johan continued. "We have already acquired permission to begin blasting. We already have the steam dredges awaiting orders to begin and divers are on standby as we speak"

The Kaiser nodded, paused then asked "How big will this island be and how many ships will it house?"

"By the time we reach our design limits in ten years, providing we do not fall behind schedule, the island will be 20 miles long and 10 miles wide giving us a land mass of 200 square miles"

The Kaiser smiled not sure whether to believe him or not; so many of his advisors had given him grand plans only to hand him disappointing outcomes. "It is an impressive plan commander. Now tell me the reality of it. Is this even possible or will we have nothing more than a pile of sand with a sail boat hidden behind it?"

Johan stood up proudly and smiled at his Royal Highness and came to attention. "We have calculated delays and if we have no delays, at all, we will have this done in seven years. Only, I have never worked on a project that didn't suffer delays of any sort. As complex as this design is, ten years is conservative allowing for delays, but certainly in the expected time frame of completion. As far as housing ships I have designed it to accommodate no less than three battleships and four destroyers under full concealment"

The Kaiser nodded. "Very well, proceed with the project. Keep me informed of progress, delays or any changes." He paused looking straight into Johan's eyes "However, if this becomes too expensive or too visible we will have to abandon the project. Germany is not in a position to wage war with the Americas and building a base in such proximity to their shipping lanes may prove difficult to explain. So, I would suggest that you keep this project *extremely quiet*." Standing straight he peered directly into Johans eyes to emphasize the fact that failing to do so could be fatal. Johan Weiss saluted his Royal Highness and left the Kaiser to his thoughts.

As the door closed the Kaiser wanted to believe but he had been disappointed too often. The idea was novel but was it plausible? Could they build this base and keep it secret? If the secret got out he could find himself at war with a great many nations and Germany wasn't quite ready for that, not yet. Though, as a landfill the construction equipment wouldn't have to be hidden and if they worked it correctly the disposal fees could make up a great deal of the cost. 200 square miles of land mass, a man-made island and a secret naval base. This would be a project that he would keep under his hat. Not even his most senior advisors would know about this one. It was a secret base after all and should remain *secret*.

—— ((O)) ——

One year later 200 miles off French Guyana

Johan Weiss aka Juan Dominges stood on the observation platform of the newly completed perimeter wall clad in Khakis and pith helmet watching the drill barges move into position. They would drill through the granite to the design depth and blast from the bottom up. A week of drilling followed by a week of carefully placing 1200 tons of TNT would, if his calculations were correct, move them a full month ahead of schedule. That is, if the custom designed, wax encased dynamite cord worked under water. He'd had it manufactured to fit onto a spool so that they could feed it directly into the holes and to ensure that there were no breaks in the detonation. Each spool held nearly 2 kilometers of dynamite cord or what he later called detonation cord.

With an incremental blast he could clear the basin and bring in the dredges to clear the debris, pulverize the stone and incorporate it into the concrete used to build the dome. Once the dome was completed they could begin building the operations base while the rest of the island was constructed around them. Leaning against the rail he took a deep breath nervous about the many variables that he may not have made allowances for. Had he missed something? Certainly, but where and when would this catastrophe surface?

So far there had been no complications and no significant delays. It was early and he knew better than to believe there wouldn't be any. It was barely two months before hurricane season and if they could build the dome in that time, work could commence on the actual base facilities under cover, safe from storms and observation. The new wall he hoped was up to the task he'd designed it for, if a hurricane knocked it down while the dome was under construction the whole project might be washed up and his career ended.

No one had ever built a base like this before. It was the first of its kind. Tactically it was an excellent idea for a nation seeking the greatest advantage in war. Ethically, it was his duty as a German Officer to create the most significant advantages possible for his country to win a war. As an officer he was pragmatic about warfare and the conduct of it. War was barbaric and inhumane at its most 'civilized'. In order to win a war ethics had to be put aside to allow pure barbarism to be expressed and in that expression, win the war.

This base was to be the tip of Germany's sword, a base so close to enemy shores they could observe them and not be seen; a base from which to strike and then hide as the enemy ran circles in pursuit of them. Not exactly a chivalrous concept, but then he hadn't concerned himself with such antiquated ideas. War had to be addressed as a purely military exercise and so it was appropriate to take advantage of the enemy where he felt most safe, near his home base. If he succeeded the base would be a masterpiece, one that he could never boast about, if he failed not only would his career be over he would likely be shot, if he didn't shoot himself first.

What delays and setbacks he'd expected never surfaced. By the end of the second year of construction orders for debris removal grew exponentially when the American Government offered Cartagena Industrial Disposal a contract to remove waste rock and dirt for a project in Panama. It was to be called the Panama Canal and dirt and rock from that dig would provide the bulk of material for the island as well as cover the remaining costs of completion. Though a boon to the cost cutting aspect of the project, it provided a strategic challenge. The Panama Canal was meant primarily for military use, to cut transit time from the Atlantic to the Pacific and vise-versa. This meant that military naval traffic would increase in the vicinity of the base, a complication but not one that would matter 'if' the island base functioned as it was meant to. It could even work to their advantage in that they could more easily observe their adversaries at a much closer range than before.

By the fourth year the tower mountain was complete. It had the appearance of the ancient tower of Babel complete with its hanging gardens, which served as erosion barriers for the soil that covered the exterior as well as providing a roadway up the mountain. The summit was massive and contained a complex of buildings ranging from the Commanding Officers residence which was a mansion designed in the Victorian fashion but which was made completely of high density steel reinforced concrete with a garden, garage and guest houses along the southeastern edge of the summit. Trees were planted along the spiral roadway to prevent trucks from being seen from the sea as well as to prevent the soil and sand from eroding in storms with grasses and shrubs planted in addition to the trees for the same purpose. Nature and the hot, wet tropical environment would do the rest. The entire mountain was covered in vegetation in less than two years.

Inside the Mountain was a honeycomb of tunnels for trucks and personnel to perform their duties under cover. Observation posts were built into the mountain allowing for a secure, invisible network of lookouts that would alert the base of any approaching ships long before their activity could be observed and give them ample time to secure sensitive equipment. Ventilation was accomplished by opening the doors above and below...with massive fans to assist with the flow of air if the wind didn't cooperate.

The main access channel was blasted clear so they could test the functional dimensions of the channel on ships. By the end of the fourth year the operational aspect of the base itself was fully functional with several ships already in the repair facility testing the capability and function of the design.

Everything worked flawlessly. The only drawback Johan could see was the time it took to drain and refill the lagoon. It was an evolution of no less than two hours. In a tactical situation two hours was an eternity and potentially fatal. To hide the ships while the lagoon drained a series of dunes were built to encircle it with trees and plants planted to break up the superstructure of any ship awaiting entry into the facility.

In the fifth year it was decided that submarines would be deployed from the base instead of surface raiders, which made better sense and automatically made the design 100% tactically functional. A submarine would easily transit the massive channel meant for battleships and enter the base without having to surface or requiring that the lagoon be drained.

To accommodate this change Johan added a rail system with a cradle car onto which the submarine would come to rest on the bottom of the lagoon. The ships screws would then propel the cradle mechanism and submarine into the main base where it would run against railroad style bump stops ensuring that the submarine was in proper position to surface inside the dome. Exiting was done the same in reverse. Three such rail systems were employed to allow multiple submarines to come and go at once. This change bumped up completion time to six years earning Johan a promotion to Captain and command of the very base he built. Like his architectural design his command could never be acknowledged; not even by the Kaiser.

When war was about to break out Kaiser sent three brand new submarines to the island base in secret. In the following months they drilled constantly learning to dive and surface quickly, scouting harbors and shipping lanes to find the best places to ambush while allowing them time to escape.

The submarines operating from the base during the war survived unscathed, due mostly to the fact that they had a place to run to after they launched an attack. Hit and run was the most effective tactic employed. By shooting their torpedoes from extreme distance on the surface then running at flank speed for 20 miles diving and running silent they left the escort destroyers spinning in circles looking for them.

Using this hit and run tactic none of the subs using the island ever came under attack. They never claimed victories, because there was no way to determine what they did sink without risking detection. Never the less the havoc they unleashed was extreme sinking dozens of ships and killing thousands of men over the years. By unloading their torpedoes into a slowly moving convoy they created confusion for the escorts who sought out their attackers who, by the time the torpedoes hit, were miles from their launch point and running for home.

During the war the base performed flawlessly exceeding all of their expectations. However, they had not been able to stem the tide of war against Germany, especially after the United States entered the war. America was far more industrialized than they expected. For a young nation they were extraordinarily capable of building ships and planes in surprising numbers. Not only were they able to adapt to wartime production they were able to adapt their tactics to 'anti-submarine' warfare within a few short months and soon began killing U-boats so efficiently that they had nearly decimated the U boat fleet by wars end.

When the war ended, due to the sensitive and illegal nature of the base, the Kaiser, who was exiled to Holland, ordered Johan to seal the base and sink the submarines in the lagoon and bury them in sand to hide the evidence of the islands purpose. The Kaiser was afraid that if the island base was discovered the sanctions against Germany would be so devastating that Germany itself may have ceased to exist. In addition to this concern was the possibility that such a base, if discovered might very well lead to the Kaiser himself getting hung due to the fact the islands very existence violated every treaty that existed at the time.

As Germans loyal to the Father Land the crews swore an oath of silence to protect their nation from further injury so none of them spoke of their service to anyone, not even their families; it was also to keep them from being killed by the Kaisers personal security, which he used from time to time to silence anyone who might have posed a threat to his survival and his planned return to the throne.

Knowing how efficient the Kaiser could be, Johan burned all his records and erased any trace of his men's identities to protect them from the Kaisers secret police. Johan Weiss, the Kaiser and Karl Donitz were the only three officers at the end of WWI who knew of the base. The enlisted personnel having been warned about the potential back lash from the Kaisers security forces remained silent for their own safety and that of their families.

Johan's final report to the exiled Kaiser occurred in Holland in 1920 confirming that the island was sealed and all record of it had been destroyed. After his meeting, Johan for reasons of his own safety, moved to Palestine where he eventually became a Rabbi. In 1933 Johan Weiss returned to Germany where he took over a Berlin Synagogue just as Adolf Hitler came to power.

However his return to Berlin was short lived. After a few weeks as the Rabbi Johan Weiss was killed in July of 1933 as he left his syna-gogue by Nazi Storm troopers who beat him to death so brutally that the only way he was identified was from the ID card they had nailed to his chest. He had been crucified in the Roman fashion and his naked body hung from the front door of the synagogue as a harbinger of the horrors to come under Nazi rule.

In 1941 the Kaiser died suddenly after Hitler refused to restore him to the throne, a gesture many attributed to Hitler refusing to forgive the Kaiser for abandoning Germany and leaving its people to the wolves as he so often stated on his rise to power.

Karl Donitz went on to command the German Navy under Hitler. It was through Donitz that Hitler learned of the Kaisers secret base. He, Hitler, then ordered it made operational again. The fact that the architect was Jewish was not mentioned to Hitler in the off chance that he dismissed this unique base as a Jewish monstrosity or some other bigoted nonsense. Donitz knew the islands potential and did not want this resource to go to waste. It would then seem that Johan Weiss's death was nothing more than a tragic coincidence, but many things in early Nazi Germany were put up to coincidence, tragic or otherwise.

From as early as 1935 Hitler had submarines operating from the island observing his adversary's and mapping shipping lanes. Like the Kaiser he had submarines seeking out the most favorable ambush sights and making practice runs on unsuspecting ships from Brownsville Texas all the way to Halifax Nova Scotia. In addition to these practice runs a feasibility study was conducted to determine whether or not torpedoes could destroy the Panama Canal in a combined operation with Japan who saw the Panama Canal as a strategic threat to its dominance of the Pacific.

In 1939 WWII began with the invasion of Poland. Once Britain and

France declared war on Germany the submarines deployed and began wreaking havoc. For the first two years of the war the American coastline was aglow with burning ships, oil fires and her beaches littered with bodies. Eventually the US entered the war. Drawing from their WWI experience and using new technology once again began decimating U-boats allowing vast convoys to get to their destination intact thereby turning the war against Germany.

Once again the U-boats deployed from the island base survived unscathed. However, each submarine mysteriously disappeared at the end of the war. It was speculated that the crews had run south to Argentina and scuttled the boats before rowing to shore. Whatever happened no submarines were found nor was anything heard of the crews ever again.

Hitler had a special plan for the island once he realized that Germany could not win the war. He assigned his most brutal general the task of initiating a South American Front and ordered him to attack the United States after rebuilding the Wehrmacht and Kreigsmarine from Argentine Germans. For this mission he was sent an untold amount of bullion from conquered nations to finance this new front. Himmler however, had other plans.

Chapter 1
A life upside down

SMOKE BOILED OUT from under the cowl of the port engine as the airport fire crew sprayed flame suppressant underneath it to prevent the fire from spreading as passengers poured out of the plane. Most of the passengers were calm though eager to get off the plane while others were in hysterics screaming and shoving their way toward the doors and slides like panicked cattle.

The last man to disembark was a middle-aged man who was more annoyed by the screaming passengers than he was the burning engine. He had the hard used look of a man who'd had enough and simply wasn't playing the game anymore. It was the look of a man who took no bullshit and gave none. Some would call him a pragmatist or a cynic while others would call him a beaten and broken man. Whatever you called him the simple truth was that he just didn't give a shit, about anything anymore.

Underneath the calm, irritable exterior was a persistent, simmering rage the sources of which were too numerous to count and which were blurred by time and heartache. Not an unpleasant man, he seldom smiled which was the reason people tended to give him a wide birth because he looked angry, even when he wasn't. This, however, suited him fine because people were too often the cause of his irritation, anger and frustration. He'd had enough of *people* preferring the company of his dog Tucker, an Airedale Terrier who was smarter than your average dog. If anything, a dog was a better companion, better friend and often, sadly, a better 'person' than many people.

A dog never deliberately sought to anger, irritate or in any way seek pleasure from your pain. Though Rick did find it irritating when Tucker helped himself to a freshly made turkey sandwich on occasion, for which he really didn't blame the dog.

He wore jeans, khaki shirt and a pair of new tennis shoes he purchased for the trip. The shoes irritated his feet and made him feel, in a way, naked, his preference being western boots. Making a fashion statement was most certainly 'not' on his list of priorities. However lacking his sense of fashion may have been, he acknowledged that boots didn't go very well with Bermuda shorts and thus resigned himself to sneakers and Dockers for the duration of his stay. But it wasn't the shoes that were irritating him at the moment it was the hysterical woman who had been sitting next to him on the plane.

Flames erupted from the port engine an hour out of St. Vincent. It was then the woman sitting to his right a 250-lbs woman from a small town in Wisconsin began to panic. She squashed him against the bulkhead and screamed at the top of her lungs while straining to get a better look at the burning engine. One of her massive tits squashed into his right ear, which saved it from damage while she let out a piercing squeal that deafened his exposed left ear. The one point of her body not layered in fat was her knees. It happened to be her knees which she pressed against his thigh placing her considerable weight on him in order to get a better look at the burning engine which caused her to scream even louder.

Her husband was asleep in his seat on the other side of the isle and apparently deaf.

Making matters worse was the fact that she was dealing with a digestive disorder that caused her to break wind incessantly with an indescribable reek that weakened the strongest constitutions. A problem that only worsened the more she screamed and the more she screamed the more noxious fume erupted from her ass causing the woman behind him to wretch into an airsickness bag.

Unable to control herself the woman got out of her seat and began running up and down the aisle screaming while spreading her fumes as well. The flight attendants with the help of an Air Marshal secured her in the back of the plane using handcuffs.

Her husband sitting across from Rick was fast asleep, or dead, because he did not in any way react or seem at all disturbed by the racket his wife was making, much less the smell. When the plane finally touched down he woke with a start. Immediately his hand covered his nose, his eyes closed and his head began to shake side to side as if asking 'Why Lord, Why?" His wife noticed and began screaming at him "Harlon! Harlon, the plane caught fire and we almost died!!! We almost died and all you could do was sleep, you useless piece of shit!!!!!!"

Seeming not to hear her vile words he noticed she was not in her seat. He looked around to find her handcuffed in the back of the plane. Smiling he asked her "Whatcha doin back there, all tied up?" Rick couldn't help but notice that his voice was a little louder than it needed to be but didn't think anything of it at first.

There was a chuckle in his voice that suggested he was more humored by her predicament than he was concerned. She picked up on this and was not at all pleased. Her reaction was, if anything, over the top and out of proportion to the situation as she cut loose with a ribbon of curses and bile that left most people red with embarrassment shaking their heads at his reaction or rather lack of one.

He didn't so much as blink or lose his smile as she railed and slurred his being from A to Z using the most disturbing words in the English language and a few clearly German curses. Mouths dropped open as she unleashed her bile and still he did not break his stale, constant smile. Rick watched the old man scratch his ear then ask "Are you done?" Straining against a full belly laugh he scratched his ear again. This however, resulted in her unleashing another barrage so foul the devil himself would have been ashamed to hear it.

The uproar caused by her latest spew resulted in the captain coming back from the cockpit to address her abusive language. He was rather stern and told her to keep her abuse of her husband private and to remind her that children were onboard who should not be subjected to such language.

The captain was applauded as she turned red, not in shame but in restrained anger. Once the captain was back in the cockpit her husband, Harlon, let out a grin and scratched his ear again. By this time Rick had figured out he was fiddling with the volume on his hearing aid. Harlon turned to whisper to Rick, man to man, "I used to think losing my hearing was a curse. But now that I can turn that old bitch off when she gets to be 'herself', I just sit there watching her say whatever she wants. Since I can't hear it...don't bother me none." He smiled wide and added "It drives her crazy".

It was then his wife piped up tired of being ignored. "Harlon, are you done? Aren't you going to tell the stewardess to untie me? Aren't you upset about how they've been treating me?"

Harlon, feeling his oats, replied "Hon, if you could control that temper of yours and keep that out of control mouth of yours from making noise or your ass from gassing the people around you, I'd say sure. To be honest, you've been a mouthy bitch for 30 years and it's about time somebody trussed you up. I'm surprised they didn't gag you." Harlon stifled a chuckle winking at Rick. Apparently Harlon was pleased that his clearly unpleasant wife was getting what he thought was her due...at long last.

Mildred, his wife turned red...but for whatever reason didn't make a sound while the plane came to a stop near the terminal. The emergency crews rolled up the ladders and deployed the slides to get the passengers off the plane. She was the first to be released and led down the passageway. Halfway down her panic took over and broke free of the stewardess and ran screaming hysterically down the aisle knocking passengers back into their seat as she passed.

Rick followed Harlon off the plane watching him as he stared blankly after his wife. The poor man watched as she ran screaming, arms flailing in the air into the airport lobby knocking no less than six other people down in the airport lobby. Standing on the platform Harlon pulled out a flask and took a deep pull and handed it to Rick who accepted it and also took a pull. Harlon said nothing but sighed in resignation before descending the stair. He walked after his wife as a condemned man might walk to his doom, though Rick had the impression that he might have preferred walking to his doom.

The taxi ride to the hotel was, thankfully, short. His taxi was a 1940's Willy's CJ2A that had seen better decades. What he had taken for camouflage paint was actually a hodge-podge of seagull droppings, rust and un-sanded Bondo covering the jeep. In fact he wasn't sure whether it was the Bondo or the seagull shit holding the jeep together. The back seat was little more than canvas over broken springs. What foam there was lay scattered about the floor blowing about in the form of foam dust, which landed on his clothes, hair and upper lip where it stuck to the sweat. His luggage stacked next to and behind him was in danger of falling out every time they hit a bump forcing him to keep hold of his luggage which caused a rusty spring poking through the seat to jab his ribs making him bleed through his new khaki shirt.

His room was a bamboo hut on stilts out over the water; like those seen in travel brochures of Bora-Bora, Tahiti and other areas of French Polynesia. It seemed the perfect hideaway to gather his thoughts and relax. But as he got closer he saw that the hut had, like the Jeep, had seen better decades. Apparently the same seagulls that had decorated the jeep had taken to perching on the railings and roof making the walk to the door precarious. Then there was the pelican, which, at first, appeared to be a decorative sculpture that turned out to be a snippy old bird that got too fat to fly after acquiring a taste for French fries and bacon the tourists threw at it.

When he approached the door the bird stood up flapped its wings in protest at having been disturbed. Instead of squawking like a normal bird this one simply belched up a French fry, waddled over to the far corner and set down with a 'whump', burping up a French fry as it settled down for a nap. It was all Rick could do to not drop his bags from laughing. Opening the door to the hut he stepped through it glancing one last time at the bird grateful for a reason to smile.

Tossing his bag onto the bed Rick took in his temporary home. At first it seemed the perfect get away, until he read a large sign posted on the deck that said 'NO SWIMMING---SHARKS!' What was worse was the fact that some of the sharks lived in and among the stilts that held his bungalow out over the water. At least one shark had the habit of bumping the stilts as he swam by. Evidently he was a large one as he shook the entire structure with each impact. That wasn't so bad until he discovered that one liked to nose up out of the water and bump his nose against the floorboards.

He then discovered that the door to the deck was permanently sealed. On closer examination he discovered why. As he stared through the glass door a large shark nosed up out of the water and raked its teeth along the wooden plank that protruded beyond the railing. The plank on which the shark was biting, already splintered and broken, splintered even more under the ripping action of the shark. Any interest he had of sitting on the deck vanished with the splinters flying through the air. Just as he was about to turn away he saw the 'big one' swim out from under the deck and out to the dark waters of the bay. The white sandy bottom contrasted perfectly with the dark gray, 12-foot shark swimming away.

Looking down at his feet Rick tested the boards for weakness and in a fit of 'Stephen King' induced paranoia started looking for signs that would indicate that the floor was rigged to drop unsuspecting guests into the shark pool below. For ten minutes he lay face down on the floor looking for any hint that the bed could tilt up and dump its contents into the shark pool underneath his bungalow. Knowing full well that he would not find anything, but not wanting to take any chances, he spent the next hour on his face inspecting the floor. Then to be doubly sure he moved his bed to the other side of the room and against the wall forcing him to crawl over the bed if he wanted to use the bathroom. Once satisfied that he wasn't going to be used as fresh chum he collapsed on the bed and fell into a badly needed asleep.

Waking early the next day he lay on the bed staring at the ceiling. "What do I do now" he thought.

This trip was meant for him to clear his head and figure out his life and whether or not to stay married or call it quits with Laurie. They had come to an arrangement to keep the peace between them for the time being, an arrangement that nobody else was to know about. Because he had been willing to let things be their relationship was, oddly enough, warmer. The situation had him spinning though. It was a compromise between the two of them in order to salvage their marriage. Try as he might to figure out how he felt about it he could not decide. He was neither jealous nor angry, hell he wasn't even upset about the situation, really. What he was however was confused. "How could I 'not' be upset about this?" he wondered.

Whatever answer he would have come up with was lost to him when the AC came on and the building began to shake as the sharks started to bash their bodies against the poles. Apparently the AC made a noise that irritated the sharks, causing them to bash their bodies against the stilts until he shut it off. Only it was summer in the tropics and he needed the AC to keep from getting heat stroke. It was almost funny, until the big one joined in, at which point the whole building shook violently as he nosed into the support stilts. However, he was the first one to quit and swim off after which the rest would follow.

He had this to wake up to for the rest of the trip that is until he had a thought to leave the AC on 24/7. They only came back once it shut off so if it never shut off, they'd stay away or so the logic ran. From then on the AC stayed on all day and didn't go off for the remainder of his vacation, turning his room into an icebox but the noise drove the sharks off. Of course he still complained to management, who cut his rate in half.

Sitting at the end of the jetty was a white 1967 Jeepster Commando with rusty rims and a new full length canvas top that the hotel had allowed him to use in compensation for giving him a room over the 'shark pond' as the locals called it. It appeared to have seen better days but the engine was in top running order and the tires and brakes were brand new. Mechanically it was solid in spite of initial appearances and drove surprisingly well. There was a kind of rugged charm about it that appealed to him. The engine was noisy but he liked the mechanical whine. Nothing sounded quite like an old jeep. Hopping in he decided to explore the island and try to relax.

It had been years since he'd truly relaxed and his health reflected it. Far from being an old man he could easily be mistaken for someone twenty years older than his current 47. From the age of 18 he had been on his own, experiencing the world on his own terms seeing the world in its raw state without a religious prism. Before that he had been raised in a classic mid-western home where conformity was expected, dad knew best and mom thought he was gay.

His parents in an effort to get him a better education sent him to Catholic school, though he had been raised Lutheran. Apparently it was their belief that he required more concentrated guilt to solidify his moral upbringing. That and they were petrified of his making them grandparents while at the same time his mother commiserated his being gay. Though he wasn't, she insisted that somehow he was and had, to his dismay, openly made the comment to many of the parents of the children he went to school with explaining a great many difficulties he encountered growing up. The fact that he was sane was a fucking miracle.

That had been his first exposure to socially engrained religious dogma. A place where the phrase "You'll burn in hell if..." was common and you finished the sentence with whatever was irritating the nun or teacher at that moment. Of course this was coupled with a sex education in which the mere thought of an act not specifically sanctioned by the church was enough to earn you a trip to hell; resulting in puberty being a blur of neurosis with bouts of penis shriveling guilt.

All of this made for a fucked up and confusing adolescence, which had he not taken life by the horns and breaking out of social conformity to look at life through his own eyes, his adult life, difficult though it was, might have been even more challenging. It did, on the other hand, give him insight into why people did drugs or drank themselves to death. Thankfully he had not resorted to either one of those stress management techniques, at least not regularly enough to do permanent damage.

What mental toughness he had, he attributed to the Navy and his time at sea on both submarines and surface ships. There wasn't a major holiday he hadn't spent at sea or on some distant, isolated coral atoll. Those times were particularly challenging but allowed him to gain perspective on what was important in life which to him was hot coffee and a warm bed to sleep in and the occasional blow job.

His time on board the submarine a 688 Fast Attack, proved especially challenging due to the fact that the captain had for some reason taken a personal dislike to him and made his life onboard a living hell. So Rick was forced by dint of circumstance to toughen up and take the abuse or lose his mind. He never understood why the captain had singled him out, at least not while on board. It would turn out that the captain was hearing another person's 'bodily functions' while Rick was at his station and had mistaken Ricks proximity as the source of the noise.

It would seem the guilty party was deliberately letting his bodily functions rip knowing full well that Rick was getting blasted by the captain for it. This he didn't learn until he was off the submarine, nor would he learn if the captain ever caught the culprit. He could only surmise by the 'kind' letter his captain sent to his 'A' school commander that he had somehow learned that Rick was not the guilty party and in his own way made amends by praising Rick in the highest manner possible. There was little comfort to be found in a letter of praise after two years of undeserved harassment.

As emotionally taxing as his years on the submarine had been they had been adventurous. Submarines were uniquely suited to the Cold War. The peace-time function of any submarine was to sneak up on potential adversaries and gather as much information on them as possible in order to obtain a tactical advantage in the event of war. Their activities included listening in on radio traffic, sneaking up behind enemy submarines and recording their sounds at various angles of approach, observing live fire exercises and naval war games of the Soviet Navy as well as various other activities that required stealth. Being in close proximity to the Soviet fleet as often as they were it was only a matter of time before they got detected, which they had been on several occasions.

The first time was while nosing about a northern Soviet port, where they were over-flown by a patrol plane no less than 4 times with their periscope up. It was obvious by the multiple direct passes over the periscope that they'd been discovered. Being a mile off the coast of Soviet Russia in 200 feet of water in a 360-foot long submarine made their situation *interesting*, to say the least.

Within minutes a destroyer was speeding out of the inlet making turns for an estimated 40 knots. This was determined by the bow wake as well as the turns the of screw as reported by sonar. In an instant the captain who'd had already ordered a heading of zero, zero, zero or dead north, muttered, "Oh Shit, we have company". Unable to maneuver effectively in such shallow water they had no choice but to drive north at 1/3 speed, just below periscope depth while bullets from machine guns rained down harmlessly onto the hull as active sonar pinged them. The bullets having been fired into the water had no force as they landed on the hull. The effect was an awful sound, like that of a huge millipede walking along the hull, as the bullets rolled into the screw, which sounded like a fork in a garbage disposal. It was the first time he'd seen his captain cringe.

Having a Soviet destroyer 'buzz' the submarine was unnerving for everyone, except Rick. In fact he nodded off during the commotion. It seemed that the danger they faced soothed him somehow. It was as if he were wired for danger, either that or he was nuts. It was during the most dangerous moments of his military career that he felt the most certain of himself and most connected to the world around him, a trait that would serve him in later life.

In spite of the adventures he experienced his personality was ill suited to a military career. Had he remained in the military Rick was convinced he would have slapped-the-stupid out of someone, likely one of the many personality defects he encountered, the list of which was long and IQ deficient. Yet he managed an honorable discharge in-spite of his urges to slap-the-stupid out of people.

However, his tolerance for IQ deficient people did not improve in civilian life nor did his urges to slap them ease. But his military experience had equipped him with the tools necessary to keep from acting impulsively. The Military experience colored his life with experience and gave him an understanding of the person he was inside, none of which made him wealthy but it did keep him out of jail.

One of the many highlights of his military career was meeting his wife Laurie. At the time neither, he nor Laurie had any interest in a long-term relationship. Both had been bruised from multiple break-ups and were in no mood to expend energy on yet another fruitless relationship. Initially they were of the mutual understanding that their relationship was temporary and that once he shipped out it was over. However, it was in letting go of expectations that allowed their relationship to flourish into something more than they had first intended or expected.

After a while, she fell for him despite his rough edges. And he, over time, fell for her though he was more reserved than she was in terms of expressing it, a fact that irritated her. Too many women had hurt him, making it seem as though he wasn't worthy of their love. As a result he reserved his expression of love in fear of *that* being the kill button in his relationships. It was for this reason he was so reserved in expressing his love.

The last thing he expected was to get engaged much less married, yet they had been married the better part of 17 years with three kids. Though he had to admit it wasn't a 'peaches and cream' marriage it had lasted longer than most, albeit tattered it was never-the-less intact.

Though never career minded he took pride in his service. It was his view that no matter how ill-suited a person might be to military life it was still an excellent experience to have. Though he would tell his kids of his adventures he'd had he would prudently keep the early days of his relationship with their mother quiet. No child needs to hear about mom and dad before they were mom and dad. The trauma from which would require far too much therapy to be affordable. Of course, he'd tell his friends all about it when his wife wasn't around. It was this thought process that began to awaken his long suppressed memories as he drove along.

Memories of his life raced through his mind waking emotions long suppressed. The people he'd known, loved and hated rolled across his memory, a movie that played out his life too quickly and-in-some-cases, not quickly enough.

A storm of confused emotions erupted from the deep recesses of his heart and brain as he drove along. One minute he was content, the next in a rage, the next sad about his wife, old girlfriends and the many mistakes made in the course of living. Not to mention the in-justices encountered while, in his mind, living an ethical, moral life. All these thoughts and more raced through his mind and heart as he drove through the streets until he found himself parked on a lonely jetty staring out over the Western Atlantic exhausted and emotion-ally raw. He had no recollection of getting there. He had just driven until he stopped.

Without warning Ricks heartache burst releasing unimaginable grief; the reason for his being on the island in the first place, his wives infidelity. The fact she had taken a lover didn't bother him as much as the many reasons for it, his lack of success as a Chiropractor. Success he had once believed would come with dedication, passion and drive, all of which had long ago burned out due to a health insur-ance system whose ethics and morality or rather the lack thereof…

made a mob hit-man appear saintly. The people he most wanted to strangle, the IQ deficient, all seemed to work for the insurance industry.

In providing service to those-in-need he discovered that passion and dedication to ethical patient care meant nothing in a world where ethics were laughed at and dedication scorned. What money he had earned, which was substantial; had been denied by a system in which his successes were credited, not to his abilities or efforts but to the residual effects of medication the patient hadn't taken in years. How does one succeed in a system so corrupt and absurd?

Too often it was a question for which he had no answer, followed by an emotional breakdown leaving him in a heap on the floor pondering his life choices and personality flaws. He was desperate to provide for his family, ashamed at not having done so, at least not in the fashion he had hoped to.

Thankfully such thoughts were fleeting. Still there was the fact that he had 'earned' the money that was being kept from him because some mindless clod didn't 'like' what he did for a living. It was this overt discrimination against his profession that bothered him the most and it was slowly killing him. Why couldn't he do what others had done so well and make money?

In spite of the heartbreaking reality of doing the work and being denied payment he felt the need to carry on in the hope that one day his efforts would pay off. Hope didn't pay the bills however and it was unraveling. Letting his head fall to rest on the steering wheel the old V6 transmitted its vibration through his brain numbing it temporarily. The effect was soothing but needing to think he put the transmission in neutral and shut the engine off.

The surf crashed along the jetty as a gentle south wind blew the resulting spray away. His forehead pressed against the steering wheel as he fought down a sudden urge to cry. Everything in his life was crumbling under his feet. The practice was not as successful as it needed to be and Laurie, his wife, had taken a lover. What hurt most was that it had been his failure behind it. Her cheating on him was merely a reaction to the stress of that reality.

Tears fell in streams as sobs erupted from his soul. His heart broke as emotions he had bottled up for decades in self-defense burst forth in one overwhelming explosion of pain and torment. It was something too few men allow themselves to do, cry. Of course, he did this on a lonely jetty two thousand miles from home where his wife would never see it, or anyone else. If anything, Rick did have his pride, for what it was worth.

His wives infidelity was, he reasoned, just a side effect of all the strain. Their marriage was far from a romance novel, where romance was depicted through the image of a strong, silent and patient lover who acquiesced to the woman's every want, never questioning her feminine authority. Generally, the men depicted in these novels were every woman's *perfect man*, a muscular, longhaired, *whipped dick*. At least that is how Rick thought of such men, reluctantly acknowledging that such men usually had women falling all over them, the bastards.

As a lover his wife was far from enthusiastic and very inhibited. There was absolutely no enthusiasm when it came to sex, none. The core issue being money, their marriage issues had always revolved around money, the lack thereof. It was the primary reason she had been denying him sexual gratification which led to her taking a lover to address her needs, needs she could not bring herself to allow Rick to address.

They could ill afford this break he was taking, but he needed to sort out his life. Something had drawn him to St. Vincent, other than the fact that it was a cheap resort. It seemed like a good place to clear his head and think. He had a lot to think about, his marriage, what to do about his wives affair and his career. She'd been seeing the other guy for several months when he discovered the affair. Rather, he was made privy to it via an accidental phone call from his wife.

They had been arguing. He couldn't even remember what they had been arguing about, yet it had been one of the worst he could re-member. Luckily the kids had been with her mother for the weekend. In the middle of the argument Laurie stormed into the bedroom and slammed the door coming out twenty minutes later wearing an exceptionally revealing dress, thigh high stockings and garter belt. The outfit was meant to send a signal of "I'm available". She was dressed so that even a blind man would get the message and she had the body to pull it off.

It was obvious that she meant to worry him. Since she had, up to that point, been so conservative sexually he doubted that she would do more than stay out late, as usual. This time was different because the clothes she wore were meant to attract attention and not just the casual sort. Still, Rick doubted that there was anything he had to worry about or so he hoped.

Around two a.m. the phone rang and he answered it expecting to hear his wife telling him to come get her because she was too drunk to drive. While it *was* his wife on the phone, she was most certainly not calling to have him come get her, not by a long shot. As her voice filled the speaker the shock of realization caused him to fall into the nearest seat. His reality was about to be turned upside down.

Apparently, his wife had accidentally dialed the home phone. The truth was she had, in her earlier rage, dialed the home phone to vent her rage some more, but thought better of it not wanting to continue the argument. Later that evening she had checked her texts to see if her husband had texted her, when she didn't see anything from him she tossed her phone back into her purse which was, at the time, sitting between herself and the man she was with in his car. It was that action, tossing the phone into her purse, where her finger hit the call button and dialed the house, a 1:100 chance but which happened none the less. She had also hit the speaker phone which increased the sensitivity of the microphone. Those two inadvertent 'accidents' would be the catalyst through which their lives would be forever altered.

Had the caller ID not identified her phone as the one calling, he would have not recognized her voice immediately because she was unusually warm and familiar with the man she was talking to. It would also appear they had known each other for a while by the tone of their conversation. That fact was made abundantly clear when Laurie, his stale, sexually unimaginative wife said "How far is it to your hotel?" The reply was muffled. "I don't want to wait that long" she answered back.

What he heard next floored him. He could not believe what he was hearing. His wife unzipped her companions fly and serviced him orally while he drove. Something she had 'never' done with him and had very often decried other women for doing, "Because it might cause and accident" were the words most often used while she put on the air of disgust and shame upon seeing a woman do-ing this.

He knew what she was doing because her phone was in such

proximity that he heard 'everything' she did from unzipping his fly to sliding her mouth over him. His moans of approval and her periodic comments of "I love doing this for you" and "It turns me on knowing you like it." left little to imagine while indicating that this had been an ongoing thing and the argument nothing more than a pretext to get out of the house to meet him.

Rick grasped the table to keep from falling over in shock once he realized exactly what his wife was doing...and saying. At first he had denied what he was hearing choosing to believe that it wasn't what it seemed because his wife just wasn't the sort of woman to do such a thing. But as the sounds continued to flow from the speaker it became obvious that she *was the sort* and it was *exactly* what it seemed. There was simply no denying it, his wife was blowing another guy and he was hearing it blow by blow...literally. The intended outcome couldn't have been clearer as she had stated her intentions verbally, though he did attempt to deny what he'd heard as a gross misunderstanding, until it became painfully obvious that he had not misunderstood anything.

Much to his own surprise he wasn't upset, not even close to it. But then he was in a state of shock, a malady requiring a stiff belt of Jack. A bottle just happened to be sitting within reach. Not bothering with a glass he swallowed the equivalent of three full shots straight from the bottle before putting it down...nearly gagging on the overload of whiskey as he forced it down. He was no serious drinker, not by a long shot, so half-way through the swallow of too much liquor he had coughed up some whiskey which now spewed out his nostrils burning his sinuses as well as his throat. To look at him he was a wreck of whiskey filled snot and confusion.

His hand gripped the neck of the bottle as if it were the only thing keeping him upright. The sounds of his wives orally amorous behavior grew more regular and more intense with each passing moment making it clear that this was just the beginning of their evening plans.

Once in the hotel his wife continued what she had started in the car with considerably more enthusiasm than he had ever encountered during their rare excursions into this activity. After 15 minutes Rick choked down another swig of whiskey as his wife completed the job more thoroughly than he was expecting her to, an act that left him staring into the speaker in utter disbelief and shock. If standing was difficult before, it was near impossible after that. "What have you done to my wife?" he muttered. At that very moment less than a mile from where he sat, his wife knelt before another man in a hotel room too preoccupied to speak.

Thanks to digital technology and a hyper-sensitive microphone he was able to hear 'everything' as if he was sitting next to them in the room and he heard *everything*. He was pissed that she wouldn't do that for him, her husband, but would do a far more thorough job for someone else. This thought forced him to pull another healthy swig from the bottle making a significant dent in the once full bottle. He then decided to put the bottle up not relishing the prospect of a JD hangover which was already threatening, a frequent side effect to his drinking too much Jack.

It wasn't long before his wife was busy again. Over the speaker he heard his wife kissing this man moaning her approval as the zipper to her dress was pulled down 'Zzzzzzpp' followed by the shuffle of her dress falling to the floor. She then said something almost too quietly for him to hear it but he managed to hear "Don't make me wait…please. It's been two weeks and I've missed you ….and…

and…I've missed your cock…so much" and she moaned out low as it became apparent that he was entering her.

He knew this only because his wife, his normally silent, inhibited 'are you done yet' wife, was moaning in bliss as her lover impaled her. It was the first time he had ever heard his wife beg for anything much less another man's cock. "Fuck me…please…God…fuck me… fuck me!! I love how you do this to me!!" she cried. It had been years since she had ever been so passionate…with him anyway'. That thought did not sit well with Rick, 'Why could she be expressive with this guy and not with me?' he wondered. A brief jolt of anger surged through him as he listened to their impassioned exchange. Part of him wanted to smash the phone while another part wanted to keep listening to satisfy his lecherous curiosity. Now she was howling in ecstasy clearly enjoying sex in a way Rick had never experience with her. "Dammit" he spat under his breath.

Stunned and still not quite believing what he was hearing Rick listened as the headboard banged against the wall suggesting that things were getting hot and heavy on the other end of the telephone line. With each bang of the headboard he heard a squeal from his wife and an exclamation of "YES…Yes…harder…*harder*! Fuck Yes!!!" exploded from the tiny speaker. It was clear that Laurie's passion was building as she was pounded hard and fast. Every moan and passionate exclamation she made were divulged through that tiny, innocuous speaker, including the most intense orgasms he'd heard come from his wife…ever.

Something deep inside him was glad she had a sexual pulse but there was also regret at not being the one to bring this side of her out. The last time they'd made love had been only a few days before, but the feeling was hollow, empty and decidedly cool. Laurie was not present in the moment and now he knew where her mind had been. After listening to three orgasms explode from his wife Rick hung up.

Staring at the phone for brief moment he decided to call her back to see what she would say in the full knowledge that she was, at that very moment, getting fucked by another man. With a drunken grin he speed-dialed her phone, which, to his surprise, she answered almost immediately. "Yes?" she said sounding less than thrilled at having been interrupted. She had answered his call because she figured he would just keep calling if she didn't.

"Just calling to check in to make sure you were ok." He said trying not to slur his words as the whiskey he'd consumed began to take hold.

"I'm fine" she said making an effort to not sound irritated but struggling to keep her voice even as Greg ground himself hard into her and grinning like a Cheshire cat. It was at this moment she hooked her heels into his ass and pulled him deeper and mouthed "Keep going" which he did, slowly and repetitively as Laurie spoke to her husband on the phone.

"Did you meet anyone tonight?" he asked. You were certainly dressed for it."

"Yes, actually' she said 'but I'm not sure you'd approve' she was daring him to guess what she was doing. She hadn't intended to say anything until that very moment. Perhaps it was the euphoria caused by the warmth of another man pulsing deep inside her body that relaxed that particular inhibition.

Yet, she remained cautious. On impulse she had Greg rollover and he was now on his back and she on top. Grinding herself down onto him she had to stifle a gasp of bliss as new levels of pleasure rose in her bosom. She covered her own mouth and pulled the phone away from her ear as she forced herself to be silent in the wake of this new and explosive position. The fact that she was on the phone with her husband made the experience that much more intense. Her excitement grew to the point where she thought she might explode in orgasm.

Looking down at Greg their eyes locked and she continued talking with her husband. "Don't worry about me. I'll be home in a bit. I'm not quite ready to come home yet so you shouldn't wait up' she said as she drove Greg deep grinding herself hard against his pubic bone stifling a gasp of bliss. 'Thanks for calling to check on me, but I'm more than fine' she said looking into Greg's eyes smiling 'Good night" and she hung up before he had a chance to reply.

Looking into the phone Rick wasn't sure what to think. Had she just admitted to being with someone? He already knew what she was doing. No...that wasn't like her. But then, it wasn't like her to actually-fuck another man, or so he'd once thought. Rick wasn't jealous oddly enough. Maybe it was for the best or maybe it was the whiskey. One thing was certain, their relationship dynamic had changed. Whether for better or worse he couldn't tell. To say he was confused was a gross understatement and the whiskey was most certainly not helping.

Staring at the phone through which he'd just heard his wife engaged in a heated, passionate and very physical encounter with another man; an encounter during which she expressed more passion, more energy and enthusiasm than she had ever expressed in nearly 20 years of marriage. Rick tried to make sense of the confusion mounting in his heart. He wasn't angry or upset, but neither was he overjoyed.

Things between them had been far too icy in recent years. Staring out the window he was wondering why he wasn't as upset about it as others would have been, for some inexplicable reason he actually liked the idea of his wife fooling around *'or was that the whiskey?'* he wondered. Whatever the case he was in no condition to decide anything, at least not while loaded on Jack Daniels, the bottle of which he was eying as he considered emptying it.

As he was already feeling the effects of his earlier indulgence to the point where walking was dubious and speech took effort with a nagging headache that suggested a hangover in the offing. It was a trait unique to his drinking Jack Daniels. As a result he could never allow himself to abuse it because it always gave him a headache and the hangovers were horrendous. He'd had far too many to look back on and had no need to experience another. Instead he downed ½ gallon of water took a shower then went to bed where images of his wife banging another man spun through his liquor fogged brain.

Across town Laurie dropped her phone back into her purse grinding her pelvis against Greg in a mad surge of unrestrained lust. She was turned on more than ever having just been on the phone with her husband while riding another man. It made her feel reckless and alive with forbidden lust and energy. Kissing Greg hard she ground herself against him while she tried desperately to take every-last inch of him into her body. Greg was the most satisfying lover she'd ever known and she could never get enough of him. No matter how often she came in his arms she'd never tire of feeling him inside her or his kisses and certainly never tired of his magnificent body grinding against hers.

She moaned softly rolling over again onto her back as his toned, muscular body ground himself into her. It was a nice change of pace to have a lean, toned, muscular body between her legs. She never tired of the sight of his 'V' shaped body pressed against her as the warmth of their connection drove her over the edge. Then there was his size, which made her brain explode when he touched her in places she never knew existed. The effect awakened feelings of being a complete woman and erased her inhibitions, all of them. They didn't talk, after six months there was no need, she simply let him take over. He was so very good at taking care of her she felt he had spoiled her for other men, especially her husband.

Looking out the window she saw her apartment building in the distance and what might have been a light on in her apartment. Her husband was awake and wondering where she was at that very moment. The thought excited her. *'What would he say if he knew what I was doing while we were on the phone?'* she wondered? She had been reckless by making the overt suggestion of what she was doing but cut short of admitting it. Reckless didn't mean foolish or stupid.

The urge to be savaged surged through her body as she focused on her apartment...wanting her husband to know what she was doing with another man. The idea of which turned her on more than she would consciously admit. Yet, she wasn't sure if he would understand. Most men wouldn't. *"Well, I'm doing it and I am not about to stop"* she thought to herself.

Laurie had been a faithful wife for 17 years but needed more than what she was getting, a lot more. The model wife and mother all those years and for what, a terminal struggle; never ending stress and a cranky, asshole husband? Life was too damned short and she had taken her life into her own hands and decided to live it, her way. She was doing things she had never wanted to before and loved every sinful moment.

A long dormant part of her sexuality had been awakened and needed to be expressed and satisfied and if it wasn't satisfied she was sure to explode in frustration and anger. '*How many years have I wasted?*' she wondered. '*No more*' she thought. Arching her back she moaned and pressed herself hard against his pelvis driving his length deeper which caused her senses to explode with unrestrained lust. Looking into the eyes of her lover...she said through gritted teeth..."Fuck me hard" and fell back on the mattress eyes locked on her apartment... which soon disappeared in a blur of motion.

Rick pretended to be asleep when she came home a little more than an hour later. Laurie couldn't help notice a strong odor of whiskey. Her brow furrowed concerned that her husband had been drinking, a pet peeve of hers. Somehow, she sensed he wasn't asleep but undressed quietly just in case he was. This didn't take long as she was naked under her dress and blouse having left her bra and thong as well as the garter belt and stockings with Greg. A habit she'd taken to as both a means of sharing herself with the other man in her life as well as a subconscious slap in the face to her husband in a reckless dare for him to catch her. More to the point it was a silent declaration of contempt for her husband.

Throwing on an overly large T-shirt, she crawled into bed next to her husband thinking of the next time she would be with Greg. Since their first meeting he was constantly on her mind and thinking about the next time they would be together, even more so since they had entered a physical relationship. So it was as she lay in bed staring at the ceiling remembering his touch and his lingering warmth...his hard, toned body...and the next time they would be together.

Slowly her hands found their way to her folds and unconsciously spread her legs taking him into her once again in her mind. The memory of his touch fed the motion of her fingers which caused her to climax over and over again mere inches from where her husband lay. Not realizing that her husband was fully awake and watching her in the mirror on the dresser. He watched as she brought her knees to her chest and brought herself to orgasm after orgasm…well into the night.

Rick had enough whiskey to dull his senses and to take the edge off the fact he had caught his wife in an affair, enough to offer up a minor hangover if he hadn't taken precautions against it. Laurie carried the faint scent of cologne along with the obvious scent of hotel soap when she came to bed indicating that she had taken a shower before coming home. What they had done in the shower Rick would never truly know but he could guess and likely not be far off the mark. Had he not known exactly what she had been doing the scent of men's cologne and hotel soap would have been a dead giveaway. That and the quaking bed from her silent, self-induced orgasms indicated that she would have stayed with 'him' all night had he, her husband, not been home waiting. The thought broke his heart and drew whiskey soaked tears to his eyes before sleep finally took him.

Over the next few weeks Rick watched Laurie more closely and noticed certain changes in her whenever *he* called. Her face would redden and she would laugh nervously especially if he was in earshot. Her answers would be quick inert one line answers like "Oh really?" "Yes he's in the office" or "No, I can't talk right now" or "Can I call you back? I'm in the middle of something". Often coinciding with these phone calls she would disappear for long lunches coming back flushed, smiling and dazed, other times smelling of hotel soap from taking a shower with him, each time minus her underwear had he bothered to check.

In spite of everything he truly did love her and didn't want their marriage to end. In all honesty he was willing to let things be if it made her happy. She was far more pleasant to be around since learning of her tryst as a result they were getting along better than they ever had before. Yet the question remained 'was it best to confront her or let it be?'

He found his lack of jealously interesting. Most men would have lost their composure had they caught their wife in the act of fucking another man. The truth was he enjoyed the idea that she was screwing around. It was something 'different', exciting and certainly not the dull, dry boredom encrusted situation they'd been mired in for so long. Since he'd been aware of her affair he had been bolder and she had been more receptive to his advances. She'd even begun doing things to Rick that she had been doing with the other guy. Still, Rick had a lot to think about and needed time to clear his head to gain perspective. So he booked his vacation a few months after discovering his wives affair for that purpose.

The night before he was scheduled to fly out he told his wife that it was ok to invite Greg over while he was gone. Using the name of the man she was sleeping with caught her off guard. Laurie responded unconsciously with "We are having lunch after I drop you off at the air---port...' pausing when she realized what her husband had just said. Laurie slowly sat on the couch turning white with shock. She didn't even try to deny it. 'H..how did you...uhmm..?" her voice cracked as a tear rolled down her cheek as the white hot sensation of 'shock' seared through her heart and limbs. The feeling one gets when truly caught and there is just no explaining it away.

Years of contempt for the man standing before her evaporated with the realization that he wasn't as 'dumb' as she had come to believe. "When....?" she uttered before shock again robbed her of speech.

Rick leaned against the doorframe shaking with excitement he couldn't explain; "A few months ago." Sitting down next to her he took her hand gently. "Remember that night I called to check on you?' he asked. 'Well you dialed the house before that and, well...I got quite an earful. When I called you that night I knew exactly what you were doing because I heard everything you did with him. I was curious to see if you would pick up.' Looking away he smirked trying not to laugh at his wives horrified expression. 'Honestly, I found it quite interesting talking with you knowing you were with another man as we spoke. I was impressed with how you kept your end up under the circumstances" He said still trying to keep a serious yet light tone.

Laurie paled even more at this bit of news not quite sure how to feel about her husband knowing so much. Her sexual liaisons were no longer a secret and hadn't been for a while. Her husband had even heard her in the act, the thought of which nearly made her vomit. What concerned her most was that she would be forced to give up Greg. She didn't want her children to find out that their mother had been sleeping around. The idea of losing Greg saddened her causing tears to fall mourning his loss as well as the loss of her 'other' self, the person she was when she was alone with him. She would miss that part of herself, a lot.

Rick saw the concern on her face and *almost* felt sorry for her. "It's ok babe' he said. Laurie hated being called *babe* but she wasn't in any state to protest. 'This is something you apparently needed so I didn't say anything.' He paused for a moment. 'If you want to keep seeing him I'm ok with that."

She didn't know what to think about that last bit looking up at him in surprise not daring to believe what she had just heard, thinking she had misunderstood him. He wasn't screaming his head off or being irrational. The whole scene felt surreal. His voice was distant and far away while blood rushed through her ears and brain throbbing as her heart beat harder yet slower or so it seemed. Time stood still as she grasped at emotional straws not daring to believe the scene playing out before her.

Rick, her asshole, prick of a husband was as calm and serene as if asking her to get his dry cleaning. It would have been less unnerving to have him flip out and throw a chair through the window. The incongruent nature of his calm demeanor in the face of her infidelity made her sick with worry. He then added "Just don't hide it from me anymore, ok?"

"You aren't angry...?" she choked out before her voice trailed off again. Shaking with nervous tension her brain burned and her vision clouded with tears of shame and fear at having been so thoroughly exposed to the one man she could keep anything from and whom she held in such deep contempt.

Moving toward her again Rick kissed her on the forehead "No" he said squeezing her hand.

Laurie's mouth dropped open in surprise and confusion. She stared her husband's hand and squeezed it hard and whispered "You heard everything we did...?" She couldn't say any more her face reddening with embarrassment and shame.

He whispered back "Yes, I heard everything you did, including what you did to him while he drove you to the hotel. That was an eye opener" He said.

Horrified her face reddened even more "Y...you...heard me...us...in the car?" she said trying desperately to retain what remained of her composure which was hanging on by the merest thread.

Rick nodded "Ohhh yeah...I heard everything.' he paused and leaned into her ear and continued with a whisper 'Everything, from when you unzipped his fly in the car to when he took you in the hotel. You made a lot of noise babe...A lot of noise!" He then went onto describe what he heard in exact detail. It was difficult to not laugh at the expression on his wives face at his clear knowledge of *everything* she had done with her lover. It was clear that there was no denying what had happened, not that she would, having been caught with her pants down, literally in this instance.

"You're not angry?" she repeated again to be clear, trying desperately to get a grip on the situation.

Rick shook his head. "Babe, we've been at each other for so long something like this was bound to happen. To be honest I expected it sooner. Especially since I gave you a hall pass, remember?" Several years earlier he had offered to let her explore sexually outside the marriage when things got strained. Rick had selfishly hoped to awaken her sexual appetites by allowing her the freedom to do what she wished but she never acted on it, at least not in the sense it had been intended.

Laurie's eyes widened "Y...you were serious about that?" she asked.

Again Rick nodded "Yes, I was serious then and I am now. But I still need to sort things out for myself." This panicked Laurie.

"You're coming back right?" she asked.

"Yes, I'm coming back' as if to answer her next question, 'No I'm not going to divorce you. I've been expecting something like this for a while. I wasn't expecting to hear it on the phone though" Rick said looking down into his hands.

Laurie looked at him for a few moments considering what he had just said "So it's okay to keep seeing...him and to bring him into our home and...be with him?" Rick nodded in agreement still looking into his hands. Laurie swooned with nervous excitement as she whispered "In our bed?" Her voice was shaking. Rick nodded looking at his wife who was smiling nervously.

Rick kissed her and said "Yes, just keep me in the loop and be safe... and change the sheets. The kids must never know about this...ever." Laurie gave him in her best 'Please, as if' look, so well-practiced over the years.

"Ok" She said both relieved and confused by his stale non-reaction to her infidelity. Had the tables been turned around the world would have come crashing down on his head, with a sure divorce to follow. Now that she was thinking about it, his lack of response made her nervous and even a little angry because it made her feel as if he didn't care. A mixture of joy, anger and confusion mingled in her heart and brain as the incongruence of the situation stormed through her heart and mind.

Looking away she thought of Greg, grateful that she wouldn't have to give him up and would again enjoy his touch, in less than a day in fact. This thought led her to think of their first meeting and their first time together in her mother's house six months before in his office.

Laurie first met Greg while searching for an estate attorney to organize her mother's assets and manage the sale of her home. She hadn't
counted on his good looks or the explosive chemistry between them.
When they first met she nearly fell over, a six foot tall blonde man
with sharp blue eyes and a loose pony tail and muscular physique
that cried out to be mauled. If his physical looks were not reason
enough the chemistry between them completely unhinged her inhibitions...every single one of them. Something about his energy
erased her marital vows in the space of a heartbeat. In fact she hadn't
felt as shameless since college or even in college and most certainly
not since getting married.

The moment their eyes met something electric sparked between
them. They both knew something would happen. The question
was 'when' and how far would it go? Had her mother not been present things may have very well started that day on his desk. Laurie
had actually excused herself to the ladies room and removed her lace
undies just in case the opportunity arose to screw his brains out.
Such was the effect he'd had on her. As it was they were both forced
to contain their lust that first day. Ironically, from that day on never
did she ever feel guilt, shame or even the slightest sense of remorse
for what she knew would happen between them...eventually.

Their meetings continued for several months with minor, mutual flirtation that grew more and more aggressive but since her mother was
at each meeting nothing happened. That is until one day, while taking inventory of her mothers' house, the sexual tension that had been
building between them exploded into a physical affair. It wasn't an accident in all honesty, they had discussed getting together several times
but neither of them knew when or if the opportunity would present
itself. Laurie, impatient to stoke his fire, had dressed to get his attention by wearing a mini skirt and lace thong with a light blue men's

button down shirt, no bra and stiletto heels. Not exactly the clothes for taking inventory of a house; attire that did not go unnoticed.

Her mother had noticed. The energy between them was palpable and obvious that first day in his office. Even then she was sure that if she left them alone for even a few minutes she suspected that she would have returned to find them thrashing about on his desk in the throes of passion. Yet, she did not disapprove or condemn her daughter for it.

She had herself wed very young and had children very young. Those two facts had done nothing to curb her lust and longing for such tawdry pursuits. However, life and social convention had conspired to force her to behave in a fashion expected of a demure woman… which she was most certainly not…at least on the inside. Denying her wants and desires as was expected and accepted in the day was likely one of if not 'the' reason she left her husband of 40 years. 40 years of self-denial, neglect and abject boredom wore her down to the point she simply had to act or go mad.

It was for these reasons she did not step in, intervene or even disapprove of Laurie's obvious attraction to Greg. In all honesty had she been a few years younger she might have been all over him herself. It was for these reasons she decided to remove herself from the garage to give them both time to do what they needed to and get things going and out of their system.

When her mother left the garage Greg moved in behind Laurie and 'accidentally' bumped his 'attraction', against her ass while pretending to reach for something overhead while Laurie was bent over the dryer writing on a pad of paper. Pretending not to notice and believing that it was an accidental bump she went about her task.

She did, however, push back against him to see what would happen, something they'd done on occasion but which hadn't gone anywhere. However this time it led to his placing his hands on her hips and grinding himself against her.

When his hands grasped her hips and took hold she realized what was about to happen and her lust exploded. She looked back at him totally giving in to her lust. She smiled pressed her ass hard against him while pulling her mini skirt up for more intimate contact. She loved how a hard man felt through jeans and relished the forbidden sensation. "Don't make any noise" she whispered keeping an eye on the door while she thought of a reason to send her mother out to give them time alone while grinding herself against him.

The amount of time depended on how far they were willing to push things along. 30 minutes would be enough if that was all they could get, but what a 30 minutes it would be. She wanted him, all of him, but she wasn't sure how far Greg was willing to take things…yet. She had no idea how deeply in love he was with her. Greg didn't say a word as his hands nervously stroked her thighs and ass wondering how far he would get before she made him stop.

Taking a quick look around to ensure that they were alone Laurie whipped around and kissed him hard on the mouth leaning back against the dryer and wrapped one leg around his. For almost 20 minutes they mauled each other. With her mother inside the house they restrained themselves, though restraint barely qualified in this instance. Had they not, they would have consummated their relationship right there on an Antique Kenmore Dryer in her mother's garage.

Restrained though they were Laurie's thong did eventually find itself on the floor and around her ankle with two of Greg's fingers exploring deep inside her intimacy with Laurie grinding herself onto them until she exploded in orgasm. She climaxed silently, biting into his shoulder to stifle the urge to cry out as spasms of bliss ripped through her body. Panting with fevered lust she stroked his denim-covered arousal, resisting the urge to rip his jeans off and take him right there.

Only after they heard her mother 'noisily' make her way back to the garage did they separate. By the time her mother entered the garage they were doing what they had been doing prior to her leaving at separate ends of the garage. Laurie's lace thong, however, remained wrapped around her left ankle, which her mother noticed once she came back into the garage. Moving in swiftly she whispered to her daughter. "You left something on the floor sweetie' then added 'Should I go shopping?"

Laurie's mouth dropped open in embarrassment having been caught in such an obvious and compromising situation and then in shock at her mother's apparent approval. She nodded vigorously 'yes' in response to her mother's question. Her confusion must have shown because her mother leaned in and whispered "Laurie, I am your mother, I know when you have the hot's for someone' She moved in closer still 'you are on fire sweetie, I'd be all over him if I were a bit younger." she whispered then said out loud, "I need to go and get us something for lunch. It shouldn't take me more than an hour or so." She then turned to her daughter and whispered "Text me if you need more time."

Laurie's heart skipped a beat realizing that she had just been given 'permission' to play out her desires without having to wait for an opportune moment. Shame and guilt were nowhere to be seen having long before reconciled the fact that she wanted Greg in every way possible. Her mother patted her cheek and smiled a knowing smile and left. Laurie and Greg stood silently staring at the door through which her mother left.

Not daring to believe their luck they both listened as they heard the front door open, close, and her mother's foot falls as Laurie's mother walked to the car. Neither moved a muscle as the engine started and idled for a minute before backing away. As the car accelerated down the street, Laurie received a text message. The alert caused her to jump. It was from her mother. *"You are welcome to use the bedroom to play, just change the sheets if you do."* Laurie gasped in shock realizing exactly how far her mother expected things to go and flushed red.

"Who is that?" Greg asked walking up next to her.

"Mom, she wants us to change the sheets" Laurie said as she put the phone in her purse resolved to the fact that she was definitely going to *change the sheets* and smiled to herself.

"But we just changed them" he said. An hour earlier he and Laurie had changed the sheets on her mother's bed and thrown the sheets in the washer as a courtesy to freshen up the room for the eventual sale of the house. Laurie shook her head and thought '*Men!*' Her heart was beating like a trip hammer knowing that what she was about to do could never be undone; which was exactly *why* she slipped her skirt off her hips and let it fall to the floor.

Wearing only her dress shirt which hung to mid-thigh, she turned to face Greg and kicked her skirt away then took his hand. "Maybe we should mess them up then" she said looking directly into his eyes and kissed him deeply as Greg lifted her up and carried her to the bedroom.

The moment they got into the bedroom Greg put Laurie down and she frantically undid his jeans and slid them to his ankles kissing him as if he were the only thing keeping her alive. She then let her hands explore his now exposed manhood. It was the first time she'd touched another man like this in nearly 20 years. What she noticed first of all was his size and length and he was not yet fully present. The idea of having her body impaled by what she had in her hand made her brain explode as years of limited thinking evaporated leaving her completely mad with lust.

On a whim, she fell to her knees and took him into her mouth. Something made her want to do *this* specifically for 'him' and found the act itself turned her on a lot more than she realized it would. Laurie was actually enjoying the warmth of his hardness on her lips and tongue. She then vowed to get better at it if only for Greg. Nothing was more important than to please him, nothing but his pleasure mattered, not even her own…at the moment.

Greg's moans drove her on. She enjoyed knowing what she was doing brought him pleasure and slowly began to move her mouth back and forth onto him. As she gained confidence and technique she began realizing how sensual pleasuring a man this way could be. For years she had thought of this act as demeaning for a woman. But as she heard his moans and sighs her desire to please the man before her grew explosively, igniting her own passion and desire.

When her own needs could no longer be ignored she stood in front of him unbuttoned her shirt and let it fall to the floor before embracing Greg and kissing him passionately. His hands on her body were like velvet causing her to explode in wanton lust. Feeling his hardness graze her she slid herself over the top of his manhood, letting his warmth mix with hers impatient to feel him inside her. Greg had other plans however.

Breaking their kiss he began moving his lips down her neck, down her shoulder working his way to her exposed breasts ravaging them with his teeth, tongue and lips. Laurie guided his movements once he reached her breasts by guiding him from one to the other. When he went further down she did not resist but remained standing as for the first time in far, far too long a man's tongue found its way into her long neglected regions.

It had been years since she let her husband do this...and wondered why she had not let him...but that was too much thinking while she held Greg's head between her legs, letting her head fall back she moaned her appreciation while fighting the urge to cry out from the intense pleasure she was receiving. Before she knew it she was blinded by a flash of light and shaken to her core by an earth shattering orgasm. Her mouth opened to scream but no sound came as spasms of pleasure ripped through her body with such ferocity she could not move, breath or think. However, instead of being spent she was even more in need of his attention.

Speaking in a quavering voice she said "I've wanted you since the day we met" and kissed him hard, whispering "Please Fuck me" into his ear before crawling on her hands and knees onto her mother's bed grasping the top of the headboard. Looking back over her shoulder she said "I have fantasized about you taking me doggy since the day we first met' then added 'If my mother hadn't been there that first day... in your office, you would have had me if you wanted me." As she said the words she realized just how true they were.

Her words were barely registering as the blood rushed to his head barely comprehending the situation. When she said 'Please fuck me' his knees nearly gave out…he couldn't believe what was happening even as he crawled up to her taking hold of her hips and was guided by her eager hand into her opening. Laurie gasped out loud "This is finally happening…it…is…really happening…" she hissed not at all hindered by it being her first act of adultery, but driven on by the fact that it *was* as she backed herself onto him one delicious inch at a time.

Stopping to let her get used to their connection he calmly asked while stroking the small of her back "What would you have done if your mother wasn't there?"

She sighed and dropped her head taking in his length and girth. "I really have no idea. All I know is' she paused and slid herself back and forth taking him deeper still 'had I known you'd feel like this' again she paused, moaning in bliss then rocked forward and then pushed herself further onto him 'I would have thrown myself at you." After their brief exchange speech was lost to Laurie. The instant his flesh touched hers any doubt or hesitation that existed evaporated in a fog of bliss.

He was more heavily endowed than any man she had known, deliciously so but not overwhelmingly, just the perfect size to satisfy her like no man had before. The feeling of this man's warmth pulsing deep within her body overwhelmed her senses, exploding in a vocal expression she did nothing to quell which carried out the open window. A flock of black birds erupted from the tree adjacent to the house as Laurie's voice carried out into the neighborhood.

The only other person besides Greg to hear her cries of ecstasy was the Postman two blocks away. He'd heard that sound before, the impassioned cry of a lonely housewife doing the UPS man, electrician, plumber or salesman and of course the mailman. He'd pretty much heard it all in his 40 years of delivering mail and was one of the reasons he'd requested the morning route, because 'he' had, on occasion, been the reason some women made 'that' noise in his youth. Stopping he watched the cloud of birds rise up into the morning sky giving him a general idea of where the sound was coming from. He then wondered 'Who was making deliveries on Saturday?' He chuckled to himself and continued on his route with a wry smile on his face.

Gouges in the wall behind the headboard bore testament to the lustful exchange that early spring morning; lust that they would express throughout the house that day and for months to come. In the two hours her mother was gone Greg took her on the couch, day bed, kitchen counter, the tool shed and on the dryer in the garage where it all began. Laurie's sexual energy seemed boundless as did Greg's, like teenagers exploring something new and forbidden. This undoubtedly fed the energy they both experienced that first day, energy that would spark whenever they were near each other from then on and which would erase all of Laurie's long held inhibitions. They did eventually change the sheets throwing the ones they'd used into the washer as her mother pulled into the driveway. Three sets of sheets were laundered that first weekend and her mother did a lot of shopping; thus the affair began.

In the months since, their interludes were limited to what few hours they could steal from their normal lives. Most often she'd meet him in a cabin he'd rented on the beach near where she worked, sometimes a hotel if the cabin wasn't available and several times he'd brought his camping trailer and parked it on a cliff overlooking the ocean where they would make love to the sounds of the crashing surf. She had slept a full night in his arms twice and she desperately wanted to again. From what her husband was saying, though she found it hard to believe, she would again and with her husband's consent no less.

Confusing her was the fact that her husband accepted the situation with a calm resolve, a fact that made her nervous because it was out of character for him. Laurie would have preferred he scream and be a huge prick about her cheating on him. As it was his lack of reaction was unnerving. He wasn't angry or even the least bit upset at discovering the affair. While her mind tried to make sense of things she felt his hand take hers again. Looking up into his eyes she saw what could only be unconditional love. "You still love me?' she said in surprise 'Even after this?"

He nodded and said "Hon, I've always loved you and I always will. Nothing will change that, nothing."

Her hand stroked his cheek as she whispered "Really?" Her heart exploded in excitement and in an all too rare 'love' for the man before her. Excitement filled her heart knowing that she would be able to continue seeing the man who awakened her sexuality and growing affection for the man who loved her enough to let her. What contempt she'd held for him evaporated and she once again fell in love with the man who had stolen her heart so many years before. She kissed him like she hadn't in years. They fell asleep in each other's arms feeling more like a couple than they had in many years.

Several days later Rick sat in a jeep looking out over the Atlantic Ocean thinking about his wife Laurie. Oddly enough their marriage was in better shape because of her affair; yet more was needed to repair the years of bitterness and anger. If that was letting his wife date another guy so be it. So far it seemed to be working, but then it was early, an experiment with no guarantees.

True love is not measured by possession and holding on but in the letting go and trusting that it is meant to be. Ironically it was precisely how their relationship had begun, free of 'expectations'. Too often a marriage becomes a prison of failed expectations. Rick had, by discarding social convention, opened his marriage to a third party hoping that his wife would be happier while they worked on their relationship. As an immediate result his relationship with his wife was more loving and caring. They were both happier for the time being and for the moment that was enough.

Chapter 2
The Rusty Torpedo

AT THE AGE of 14 Rick had a unique view of the world. One of the many influences on his upbringing was his unique experience of nineteenth-century farm life on his great-grandfather's farm. His great- grandfather used his horses until the late 1970s when his two horses died. Prince and Charlie were shires, draught horses that made a Clydesdale look like a pony. He'd inherited his farm from his father, who had inherited it from his father and so on, dating back to the early 1800s.

What mechanical implements he had were ancient tractors that dated back to the late 1940s, and those his grandpa referred to as the "new tractors" that he used only to spare his horses when the weather was bad. Sitting in a barn situated in a dell deep in the timber was a Case steam tractor. It had been purchased new in 1912 and was used regularly, mostly in the winter or when they needed to bale hay or to plow a field that was too big for the horses to plow efficiently. The barn had been built around it by his father when they first bought it when they realized, that it was too wide and far too heavy for the driveway. At first they kept it in the dell, covering it with an old canvas tarp to keep the cab dry. As it was one of the more expensive pieces of farm equipment, an investment in the farm's ability to make a profit, a barn was built around it to keep it from rusting away.

During the hay season, it was hooked up to the hay elevator and used to load hay bales in the loft. In the winter, it was hooked up to a wood splitter and used to split the deadfall trees they used as firewood, both for the tractor itself and to heat the house. In its day it had been an indispensable work- saving device that increased the farm's productivity. Yet the tractor itself was a labor-intensive piece of equipment and was, after the purchase of the new tractors in 1948, relegated to winter plow duties and hay-bale loading.

It was in this barn, sitting in the cab of the ancient steam tractor where Rick often thought about his future. It was in this place of peaceful solitude that he developed his sense of who he was while planning his future, which, of course, included becoming a million-aire, marrying a hot wife, and fixing the ails of this world. Being that he was a teenager, his thoughts most often dwelled on naked women, girls, and whether or not a knothole would make a passable substitute for a pussy.

Bees were a strong argument against *that* idea, as was having to ex-plain a bee sting to his particulars, as well as possibly having it swell up and get stuck in the knothole, pretty heavy thinking *for a teenager*. His most cognitive times, he had other things to contemplate, such as social morality and the many doubts he had discovered in school, specifically in the church basement while on the many detentions he spent there.

Earlier that year, he found himself in the church basement on a lunch-time detention assignment, reorganizing National Geographic magazines in order of their publication date. It was punishment for guzzling a Pepsi then belching into Cindy Cybarts' new perm. It was a perfect three second carbonated explosion that he hadn't really intended but did nothing to stop after she had whipped her new frizzy perm in his face while getting into line for lunch. Her curls had settled onto his face and nose just as the gas bubble erupted from his stomach in a three-second blast of carbonated revenge.

His friends thought it was hilarious, the teacher, not so much. Neither did Cindy, she ran into the gym showers screaming as if her air was on fire to rinse the Pepsi residue from her curls. The laughs he got were worth the detention he received, not to mention a satisfactory bit of revenge on Cindy for spitting in his lunch the day before. He often wondered why they never became friends.

There were at least 2000 magazines to organize, with duplicate issues from donations over the years. It was a mindless, time consuming task that he worked at for two hours straight before taking a break. It was then he heard voices and footfalls on the far side of the basement.

He recognized the voice of the Pastors wife who was a busty, attractive woman. Rick always had a weakness for big tits. She dressed in attire commensurate to her status as the pastor's wife and her demeanor was equally conservative in public, if not in private as he was about to learn. At first her voice was normal but the echoes of the basement blurred her words as they came down stairs. A male voice laughed softly as they both entered the basement and closed the door behind them. The lock being set echoed loudly.

"Hank, go lock that other door, do it quietly. If it's locked they won't be able to get in unless they go get the key in the office'. She giggled...'and I have it in my pocket. So...' she said coyly 'we have at least 30 minutes to ourselves" The man was a leading member of the church and a local banker; a handsome and clean-cut man whose wife did not believe in recreational sex. The preacher was of the same mind. So each having needs and none of them being met they took to the church basement on weekday afternoons as school settled in for lunch to address their needs, forbidden though they were.

Rick got an earful as the Preachers wife and the banker abused a bingo table that autumn afternoon. Bingo would have a very different meaning for him after that. Especially after seeing the preachers wives tits jiggling and open to the air as she got pounded. The banker's amorous grunts reminded Rick of a dying squirrel. He hoped to God that when his time came he didn't make noises like that.

He did not he say a word to anyone about it because he wanted to see if he could catch them at it again with earplugs if possible because the noises the banker made were not noises he needed to hear again. He never did catch them again but he did find the basement doors locked on occasion with the faint sound of a dying squirrel within.

His wife apparently needed something similar to what the preacher's wife needed. It had been that event he'd considered while listening to his wife on the phone with 'Greg'. He remembered how sad the preacher's wife seemed even as she took the banker into her. A sadness that her life expectations had not measured up forcing her to take measures she didn't approve of to satisfy her needs as a woman. The preacher had been an old fud and considerably older than she was. It was assumed that he couldn't do the job, though a later incident would prove otherwise.

The preacher's wives infidelity had not been an isolated incident as

Rick would later find out. Having an affair was, it seemed, a favorite pass time in his old home town. First the preacher got caught by his wife with the same banker's wife, the church organ player and two members of the choir, at the same time on the same bingo table, which they had apparently broken in half. The preacher was said to have nearly broken a hip and limped about the town for weeks afterward. The banker's wife also walked sort of funny for a while because she was riding the pastor when the table broke.

Then it was discovered that three wives in the congregation had been sleeping with the same high school football player, who wasn't just mowing their lawns, he had been plowing their gardens as well. That story broke when one of the women got pregnant after her husband got a vasectomy and hadn't told his wife.

A host of tawdry tales kept the gossip channels fired up. Ole Richmond wasn't the sleepy little farm town initial appearances would suggest. Yet the pretense of a respectable, conservative church going community continued on as if everything was just fine. It was in witnessing these many acts of 'hypocrisy' that began to turn him away from the 'sheep' mentality that Rick had come to recognize as a social plague. His mind had been opened to more diverse methods of conducting life leaving hypocrisy of 'church' and 'socially accept-able' behavior in the dust that covered those national geographic magazines.

As the years went by Rick grew intolerant of the bullshit that went with social decorum, so he became a loner. After a while he came to prefer it because being alone he didn't have to change to suit some-one else. This changed however, when he discovered 'older women' who knew how to change a man's mind. An older woman did not play games and knew what they wanted and made no bones about it.

Not only were older women less stressful to date, they tended to be less inhibited and far more adventurous in the bedroom not to mention more assertive where their wants were concerned.

His adventures with older women weren't limited to the bedroom either. In fact the bedroom was rarely visited whereas open fields, restaurants, theaters, public piers and on one occasion inside the shrubbery of a busy mall on a Saturday afternoon. The ability to speak, walk and think often escaped him thanks to the ministrations of a well-practiced and artfully minded woman. It was during this period where he came into his own way of thinking, being and doing. The simple act of dating a woman who didn't play games and who allowed him to be who he was enabled him to develop into a more functionally mature adult.

However, this also included a few close calls where the women he dated turned out to be married. Too often he'd found himself leaping naked from the second story window of a woman's bedroom when her husband came home early. The phrase "Oh god my husband is home" was, for a while, a common phrase to be heard as he addressed his growth into manhood, a phase he luckily survived. He did not hold it against the women however. Clearly they needed something their husbands weren't able to provide anymore. Either that or marriage hadn't lived up to their expectations. They had become disillusioned, bored and completely dissatisfied with life, so in desperation, boredom or whatever it was that drove them, these women sought the excitement taking a lover provided. Insights he'd obtained from talking to and dating older women.

Women were not unlike men and shared similar reasons for cheating, though a double-standard plagued women with unreasonable expectations that they were somehow immune to such tawdry, selfish desires. Nobody wants to think that mom ever fooled around, whereas it was sort of expected from dad. Though few people would actually put it to words, it was an unspoken and accepted double standard. Some were divorced and from them he learned what 'expectations' had been forced upon them as girls and on and how difficult it was to express their wants without being labeled a slut, whore or whatever else society labeled a sexually independent woman.

Too many women placed importance on what society expected. Even in the 21st century women were held to the same double standard that weighed heavily on their abilities as functional members of society. It was most often while he lay naked next to these women panting and covered with sweat where he learned just how complex and sensitive they were, something that he found intoxicating and alluring.

Another thing he appreciated was the way they actually talked to him like he had a brain and could understand English. Too often the younger 'girls' he'd dated were themselves trying to find out who they were and had no clue how to be natural. So either they emulated some person or character they wanted to be like or they overcompensated by being 'bitchy' as a means of putting on the air of independence. After dating several self-assured and sexually independent women Rick was done dating women under 25. There was no room in his life for bullshit, until he met his wife.

For some reason his independence went out the door with her. She got away with 'some' BS but not much. They seemed a good match for each other, as life would have it things got tougher and tougher as they each learned what they would and would not tolerate. After a while Laurie seemed to expect him to knuckle under while Laurie felt Rick wanted her to whore up a bit, which he admitted was true. C'mon…*what man doesn't want that*…really?

The word was compromise…after a while the word meant nothing to either of them and so each began building up defenses against what they each saw as an attack on their 'independence.' The result being a total breakdown in their relationship to where Laurie found absolutely nothing wrong with seeking out and engaging a lover and where Rick was content to hide from his marriage by staying at his office hours and hours after he had closed up. This was how Rick found himself sitting on a lonely jetty 2000 miles from home while his wife enjoyed the company of another man in their bed.

After two days of abject boredom and soul searching Rick was getting restless. It was his habit to avoid tourist traps and crowds, but on this day he decided to mix it up and see what the 'tourists' were doing. After checking out a submarine tour in which a two man mini sub was used to drive in circles on the bottom of the lagoon he opted for renting a kayak after he found the sub cost $150.00 for a 20-minute ride. Renting a kayak was more to his taste and wouldn't wreck his pocket book. Also in a kayak he could be alone and not be bothered by other people.

His thoughts were with his wife as he drove to the beachfront. They'd had a long talk that morning. She was growing more and more comfortable with discussing Greg openly while not their activities. Because of this new found freedom she felt like a new person, more alive and more adventurous. No longer trapped in her marriage she began a new chapter in her sexuality and her marriage. That morning they had agreed that she would see Greg when she wanted to but not when the kids were around.

As it happened the kids were at her mother's for the weekend giving her the freedom to invite Greg over. In fact he was lying in their bed sleeping off their evenings activities while they spoke over coffee that morning. Laurie didn't bother to mention 'that' on the off chance that Rick might, in fit of jealousy, change his mind about letting her see Greg. They both agreed that their new lifestyle would be kept from her mother, a point they both chuckled about. Laurie chuckled knowing that her mother already knew of her tryst. But she didn't share that with her husband and was not quite sure that she would. It was the first time they'd laughed together in a long time, granted for very different reasons.

Laughter was something they both needed and it helped them to realize, down deep, that they still loved each other. It was a new dynamic for sure but it was easier, less stiff and much less angry. For the next hour they talked and had their morning coffee over the phone, like an actual couple and not an old married couple biting each other's heads off; Laurie in her robe at the kitchen table and Rick 2000 miles away in a bungalow, watching sharks rip the wood off his deck. It was the start of a warmer and very different sort of marriage for them, no less loving, just unconventional, very unconventional.

Later while walking along the beachfront Rick was looking at dive shops and kayak tours. He heard rumors of treasure galleons loaded with gold and silver which kept the dive shops busy. Enough gold was found to keep the stories alive. In truth the dive shops dumped hundreds of cheap counterfeits all over the bay to give their clients something to find.

He was about to rent a Kayak when the beachfront was closed because of a shark attack. Apparently a large Bull Shark bit into the hull of a kayak and panicked the occupant who happened to be the same woman who had deafened him on the plane. He wondered how she ever fit her huge ass into a kayak without sinking it, then thought "Poor shark".

Since he could no longer do as he had planned he decided to drive along the coast and up the mountain if he could find a way up. One of the tour guides had warned him to stay on the roads and away from the interior of the island because the police didn't patrol out there, so if he got stuck he'd have to walk back and that it was private property. It was a large island but the bulk of activities were confined to one corner of it leaving the rest of the island uninhabited and untouched by development, ripe for exploration. Being a bit anti-social it was a perfect situation for Rick.

On initial observation it didn't seem as though there was any reason to prohibit development. On the southern end of the island was a conical mountain of about 1000 feet if he had to guess. It was covered with foliage from the base all the way to the top. There was something that appeared to be a spiral roadway up the mountain but it didn't appear to have been used or maintained in a very long time, if it was even a road. As he was turning to watch a boat leave the harbor a gust of wind caused the trees on top of the mountain to sway exposing what appeared to be the roof of a building, sparking his curiosity.

He was feeling irritable after eating breakfast so he paid his bill and left the Jeep parked to walk off breakfast and settle down. He was in the process of debating whether or not to buy a T-shirt with geckos in various sexual positions when the 50 dollars price tag killed any interest he had in it. It was one thing to pay 20 bucks for a shirt to wear on vacation but paying 50 bucks for a T-Shirt wasn't happening. He dropped the over-priced T-shirt unceremoniously onto the pile eying a rack of brightly colored Hawaiian shirts for $20.00. "Now that's more like it" he muttered and bought two.

Tossing the two shirts in a shopping bag he made his way down the street where piles and piles of useless 'made in china' crap filled the available space. It was disappointing to discover that it was all the same type of cheap crap he could buy at the dollar store. As a result it wasn't long before he tired of being jostled about by fat, sweaty tourists and rude clerks with fake Jamaican accents.

Stepping out into the middle of the square to be clear of the crowd he stood alone for a moment deciding what to do next when he spotted a church. The white stucco exterior and red tile roof and a belfry made it stand out from the newer commercial buildings surrounding it. The church dominated the square leaving the lesser buildings diminished by its character.

It was then he noticed a mid-western family with mom leading the way and dad slugging behind two pre-teenaged daughters looking as if he'd rather be taking a nap or playing golf, *anything* but what he was doing but knew better than to say so. Rick grinned in sympathy for the man feeling his pain. "Oh look' his wife cried 'A maritime museum!!" and she pointed at the church. It was then he noticed a small sign that said 'St. Vincent Island maritime museum' Est.1985.

Watching the family walk by he noticed an elderly man, dressed in a linen suit sitting on a bench immediately in front of the church. The old man watched the woman letting a good-humored smirk surface as she passed. He had close-cropped hair, which gave him the look of an old soldier, but his demeanor also suggested that he'd been military, as many of his generation had been. Rick guessed his age to be about 80 or more. There was vitality in this man that age had not erased. Clearly he'd been an impressively built man in his youth. Even now, he appeared to be well muscled and toned. He watched the man as he in turn watched the woman.

When the old man turned his head back their eyes met briefly and a glint of fear surfaced in the old man's eyes. Rick smiled then nodded at him to ease the tension and turned to observe the woman they'd both noticed. On impulse Rick decided to go inside the church/museum to see what was inside.

The late morning sun was blazing overhead as he stepped into the dark entry hall. Rick was immediately aware of a heavy, musty odor typical of poorly ventilated buildings in the tropics. He stood in the doorway letting his eyes adjust. To his right he spied the donation box typically found in a church alcove. On it was a white plaque that said. "The museum is open to the public, but we rely on donations to keep our doors open Thank You."

The old man on the bench watched Rick disappear into the museum. Once the man was out of sight, he got up and moved quickly down the street and away from the strange man. His heart began to pound painfully in his chest as he did so forcing him to take several deep breaths to help calm his heart down otherwise he risked his heart going into v-fib.

Back in the museum strolling through the dimly lit displays Rick saw very few items that interested him. In one case were the corroded remains of a flintlock pistol or musket. The wood had long since rotted away leaving the brass fittings covered with bits of coral and corrosion. Each case seemed to hold similar sorts of items. After 20 minutes he was ready to leave. Nothing interested him and there were other things he would rather be doing.

In a moment of indecision he spied the family he had followed into the museum. The kids were standing around obviously bored as they followed 'mom' as she moved excitedly from one display to another gasping and oohing at the thing's she found interesting and exciting. It was clear that she had never been anywhere and was relishing the newness of her discoveries oblivious to the sighs of impatience from her daughters. Her husband, a tall lanky mid-western auto worker by the looks of him was eyeing the exit with his hands shoved in his pockets clearly 'not' interested in 'crap' found on a beach, which is what most of the stuff was. But he knew better than to put these thoughts to words, wisdom that comes from being a married man who wants to keep his balls attached to his body.

Just as he was about to leave, on the far side of the room, he saw a rusty torpedo. The sign on the case said that it was a German WWII torpedo found by a diver in a coral trench a mile off shore. The Coast Guard removed the warhead then donated the casing to the museum. In a case next to it were items found in the vicinity of the torpedo, a rusted German helmet, a boot, belt buckle and a hunk of corrosion that had once been an MP40 machine pistol. The clip and gun had been rendered useless by corrosion. The only way one could tell it had been a gun was by the general shape of it otherwise it appeared to be nothing more than a misshapen bit of rusted metal laced with coral and barnacles.

The sign in front of the display was a brief description of the items and their suspected uses and a brief statement as to why they believed the items were found in the Caribbean.

The torpedo was an electric drive torpedo used by the German navy in the late stages of the war. It had been armed when found though the years of saltwater exposure likely rendered the warhead inert; was disarmed by the Coast Guard EOD team and detonated at sea with other ordinance set for disposal. It may have been fired by a Type 7 U-boat Germany's most successful design. Type-7s were capable of trans-Atlantic crossings and operating for several weeks along the coast or briefly deep into the Gulf of Mexico. (See map on wall to your left)

Though there were no reports of any attacks in this vicinity during the war it is speculated that the torpedo seen here was fired at a merchant ship and missed. No engagements were recorded in the area other than a depth bomb attack on an unconfirmed sighting of a submarine cruising on the surface, a few weeks following the surrender of Germany.

Upon discovering the torpedo several attempts were made to locate a sunken submarine with no success. Given the timing of the sighting 'weeks after VE day' it was likely that a diving whale had been spotted by the inexperienced crew had mistaken for a rogue submarine. There is no doubt that German submarines did operate in the area during the war but there is no record of an engagement near St. Vincent; The helmet, boot and machine pistol were likely worn by a sailor who was washed overboard in a storm.

Rick had always been interested in WWII, particularly where German submarines were concerned, especially since he had been a submarine sailor himself, albeit on a nuclear submarine. His interest peaked as he contemplated the poor sailor who had once worn or used those items. Moving to the next case he recognized the shape of a Luger pistol, again corroded beyond use but still retaining the distinctive shape of a Luger. Next to it lay the dried out, rotted remains of its holster and web belt along with several clips for both the machine gun and pistol. All of these items were found near where the torpedo was found.

Rick was beginning to doubt that it was mere coincidence that these items were found so close together. Clearly something had happened that caused these items to fall into the sea, something catastrophic, but what? The sub had not been sunk, at least not in the area, which is what you'd expect. Was it damaged but not sunk; did it sink later? So much time had passed that an answer was not likely, not now. There was the fog of war itself, the aftermath of war and the many years in which hurricanes struck and millions of fish had nibbled bits and pieces of evidence away and shit them out among the countless crevasses in the coral reef that had grown, died and been broken off since these items fell to the bottom. "Too much to contemplate while on vacation" he thought.

His attention turned to the wall map behind the display cases. It was a chart of the Gulf of Mexico. On it were pins of various colors indicating the difference between a submarine 'sighting', an attack by a submarine and confirmed sinking of a submarine. White pins indicated a confirmed sighting of a submarine. Red pins indicated an attack by a submarine. The Red pins were often accompanied by a yellow pin indicating sinking that resulted from the attack; Orange pins indicated an attack on a submarine but no sinking, where Black pins indicated attacks on U-boats with a confirmed kill.

Studying the map he noted that there were a lot of red pins in the western Gulf, more than he would have expected. There were a lot of yellow pins on shore indicating that the sub had either shelled the facilities or fired torpedoes at the oil delivery systems that loaded tankers that were later to link up with convoys heading to either the Pacific or Atlantic.

On the Texas coast the yellow pins were concentrated most heavily in Brownsville and Corpus Christi. Moving north towards New Orleans, Mobile, Tampa and other Gulf Coast cities where ships had congregated to take on supplies, fuel and other war materials needed at the front. Submarines were sighted and attacked with relatively few kills confirmed. The center of the map was clear of pins with the exception of a few white pins. Scanning the map he noticed a grouping of white pins near the very island he was vacationing on.

There were about six pins indicating sighting of submarines transiting the surface dating back to 1940 all the way through 1945. One pin caught his attention. The last sighting had been dated June 7th 1945, a full month following the surrender of Germany, sighted by a soldier on a Liberty ship heading for Galveston Texas.

However the person making the report wasn't taken seriously until ten other passengers and crew reported the same thing. By the time a search was mounted the submarine was long gone. "Fugitive Nazis heading to South America no doubt" he said to himself. He then noticed an old man walked into the room from what had once been the church office but which now served as museum administration.

Looking around the mid-western family had gone and he and the old man were the only ones left. The old man walked with the vigor of a much younger man. Stepping in front of the torpedo he pulled out a book and turned to a page and looked at something in the book and then something on the torpedo. He stared intently at the torpedo as if hoping it would somehow speak to him. Without warning the old man threw the book at the case and swore viciously.

The book landed at Rick's feet as the old man leaned angrily against the case staring at the torpedo, clearly frustrated. Picking up the book he walked silently toward the old man and laid it on the counter next to him. It was a moment before the old man noticed he was there. "Oh, er...uhm..Sorry about that I wasn't aware that you were still here son. I do apologize for that little outburst" He said. "I had a bet with a friend about the serial numbers and it turns out he was correct. It cost me a $100.00."

A man of about 80 stood before him wearing the clerical collar of a protestant minister. He like the man outside had the close-cropped haircut and the hardened appearance of a soldier for whom the war would never be over. His hard steel blue eyes were alert and did not betray the 80+ years of living behind them. "My name is Archie, Archie Davis. I was once pastor in this church before the congregation left and the tourists moved in. However, the diocese did not wish to lose the property and thus converted it to a public charity. I was retained as caretaker and curator" he said waving a hand around indicating the old church. "Not exactly the sort of retirement I'd planned, but it could be worse".

Archie moved up to the map and stood before it. A hard look of knowing surfaced "I noticed you looking at this map rather intently earlier. Did you notice anything 'strange' about it?" he asked with a look of cunning.

Without hesitating Rick answered "Yes, I saw that there was a submarine sighted off this island in June of 1945 a month after the war in Europe ended. Very likely a boat load of fugitive Nazis escaping to South America" he said.

Archie nodded approval "You are among the very few who would see that pin and realize what it *might* mean' he paused then continued 'It's a sad testament to the education our youth has been receiving of late." Then waiving a hand at the map he said "You are partially correct about fugitive Nazis but not in the way you might think. Why, if they were heading to South America would they be here when it was much easier to remain far out to sea and head straight to Argentina?"

Rick knew that German Subs could not make the transit from Norway, which was where that sub had to leave from, to Argentina without refueling. "A refueling stop?" he suggested.

At that Archie clapped his hands in delight and exclaimed "Precisely. They had to be here only for a refueling stop if they hoped to make it the rest of the way to Argentina, That is' he paused *'if they were going to Argentina."* He added with emphasis giving Rick a look that suggested there was more to the story.

He paused for a very long time staring at the map and then back at Rick as if debating something in his mind. Then without warning he pointed at the map "Very seldom did the Germans ever follow the same route twice. Yet, here we have a series of sighting in exactly the same place. That seldom happened unless the sub was entering a port or heading somewhere specific so that they 'had' to follow that route to get there. Each of these sightings placed the sub no less than a mile off shore of this very island on the surface. At no time were they seen again...once disappearing past the point 'here'" and he pointed to a finger of land that represented the southern tip of the island.

He looked directly at Rick and asked "What do you suppose happened to them?"

Rick shrugged. "It's obvious they dove, but on battery power they'd have to surface somewhere. Unless they had a base they could reach under battery power" he said. Then it dawned on him that this island might be where they were headed...but that was too fantastic, so he said nothing.

Archie nodded agreement "With the exception of these six sightings no other sub was spotted within a hundred miles of this island and they weren't snorkeling and making a bare ten knots vs. their usual 20 knots on surface. That and no attacks were launched within a one hundred mile radius from the island center." Again Archie looked at Rick as if deciding something. "There is a lot more to this story to tell but there are few people who would appreciate the sort of thing I have to tell, if you have time to hear it." Rick nodded eagerly.

"Ok, then why don't we retire to my residence and I'll make us some tea. Then I'll fill you in on the rest of the story."

Chapter 3
The Old Soldier

STANDARTENFURHER HANS BECK of the Waffen SS, veteran of the Winter War and countless engagements during the war, walked the sidewalk of St. Vincent village with the fluid ease of a much younger man and not one of 88 years. What vitality one might observe on the outside years of living on the run had worn down on the inside. He could no longer get agitated or angry because of his heart condition. It went bad while living in Switzerland, when he realized that Odessa, an organization of former SS, was on the hunt for him. They were looking to take the money he made on the black market during the war and punish him for not joining in the guerilla war Hitler had ordered.

It was Odessa's view that his black market activities were not SS sanctioned therefore subject to seizure once the bank account numbers were beaten out of him. He would then be shot. The fact was that most of the SS failed to join the guerilla war to keep from getting hung. The absurdity of their behaving as if they had the 'authority' to punish him both angered and offended him as a German. Their hunting him was out of greed and nothing more. The 'excuse' they were using was just that, an excuse to behave like the animals they were. That he had been one of them sickened him like poison.

Also the fact that he had been on an island in the middle of the Caribbean Sea on a mission for the SS would do no good since he was the sole survivor with nobody to verify his story. Then there was the fact that it was such an insane mission that nobody with a grain of sense would believe him anyway.

His pulse quickened and his heart beat painfully in his chest. "Calm yourself Hans" he said taking another calming breath. "He might just be a tourist, only a tourist" His hands were shaking with early Parkinson's as he walked to his car, a malady that got worse the more agitated and nervous he got. Parked next to the beach sidewalk was a powder blue 1973 Fiat Spider he'd restored. It was one of many cars he'd built over the years. He'd never owned a 'new' car and was always drawn to the cars that stirred him. To Hans a car was an extension of the person within and was something you couldn't just 'buy' on a lot somewhere. To him you had to find the car connect with it and then make it 'yours'.

When he'd tire of a car he was driving he'd sell it to a museum or a collector who he knew would 'save' the car for generations to come, never to a person on the street. Cars had always been a passion of his, almost a religion, especially sports cars, the faster the better. As he got older his needs changed to dependable easy driving cars that caught his fancy. This one he had found in Florida on one of his many trips there. He often traveled to Florida just to drive along the American Highways and to visit his chiropractor to keep himself mobile.

He transported it back to the Island where he worked a full year rebuilding it to its original state. Only he had added a German electrical system and ignition system to ensure it was reliable. Fiats were notorious for their poor electrical systems. "Almost as bad as the

Brits" he thought to himself. It fired immediately and ran perfectly as he had come to expect with cars he built.

One of his absolute favorites was a hybrid sports car combining the style of a Triumph Spitfire and the drive train of an Buick Grand National and of course a German electrical system. The combination resulted in an insanely fast car with a proper growl and a power band that never ended. He never tired of driving it. In fact he refused to sell it because he enjoyed driving it so much. It was the car he kept in Florida. The Fiat Spider was perfect for the island. Not too big, not excessively powerful it was just right for running about. But he had other things to be concerned about and it had nothing to do with cars.

His concern was that Odessa had found him again. It had been over 30 years since his last run in with them and he was in no hurry to meet them again. Pulling into the driveway of his villa he remained in his car considering his options. The man outside the church hadn't seemed threatening but then he couldn't take any chances either. So he decided to drive up the mountain and lay low, just in case.

He had taken to spending weekends on the mountaintop and found it to be a peaceful getaway. Also the temperatures on the top of the mountain were cooler and the breezes more constant. Also unwanted guests could be seen coming miles away. That and the only way up the mountain was secret and all other entrances were sealed off, inaccessible or hidden.

Ten minutes later Hans tossed his pre-packed duffle bag into the trunk and a Luger pistol in his glove box. That morning his friend had called him saying that he was being watched by two suspicious men, hence the immediate apprehension of seeing the strange man outside the church. He'd fit the description of one of the men his friend suspected of watching him and both had good reason to be wary. The secret they shared was one that if compromised could lead to the rise of another Nazi regime, something neither man was prepared to allow.

Hans phoned his friend and let him know that he intended to lay low on the mountain for a few days and suggested that he do the same. That done, he drove directly out of town and onto a secret roadway they had created for the purpose; a private road hidden deep in the scrub that covered the island. On the drive up he let his mind drift to his wife Sarah.

***Switzerland 1970 ***

Hans was elbow deep in grease working on a 1936 Mercedes Benz SSK Roadster he'd found in a barn a year before. It was almost completed and he was impatient to take it for a drive. Looking at his watch he was startled to realize that it was nearly 2am and he'd told Sarah that he'd be in by dinner. Sarah was not the kind to be upset or angry for his lapses. They'd been married 20 years and had yet to have a single disagreement much less a fight. They met in 1948 and married in 1950 never to spend a single day apart again. Sarah was barren due to a bomb blast in 1943 that had ruptured her uterus forcing doctors to perform an emergency hysterectomy to save her life as a result they had no children.

They had purchased a farm along the German border in the spring of 1951 and lived a simple peaceful life in the Alps. Every year they'd travel to Greece, Portugal and the South of Spain to enjoy the warmer climes they offered. Hans had even purchased a villa in Portugal overlooking the Atlantic so they could stay for extended periods if they wanted. But their favorite place was the farm and when there they seldom left it spending most of their time making love. Sarah was an uninhibited lover as well as a shameless exhibitionist. He loved her with all his heart and she him.

Putting the wrench down, he wiped his hands with one of the many rags he'd had lying around the barn and headed for the door. Turning out the light before he opened the door had saved him. When he stepped out into the yard he saw three men dressed in black carrying what he recognized to be MP40 machine pistols running across his lawn and into his house. Without thinking he rushed to his footlocker and pulled out his own MP40, which he had kept close by since learning of Odessa being on the hunt for him. His was modified to shoot .357 magnum rounds with a silencer permanently mounted. He wanted a gun that punched harder and went further but which nobody could hear. This gun had been known to knock down adult pine trees with three shots at 100 meters.

Grabbing several clips he shoved them into his pockets and rammed one home and pulled back the slide and flipped off the safety. With the skill of an old soldier, remembering his war experiences he crouched and ran to his house. The door was open so he went through, just as he passed through the kitchen he heard their boots kicking in the door of his bedroom, Sarah who had been asleep screamed and was immediately shot. Hans knew she'd been killed when her screaming stopped cold. Tears filled his eyes as a deadly resolve surfaced. He might die and gladly to be with her...but every last one of those bastards would die first.

Steeling himself, he knelt down in the shadows of his kitchen shouldering his machine pistol as tears clouded his vision. Her death was his fault and the consequences of his past had caused her to die by mistake. He was about to break down completely when he heard their voices in his room. "Dammit Stephen, you didn't have to shoot her. I thought you said he'd be here Paul. Where is he?"

"He never left. I saw him enter the house. His car never left the park and there isn't any way off the property except through the gate and nobody left" replied an excited, quivering voice.

"Then he must still be here, radio Bruno to keep an eye on the gate. He may be in the barn working on one of his cars. Maybe he fell asleep out there. One by one they left the bedroom leaving their machine pistols dangling from their shoulder straps as they descended the stairs in single file. A silenced Phoot, phoot, phoot filled the night as each of the invaders took a bullet to the head spraying gore over the wall. One by one they fell in a heap on the foyer. With the steady, cold hands of a soldier Hans took their weapons and their clips and added one extra bullet to each skull to ensure that he had finished them.

Slowly he climbed the stairs hoping that Sarah was alive, knowing that she wasn't. His brain would not allow that idea to form until he saw for himself that his love, his reason for living, was gone. Entering his room, pushing the door open he gasped in horror seeing the blood from his beloved wife sprayed on the wall behind her. Sarah was sprawled on her back with a bullet hole in her forehead, eyes open and the look of terror etched on her face as she saw three armed men enter her room.

She'd put on her favorite nighty, thinking of seducing him when he finally did come in from the barn. Hans fell to his knees next to his wife "Sarah? Sarah? Please...don't be dead...Please let this be a bad dream...God let me wake up...Please let me wake up!!" he sobbed.

He cradled her in his arms until the cold, gray dawn lit up the eastern sky.

Cold salt stains from his tears covered his aged face as he stared blankly into his life without Sarah. Laying his wife on her side of the bed he pulled the blankets over her, still hoping to wake from this horrible nightmare. Perhaps, if she is in her bed...she'll wake up next to me. Perhaps yet...I'll wake up and this whole thing will be over. She was not to wake and his nightmare was not to end. Sarah his love and reason for being was gone.

Out of the corner of his eye he saw at this front gate the cherry of a cigarette being tossed away. He'd forgotten about the ones at the gate. Fresh, angry tears fell as he reached for his gun ramming home a fresh clip. Calling the police to report what had happened he hung up and marched directly and deliberately out his front door ready for his life to end but only after he'd finished with the bastards who had invaded his home, his life.

An insane rage filled his heart, rage he'd not felt since the day his family had been killed by an American bomb. Then his anger had been directed at the Americans, now it was directed at the men at his front gate. Three men sat in a black Mercedes sedan. He'd grabbed the radio of one of their comrades lying at the foot of his stairs. The radio crackled as they called to their friends...now dead.

The dark of the early morning kept Hans from being recognized until it was too late. "A window opened. "Did you get him? Did you find out where his money is?" The driver asked as he puffed on a cigarette. "Well? Where is it, where are the others?" the voice demanded.

Hans stopped. "Money?!!! Is that why you killed my wife?!! He yelled lifting his pistol "You bastards!!! You came here, to my home for money? You killed my wife for money?" Han's body shook with inconsolable rage as he stood staring at the men in the car. The driver took a long drag from his cigarette, fear nowhere to be seen, a true psychopath, a perfect Nazi.

Hans caught movement in the corner of his eye and his soldiers reflexes instantly raised the gun barrel to the perfect height and sprayed the back seat with bullets killing the two who had trained their guns on him. Still the driver didn't so much as flinch or even dodge the bullets flying inches from his face. He didn't even blink but raised his cigarette to his lips and looked out the window as if talking to a neighbor or a friend.

"Yes, Standartenfurher, Odessa is displeased that you made money on the back of the war. It is our view that you 'stole' from the Reich contributing to its defeat and dishonoring the SS." His tone was that of self-righteous indignation.

Hans let a chuckle of insane rage escape his lungs. "What money I made on the black market was from our leadership exchanging gold for cash to escape the gallows. They were rats abandoning a sinking ship, a ship they sank and you dare to accuse me of contributing to Germany's defeat? I fought in the Winter War witnessed horrors 'you' have never seen, dedicated my life, my troops and my actions to saving Germany" his barrel leveled at the driver. "It was you and your kind who defeated Germany before the war even started. Now your insane dedication to a cause that killed millions of Germans just killed my wife...for money." His rage was ready to explode but he resisted his urge to cut the man in half only because he was curious to know why, after 25 years they had bothered with him.

The driver turned off the car and opened the door getting out as casually as if it were any other day. It was still too dark to see the drivers face. "Hans, The SS dedicated itself to Adolf Hitler...not to Germany. Our cause was to see his vision realized, a pure Arian race leading the world to a greater tomorrow. We are doing that as we speak, even now...we SS are leading the world by the nose directing governments to do our bidding. We've been able to do so much more...as a shadow government. We control the British Parliament, the American Congress even the President of the United States. And it is through 'money' that we are able to buy and sell these 'politicians' so easily.

Who do you think really had Kennedy Killed? I'll tell you this it wasn't that communist dolt Oswald. He was set up by our Russian contingent. Kennedy resisted our efforts to turn him so we had the soviets set up Oswald then we had two French Comrades from the War shoot him one from the storm drain in the street and another under a tree on a grassy knoll. We have them on assignment in South Africa containing troublesome Africans for our friends there. The Soviet Government has long since been ours" taking a drag from his cigarette he inhaled enjoying his smoke. "Yes, we've discovered that the Russians hate Jews even more than we do and are better at killing them to. Of course it's a much larger country so hiding the ashes is much easier." The driver casually leaned on the fender of the car, crossed his ankles and continued. "Since the forming of Israel we've been funding the PLO and other Arab nations in their effort to eradicate the Jewish state."

"So the Six Day War was you're doing?" Hans asked.

The driver nodded. "Not exactly the success we were hoping for but what can you expect from Arabs? They're usually fighting among themselves if they're not attacking Israel. The Israelis on the other hand have discipline, training and American money, tanks and aircraft to help them".

Hans scoffed "So, the fact that they were surrounded on all sides and still managed to beat back a simultaneous attack from Jordan, Syria and Egypt was due to American backing? I'd say tactics and dedication to a worthy cause was more like it."

The driver looked up clearly affronted by his SS comrade's praise of the Israelis. "What cause could the Jew have that was 'worthy'?" He retorted.

Hans never wavered nor did he drop his gun for a moment but pointed it more directly at his antagonists' chest. "Protection of their families for one, Jews love their children and wives just as fiercely as anyone else, you've dedicated your life to murdering a race of human beings simply because you bought into that 'Master Race' shit. My God, you are pathetic. That I counted myself among the likes of you disgusts me." He hissed as his body seethed with rage and anguish finding it more and more difficult to restrain his trigger finger.

The driver lowered his head menacingly and said in a low, dangerous voice "Careful there, you forget that you are SS. I could have you shot for that".

Hans laughed bitterly at his antagonist. "We are no longer SS!! The War is over and the Reich is no more. Odessa is a criminal organization filled with psychopaths and malcontents who still believe in a dead man. The world killed the Reich because of inbred morons like you believed they deserved to rule because they had blue eyes and blonde hair. Hitler was insane!! We all followed him because we were desperate. Only he destroyed our homeland and many others for his vision of racial purity and a non-existent Master Race. Look at you; you had to raid my home to find money you believe was yours to take because of that insane 'oath'. An Oath that ceased to have meaning the moment Hitler shot himself in the mouth." Hans felt the rage build as this insane man stared at him.

The driver was losing his patients but kept his composure. "I'm sorry to hear you say that. I still believe in the ideal he stood for. It is clear that you were not as dedicated as the rest of us Hans, pity. Anyway, getting back to Israel...Apparently those we control in the American Congress haven't been able to remove US aid to the Israelis. The KKK is no longer as influential as it was when we first infiltrated it. We've had to expand to more sophisticated and less obvious sources for support. Still, the Jews have a steadfast ally in the United States, but not for long."

Tossing his cigarette on the ground the distant sound of police sirens broke the morning quiet. "You've called the police?" the driver asked sounding astonished and even worried. "You fool!! I was going to give you a reprieve if you turned over the money and bring you back into the fold, but now...you've signed your death warrant" He hissed.

A Luger came out of nowhere and Han's gun, already trained on the drivers chest erupted in flame spraying lead into the driver's chest and head. Bruno's head exploded like a grape then fell like a rag doll onto the roadway. He took time now to look at the driver. At first he did not recognize him as it had been over twenty-five years since he had last seen him, that and his face was now somewhat mangled from the heavy caliber bullet that had destroyed his skull. It was Bruno, the driver who had driven Frederick and himself to Norway in 1945.

He'd never given their driver much thought but then he wouldn't have given the circumstances in 1945. Apparently he wasn't the type to let go of losing the war. There were many who had joined Odessa when they couldn't bring themselves to surrender. Some because a noose awaited them, while others couldn't accept defeat. The idea that he had fought alongside such men sickened him. He stared at the man for a long moment not knowing how to feel. He did not regret killing these men it had been a long time since he'd killed any-one. What he realized was that he felt no remorse at killing these men. The distant sirens broke his revere, he stood and looked off in the distance assessing the situation and how best to manage it.

The police were a mile distant. Running back to the barn Hans stashed his MP40 to keep the police from confiscating it. It was clear he would need it, especially now that he had killed members of Odessa. Not that he regretted it he would kill them all if he had to, every last one. For that he would need his gun.

He then took up one of the other guns they'd brought with them. Returning to the car he fired a few rounds into the front seat to show that the gun had been fired to make it appear that he had taken one of theirs. The caliber of wounds might give that away, but then they were each a mess so maybe the mess would delay their discovering the fact they'd each died from being shot with 357 rounds.

He stood in the driveway of his home with the gun hanging from his hand as he smoked a cigarette. Something he hadn't done since he'd met Sarah. She made him stop because she wanted him to live a long life with her. Now that she was dead he had no need to live a long life. At this thought his heart broke and tears fell as he slowly sank to his knees sobbing bitterly as his hand covered his eyes in vain hope that this whole nightmare was just a bad, bad dream. He didn't notice the Citroen police car pull up to him he was sobbing so bitterly. He didn't even notice the police officer removing the MP40 from his hand as he wept.

Looking out the window of the ambulance he looked upon his farm as he rode with his wife to the morgue. He would return only once before he sold the farm and that was to retrieve his unfinished car and guns in the barn. He never again stepped foot into the home he shared with Sarah, his heart simply couldn't take it. Driving up the roadway to the mountaintop Hans wiped his eyes because he needed to see the road. He sobbed openly now. "I'm so sorry, I am so very sorry" he said to the wind. His skin tingled and an icy/warm touch met his arm. Sarah had always been with him and it was her spirit that watched over him. Even in death she could not bear to be apart from the man she loved and had remained as his guardian. Hans felt calm and at peace knowing his wife, his love was near. "Sarah…I love you…I miss you"

Chapter 4
The Ghost of SOE

BEHIND THE CHURCH/MUSEUM in the Vicar's residence the Reverend Davis made tea on a gas burner installed on an ancient wood stove. Noticing the curious glance Rick made to the gas line he explained. "I had a gas line hooked up ten years ago when I got tired of stoking the fire whenever I wanted tea." He grinned warmly as he poured them each a cup then sat down with a sigh.

From a bookshelf next to the table he pulled out an ancient, weather beaten, leather brief. On the flap of the brief were the faded letters SOE or Special Operations Executive the British intelligence agency that came into being prior to WWII, an organization that organized resistance against the Nazis during the war. From the brief the Reverend pulled out several-faded files including a brown leather satchel that had the appearance of having been water logged at one time, but was now dried, cracked and deteriorated.

"Before we begin I should tell you about myself. I am not an ordained minister and never have been. The closest I came to being clergy was as an altar-boy." He shoved the pile indelicately to the side and reached for his tea. Rick gave him a curious grin as if being teased but said nothing. Reverend Davis smiled patiently sipping his tea before continuing.

"This' he said, gesturing to his garb, 'is deep cover, the story behind which started back in 1940 when I was recruited by SOE out of basic training with the Royal Marines. I was interviewed on numerous occasions throughout training as we all were, but the same man, an American Colonel, always interviewed me. McKenzie was his name, Col Richard Kane McKenzie. He apparently saw something in my looks and demeanor that suited SOE" he said stopping short as Rick interrupted him.

"An American?" he asked.

Archie nodded "Yes. He was the man who recruited me, trained me and gave my call sign "Ghost". He liked the way I could blend into a crowd or a wood and just disappear. He wasn't looking for anyone flashy or daring, no, he was looking for a cautious young lad who wasn't going to do something stupid. Anyway, back to his being American. There were a great many Yanks in SOE early on. American involvement in the war was inevitable so the Americans sent personnel to work with us so that when the time came they could hit the ground running and not waste time training operatives. Col McKenzie had been with SOE as an observer since the Expeditionary Force deployed to France in 1939. That changed when the Germans introduced us to Blitzkrieg in May 1940.

McKenzie was accompanying a squad of Royal Marines to observe and report on increased German activity. Hundreds of Stukas' filled the skies followed by fighters and bombers. They were the first to report the Blitz giving our troops the heads up to get under cover or pull out; had it not been for that early warning history would have likely read very differently because the attack would have decimated our troops. Dunkirk would have never happened and Britain would have been invaded and occupied. The War may have ended before it ever got started. His early warning allowed our forces to survive.

Most of our forces were dug into WWI style trenches. Some of the older commanders were expecting the same sort of business as WWI and were caught flat-footed. Those troops not over-run by the blitz pulled back and never stopped until Dunkirk.

McKenzie and his squad of Royal Marines found themselves behind enemy lines before they realized it. So as the Germans advanced they reported their movement. Churchill himself inducted McKenzie into the British military and put him in operational charge of the squad due to his rank. He was part of SOE operationally from then on. He kept our troops one step ahead of the Germans. Once our troops were encircled at Dunkirk he was ordered to make his way back to England any way he could. This he did by stealing an airplane from a Dutch flying club that hadn't been overrun by the Germans yet. I think he said it was an American Curtis Jenny, a slow but serviceable aircraft. Whatever it was it got him back home.

He had been with SOE less than a year when he began interviewing me. He liked my looks. I wasn't striking nor was I bad looking. I was, as he put it, plain. They wanted someone who would blend into a crowd and be easily forgotten if seen. It didn't hurt that I could speak and read German." He paused sipping his tea.

"Most importantly I was not on the German list of known agents. Thanks to several high ranking British Nazi sympathizers many deep cover agents were unwittingly exposed. In the weeks leading up to the war we learned that the Gestapo was planning to arrest and execute them in public once hostilities broke out. Thankfully we had a mole in the German Embassy feeding us intel allowing us to pull them out just in time.

He was a German Jew who had immigrated before the Nazis took power. A friend of his knew what was coming and warned him to leave. He packed up his family and fled Germany in 1933. The only job he could get was as custodian in the German Embassy because he spoke very little English. Anyway he spent his days in the basement of the Embassy listening to conversations through heater vents." He shook his head and laughed softly. "This bloke fabricated a listening post by creating a fan room using a prefabricated green house in which he mounted ventilation tubes both in-coming and outgoing.

Being made of glass he could see the guard coming and get about his business and they'd never be the wiser. All he had to do was switch the fans on high and the noise in the room was deafening. He'd made us aware of Germany's plans to attack Poland a month before it started, which should have been plenty of time to avert hostilities." Archie shook his head in disgust. "Even so the attack on Poland took us by surprise because the brass didn't trust the intelligence of a Jewish custodian, who we later discovered had been with German intelligence during the Great War, a high ranking bloke. WWII could have been avoided. The whole bloody mess averted or at the very least limited to Poland had they but listened to this man."

Then in a flash of anger similar to what Rick had witnessed in the Museum Archie slammed an open palm on the table. "The whole world went to war, millions killed, entire cities and countries destroyed because some general didn't like this man's religion!!!" He stood and for a moment it appeared as though he might smash his cup against the wall in anger and frustration. The look on his face was terrible. He was tormented by horrors of a long ago war, torments that time had not erased or softened. Rich looked up at Archie knowing well enough to leave the man alone. Archie was experiencing a flashback ad such moments were often dangerous. Archie had lost his 'old man' for the moment and had the appearance of having great vitality in that aging body. His face was white as death and his muscles were keyed and ready to strike out at whomever it was he was facing in his mind. In an instant Archie was back in the present and sitting at the table, breathing heavily.

"I, I'm sorry about that" he said wearily. "That hasn't happened in years. Then I haven't spoken to anyone about this in years, that's probably why" he said laughing softly. He was instantly serious, frightfully so as he continued "Nobody has ever heard what it is I'm about to share with you and I am going to tell you because I'm afraid I may not live long enough to find a replacement." Archie sipped his tea and stared out the window looking back through the years. His features changed as his thoughts reached back in time. When his eyes came back into focus on the present he smiled and continued on with his story as if there had been no interruption.

"We had a few agents in France and her south American and African colonies. They operated pretty much out in the open and managed to feed us good information until the Viccy government arrested them and turned them over to the Germans. He sighed and shrugged before proceeding. "Most often they were simply attaches to the embassy, none of whom were trained but were simply asked to 'gather what they could because our trained agents had been pulled out of country." He looked darkly into his tea, which had turned cold.

"We were short of trained agents. Part of my job was to drop into France or wherever they needed me to infiltrate and report back on what I found. It was usually stand-off work watching from a distance and reporting in. Usually it was something specific like observing a bomb run on sub pens or to count submarines coming and going and report any damage to them or changes in their hull etc. One time I spent an entire week camped out in the dunes near Brest as our bombers plastered the pens causing little or no damage. They even tried their first bunker buster bomb there' he smiled a wry smile of a man remembering a bitter memory, '5000lbs of high explosive detonated rather impressively but did nothing more than dust off the surface of the pen. I don't even think it scratched it. As I gained experience my missions became more challenging and more involved and certainly more dangerous. But I digress. My usual job was to observe submarines entering and leaving the pens then informing them about subs leaving in numbers greater than two or three at a time. That would signal a possible wolf pack forming up. Wolf Packs were the worst." He said.

Gathering his thoughts again he sipped his tea. "When a wolf pack attacked it was hell. They'd spread themselves over the shipping lanes and waited for a convoy to pass by. Once a convoy was spotted they'd radio their position and the pack would deploy in staggered formation to attack all at once to get as many of the ships as possible before they scattered.

It was particularly bad when the escorts were hit. Once the escorts were out of commission the U-boats had free reign until the destroyers in the rear of the convoy came steaming up. Then if there were enough U-boats they'd tag teamed the destroyer until it was either sunk or drawn away from the kill zone. One terrible night half of an inbound convoy was lost within sight of Portsmouth."

His eyes glazed over as the memory of that night came back to him with horrific clarity. "I had just completed my first month of training as an SOE operative and was out enjoying a three day pass. I was standing on the point looking out to sea taking in the cool breeze and watching the convoy approach Portsmouth. The lead ship was three miles out when the first torpedoes struck. I lost count after 50 explosions. After that the explosions came in rapid succession. You couldn't tell which explosions were from torpedoes and which were from exploding ordinance. Entire ships exploded as I watched help-lessly from shore. The night sky was bright as mid-day and might have been pretty had it not been the life blood of Britain going up in flames and the awful screams of the lads in the water. Their voices carried a long way in the dark. One voice in particular haunts me to this day, a young lad crying for his mum, whimpering into the night as the current carried him out to sea. It tore at my heart knowing that he was never going to see his mum again or she him. I could do nothing to save him but pray, which I did." A tear fell from his eyes, which were again clouded with distant memories. "I fell to my knees, clasped my hands together and in earnest supplication to the Lord God Almighty and prayed for that young man's salvation from death."

His eyes squinted as the memory pained him and he wiped his nose with an old, disgusting handkerchief. "I'll never get his voice out of my head, never." He whispered. After a moment of silent remem-brance he perked up again and continued his story. "That was the night I saw my first U-boat. It was only a few hundred yards off shore, so close I could hear its diesels thumping." He smiled. "Mad with anguish and rage I pulled out my pistol and emptied the clip into the night in the general direction of the U-boat.

As I was changing clips they fired the machine gun in my general direction. I had their attention. I took after them along the coast running and firing into the silhouette. I don't know if I hit anything but I like to think I did.

They returned fire and I emptied the few clips I had on my belt and ran back to my car. I drove the car to the farthest point I could reach and searched for the U-boat again. By this time I had grabbed the Sten-gun from the trunk and threw a few clips in my coat pocket. They had come in closer to shore and were searching for me calling out to me in German hoping to draw my fire. In my foolishness I did what they wanted and opened fire cussing and swearing for all I was worth emptying my clip into the silhouette.

As I changed clips I felt the whizzing of bullets near my face before I realized that they were shooting at *my* silhouette, which was outlined by the headlamps of my car. Dropping to the ground they riddled the air with bullets hitting my car several times. Luckily they didn't' hit anything vital, on the car or me. I honestly don't know how they could have missed. When they finished I heard one of them calling in English "Stand up...stand up so we can finish you" From my near flat position I fired at the voice emptying my last clip into what I hoped was a German sailor. Whoever it was swore in surprise and returned fire. My bullets must have come a little closer than they expected they would." He was smiling to himself as he remembered his one on one confrontation with the submarine.

"With my bullets gone my bravado faded as the stupidity of my actions came into clear focus. They idled off the coast waiting for my reply. I started to crawl backwards and out of the light of my cars remaining headlamp. Just as I reached a small depression they opened fire again. They filled the air with bullets and kept up the fire. I flattened myself into the heath so deeply that I must have left an impression. A squad of Royal Marines heard the commotion and drove out to investigate. Then someone switched on a search lamp and caught the U-boat in its beam.

The U-boat accelerated and quickly left the scene as the Royal Marines fired on the sub with mortars and submachine guns. 'FOOM...FOOM.... FOOM' three shells were in the air before the first one hit. BOOM!! BOOM!!! KA-BOOM!!! The last one hit the hull at an angle that tore up the wood decking of the U-Boat but it was otherwise undamaged."

He paused. "Unfortunately it was an anti-personnel projectile and didn't have the power to damage the steel hull. It got their attention though. They wasted no time leaving. I could hear the diesels wind up as they accelerated and disappeared into the night. The fire team kept up the barrage as long as they could hear the diesels. But they never hit it again" he smiled remembering the sergeant swear like an old parrot when he was ordered to cease-fire. Archie sighed as his eyes came back into focus.

"Their U-Boats were a concern early on; which is why I was assigned the task of observing them. But I was among a very few, most of whom were caught and killed. The Germans weren't keen on putting spies in POW camps figuring their training might aid escape attempts. At one point I was the only field observer for the entire coast of France. I had managed to maintain my freedom by using a motorcycle and German uniform. In fact I'd stolen the bike in Viccy France and was given the uniform of a German MP killed by French resistance.

That was my first and only collaboration with the French because McKenzie told me to keep my contacts to a minimum. Too many

French were in sympathy with the Germans to allow me to trust anyone. So my strategy was to remain independent and free roaming. I had three radios pre-positioned, stashed by me. I even stashed one' he grinned broadly 'in the German warehouse across from the Brest sub pens. When I needed to broadcast to make a report I'd walk into the building like I owned it and disappear among the boxes and crates then crawl up into the rafters above the lights and transmit my report from inside their own building. I'd then leave through the roof top access hatch. Another radio I kept buried in the dunes in Cherbourg just out of sight of the pens but where I could observe the subs coming and going.

My last radio was in St. Nazaire hidden in the floor of a church just in sight of the pens. The Germans never discovered my hiding places as far as I was aware, but I prudently quit using them when my instinct told me to. It was by listening to that voice that kept me from being captured and killed. But I was only one man and we needed literally hundreds of operatives to keep tabs on Gerry. My puny efforts weren't enough.

In fact had the Japanese not bombed Pearl Harbor and brought the Americans into the war Britain would have been occupied. There is no telling what Hitler would have done had Western Europe been 100% secured. Russia would have likely fallen eventually and the steps of Asia would have been Germanys. I shudder to think what that lot would have done had they won."

"So as bad as Pearl Harbor was for the Yanks it was a Godsend for us." He paused and sipped his tea then looked at his watch. "Would you mind if I had you over for lunch tomorrow? I've an appointment this afternoon that I cannot miss", he said.

Rick nodded and shook hands "Thank you for the tea. Yes, I'd like to have lunch with you tomorrow" Pausing a moment he turned back to Archie "Before I walked into the museum a gust of wind blew on top of the mountain. I thought I saw a building up there. What's up there?" He asked.

Archie's smile faded momentarily as if trying to remember something. "Oh, that's been there as long as I can remember. In fact nobody has been up there in years. I think the road is too dangerous or something. That's why the owner of the island blocked off the roadway. Some poor soul attempted to drive up and ended up driving off the side of the mountain. Besides nobody is allowed on that side of the island, I'd forget about doing any exploring" he said giving Rick a quick pat on the shoulder. "I'll see you tomorrow for lunch, about the same time?" Rick smiled and nodded agreement then handed Archie his room number and then saw him out as a good host.

Chapter 5
King and Country

1941 Brest, France

FLIGHT LIEUTENANT ARCHIE Davis sat astride a BMW motorcycle just inside the tree line overlooking the Brest Submarine pens. He was dressed as a German Army courier in order to be inconspicuous. Couriers were always running about and had no specific place to be other than delivering messages and they usually held priority in terms of road blocks and ID checkpoints. They were very seldom stopped for fear of being blamed for delaying vital information. As a result he had pretty much free reign to go anywhere the wanted. The goggles and helmet kept his features covered well enough to avoid being recognized too often. However he did make it a point to not repeat his routes too often in the off chance that he might somehow be recognized or remembered. In his line of work being inconspicuous and anonymous was vital to not only performing his assigned tasks but survival.

Rain pelted his helmet as he watched the construction activity through field glasses. The rain was cold making him regret choosing the motorcycle, at least for the moment. A Kubelwagon would have been warm and dry but was not swift and he needed the swift maneuverability of the motorcycle more than he needed comfort, catching a cold was preferable to getting shot.

From a distance the motorcycle wasn't as visible as a car or truck giving him the advantage of being able to vanish into the country-side if needs be. He'd been in country for several months and had memorized the roadways along the French coast. So much so that he'd taken to driving at night without his headlight to minimize his visibility even further. In the months previous he'd been to all of the sub pens and reported in turn their various states of construction and the number of submarines currently housed in them. He had pre-positioned four radio sets along the coast so that he didn't have to carry one with him. A radio set, even a German one would be suspicious if in the possession of a low ranking German soldier, especially one driving a stolen motorcycle. The stolen motorcycle would be hard enough to explain, ad a radio to that and he'd find himself dead, but only if he was lucky.

Archie shook his head as if to dismiss the thought. He had no intention of getting caught, but then neither had the others who had jumped into France with him and they were all dead. Again Archie shook those thoughts away swallowing the mounting fear such thoughts generated in him. It would start as a gnawing burn in the pit of his stomach robbing him of hunger, which eventually would weaken him if he allowed the feeling to persist. Fear in this line of work was normal and it would be fear, if properly controlled that would keep him alive. However, panic could get him killed.

Archie was on the ragged edge of controlled fear and panic. His loose bowel that morning was testament to that fact but it was also the reason he had taken so many precautions and wasn't in the habit of being reckless. The other agents who had been dropped into France with him were gone out of sheer stupidity, arrogance, foolishness or a combination thereof.

For security reasons they'd been kept separate during training and were not allowed to get to know any of their fellow agents for reasons of field security. They were even made to wear masks on the plane and were not allowed to speak to each other. Each man was assigned a Royal marine who was tasked with the job of keeping each agent separated from the others on the plane. It was early in the war and nobody knew just who to trust so every precaution was taken to ensure that each mission operative was given as much anonymity as possible in case they were captured in order to minimize collateral damage.

In less than a week the first agent had been killed. He was a head strong dolt he knew only as Tom, which he knew only because the Marine tasked with guarding him let it slip just prior to take off, had attempted to bluff his way through a road block near the port of Calais. In a moment of panic he had bolted through the road block killing a soldier with a burst of machine gun fire. A tank sitting in the shadows took out his car. One shot and his car disintegrated. He heard that the Germans simply took the wreckage, body and all, to a foundry where the car was turned into molten metal and what was left of his body burned away and skimmed off as slag.

The other two died weeks later in the courtyard of a French farmhouse after having been captured. Archie had killed them himself while they were being dragged, after having been beaten unconscious, to a waiting car to keep them from being tortured to death. They had received a radio message requesting a meeting with the local resistance, a message that made Archie immediately suspicious.

They had been warned that very morning against accepting such requests, a common tactic used by the Germans to draw agents out. They would monitor the radio frequencies the allies were using and then transmit messages of their own generally in plain language vs code. That alone should have alerted the agents that something wasn't right. But the vast majority of the agents in the field early on were poorly trained in a desperate attempt to stem the Nazi stain oozing over Europe.

Archie had attempted to reach them by radio to warn them not to go but neither acknowledged his transmission. He then raced to the rendezvous in an attempt to intercept them and hopefully prevent their capture. The whole things smelled like a trap and not even a well-planned trap. He hoped the other agents were on the ball and paying attention to their instincts. Never the less he knew that neither of them would withstand the kind of questioning the Nazis were known for. There weren't many who could.

Cain himself had cautioned them against relying too heavily on the French Resistance due to the high rate of collaboration. Every morning at 6am Cain would signal and brief them, in code, on changes to their orders. No response was to be given except a solitary click of the 'mike' in turn to not give the Germans time to triangulate their position. The Germans equipment was good but nobody knew just how good so every precaution was taken against detection and triangulation.

Archie took up position on a hilltop a 1/2 kilometer away from the farmhouse and began observing the scene. At first he believed that maybe his fears were for naught when, to his dismay, his fellow agents showed up. Walking up to the door of the farm house they didn't even have time to knock before they were surrounded and taken into custody by a squad of SS who poured out of the house and surrounding trees. Archie having qualified as a sniper during training assembled his sniper rifle in seconds. In a moment he considered his options. Kill the guards and give the agents a chance to escape or create a diversion.

He had only five bullets in the clip so that wouldn't do much good because they'd kill the prisoners almost immediately in retaliation before he could reload. The guards were already beating them savagely as they shouted questions at them in French and English. One body blow to the shorter agent apparently ruptured his spleen because he collapsed and immediately spit up blood and fell unconscious to the ground. It wasn't long before both men were on the ground unconscious and bleeding from their mouth, ears and nose.

Archie in that moment realized they would not survive questioning. Two SS guards dragged each man bodily to the Mercedes Saloon parked in the farmyard. Already unconscious from the beatings neither man showed any signs of resistance. If they reached the Mercedes both were as good as dead or worse. It was then that he decided that a mercy killing was best, that and it was necessary to keep them from divulging vital information in case they couldn't resist or if a truth drug was used on them. He didn't know what they knew or didn't know and Britain could ill afford anything vital to fall into German hands, not at that stage of the war.

Archie said a silent prayer for each man, thanking god for their being unconscious, raised the rifle and took aim at each man in turn and pulled the trigger. In a haze of red mist the head of each agent exploded with the bullet passing through their skull and into the body of the guard opposite. The agents were both dead immediately, the guards not so much.

One guard dropped his charge and looked down at the blood on his tunic not realizing that some of the blood was his own. He then lifted his MP40 machine pistol and began raking the woods with his comrades before collapsing in a heap having bled to death, his aorta severed. The second guard lay screaming in agony from having a bullet tear through his entrails lodging deep inside his liver. The resulting injury would dump toxic blood from the liver into his body cavity and if he didn't' bleed to death would develop sepsis and die of the infection, painfully.

Once the second agent hit the ground Archie's training took over. His rifle was disassembled and in its case in seconds, the spent casings were caught as he had fired them so not to leave any clue to his location. Taking a downed branch he began scraping over the spot he'd been laying and erased any sign that he had been there. If they had his exact location pinpointed they could use dogs to obtain a scent and track him but only if he was on foot. His motorcycle would break up the scent sufficiently to give him time to hole up somewhere safe. Stashing the rifle in the saddlebag he then pushed the bike to the road.

He let the bike roll downhill a full mile before he popped the gearbox and clutch to start the bike then riding as fast as he dare. Distance was his greatest ally at the moment. The more distance he put between himself and the Germans the better. He needed to get under cover quickly so he headed for the nearest cache bunker along the coast instead of heading to his usual hole-up in Vichy France.

Vichy was the pro German government in unoccupied France. Being unoccupied by the Germans it was relatively easy for Archie to hole up, provided he wasn't in German uniform. The French people, in spite of their pro German government, weren't inclined to leave a lone German soldier unmolested and Archie wasn't into pushing his luck…too far.

The bunker was only a few miles away and the sooner he got under cover the better. When the Germans went looking for someone they tended to pull out the stops. He knew he'd made the right decision when he'd spotted a halftrack blocking the roadway a mile ahead. Next to it was a kubelwagon and a squad of soldiers. He'd seen them moving into position as he topped a rise. He immediately killed the engine and pulled off the road and into the woods.

The Germans knew that he was in the area and would be turning over every stone in the search for him. Thankfully it was a moonless night and it would soon be raining which would make it that much more difficult for them. Once it was light there would be spotter planes and ground troops deployed to search the immediate area. Eventually they'd discover something that would give them an idea of which direction to look. Even brushing away tracks left signs that a trained eye could detect but brushing away tracks was far better than not because it did buy him time and every second counted. As he finished brushing his tracks he heard a dog barking in the distance. "Damn!" he whispered to himself. If they were using dogs his prospects of survival had just diminished considerably. Sitting still would not do, he had to move.

Just as he turned into the woods he heard the rumbling of a pair of motorcycles racing down the road followed by a kubelwagon and the Mercedes saloon his friends were meant to be riding in followed by a truck carrying a squad of SS. In the truck he could hear the guard he'd shot screaming in agony as the truck drove by. It was the agonized cry of death. It was too dark for Archie to see any faces but he sensed that they were angry. He froze in place not moving a muscle knowing that any movement, even in the dark, could be detected.

He could feel the eyes of the troops scanning the woods. Careful not to stare directly at any one as they drove by because of the training he'd received. He looked down into a clump of grass allowing his peripheral vision to watch the motorcade drive by. Staring at them directly would have drawn their eyes to his position.

———=((•))=———

Six months earlier Col McKenzie told him "If you look directly at someone and stare, there is something that lets them know they are being watched and from where. So you mustn't stare at anyone for more than a second or two. In fact if you are hiding its best that you never look directly at anyone at all...period. Especially if you find yourself hunted." After that McKenzie took him to Piccadilly Circus dressed in the plain clothes so his uniform wouldn't draw the eyes of anyone and told Archie to find a person at random anywhere in the area, no matter how far they were and stare directly at them.

It took him less than a minute. She was a nurse, apparently just off her shift as she had the appearance of being exhausted and drained like many Londoners in those early days. The Blitz being in full swing spared few the horrors of indiscriminate bombing. The look in her eyes was that of a woman who'd seen death come too often in horrible ways to far too many people. It took less than ten seconds for her to look up and directly into Archie's eyes. From a hundred yards away they locked eyes on each other. For a brief moment Archie knew her and she him. She smiled a warm, exhausted smile then turned away and stepped onto a bus, which disappeared into the depths of London.

Col McKenzie walked up satisfied that he'd proven his point. "You see, she didn't know you and probably wouldn't recognize you if she saw you again, but she did feel you staring at her, didn't she?" Archie simply nodded not knowing what to say. "Nobody has been able to explain it to me better that an old Apache I knew growing up in Arizona. He said "A human being is still in his heart an animal in spite of all we know and learn. We still have instincts and senses that we may not truly understand for our educated mind clouds these senses. In war these senses come to life and those who pay attention to them survive, those who do not…die" Col McKenzie looked hard into Archie's eyes to emphasize the last word.

Archie straightened up realizing for the first time that this war could kill him. Most young men do not believe that they will die, even in the most brutal of conditions. Up to that point he had never considered death as being real, that it would never reach him or touch him. In a sense he'd grown up and he didn't like it, not one bit.

———◦((◦))◦———

Archie's thoughts drifted back to his present situation and the passing motorcade. The brakes of the truck squeaked loudly in the night as orders were barked and soldiers tumbled from the truck. They were too far away for him to understand anything they said but it didn't sound good.

Someone was barking orders, which were acknowledged with sharp enthusiasm. The cries of their wounded comrade pierced the night as his agony increased with every breath he took. A shot rang out and the agonized screams stopped. They had killed one of their own just like he had done for much the same reason, to spare them the misery of dying in pain. That he was dying was obvious. Where he'd hit him made that a certainty. If he didn't bleed to death he'd have died of an infection that would have no doubt killed him in a few days if not hours.

Archie did not waste a second getting to cover making his way to the bunker keeping to the trees. Luckily he was less than a half a mile from his destination, which was downhill. He rode the bike with its engine off in neutral through the woods and up to the entrance of the bunker that lay hidden under an outcropping of sand stone. A narrow path just wide enough to accommodate a bike skirted the cliff face and could not be seen unless you crawled up to the edge of the cliff and hung your head so far off the edge that you risked falling.

Most soldiers weren't so dedicated to their tasks to risk death in the search for a resistance operative or a spy. Such people tended to shoot back, so the enthusiasm to locate them generally waned when personal safety was on the line. Not out of cowardice but who wants to die because he stuck his head down a hole? Most soldiers would prefer a straight firefight where the odds were even. Sticking your head into a hole where your enemy might be hiding...reduced the odds of survival considerably, at least that is what McKenzie said, Archie hoped that he was right.

After stowing the bike in the bunker he went about erasing the tire marks from his silent ride through the woods. Rain was beginning to fall but not enough to keep planes grounded, at least not yet. But he knew the storm that was supposed to hit the coast would wipe any trace of his movement away while reducing the enthusiasm of the soldiers searching for him.

Once satisfied that he was safe he let the tension ease as he made himself some tea, which he found in the stores supply. The bunker was cold but had plenty of supplies and to his astonishment a fully furnished bedchamber complete with mattress and quilts. Apparently somebody decided that living in a hole should have its compensations.

Once his tea was done he added sugar and canned milk from the stores and took up station at the view port to check on the activities outside. The view port was a modified periscope that allowed a 360' view of the surrounding area. It acted like a miniature turret like those found on the Maginot line. When opened it could not be seen unless you were immediately next to it and then only if you were looking for it. When closed it would appear to be part of the earth with grass and weeds to keep it hidden. It was clearly not a tactical bunker but more of a fortified safe house with an escape hatch leading to a cave that opened to a sheer cliff face. A rope was the only way down. It was a way out with little chance of immediate pursuit if discovered, especially if he placed a mine or two in their path.

As he sipped his tea he smiled "You have to admire the French' he thought ' they do know how to live" Just as he was about to close the port he saw several German soldiers coming out of the woods. It was a line of 20 soldiers in a standard search pattern. He was also aware of the wind picking up and the sprinkling of rain.

If anything a soldier liked his comfort, in small doses perhaps, but he didn't like being wet, cold or miserable if he didn't have to be. As long as a soldier's feet were dry, his cloths warm and his bed soft he would live a Spartan life with few complaints. A content and comfortable soldier will seldom get into mischief or become unruly for fear of losing that source of comfort. It was a truth all soldiers understood dating back to Alexander the Great, an axiom Archie hoped the officers leading these men were well acquainted with.

One group would walk north to south while the other group walked east to west ensuring that they missed nothing in their search. He was relieved to see that they didn't have any dogs with them. Still they were too close for comfort and he didn't know for sure if he hadn't somehow given away his position. Slowly Archie put the periscope down in its hole and stopped breathing. Moving toward the hatch he strained his ears listening for any sound. If he heard so much as a scratch he was going to bolt down the cliff and make his way to the next safe house on foot.

There would be no time to radio London until things cooled down which could be several days or several weeks depending on how badly they wanted him. It was then that he began to fear that someone in the French Army might know of these places. How man on the Vichy side would divulge such secrets to their Nazi masters?

Sweat trickled down his brow though the bunker was freezing cold. Had he opened a can of worms killing those two agents? They knew too much and they could have been injected with scopolamine a very effective truth drug that removed the brains higher function leaving them unable to resist questions especially if the questioner was sweet and kind to them. "A healthy cleavage wouldn't hurt," he thought.

Most men he knew had a weakness for tits and would gladly allow themselves to be smothered to death in a woman's bosom. "If only" he thought with wry smile. More realistically they'd have been tortured brutally and then butchered like cows. No, it would have been a can of worms had he *not* killed them. This way they only knew of him but not if he was French underground or another British agent.

He knew that he'd made the correct tactical decision but did he leave behind a clue that led them to him? His mind raced with possible blunders that he systematically imagined he'd made.

For the next 4 hours Archie waited for the slightest sound of entry. Though hidden by a bush he didn't dare use the periscope for fear of a German soldier being at just the right place to see it or worse feel it move under his bum if he happened to be sitting on the mound concealing it. He was stuck waiting it out. Tired though he was he could not afford to sleep until he knew that he was safe. Hours later he was jumpy, keyed up and exhausted. He decided to wait another 12 hours before using the view port. Exhaustion was wearing on him and if he were forced to flee he wanted to be rested for the effort.

Tempted to use the bedchamber he opted for the cold floor near the cave entrance in case he needed to escape quickly. Sleeping in the bed would be comfortable, too comfortable for the situation. The last thing he wanted was to fall into a deep sleep. If he were compromised he needed to react fast.

He woke every few hours to noises that echoed from the cave below. When he'd go to investigate he'd find it was a seagull plucking at the carcass of a fish while fending off other seagulls. By dawn he was so exhausted it was as though he hadn't slept at all. Fatigue was as dangerous to him as a gun to the head. Raising the periscope to its lowest functional height and scanned the area around his hole. A quick 360 scan let him know that the soldiers were no longer around but he checked again, twice to make sure. He left the periscope up for a full five minutes in the direction he thought most likely to hide a body of men to see if he detected movement. Breathing a sigh of relief he put the scope back down and decided to try out the bed. He was out before his head hit the pillow.

For the next three days Archie remained safely tucked away in his hole. In that time he rehashed the killing of the other agents over and over. They weren't his friends so he didn't have that kind of remorse for his actions but they were Brits. Was his motivation noble or selfish? Was he simply looking out after himself or did he act for the best of everyone involved? That they would have been killed was certain. Would it have been better to let them suffer through the questioning and perhaps resist to the bitter end for the sake of honor or did he do them a favor by ending their suffering? It was a question he would ponder for the rest of his life with no resolution.

At midnight of the fourth day he emerged from his hole and rode to his safe house in unoccupied France where he radioed McKenzie and informed him of the situation. What he had done was praised by his chiefs as necessary in light of what they, the agents, were to face otherwise. For the next few months agents were not dropped into France leaving Archie the only field agent in country, at least the only one they trusted fully. During his brief radio exchange he expressed concern about how many people knew about the 'cache bunkers' and his concern that the French were compromised.

It had been the Free French forces in Britain who had informed SOE of caves and weapons caches they'd positioned in preparation for their own return to France prior to Dunkirk. In the weeks leading up to Dunkirk when it became apparent that the Germans would not be stopped French engineers built each cave as if it were a bunker including hidden access ports concealed so well that you wouldn't know it was there if you were standing on it. Each bunker included bunk facilities and even a functioning toilet and shower albeit cold. He could easily avoid capture by locking himself in the bunker and wait for things to cool down if they ever heated up like he had already done. Of course he chose not to put any radio transmitters in the bunkers figuring that a fixed location might be too easily triangulated. There were 12 such sites he could use but he chose to use only three leaving the rest as back up if any one of his regular safe houses were compromised.

A month later he found himself overlooking the construction of the Brest sub pens taking note of its size and determining the date of completion. He would make his report to Cain that afternoon. The submarine pens were all operational if not finished but capable of practically rebuilding a submarine completely under cover. He over saw the allied bombing missions on the pens reporting the damage done. On his suggestion they did try taking a used up B17 loaded with explosives and crashing it into the Sub pens at St. Nazaire.

They had even devised a radio control mechanism to fly the plane remotely from a C-47 transport. All the tests seemed to work fine. However when the pilot armed the drone prior to bailing out the plane blew up. The explosion was so powerful that Archie felt the blast wave 1.5 miles away. As a result the Germans now had permanent picket barges armed with AA guns as a barrier against any further attempts. The Brits never attempted it again because the risk was too great and the benefit too questionable.

Not long after that Archie was called home. His mission had been to gather information so the brass could determine a course of action. His mission had been to observe only and to not participate in any espionage activity that would compromise his safety. The months he'd spent in the field did however awaken the brass to the fact that there was no quick return to Europe. The Germans were dug in deep and would not give up any of their territory without a fight.

Archie was flown out of France on a moonless night. His mission had been considered a success though he didn't feel that way about it. France was still occupied and would be years before an invasion could be mounted. In that time he knew that the Germans would be building fortifications against invasion, which would prove costly to the Allies when the time came.

Over the next four years Archie dropped into France and Germany for the purpose of locating the precise location of munitions and aircraft factories, ammunition dumps and even ball bearing factories. There was only so much an aerial photograph could tell even with high-resolution images. Hard intelligence was needed on the ground to identify the factory on the map and even verify the destruction of the facility. The brass didn't need him complicating his missions by blowing up superfluous targets. They needed hard intel they could rely on.

Then on the night of June 5, 1944, Archie was headed for France in a blacked out Lysander. Due to miscommunication he found himself in the middle of thousands and thousands of C-47 transports. Looking down he saw thousands of ships crossing the channel. Realizing the folly of his mission he was about to tell the pilot to turn back when the radio crackled with a plain language message for them return to base immediately. The signal was so powerful that the pilot nearly threw off the headset but immediately obeyed the order and threw the plane into a steep left turn diving to 1000 feet to avoid colliding with any other planes. From 1000 feet Archie could see the endless wakes of the invasion fleet heading east across the channel. The invasion was on.

When they landed his CO sheepishly informed him that the message to cancel all outgoing flights had been sent by courier to keep technical communications off the airways on the chance that the Germans would catch on. A truck on its way to deliver last minute equipment vital to the invasion had hit the courier, killing him. Due to the sensitive nature of the cargo they were not allowed to stop. As a result the accident wasn't reported until they got to their destination. Thus the message the courier had been carrying had not been delivered until it was retrieved from the morgue where his body had been taken. With that Archie's wartime forays into Europe ended, for the time being.

Chapter 6
Strange Discovery

TEN MINUTES AFTER leaving Reverend Davis house Rick drove out of town. He had never been one to follow rules or take advice. In fact he never saw the point in having rules if one could think around them. He laughed at himself realizing that he had forever defied authority where he could get away with it and here he was doing it again. "You are a born anarchist Richard" he said to himself.

Twenty minutes later Rick was bouncing down the coast road. Intent on driving to the top of the mountain, but as he approached the far side of the island he noticed that the pavement was crumbling and littered with debris that would rip his tires to shreds if he wasn't careful.

The state of the road forced him to slow to a crawl and dodge trees and bushes that had grown up in the middle of the disintegrating roadway. At the base of the mountain he found a road blocked by a fallen tree he could not push out of the way or drive over so he got out of the jeep and walked past the tree to see if it would be worth exploring later. It seemed the tree at the bottom of the road was the only one blocking his way so he decided to try again later.

Backing down the narrow roadway he headed back toward town. About half a mile down the road he began to feel the coffee on his bladder and pulled behind a bush to pee. As he watered a tree he turned his head to make sure nobody could see what he was doing and noticed an old roadway heading inland. Having all day and not wanting to go back just yet he decided to follow it. Had he not stopped to relieve himself he would have never seen it. It was surrounded by foliage with a canopy overhead, which kept it from view of low flying aircraft. From the looks of it, it had been deserted a very long time.

Evidence of past heavy use presented in the hard packed gravel where the tires had pressed it into the earth. The center of the roadbed was overgrown with smaller plants that had pushed up through the hard pack. In several areas he could see adult trees growing in the center of the road confirming its age and lack of recent use. Hopping back into the jeep he drove along at 25 mph weaving in and around the trees and bushes.

Passing the first clump of trees he came upon an open meadow. The canopy had grown over most of the meadow creating semi-permanent shade. Rays of sunlight poked through the canopy allowing enough sunlight to see his way down the road without lights but he turned his lights on anyway. It was here that he began to notice junk piles off to the side of the road. As he drove he began to notice that these piles were neatly spaced and not simply tossed to the side like most junk. They were also covered with canvas or had been once. Most of the canvas had rotted away long ago but enough remained to suggest its presence.

A few miles further down the road he found artillery shells neatly stacked. Plants were growing through the gaps in between the casings and around the warheads. The visual effect was surreal as nature consumed the corroded weapons suggesting in its own way the futility of war. Looking up from his find he noticed another pile and another. He had stumbled into what appeared to be an ammo dump that had been forgotten. Knowing a great deal about old ordinance he backed away understanding that unstable explosives could go off 'just because' and if one went off there was a good chance he could be caught in the middle of a chain reaction explosion. Sweat trickled down his upper lip both from the humidity and the instant tension created by his knowledge of old, unstable explosives.

In spite of his knowledge of explosives he continued driving down the road noting how the piles of shells got bigger and more numerous. He then realized the junk near the edge of the meadow were the guns that had rusted and fell apart where they were stored. He made a mental note to give them a closer look later. Coming to another open meadow he noticed a roadway that skirted the trees and mountainside instead of going straight across the meadow. Apparently whoever laid out the road had intended that it not be seen if a plane flew over. This portion of road was almost perfectly flat and devoid of growth except for the canopy overhead. Picking up his speed he cruised across the meadow. Just as he was about to enter the next stand of trees he spied a car lying on its side. Pulling up to it leaving the jeep running and on the road he got out and walked over to it.

As he approached it he began to recognize it as a Volkswagen, but as he got closer he recognized that it was a Kubelwagon, the Germans version of the jeep, which VW had built during the war. The paint was badly faded but he was able see the remains of the German cross on the door and hood. As he walked around the vehicle he thought that maybe it was a converted 'Thing,' which is based on the Kubelwagon. But as he inspected the remains further a few details

jumped out at him that made him believe it was an honest to goodness Kubelwagon.

One thing that stood out was the amount of decay and the obvious
military service tools still attached alongside of it. The most telling
detail were the bullet holes that perforated the hood, seats, gauge
cluster, floorboards and rear facing bonnet lid. From the looks of it
the car had been hit from behind by machine gun fire. The bullet
holes were too small for anything but a hand held weapon, aircraft
strafing would have destroyed the car altogether. The car was lying
on the driver's side as if it had been driving away from where Rick
was headed. It appeared to have been on its side for a long time
because bushes and a small tree grew through a rust hole in the side
of the back seat and where the front passenger seat had been was a
bush growing out of the frame itself.

He was thinking that it was a souvenir brought back by some G.I. after WWII. It wasn't out of the question as all manner of contraband
had been sent back by all manner of personnel. There were quite a
few captured Kubelwagon's to take parts from. Apparently whoever
had taken this home did so for the bullet holes. A rather unique war
prize showing battle damage was a hot item as were Luger pistols,
hand grenades and machine pistols. As such he didn't think it odd
that a German military vehicle had found its way to the states in the
years after the war. There was one instance where a General acquired
a King Tiger Tank captured during the Battle of the Bulge, shipped
it back with ten other tanks and lost it in the paper work then kept
it in his barn in Ohio.

Then he remembered the military gear and artillery shells. He figured that it was an old military dump/storage facility and this was
one of the vehicles brought over by the military. It wasn't unheard of

to use enemy equipment. It was a practical solution to some logistical problems. But that did not explain why they had abandoned the base full of ordinance. It should have been fenced off and signs put up warning people of the danger.

Tired of trying to make sense of a Neolithic example of monstrous stupidity, he searched the vehicle for a souvenir of his own. The seats had rotted away leaving only the bare frame and springs. Nothing inside the passenger compartment was salvageable. The gauges were cracked and permanently damaged from years of exposure. The knobs were not much better as most simply cracked into pieces when he touched them. Evidence of small rodents remained in the corners protected by what remained of the vehicle. The boot was rusted shut. He forced it open using what appeared to be the tire iron. The interior of the boot was dry and so whatever was inside was likely salvageable. An old canvas lay crumpled on the side of the overturned vehicle.

Using the tire iron he pulled it out of the boot and spread it out, aware that such places often housed spiders and snakes. He was not aware of any venomous snakes on the island but he was not going to take any chances and he didn't like spiders any better than snakes. Pulling the canvas open several items fell out onto the ground, two German potato masher hand grenades and lying next to them in surprisingly good shape was a black briefcase emblazoned with silver SS runes on its face.

Rick stood staring at the grenades and brief case lying at his feet. He had seen a few souvenir grenades in his Grandfathers gun collection, so recognized them for what they were. He bent over to pick up a grenade. It was broken near the base of the casing and kind of loose not worth taking home so he pulled the pin. It came out easily, too easily…smoke. In a moment of panic he tossed it into a nearby bush as he threw himself to the ground. KA-BOOM!!! Leaves, sand and what was left of the bush fell to the ground pelting his head and neck as he crawled under the jeep.

Choking on his heart beating in his throat he stared back at where the bush had been, now a blackened crater with blue smoke hanging low over the hole. At first his reaction was to cuss the fool who had brought home live grenades, but then he remembered the ordinance and slightly freaked out realizing he could have set off the entire field. Cussing himself for a fool he crawled out from under the jeep and got to his feet. His legs were like Jell-O. He poked a finger in his ear to clear it of the buzzing and to check to see if there was any blood indicating a ruptured eardrum. No blood. "Good" he said out loud to see if he could hear himself.

Staring at the remaining grenade Rick left it sit while he searched for a place to dispose of it properly and not set off anything else. He found a ravine about 50 feet deep that seemed to be a watershed from a recent storm. Walking back to the car he gingerly picked up the grenade and walked over to the watershed checked to make sure he could get out of the way he pulled the pin and tossed it down the deepest part of the ravine. He then dove behind a tree stuck a finger in each ear and waited. Nothing…he waited…nothing….just as he stepped out from behind the tree it blew up with very intense explosion at least three times as powerful as the first. The ground shook and sand flew into the air as did several twigs and whatever else had been in the ravine.

Curious he walked over to see a blackened hole with blue smoke rolling up hill as if from a volcano. This was weird, a WWII German car with two live grenades in the boot, an entire arsenal of field artillery with enough ordinances to fight a protracted war sitting on a Caribbean island thousands of miles away from any known base. This did not have the appearance of being a relay station for escaping Nazis. It appeared to be more of an operations base, or a storage depot for weapons. "What the fuck is this? This shouldn't be possible" he said.

Head buzzing from the first explosion he decided to check out the brief case. At least that might make an interesting souvenir. With proportionate paranoia Rick took a long stick and opened up one clasp then the other and slowly opened up the brief case, it did not blow up. Instead of finding booby traps he found papers, in German and what appeared to be a shipping manifest. On top of these pages was a Walther PPK with SS runes on the handle. There appeared to be very little rust on it but the mechanism didn't work very well so he pulled out the clip and with effort emptied the chamber of the last corroded cartridge which he let fall to the ground.

Closing up the brief case he placed it gently on the floor in the back of the jeep and hopped into the driver's seat and pulled away. Looking back he had come roughly 6 miles and it was still early so he drove down the roadway further inland. Here the road was smoother than the rest and he accelerated to 40. He had gone another 2 miles before he came to a clump of trees where the road curved and disappeared.

Just as he was coming out of the turn the road disappeared into a mangle of bushes and into what was apparently a cliff face. Mashing the brakes the jeep began to skid but he was traveling too fast. There was no time to bail out so he held on and stood on the brakes. A sickening screech from his tires was punctuated by a crash of bushes soon to be followed by the crunch of metal.

Where he expected to hit rock the jeep crashed through the over-growth and into a dark cave --- a man-made cave or more accurately a tunnel. Only he didn't notice it right away being that he was once again working out whether or not he was alive, dead or injured. As he determined that he was not dead or impaled on a branch he began to notice his surroundings with more clarity and detail. Being charged on double load of adrenaline tends to fuel both caution and attention to detail.

He could smell old oil and machinery mixed with mildew and tropical rot. A large branch lay across the hood as the engine idled. Not wanting to shut off the jeep more for the security of knowing it was still able to move he put the brake on and put it in neutral and began pulling branches and leaves off of the jeep and himself. This gave him time to think and calm himself and inspect the jeep for damage. Twice in twenty minutes he had nearly choked on his own heart. He needed to be more careful he told himself.

Mildew and moss hung from the walls and overhead adding an air of decay and long disuse to the dark tunnel. Calming down enough he decided that it was safe to explore the tunnel. Only he was going to go extremely slow in the event he discovered otherwise.

He did not pay attention to how far he went only that it seemed to go deep into the mountain a long way before curving to the left and then down. From the top of the ramp the sweet, sick fume of old oil and machinery was over powering. It was obvious that he was getting closer to the source. At the bottom the road it turned right emptying into a vast, cavernous space where evaporated sea water mist and the fumes of old machine oil taxed his lungs threatening to gag him with each breath. The Jeep was equipped with off road floodlights so he flipped the switch and the cavern was pierced with a beam of light.

Sweeping the light on his left using the handle the light cut through the misty haze until it fell on an object that caused him to gasp in surprise. He did a double take not trusting his senses because what he was looking at defied logic. It simply wasn't possible, not here, not now. What his light had revealed hidden in the mist was a German U-boat moored to a pier with another one out board the first, two WWII German supply subs or Milchows'. A larger un-armed variant of the U-boat used to re-supply subs on patrol early in the war. None were supposed to have survived. Every Milchow on record had been sunk either in port, on patrol or as it left port and usually with all hands. The Germans quit building them in 1943 once they had improved the Type-7s.

Milchow's were easy targets because they were slow and cumbersome and did not dive as quickly as the boats they were meant to support and the metal necessary to build one Milchow could build two Type 7s. Rick was no historian but had a curious fascination with German U-Boats and was therefore aware of certain aspects of U-Boat history. Apparently at least two had survived the war and the reports of their destruction were meant to throw the Allies off their trail. Why track that which has been destroyed?

The nearest one was German Military gray with the standard Kriegsmarine markings and a swastika on its commissioning ensign. Aside from having no hull number, which usually resided on the conning tower it was a normal boat. The other submarine was black, with a polished but tarnished metal, deaths head insignia welded to the front of the conning tower. Silver SS lightning bolts were welded to the side of the conning tower surrounded by a wreath of Oak Leaves. A bright crimson ensign displayed the swastika prominently on the prow.

Inching the jeep closer he could see that both subs were in a make-shift dry-dock. By all appearances the two boats had been moth-balled or placed in long-term storage. Clearly nobody had returned to retrieve them.

Taking the flashlight from the glove box he got out and walked to the edge of the pier. At the bottom of the dry dock he could see two hatches where water would be let back in when the time came to float the subs. As he walked the length of the pier he noted the water intakes or where they should have been were covered in oilskin and coated with a thick layer of grease, obviously meant to keep moisture from corroding the vitals of the submarine. He was awestruck by the thought that they might actually be operational. Carefully inching closer to the edge he saw the gangplank.

The gangplank was metal and had the appearance of being solid but he tested it very carefully to make sure that it wasn't booby trapped or weakened by corrosion from exposure to years of moisture. He wasn't keen on falling into the bottom of the dry dock. His initial scan of the dam didn't reveal a way to climb back out if you fell in and weren't killed. But then he had not inspected the whole thing. He wasn't about to push his luck, not with his recent close calls fresh in his memory.

Grabbing a rope from the back of the jeep he tied one end to a piling and carried the other in his right hand while holding the flashlight in the other. Taking easy steps and testing each one before taking another he made it across the gangplank in a few seconds. Once on deck he tied the loose end of the rope to one of the stanchions along the deck.

The deck was made of wood slats that were meant to allow the water to wash through them and over the side. To his astonishment the wood underfoot was solid as the day it was installed. Taking no chances he walked gingerly to the ladder that went up the conning tower and then behind the surface bridge. It was at this point that Rick took notice of the overall condition of the boat. In spite of all the moisture in the cavern the boats had little rust. When he went to grip the hatch he realized why. The entire surface of the boat was coated with a thin film of grease mixed with something like oil but it wasn't any oil he was familiar with. Taking a hold of the wheel he used a great deal of effort to open it, but it wasn't necessary and he skinned his knuckles on the hinges of the hatch as the wheel devoid of any corrosion gave way instantly.

Once the dogs were free the hatch sprang up nearly hitting Rick in the mouth. A rich, stale odor wafted up from the blackness of the hatchway. An innate mixture of excitement and fear jumped into this throat as he pointed the light down the hatch stopping at the deck plate. With heart pounding he spun around and went feet first into the depths of the submarine. How long had they been there and what were they doing in the middle of the Caribbean? Remembering the ammo dump, the Kubelwagon, live grenades, brief cases emblazoned with the SS runes, manifests of lading, he began to understand the impossible; this had been a Nazi secret base. But that was just too fantastic to believe, it was *too insane.*

His head began to spin with ideas of what this could mean. Obviously nobody knew of this place and those who did were either dead or the next thing to it. He let his light find its own way as he stood at the foot of the ladder wondering if he should listen to his adolescent fear and run for the jeep and keep going until the saw light or keep moving into the depths of the sub and see what secrets it might hold. He wanted desperately to run. But the damnable curiosity that had always plagued him tended to over-ride his inner child and he took a step toward a ladder well that went down.

Walking down the ladder he found himself in a massive hold packed tight with boxes, which were covered with a heavy canvas tarp. On closer inspection he noted that the tarp had been soaked in the same mixture of oil used on the external surface. Only the tarp was protecting the boxes underneath. Taking a pocketknife out, cut the ropes holding the tarp in place and flipped it over as far as he could. Wooden ammo crates were stacked from bulkhead to overhead leaving only enough room for a crewman, a skinny crewman, to check the bonds during whatever voyage they had planned to take or had already taken.

His nervousness was growing. Turning he let his light fall on the passage he'd come down and into any corner he couldn't see. It was clear nobody had been in this hold since the end of the WWII or shortly thereafter. Something made him nervous about being in a place nobody else had been in seventy years. Somebody had put them here and they had taken great pains to preserve them, so why leave them? Using the screwdriver of his pocketknife he began to pry open one of the ammo crates. Considering the amount of ordinance he had seen out in the meadow he expected this was more of the same only for smaller weapons or probably crates of grenades like those he had found in the Kubelwagon.

Hesitating only a moment he worked more carefully not wanting to accidentally set off anything that might be inside. One board free, a second and he then opened the crate finding more greased canvas and oil paper like that used for wrapping up and shipping machine parts all of it packed in a straw like material. This was a practice common in WWII as most equipment was shipped by sea every precaution needed to be taken to protect the parts from corrosion. Taking his knife he cut the canvas and tore away the paper. Rick felt a hard metal object, smooth, cold and solid. Taking the light from the perch were he had laid it he pointed the beam onto the metal. In shock he stood up and slipped backwards hitting his head on something very hard nearly knocking him unconscious.

Gripping the back of his head he cussed in pain and waited for the stars to clear then tested his bump for blood, nothing wet and he could still see straight.

After convincing himself he wasn't going to drop dead and that he didn't have a concussion he crawled slowly back to the crate. His light hit a shiny bar of silver metal at first he thought it was silver but then the noted the letters stamped into the center of the bar PLTM 2kg. The crate held 10 bars each weighing in at 2kg. He opened the next crate and found 10 bars of platinum. He opened five boxes total and each had 10 bars of platinum. Thinking of the manifest in this jeep he grabbed the first crate and headed up the ladder. It was too heavy so he managed to take each bar one at a time and carry it up to the base of the conning tower and up into the battle con, or what would have been the battle con had this been an armed submarine.

In ten minutes he had all ten bars up the ladder and in twenty minutes had the bars in the jeep and inside the crate. Half an hour later there were four crates in the back of the jeep. In spite of the weight the springs didn't show signs of strain yet he knew that the weight had to be considerable. His fear having long since evaporated he decided to check out the other sub. There were two subs and both were Milchows' and each must be loaded with something.

After securing the load in his jeep he crawled across the gangplank once again and found a second gangplank connecting the outboard sub with the first. Again he tested this gangplank and found it secure. The second boat was coated with grease and oil but the second was treacherous where the first was not. His feet slipped under him threatening to up end him with every step with the entire boat coated in a double layer of the oily, protective coating.

The second boat was the same in layout as the first only the second was far more impressive in terms of cleanliness and décor. Someone had gone to lengths to make this look and feel like an SS boat and not a Kriegsmarine boat. Death heads and swastikas were everywhere one looked. Martha Stewart would have gagged at the sheer over-kill of the Nazi Reds and Blacks. Silver SS lightning bolts emblazoned every non-moving part and several moving parts, a twisted sight.

Shaking the macabre imagery from his head Rick headed down to the hold. Again he found a pile of crates covered in the same treated canvas as the other sub. He opened another crate. This crate had a mix of platinum and gold bars each 2kg and again holding ten. The second sub held as much as the first only this one appeared to be packed more tightly, so that even a skinny sailor couldn't have fit between the bulkhead and the crates. Indicating that there might be a few more crates on the second boat.

He had discovered a Nazi treasure horde. There was no need to open another crate, the odds were good that every crate on this one was loaded with bullion. The why and what for were outside his ability to answer, not that it mattered. He was rich!! His debts were effectively gone with 'one' crate. With what he had here on these two submarines would change his world in ways he could not begin to imagine, though he would try.

He left the open crate where it was and headed back up. As he approached the ladder something made the hair on the back of his neck rise up. Turning the light on the rest of the control room to confirm that he was still alone his inner child began to awaken again. Turning back around his light fell on the passageway beyond the ladder. Stepping around the ladder his light beam led the way.

Some innate curiosity drew him forward in spite of the urge to run. It wouldn't have taken much at this point because his unreasonable, irrational childlike fear had surfaced and was screaming desperately to run, but he did not. Sweat trickled down his brow and down his nose as his heart beat like a hammer and threatened to climb up his throat, again. Two steps further brought him to the first birth. Moving the curtain aside he pointed the light beam into the darkness. What he saw shocked him so severely that he jumped back involuntarily nearly dropping his flashlight. Though shocked by what he saw the urge to run didn't take hold but curiosity planted his feet firm. Luckily his bladder had been empty otherwise he would have pissed himself in shock.

Moving forward he let his light find its place again. The space was a birth typical of officers on board a submarine, one birth stacked on top of the other to save space. In the corner of the birth was a desk with a fold away seat underneath it. But it wasn't this that drew his attention. Lying in the bunks were two fully clothed skeletons; both in dress uniforms of an SS Officer. Stepping into the birth he noted their guns hanging from the bunks still in their holsters.

Each skull had one bullet hole to the temple. Yet both skeletons were lying as if they had been sleeping peacefully. "Were they killed in their sleep?" he wondered. Sleeping in full dress uniform? 'No', he thought, 'this was a ritual suicide'. Moving the light beam to see more he noted a dark patch against the far bulkhead opposite the skull. He surmised that it was dried blood.

Directing his light beam into each birth and found all the bunks filled but one. Most of the remains appeared to have been resting as they died. Several appeared to have fought death as their arms were gripping the pipes and fixtures within reach. One body was face down with his arm hanging down off the rack as though he had changed his mind, too late.

In the Captain's quarters, a grandiose and gaudily decorated space contained the body of an SS General again lying peacefully on his bunk hands folded on his stomach...with a bullet hole to his head. His skull had its mouth agape and something in the mouth reflected the light from Ricks' flashlight. Slowly losing his fear of the dead he reached into the mouth and pulled out a glass vile that had been bitten in half. Not knowing how long Cyanide poison remained toxic Rick carefully let the broken vile fall from his fingers.

He found 13 skeletons, each with a bullet-hole in the temple and each with a broken vile of cyanide that each had obviously taken voluntarily. The evidence suggested the presence of a 14th man who was not among the dead. Clearly someone had put a bullet into each of these mens' skulls and not his own by the absence of his body.

His mind raced as he considered the possibilities. Were these the last men to know of this base? Was their suicide meant to ensure its secrecy? He was no scholar in terms of the Third Reich but he was aware of the fanaticism of those who followed Hitler. Most were so devoted to his ideals that they emulated their beloved Fuhrer by killing themselves in the same manner he had, a cyanide pill and a bullet to the brain. But none of these men had used their own guns as Hitler had.

Someone else had seen to it that they were truly dead. Who shot them and why shoot them if they'd already taken cyanide? The answer was obvious; to make sure that none of them had faked their death like he had.

Checking each bunk he found that they each had their service holster and pistol hanging on the hook by their bunk. Each holster had a gun, except for the one bunk that was empty. The holster remained but the pistol was gone as was its owner. Clearly someone had second thoughts about suicide. The gold was the obvious reason. But the gold was left untouched…he never returned to claim it, at least not all of it.

Nearly 70 years had passed. Any number of things might have befallen him like falling ill and dying before he could return. Perhaps, being SS he found himself under arrest, imprisoned and possibly hung. He might have been working with someone and they decided not to share this vast wealth and killed each other. The one thing that Rick knew for certain was that whomever it was had not come back and they weren't likely to, not after 70 years.

Where was the other crew? Were any of that crew alive or were they killed? Rick knew the answer before he finished the thought, they had been killed. They had to know what they were carrying or at least suspect. There are few secrets on a submarine. One cannot live in such close quarters and have many secrets unless he is very careful and gold is something that erases caution and the amount of gold present on these two submarines would have vaporized it.

It was clear that these men had committed suicide. The other crew had been killed because the gold remained untouched. Had they been alive the gold would have long since been looted. Why? This question repeated itself over and over again. The sheer lunacy of taking ones' own life when they could have easily taken a share of the gold and disappeared to live out their lives in the lap of luxury confused him. He'd heard of dedication to duty and country. But to be so dedicated to a cause, especially a cause as vile as National Socialism that you could not bear to live in its absence did not make any sense. Luckily for Rick he could not understand, a sane and rational person wouldn't.

On his way out his light fell on a two movie reels and an old projector on the navigation station. He took them and climbed the ladder. Perhaps this would answer the questions he had storming through his mind. His heart raced with excitement realizing that he had more than enough bullion in his jeep to keep him very well off for the rest of his life if he chose to keep what he had. He laughed at the idea knowing that he intended to keep this find and all of the gold he had located. But before he could do that he had to secure it and make sure nobody else could find it. With that thought in mind he accelerated up the grade and tore up the main passage out of the tunnel.

It was late afternoon when he cleared the tunnel. He first made sure that there wasn't anyone who would see him leave. Being seven miles inland and under a dense canopy he didn't believe anyone would, but now that he was in possession of tons of gold, silver and platinum bullion he wasn't about to risk losing it. After years of self-examination Rick was aware of how he had already changed inside as a result of having wealth. Even so, he did not allow himself to daydream about spending it until he had it secured.

Something down deep had awakened in him, unlocked by the release of stress caused by the knowledge that now he had enough money to do what he wanted no matter what. "So it is true, money does change you." He thought out loud. He smiled liking the change he was experiencing. While he was covering the entrance of the tunnel he paused as he realized that the 14th man may have decided that he had enough to live on for the rest of his life and if he needed more he knew where to get it. What he had here was better than a bank. Whatever the case whomever had killed those men or made sure of them had never returned. What happened to him? Who was the 14th man?

Chapter 7
The 14th man

March 1945 50km north of the Swiss/German Border: Midnight.

IN THE CLOSING months of WWII the allied bomber offensive intensified significantly after the Battle of the Bulge, what the Germans had called the Winter Offensive. Germany had taken to launching V1 Buzz Bombs and V2 rockets at London months before the offensive in a desperate bid to force the allies to sue for peace. Instead however, the population, weary and spent pushed their leaders to finish Nazi Germany once and for all *without mercy.*

Germany was, as a result, utterly destroyed city by city. Fire bombings of cultural centers like Dresden and other non-military targets was the allied answer to Germany's brutality. Firestorms and carpet-bombing of entire cities killed tens of thousands and left once magnificent cities in ruin. Germany's military leaders could not do a thing to stop it.

Weary military units were left to watch and wait as their war came to an end. Some would die in a vain effort to save their homeland; others would surrender so that they could survive and rebuild Germany from the ashes. Others, knowing they had nothing to expect but the gallows committed suicide, others ran to South America while more dedicated or psychotic individuals, mounted a guerilla war against the allies in an effort to reestablish the Nazi regime. The more pragmatic individuals however, used the chaos of war as a means of profiteering so that they could end the war on their terms and live out their lives in luxury and save as many of the men under their command as possible.

One such man, Oberst Hans Beck stood in the cold night air listening to bombers fly overhead. His great coat and its woolen collar were pulled up against the bitter cold of March. His eyes were haunted by years of war from the Poland, Dunkirk, North Africa and most especially the Winter War. "They're loaded heavy tonight" he thought. He pulled out a fresh pack of Lucky Strike cigarettes he had been trading on the black market, pulled out two handing one to his driver. "Here Gunther, let's put that piece of shit you are smoking to good use and light these."

Gunther, barely 18 was no longer a boy but a man with the hard-used look of a soldier. A soldier who had seen too many of his friends die, many horribly. He eagerly reached for the American cigarettes and lit them both handing one back to his commanding officer. "Danka Herr Oberst" he said gratefully. Once his cigarette was lit he dropped his German cigarette unceremoniously into the dirt and stomped it out.

They stood in the bitter cold smoking in silence appreciating the simple pleasure of real tobacco. "Thank God for the black market and Lucky Strike" Gunther said looking up into the black sky into what would have been hundreds of bombers had he been able to see them. "Do you think they are going to hit Singen again sir?" he asked. Beck nodded but said nothing.

Singen was the target, his boyhood home. His parents and brother were killed in the very first raid on Singen. Like many of his countrymen his heart had hardened against death, more out of self-preservation than anything else. Those who were unable to cope went mad after watching helplessly as their families perished in the firestorms the allies were now adept at creating.

There had been nothing left to bury, nothing to identify them as human beings much less members of his family. What he found were his parent's wedding bands, very near each other indicating that they had possibly been holding hands when the end came. Of Joseph, his brother, nothing was found. A genius with a violin he could make such music that made the most experienced players jealous. He could have been one of the greatest violinists in the world had he lived. Joseph had been 12 and dreamed of moving one day to the United States. He loved Americans in spite of the war. Ironically it had been an American bomb that killed him.

The day he arrived home on leave he had found his home a smoldering ruin. Nothing was left that could be identified as a house other than the pile of bricks that had once made up his family home. The bricks had collapsed inward into a pile. Such was the effect of a firestorm. The buildings would burn from the inside and suck the rest of the building into the vortex that was created by the extreme heat.

When he dug around looking for his family he discovered that many of the bricks were glowing red. If the fire had been that hot nothing would be left of his family he knew. Never the less he kept looking until he found the rings. Hans wanted nothing more than to collapse and die in the place where his family had died so that he could be with them. Had it not been for his father's words a year before he would have un-holstered his pistol and ended it all right there.

"Hans, the first war did not go well for us because our leaders started a war on the ego of one man, the Kaiser. Now Hitler has led us into another mess" he grabbed his arm and looked into his sons eyes. "I am proud of the man you have become. Many people are dying from the bombs the British and Americans are dropping on cities all over Germany. It is only a matter of time before they bomb Singen. We have no place to go so we must remain and pray that we survive the bombs that are certain to come. If we do not and if you somehow are able to survive this madness, promise me that you will live on and give me grandchildren to carry on our family name. Germany has nothing more precious than its sons and daughters, I want you to live, I want you to live, never forget these words...never forget I love you...and remember that I have been and will always be proud of you".

The rest of that visit had been as warm and loving as any he could remember. He had last seen his father a month prior to the bombing. In the last moments before he drove away he had shared a silent, knowing good-bye with his father. Somehow they both knew they would never meet again, but neither could bring themselves to say it. They held each-others gaze as his father took his sons hand for the last time. "I am proud of you Hans, very proud...I have always been so" Hans knew that it was all his father could do not to break down as he pulled away.

Hans looked up into the sky as hundreds of bombers flew overhead. The memory of his family was fresh as were the last words his father spoke to him. Tears streamed down his cheeks knowing that soon families would be ripped apart, forever altered and a piece of German art, history and culture would be soon wiped from the face of the earth. Singen itself was of no military value. There were no war factories, no munitions dumps and no troops. Therefore it had not been defended properly as there had been nothing to defend. Apparently people were not worth defending.

What Hitler had not counted on was the wrath of the Allies turning on Germany with the same ruthlessness he had unleashed on the world. The Allies were destroying Germany city by city because Hitler had been unwilling to be humane in conducting the war, if war could ever be humane. His insane actions had provoked the anger of the world, which now sought the utter and total destruction of the country that put him in power. He could see their point. Hitler was insane as were most of those who followed him though this wasn't apparent early on.

Like so many Germans Hans had been caught up in Hitler mania. At first it seemed that he was what Germany needed to pull them out of those desperate and dark days following the Great War. At first he seemed a genius with a vision for a greater, more powerful Germany. Everything he touched turned to gold or so it seemed. That was why Germany went willingly to war believing that he would make Germany the great empire it had once been. Their early victories seemed to prove to the world that he was invincible, that Germany was invincible.

Poland fell in a few short weeks. It was not unexpected considering that German Panzers and Stukas' were mowing down horses and mules. What air battles there were had been short and non-dramatic. Considering the Polish air force was small and its planes hopelessly out matched it was to be expected in spite of impressive victories by a small number of skilled pilots. It did not help that most of the Polish air force was destroyed on the ground before anyone knew what was happening.

Then came the Phony War, the British and French had declared war but nobody attacked, at first. The British sent planes, tanks and troops to France. France built up the vaunted Maginot Line in preparation for a repeat of WWIs, trench warfare. It was the product of classic, antiquated military thinking preparing for what they had experienced before and not making allowances for the changes in technology and tactics that the Germans had used to sweep over Poland. That the Maginot line was built between France and Germany while leaving their borders with Belgium and Holland unprotected spoke to the limited mentality behind its construction.

The Maginot Line was built with the thought that Germany would have to cross over the line to enter France not once considering the fact that Germany had swept across the low lands in WWI to invade France through Belgium. For whatever reason the French didn't expect that Germany would do the same thing twice.

When Germany finally attacked they swept over Holland and Belgium and from Belgium into France bi-passing the Maginot line entirely. Nothing could stop the Germans. Entire countries fell before German tanks and planes like grass to a scythe. Dunkirk should have been the end of the war had the British people not come to the aid of the British and French armies. They arrived in military and civilian craft saving the bulk of the British and French armies from certain destruction. Yet, it was a great and massive victory for Germany. The war had been won. All they need do was to wait out British supplies. No invasion would have been necessary had they simply kept the pressure on the British and starved them out.

The British would have been forced to accept a peace treaty and a token occupation force of a few hundred thousand troops effectively securing their western frontier, which would have allowed Germany to consolidate its industrial might. Then from a position of power and control they could have negotiated a land deal with Russia without opening hostilities and the hell that had been the winter war could have been avoided.

Hans worked his hands as the memory of the Winter War shot through them. They could not tolerate the cold after having been so badly frost bitten. His feet were no better. Yet he counted himself lucky because he still had them. Many had lost fingers, toes, hands and even limbs to the cold of the Russian winter.

His mind drifted back to that brutally cold day when an artillery shell blew his Kubelwagen into a ditch filled with bodies and blood reddened water. Knocked unconscious in the blast, he woke covered in ice from head to toe after having been pulled from the wreckage by a soldier who had seen it happen. That soldier lay across his chest dead, killed by a Soviet sniper as he pulled him from the wreckage then fell on top of him. The bullet had entered his head between the eyes blowing out the backside of his skull killing him instantly. It was likely his body that kept Hans from freezing to death.

When he came to his hands and feet were frozen to the ground. It took nearly an hour for a patrol to find him. Luckily the sniper who had killed his rescuer was no longer around. It took them another hour to separate him from the ground. The pain was indescribable. Yet, he refused to cry out knowing that his cries would draw soviet troops to their location. Luckily he passed out before his resolve broke. He woke in hospital screaming in agony feeling as though his feet and hands were on fire.

How they managed to save his hands and feet from amputation was a testament to the skill of the surgeon who tended to him. Though he remembered begging the doctor to cut them off as he was immersed in what felt like boiling water. He was knocked unconscious by a soldier on the orders of the doctor as a crude means of anesthesia having no drugs available. Mercifully he was out for several days.

He woke on a blacked out train headed to Germany in a morphine-induced haze. His head felt strangely separate from his body. He felt the pain even with morphine but his brain did not seem to register it, as though it was someone else's pain and not his own. Through the haze he noticed that most of the others were also frost bitten. It made sense to triage the patients like this to keep their care as simplified as possible. Each car was a ward for specific types of wounded from combat injuries, frost bite, and battle fatigue.

Most of the battle-injured were unconscious from either medication or shock. Those who were frost bitten were often medicated in severe cases. Less severe cases were left to deal with the pain as best they could with drugs being scarce. Allied air raids were hitting specific targets like drug manufactures that were using the pharmacy labs to produce certain types of high explosives alongside narcotics and a new drug called penicillin. It had been done in the spirit of efficiency to keep from having to build separate facilities to develop and manufacture explosives, which in turn made it that much more 'efficient' for the allies to destroy two vital plants in one bomb run leaving Germany with a shortage of the medicines needed to reduce the suffering of its soldiers. Yet no matter how bad things got...they always had explosives.

The train trip lasted an entire week due to having to travel only at night and at 25mph, to both reduce noise and smoke from the engine, which could attract bombers. A moving train by day was an invitation for attack. That and the fact they were on a well-known rail system the fighters need only follow a track before they found a train to shoot up. Where possible they parked the train in tunnels. Most often they stopped in heavily wooded areas and covered the train in camouflage. Where there were long stretches of open area to cross the train would make a mad dash across these open areas but only at night. For such high speed runs a special tube was fitted over the stack to dump the smoke down under the train to minimize their visibility further but which filled the cars with smoke.

It was while on the train that he decided to focus on his black market business to secure a future for himself. His plans formed while staring out the window as the darkened countryside moved by. The war was all but lost he knew, as did most any soldier who had been on the Russian front. As early as 1943 he began to suspect that the war was lost, though he would not dare put those thoughts to words knowing full well that it would get him shot.

He expanded his Black market operation to include smelting gold and silver. Ingots were easier to handle and were much more marketable than silverware or gold jewelry because with ingots you didn't have to explain where it came from, especially if you had a bank mark on it; stamps a banker fleeing to Spain had sold him.

This turned into a black market money changing operation and was highly profitable especially with the end of the war being so near and fleeing Nazi leaders needing cash to pay for passage to South America. He accepted anything that could be changed into money. However, he did not accept Deutschmarks. It was so worthless that many people were using the bills as fire starters in their stoves. People were shedding their German marks for dollars and pounds simply to survive on black market goods, a fact that he capitalized on handsomely.

Inhaling his cigarette, he enjoyed the North Carolina tobacco. His thoughts drifted to the Swiss border 50 kilometers away and making an end to this war for himself and his men. He had in recent months heard rumors of the Allies intention to prosecute members of the SS. However, he doubted the rumor applied to those who acted within the confines of the Geneva Convention. Yet he wasn't ready to test this theory. He knew all too well of the atrocities many of his colleagues were guilty of and this knowledge might be enough to include him among the guilty. He also knew that if he were called to testify in a war crimes tribunal he'd likely be murdered in his sleep by Odessa.

Odessa an organization of SS formed to protect and aid in the escape of Nazi fugitives, was highly organized and ruthless. Their intention had been originally to spirit away senior Nazis to South America to rebuild reorganize and continue the war by invading the United States. It was a plan born of desperation. More accurately it was a convenient excuse for them to escape with their lives, especially those who had ordered or had done the deeds fueling the anger of the allies. The most recent and by no means the least was the slaughter of American Prisoners captured in the Arden during the winter offensive, what the Allies were calling the Battle of the Bulge. That was nothing compared to what they would find once they crossed into Germany and discovered the death camps.

Hans had known of them since he had visited Dachau and Auschwitz when they were first built and empty. The camp commander had described the function of each building with disturbing enthusiasm. He actually seemed giddy at the prospect of murdering thousands of people in a single day. Hans remembered feeling sick as he fought the urge to un-holster his pistol and empty it into the bastards head. Wholesale murder was not something he wanted Germany remembered for. That had been the day he first saw Himmler in the flesh; a notably unimpressive man with a weak chin and pot belly reminding Hans of an unpleasant schoolteacher.

Shaking himself back into the moment he finishing his cigarette, then debated whether or not to smoke another. It wasn't really a debate more than a conscious effort to resist the urge he feared was becoming a habit. A bad habit born of addiction he was mildly aware of from his brief addiction to morphine following his stay in the hospital. After he 'wanted' the cigarette and did not need it he lit another cigarette.

Reaching for the packet he took out two more. On a whim he reached into the backseat of his car and pulled out a new carton tossing it to Gunther. "Here, go hand these out to the men. We may be here a while. The night fighters can see movement a little too well for my comfort. It's almost as if the can see us at night, and the allies are getting a little too good at aiming their bombs.' Gunther nodded but said nothing, knowing what his commanding officer said was true. 'We'll move out once the air-raid is over".

Gunther saluted his Commanding officer in a classic Prussian military salute and not the 'Nazi' salute, knowing well that his CO was no longer enamored with the inane, pointless displays that meant nothing outside the fevered minds of Hitler and his devotees. "Herr Oberst" and went about dispensing cigarettes among the men.

This was his third shipment to his bank in Switzerland. He had enough in the bank to keep him well off for several life times already. After this shipment he would retire and buy that Mercedes 540K he had his eye on. A Jewish banker had driven it to Switzerland before the war and sold it before leaving for America. It was in fine shape, red with a black top and black leather interior. It would make a nice drive up to the mountain house he had rented. He planned to remain there until the wars end and for several years after to wait out the post war chaos that he knew would consume Europe, Germany in particular. It was a thought that filled him with immense satisfaction.

Once he'd established residency in Switzerland he could apply for citizenship and then a Swiss Passport. Once that was done he could return to his barn high in the Alps and safely remove the remaining crates of cash. But that could wait until things calmed down and the occupation armies settled in to their routines. It would also give him time to acquire a second home in Spain or Portugal. His chalet was a rental; it was a temporary home only, albeit a comfortable one. Maybe he'd buy it. He laughed. "Don't spend it all before you've had time to enjoy it Hans" he said to himself.

Taking a drag on his cigarette as he let his plans form, his eyes closed as an image of a walled hacienda on the Spanish Riviera with a private beach and scantily clad housemaids dashing about seeing to his every need. He laughed out loud to himself. "Hans, you're a pig." He laughed again deciding that three housemaids would be sufficient, nymphomaniac housemaids. Again he laughed with satisfaction that his life was set and this fucking war was over, for him anyway.

The thought of ending the war on his terms with three Spanish housemaids to assist him made him smile. They would certainly be a distraction from being a soldier of a defeated army. That was the least of his concerns because he had long since accepted the fact that Germany had been defeated. He had hoped for an honorable peace, which was what the Winter Offensive was supposed to have achieved.

It was meant to turn the tide so Germany could at least negotiate a ceasefire and eventually return to pre-war borders. That was the plan as far as he knew. He had thrown himself and his command behind that effort only to lose 60% of his force in an air raid the day the weather broke. The remaining survivors were with him now heading to Switzerland. Most of them had taken part in his black market operation and had profited nicely. In each truck were the surviving member's assets that remained in Germany. He had given them the choice to surrender to the Allies or to drive to Switzerland and 'retire' as he had termed it.

Desertion was the more accurate term. However, each man had given their heart and soul to the madmen running Germany. They also knew that the war would not end for several months. If he followed orders and reported to the nearest command post his men would be dispersed as replacements on the Russian front where death was all but guaranteed. Those who managed to survive would spend long miserable years in a Russian gulag in Siberia and likely be worked to death. His men deserved better than that.

The Russians were on the march. There would be no stopping them and mercy was not to be expected as Germany gave none on its march east. The Soviets wanted revenge and nothing could prevent them from having it, not now. His countrymen would pay a brutal price for what Hitler and the Nazis had done. Hans shuttered in frustration knowing that throwing his men into the fight now would accomplish nothing and waist their lives in the bargain.

The plan was to deposit money into a Swiss account then travel into Spain and back into France where the Allies were well established and surrender. That way when the war was over their legal obligation to Germany would be fulfilled and they would qualify for pensions and be able to live in Germany without shame. Germany was in ruin and the Nazis in control knew their lives were forfeit and were continuing the fight to stave off the noose that awaited many of them. He wasn't about to waste the lives of his men for them. One of his men was worth a hundred filthy Nazis. Yet he wasn't sure that was a fair assessment as the Nazis in many cases didn't qualify as human, in his opinion.

Germany had expended its last resources on the Winter Offensive. They were building all the tanks and planes needed to fight a war but had no fuel to run them or men to fight them. In disgust he threw down his cigarette crushing the embers under his toe. Germany's greatness had been squandered for what? The most he could do for his men would be to get them someplace safe so they could grow old and raise families and not waist their lives.

He lit another cigarette as the horizon lit up with orange flashes signaling that the bombing of Singen had begun. He felt the ground shake under his boots as bombs exploded miles away. Looking down at his feet he felt each bomb blast. He'd felt this before when the Luftwaffe bombed Amsterdam. It was a very different feeling then. Germany had reclaimed its greatness and asserted its dominance over Europe with unquestioned authority. It seemed that Germany had finally reached its proper place. Then the vibrations filled him with a warm glow because the war was over and Germany had won.

However, since then, countless acts of stupidity had brought Germany to its knees. The same physical sensation now had a very differ-ent emotional connection because it was Germany being bombed. Those were British bombs exploding on a German city creating a very different feeling indeed, a feeling that chilled him to the bone. In a fit of nervous irritation he felt the need to be moving, to be the hell away from the torment of the bombs. Movement, even at night was easily seen so he had to fight the urge to move his men. In his irritation he decided to check on them if only to be doing something. Approaching the trucks parked along the side of the roadway, he realized that they had stopped at a cross roads, a bad place to be stationary. That he hadn't noticed it before irritated him. This was the sort of mistake that got men killed, he admonished himself making a conscious note to be mindful of such details in the future.

The Allies were bombing crossroads to disrupt the transportation of weapons, fuel or whatever needed to be transported by truck. Trucks did not move very well over bomb craters, especially when carrying explosives, ammunition or rockets.

He'd driven past what was left of a V2 mobile launcher a week before. Apparently someone had fueled the rocket 'before' loading it onto the trailer. Not an uncommon practice given their need to be quick to launch, the less time at the site the better. They were transporting it for immediate launch after which they were to vacate the area. Once a V2 was launched ground attack aircraft would soon follow because a V2 Rocket was easy to see from the air even from 10,000 feet, either before a launch or after, especially after with the white smoke pointing directly at their launch position.

However, the driver had driven too quickly over a bomb crater. The resulting blast cleared trees, trucks and personnel for a 50-meter radius. Trees that were not obliterated were knocked down and on fire igniting other trees. Wheels were embedded into the trunks of trees and the truck itself or what was left of it was located a half mile away 50 feet up in a tree with the driver missing his upper torso. Thankfully that was a spectacle he'd not seen himself. He'd seen enough of that and needed no more. With this in mind he directed the trucks nearest the cross roads to move along the tree line away from the center of what would be the target area if bombs were dropped. Once that was done he ordered everyone to remain near their trucks ready for a rapid departure in case they were spotted. Once satisfied his men were ready he walked slowly back to the Kubelwagon.

AA fire was illuminating the night sky over Singen. Someone had moved AA guns to the city center. At least the city could now shoot back. Looking up at the flashes he could see shadows of Lancaster bombers beneath the flak bursts. Just as he was about to drop his gaze he saw a burst AA fire hit a plane and the red-orange flash of fuel igniting followed by the death whine of a bomber falling to earth. A second bomber was hit in the bomb bay and a massive ball of fire filled the air as the plane disintegrated. The first bomber was spiraling down to earth trailing fire as three parachutes popped open.

The spinning bomber brought back memories of his early days as a young officer searching for downed RAF pilots. It was December of 1939 when he'd discovered the barn high up in the Alps. He was on a patrol searching for downed aircrew from a British bomber that had been shot down the night before.

He was searching what appeared to be a stand of pine trees when he tripped on a protruding root and fell into the center of the trees landing hard against the wooden timbers of an old barn. Even from feet away nobody could see that there was a building hidden behind the pines. There was just enough space behind the trees to allow him to move and search for an entrance. His original thought was that it was a perfect hiding place for a downed aircrew.

He found the door and opened it. The door opened with some difficulty as years of needles and broken pine boughs littered the ground. It was apparent that it had been years since anyone had been there. From the look of the trees surrounding the barn it had been centuries since the barn had been built. The trees had apparently been planted around the barn to keep the animals housed inside warm. Alpine winds were harsh and would suck the heat from a building without a windbreak to diminish the winds effect.

Stepping inside the barn he noted the musty smell of a poorly ventilated space. Standing in the door he noted the barn was packed full of crates and other items he could not identify in the dark. Reaching for his flashlight he flipped it on and started to search the barn for any sign of a hiding bomber crew.

To his astonishment he realized that he'd just stumbled on a weapons cache complete with cannon, muskets and battle ensigns from the late 18th century or early 19th century. Reaching for the nearest flag he unsheathed it and discovered a highly adorned tricolor flag of the Imperial French Army of Napoleon Bonaparte. He had been a history major in Berlin University and was well acquainted with Napoleons march across Germany and knew that he had marched his army through the valley below on his march to Russia and again on the long march back as a defeated army.

Somehow in the fog of war this weapons cache had been forgotten. In any event nobody had come back for these weapons or supplies for nearly 150 years. The historical significance of this find was, to him, profitable. Historians and museums would pay handsomely for such rare, pristine artifacts from that long ago war. He also knew that Hitler himself would prize such items as he viewed himself as a modern day Bonaparte. However, his second thought on the subject was that this barn was impossible to see from the air and even when standing feet from it. Hans wanted money and knew how to get it. This would be a perfect storage warehouse for his black market goods, once he sold the contents of the barn.

As in any war the black market was a profitable endeavor. He had already acquired a source of American Cigarettes and had begun selling them to troops. As the war progressed he expanded into cash exchange and gold and silver smelting. By the end of the war leading up to the Winter Offensive of 1944 he had amassed a healthy sum of well over 50 million American Dollars and that was what he'd deposited in the bank. He'd not been able to count what he had yet to deposit, which appeared to be an equally vast sum, which he kept in a bunker under the barn.

As he stared at the horizon his thoughts were broken by the all too familiar sound of planes diving. Two Mosquito fighter-bombers tasked with escort duties had spotted the convoy and broken formation. Looking around he saw nothing that would have given them away. In the split second it took him to evaluate the situation he acted as only a battle hardened veteran could crying out "Scatter!!!"

As one the trucks scattered into the woods and down the road like rats before a plow. Once his men were safe only then did Hans get into his car as Gunther gunned the engine and raced for all his life was worth away from the bombs. As his car reached speed the whistle of a falling bomb reached his ears followed by a blinding flash followed by another...and another. All was silent as they tumbled through the air, time stopped, followed by a sickening crunch then everything went black.

Two Thousand feet above two British Mosquito Bombers flew in tight formation. "Bloody Hell...they scattered!!" cried the bombardier staring into his new night vision scope. "Ah well, we at least got that bugger in the car...he must have been an officer, looks like he's had it. Ok, head for home, we're done here" With that the two mosquito bombers turned hard right and headed for their base just inside the French-German Border.

Chapter 8
An Old Spy

ARCHIE SAT IN his study considering his new friend Rick. He would be 89 years old in a month and he had nobody to leave the property to. Rick seemed to be a person who would keep a secret. He certainly wasn't going to turn it over to the bloody government. 'Vultures' he muttered quietly to himself. He planned to tell Rick of the gold at their next meeting. Archie smiled, Ricks desire to keep the gold in his possession would certainly fuel his caution. That and Rick appeared to be a person who could use the money. Also the cancer was spreading fast and the morphine was hardly working anymore.

His doctor told him he had six months to live two years earlier. A year was too much to hope for and innately he knew that he wasn't long for this earth. With luck he would die in his sleep and not suffer badly. However, that was the least of his concerns at the moment. He had to leave the bullion with somebody, preferably moving it from its present location, something he should have done long ago. But if he had, would he have found someone to leave it to? "Clearly God intended this to happen this way" he thought to himself.

The bullion had to be kept out of the hands of the Nazis. He had put off moving it far too long. If a developer discovered the gold the courts controlled by Odessa would freeze it long enough for their teams to retrieve it. Anyone unlucky enough to be present when they showed up would be killed. At best the money would be lost to greed at worst it would fund the rise of Nazi power wherever they had a toehold. Such a thing was not to be tolerated. His memory of the death camps was too vivid even these many years later.

Ironically it was the younger generation of Neo Nazis who had become fascinated with the resurgence of Nazi power. Skinheads were leading the charge and they tended to be far less refined than the 'Old Guard' had been. As brutal as Hitler and his original henchmen were they at least hid their brutality behind a facade of social decorum that succeeded in pulling the wool over the eyes of the world; until it was too late to stop them. Skinheads were thugs barely capable of generating thought and were used primarily as muscle by Odessa. The remnants of which was still led by original aging members of the SS who held sway over governments through bribery, blackmail and murder and who still believed in Hitler's vision of new world order.

Hitler saw National Socialism as a means to purify the world of the unclean races and to grant the world a master race. At its most refined it was nothing more than base racism wrapped up in psychotic dogma and a pretty uniform. Sadly humanity had a great deal of evolving to do before racism, bigotry, hate and the stupidity associated with such ideas were no more.

Archie's life had been exciting and adventurous, for that he was thankful. Though he had only adopted the role of a preacher, he had, over the years learned much about the Bible, Jesus Christ and God. He had learned enough to know that being ordained wasn't absolutely necessary to be a man of God if your heart was truly of God. But it was his mission that concerned him. Archie smiled 'I'm still thinking of it as a mission. God help me.' He thought. Archie was one of two men who knew of the location of the base and what it contained. Others knew of its existence but not its location, knowledge they would never possess if he and his friend could help it.

That thought brought him back to the two men he'd seen watching him that morning, men who caused his hackles to rise in warning. Archie noticed the two bald, tattooed men who had been following him. He had tailed enough people in his time to recognize it. They weren't very good at it because he'd seen them long before they saw him. Two short, muscular bald men with that fresh out-of-prison look each with a frown permanently etched on his face.

When they walked he was reminded of two gorillas taught to walk upright, typical hired muscle. Who did they work for? He wondered. Initially he hadn't even considered Odessa as it had been so long since he'd last heard of them in any active capacity. His long dormant instinct told him that these two men were dangerous. Just looking at them told him that. It had been years since this feeling had surfaced, not since the war in fact. He smiled at the feeling it generated in him, a tingling sensation that excited him and made him feel more alive than he had in many, many years. The feeling meant danger was near and was not to be ignored. It was for that reason that he called his friend to warn him of the danger he sensed in these two men.

Hanging up the phone he relished the sensations that caused the hair on his neck to stand on end. It was a vigor he'd not felt since the days he trolled around Nazi Germany and occupied France, the game was on. Though he wouldn't admit it to anyone, not even to himself, he enjoyed the danger. Something about it made his pulse quicken and his heart beat with a force that only those who thrive on danger can understand. To Archie Davis danger was like a drug, a strong and addictive drug for which there is no rehab. It is an addiction that only death can cure and is one of the many reasons 89 year old spies are rare.

His age fell away as he strode about getting ready for his day. Joints once stiff and sore moved freely and his aches and creaks seemed to disappear the more he moved. It was as though his age was reversing itself simply with the ignition of long dormant purpose. Smiling to himself he knew too well that what he felt in that moment would pass far too quickly. He also knew that his aged body would not fare well by it. So he decided to enjoy it while he could and live in the moment, mostly because he didn't have many 'moments' left.

The rest of the day was spent going about his normal routine to see if in fact he was being followed to make sure that he wasn't imagining things. He wasn't imagining anything, everywhere he went they went. Where he'd give them the momentary slip, they'd frantically search to reacquire him. So he confirmed to his own satisfaction that he had not imagined being followed. Before he left to meet Hans he had to lose them. Hans had suggested they both retreat to the mountain top and stay there until their visitors lost interest. If he and Hans disappeared; it was likely the two men would go away with nothing to follow.

His friend Hans was always looking over his shoulder worried that Odessa would find him again. But according to the few remaining contacts he had at MI6 and the CIA Odessa was long ago defunct with its senior members either dead or so far gone in dementia that they were no longer worth the time to prosecute. Not even Israeli Intelligence wanted them anymore. If the Israelis weren't interested nobody would be. So who where they working for? Archie knew enough to know that Odessa had likely reorganized under a different name and incorporated younger more virile membership. But that did not answer the question of why he was being followed, though he did suspect the secret he and his friend shared had a lot to do with it. In fact he knew it had to be there simply was no other explanation for his being followed.

Being near 90 years old there was no way he could out run the two men tailing him, but that didn't mean he was helpless. He kept up some of his old training and with the help of some senior Tia Chi he could possibly out maneuver and get the jump on them. Archie kept to the public walk ways as he headed to his meeting with Hans. As long as he remained in public view the two skinheads kept their distance. Archie decided to see if he could shake them. He made a quick turn into a shop where he knew there to be a back door.

He emerged from the back door and immediately started moving in the opposite direction and into another door and back out onto the plaza, looping behind his tail. Leaning against the post of a shop he watched the two gorillas standing outside the shop he'd disappeared into. The minute they noticed the back door they ran helter-skelter through the shop. Taking two quick steps back into the shop he saw them rush out the back and begin searching for him, clearly upset at having lost him. He had already established the fact he was being followed but until he could shake these men meeting with Hans was not advisable. Calling Hans he suggested that he should go up the mountain without him and wait and that he'd join him later.

They were supposed to meet and discuss transitioning of owner-ship of the property to somebody who could be trusted to keep it secret. Neither one of them wanted their secret found by anyone. Governments would squabble over it for decades giving what re-mained of Odessa time to organize and steal it. Even if they no longer existed as an organization the people who had been with it were still dangerous and very real. That was the only real plausible explanation he could come up with to explain why he had been fol-lowed. Someone had done their homework, someone with extreme intelligence and attention to detail or they had guessed very well.

As he put the phone back and looked up the saw the two gorillas again running down the alley he'd used to escape them. Calmly walking down the plaza again he stepped into the shop he had used to get away and bought a bright yellow Hawaiian shirt and changed out of his clerical garb being too easy to spot in a crowd of tourists. He also donned a broad brimmed beige fedora. Archie smiled at his reflection and decided he liked the look, though he couldn't bring himself to buy Bermuda shorts. He didn't want to afflict innocent tourists to his knobby knees and pasty chicken legs. Such a sight would be too cruel.

Dropping his clerical garb into the bin Archie stashed his service .45 behind his belt and made sure the shirt covered it fully before he once again emerged onto the street. Stepping deliberately into a stream of people he made his way across the plaza and toward the garage where he kept his jeep.

It was a 1950 CJ 2A painted in Luzon Red with a dark gray canvas top with black seats. He did not drive often, less than once or twice a month, usually when he and Hans drove up the mountain. Just as he was about to reach the garage the two skinheads came running around the corner. It was a moment before they recognized him and skidded to a stop.

On a rooftop across the square, a sniper, one of three known as the Trio had been watching the skinheads following Davis. The others knew him only as 'J'. From his vantage point he was able to see Davis leave his compound with the two skinheads in tow. He spied Davis entering the shop and could see him leave out the back door. After which he saw the two skinheads waiting for him to come back out. When they discovered the back door they both seemed to panic try-ing to re-acquire him. "J' to Mom, target has acquired a tail. But it appears he is aware of it because he just gave them the slip"

"Mom to 'J' Keep an eye on Davis. I've worked with these men be-fore and they are rough characters. We can't afford to lose Davis if Beck has gone to ground. Take them out and dispose of the bodies" She said with sufficient urgency to convey the importance of the situation.

"Roger that. Send M to the garage with a truck. Once they drop we'll scoop them up and feed the fish" All the while this conversa-tion took place he watched the skinheads run amok. Doing a quick scan of the storefronts he spied Davis leaning against a wall watch-ing the two men scurry about. 'J' laughed to himself. "Smooth old man, smooth"

"J to Mom, I'm beginning to like Mr. Davis. He's watching our two friends from a storefront. He definitely knows he's being followed."

"Right, keep an eye on him, if he is aware be prepared to lose track of him. He didn't get to be an old spy by being predictable." Patrice the Trio's mission leader was on pins and needles now watching from the far side of the square at the storefronts instantly seeing Archie Davis leaning against the wall as he casually watched two of the most dangerous thugs in Europe try to find the most elusive British field agent of WWII.

Davis then casually strolled along the storefront re-entering the store he'd first entered and re-emerged five minutes later in a Hawaiian shirt and wide brimmed hat. He then made his way across the plaza to a public garage. Just as he was about to go in she saw the Dutch Skinheads come running around the corner. "Shit" she muttered. "'J' do you have Davis?"

"Yes, I have him. He's in trouble."

When you have a clear shot take them out" she muttered through gritted teeth.

"Roger" replied 'J'. He'd been watching through the scope of his rifle from the moment he began watching the action. From his vantage point he could see Davis move away from the building then say something to the men whose postures were clearly threatening. Davis said something that made the big one tilt his head to the side and hunch his shoulders as if to strike. If it hadn't been such a tense and dangerous moment J might have laughed.

Before 'J' could do a thing Archie pulled out an antique, Colt .45 1911 from the back of his pants and shot the big skinhead in the chest. The second one moved to pull his own gun out as he put the cross hairs on this forehead and pulled the trigger. In slow motion the second skinhead fell backwards but the gun in his hand was already on its way up so that when he fell the gun fired hitting Archie in the side. "J to Mom…Skinheads are down but Davis is hit, repeat Davis is hit"

Moments earlier Archie found himself facing the two men he had hoped to evade. The bigger one 'Olaf' smiled unpleasantly as he recognized Archie. "So, reverend, you thought you could get away, eh? Zig here and I,' he indicated the other skinhead, 'want to know where you have hidden the gold bricks. Tell us now and we will only kill you. Don't...and we'll make it hurt...a lot" they both laughed unpleasantly.

The smaller one, Zig, moved in behind Archie ready to grab him. Though it had been seventy years since he'd seen any real action Archie's SOE training began to dust itself off. He knew he could not win a fight. So he began to move himself away from the building. He mustn't get pinned down. If he was going to do something he needed room. Running wasn't an option. At 89 he had nothing but his guile and experience, which against two meatheads should be more than enough.

Archie smiled at him and thickened up his best 'Welsh brogue' and laid it on thick.

"Nae Byes, ye dun wan nunna mey mooney, I'm an auld man who dunna wan trooble with the leeks auf ye heathen *bastards*" The last word was well pronounced and clearly spoken in the Queen's English, so they would at least know they'd been insulted. From the looks he received they didn't understand a word he said, except the last one, which is what he wanted. Archie couldn't help but laugh at the expression on their faces.

Olaf squinted and tilted his head like a dog hearing a whistle for the first time. "What the fuck ju say?"

Archie, while they were trying to figure out what he said, pulled out his service .45, flipped off the safety and shot Olaf in the chest before he could bring his head straight again. He fell like a tree flat on his back eyes open to the sky. Zig caught off guard by facing down an armed old man…began pulling out his own gun… before he could bring it to bare a bullet from somewhere in the distance blew a hole in his forehead leaving him standing there wondering what had happened before his eyes went black. As he fell back the gun in his hand went off hitting Archie, digging a nasty furrow into his side knocking Archie down.

The pain was incredible but Archie didn't have time to worry about it or wait for his rescuer if they were indeed a rescuer. It was possible he was the next target, though he knew that was unlikely because whoever it was needed him alive to tell them what he knew. The two thugs had let *that* cat out of the bag. His worst fears were coming true, they were after the bullion. Complicating matters was the fact that there were at least two competing parties. Who were they and how did they find them after so many years?

A stab of pain nearly brought him to his knees cutting off his thoughts instantly. Stifling the urge to cry out he began to move unconsciously to the jeep holding pressure on the wound with his left hand, which did little to stop the flow of blood but it did ease the pain somewhat but he had to keep moving regardless of pain.

The questions racing through his head were disorganized and fogged by the pain of his wound and loss of blood. Though the wound was minor and hadn't hit anything vital, the loss of blood was enough to be a concern. He wasn't a young man anymore and at his age things didn't heal as quickly as they once had and blood loss was not something anyone of any age responded well to.

An eternity later Archie fell onto the seat of his jeep and clawed his way into it. Sitting brought a measure of relief to his wound allowing him to breathe without pain shooting down his side. The momentary respite from the pain allowed him to fold his hanker chief over it and press it against the wound. Thankfully it was clean and had not been used. He didn't need an infection on top of everything else. Testing the clutch with his left leg he found he could use it without pain, he then started the jeep.

In no time he was driving the jeep out the back door and down the alley to the nearest street toward Rick's bungalow. If he went to the emergency clinic the police would get involved and questions would be asked, too many questions. The fact that he had shot one of the men would be hard to explain since guns were not allowed on the island due to its history with drug cartels. Possession of a firearm on St. Vincent was an automatic six months in a French jail in Guyana, the nearest legal jurisdiction with whom the authorities had made arrangements to address crime because there wasn't any room for a jail on the island.

He had to get his wound tended to. The blood loss was significant and he felt his body weaken from the shock. The bullet had gone through him. He'd seen worse, but that didn't make it hurt any less. In all of his years of service to the Crown he'd never been shot, not once. He'd been shot at numerous times, not a single bullet had ever touched him. He noted that though his body might be slower and less agile his nerves seemed be working quite well by the pain they were transmitting. As bad as the pain was it was keeping him focused and alert allowing him to navigate the jeep through the back streets.

When he arrived at Rick's bungalow he was disappointed to find

Rick gone. So he parked the jeep in a space between two large man-groves, a tropical plant that skirted the island immediately adjacent to salt water. These plants grew together so that you couldn't tell where one plant ended and the other started. Under the canopy branches wove together like vines reaching for the sun where they could find space. The effect being a canopy 8 to 12 feet above the ground so dense that water and sunlight seldom reached the ground underneath. Locals took to cutting holes in the mangroves adjacent to their homes turning them into makeshift garages to keep the sun off their cars and bikes.

It was in one such cutout that Archie backed the jeep into to keep it out of sight. Moving around the edge of the bungalow noting one or two shark fins in the distance, causing him to grip the rail just a little tighter. Though foggy from pain and blood loss he did notice that the sharks seemed to be repelled by some invisible bar-rier, because they would approach to a specific line and turn around as if repelled.

Reaching the deck he collapsed onto the chair. He was too weak to care that the seat had not been cleaned off in months if not years. Reaching for his handkerchief, he began addressing the wound and pressed hard against the hole in his side. The pressure felt surpris-ingly good and he allowed himself a relaxed breath with the decrease in pain. Taking his belt from his pants he used it to secure the hanky to his wound and settled down to wait for Rick to return. Relaxing in the evening breeze he let the lapping of the water lull him to sleep.

Archie fell into a deeper than usual sleep due to his blood loss. He had fallen so deeply to sleep that he didn't stir when Rick returned with the bricks of bullion he'd retrieved from the submarines. It wasn't until 5am that he woke up from the searing pain his wound caused him when he shifted. Though weakened he was able to get back to the front of Ricks Bungalow and knock on the door, only when he did the exertion had drained him and he fell onto the floor when Rick finally opened the door.

Chapter 9
Quest for Answers

April 1945

FROM THE FILES he'd gone over in the closing days of the war Archie learned that Odessa was searching for something that had been shipped over-seas in the last two years of the war. A total of six shipments were sent via submarine two shipments from Brest France, others from St. Nazaire and Lorient with two final shipments from Bergen Norway in March of 1945, with a reported 20 other shipments sent via Spanish and Portuguese ships earlier still. The bulk of 'material' was shipped via Spanish and Portuguese cargo ships, which were conveniently, manned my German crews.

It was the last two shipments and his investigation of Hans Beck that lead him on a journey to Beck's Alpine warehouse and knowledge of Odessa. An organization of SS fugitives whose mission it was to spirit away senior Nazis to South America and to organize resistance to Allied Occupation, a guerilla war against the allied armies initiated on Hitler's orders in the closing weeks of the war. The intent being to buy time for the Third Reich while the South

American Front was established, a front that never materialized to the rage and disappointment of the Nazis remaining in Germany.

In the closing months of the war several delegates were sent to encourage Argentina to enter the war and attack the United States. There had also been an appeal to the Mexican Government as well, just as in the first-world-war, offering the Mexican Government the return of their former territories of California, Arizona and Texas in exchange for their support in attacking the United States.

Luckily the Mexican government considered itself an Ally of the United States, but more importantly understood that attacking the United States was insane. Mexico lacked the industrial capacity to wage war much less against an industrialized nation, a nation already on a war footing. More to the point many Mexicans had joined the American Armed forces following the attack on Pearl Harbor. Many Mexicans viewed the United States a brother nation and to attack it was to attack them. For those reasons the Nazi appeal to the Mexican Government fell on deaf ears.

Once Archie transported all the cash from Becks barn to a bank in Switzerland, he went about his duties. Like many he assumed that Beck had escaped to South America. However, once Archie discovered the barn and made away with the contents nothing remained of Beck in terms of evidence. Not a scrap or clue to his whereabouts was found at the barn. Clearly Beck had not wanted anyone to follow him in the event the barn and its contents were discovered, most of it evidence that would get him hung. Beck had been far too careful for that.

After he had returned to England having failed to locate Beck, or rather having disposed of what evidence that remained of Beck,

Archie found an old dispatch sitting on his desk. It was a report indicating that a merchant ship sitting at anchor in Huelva Spain with Portuguese registry, but known to be a German tanker, was riding higher in the water than she had been the night before, at roughly the same time two German U-boats were seen cruising the surface in the Dover Straights. A strong indicator that the submarines spotted in the Dover Straights had made it as far as Spain and had managed to refuel. That stop gave them fuel enough for an Atlantic crossing. Yet nobody saw either submarine enter the harbor or leave it. What was certain was that they had been and gone, but where did they go? That was a question for which he had no answer.

Having lost Becks trail Davis was assigned the task of interrogating captured members of the Werewolf division. A formation of SS who refused to surrender and who were waging the Guerrilla war Hitler had ordered the day he died. Most of their targets were provisional authorities empowered by the Allies to govern their respective cities and towns, usually killed in their sleep.

Odessa would surface as the organization behind the Werewolves. They proved elusive, so much so that when he brought up their existence to his superiors he had been rebuked as paranoid and overly aggressive which led to his being 'retired' with battle fatigue. The powers that be didn't want to believe that a secret Nazi organization was at large and waging a clandestine war against the occupying powers. Such a development would be inconvenient and possibly interrupt the flow of money being sent by the United States to rebuild Germany and France. So Archie was silenced via retirement. McKenzie believed him however and pushed the matter forward believing that Odessa should be taken more seriously and was himself reassigned State side for his effort.

Immediately after the war Archie spent several years in Portugal. McKenzie had asked him to keep an eye on individuals suspected of organizing Odessa and assisting high-ranking Nazis escape to South America. He was from that point on a 'contractor' for OSS which would later become the CIA. Unlike the Europeans the OSS was monitoring Odessa concerned with a resurgent Nazi regime putting McKenzie and Davis in charge of hunting Nazis as an independent team.

Years passed and the threat of a resurgent Nazi government diminished with each successive year following the Korean War. A nuclear-armed Soviet Union replaced the Nazis in terms of priority especially after Cuba became communist. Also with stories mounting of Stalin's atrocities it would seem the threat of a Nazi regime paled next to a communist leader who made Hitler look like an amateur with only a few million deaths to his credit when Stalin could lay claim to 30 million in just one incident alone. So Stalin replaced Hitler and the world changed again.

The FBI had other priorities as well. Civil rights activists and organized crime became their focus leaving the hunt for Nazis to Simon Wiesenthal and Israeli Intelligence, who seemed to be doing the job well enough to allow McKenzie to enjoy well deserved peace-time retirement, if the Cold War could be considered peace-time.

When clearing out his desk McKenzie discovered a seemingly unimportant file that nobody had bothered to unseal. A classified file from the British Admiralty dated 1917, which had somehow found its way into his piles of wartime documents which had never been examined for various reasons. It was a report from a naval commander expressing concern about the heavy U-boat activity in the Gulf of Mexico and Caribbean.

It was his opinion that no German U-boat could transit the Atlantic and have sufficient time in the area to do much more that turn around, much less patrol the entire gulf region and then actually sink ships. Given his operational understanding of the capabilities of the WWI German U-boats he was convinced that there had to be a base in the region supporting them and giving them refuge or at least a ship at anchor hidden among the mangroves.

His calculations put their effective range from Germany no further than the Florida Keys at which point they would have to turn for home. He cited reports of U-boats being sighted along New Orleans, Brownsville Texas with 50 visual reports of U-boats running on the surface in site of land, 50 Confirmed sightings. There were many more sightings but none of them had been confirmed because in those instances only one person had seen them and confirmation required no less than three individual sightings.

The report went on to speculate that there had to be a German base somewhere in the region. The commander had done his home-work and speculated that there were three possible locations that bore investigation. One site he suggested was French Guyana in the mangrove swamps, the southwestern coast of Cuba, where the population was least dense and St. Vincent Island a privately owned commercial landfill. However, even the commander noted the likeli-hood of the island being a base was remote, but had been included because he could not rule it out completely.

The report had been reviewed and passed through the admiralty as a plausible explanation to their U-boat dilemma in the Gulf of Mexico. Yet nothing came of the investigation. Britain was on the verge of economic collapse because of U-boats in the Atlantic. As a result they simply didn't have the resources to expend on a full-scale investigation to U-boat threats in the Caribbean. What they did was send signals to their fleet bound for the region to look for any such activity in the regions noted, but only if they had time to do so. That was the last entry in the file with nothing beyond the field order. Apparently nothing had been seen or discovered to justify any further entry.

McKenzie sent the file to Archie who he knew would at least look into it. Sending it back to Britain was useless and the idea of a secret sub base would intrigue Archie and give him something to do in retirement. McKenzie knew too well that Archie, his best field agent, needed something to keep his brain going. He had thrown Archie into the hornet nest of occupied Europe fully expecting him to be dead in less than a month. Everyone else had died in less than four weeks but Archie…he made it through the entire war without getting so much as a sliver. Not once had he taken more than 48 hours R&R before he was back in the thick of it, often volunteering for missions before the orders were cut. He had created a monster, so to speak and now he had to feed it to keep it alive or 'he' Archie Davis would die of boredom. If such a base existed Archie would find it or die trying.

Archie received the report and read it through several times before he began traveling to these regions looking for anything that would have potentially housed a submarine base. Nothing was discovered in Cuba. Too many fishing villages dotted the coast for a submarine to have operated without being spotted. The same with French Guyana, the mangrove swamps were too inhospitable and far too shallow for a submarine to operate from, those regions deep enough for such activity housed a dense fishing population where any submarine activity would have been easily spotted. That left St. Vincent, where he arrived posing as a preacher and where the church lacked a pastor in 1970.

Within a week of his arrival having taken up the post as church pastor, he was met late one night by one of his parishioners who'd lost his wife just a few months earlier. On introduction Archie immediately recognized Hans Beck, the SS Officer he had been sent to locate at the end of the war. He'd seen so many photographs of this man that he had recognized him the instant they met in spite of the 25+ years that had passed since the end of the war.

Struggling to contain the urge to barrage Hans with questions he listened as Beck released his heartbreak. Pity for this man grew as he sobbed telling how he had lost his wife and the circumstances leading up to it. It turned out that Archie had no need to ask any questions as Hans readily filled in the blanks in one night of heartfelt expression of a life full of adventure, terror and heartache.

That first night was spent listening and praying with Hans who he'd put up for the night on the Murphy bed in the guest room. Next day Archie having secured Hans trust told him of his wartime adventures and how it was he had come to be on the same island. When he admitted to finding his stash and taking it Hans, instead of getting angry laughed heartily, glad that someone other than some gestapo prick got his hands on it. He told Archie that he had not been to the barn since the war, because he had no need to. Their friendship blossomed as two old soldiers from opposites sides of the same war became the closest of friends, helping each other heal as no therapy could. In time each man knew the other as they knew themselves and grew to depend on each other as one depends on air.

Chapter 10
Broke no More!!

IT WAS LATE afternoon when Rick cleared the tunnel making sure that nobody saw him leaving. Being that he was in the middle of the island under a dense canopy it was unlikely that anyone would. However, now that he was in possession of a horde of bullion that would change his life forever he was not going to take any chances. The thought of not having to work again made his head spin. He would continue practicing of course, but the stress of 'having' to make money would ease the burden considerably. In the years to follow, due to his light-hearted demeanor, the office would become a serious moneymaker.

As he drove along the roadway passed the K-wagon, where the faint smell of gunpowder still lingered, it dawned on him that he couldn't just fly home with several hundred pounds of gold in his suitcase. Where would he open an account and change the bars into cash? His excitement turned to concern and a measure of worry. The last thing he wanted to do was leave it because back home, his accounts were sucking air and without the immediate cash flow to come back, he could very easily lose this find to some other individual with a curious streak. Who would he call, a bank, if so which one? He certainly couldn't just waltz into a bank and throw the bars on a desk most especially 'not' on the island. The stampede that would result would cost him everything and leave him broke if not under arrest for trespassing. 'Maybe I could ask the preacher' he thought. It was a step in the right direction and with that first step figured he took a relaxed breath and let his mind wander on the possibilities before him.

He reached the bungalow well after dark having driven slowly so not to risk puncturing the tires with the heavy load he now had on board. His caution was spurred on by the fact that he, while loading the bullion, realized that there was no jack so if he punctured a tire he was stuck. As a result he drove along the torn up roadbed dodging anything that might even hint at a punctured tire.

The narrow walkway from the lot to the bungalow made carrying his bars difficult but he did it and loved every muscle strain he encountered as a result. Once inside he piled the bars on the floor in a pyramid and stared at them. His first impulse was to wonder how many of them there were. The pile of bricks on his floor was enough to change his life what was in the subs could change a few thousand lives.

He needed an attorney to help him acquire the land on which the two submarines sat. Once that was done he could quietly remove the bullion from the subs and deposit them into a bank vault where they would be stored and sold as the market indicated. That thought raised the question as to exactly how much of it he would have to move. It was then he remembered the manifest in the brief case in the jeep. "I wonder if...." He paused. "Can't hurt to check" he said opening the door and rushed to the jeep.

Back inside he opened the briefcase and began looking for lading bills. Finding nothing that named a vessel he discovered two ship-ping manifests. One was for #332 with special cargo numbering 32,000 units. Following this entry was then entry PLTM. Ricks eyes darted back to the pile of precious metal on the floor. His mouth dropped open unconsciously "32,000?!!" He looked back at the manifest and gasped in surprise. That was only one shipment and there were two ships both loaded with Gold and platinum bars. Rick jumped up in nervous excitement both elated and frightened at the same time.

His fright came from not knowing how he was going to hide it all. The question of where the gold and platinum bars came from would no-doubt surface. If the authorities learned of the submarines the international courts would tie up his wealth for years even decades rendering his find untenable. That was the last thing he wanted. Then he remembered his resolution to talk to the preacher in the morn-ing. His worry once again transformed to excitement. Realizing his quandary and the ups and downs he'd just gone through he smirked to himself 'You're going to drive yourself nuts' he thought then took another deep breath and tried to relax.

Too excited to sleep though he badly needed it, he just could not drift off. Sitting up he decided to watch the films. It was then he realized one of the film canisters was dated July of 1945 two months after the surrender of Germany in Europe. He decided to watch that film first. As he began setting up the reels he realized that he was about to see something filmed by the Nazis that was likely never seen before. That fact made him nervous because the Nazis weren't ashamed enough to censor their brutality, hence the Nuremburg tri-als, where their self-produced evidence got most of the Nazi leaders hung or life in prison.

The projector worked well. The Germans had very seldom taken half measures and were usually keen on quality. Unfortunately it was that same attention to detail that had caused them to take too much time building their aircraft, tanks and other high-end weapons that had cost them the war. In contrast the Soviets T-34 main battle tank was built for rough use and ease of field maintenance, which made it easy to build in huge numbers. The ease of construction had nothing to do with its quality however, as it was the T-34 was among the most survivable, deadly and dependable tanks of the war, whereas the German Tigers were prone to break downs and required garage facilities with specialized equipment to do basic maintenance and were not easy to build. The Germans built little over 1200 Tiger tanks during the war where the Soviets had built well over 20,000 T-34 tanks. The math was clearly on the side of the Russian approach to wartime production.

The film began to flicker against the wall and his thoughts were redirected to the image on the wall. What struck him at first was the quality and color of the film, especially after 70 years in a damp submarine. The opening scene was that of the same cavernous space he had just discovered but 70 years earlier. Then it was clean well-lit and very organized. Both subs were decorated in tiny triangular flags each sporting the Nazi swastika. One huge crimson swastika was hanging from the center of the cavern with every spare light pointed directly at it making it seem that much more impressive. Standing on the prow of the black SS submarine was the commanding General. He was dressed in an immaculate dress uniform with his Nazi armband prominently displayed. The audio failed on the projector so Rick heard nothing.

Based on the gesticulation of the General he was admonishing the Kreigsmarine crew for something. Then the camera turned to a floating barge on which stood Kreigsmarine ratings and officers who were shackled to it. Behind each of these men were two SS officers with machine pistols. With the wave of an arm from the General one SS officer disappeared into the hull of the barge and then reappeared a few moments later. A second later one of the ratings began pulling frantically on his chains and screaming something at the General. At this point Rick was grateful that the audio had failed.

A launch pulled alongside the barge and pulled away leaving the Kriegsmarine crew shackled to the barge. It soon became apparent that the barge was sinking and that the officer who had gone below had opened a scuttle port. The barge sank in agonizing slow motion as the crew fought desperately against the chains. Rick did not finish watching as he knew that the crew had certainly died. Speeding up the film he closed his eyes to shield his mind from the awful scene that had been so carefully filmed.

When he opened his eyes again he saw the SS General. Before him stood the SS crew most of them officers with a few non-commissioned officers. Again he gesticulated with great emotion only this time it was in pride and honor of his men. A close up actually caught a tearful SS General bidding his comrades farewell. With a final Nazi salute, which was enthusiastically returned by the crew, he turned on his heel and marched solemnly down the prow to an open hatch and went below.

Once the general was out of sight the crew in an equally solemn manner walked up the gangplank and descended below decks. Below decks the film resumed in the control room with the general handing out cyanide capsules. One by one they took their capsules, saluted the general and disappeared into their cabins. The last man to take a cyanide capsule was the general who went to his cabin and pulled the drape as the picture faded to black and Sieg Hiel flashed onto the screen just before the screen went white.

Ricks heart raced not sure what to make of the horrifying scenes he had just witnessed. If he thought sleep was elusive before it was long gone now. There were two other reels in the pile, dated several months earlier. He wasn't certain whether or not he wanted to watch them now that he had seen the ultimate end of each crew. Shaken by what he just witnessed he felt suddenly unclean and tainted by the horror of watching the calculated murder of innocent men and an equally insane mass suicide, for what?

He had been sweating all day and was now ripe with the stink of stale oil and mildew. Deciding to take a shower and get clean, it would offer him time to relax and clear the images of dying men from his mind. But the question of *why* it had been done persisted.

Deliberately he forced himself to think of disposing of his bullion, if only to cleanse the images of panicking, doomed men from his thoughts. How did you dispose of so much gold without drawing unwanted attention? Perhaps an idea would come to him if he re-laxed. Hot water rolled down his back as he let the tension of his dilemma fade. The first thing he had to do was extend his vacation to give him time to take action. Next he had to acquire the land containing the base then he thought "and the mountain" he said out loud. He drifted off to an uneasy sleep. Around 5am a severe knock-ing and a hushed cry of pain awakened Rick. Looking through the hole he saw Archie, he didn't look good.

Opening the door Archie fell through it landing hard on the floor groaning. Rick picked him up and noticed that he was damp and sticky when he turned on the light he saw that Archie had been shot in the side. In his left arm was the briefcase he had shown Rick the previous day. Gasping for air Archie spoke in rasping, ragged breaths "Got jumped by two men looking for something of mine". The two hoodlums meant to rob me but got nothing. I still have a few tricks up my sleeve...just forgot how to dodge bullets." His eyes moved around the room and fell on the bricks. He smiled "You should hide those better. The cleaning staff will rob you." Rick then helped him to the bed and set him back on the pillows, a little too low but Archie was too weak to move at the moment.

Rick, shaken, reached for the phone to call for an ambulance. "No!" Archie said with a bit more force than was necessary. Placing a hand on Ricks "Don't call the ambulance I have to...'cough' have to tell you what to do. If law enforcement gets involved what you found will be lost to you." his voice trailed off breathing heavily for a few minutes. "I know where you got those bricks" he said. "What is on board those submarines is...is nothing compared to what is stored on the far side of the lagoon and inside the mountain itself. Look in the warehouses when you go there again."

He took a deep breath to calm himself. "I think I'll be ok if I can rest a bit. I am too old to be dealing the gunshot wounds" he said laughing softly. "Good Lord this hurts! I need you to listen to what I have to tell you, do not interrupt, please" he said. Setting himself up on the headboard he brought the brief case up on the bed and laid it next to his thigh. "I found the base many years ago. I bought the land and kept it undeveloped to keep it hidden from the evil men who are looking for it, people who would use that wealth to start another war or worse bring back Hitler's legacy."

His hand grasped Ricks forearm with surprising strength as a spasm of pain shot through his body.

Panting Archie continued "What you have found is dangerous. The Nazis who put it here killed everyone who knew of its existence and then themselves to keep it secret" Archie was breathing more raggedly. "Bear with me" he said in a raspy voice. "In this brief you will find the deed to the island. Once I heal up from this scratch my partner and I will help you move the contents of the warehouses to a safer location. The men who did this to me knew of it, they're dead now but the ones who put them on clearly know or at least suspect that the bullion is here. I made provisions years ago to move it in the event they found it but we never did move it."

Rick nodded and asked "Who are they?"

Archie gave Rick a fierce glare. "Odessa. Though the Nazi Party is no longer a serious political threat they are highly organized and are no less dangerous I'm afraid. Too many of our governments Britain, Russia and the United States are tainted. Bribery is their most effective means of influence. Of course they don't call themselves the Nazi Party as that would be political suicide for anyone associated with them and they need their allies.

Lobbying firms in Washington and Britain and most western powers have been infiltrated and have been slowly taking control of the political apparatus. Once a politician is hopelessly compromised they are blackmailed and forced to act on behalf of Odessa through a series of corporate fronts. Of course the politician is never made aware of the fact that they are working for a Nazi organization because the backlash would be so severe that Odessa would be hunted down and destroyed. As it is they enjoy the functional anonymity of being a true shadow organization through which they control most of the more powerful political parties."

Archie looked out the window as the sun rose. "I've lived 89 years and lived them well with few regrets. That said I cannot take any chances that I might die and have this property come onto the market. Any development would expose the find to the world and Odessa through their corporate fronts would engage in legal, political and even criminal behavior to obtain this horde. They must *never* find it." he said in a near whisper.

Handing him a towel Rick helped him clean off the blood. Archie had dressed his own wound to stop the bleeding. Rick, though knowledgeable about such wounds from his naval training as a corpsman, thought better of changing the bandages fearing that Archie had already lost too much blood. Though the damage was not severe a man half his age could easily survive the wound. At 89 such a wound raised a question, especially if an infection took hold. Archie closed his eyes and asked for water. Rick jumped up and got him water from the fridge and helped him with it. The water seemed to help revive his energy somewhat giving him the ability to continue.

Handing Rick the briefcase he said "In this is my will and a deed to the property. I've already signed it all over to you. You need to sign where I've marked it. My attorney is already aware of the changes I've made. There is a compound on the top of the mountain that should interest you. You can access it through the base you found yesterday. The whole mountain is man-made as you will see once you drive up the road. If I can I'll show it to you myself" he said with a sigh. Clapping his hand in Ricks he said "Congratulations, you are a rich man. Now, if you wouldn't mind I need to take a nap. You might want to raise my legs up a bit and cover me up I'm cold." Rick propped him up on the pillows and raised his legs up to help prevent shock or reduce it. A heavy blanket was tossed over him with the water bottle in easy reach.

"Ok, I'm going to be fussing over you to make sure you are still breathing ok?" Rick said using his best bedside manner. Archie smiled pleasantly and nodded too tired to speak. Rick checked his pulses, which were steady but weak and his breathing was more regular and less ragged. Rick knew too well that this could quickly change. He watched over Archie for the next several hours to make sure he had been stabilized; only when Archie was holding his own did Rick pull up a chair and allow himself to sleep.

Two hours later Rick woke and found Archie sleeping soundly his pulses stronger and his breathing regular and deep though raspy. Making himself some coffee Rick looked over the paperwork Archie had brought him. The deed of the property was filled out, signed over and notarized. The official seal of the local magistrate was stamped on the receipt making the property transference official. In a matter of a day he had become a billionaire and property owner as well as trustee of a deadly secret. In the will Rick was instructed not to develop the land until all the bullion was disposed of or removed from the island. The provisions for which would be disclosed at a later date. Among the papers was an ancient blue print of the island itself. Curious he pulled it out and unrolled it on the table, careful not to tear it or damage it.

Several layers of translucent plans showed a comprehensive, highly detailed design from the base dug into the coral reef to the pump systems and the inner and outer lagoons, all the way to the mountain top compound, including the buildings. If the plans were accurate the road he had traveled down the day he had discovered the subs had once been a service road for the external harbor. For some reason it had been filled in with sand. Over the years grasses and trees took root and helped to firm up the surface layer. According to the plans it had been 60 feet deep with the outer lagoon 150 feet deep.

Along the edges of the blue prints were drawings of old style battle ships complete with their dimensions from overall length, beam, draft and mast height. That explained why the base had been so massive. It had been intended to house battleships but that raised more questions as to how they would get into the base, he had seen no doors or entrances large enough to allow a battleship to pass through.

Flipping to the next sheet answered that question, but only after he had made sense of the pumping system that apparently drained the lagoon exposing the doors, which would then open allowing the ship to enter the facility. The lagoon would then fill back up again hiding the base entrance from prying eyes in the event that someone came snooping. He laughed softly and whispered "Genius, just plain genius" he said.

Little did he realize that Archie had awakened and was watching him as he figured out the plans without his having to explain them' It was enough to Archie's mind, that Rick was the best steward of the secret they could find and drifted off to sleep in peace.

That afternoon Rick hung the "Do not disturb" sign to keep the cleaning crew out for the day. Even then he refused to leave Archie alone. Every few hours he'd make him drink water and check his pulses. For nearly two days Archie rested and was getting stronger. He had been conscious only twice since he'd first gone to sleep and then only for a few moments of barely lucent speech. By the end of the second day Archie had been awake long enough to sign the remaining documents over to Rick before collapsing once more into a deep sleep. He was getting stronger. The next day Rick woke early, checked Archie's pulses and breathing to ensure that he was strong enough to be left alone for a few hours. Archie had been half awake when he left so he told him that he was going to check out the mountain and the summit. Archie, who was not quite awake enough to understand the words being spoken simply nodded and fell back to sleep.

Waking a few hours later taking a deep breath Archie moved slowly but steadily to a sitting position. The pain was excruciating, but the bleeding had stopped and he did have more energy, but he was still weak. Once he'd awakened fully only then did he realize the Rick had left and vaguely remembered him saying something...like... heading up the mountain.

"Bloody hell" he muttered reaching for his phone which he realized was gone. Looking over on the bed stand there it sat smashed by the bullet that had grazed him. Using the hotel phone to call Hans, there was no answer and his voice mail was not set up. 'He'd never learned how to set that damned phone up' he thought and spat "Damn!" He knew that Hans was on the defensive and if Rick had gone up the mountain he might be mistaken for one of the men who had been following them and Hans being the old soldier he was wasn't likely to be cordial or in any way inviting to a perceived 'intruder'.

He would have to drive up the mountain. Luckily the keys to his jeep were on the table next to him and he once again steeled himself to move and in one slow, steady movement stood. "Not bad, this time around." He thought. Walking to the door Archie opened it and looked out to see if anyone was about. His jeep was still in the space between the trees where he'd left it.

He walked as normally as he could so not appear wounded or hurt in any way. The more he moved the better he felt, except when he got into the jeep. That moved him in the wrong way sending shooting pain down his body and legs so that he nearly went to his knees.

But he managed not to cry out or feint. Once in the jeep he panted and breathed slowly to ease the pain. Once things calmed down he started the jeep, put it in gear and slowly drove down the road. As he did so the storm that had rolled in unleashed its fury on the island making Archie glad he hadn't taken down his top.

The road that Rick had taken wasn't the one Hans and he had used for so many years. They had created an alternate road behind the many trees that skirted the base of the mountain. The road wasn't really a road so much as it was a worn down track from their driving over it over and over again. It led to a roadway up the backside of the mountain that ended just behind the basement garage area of the house. He saw the open door and surmised that Rick had been there. He looked inside and was about to go up into the house when he heard the faint sound of a gunshot emitting from the basement garage. "Shit!" he muttered entering the basement garage through the open door he slapped the giant garage door button and it slowly began to open up. This gave him ample time to rip the canvas off the G4 sedan. The massive Straight Eight Cylinder engine started on the first go and roared to life.

Chapter 11
Berlin: March 1945

(The Fuhrer Bunker)

HIGH-RANKING NAZIS WHO had ordered and partici-
pated in the murder of millions of Jews, Gypsies and homosexuals
throughout Europe were transforming the Fuhrer bunker into a lunatic asylum.

The war was lost and the allies made it clear that the guilty parties would be tried for war crimes and hung. Desperate to stave off
the hangman and to buy time in order to escape to South America,
imaginary battalions were formed from troops long since captured
or killed. Generals were given command of non-existent divisions
and then executed for not attacking when ordered to with their
imaginary troops. It was the beginning of the end and it would get
worse before the end, much worse.

One of the few people not panicked was an SS General who sat in
his office quietly smoking a Russian cigarette, enjoying its harshness
as he watched the panic unfold around him. General Horst Krupp
was to have been the heir of the Krupp ship building fortune, the
primary ship builder of U-boats for the German Navy.

Though Horst had never seen combat he was horribly scarred from a bomb blast meant for Hitler the previous July. He'd been in the 'Wolfs Lair' standing next to Hitler when it blew up knocking him unconscious, waking weeks later in a Berlin Hospital blind in his left eye, lost when a piece of steel rebar lodged in his skull, through his eye socket. The wound gave him a sinister look which the eye patch enhanced belying his genteel, aristocratic nature.

With the defeat of Nazi Germany and the war crimes tribunal listing his uncle as a war criminal and himself among the top most wanted for his close association to Hitler, any inheritance was long ago forfeit. Of course he was far from destitute having poured millions and millions of pounds from his shares of Krupp into Swiss Banks. This was done immediately following Hitler's attack on Russia. An act he and his uncle both viewed as a massive mistake, knowing that it would cost Germany the war.

Germany had not been prepared for a two front war or a winter engagement on the Russian Steppes. As a senior member of Hitler's logistics staff he was in a position to know what Hitler had planned so that he could acquire the appropriate equipment for the engagement, which would have worked out well had Hitler been rational. However being an impatient drug addicted psychopath Hitler had usually acted on impulse and on the advice of his astronomer.

General Krupp had advised Hitler from 1936 up until the Battle of the Bulge, when he was fired from his post on the advice of Himmler whom he distrusted. Krupp urged Hitler to wait for the equipment to be ready before attacking. If Hitler had listened he would not have attacked Poland until 1943, when Krupp ship yards would have completed 250 submarines for use against Allied shipping.

Not only would they have had enough submarines to blockade Britain and the east coast of the United States they would have had two battle ship squadrons of 20 each completed as well as two Aircraft Carriers and a fully modernized Luftwaffe complete with ground attack as well as long range bombing capability. In other words Hitler had, in his impatience, attacked Russia before he was tactically prepared for a two front war, much less a winter engagement on the Steppes of Russia where no modern Army since Katherine the Great had survived much less won.

However, in March of 1945 everything that was or would have been was now a smoldering ruin. Being on Hitlers advisory staff he had been privy to the decision making process or what passed for decision making in Hitler's psychopathic brain. Decisions usually came in the form of a temper tantrum that precipitated military action that inevitably ended in catastrophic failure, thereby causing another temper tantrum. Because of Hitler and his need for immediate gratification, what had once been Germany's greatest achievement, the total conquest of Europe, was lost under the influence of profound psychosis, narcotics and fear or any combination thereof.

Himmler had exploited this fact more often than he cared to remember. It was something he'd witnessed over the years. Apparently Hitler had been addicted to cocaine when Himmler advised him on supporting Spain in their Civil War after he had brought him tea or coffee, an act Krupp found suspicious. Himmler was far too imperious to do anything for someone else unless he had motive. Coinciding with these 'favors' by the ReichsFuhrer, was a Hitler temper tantrum soon followed by an insane command that in some way favored Himmler's immediate needs.

Krupp made the mistake of sharing this observation with Martin

Bormann, because within a week he had been sacked, via Hitler temper tantrum induced by whatever had been served to him by Himmler. It then became clear to Krupp who had squandered Germany's victories. Himmler, through a drug reactive Hitler, had led Germany to defeat pursuing his own selfish interests.

Because of this he took satisfaction in knowing that Himmler's recent attempts at negotiating peace with Eisenhower had been rejected. Not only rejected but Eisenhower made it clear that he intended to have Himmler arrested, tried and hung. He then added that he would weave the rope himself and hang 'that goddamn chicken farmer' from the nearest tree 'himself' if he saw him again. According to his sources Himmler nearly wet himself and very nearly fainted getting back into his Beige Mercedes G4 following the confrontation with Eisenhower.

Krupp took a drag from his cigarette and smiled to himself as he watched Himmler in full dress uniform stride past his office looking pale and sick as he conferred with Bormann who also had a rather sickly green complexion. Though speaking in low tones he heard the words 'Peron, Argentina, Bergen and submarines'. Krupp smiled broadly as he blew Russian tobacco smoke into the air chuckling. "The fuck is running to Argentina."

Being the Reich logistics coordinator he didn't have to hear Himmler speak to know his plans. He had in front of him a report that told him that several massive shipments of gold, silver and platinum had been shipped to Norway and subsequently shipped to an undisclosed location. Anyone who understood what was going on knew that senior Nazis were fleeing for their lives now that the last breath of Germany had been spent. They needed money to live on and they wanted to live well, apparently.

By his calculations the amounts of Gold, Platinum and Silver bullion in one shipment alone exceeded 50 billion pounds sterling and that was only a fraction of what had been sent so far. Again he chucked noting that the wealth had been calculated in pounds and not Deutch marcs. He'd been using Marcs in his fireplace when wood wasn't available; an example of how worthless the Reich currency was in 1945.

Putting his feet up on the desk leaning back he felt a rush of euphoria as he looked at his wristwatch. Horst Krupp was planning to leave. This was mainly because his knowledge of Himmlers death camps would count him as guilty and his prolonged association to Hitler guaranteed him a noose if not a life-long stay in prison. Neither of which he had any intention of facing. In less than 30 minutes he would take up his brief case and leave the Fuhrer Bunker, walk down a rubble-strewn street to a Mercedes sporting RF-SS insignia and drive it to a field twenty kilometers south of Berlin.

Parked in that field was a Fiesler Stork spotter plane fitted with long range tanks for the long flight he had planned. Not a fast plane it did have a long range and could get him to Italy and then Spain. It was also easy to fly and with the loss of an eye he would need an easy bird to fly without depth perception, particularly when landing. From Italy he would fuel up and load extra tanks for his flight to Spain. He didn't believe that a lone unarmed spotter plane would attract attention. As a precaution he planned to fly low and hope that he didn't run into a destroyer along the way. It figured that if he stayed far enough out to sea he wouldn't be bothered. He would fly at night and stay low and away from known radar stations reaching the Spanish coast at dawn the next day.

His plan was to remain in Spain for five years while the aftermath of the war played out. If he stayed out of sight and off the radar in five years he could take up residence in Argentina and live quietly as he had originally planned to do before Hitler screwed up his plans by starting a fucking war. Unbeknownst to Krupp the orders to build a home supposedly for Himmler to live in would be a brick by brick reproduction of the Castle in Wewelsberg Germany, the HQ of Himmler's SS. Complete with inlaid onyx swastikas and cremation pits and urns to hold the ashes of the fallen.

Krupp placed his files and bank information in the false bottom of his briefcase and then closed the flap. Horst was tapping his fingers impatiently on his desk irritated by the exceptionally loud ticking of the clock on the file cabinet, which seemed to be ticking rather more loudly than usual. It was then he realized that the halls outside his office had gone quiet. Nobody made a sound except for a strange murmuring group of voices.

Shuffling footsteps got louder and before long he realized it was Hitler. He had emerged from his offices deep in the bowels of the Fuhrer Bunker and was heading topside for some air. Next to him was Bormann and following close behind was Himmler paler than before with beads of sweat trickling down his temples, the very image of a defeated, fearful man facing his mortality.

Hitler was rambling on about something incoherent as his beaten and sickness ravaged body shook from some unknown malady that had plagued him since before the war. Most noticeable was the left hand that shook constantly now. He often had it in his pocket to keep it still. Today however, it was out and shaking worse than ever.

Something near pity surfaced for his Fuhrer but not enough to sway him from his path however. No, he had no desire to die for crimes he had little to do with much less the ability to prevent. The Allies apparently did not care about such trivialities. They wanted blood and would take it from the top down and he was in no mood to accommodate them.

Watching silently from his desk the three leading heads of the German state shuffled down the hall and up to the courtyard where they would stroll around and talk. The moment he heard the steel door open he grabbed his brief case and left before they could close it again which they wouldn't while the Fuhrer was outside. Yet, he felt an urgent need to make his escape. Something told him that if he didn't act now his chance to escape might very well vanish.

Reaching the doorway the guard recognized him saluted and let him pass. "Der Fuhrer is on the far side of the courtyard Herr General." The guard said assuming that Krupp was rushing to speak to Hitler. He merely nodded and headed off in the direction of the Fuhrer. When the guard was no longer looking he made a run for the street. It was late afternoon so the British bombers wouldn't be in Berlin for another two or three hours, plenty of time for him to make it to his air field and be long gone. In less than five minutes he located the garage in which his car was waiting, rather Himmler's car, a satisfying bit of revenge on the prick while making his ride to the airfield more pleasant. He'd always liked Himmler's car...it was much too good for that sniveling prick. A thought he wisely kept to himself.

Tossing the brief case into the passenger seat he started the car to let the engine warm up. From the trunk he pulled out the flags of the ReichsFuhrer staff and placed them in the flag mounts on the fenders. He had chosen Himmler's personal car for the convenience that it provided. No one dared stop or question the ReichsFuhrer or his staff, not if they expected to live.

It was his hope that the RF-SS insignia would be enough to get him by the checkpoints and the Beige G4 Mercedes was well known, a fact that could pose difficulties if Himmler noticed his car missing. He could have the entire SS on his tail if he wasn't careful. Horst looked out of the small window of the garage door to ensure that the coast was clear. Seeing nothing he threw open the doors and pulled the car out onto the street and headed directly out of town. Weaving the massive Mercedes through the streets he maintained a healthy pace as he worked his way out of Berlin.

Sadly he realized that he would not see Berlin again but the desperation to be away quelled his desire to stop and say goodbye to this hometown. A tear rolled down his cheek as the powerful engine pulled him along. To see Berlin in such a state broke his heart. What hurt worse was that he had been part of the reason Berlin now suffered the wrath of the world. Germany would rise again he knew…but he could never be part of that renewal, he would forever be a fugitive and his scar guaranteed that he would never step foot in Germany again. However difficult his leaving was, staying just wasn't an option, not if he wanted to survive and the voice inside his head was screaming to leave now as he somehow sensed his time was running short. This 'urge' caused him to press his foot down onto the accelerator.

At that very moment outside the Fuhrer Bunker Heinrich Himmler excused himself as the Fuhrer disappeared into the depths of the bunker. There was the briefest glimmer of sadness for his ailing and defeated Fuhrer, brief in this instance being the space of a single heartbeat.

Hitler had just rebuffed him for suggesting that he make overtures of peace to the Allies.

Perhaps a word from him and the world might once again fall in line as they once had. Only Hitler had lost his spark, that and his physician Dr. Morrell had him on a cocktail of narcotics that had the effect of dulling his pain as well as his once sharp mind. Hitler was, at that very moment, suicidal and intended to take Germany with him, "If Germany isn't strong enough to survive then it will die with me." he said turning to descend the steps into the depths of his citadel, the last place of refuge for National Socialism…a deep dark hole under a bombed out city.

Less than 24 hours earlier Himmler had been facing Eisenhower in a secret location outside Bonn Germany. He had offered to kill Adolf Hitler in return for negotiated peace and return to prewar borders. However, with the death camps being liberated and the recent murder of American POWs by the SS in the Arden during the Battle of the Bulge, Eisenhower was in no mood to negotiate anything more than total surrender and the hanging of those responsible, which Himmler was, very much so.

Himmler had directed the construction of the death camps and it had been he, himself who had issued the orders to eliminate POWs during their offensive to Antwerp. Eisenhower apparently knew this and made it clear that Himmler would not be allowed to negotiate his neck out of any nooses and that he should put a bullet in his own brain if he wished to avoid that end for himself. In fact Eisenhower lost his temper when Himmler persisted, offering to get the rope himself if he, the ReichsFuhrer, uttered so much as another syllable.

The meeting had not gone the way Himmler had anticipated not even close. Nobody had ever dared speak to him like that, not since he had been a corporal and certainly never as the ReichsFuhrer. He had badly underestimated the Allies desire for peace. They didn't want just peace they wanted the total and absolute eradication of the Third Reich. Heinrich Himmler unconsciously massaged his neck as one by one thousands of faces he had sent to die danced in his memory, taunting him as his own death approached much too quickly.

He had believed that he could negotiate a truce with Eisenhower. His delusion was that his status as head of State Police would grant him immunity provided he assassinated Hitler. They would then negotiate a cease-fire and a return to prewar borders. To him the whole thing seemed simple enough, but he had not anticipated the Allies anger. The Nazi 'total' war mentality and the murder of millions for the sake of racial purity had not been viewed as acceptable, this confused him. Nobody had ever liked the Jews, Gypsies, homosexuals or other lesser people.

He couldn't understand why the world was so angry at their efforts to rid the world of people nobody liked. "Why would they not see our plan was for the betterment of humanity? Why would anyone be annoyed with the death of a bunch of Jews and filthy gypsies?" He believed their actions were necessary to ensure racial purity and Arian strength for future generations of humanity.

During his ponderings he found himself wandering to the garage where he had parked his car, the beige Mercedes Hitler had given him on his birthday in 1942. Looking up he saw that the garage door was open and his beloved car gone. Not that he was upset with its loss as a possession but as a means of getting his ass away from Berlin and onto a plane bound for Lisbon, a fact he had not announced to his peers for obvious reasons.

His plane was supposed to leave in less than three hours. It was clear that nothing could be done to obtain an honorable peace, at least not one where he could be allowed to lead Germany or retire to his farm in Bavaria or even live. It was the idea of getting hung that concerned him most. He would be satisfied with living as a civilian if that is all he could get. But getting hung scared him like nothing else, he knew how terrible it could be if it wasn't done properly.

Himmler had already made arrangements to leave the country, prior to his meeting with Eisenhower. It was clear to him now that he should have, immediately following the meeting with Eisenhower, headed straight to the plane and Portugal where a ship would take him to Argentina. Contingency plans had been made by shipping tones of bullion to a base from where they would finance their lives in hiding. But that was on hold now that his car was gone. Immediately he ran back to his offices in the bunker and called his Gestapo chief to report his car stolen and ordered him to find it and have the person driving it shot.

Once done he began taking roll of those persons in the bunker and those persons who had recently left, he soon discovered that General Krupp had followed himself, Bormann and Hitler out of the bunker but had not come to see them. It was clear then that Krupp was the one who had taken his car, or was at least a strong candidate, being the only one to have left the bunker in the last hour and the only one besides himself to know where his car was. Krupp, the person who had seen through his scheme to control Hitler and through him take control of the war and whom he had fired because of it, had taken his revenge by stealing his car to escape himself. He would see to it that Krupp was shot. Something he should have done long ago.

His phone rang. Answering it he was told that his car had been spotted less than 30 minutes earlier heading south and that a car was already in pursuit to intercept Krupp. The order was given to shoot him immediately upon capture. That would tie up that loose end. Not that it mattered, the war was lost and Eisenhower made it clear that he was facing a noose with no possible way to avoid it other than to run or take his own life.

Strangely it was that 'choice' that brought him a measure of peace. He reached into his desk and pulled out a black leather box with silver SS runes mounted on its face. Opening it revealed, 4 vials of cyanide poison nestled snuggly in red satin cloth protecting each vial. He let a sigh escape his lips as his fevered brain accepted the possibility of taking his own life versus being hung on the gallows. Placing the box in his breast pocket he would carry it for the rest of the war and use it only if he were unable to avoid capture.

In late May of 1945, dressed like a common laborer having shaved off his mustache Hienrich Himmler, Hitlers second in command, the man responsible for the deaths of millions of innocent men, women and children was captured. He was not recognized at first and was nearly let go until he was recognized at the last minute by a woman whose son had been hanged on Himmler's orders for throwing rocks at a tank, a five year old boy.

Upon being formally arrested Himmler bit into a cyanide capsule hidden in his cheek and died on the floor looking up at the woman who had recognized him. Without a word, she walked up to him looked him in the eye just before he died and spit on his face. His last cognizant view of the world was that of an angry, vengeful mother with her spit in his eye.

****** Krupp's narrow escape *******

The insignia worked flawlessly as not one single guard had the courage to physically check the car. The moment he was outside the Berlin city limits where the roadways were no longer littered with debris he punched the gas and made the 20km journey in less than 15 minutes. Horst pulled the car up to the aircraft, which was covered in camouflage netting to keep it from being seen from the low flying allied aircraft. He then transferred his luggage from the car to the plane and covered the car with the camouflage netting.

When he was through it appeared to be a large car shaped bush inside the trees. Nobody would see it unless they were feet from the vehicle. Horst waited until just before dusk to push the plane onto the roadway. He didn't want to risk the Allies seeing him take off and shoot him down. His plan was to take off just as the sun set. It would be 4 or 5 hours before he could touch down in the mountain valley where he had pre-positioned his equipment.

The engine started instantly. He nodded with pride and frustration in German engineering. "How is it we can build such magnificent machines and still not win a fucking war?" he whispered to himself in bemused dismay. While the engine warmed Horst lit a cigarette wondering if it was wise to smoke in the cockpit. In WWI he knew it was a bad idea to smoke in the cockpit of his DR1 because the tank was sitting in his lap, yet in spite of the danger he did anyway. "Bah…another war we lost" he whispered. Shrugging he threw caution to the wind and inhaled deeply on the Russian cigarette.

This was his last pack and he considered how he would miss the pungent stink and their burning, acrid flavor. Eyeing his instruments in the low light he flipped on the dash lights and dimmed them to the appropriate setting so he could see them and still not give himself away at night. The engine temperature was coming up nicely. He ran through his planned route in his head over and over to see if he had memorized it properly. He was flying the route at night and on instruments because he could not rely on landmarks so he could not afford to make mistakes. He wanted to make it to the meadow in Western Italy by midnight. That would give him all night to rest and all day to go over his flight path for his flight to Spain the following night, if he chose to leave immediately.

Using official bases was too risky. He wasn't sure if anyone would notice that he had gone or even if they'd care. He smiled thinking that Himmler might miss his car. 'How long would it be before he noticed?' He wondered. Laughing to himself he imagined how the sniveling miscreant might look when he discovered his personal car was missing when he abandoned the Fuhrer. 'That might get his temper up' he thought letting out a chuckle. He went through the checklist and then stepped outside to remove the chalks.

Looking behind the plane having seen something in the corner of this eye and got instantly serious as he looked behind the plane and saw the distant flashes of blacked out headlights of a motorcar speeding toward him. The back road he was on was not normally traveled which was why he chose to hide the plane there. Himmler apparently missed his car and put two and two together much more quickly than expected. How they'd found him was a question he didn't need or want to have answered.

It was likely they had radioed all the bases and would be looking out for him with orders to shoot him on sight as a deserter. That is if Himmler gave the order. If Hitler gave the order it would be to have him returned for trial and then have him hung with piano wire, a sight he'd seen too many times. Just then he heard the 'pop-pop-pop' of gunfire and the telltale sound of bullets passing by his head followed by a 'tink-whine' of a ricochet. "Well at least they don't plan to hang me" he said to himself climbing into the cockpit.

Turning his head just for a second he spotted the black Mercedes Benz sporting SS runes racing from the woods attempting to block his escape. Gunning the engine to full throttle the Stork jumped forward surprisingly quick and in a matter of seconds had its tail off the ground and was airborne no more than a minute from when the first bullets had whizzed by his head.

Climbing to 500 feet Horst took out his torch and examined the wings for bullet holes. His tanks were not leaking. As he searched for damage he circled the meadow he'd just taken off from as the squad of SS fired wildly at him, their guns not powerful enough to reach him even at such a low altitude. Still he'd tempted fate long enough and pointed the Stork on the heading that would take him directly over his mountain meadow. He did not worry about night fighters because there were none close enough to be deployed in the time necessary to intercept him. By then he'd have altered his course anyway. Still, it didn't hurt to be cautious.

On the ground the Gestapo troops stood silently watching the plane disappear into the night. After a minute all they could see of the plane was the blue flame of the exhaust as it leveled off at 1000 feet. Each man was numb and dispassionate about doing their job, all of them except for the SS Lieutenant who was a deeply fanatical devotee of National Socialism. He swore viciously at the Generals plane now out of range, yet he un-holstered his pistol and emptied the clip into the dark silhouette in frustration. The Lieutenant had not yet lost hope. He was convinced that the Fuhrer had more won- der weapons hidden away to use on his enemies, weapons he was holding in reserve until the last minute. They had already won the war, several times…and they would do it again, one last time.

Holstering his gun he looked at the Sergeant in charge. "Look over there for the ReichsFuhrers car. It should be in those trees. In a minute they found it and uncovered it. It was undamaged. "Excellent, the ReichsFuhrer will be pleased.' Pointing to a corporal he said 'You drive it and follow behind us. Do not damage that car or you will be shot" he said and got into his own car. Less than an hour later the Lieutenant was put against a wall and shot for failing to kill Krupp…the madness had begun.

Meanwhile…Leveling off at his chosen altitude Horst set the trim and flipped on the autopilot, which was really just a cable that kept the stick still and did nothing to correct for wind or the Earth's rotation. What it did was give the pilot time to either eat a meal or drink something or to deploy the relief tube, which allowed a pilot to relieve himself in flight. This time he needed to calm himself. His hands were shaking from his recent brush with death.

Horst reached for the loose pack of cigarettes on the passenger seat. Lighting the cigarette he once again threw caution to the wind in the need to settle his nerves. Cracking the access panel just enough to let the smoke out he inhaled deeply and sighed in relief. Scanning the sky around him his ears were alert for the sounds of another airplane or worse gunfire from another airplane. Thankfully he heard nothing. But then it had been why he chose this spot to take off from. It was close enough to Berlin for a quick escape and far enough away from air bases to avoid pursuit.

Six hours later Horst Krupp, SS General, former heir to the Krupp shipbuilding fortune and fugitive of both the allies as well as his own, soon to be defeated Government landed on a tiny mountain top meadow in Northwestern Italy. A drover's shack provided him with shelter and the stove inside warmth. His plane he covered with netting to keep it hidden from both allied and German aircraft now that he was a fugitive of both the Allies and Germany. It was not a major concern because he knew, perhaps better than they did that there weren't enough resources left to expend searching for one lone man. He also wasn't that well known. Yet he took precautions against discovery never the less. Not to do so would have been fool-hardy in the extreme.

During the night cloud cover blanketed his alpine meadow adding a measure of protection against discovery allowing him to sleep soundly. The next morning a solitary single engine plane flying high overhead woke him. Instantly he recognized it as an American spotter plane but it was flying in a straight line heading south. It was not in a position to see his meadow or the netting along the tree line covering his shack and plane.

The rest of the day he spent refueling the plane, napping and reading a German translation of a Louis L' Amore western 'Hondo'. As he read he found himself regretting not being able to visit the American West again as he had done in his youth. It would have been nice, he thought to build a 'ranch' deep in the Arizona desert raising mustangs and living like an American cowboy. Shaking his head he laughed off his childish impulses, nonetheless his regret remained.

The next evening he landed on a patch of land along the Spanish Mediterranean coast where he parked the Stork inside his barn on the Hacienda estate he had purchased immediately following his decision to vacate Germany. He would remain a reclusive hermit on his estate while the war came to an end and the allies hunted for his former colleagues and himself. A fact he was forced to remember from time to time when he had urges to 'escape' his self-imposed prison.

For the next five years he watched the world from a tower separated and safe from discovery. It would be from this estate that he would consolidate his power and control over Odessa, particularly after the Nuremburg trials. Up to that point the SS expected short prison sentences of their leaders and a possible return to power with their release. When the bulk of them were sentenced to hang or to lengthy prison sentences, then and only then did the SS abandon hope and flee. By creating a pipeline for escaping SS he created a loyal power base in Argentina that would facilitate his control over the entire organization in the years to come.

Chapter 12
Bahia Blanca Argentina: Present Day
The new face of Odessa

PATRICE VERGA SAT in the back of her 600 series Mercedes limousine smoking a cigarette enjoying the passing scenery. A tight bodied blonde with ice blue eyes and a figure that turned heads she had been a small time crime boss in Buenos Aires who did remarkably well with two brothels and a legitimate trucking company as a front for cocaine distribution. She was able to place herself as a go between for the Columbian Cartels by keeping the shipments small and her drivers on a 24-hour delivery cycle. The small yet consistent deliveries kept her operation off the police radar. Her brothels were a source of information that kept her nose clean because most of her regular clients were police officers who liked to talk especially when a woman was pleasuring them orally. It was an incredibly effective interrogation technique and when properly applied, was better than any truth serum.

It was her talent for staying off police radar that drew the attention of The Operation who needed a discreet, connected administrator;

someone who was morally flexible and knew when to look the other way. She had been brought in as a go between to help them develop connections overseas. Patrice had a particularly effective manner that made the person she was negotiating with believe that 'they' were making the rules when in fact she had skillfully pulled them into her web. As long as they believed they were in charge and she got what she wanted it didn't matter what anybody thought. She was so effective at developing connections that she rocketed upwards to senior advisor of the head of the organization, an ancient German who had clearly once been a Nazi.

Initially the old men were interested in the visual entertainment of watching her give presentations, as many were aged male chauvinists who could no longer enjoy the physical attentions of a woman without their hearts exploding. However, they soon gained a new respect for her when she began providing them with toeholds in markets they had once thought out of reach. As the senior members began to die off she gained position until finally the last surviving member of the original organization promoted her to his right hand and supposedly was second in line to head the Operation, or so she had been led to believe.

Patrice was on her way to make her quarterly report of the organizations activities and to report a new development. A person of interest to the organization surfaced unexpectedly on an island off of French Guyana, a person believed to be dead. Hans Beck was last seen in Switzerland in 1970 prior to an altercation with 'Odessa', an altercation that left six Odessa operatives dead along with Becks wife Sarah. Beck then vanished along with the 150 Million dollars they'd been after. Money he'd supposedly made on the black market during the war, which Odessa decided was rightfully 'theirs' as he had been in the SS while making it.

Nothing more than an excuse to justify robbery as moral and just to the surviving members of the SS. Truly hard core Nazis died with their Fuhrer immediately after the war either by suicide or by the gallows, death before dishonor on their lips as the trap sprang, or as the hammer fell on the bullet that ended their twisted, miscreant lives.

The money they were after was transferred to a bank in Costa Rica and cashed out, 150 million dollars US. Odessa searched the entire South American banking system for large sums being deposited. Nothing turned up in the quantities they were seeking. Hans Beck simply faded into non-being, in the traceable sense.

What they didn't realize was Beck had flown back to Switzerland with the cash in courier containers and deposited the money back into the same bank under four different numbers over the next six weeks. Since Hans had been aware of their watching the bank he removed the money thereby removing their interest in his bank, never once suspecting that he would double back and deposit the money into the same bank, a fact to which they never caught on.

No trace of him was seen again until a senior member of the organization Christophe Lutz, a former Gestapo agent, Nazi fugitive and renowned pervert had recognized Beck while on vacation on the island of St. Vincent. He had been part of the team sent to arrest Beck the day he arrived in Singen in March 1945. Later that day Beck escaped following a firefight that killed two Gestapo agents. Lutz, having lost his commanding officer and with Germany in disarray and himself on the Allies wanted list, decided to drive his Mercedes to Switzerland, purchased a ticket to Spain where he lived quietly until the late 1960s when Mossad came calling. Odessa had warned him mere hours before he was to be kidnapped and taken back to

Israel for the rape and murder of ten Jewish women. Convicted in absentia he was sentenced to hang but was never apprehended.

Patrice shook her head in disgust. She knew Lutz from her dealings within the Operation. He was a low level grunt used to do dirty work and wasn't all that bright. Also being a fat slob no self-respecting woman would let him touch her…voluntarily. That aside Patrice had her doubts regarding the validity of his sighting Beck. Lutz was the sort to invent a story to make himself look good. Yet it bore looking into given that it was the 'only' lead to surface with regard to Beck in 30 years. Weak as the information was it had to be reported, but the other details she discovered were enough to form a possible hypothesis.

Long since disenchanted with her employers she had grown even more so having learned that the 'Operation' was a front for Odessa. "I work for a bunch of fucking Nazis" she muttered to herself. She had no choice but to do their bidding because they had her by the balls, so to speak. She was in too deep. Clearing her head she focused on the file in her lap.

Thumbing through the file she found it interesting that the island itself was apparently an early 20th century landfill. The bulk of its mass apparently came from the digging of the Panama Canal. The origin of the island wasn't as strange as the personal history of the builder a serving naval officer of the German Imperial Navy, Commander Johan Weiss whose specialty was building naval bases. The fact he had been using the name Juan Dominguez bore up to more careful scrutiny.

That discovery had been pure luck because she had his photograph traced out of curiosity. It was this curious find that prompted her to report the sighting of Beck to her boss. A land fill island built by a serving Imperial German Naval Officer in good standing before WWI who was using an alias clearly for the purpose of creating a cover was a detail that could not be ignored. Also with Beck being sighted on that very same island, the odds of coincidence were low, but then the reported sighting was from a person known to fabricate stories though Lutz did not know why Beck was wanted by the Operation. Mistaken identity was the most likely answer to this and yet she had nothing but supposition, speculation and a curious find that could merely be a strong, weird coincidence.

The old man, as he was called by those around him, but never to his face or within earshot of him, made her nervous. Not that he had ever done anything to make her so; there was something about his demeanor that filled her with dread and even a sense of loathing. She could not put her finger on it other than the icy chill that ran down her spine whenever she was in his presence. Patrice put it down to female intuition. Yet, it was not that either. Whatever it was she dreaded being near him, his being a Nazi didn't help.

Patrice was the administrative head of the organization or 'the operation' as it was known. Her current position was more by default because the other administrators had died of old age, supposedly. In the ten years she had been with the operation she had gone from a street level operator to administration of the Operations worldwide projects, as such she knew far too much about the operations inner workings to be allowed to leave the organization…alive. Little did she realize that her knowledge alone made her a liability in the chauvinistic mind of the old man, her boss.

Her position gave her wealth far greater than she had when she was the sole owner of her own businesses. She had farmed out their administration to a colleague when she could no longer run them herself. This kept her in touch with police and where they had their focus. Yet, the operation wasn't about to let her go and retirement was out of the question. She had floated the idea once to see what would happen. It was made clear that she could retire whenever she wanted.

The next morning she found a bullet on her bedside table with her name engraved on the casing and the words "retirement plan" under her name. So it was implied that if ever she decided to 'retire' she would be *'retired'* by the organization permanently. Thus her plans for retirement were nixed.

Odessa, was an organization formed by former SS officers to spirit away their leadership at the end of WWII. Odessa had originally operated out of Germany until the de-Nazification effort by the Bonn Government made that difficult. They moved their center of operations to Buenos Aires where they provided security for their former bosses hiding in the Argentine outback and other South American Nations.

As the original members aged and died off the emerging leadership found itself less dedicated to the 'cause' as much as they were to expanding 'the operations' reach. The ideals of Hitler's National Socialist Party were no longer convenient and often problematic when it came to doing business. Even the Columbian Cartels wanted nothing to do with Nazis. So it was decided that Odessa fade away and a new organization be formed in its place, quietly.

These changes did not sit well with the old guard of the SS who had originally hoped to form a 'Fourth Reich' in Argentina. That had been the intent in 1945 when the Nazi leadership first began arriving in Argentina. The first and only 'official ' delegation arrived in Buenos Aires in early 1945 when it was clear that all was lost. They had arrived with full military pomp with flags waving and dress uniforms pressed ready to 'allow' Argentina the 'honor' of hosting their exiled government and entering the war on Germanys behalf.

What they hadn't counted on was the publics' reaction to their presence. The motorcade made up of a G4 six wheel drive Mercedes sedan, four Kubelwagon, two troop carriers and a motorcycle escort, was pelted with produce and dog excrement by an outraged crowd who was howling hate filled insults at them. Not the reception they were expecting from a formerly friendly nation.

Two officers walked up the steps of the Capitol for a meeting with the President of Argentina. That meeting ended suddenly with the Nazi delegation escorted from the Capitol under armed guard with full military escort back to the German consulate where they were asked to remain for their own safety. It was made clear that the Argentine Government had no interest in entering a war on behalf of Germany, not since the death camps had been liberated. No government wanted anything to do with Germany or the Nazis after the extent of the atrocities were made public.

Prominent Argentine Nazis found themselves unwelcome at social functions and increasingly ostracized by once friendly Argentine society. This change of tone by their hosts forced many prominent Nazis to literally fade into the woodwork and disappear among the German populace, adopting Spanish names and ditching anything that could identify them as a Nazi.

Many had hoped to live openly in Argentina as refugees safe from prosecution under the protection of the Argentine Government. What they discovered was that Argentina would 'tolerate' their presence and allow them to live there, but they would not be allowed to exercise their politics openly or even hold public rallies to show their allegiance to Adolf Hitler. In short they had been told to shut up, be quiet and not make trouble, an inauspicious end for men who had once conquered the whole of Europe.

At the end of the war an Allied contingent made up of British Royal Marines entered the consulate compound to arrest the Nazi officials there. Upon arrival they found all German personnel gone and a tunnel that ran from the garage facility to the commercial wharf a half-mile away. Reports began to surface of a curiously large submarine mooring up to the wharf late at night as personnel and equipment were quickly loaded on board. It was seen by enough people to be taken seriously, but reported too late to do anything about.

The building was completely empty with a heavy layer of dust suggesting that they had vacated the consulate weeks before. Over the next few years fugitive Nazis would flood into Argentina, Paraguay, Chile and Bolivia where they would blend into the ex-patriot German populations. Argentina having the heaviest German population bore the brunt of that invasion.

Among them a battle scarred SS General with the economic resources necessary to buy off public officials and to buy a remote piece of land on which to build his personal retreat. The gate of which Patrice found herself facing while a security detail of blonde, blue eyed German speaking, machine gun toting, young men inspected her car for bombs, cameras or anything that could be used to harm their employer.

Patrice was the only person within 'the operation' allowed to see the old man in the flesh that she knew of. He had to be nearly 100 if he was a day but with none of the usual age related debilitation. Even his black hair had retained its youthful appearance. His body was heavily muscled and vigorous belying the age his face betrayed. On initial appearances he seemed a normal old gentleman. A scar ran from deep under his hairline down through his eye and into his left cheekbone giving him a menacing appearance. The left eye was covered with a black eye patch, which, according to her sources was lost in a bomb blast.

She knew little of him except that he was German and had arrived in Argentina several years after the war in Europe. He arrived with enormous wealth with which he had purchased 3000 acres of land on which he built a castle, an exact duplicate of Himmler's personal retreat, or so it was rumored. No one outside his group had ever seen it due to its remote location. If you were 'invited' you had to agree to wear a hood to keep its exact location secret. The castle itself was built deep within a canyon so that it could not be seen from the air or from the sea. This fact spurred speculation that Himmler himself had commissioned its construction and expected to take up residence when he escaped Germany, which he obviously did not.

It didn't take a rocket scientist to figure out that he was a Nazi. Argentina was full of them, or had been. Most of them had either died off or had been captured by the Israelis. It was something Argentina had to accept having been officially neutral but sympathetic to Germany with a heavy German expatriate community. In fact there were more Germans living in South America than there were in Germany, particularly after the war. Argentina simply chose to ignore the Nazis and made token protests to the Israeli government after they kidnapped a fugitive Nazi.

RICHARD BEND

In truth the Argentine Government was glad to see the bad ones go. Their presence in Argentina was a source of shame for most Argentines of good conscience. Yet, those who remained were either exceptionally dangerous or simply not important enough to bother with. Patrice had reason to believe she was working for one of the more dangerous Nazis.

She knew his real name, but wasn't supposed to. She as a result feigned ignorance for her own safety. He insisted that she refer to him as 'Mein Fuhrer'. Even then she was not allowed to look him directly in the face, she imagined it was because they didn't want to run the risk of a sketch artist getting a hard fix on his identity if ever she were picked up and interrogated. Though she surmised the scar would have to be a dead give-away. How many old Nazis had such a distinctive scar? She put up with the charade because she had no choice, got paid well and was allowed to live her life without interference.

Patrice kept her private life very private and enjoyed a vigorous sex life with few taboos. She enjoyed the company of men only when she felt the need, preferring the sensual touch of women because they were far more sensual than a man and tended to keep up with her. It didn't hurt that there were devices that allowed her the plea- sure of a 'man' without ever having to deal with the vulgarity or the physical limitations of one. Men could only 'keep their end up' for so long before being a useless panting object in her bed, women had sensuality and stamina. But there were times she wanted the aggres- sive vulgarity of a man to remind her that she was a woman, but only when she was in the mood for it, which she was at that moment.

Once her car cleared the gate she was searched rather extensively by two of the young men guarding the gate. She didn't mind their roughness. In fact she enjoyed it, especially when Werner frisked her. A brutally handsome man of about 30 with platinum blonde hair, broad muscular shoulders and a tiny waist that drove her mad with lust, what lust she could have for a man, anyway.

On several occasions she had been taken to the back room for a more thorough search that usually culminated with Patrice bent over the 'interrogation' table with her skirt hiked up over her waist and Werner pounding his rather impressive self into her. This time she wore a garter belt and no panties so that he knew to interrogate her more thoroughly. A smile curled her lips as she felt his hands begin the search.

Twenty minutes later Patrice was standing in the main salon waiting for 'Der Fuhrer' to enter the room. She gazed into the fire savoring the warmth of Werner's recent 'interrogation'. He'd been particularly brutal this time. When he discovered her lack of undergarments he grabbed her by the wrist and dragged her to the 'room' where he then threw her onto the table. "Spread em' he said. When she did he dropped his pants, grabbed her ankles and took her savagely ramming himself into her slamming the table against the wall. This time Werner made her bring herself to climax while he took her. He always lasted a long time, for a man, which is why she liked his attention so much. In fact he was the only man she'd allowed to fuck her in several years. Her orgasm was so powerful that she cried out which caused Werner to cover her mouth with his hand as she convulsed in orgasm as his girth and length burrowed deeper and deeper before he himself climaxed.

They both left the room as if nothing happened. He shoved her hard against her car to give her one last 'frisking', which for Werner was 'thank you'.

When she heard the door open she automatically moved her eyes to a spot that would guarantee that she could not get a clear facial view of her boss. Out of the corner of her eye she watched the tall, lean man move to his seat. "Hello Patrice" he said in a voice that always chilled her. No matter how kindly he spoke to her there was something about this man that unsettled her.

"Good After noon Mein Fuhrer" Patrice said keeping her voice even and absent of emotion.

"What have you to report?" He said.

"Mein Fuhrer, We have had a new development in the project which you assigned me last year when you tasked me with locating an SS fugitive by the name of Hans Beck. Up until now I've had nothing to report. Last week one of our operatives took a photograph of a man who fits his description living on an island called St. Vincent off the coast of French Guyana. It's an obscure island with a small permanent population. It started out in the 40s and 50s as a pirate colony for drug traffickers, fugitives and political refugees'. She paused then continued.

'While researching the details of why he might be on this island, thinking that there may be family ties to property we discovered that the island itself was actually a land fill in which a Columbian firm 'Cartagena industrial waste Disposal' was given a permit to build it as a land fill site to dispose of industrial waste from the Gulf region starting roughly in 1900. The company itself ceased to exist sometime in the 1920s, but the title to the island itself remained in their name until the mid-1970s when a church based in Costa Rica bought the property"

Sighing impatiently Krupp said. "So what does that have to do with anything? So he is on an island that was man made…so what?"

Swallowing nervously she continued, "I'm getting to that Mein Fuhrer. In our background search we discovered an old photograph of the owner of the company one Juan Dominguez who didn't appear to be a Columbian or even a European Spaniard. So we ran a computerized search of his photograph and found a match. An Imperial German Naval Architect by the name of Johann Weiss', she paused for emphasis, 'His specialty was naval base construction." she paused.

"Again…what does this have to do with locating Beck?" he said growing impatient making Patrice cringe.

"Sir, you also tasked me with locating the possible hiding places for a stock pile of bullion worth several hundred billion pounds in1945. If such a horde does exist, the net worth of that horde is easily 100 times the 1945 estimates." She felt her heart race not knowing how he might respond to this news.

"Go on" he said quietly.

"Yes, the question raised was, what was a 'serving' line officer in the Imperial German Navy doing in South America posing as a Columbian businessman building a landfill when his specialty happens to be naval base construction?" She swallowed then continued. "Sir, this could mean that the Kaiser commissioned this officer to build the island as a secret naval base that was later used by Adolf Hitler as a forward base as well as a storage depot for a vast quantity of bullion. This island may be where the missing bullion is hidden and why Beck may be there. It may be a coincidence but I'm not inclined to believe so. Because of all the places Beck could choose to hide, why this one specific, obscure island?"

Horst, nodded his head. "Beck disappeared with the bullion when it was shipped to an undisclosed location. He was part of the transport team that was meant to disperse the funds for whatever uses were deemed prudent as directed by Hitler. Only the gold and those attached to the mission disappeared." He said with some irritation.

Patrice continued her report after he had finished his thought. "None of those men ever reappeared except for Beck who was located in Switzerland in 1970. The money he had was the same money he'd acquired on the black market and was nothing close to the amount he helped transport, that and it was already in a Swiss bank 'before' the war ended. Gold hitting the market in quantities like that is hard to miss. According to the records you allowed me access to, Odessa watched the commercial smelters for years and nothing of that magnitude was seen. That and as I said before bullion of that quantity hitting the market would eventually drive the prices of bullion down possibly crashing the markets."

Horst looked up suddenly in surprise and anger. "Who told you about Odessa? I never gave you access to anything that indicated we belonged to that organization" An icy menace filled the room that chilled Patrice to the core. She began backing away as her fear rose, realizing that she had stepped over some invisible line. Before she could say a word he stood up and slowly turned to face her directly.

A calm, icy and extremely dangerous voice filled the room forcing Patrice to grasp the back of a chair to keep from collapsing to her knees in fear. "I commend you on your diligence Patrice, but I must apologize for my negligence. Yes, Odessa was once an organization

I belonged to and led…for a time. It no longer exists and it would be wise to never make reference to it again.' He stalked closer and looked down at her smiling but the anger in his one eye made the smile seem vile and evil. 'The operation has avoided the attention of Mossad for quite some time. It would be inconvenient if we had Israeli intelligence interfering with our enterprises."

He grabbed her by the arms and with surprising strength pushed her hard against the wall so that her head collided violently with the paneling. The impact of which nearly knocked her unconscious. Grimacing so that Krupp appeared to be a flesh covered skull and hissed in a low, venomous oath "Odessa is a name that must be forgotten. It must never be mentioned, hinted at or even suggested that "The Operation" is or was Odessa. Even in the underworld Odessa represents something abhorrent to even the most bloodthirsty crime syndicates. We had to disband officially and reform under another name and refit our image so that we could see to the advancement of the cause set forth by our beloved Fuhrer on the day he sacrificed himself for the fatherland. That is why we hired you,' he hissed. 'No woman could be seen as leading Odessa. You, my dear, have provided us with an effective blind."

Sweat suddenly appeared on his temples and forehead as a look of confusion and shame contorted his facial features. He then put her down suddenly. Turning away he stumbled back to his seat and fell into it drained of what energy he had prior to his agitation. His face fell into an open hand. "We once had control of the world governments. We dictated policy through corrupt politicians who we'd blackmailed. Our influence was worldwide and we had money pouring in from many different sources. Our influence peaked with the igniting of the Six Day war in 1967. We were instrumental in that endeavor." He sighed wearily.

"The existence of Israel was a slap to the face to the SS because 'we' were used as an excuse for its creation. If 'we' were responsible for Israel's existence as a nation, it was our duty to erase it. It took a great deal of work to organize the Arab nations," he said shaking his head and laughed humorlessly. "It was that action and the careless talk of our members that got Odessa noticed by Israel. Mossad was all over us after that. Robert Kennedy supported Israeli efforts to hunt us down cutting down our web of influence in the American Congress one string at a time. We had him killed in hopes that his death would stop the Israelis. We had not anticipated that the Israelis would double their efforts as a result.

We disbanded officially in 1980 and reformed as 'The operation' once the heat died down. You were brought in as we were re-establishing our former influence." He sighed wearily and seemed to sag in his chair. "If we are to strengthen our grip and shape world events as we once did, we will need money. Which is why I put you on the task of locating Beck; he is the only one who knows where the bullion is. If he is still alive, we must get our hands on him and see what he knows. You needn't worry about us creating another Reich. We simply use our 'Nazi' past as a means of blackmailing honest politicians into behaving in our interests. The last thing any of these spineless men today want is controversy that might interfere with their career or rather the money associated with their career. We simply use that to our advantage when and if the need arises."

He was silent for a long time, so long that Patrice thought maybe he had fallen asleep. Just as she was about to leave he started and looked into the blazing fire. "I did not dismiss you. Finish your report and then you may leave. I don't want to hear of you mentioning Odessa again. Is that clear?"

Patrice nodded and said "Yes, Mein Fuhrer, I understand." Her voice shook with a combination of rage and fear. She had known he was a Nazi, but to have been used in such a way enraged her. She was ashamed at having been used in repositioning them to peddle their influence on the world. With her heart sinking and her head spinning Patrice struggled to regain her composure.

"You may finish your briefing miss Verga" His voice was once again the icy rigid voice she had once been used to but now that she knew his truest nature, jumped in fear as the voice echoed.

Swallowing her heart she looked over her file. And with a forced effort swallowed the rage she felt struggling to keep it out of her voice. Then with a forced calm she pushed forward as if nothing had happened. "Yes, Mein Fuhrer, where was I? Ah yes. If this gold was never put into circulation we can assume that most of the original shipment is still on the island."

Horst piped up "That is if they took it to this island. What you say is pure speculation, nothing more. The fact that Beck is there means nothing it's a tourist spot and has been since the 1950s. It's been loaded with people for all that time and if nobody located a massive mound of gold bullion by now it is likely not on the island."

"Mein Fuhrer the town 'St. Vincent' is actually leased by the inhabitants and owned by a corporate firm in Costa Rica. The corporate firm is actually a Presbyterian church giving it a tax exemption while allowing shares to be sold. However, there is only one shareholder by the name of Archie Davis. We did a background check on him and it turns out that he was a Royal Marine recruited in 1940 by SOE as a field agent. His service record is blacked out and sealed from 1940 to 1944. In June of 1944 he was attached to the administration offices of SOE and spent the next few months researching the whereabouts of missing Nazi personnel who were not listed among the dead, missing or captured."

"In April of 1945 he was assigned the task of locating Beck who was reported seen in Bergen Norway in March of 1945. He first went to Singen Germany where Beck was officially posted and from where he was last seen leaving his headquarters under fire from Gestapo agents two of whom were killed. The details surrounding this event are unclear. But an arrest warrant was issued for Beck around this period. At the end of the war Flight Lt. Davis is forcibly retired from active service apparently for being too aggressive in his hunt for 'Odessa', which the allies were not willing to acknowledge. He turns up ten years later disguised as a Presbyterian minister in Cuba and later in French Guyana. The church in which he preached owns the island and Archie Davis owns the church." Patrice smiled... Reverend Davis...is worth at present $300,000,000 dollars US. It is also interesting that Mr. Davis has never attended Seminary school of any sort anywhere.

Horst sat up suddenly "$300,000,000 dollars US?" he asked. It was clear that he had not heard the last sentence having latched onto the dollar amount in his account. Patrice merely nodded. "Very well, I'd say this needs looking into.' He paused, 'This Davis fellow clearly has access to the bullion if what you say is accurate. Not that I doubt you Miss Verga. I trust that what you say is true, but I am not inclined to expend our resources until we know for certain."

He stared thoughtfully into the fire. "This needs to be done quietly Patrice. We can ill afford to miss this opportunity or have the authorities involved." He turned to face her. "Since you have not said anything of this to anyone before today, I will keep Werner on his leash, for now." Patrice went cold inside as he stared at her with his one good eye then said without blinking "To be fair to you Patrice, if you ever see Werner anywhere but at the front gate you might want to run. That would be a pity, because he likes fucking you. That will be all Miss Verga. Keep me posted…Good day." He then left the study without saying another word. It was all she could do not to throw the file at the back of his head as he walked away from her.

On the drive back to her beach front home Patrice emptied a bottle of Champagne and was half way through a second when her driver pulled up to her home. Having her life threatened was nothing new, but the revelation that 'he' knew of her dalliances with Werner sickened her. Her stomach twisted into a knot thinking that the one man she wanted physically might be sent to kill her. It was an unsettling thought to say the least. She had to find a way out or end up dead.

That morning she had been 'she thought' second only to Der Fuhrer. Now she was just another tool to be used and discarded. She felt trapped before but now she felt violated.

The next morning her head ached as her private jet taxied down the runway before heading to St. Vincent island. Each jolt and bounce made her want to vomit. But that was nothing compared to the despair she felt knowing that she had been instrumental in furthering the agenda of one of the most dangerous organizations in the world. The only thing that brought her comfort was the new flight attendant Lisa who provided her with adequate distraction on the flight.

Chapter 13
The Compound

THE TREE LYING across the roadway had apparently rotted in place and crumbled as the bumper of the jeep pushed through the bark. It wasn't nearly as solid as he had originally thought, though he had been pushing it with his hands the last time and didn't know what to look for. As the Jeeps bumper pushed right through it he noted that termites had made quick work of the trees interior which was little more than sawdust that crumbled under the weight of the Jeep.

The road itself was not nearly as bad as he first thought. There was a natural canopy created by the trees that lined the roadway keeping it hidden from low flying aircraft. On the other side of the tree line was a cliff that would allow you to free fall several hundred feet before you hit anything. However, Rick did notice that the road was made of solid concrete. The road bed was as solid as the day it was first built albeit with occasional slippery patch of moss or some tropical variant which proved unnerving when the tires spun over the patches. The shallow grade was designed to be easily traveled and wide enough to accommodate large trucks and automobiles. As wide as it was it would be impossible to back out of the way of any opposing traffic, not that he expected any. This led him to believe that the designers had likely provided another way down. They had to because a traffic mishap on this road could prove fatal.

Driving up the mountain took 30 minutes because he was being cautious not wanting to make himself a statistic of poor judgment. The incidents from several days before were still fresh in his memory feeding his caution. Once on top he discovered a clearing surrounded by bushes and trees that were planted apparently to maintain privacy. As unkempt as it was the atmosphere proved inviting and somehow calming. It was immediately apparent that the temperature at this altitude was at least ten degrees cooler, that or the humidity was lower. In either event it was much more comfortable on the plateau. The driveway was circular and circumvented the plateau. What plant life there was had over taken the buildings entirely with the exception of the one corner of the house he had spotted days earlier before meeting Archie. The compound had been purpose built though moderately stylish.

To his right a large garage facility stood erect and overgrown with no less than three bays large enough to house a Deuce and a half. To his immediate left he noted a boxy concrete shed or what he thought was a shed, which on closer inspection turned out to be a pillbox with the slits open to the north, south and east the entrance of which was, of course, on the west side. The main residence appeared to be a three-story mansion made entirely of high density concrete. The kind used by the military to build bunkers and pill boxes so that they are resistant to bomb damage.

Pulling up to the mansion Rick stepped out of the jeep and took a closer look. It was a house with Roman pillars and a full width porch that gave anyone sitting on the porch a view of the northern end of the island. He saw that it had been painted once but years in the tropical sun and weather had cleaned away the white wash. The door was made of a dense wood with copper sheathing around the edges to protect it from damage. When he tried it the door lever moved easily and aloud 'click' suggested the door mechanism was functioning well in spite of many years apparent disuse. Opening the door the hinges squeaked mightily and echoed through the dark and stale entry hall. It was dark enough to require a flashlight which he retrieved from the jeep.

Returning to the entry hall Rick noted the richness with which the previous owners had decorated the space, opulent yet sparse. To his right the circular stair was made of concrete but each step had wood inlay to soften the concrete overtones. The banister was made of concrete supports, which were at least 6 inches in diameter with a dark wood top rail. Though it had been years since anyone had lived in this place the only sign of wear or age was with the mold that had accumulated on the walls in the absence of air flow and general upkeep.

The floor was made of the same dense hardwood as the door and save for a few bits of debris, paper and leaves...appeared to be solid as the day it was put in. Walking directly into the back of the foyer he walked through the open door and into what appeared to be the main salon or living room. A massive fireplace with a wood mantle dominated the room. The one piece of furniture in the room was the couch, covered with a heavy canvas sheet a throw rug lay between the couch and fireplace. On the far side of the fireplace another stair identical to the one in the foyer wrapped around the fireplace and disappeared upstairs. The southern wall was made of French doors that opened out onto a balcony overlooking what appeared to be an expansive and once impressive courtyard with several defunct fountains now overgrown with plants and vines. The trees had created enough of a canopy to hide it from aircraft.

To his left a large dining table sat covered by canvas under a massive chandelier that, even with a coating of dust was an impressive sight. Turning again to his left he saw a door that obviously went to the kitchen and servants quarters. Through the door was a narrow hall with three doors on the right and one on the far end of the hall that went into the kitchen itself.

A dusty hall rug had clearly not been used in a very long time. His foot prints were the first to disturb the coating of dust. Checking the first door to his right he found it unlocked. As he suspected it was a small apartment for the day staff to live in while on duty. It was certainly not large enough to live in full time, just a place for a bed and a wash-basin with no window. Each room was identical to the first each tidy and fairly comfortable but not too comfortable.

Entering the kitchen he found it agreeably neat and clean in spite of decades of dust accumulation. White tile covered the concrete cabinets and center island that served as prep station for the foods that came out of the two impressively large gas stoves and ovens. Whitewashed cabinet doors were closed tight. Kitchen implements were put in their place and left as if the staff had one day cleaned house as usual but never returned. To the right of the doorway in which he stood was another door mostly made of glass panels that went to a stair well and down to the pantry and a back patio that was covered with overgrowth.

Rick decided that he would explore the patio later. Entering the living/dining room again he walked over to the stairs. As he reached the stair he noticed the room on the far side opposite the living room. The room was as large as both the dining room and living room combined only it was furnished by an extremely ornate carved oak desk that faced the balcony. Behind the desk was a large map of the South

American continent. Colored Pins and strings covered the map indicating routes and places that meant something to the person who once occupied the desk. The desk was covered with a canvas sheet.

Stepping into the room he noted that another fireplace opposite the one in the living room though not as large. The only furnishings beside the desk were two leather chairs equally spaced in front of the desk. Hanging from the ceiling was a fan that had once circulated the air. Looking out of the French doors he heard the rumblings of a storm brewing. The Jeep was exposed and he did not want his seats to get wet, so he quickly ran outside to put up the top. As he struggled with the stubborn top, which apparently had never been put up and had locked into place from rust he then remembered the garage and decided to take advantage of it.

Pulling the jeep into the garage he left the door open to allow fresh air in. It had been closed for a long time indicated by a strong musty odor of mold and jungle rot. As he stepped toward the door he noticed a diesel generator in the corner but paid it no mind. He entered the house through the door from the garage to find himself back in the map room with the large desk and chairs. Having already inspected this room he walked deliberately over to the staircase reaching the top landing as the first clap of thunder shook the island followed by torrents of rain and hurricane force wind.

Finding the upstairs oppressively stale he decided to go back down stairs and open the front door and a few of the French doors in the back to create a cross breeze in hope of circulating the bad air out. Unfortunately the initial effect of this action was to cause the dust that had settled on everything to blow around and fill the air making it impossible to breath. So he stepped out into the balcony to allow the air and dust to blow out.

Ten minutes later the air in the house was breathable again. Outside the rain was coming down in torrents and the wind was near hurricane force with sustained winds of 60mph or more if he had to guess. It was then he decided to climb the stairs which he did testing each step for weaknesses. Being the stair was made of concrete and topped with a wooden slab he didn't' expect anything to collapse underfoot, but with the multiple close calls in recent days he was taking no chances. Reaching the top stair he sent a beam of light down the hallway. No less than four doors were on the left while the opposite wall was covered with paintings that were covered with canvas.

Like the doors previously these were not locked. A canopy bed sat against the wall with a chest of drawers opposite with a simple lamp table on each side of the bed. To the left was a bathroom with full bath and toilet with a sitting/dressing room attached. Each room had their own balcony that over looked the courtyard in back.

The only difference he noticed with each room was the color of the quilts on the beds. Otherwise each room was identical to the first. At the far end of the hall was the landing from the front foyer where he had first entered, to the left of the landing was another set of stairs that led to the third floor. Eight steps led to a door that open into a glass enclosed roof top patio which was attached to a single room that turned out to be a very elaborately decorated suite with a fireplace opposite the bed covered with a deep, rich red velvet quilt piled high with red velvet pillows all covered with decades of dust. To Rick the room reminded him of a French Bordello, either that or the man who stayed in the room was very, very gay.

The view from this room was to the north end of the island. A stair well accessed another room that was a kind of glass observation tower. The tower itself was completely overgrown with trees so that nothing could be seen but trees. Of course this resulted in the tower being completely obscured from view from the rest of the island.

Someone had taken the time to build this house to be comfortable and long lasting but didn't waste a lot of money on creature comforts like over-stuffed sofas and lounge chairs. He also noted that there was no library, but then he hadn't explored the lowest level of the house either. It reminded him of the admin buildings on the military bases where he'd been stationed in the Navy. It was similar to the stark, official décor that you'd find in the living quarters of a General or Admiral, comfortable yet austere with a hint of opulence, just enough to take the edge off the rigors of military life.

Rick liked the way they'd done things. In fact he could see himself living in the house quite comfortably without changing a thing. Closing his eyes he listened to the rain hit the glass. The sound was pleasant and soothing. He soon found himself wondering how difficult it would be to get a hot tub put in and decided that it would be perfectly easy. Opening his eyes again he turned to look around and noticed another door with a small window in the middle. Taking a few quick steps over to the door he opened it to find a white tiled steam room that was good for six or seven people. Of course it hadn't been used in years. Closing the door there were no other doors to open or rooms to explore. Standing in the middle of the glass room he watched the wind blowing the trees around him. Water lashed the glass removing the grime that had accumulated since the last rain.

Rick stood looking out over the island wondering why the previous occupants had never returned. He then reminded himself that this place was likely a base used by the people who had hidden the submarines. But the place couldn't have been abandoned for 70 years it was too neat, too clean for 70 years of neglect. Someone had been here since, easily in the last decade, if not the past few months. He thought about the dust and the heavy canvas covering the furniture. People usually put sheets over furniture if they were leaving for a while in order to keep dust from their fabrics and things, they didn't usually use heavy canvas.

Returning to the main level he found the rain was coming down in sheets. It was clear that he was stuck on the mountain until the storm passed and the roadway down the mountain was dry enough to be safe. Especially since he didn't know the quality of the Jeeps drum brakes knowing that drum brakes tended to be less effective in heavy rain. It was only mid-afternoon but the storm had darkened things up enough to make seem much later.

The rain got heavier and heavier and the thunder was nearly constant. After an hour the storm was far worse though he didn't think it possible. He was stuck up on the mountain till it blew over. It was then the generator caught his eye. "Did it work?" he wondered. Using the flash light to check it out he had doubts considering the fact that the fuel was likely gelled and useless. But he gave it a look anyway.

The tank he noted was full and the diesel fuel appeared ok enough... certainly not gelled...at least not that he could see. The battery had been stored properly...but he doubted that it held anything close to a charge. When he connected the leads to the battery and a spark jumped as the positive cable came into contact with the battery.

Pressing the start button it turned over easily, but it didn't start up until the third attempt. It ran beautifully. As it warmed up he heard the whine of the generator begin to produce electricity. In five minutes the lights in the garage were flickering. In ten minutes the lights in the garage were fully lit and he could see the interior of the garage clearly for the first time, it was too neat, too clean no self-respecting home mechanic would be caught dead with such a disgustingly clean space. There wasn't even a work bench to lay tools on. Rick shook his head in disgust. "Neat freaks" he muttered.

Rick decided to go back in the house to see if the lights worked and to his astonishment he found that the lights did work in every room but one. However he also found that the generator had limits as the lights began to flicker on and off when the generator couldn't keep up. Turning off the lights stabilized the flicker and the more lights he turned off the more brightly each bulb seemed to burn.

He was careful to leave the lights on the north side of the house off because was trespassing on private property forgetting that he was, at that very moment, the owner of the very ground on which he trod, left to him by his friend Archie, as well as a sizeable amount of bullion.

The enormity of which had yet to fully sink in and register in his brain as 'reality'. Part of him was reluctant to believe it, fearing that if he were to fully comprehend what had just befallen him he'd wake up and find himself in the same shitty mess he was in the day he landed. So in denying the reality he feared was a dream he staved off disappointment, because if this was a dream he wanted to savor it and keep it alive for as long as he possibly could.

Shaking the doubt from his mind he decided to brave the exterior staircase and see if he could get to the basement level. He found it interesting that they hadn't built an interior access door to the basement. But then he figured it doesn't storm 'that' often therefore wasn't deemed necessary.

Checking his batteries of the flashlight he walked through the kitchen and to the door opened it and took a blast of wind and rain in the face as he stepped through the glass paned kitchen door. Closing the door behind him he walked carefully down the steps. The last thing he needed was to break a leg in a place nobody had visited recently. Upon reaching the bottom he faced two large plate glass windows each no less than twenty feet high and twenty feet wide behind which were crimson draperies blocking his view of the interior.

Wind and rain lashed him intermittently. He was drenched and feeling cold. The door was locked. He used his flashlight to break a small pane of glass reached in and unlocked the door. The room was totally blacked out and incredibly stale making it particularly hard to breath at first. Standing in the door he let his eyes adjust to the dark. The faint smell of old machine oil met his nostrils. It was the smell often associated with a closed up barn filled with old tractors and farm implements. It was similar to the odors in the cavern, where the submarines were stored. The fact was that it was the very same odor though much less intense.

Stepping into the dark he became aware of the immense size of the room itself. Shining the light to his right he saw a massive bookcase filled with leather bound books and a large couch, covered in canvas like the rest of the furniture in the house. Sweeping his light left he saw the corner of the bookcase sweep around to another that ran against the entire opposite wall, each filled with books. In the far corner of the room he saw what was obviously an old car covered with the same canvas used to cover the furniture.

His excitement grew as he was a long time motor head who had fantasized about finding an old car in a barn somewhere. He stepped closer and carefully he removed the tarp exposing the front. Rick gasped in excitement as he realized what he found was a Mercedes Benz. Stomach muscles contracted as his excitement grew as he uncovered the massive vehicle. He noted that it was taller than other cars but as he uncovered the fender he noticed a place for a flag. Once he uncovered the door a pair of SS runes appeared on the passenger door.

Stepping back he forced himself to calm down. Uncovering the rest of the car he noted that it was a Mercedes G4 command car, sedan. These cars were usually convertibles; the hard top made this car exceptionally rare, though he wasn't sure about how the SS runes would play in the collectors market. Rick opened the door and sat in the back seat. The interior was clean but musty, something to be expected in an old car, particularly in the tropics. Someone had put a lot of time into keeping the car pristine. Behind the car was a massive garage door that appeared to lead into the mountain. He stepped carefully over to the garage door. Next to it was a smaller door for human traffic and he opened it.

The door swung opened as if the hinges had been oiled and used frequently but this meant nothing. The hatches had opened on the submarines just as easily. A blast of cool, dank and musty air hit him as the door opened. It was the very same moist, oily smell that filled the cavern where the submarines were stored but not nearly as strong. Stepping through the door he noticed a dark lump immediately to his left which appeared to be another car covered with canvas. Peeling the canvas off the car with some effort he discovered a completely intact Kubelwagon.

It was painted in a German Military Gray complete with German Crosses on the doors and all the field implements. Even the tires seemed in perfect condition and still full of air. But that didn't register immediately because his excitement at discovering the gold horde was still with him. He would have to tell Archie. Perhaps when he recovered they'd take day trip and explore the summit, again forgetting that it was Archie who had owned the property before himself.

Walking several feet down the ramp he confirmed it was a circular ramp that likely went all the way down to the cavern. It was too far to walk and he didn't know how long the batteries in the flashlight would last. Remembering the generator he looked for a light switch. He found one by the door he came through and flipped it on. A single cone of light filled the landing giving Rick enough light to put up the Flashlight. The ramp remained dark however. Stepping back over to the Kubelwagen he was able to see a set of keys in the ignition. "No" he said to himself. "There's no way..." but he hopped behind the wheel and tried it anyway. To his surprise it started immediately on the first turn over and ran perfectly.

Stunned Rick sat with the engine vibrating through the seat. No vehicle could sit for decades and start up immediately, not even a German vehicle. But excitement and curiosity overrode caution. Rick flipped a few switches on and off until he found the head lights which lit up the whole tunnel with an unusually bright beam. Everything in the Kubelwagon was like new certainly not something that had been sitting in a damp tunnel for six decades. Still the house didn't appear to have been lived in for a very, very long time. Throwing caution to the wind Rick put the car in gear and moved forward toward the tunnel. He shifted to second gear as he hit the downward slope deciding that second was fast enough for the time being. The memory of crashing through the brush was fresh so as reckless as he felt he wasn't about to tempt fate.

The engine echoed in the enclosed space. One hundred yards down the tunnel the first of many large garage doors appeared on his left. Next to each large door was a secondary door. At the level of each door a flat slab provided a parking space that was perfectly sized for the vehicle he was driving. Again curiosity gained the upper hand. Pulling into the space he decided to leave the car running just in case it wasn't in as good a shape as he thought. The smaller door opened easily. His flashlight beam fell on a warren of smaller rooms, about eight if he were to guess, though he didn't bother to count them. Instead he stepped over to the nearest one and opened it. A bunk-room with six individual bunks presented. Against the far wall the exterior wall if he were to guess was a boarded up window.

On the opposite side of each garage was a storage facility. He counted about 40 separate sets of living quarters and storage depots. Most of which were filled with crates like those on the subs below. What that could mean didn't register until he reached the bottom of the ramp where he found a mountain of crates stacked 30'x 20' that ran the length of the cavern opposite where the submarines had been moth balled.

Driving into the main cavern his headlamps were not impeded by mist unlike his earlier exploration. His opening the doors above had likely created a draft sufficient to ventilate the moisture from the cavern. His brakes squeaked as he came to a halt. Grabbing the flashlight and a tire iron Rick stepped over to the pile of crates and pulled one from the pile and opened it. Like the crates on the submarine he discovered ten 32oz bars of platinum. Shining the light on the crates he began noticing that these had been marked. Gld, Slvr, Pltnm, had been painted on these crates designating their contents. The enormity of what he'd discovered made his heart race. What he'd found on the submarines could have potentially erased the national debt, or at least make a significant dent in it. What stood before him could easily erase the national debt of several nations.

It was then that he realized that the storage depots he'd checked on the way down were stacked to the ceiling with crates just like these. He'd counted no less than 40 such rooms. Though he hadn't checked them all, those he had checked had been packed full. Where they all full?

Rick had to sit down to get a hold of himself as his excitement grew as did the fear. He had no idea how much this find was worth, what would he do with such an enormous amount of precious metal? How many banks would he need? How would he keep this secret?

As he pondered this dilemma a shot rang out from the far end of stack of crates with the bullet barely missing his head as splinters of wood tore into his skin. Instantly he was on his belly moving behind the car to put it between himself and the shooter. Strangely fear was not present but a very profound clarity had surfaced allowing him to focus on the task at hand, survival.

Once hidden he focused his attention on the shooter whom he could see, was walking slowly along the pier hugging the crates as if he expected to be shot at himself. As the figure entered the edge of his headlight beam a voice spoke with a soft yet distinct German accent. "So Odessa found me again. The last time they sent six men, they killed my wife and I *killed them*. Now they send only one? They came for my money. They killed my wife looking for it. You and your Nazi friends will never get this gold, not if I have anything to say about it." He hissed in a low determined voice, "I thought they'd learned to leave me alone."

Rick crouched behind the car shaking like a leaf. 'Nazis?' he thought. The shooter stopped. "I see you have no gun. You weren't anticipating my being here, were you' he paused 'If you put your hands up I won't shoot you."

"Are you out of your fucking mind?!!!! You took a shot at me and barely missed. I don't think that was a warning shot *pal*." Rick screamed. Looking under the car, lying flat on the ground Rick saw the feet of his attacker attempting to sneak up on him and stop suddenly.

"You're an American? Why have you been following my friend and I?" he asked.

"I haven't been following anyone. I came here on vacation and got bored and went exploring. I accidentally discovered the tunnel several days ago while exploring the island interior. Before that I saw a building on top of the mountain here, got curious and decided to check it out. I found all this by accident." Rick said watching his attacker's feet from under the car. He had stopped walking.

"So…you are not with Odessa? You have not been following me?" he asked nervously.

"No, if I were following you I'd have known to carry a gun and be shooting back." He said trying not to sound afraid. Suddenly a loud roar came from the tunnel and the Mercedes G4 came to a screeching halt with headlights blazing into the cavern

"Hans…don't shoot. He's a friend!!" It was the weakened, raspy voice of Archie Davis standing on the running board of the massive Mercedes.

Chapter 14
Change of Plans

March 1945

HANS CAME TO on his back inside his car, which lay on its side against a tree. Dazed and disoriented he assessed his condition before attempting to move, a habit formed from years of combat. He had all his fingers and toes and they all moved. His head was bleeding but not badly. Looking forward he saw Gunther. It was obvious that he was dead before he did more than look at him. The steering wheel was draped around his shoulders with the steering shaft sticking out his back.

Gunther hadn't suffered, he was glad for that. Over the years he had seen worse, much worse. He'd seen men with both arms and legs blown off from Russian artillery screaming in agony unable to move begging someone to finish them, which he had done more than once. It was the merciful thing to do. What life could they expect with no arms and no legs? He also knew if he didn't do it they would either freeze to death or be eaten alive by wolves. A corporal, whose name he never knew, had been cut in half at the belly button. The young man was stunned and unaware of the fact that his entire lower half was no longer attached to his upper half, which he was dragging along with several feet of his intestines attracting the gaze of a large, male wolf.

A pack of wolves had already begun eating his lower half, which was likely the reason the stunned corporal was dragging is ripped upper torso through the snow. Hans had driven up in a commandeered Russian GAZ field car to see if there was anyone still alive only to find one survivor, who was dead already but didn't know it. Out of mercy and to keep the young man from realizing the horror of his wounds Hans walked deliberately behind him and put a Mauser to his head and pulled the trigger.

Pale from the shock of what he had just seen Hans fought down the urge to vomit as he pulled away driving as fast as he could, desperate to be away. The dead were being mauled and eaten by starved Russian wolves. By morning the bodies would be gone and nothing but blood and snow would remain, if that.

That was not the most horrific spectacle in his memory. The worst had been the headless General. A tank shell had taken his head off as he walked along the sidewalk behind a trench line dug into the roadbed. His corpse continued to walk for 50 meters before he stopped and turned as if to look toward the Russian lines and lifted field glasses to eyes no longer present, stood for 30 seconds before collapsing into a trench landing on top of a young soldier who had been sleeping.

The nearest the doctors could manage to a reasonable explanation for the animated corpse was that the general had been near hypothermia when he was struck. It certainly had been cold enough. The fact that his neurological systems were slowed and the blood was

flowing more slowly than usual enabled the body to continue marching after the brain was no longer firing orders to do so. That and the
General had walked that same road bed hundreds of times in the
months previous almost identically each time so it was surmised that
the 'habit' had been neurologically embedded in his muscles and
nerves so that when he had begun his 'habitual' inspection of the
trenches his body simply continued to do what it had done many
times before, which made it all the more horrific for those watching
it happen.

Regardless of the reason for this anomaly the sight of the headless
corpse walking as normally as if nothing had happened was disturbing even to the most seasoned veterans. There were few sober men
on the line that night, including Hans. He had been standing mere
feet from the General when his head exploded off his shoulders,
the splatter from which sprayed him and several others with blood.
The General marched by him at the same pace he'd been walking
before the shell took his head off. As horrific as the sight had been,
it proved a saving grace for the men under the Generals command.

Those Soviet soldiers, who had seen his body walking, determined
that the General was an earth bound demon and that his demon
spirit inhabited the bodies of the soldiers under his command. This
idea was reinforced when the Generals body stopped walking, turned
and lifted the field glasses. It was reported that at that very moment
a private died when the general looked directly at him through the
glasses, a fact which added to the horror of the Soviets earning Hans
Regiment the nick name Demon Regiment.

The Soviets refused to engage them directly, ever again. They would
shell them constantly...from a great distance but never did a soviet
soldier venture within a mile of them again such was the terror the

headless general had created. When the German Army surrendered the Soviets demanded that the Demon Regiment be sent home... never to return to Soviet soil again. Hans had been in a Berlin hospital when he'd heard of the surrender and of the Soviets strange request of his old regiment. He laughed when he heard it, wishing the same fate had been bestowed on the 300,000 other troops who had surrendered. Most of them would die in POW camps in Siberia. Those who survived would not see Germany again until 1955.

Most of the Demon Regiment had been posted on the western front along the Normandy coast. Where he would rejoin them and where they would face the D-Day invasion in June 1944. Their Eastern front reputation had not saved them from the Allies as it had with the soviets. Those who survived were under his command and with him now heading to Switzerland or rather 'had' been. At least 50 men he knew were in an American POW camp in Georgia.

He would later learn that most of them had applied for American Citizenship. Hans smiled knowing that they would live out their lives as American Citizens living as freely as they chose raising children in homes far away from war torn Europe. Sighing to himself he began to relax and accept the idea of being through with war. He'd had enough and wanted peace, children and a quiet, easy life where he could get fat and live out his days trying to forget the horrors of war that would forever be part of his life.

Coming back to himself Hans stared at his young driver's body saddened by his death at such a young age. "You were a good boy Gunther; No, a good man. I wish I could have gotten you out of this sooner. I am sorry" he whispered "I'm so very sorry". At least Gunther was in a place where peace reigned and his suffering was no more. "Be at Peace Gunther" he said came to attention, clicked his heels in the Prussian style and gave him a civilized and honorable salute vs the perverted Nazi salute. "Good Bye my friend".

Stepping back from the wreckage he took stock of his situation. The car itself had been tossed into the trees nearly torn in half by the blast that sent it there. None of his trucks got hit as far as he could tell but they had scattered and wouldn't reform until they approached the border. He was on his own.

He was 50 kilometers from the Swiss border. It was too cold for him to be walking that far. He remembered a bombed out village they'd passed through ten kilometers back. He thought he'd seen a car in a garage. With luck it would run. If necessary he could use his rank and commandeer a car or truck and head south.

An hour later he came up on the village and the house with the garage. On closer inspection the house had been bombed and his heart sank. It was likely the car inside the garage was destroyed but he went ahead and checked it out. To his amazement the car was untouched. It was an older Mercedes Benz saloon.

The people in the house apparently had been preparing to run for the border if and when the Russians came. It appeared that the house imploded from a single bomb blast killing the family inside. Looking through the rubble of the house it was clear that nobody had survived, which appeared to have happened some time before. No bodies were evident but since the car remained it was likely they were killed, as any surviving family would have taken it and fled. How the car had remained untouched was a miracle and he thanked God for it. He did so, silently as God was not officially sanctioned by the National Socialist regime. It was a habit he vowed to break the moment he was able to openly acknowledge his Lutheran faith.

He actually looked forward to going to church but he had other things to consider before that could happen.

Clearing a path to the car he found the keys in the ignition. It started without hesitation. "Typical Mercedes" he thought to himself with some pride. "At least we do that well". He let it run to both warm up the engine and to ensure that it would continue to run. Once satisfied that it wasn't going to die he began clearing debris from behind the car. It was during this time that he decided to return to the barn high in the mountains and load the car with as much cash as he could fit in the boot and back seat before he would finally 'retire'. A tiny voice in the back of his head told him to head to Switzerland now and get the money later. But greed won out and he pointed the Mercedes north.

Dawn broke over the Alpine forest as Beck loaded the last crate that would fit into the car. He was tired and needed sleep but sleep was the last thing he wanted right now. He had evaded the clutches of no less than three SS death squads by bluffing his way through. It was easy as he was then headed toward the fighting. Now he had to find alternative routes around the checkpoints heading toward Switzerland. Checking his watch he decided to make an appearance to his office in town and hopefully generate a set of orders to get him by the checkpoints.

The city was nearly destroyed and buildings were little more than piles of smoldering rubble. Armored personnel carriers rolled through the streets looking for deserters. Black Mercedes Benz with SS flags raced through the streets as though their presence meant something. The sounds of firing squads were everywhere. Hans started to rethink his decision to visit the barn, too late. He cursed himself realizing that he could have been in Switzerland driving up to his mountain house in that beautiful Red Mercedes SSK. For an instant he debated pointing the car south and making a run for it. It was only 100km to Switzerland. Then he remembered his cargo. If anyone saw what was in his car they would seize the car, shoot him on the spot and likely head for Switzerland themselves.

He pulled into an abandoned garage two blocks from headquarters. He didn't feel like explaining why he had a car full of cash and petrol when it would be obvious to any dolt that he was preparing to leave the country. Walking the two blocks to HQ he noted the panic in the eyes of those who had not already left. At the bottom of the steps the once proud building showed bomb damage. As it had been built as a bomb shelter to resist fire and bombings it was one of the few buildings left standing, marking it as a target for stray fighters or bombers that happened to see it. Hans stood at the bottom of the steps and viewed what was left of the city. Anti-aircraft batteries lay in ruins among the buildings they were meant to protect, downed aircraft lay among the ruins as well both allied and German alike.

He remembered feeling joy at the sight of a squadron of Me-262s flying in V formation and into battle. It had been an awe-inspiring sight. Their speed alone was enough to swell his pride as a German and the sound of their engines was frightful. For the briefest moment hope that Germany could extricate itself from disaster filled his heart.

When all 15 planes returned from combat none of them were damaged, not one, but were all destroyed by a squadron of Mustangs that had followed them back to base, shot down as they landed. The jets were running out of fuel so could not gun their engines to escape. The destruction of the most advanced fighter in the war was caused by the one weakness of any fighter, its thirst for fuel, one thing Germany could not make enough of. If such an advanced fighter could be defeated simply because it was out of fuel, he knew the war was lost. This was due to his knowledge of how little fuel they had and how difficult it was to produce without oil.

Shaking his head Hans walked up the steps and down the hall to his office finding the building all but deserted. Desperate citizens were chopping desks into firewood while Military personnel burned classified documents. No command personnel remained that he could see. His typewriter was gone so he couldn't even fake a set of orders for himself. "Damn" he hissed.

He was about to leave when he heard someone call his name "Hans? Is that you?" A hand clapped onto his shoulder in a firm but friendly grip. Fredrick his best friend turned him around and clapped him firmly on the shoulders. "Hah, it is you!! Thank God!! I thought you were killed in December" he said in astonishment. "I saw what was left of your battalion and thought the worst. My own battalion was hit as well', his face darkened as the memory of that day replayed itself in his head 'Their bombs threw our tanks, our King Tiger Tanks into the air like they were toys!!! The largest, most heavily armored tanks in the world were smashed like eggs under a hammer. I am amazed any of us survived it" slapping his friends back in genuine happiness he said "I'm glad you were not killed".

Hans was happy to see his friend but felt a pressing need to be away, far, far away and the need grew more desperate the longer he and Fredrick remained in the building. Fredrick looked about the nearly deserted building with a wry smile. "It would seem our leadership has vacated the premises or rather deserted." Hans detected a menace in Fredericks voice and demeanor. Had Fredrick become a true Nazi fanatic? He wondered. His menacing grimace seemed to consume him momentarily. He brightened turning to his friend. "I'm glad to find you here at your post. It would be unpleasant to have to shoot you" he said with a friendly smile, 'especially after what we've been through".

"Is that why you are here, to shoot me?" Hans said smiling as the icy grip of fear began to churn deep inside his heart. Something wasn't right. Some unknown danger seemed to fill the space around him. But the danger was not coming from his friend, it, however, was close.

Frederick smiled and shook his head. "No, I was tasked with a special mission for the Reich as well as transporting General Dietrich's staff car to Norway. I've been instructed to recruit as many men to the mission as possible. I can think of no one better suited to assist me than you Hans." Frederick placed a hand on his friends shoulder. "As much as I hate to admit it, we are unable to continue the war from Germany. We have to begin another front so that we can once again gain the upper hand." At this Hans began to unravel from the inside barely managing to keep his composure.

Shaking his head in despair "From where Frederick, Spain, Norway, dare I say it...Argentina?" He knew that he was treading on thin ice but he was no longer himself. He was angry because he realized looking at his watch that he would have been in his new SSK driving up a lonely mountain road at that very moment. Heading to a chalet where he would have made himself a pot of 'real' coffee, started a fire in the fireplace and 'retired' from the war a wealthy man.

That was now crumbling before him sickening him like poison. In a flare of anger he looked at Frederick "Another front? We have more tanks than any nation has ever had, we have the best planes and more of them than any other nation…but we do not have the fuel to operate them nor do we have men left to man them. We've even used up our 'Hitler Youth' on the front. We are sending 12 year old boys to face Russian tanks and dive bombers…because we've run out of men!!!

Old men, men who should be resting at home enjoying peace and quiet are shouldering weapons they can barely carry much less fire." Waving a hand to indicate the city around them, "Every city in Germany looks like this one Frederick!!! Every City!!! We managed to wreck Warsaw and London…and not even to this extent. They, our enemies, have the bombs to destroy our entire nation…and they are doing it one city at a time…burning them…killing our people…. burning our children…like we burned theirs!!!" Hans, felt exhausted and no longer cared if he lived or died. In fact he hoped his friend would end it for him.

Frederick was not the fanatic he played himself out to be. He, like Hans had learned to survive and he had to behave like a crazed lunatic, particularly around other crazed lunatics. So he simply stood there with a mild, fanatical grin and a dangerous glare in his eye, acting the part in case he was being watched. "Hope is a commodity we can no longer afford. All we have is our ingenuity, cunning and daring to renew our nations pride and hope" He paused "It is that mission I've devoted myself to Hans. Germany is paying a heavy price for its greatness. Hitler, as great as he is, is still a man. I know, as many do that this war will be the end of him. But we must carry his vision to the future. In time the world will see his greatness, perhaps not for a long while which is why we must carry on and be there for the future so that National Socialism can be reborn and made even better than before."

Hans had not known Frederick to be a Nazi fanatic and wondered if he was joking as he continued. "I am willing to commit myself to the mission in which my death is a known outcome. I am willing to die for my Fuhrer Hans, as you are. I will let this moment pass as Battle Fatigue knowing what happened to your battalion and mine." Turning his back on him Hans for a brief moment considered killing his friend. But they had grown up together. Lived next door to each other and had even fucked the same women, often at the same time. Frederick was as close to a brother he had left in this world. Killing him simply wasn't an option, though the thought lingered.

He collapsed into the chair behind what was left of his desk. Frederick turned around again, pulled out a packet of Russian cigarettes and leaned against the doorframe. Looking at his Russian cigarette he eyed Hans hopefully "You wouldn't happen to have a carton of Lucky Strikes would you?"

Hans smiled though he didn't feel like it and pulled out a pack tossing it to him "Keep it".

Frederick tossed his Russian Cigarettes onto the wheel barrow pushed by an old man carting out chunks of wood down the hall and out of the front of the building. He lit the cigarette and inhaled deeply, savoring the smooth Carolina tobacco smoke letting it fill his lungs with a deliciously toxic euphoria that only a true smoker can enjoy. "If ever I am placed in front of a firing squad Hans I hope I am allowed a last smoke...and I hope it is one of these damned American Cigarettes". He looked at the smooth paper wrapper and smiled ruefully at his weakness.

"You know my friend. If I knew that surrendering to the Americans would mean a few years in an American prison camp I'd willingly drive to the Western front and surrender myself if only for a pack of these cigarettes. However, I've heard rumors that we, the SS, are to be tried as war criminals, regardless of our individual involvement." He took a long, sensual drag from his cigarette. "You and I are sensible and usually do not trust rumors, but I'm not willing to risk that rumor being true...are you?"

Hans was not listening but nodded as if he had been. His mind was on idle, life meant nothing...he was being recruited for a fucking suicide mission...for what?!!! His rage was about to break its containment when Frederick spoke. "Hans! I was kidding about the suicide mission." He laughed out loud at his friend's expression. "Honestly, Hans, do you think I want to die? In the meantime we are bound by our duty to follow orders. Believe me Hans, the Gestapo is searching for any reason to shoot people. If you are in uniform and without orders, they will assume you are deserting and shoot you on the spot...regardless of rank"

Frederick smiled a sick smile as he watched the peasants rummaging through what had once been a bustling administration office for the Reich. "Our time here is finished Hans. Come with me, *quickly!*" he said with sudden urgency.

The urgency his friend had adopted caused him to follow without question because in that moment men in black leather coats kicked in the back door of the building. They each carried machine pistols. "This is the property of the Third Reich! We are not defeated... cowards!!!" They screamed in a maniacal tone that indicated they'd long since lost any hope of surviving the war and opened fire killing everyone in sight.

As Hans ran down the corridor bullets struck the walls and door as he passed through it with his pursuer close behind. When Hans was halfway down the steps he saw Frederick standing next to a Mercedes G4 sedan, a six wheeled sedan painted in flawless black paint with SS runes on the door and two red flags on the fenders with Nazi Swastikas blowing in the morning breeze.

Fredrick had drawn his pistol as Hans ran toward him. In a moment of surprised panic as Frederick fired. For a brief moment Hans believed his friend had shot him. It took a moment for Hans to realize that he had not been shot. Time seemed to slow for him as he looked at Frederick who was not looking at him, but just behind.

Hans turned to see a Gestapo agent fall face first on the steps. Grabbing the machine pistol he pointed it up the steps just as two more Gestapo agents ran through the door firing wildly at anything that moved. Each man fell before they knew what had hit them. Hans took their weapons and what ammunition they had and climbed into the back seat of the sedan.

Unloading the guns Hans put them on the floor knowing too well that guns often went off for no good reason and he had no desire to have his foot blown off. Then turning to his friend he said in a tone of exasperation "I'm glad to see that you've at least camouflaged the car Freddy. Christ!! Could you have picked a more conspicuous car? How do you propose we get to Norway in a car that will draw the attention of every allied fighter on the western front?" he said heatedly.

Frederick smiled calmly. "There is a Luftwaffe base in the woods near here. I plan to stay there for the day and drive by night down the Autobahn"

Hans shook his head. "Night fighters?" he asked.

"Hans, night fighters are looking for aircraft. They aren't set up for ground strafing especially at night. Besides where we are traveling there will be no targets for allied bombers to hit. We've evacuated that sector because of bombing. They won't be wasting time following a single car traveling at night. We will of course not be using our headlights will we Bruno?"

The Driver shook his head and said "No Standartenfurher, we will not be using head lights."

Frederick reached into his coat and pulled out a flask and took a pull from it then wincing in disgust at its contents "Blah...American whiskey. I believe it's Jack Daniels if memory serves me" he swallowed again and handed the flask to Hans. "Here, if it doesn't kill you, you should live forever."

Hans took it and looked at the engraved markings on the flask. Lt. Jasper USAAC. "DOGMAN" was engraved into the silver plate. Taking a pull from the flask he found that he enjoyed the burning sensation of the American Style whiskey. "Mmmmm. Where did you get this Freddy?" he asked savoring the smoky harshness as it warmed his throat and stomach.

"I took that off an American Mustang pilot who strafed us several days ago. Our gunners got him and he belly-landed his plane perfectly in a field. Smoothest landing I'd ever seen. When we got to him he was sitting in his seat perfectly still and not a blemish on him. He might as well have been asleep. But he was dead. Our medic examined him and found nothing to suggest a cause of death.' Hans said with a wry grin 'Perhaps, he drank too much of this" as he took another pull from the flask.

Freddrick nodded "We buried him with honors and I kept this. Still, I'm not sure if I like it better than schnapps. It seemed a pity to let it go to waste" and took another pull wincing less this time having grown used to the taste. Neither spoke for the next hour as they drove to the airbase, each looking for fighters diving on them but none came.

Two days later they arrived at a German naval base in Denmark where the car was loaded onto a destroyer. Hans was given a birth near the Captains quarters as was Frederick. Bruno their driver was placed in crews birthing where he fell instantly to sleep as he had not slept in nearly three days. Neither Hans nor Frederick was in a mood to sleep. They were suffering from nervous energy in the understanding that in a matter of months or even weeks they could be facing a firing squad or the gallows simply because they were in the SS.

Hans was angry, depressed and frustrated with himself more than anything because he had allowed his greed to get him into this mess. Had he simply followed his original plan he would have been sleeping in a nice warm bed, wearing nice new pajamas and living high in the Alps a retired, rich gentleman with the horrors of war a distant memory. Now he was on a mission to transport a fucking car to an egotistic General in Norway and then escort him and his staff to Argentina to attack the United States from South America, a fool's errand.

Beginning a fourth Reich from Argentina was not going to happen no matter how sympathetic Argentina was to the Nazi cause. To move an entire attack force from the southern end of a continent to the northern end through some of the most dangerous and hostile environments known to man was the definition of insanity. Of course to expect such an endeavor to be kept secret was foolish in the extreme. Hans felt his heart sink as the lines were cast away and the destroyer nosed out of the birth and into the channel heading for the North Sea.

For hours he stood on the lookout deck staring into the blackness letting it fill his heart. He no longer cared if he lived or died. The war, its trials and his personal defeats had numbed him from fear of death. In fact he hoped for it. He didn't even feel the cold anymore it was as if he ceased to exist. As his mind stormed he noticed a white streak heading at them from out in the distance. A Torpedo!! He watched it approach as the lookout hit the alarm...too late. The night was pierced by the clang, clang, clang of battle stations.

He watched the torpedo approach in numb disbelief both hoping and fearing that it would kill him in the same moment. His hands gripped the railing as he watched it hit the hull directly below his feet closing his eyes expecting the merciful, terrible explosion that would end his suffering forever. He had accepted his death just as the torpedo hit the hull with a dull 'thud'. It hit hard enough for him to feel the impact of it through the hull but no explosion came. The bent torpedo simply floated briefly on the surface as the ship it was meant to sink kept going.

Hans felt the ship pick up speed as it accelerated to avoid a second torpedo that passed just aft. A third torpedo came from the opposite side and missed because the ship turned into the oncoming missile. The destroyer was now moving at flank speed doing a healthy 40 knots through the North Sea. Hans was still gripping onto the rail as the sea spray hit him on the back of the head as he watched the last torpedo disappear into the night and aft of the ship.

Bruno was soon standing next to him on the bridge white as a sheet and shaking like a leaf. Frederick was smiling in an attempt to hide the fact that he had just faced his inner demons through the specter of death. His earlier bravado was now gone and the pretense he hid behind was also gone. "That was close" he said at last looking out into the darkness "Too close".

Bruno said nothing but stood there shaking. The torpedo had struck exactly where his bunk had been. He woke the moment it had struck and noticed the hull dented where his head was lying. The knowledge that he could have been vaporized by the blast of a torpedo had shaken him so badly that he didn't speak a word for nearly a week. That night they steamed into a fjord and anchored next to an island to wait out the day before proceeding to Bergen at night. Making a passage at night was bad enough with submarines. They didn't need to compound their difficulties by adding air attack into the mix traveling by day.

It took them two days to reach Bergen Norway. Bruno had recovered sufficiently to resume driving duties and drove both Frederick and Hans to the submarine pens where General Dietrich was eagerly waiting delivery of his new staff car.

Chapter 15
Hope Returns

FOR TWO WEEKS Hans and Frederick rested in their quarters awaiting the General to summon them. They had been given strict orders to remain in the compound due to increased resistance activity against German personnel. Hans suspected it was meant more to keep desertions down. It was clear to everyone that the war was over. There simply was no desire on the part of the 'sane' personnel to die for a lost cause. Had there been a chance of a German victory, perhaps but any hope of victory had long since faded.

Desperation had replaced confidence among the hard core Nazis who had directed mass murder at the height of Nazi power. Almost daily solitary pistol shots could be heard in the compound signaling a suicide. The radio was full of reports of concentration camps being liberated and the horrors of their individual actions were being documented and broadcast throughout the world. Eisenhower made it clear that those responsible for these camps would be prosecuted by a military tribunal, if found guilty hung by the neck until dead.

Air-raids were a daily occurrence, weather permitting and the American and British Navy destroyers and cruisers were patrolling along the coast off every German naval base waiting for any ship foolish enough to venture forth. In the last month no submarine had survived more than an hour after leaving port, even if they left the harbor submerged. What was worse was the fact that those scheduled to leave port were able to watch their comrade's fall under attack and sink within sight of shore. The tension created by witnessing a fate they themselves might suffer accelerated the suicide rate as each man's departure date approached. It was understandable given the brutality with which these attacks were carried out.

One such attack was so terrible many submarine crews simply deserted. Three destroyers had steamed up and taken station around the submarine. As one all three destroyers dropped ordinance on the submarine. It was immediately apparent that they were making direct hits as the wood planking began floating to the surface. When the submarine surfaced to surrender all three destroyers opened up with deck guns and utterly destroyed the submarines superstructure at point blank range forcing it to dive at which point depth charges were again deployed. One sailor counted no less than one hundred explosions before he quit counting. They knew the moment their fellow submariners were killed when a bubbling mass of oil and air boiled to the surface. Not one of their shipmates made it to the surface alive.

Hans was standing atop a gun tower when the attack occurred. He watched the submarine dive just before it exited the harbor out of sight of the picket destroyers. He saw the wake left behind the submarine as it cleared the nets. The water was so clear that he could literally see the submarine for several hundred yards. When they had reached the half-mile mark the destroyers took up station and attacked.

He was shocked at the brutality of the allies. It was clear the sub had surfaced to surrender but had not been allowed to. No quarter was given and certainly no mercy. Three submarines had been destroyed in this manner in two days. The one surface vessel that attempted a break out was bombed, torpedoed and bombed again before sinking within minutes of clearing the nets. Immediately following this attack Hans heard no less than three pistol shots in the officer's quarters indicating that they too had seen the attack and had no stomach to face a similar fate.

He couldn't blame them because he was suicidal himself. Beck cursed his stupidity and bad luck as he thought of that warm chalet in the Swiss Alps waiting for him, knowing that it would go on waiting. Had he simply taken that damned car south and come back later. He beat a fist on the concrete wall in frustration and anger thinking of the cash he had already put away. "More than enough to live on for several life times' he thought. "And I had to get just a little more...Stupid!!" he muttered under his breath.

One bad decision found him stuck in Norway awaiting transport to Argentina for some idiotic mission that had no chance of changing the course of the war. It made him sick to think that he might well be on the next ship or submarine that attempted a breakout and die in the arctic waters off Norway. Hans looked toward the airfield hoping to see an aircraft lift off and engage the destroyers in revenge for this most recent attack knowing full well that the Luftwaffe was no longer able to protect anyone.

The Stuka's that would have normally protected the harbor entrance and attacked the destroyers while their ships made it out to open sea were parked on revetments out of fuel and out of ammunition with no fuel shipments planned or expected. That is, those aircraft that hadn't been bombed, strafed or stripped for parts.

Leaning against the railing of the gun tower Hans looked once again out to sea as one last bubble of air breached the surface marking the grave of 40 brave men. He saw the crews of the destroyers walk solemnly to the rail of their ships and look down at their handy work. It seemed to him that they were not happy with destroying their enemy. None of them were cheering, he saw several men take off their caps and bow their heads.

They were men doing a job, following orders and did not take joy in killing a defenseless enemy. Even so, the submarine was sunk and the crew aboard her was dead regardless of how the American and British sailors felt about it. Soon it would be his turn to chance a breakout, that is unless he could get away and somehow make his way back to Germany...or better yet Spain. "This time' he thought, 'I will not be so foolish. This time, if I am able, I will head directly to the Swiss border and stop for nothing."

He let the thought linger as he considered the possibilities. "Perhaps, I could get to Spain and make my way to Switzerland, perhaps southern France or even northern Italy where Germany still had a firm grip. But as he considered his exit routes he fell into a depression knowing that he was running out of time. First he had to find a way back. If he went by boat he risked being torpedoed in submarine infested waters and he had already had a close run there, far too close. Flying back, even if he could find a flight, meant facing a hornet's nest of allied fighters both day and night. Both modes of transport were dangerous to say the least, suicidal given the fact that the only German planes flying at the moment were the ones ferrying fugitives to Spain and Portugal from where they were buying passage to Argentina.

He could buy Argentina if he wanted to with all the money he had in Switzerland. Yet here he was stuck in Norway waiting on orders to board a doomed ship that would likely end up on the bottom of the Atlantic. It had been two weeks since he'd arrived in Norway. He had daily taken watch on the gun tower to witness the loss of at least one ship each day. In those two weeks the Gestapo was clamping down on unauthorized excursions outside the compound. An officer was shot earlier that day at the gate because he was caught carrying ten thousand dollars in American money and a satchel of civilian clothes with a forged passport and a ticket on a Swedish passenger liner bound for Spain.

Yet a glimmer of hope did arise when several submarines did finally escape over the next few days. They had radioed back that they had successfully evaded the picket destroyers and were now on their way to Spain where a tanker would fuel them before making their way across the Atlantic. Hans had no idea where they would be going because most of the submarines he was aware of didn't have the capacity to make the journey non-stop to Argentina, even from Spain.

They had escaped because they had submerged in the harbor, made their way through the nets that their divers had cut away rather than have the tugs open. It turned out that the destroyers were standing over the horizon with high magnification optics mounted on their highest mast to observe when a ship was leaving port. Using the tugs as an indicator they'd launch themselves forward and reached the channel opening just as their quarry was leaving port, but in shallow enough water that prevented the subs from diving to safety.

The shallow depth combined with the sheer volume of explosives amassed on one target virtually guaranteed total destruction of the submarine without the need of a direct hit. The concussions in the shallow water would be enough to shatter seams as well as nerves in the poor, doomed vessel they were attacking. It was also clear that they were to give no quarter, accept no surrender unless Hitler himself offered it. Until then they were under orders to destroy utterly any vessel, especially submarines, attempting a break out to open sea.

So the captain of the submarine having observed this pattern decided to violate orders and have his divers cut the nets below the water line leaving the floats in place to give the appearance that the nets were still closed. He would then dive in the harbor and navigate through the net and set themselves on the bottom among the rocks. After several hours they came to periscope depth. Still flanked by the banks of the fjord they cruised along at one knot so not to make a wake or make noise of any sort. Their escape was to follow the contours of the Norwegian coast to hide their periscope and to use the tides to hide the noise of their screws. 12 hours to go 12 nautical miles yet it was enough to allow them to get away. From then on the subs followed that same tactic and got away.

Hope had returned the day they were summoned to the Generals Office and given instructions to be ready for immediate deployment. General Dietrich sat them down in a map room clearly excited about the mission he was charged with overseeing. "Gentlemen, we have been charged with a mission by the Fuhrer himself. Our mission is to proceed to Argentina where our comrades are already seeking an active alliance with the Argentine Government from where we plan to build an army and attack the United States. Our first objective is to attack the Panama Canal, once an army has been outfitted and trained. It will be necessary to prevent the Pacific fleet from interfering with our Central American Front and our march into Mexico.

Our plan requires that we train in Argentina and in Paraguay out of sight of our Enemies. We are to rebuild our navy deep in the

Jungles along the deepest parts of the Amazon River. These regions are so remote we will be able to successfully build our navy back to its former glory" he stood at attention and saluted the painting of Adolf Hitler. Returning his attention to the two men "This is a great honor the Fuhrer has bestowed upon us. We three shall be the leaders of the new Reich and I shall take my place as Fuhrer." When he turned to face the map both Frederick and Hans looked at each other with concern and mounting dread. They were beginning to realize the General was insane.

Chapter 16
The Mission:
Attack the United States

THE GENERAL WAS a hardened veteran who had served from Poland, France, North Africa, Greece and the Russian offensive. He was responsible for murdering hundreds of thousands of civilians on his rampage to Moscow. When his murderous rampages became too much for even the Nazis, he was removed from command. The General was a tall, muscular man who had trained with his troops so that he was able to lead them on the ground himself if needs be. An admirable quality in most generals but in his case it meant that he could oversee the mass murders he was almost single handedly guilty of perpetrating.

Hans did not like the 'gleam' in General Dietrich's eyes. It was the same gleam he'd seen in the eyes of the commandant of Dachau, that of an unhinged sociopath. "Ah Standartenfuhrer Beck' he raised a hand to an unspoken question 'Yes, I've seen fit to promote you. We will need men like you on the South American Front. Your first task will be here' and he pointed to an island off of French Guyana. 'The submarine crews, my staff, not even the Captains are aware of its location, not yet, anyway. You are the first to be aware of its existence.

I must emphasize the importance of your keeping this to yourselves' he looked seriously at the two of them and whispered 'not even in the privacy of your room must you mention this' he said. 'If so much as a rumor of this islands existence escapes this base, it may cost us this last hope at victory'. Pausing General Dietrich meditated on the map for a few seconds as if deciding whether or not to say any more and then apparently decided to continue on his original train of thought 'This island was built by an engineering genius before the first war as a forward operations base for raiders and was modified during our peace time resurrection as a forward submarine base. Your job is to oversee the construction of ten new submarines for our glorious Reich then we are to deliver them to our bases along the Amazon River."

Hans was quickly losing patients with this foolishness but kept his growing anger at bay. "Sir, the Amazon is not anywhere near Argentina, and many of the countries that it flows through are neutral and sympathetic to the Allies. How are we to persuade these nations to allow us to build bases along their river?"

The General turned slowly on his heel, raising an eyebrow giving him an even more maniacal appearance. "That, Standartenfurher Beck, is not your concern. I will tell you that as Germans we will do what we must to ensure that we have those bases. Treaties are easily made with savages. Brazilians and Columbians are little more than Spanish Gypsies easily bought off with trinkets and promises." He said waving off the thought as if it were a fly buzzing in his ear. He finished the thought with "You needn't be concerned…you have your task. Leave the rest to me."

Turning again to face Frederick "Standartenfurher Prussien you shall be in charge of dispersing the funds we have allocated for this project, which brings me to the purpose of your being here rather than in Spain or Portugal. This is our last port facility with immediate access to the Atlantic. We have been, over the past two years, accumulating Gold, Silver and Platinum and smelting the metal into ingots for ease of transporting and conversion to cash.

Banks are starving for precious metals and have no interest in watches, necklaces and earrings. As result of this we've taken to mining for gold, platinum and silver in regions we've conquered and that metal was shipped by the ton here to this base. In the past year we've shipped no less than six submarines full of bullion to our island sanctuary, and many more shiploads. All of the personnel who knew of the bases location have been killed for security reasons and the crews responsible have been sent to Argentina as a forward contingent. They will be waiting for us at the legation in Buenos Aires.

Our last shipments are on board two submarines sitting in the pens as we speak. We are to accompany this last shipment to the island and await orders to proceed to Argentina." The General hopped excitedly on his toes hands behind his back. "While you are doing your duty I shall be organizing the recruitment of a new army which I shall personally lead to victory over our enemies." He said the last sentence with such enthusiasm that it was almost believable had it not been for the fact both Frederick and Hans were convinced the man before them was out of his fucking mind.

At this both Frederick and Hans glanced at each other with eyebrows raised but only when his back was turned. It was then that Frederick began to have misgivings. The General was clearly delusional and the tasks they were assigned were possible if you had a highly organized industrial infrastructure to collect the steel, process it into workable ingots and then into sheets, from sheets to the stamping mills in order to create the basic components for ship building. Simply having a dry dock and men to do it...wasn't enough. Then the construction of naval facilities in the dense jungles of the Amazon basin without the governments getting wind of it was impossible.

The ships required to carry equipment to the sites would be too large to miss and would draft too deeply to travel much past the Amazon delta. There was no way to drive a submarine that far down river submerged or surfaced.

For an hour the General kept them in his office painting a picture of grandiose and fantastically impossible scenarios of German victory in the Americas. He expected them to produce their first submarine six months after arriving on the island and he expected their first expedition through the canal to occur in less than two years.

At the end of the meeting Hans and Frederick walked silently to their quarters both deep in thought, Hans admonishing himself for not leaving the country when he had the chance. Frederick on the other hand was badly disillusioned. He had truly believed that this had been a sanctioned and organized effort with most of the facilities already under construction. He had no idea that he and Hans were expected to create a fantasy army, navy and air force out of thin air and in the middle in the South American jungle no less.

"Hans' Frederick said quietly 'I believe the General expects a miracle. I was under the impression that all this had been planned and implemented several years ago' Frederick walked in silence for several moments before continuing. 'Frankly, even with the money we have and the facilities present we lack the economic support and infrastructure necessary to do what he has asked of us. Building a shipyard in the middle of the jungle will take years…let alone building an entire fleet of submarines. We aren't enough Hans!!!" Hanging his head low despair replaced the hope he'd had of turning Germany's fortunes around. His reality was crashing like glass at his feet.

Once they were alone in their quarters he threw his hat on the desk in frustration and mounting anger but said nothing knowing that the Gestapo had likely bugged their room to make certain any plan to escape was thwarted or any complaints recorded and complaints were considered treason and punishable by firing squad. Not to be out done, he grabbed a note pad and wrote.

"I do not want to waste my life on some useless mission that will accomplish nothing but get us killed".

Hans answered back, also in writing, *"It seems we are currently at the mercy of the Reich, unless we can find a way home. I'd rather take a chance at the hands of the Allies where we have a hope of reprieve whereas here…the general will likely have us shot by his fanatics if we fail to do his bidding."*

Frederick read the note and nodded agreement taking up his pen again to reply *"I agree. I'm afraid we have few choices left to us at the moment. The Gestapo will not let anyone leave the compound. The base is on lock down. Did you see our escorts following us?"*

Hans read it and nodded. *"What do we do?"*

Frederick replied *"That is a good question my friend"* he put a hand on his friends shoulder and whispered *"I am sorry for dragging you into this"*

Hans smiled and wrote *"We have the fog of war to help us, perhaps an opportunity will present itself and we shall be able to extricate ourselves yet"*

Frederick nodded and took a deep breath writing *"I am glad you agree, I've had to put on this SS pretense for too long, it's been absurd and tiresome for too long...It's time for peace...my hope lies in our rebuilding Germany and reclaiming it from these fools we've been made to follow for so long."*

Frederick whispered into his friends ear..."We need to burn this note. The Gestapo does not approve of such communication. I suspect that they shall come to check on us before long. We would do well not to have this on us."

Hans provided a Zippo lighter and lit the corner of the paper as well as a cigarette for each of them to mask the odor of burning paper. Frederick allowed the paper to burn in the bathroom while turning on the shower so that the steam dissipated the smoke even more. The ash fell into the toilet and they flushed the evidence of their conversation away.

Within minutes they heard the abrupt footfalls of two Gestapo agents marching with deliberate authority directly to their door. "Actung!!!' open the door for inspection." Their suspicions had been confirmed. There were listening devices in the room and their lack of verbal communication and possibly the sound of scratching on a note pad alerted their overseers to a possible desertion attempt. In preparation for this expected eventuality they had each taken up a post in the window with field glasses to make it seem as though they had been observing movements in the harbor. Before they could open the door the Gestapo men kicked it in pistols drawn.

Frederick and Hans both looked at the men with contempt. "Exactly what is the problem?" Frederick asked putting on the air of a truly offended aristocrat typical of an SS officer.

"We heard you writing on a note pad. We want to see what you have written. Now!!!" they both demanded in one voice. Frederick had the foresight necessary to tear off several pages and burn them knowing that what they'd written on the top page would indent onto the second and third pages. He also made notes of observations made while looking through the window at the harbor entrance to obscure what may remain in terms of incriminating evidence.

The lead Gestapo man took the pad roughly and gave Frederick a menacing glower which had the effect of making him look more like a barely evolved Neanderthal. Frederick choked down the urge to laugh so not to aggravate the situation. Though the situation was not at all funny the lunatic standing before him was anything but impressive, at least to Frederick. As unimpressive as the Gestapo man appeared, he was known to be an unbalanced psychopath with a penchant for extreme violence.

Berger took a pencil lead and shaded over the page looking for indented writing but found nothing but what the Standartenfurher had said he would find. Disappointment or the closest thing to it that Berger could feel surged into his consciousness. He examined the pad of paper with clear hope of finding enough evidence to have these two men shot, a duty he fully intended to perform himself. Tossing the pad of paper onto the bed he looked around the room for anything that he could use as evidence but saw nothing immediately obvious. Beck had been his intended victim. He was aware of Becks black market operation and that he had spirited away millions of pounds in Swiss accounts. In fact he was surprised to find Beck in

Norway. He had expected him to disappear into Switzerland once the game was up and it had been for months.

Turning his back on the two men he closed the door behind him and walked briskly toward the courtyard and to his listening post hoping to find a reason to return and empty is magazine into the two of them. Berger's devotion to Adolf Hitler was absolute. Hitler had given him the ability to serve Germany while exercising his blood lust by killing Jews, by the hundreds on occasion. His calling and purpose for living was to kill for Adolf Hitler.

Berger had little problem killing non-Jews, in fact, he didn't care who he killed. A twisted smile curled his lips as he marched to his office finger twitching on the trigger of his MP40. He brightened as the entered the room knowing that someone in the compound very likely had condemned themselves and his blood lust would soon be satisfied.

He had been imprisoned in the 20s for murdering a family while robbing their home. In fact he had murdered no less than ten families, all of them Jewish, all of them wealthy. He was a sociopath who enjoyed the screams of his victims. It gave him a rush of power. The more they screamed the more enjoyment he derived. To him a person writhing in anguish gave him a rush of euphoria often associated with sexual orgasm. Being a true sociopath fear was not in his psychological profile. He would take his final months and enjoy himself by exercising his blood lust and then take his own life, which was his ultimate fantasy.

Hitler had been the nearest thing to a deity he ever encountered in his tragic and loathsome life; a petty criminal from the age of ten when he started stealing food to survive graduating to burglary at age fifteen. Convicted of a minor burglary at age 17 he was given the choice of enlisting in the army or spending the next several years in prison. That was 1915 one year into the Great War. He had been wounded twice in the first six months and served with distinction. Then in 1918 he was gassed with French mustard gas.

It was the gas attack that made the most significant change to his psychology. After his recovery he was no longer able to feel fear, remorse or compassion. His frontal lobe had been neurologically fused from the scaring caused by mustard gas he had inhaled through a small tear in his gas mask that he discovered too late. An underlying anger simmered in his soul from then on, anger that he had not died in that trench, anger at having survived in a world he no longer wanted to live in.

With the end of WWI and Germanys surrender many soldiers felt betrayed. They had already won the war against Russia and had expanded their eastern boarders. The eastern front was a total and utter victory there was no reason for them to surrender in the West. They felt a negotiated, honorable peace was the better option now that they had won in the East. That was what they expected but instead they found that their leadership had signed an armistice with the western powers forcing Germany to give back their Russian lands and repay the allies reparations. A general surrender when there was no need of one was considered a betrayal of their sacrifice to the Fatherland. It was that betrayal that provided a springboard for Hitler's rise to power.

The economic collapse of Germany forced Berger back into the life of crime he had hoped to leave behind. The purpose he felt in serving Germany as a soldier had given him a pride he'd never known before. No longer able to remain in the army due to his battle injuries he was forced to make a living the only other way he knew how and that was to break into homes and rob them. For nearly five years he survived quite well, obtaining enough cash to sustain a decent if not opulent life style robbing one or two homes a year until he was finally caught. He had been convicted of robbery and murder and was serving a life sentence when Hitler was imprisoned. In prison he and Hitler became acquaintances, not quite friends. However, it was enough to earn him a reprieve when Hitler took power. This was the catalyst for Berger's devotion to Adolf Hitler whom he revered as nothing less than an earth bound god.

He was given a job in the newly formed Gestapo investigating black market activities. Anything that took revenues from the Reich was not to be tolerated. His devotion to Hitler drove his mission to eradicate all Black Market operations for the sake of his beloved Fuhrer and Beck was the worst offender he knew of. When he couldn't stem the flow of black market goods he was reassigned to Norway and effectively exiled for his lack of performance.

Returning to his office following the disappointing encounter with Beck he placed his machine pistol on the desk petting it as if it were a pet. An envelope was resting on his blotter. It was from General Dietrich. He and the General had an excellent relationship because both understood the other both being veterans of the Great War. Berger, being unable to feel love held the General in the highest esteem he was capable. Taking the envelope up and opened it with a recently confiscated SS dagger from the body of a recent suicide. He currently had twenty such daggers in his desk drawer. He opened the letter and began to read.

Victor

With the end of the war, our beloved Fuhrer has tasked me with a mission that requires I relocate to South America to see it through. The details of this mission I cannot share but it is important that Standartenfurher Beck and Prussien be given every courtesy and protection for they are key to the success of the mission. I want you to ensure that they are both onboard U–SS1 one hour prior to its departure this evening at midnight. We are breaking out this evening through the hole in the net. Both U–SS1 and U–SS2 are leaving for an undisclosed destination. Burn this letter immediately and watch that it burns completely. It is likely we shall never meet again old friend.

Good bye and Good luck
Your Friend
Werner

P.S. This knowledge must be kept in the strictest confidence. I am trusting that you will do what must be done to keep this secret. It is essential to the success of the mission and the survival of the Reich. Hiel Hitler

Berger read the note twice as his disappointment rose like bile in his throat. He'd wanted to kill Beck not play nursemaid to him. His psychopathic mind boiled with resentment that this criminal had been chosen to serve his beloved Fuhrer and not himself, his devoted disciple. Had this request come from anyone but General Dietrich he would have ignored it completely. Out of respect for the General he would see to it that his wishes were carried out, regardless of his feelings in the matter. Still the feeling of ultimate betrayal broiled his guts in acid nausea.

He knew that there were two Milchow submarines loaded down with crates, heavy crates that were loaded under extremely high security. The laborers used to load the cargo had been shot immediately after the last crate was secured and their bodies dumped in molten steel at a local foundry. Nobody was allowed within 100 yards of the pen where the two subs were now birthed. The General had ordered the remaining Stukas be fueled and readied to attack the destroyers. Five Stukas were armed and ready but there was only fuel for one plane, the fuel was later confiscated by the Gestapo and put in a plane, a long range transport, they had parked in a hanger on the far side of the base, their intentions were quite clear….they were going to abandon the base at the first opportunity.

Five planes were barely enough to do the job and that was if the pilots were willing to commit suicide once their ammunition was gone. One plane was as good as none at this point and without fuel it was less than nothing it was nothing more than a target for the allies to shoot up.

Following his friends orders Berger took a lighter and burned the letter, then took the ashes and flushed them down the toilet to ensure that nothing remained of the letter not even ashes. He could do little about the smoke but nobody could read smoke and he had simply been following orders. If anyone were foolish enough to question him about it, he could just shoot them. Berger smiled sadistically and let out a self-satisfied chuckle. He knew that none of the men under his command would dare question anything he did.

Lighting a cigarette he glanced at his watch, it was 9pm. Outside was barely dusk and the sun wouldn't set until near 11pm this far north and then for a few hours only. Long enough for the subs to escape the enclosure and make it out to sea. The dark wouldn't hinder the navigation of the subs if they left the harbor submerged. He knew through his sources that the nets had been cut away to give the remaining submarines a chance of escape by leaving submerged. This tactic had been successful so far. However, it was only a matter of time before the Allies caught on, hopefully not before the General got away. The fate of anyone else mattered little as the General was the only friend he had left in the world and Hitler, who was his reason for existence.

Chapter 17
Western front Verdun France 1917

Berger's Story

IT HAD BEEN raining for nearly a week flooding the trenches and shell holes in 'no man's land', the strip of land between the German and Allied trenches, a place where men went to die, *if* they were lucky. Shell holes, barbed wire fencing with decaying bodies hanging on them, body parts sticking out of the mud, bits of aircraft with their wings and tail sections sticking out at perverted angles showing German crosses, British Roundels' and French Tricolor insignias.

It was the very image of hell, a paradise of Satan's own design at the center of which lay two soldiers, one German and one British facing each other in death as they had in battle. Their helmets a British Tommy helmet and a German Spiked helmet made for a surreal sight in the middle of this already hellish landscape.

Berger had been leaning against the wall of his trench smoking a cigarette and staring out at this spectacle. He'd known the German soldier very well. Otto is all he knew him by, never knew his last name or was that his last name? Not that it mattered; they'd been friends only a few months. In that time they'd gone over the top together attacking the Brits one day and French the next. As a team they seemed invincible killing every allied soldier that came near them. At night they'd play cards and drink wine and beer they'd stolen from the officers mess or from the body of one of their comrades laying somewhere along the trench.

A soldiers' friendship made hell livable with a friendly laugh or a sympathetic nod. His friend had been lying in the mud with a bayonet sticking out of his back for two weeks. Three other soldiers lay dead in line with his body killed when they attempted to bring him back for burial, now four of his friends lay dead in the mud unable to be buried, each killed by a French sniper. Thankfully the rain subdued the smell of rotting corpses. He had started smoking to keep from vomiting from the smell; it also soothed his nerves and kept his mind and hands busy.

Otto had convinced him to remain in the army once the war was over. He said that he was a good soldier and had a good head for leading men into battle. This sentiment was seconded by a visiting corporal who'd been temporarily assigned to them for several weeks until his regiment could be reformed having been decimated in a shelling in the opening weeks of the war. He was a lean, wiry man with a strong charismatic personality and a bitter hatred of Jews. He was a corporal named Adolf Hitler.

Hitler was a soldiers soldier and exceedingly brave in the face of the enemy. When he, Hitler wasn't fighting, he was lecturing the troops on politics, with a deeply held passion that left many awestruck and others nervous. He was, if anything inspiring and charismatic and knew how to inflame the passions of those with whom he spoke.

For weeks they'd fought together and talked together until Hitler was transferred back to his newly reformed regiment. He considered Adolf a friend by the time he left.

Otto on the other hand did not care much for Hitler. He found him to be too regimented too military and too 'fucking perfect'. Otto, though a career soldier didn't hold with the starchy military codes of conduct. He had a more pragmatic idea of what a soldier should be and do. According to Otto a soldier's duty was to kill the enemy and follow orders when he had no other choice. When he was able he should get drunk and fuck as many women as he was able because he could be dead in the next day or hour.

Hitler had been a rigid devotee of Prussian military ideology. Seldom, even in battle was his uniform out of order. He brushed the mud from his boots, and tunic incessantly. Even in the impossibly muddy trenches his uniform was cleaner than most in spite of his being in the thick of the battle alongside his comrades. Hitler had taken his identity as a German soldier to heart and made it part of his being, he would live and die as a German Soldier. He had believed in total victory for the Kaiser and nothing less. When the Kaiser abdicated his thrown and exiled himself to Holland it is said that Hitler sobbed like a child and refused to forgive the Kaiser for what he saw as a betrayal of the German soldiers who had died serving him. It was a betrayal he carried into his political career.

Berger took one last pull on his cigarette and tossed it in the mud at his feet. He was looking at the back of Otto's helmet watching the water drip off the spike creating a stream that flowed down the open collar of his tunic. Otto's face was now black and swollen from the heat and rain with bits of his flesh now falling away from the bone. His jawbone was now visible thanks to a ricochet bullet. A portion of his spine now lay exposed from that same bullet. Yet, he remained tangled with the British soldier who looked much like Otto now, only his helmet covered his face.

"How long will they remain upright like that?" he asked himself. The loneliness of losing his friend was weighing on his mind when the concussion of a distant artillery barrage quaked through his feet. "Whose, guns were firing and at whom are they firing?" he asked himself as the quakes increased in frequency. In less than a second he heard the telltale whistle of multiple shells inbound. Not knowing where they were coming from he screamed "In coming!!!" and dove to the nearest shelter.

As he stepped in he allowed himself one last look at no man's land and watched the line of explosions mark their path along the trench line, some landing in the trench some outside the trench. Just as he ducked into his shelter a massive shell which sounded like a freight train hit the spot where Otto and the Brit lay obliterating them both in a massive explosion so that nothing remained but a smoldering hole. His friend had finally been buried, that is what he told himself and in that found comfort.

Shells fell like rain as he stepped into the bunker and into the deeper chamber where the sound of falling rounds was muffled. Only when he took a seat on the bunk did he realize that he was the only one in the bunker. He hadn't seen anyone else for a while. Had he missed an order to move out or had they scattered once they heard the shelling begin? Whatever the case, he wasn't going outside, not now. It didn't really matter if he were inside or out because a shell, especially the heavy shells raining down outside could easily crater his bunker and kill him. Berger hadn't felt fear in the normal sense, not for several months. He could thank Otto for that. He smiled remembering his friend lecture him on what a waste of time fear was for a soldier. "Victor, it is a waste of time to worry about shelling. There isn't a thing you can do to stop it. You can run but where would you run? They drop shells at random because they cannot find our exact location. You are better off staying put because shells never fall in the same hole twice, generally. See this bunker? It is built deep because a general came to visit us a few months ago. They built it twenty feet down layered the roof with six layers of logs which make it 12 feet thick with four feet of earth above that. If a shell penetrates that it will have to be pretty big and if that happens we won't know it anyway so why worry?"

After that they discovered a forgotten case of wine under the generals vacated bunk. Twelve bottles of wine and an 8 hour artillery barrage made for a fine evening. They invented a game called 'artillery dice' in which they took dice and laid them on the floor and let the artillery concussions roll the dice for them. They would then wager on which side of the die would come up. It was a creative way of distracting themselves from what would have otherwise been a miserable time. He had never enjoyed a shelling before. However, the resulting hangover made the next days' shelling less pleasant with each of them vowing never to drink again. Berger's future hangovers would be less enjoyable without Otto.

Berger decided that being killed in a warm and dry bunker would be preferable to dying in a wet, muddy trench. With that he lay on his pack which made a serviceable pillow. He then realized that it had been nearly a week since he'd slept at all. He fell asleep instantly in spite of the shelling and slept for two days.

Victor woke to a sudden and chilling silence. It had been the lack of shelling that woke him. For two days he was lulled to sleep by the shells falling around him. When the last shell exploded he was instantly awake. That last explosion hadn't been 'right'. Instead of a concussive boom he'd heard 'thump….Pop..pop..pop…hsssssssss' that made him nervous. He'd heard that sound before and knew without thinking what it was…mustard gas. Getting his mask on he'd missed the tear between the canister and the rubberized canvas. A tear caused by falling on the mask in an effort to avoid a machine gun burst almost a month before had expanded enough to allow gas through, but wasn't big enough to notice, not in the heat of the moment.

Feeling secure he began wading through the waist deep yellow gas making his way to the trench where he planned to climb out and head to the nearest German position. However, before he could reach the door he found himself gagging and reeling from pain at having taken a deep breath full of mustard gas that had leaked through the tear in his mask. His eyes watered and burned as the gas choked the life from his body.

Without realizing it he found himself on his knees unconsciously working the straps of his mask trying not to vomit into the one thing that would save his life. Nothing helped as his eyes began to fade to black the fire burning in his chest, mouth and sinuses caused him to scream in agony as he fought for life while at the same time praying for death. He fell not quite into unconsciousness and vaguely remembered being carried from the bunker. He was in and out of consciousness rolling and pitching in the ambulance that was carrying him from the front. It was during the ambulance ride that he had finally faded out into the coma from which he would awaken six months later.

His mustard gas inhalation hadn't been enough to kill him but it had been enough to permanently alter his brain function as the gas had neurologically fused some of his brain tissue erasing his once cheerful, caring and polite demeanor and over time transformed him into a psychopath with a face wrinkled in a permanent snarl making him appear permanently angry. This puckering was the result of the mustard gas scaring the internal mucus membrane in his sinus cavity.

After nearly a year in hospital he wanted to return to his company but his company had been wiped out in the attack that had nearly killed him, that and due to his injuries he was no longer fit for duty. The mustard gas had damaged his brain sufficiently to cause him to black out. Only when he blacked out he became unspeakably violent attacking his doctors and nurses in fits of uncontrolled rage that he wouldn't remember. It was a common side effect of mustard gas poisoning…if you survived. Over time these fits would cease but not before the war ended. He would finish his hospital stay under Allied supervision and was released from active duty on Christmas day 1919.

Having no money to his name Victor roamed the streets a vagrant taking up residence where he could for nearly a year before he moved into a warehouse abandoned by an industrialist who had moved his money and factory to Switzerland to avoid having to pay war reparations.

Other homeless veterans had formed a group dedicated to saving their comrades where they could and had secured the building for that purpose. Each man was allotted a space of 12 x 12, affording him privacy and a bed. It would be his home for the next few years.

Victor sat on the edge of his bed suffering yet another hangover from another binge drinking session. The few jobs he'd been able to get over the previous three years had been temporary but his injuries made permanent employment almost impossible. Germany was in no position to look after its soldier's. Many were like him, destitute, homeless and permanently injured and unfit for further duty.

The warehouse was a shelter from the wind if not the cold. Heat came from stoves when wood or some other fuel was available, which wasn't often. Other soldiers had taken residence there and did their best to make it a home. His bitterness would grow and foment as he struggled to survive the brutal economic conditions that befell Germany after the war.

Werner Dietrich had been a corporal when he'd rescued Victor Berger from the gas attack. He'd been temporarily assigned to ambulance duties tasked with retrieving survivors from various battles taking place along the front. Being a veteran of the front he was suited to the task of collecting only those who could be saved. That and he would not shy away from a horribly mangled soldier having been hardened to such sights.

Berger was among the many millions of Germans who could not find work and what work they could find was back-breaking and paid barely enough to keep a person from starving to death. What jobs he did get were through his friend Werner the man who had saved him from the gas attack in the war. However, he didn't know how to feel about that exactly. What had he saved him from.... death? Death, he often felt, would have been better than the shit life he was currently living. Then again, he was grateful to him for saving him from the enigma of death. This confusion was one of the early symptoms of his developing psychosis.

Circumstances forced Berger back into a life of crime if only to survive. A life he had hoped to leave behind, but his battle injuries made remaining in the army impossible, they also made permanent employment impossible. But crime, disgraceful as it was, provided him a decent living, until he got caught and was sent to prison where he was reacquainted with Hitler. Hitler had attempted to over throw the government alongside many of his WWI comrades. It was this association with Hitler that would change his life and give him a sense of purpose and belonging he had long since lost.

The year Hitler was elected Chancellor of Germany Berger was released from prison and sent to train with the Gestapo. Only once did Berger meet the Fuhrer after he was elected chancellor. He had been invited to meet Hitler who awarded him the blood stripe for his time in prison with Hitler. It was at this interview that Hitler spoke to him as an old soldier to another and brought him thoroughly into the fold as a true devotee of Adolf Hitler.

"You and I are comrades in arms. We share scars of war and the burdens they bring. It is for that reason Victor that I have chosen you to serve the Reich as my personal representative in all tasks assigned to you in the coming years. We may never meet like this again due to the duties of state, but know that you have my trust and my gratitude as one German Soldier to another. Good luck." With that they shook hands and parted never to meet face to face again. Berger was satisfied with that, his Fuhrer had spoken to him as a soldier and that was enough, he was the Fuhrers man from then on.

Chapter 18

The Piening-Route

GENERAL DIETRICH EYED the map on his desk seeking out a more suitable route if he could. There simply were no other choices left to him, especially with two large, slow heavily laden submarines. The entire North Atlantic was covered from coast to coast with ships, bombers, floatplanes, blimps and countless, uncharted buoys each with passive sonar mounted to create the very first sonar net. The fact that 80% of their sub fleet now lay on the bottom was testament to the effectiveness of this system.

A breakout into the Atlantic was suicidal. There simply was no way for a slow, unarmed submarine to survive in the Atlantic without taking special precautions. The planned route to The South Atlantic was a modified version of the Piening-Route so named for the Submarine Captain who had hugged the French and Spanish Coast line in 1943 to avoid Allied Bomber patrols. It was effective but time consuming and used up precious fuel reducing their patrol time.

To counter this they had pre-positioned several German ships in Spanish and Portuguese ports where the subs would sneak in under the cover of night and refuel. Spain though neutral was sympathetic to Germany and feigned ignorance. However, once it was clear that Germany was losing the Spanish were forced to put a stop to this abuse of their neutrality in fear of being declared a hostile state.

Even with Spain enforcing its neutrality Germany continued meeting their ships in Spanish ports though much more carefully. A mid Atlantic rendezvous was out of the question with the allies having the entire Atlantic secured. With the Spanish being recently less cooperative sneaking a massive sub into a neutral port was going to be dangerous, especially with two, but it was the most secure option available to them. Actually it was the only option when you really looked at it.

He had conferred with both captains on this matter and they both agreed that if they could transit the surface of the English Channel under the cover of a storm it would be their best chance to reach the French coast. Rounding the point just before Brest under the cover of a storm they would then submerge and hug the French Coast line using their snorkel to recharge the batteries. Their hope was that the sound of the crashing surf would be enough to mask their diesel engines

So far three other submarines had made the dash and all three had survived. He knew this because they had all three radioed signaling that they had each made their destination. "Mother of God 1 home", then two and then three etc, just one simple message from each boat was enough to let them know that all three boats had reached their destinations using the same predetermined route. So it was decided that they too would use the same route as well. The only difference was the fact that the other three boats had been able to transit the English Channel submerged. They were Type 7s and faster under battery power than the two cows were. But they had also charted a new channel through the minefield, which could only be transited on the surface if the weather was rough. In calm weather only a type 7 could transit the channel submerged. These were sent in the open using an addendorf cipher, the key being in the possession of General Dietrich.

They could transit the channel under the cover of the storm and that would be sufficient to mask their noise. Sighing in relief he once again phoned each captain and conferred with them on the matter to ensure he hadn't missed any details that they might see. The success of the three boats in recent weeks propped up his confidence.

The one remaining doubt the captains had was whether or not the submarines would have sufficient speed and endurance to keep up with the storms projected speed of 8 or ten knots. If they transited the surface, they could but the question remained if the electric motors would keep up.

The two captains each let out a sigh of relief as 'finally' a rational thought escaped the Generals fevered brain. His original idea of transiting the channel on the surface was insane. If they could transit submerged under the storm they could greatly extend their range and prolong their safety. Following a slow ship could only improve their chances if they happened to meet one. If not they would simply wait for the storm to hit and then follow along under the waves hugging the bottom of the known shipping channels and that would only be if they happened to escape their harbor undetected. Only time would tell.

Hopefully the Allies would not get wise to them before they'd reached their safe point. For General Dietrich that would mean safe in port on St. Vincent and fully under cover in the sub base there.

Driven though he was, he was no fool. The odds were steep and he had his misgivings.

They needed the ship building capacity of the Argentine Government to make their plans of building a new Navy a reality. There simply was no way to build a ship without foundries, presses and skilled labor to do the job he had asked of Beck and Prussien. They were aware of this, but it was in his interest to make them believe that he was insane or bordering on it to keep them in line. A crazy man is unpredictable and deadly and so must be kept at his ease lest he act on his 'insanity', Hitler being a prime example of this paradigm.

Beck and Prussien would do as they were told to keep the project on tract if he could somehow secure the support necessary. It was a long shot but it was their last best chance to prolong the war in order to regain the upper hand. He hadn't the stomach to lose another war, especially not one that had already been won and then squandered.

Had they but waited out the British consolidating the western front it would have allowed them to negotiate a land deal with the Russians. Then, if that didn't work a properly planned and executed invasion would have had a far better chance at succeeding. Turning in his seat to the map of Europe and Asia he eyed it as if to plan another invasion of Russia the way 'he' would have done it.

"If I had planned it we would have invaded in late winter or early spring before the ground had time to defrost" he thought. "We could have then used mechanized infantry and tanks to cross the Steppes of Russia and take Moscow securing a strong hold from which to launch an offensive into their manufacturing centers before they'd could ramp up their armaments production." He stood up and stepped over to the map and tapped the Baku region. "Once their manufacturing base was secured then we would have driven south to the Baku and secured their oil fields and Black Sea ports." Had it been done that way the Russians ability to launch an offensive against them would be erased and Germany would have secured their eastern frontier. The rest of Russia would've been theirs in time." This entire dissertation was recited out loud as if he were actually giving the presentation to the Fuhrer himself.

General Dietrich starred at the map knowing that such ideas were no longer possible under the circumstances. His focus was to procure support from Argentina so that he could later implement his plans for the conquest of Russia. That is 'after' they had secured the industrial might of the United States. Hitler would no longer interfere or interrupt military strategists in their efforts to move Germany to genuine victory. Would Hitler's Germany be able to hang on that long? He doubted it, but Germany was resourceful and in war nothing was certain.

Hitler's trust in 'wonder weapons' was foolish. They were of little strategic value other than to enrage the enemy. They simply weren't precise enough to be strategic. Men, tanks and planes were needed so that they could physically take possession of the territories conquered. If the V1 and V2 could be guided to precise targets ahead of an advance then maybe they could be useful, but until then their use was a huge waste of resources.

General Dietrich in that instant felt his heart sink. He knew, without a doubt that Nazi Germany was defeated and merely fighting for time. Argentina though sympathetic to Nazi Germany wasn't about to throw in its lot with a dying regime, not at this late date. A tiny, frantic voice was screaming in the back of his mind. A panicked, desperate voice of a man who wanted to live but knew he could not, at least not in a world without his beloved Nazi Party. He would die with Nazi Germany and if his Fuhrer were to die…he would follow him in death and forsake the mission. Shaking that thought from his mind he muttered under his breath "Only after I have done all that I can to prevent it."

The General began to consider the fate of the remaining personnel. They each were destined to surrender and face the defeat and occupation of Germany and possibly the dismantling of her infrastructure leaving Germany a third world country. Whatever Germany was to face it would need its people, as many as could be spared to drag Germany out of the post war muck, as all warring nations must, victorious or otherwise.

He had ordered the base sealed and all personnel confined to base for their protection from Norwegian resistance forces that had effectively retaken the town. The Norwegians wouldn't take their revenge on the innocent, enlisted personnel he knew. It was the officers and the SS guards and Gestapo that faced the wrath of the population they had brutalized. Their lives were forfeit the moment the allies took the post and it was this knowledge that would drive the lunatics over the edge and massacre all German personnel in revenge for not winning the war for their beloved Fuhrer.

He had to ensure that the lunatics wouldn't act. None of them were leaders except for Berger and if there were no leadership there would be no organized massacre. It was with that end in mind that he had hopefully manipulated Berger to address this dilemma himself by putting a bullet through his own brain.

He and Berger had been friends in the beginning but over the years Berger had become violently insane. It was an unfortunate side effect of mustard gas. Too many of his comrades had been killed by the gas and those who had survived either went mad or had committed suicide from the extreme pain caused by the scarring of their lungs and sinuses. Berger did not suffer pain. Apparently the portion of his brain that allowed that sensation had degenerated along with the portion that generated restraint the lack of which drove him to become unspeakably violent and unstable.

As the allies approached, Berger would kill the entire garrison. He enjoyed killing so much that in the event of his known capture or death he would engage in a murderous orgy, and for Berger that is what it would be, an orgy; another side effect of mustard gas scarring his brain.

It was for this reason that he had let slip a minor tidbit of information that seemed important and then suggested that he keep the 'secret' at all cost. He was confident that Berger, devoted as he was to the Fuhrer would put a gun to his own head. A sniper would be given orders to kill Berger just in case he did not. This was a situation he did not wish to trust to luck or chance. Berger had to die one way or the other for the sake of those left behind. He was just too unstable and Germany would need her remaining sons to rebuild if he failed in his mission. Yet the squealing frightened voice repeated over and over again "You are going to die, you are going to die."

Shaking the voice from his consciousness he took one last look at the map and chart then rolled them up. He then placed them in a tube and began packing up what remained of his personal items most of which were already on board U-SS1. It was then he noticed his hands shaking and beads of sweat trickling down his temple though the room was frigid and damp. Clenching his fists he stood behind the door of his office as he gained control of himself "No" he whispered through clenched teeth as he regained control over his nerves once again. Since learning of the Allies intent to prosecute 'him' specifically as a war criminal he'd become nervous. He could handle a prison camp and repatriation like in WWI. But to be tried like a common criminal, stripped of his honor and then hung was something he feared above all else. It was that fear he was forced to contain.

Leaving his office for the last time he spoke to his orderly giving the order to have Standartenfurher Beck and Prussien escorted immediately to the pier, emphasizing that they were to be 'unharmed'. The orderly saluted in a crisp well-practiced Nazi salute, clicked his heels and turned to carry out his Generals orders.

The Generals personal Kubelwagon was waiting with its engine running. The Canvas top was up against the rain that was beginning to fall. He smiled at his luck. Rain would help hide their screw noise as they passed out of the fjord and out into the Atlantic. It was the leading edge of the storm that was to shield them while transiting the English Channel. His timing couldn't have been more perfect. "Maybe God is on our side after all" he said to himself.

Tossing the charts and maps in the back seat he then climbed behind the wheel and drove to the pier. The rain fell harder and harder as he drove. He slowed his pace both for safety and because he had always enjoyed driving in the rain. It was peaceful and relaxing to hear rain thundering on the roof of his car. He especially loved the sound of rain on the canvas top. "Will I ever enjoy this simple pleasure again?" He asked himself.

Such thoughts are typical of men facing death. He'd often asked such questions prior to going over the top as it was called when they poured out of the trenches time after time to retake no man's land. It is this morose acceptance of death that makes a soldier such a pragmatist. It is also those same men who could teach Dante a thing or two about hell and why such men enjoy simple pleasures like cigarettes and hot coffee. These simplest of comforts satisfy old soldiers and sailors better than the finest wines or cigars. It was these simple pleasures that kept them sane while living through a living, breathing hell.

As he approached the bunker General Dietrich decided to pull over and smoke a cigarette. He'd procured several cartons of cigarettes from Beck, a fact that irritated Berger who despised the black market and those who perpetuated it. The Black market was a reality of any war and he saw no reason why a person with Becks ingenuity couldn't take advantage of that reality. Besides German cigarettes were shit and the Russian Cigarettes he'd been forced to smoke were worse than shit as far as he was concerned. Why not smoke an excellent American cigarette if you had the choice? Reaching into his pocket he took out a Zippo cigarette lighter he'd taken from the body of a bomber pilot who'd belly-landed after being shot down. He looked at the lighter remembering the day he'd found it.

The crew of the bomber had bailed out but for some reason the pilot stayed with the plane. Perhaps he thought he was too low to bail out so he drove her in and belly-landed. He had come in too fast and nosed into a growth of trees and was catapulted through his windscreen killing him. He was found hanging by a leg with his boot wedged in between two branches of a tree. The lighter had fallen from his pocket and was lying under his head when he had found him. There was a look of sheer terror on the pilots face as he hung there his body rigid from the stress of his last ordeal on earth.

To face death, beat it and then face it again at the last moment had to have been a shitty way to die. It was this thought that passed through the Generals mind as the Zippo ignited. Shaking his head in sympathy for the dead pilot he lit the cigarette. "At least some good came of his death" he thought and took a long drag inhaling deep on the cigarette smoke.

Twenty minutes and three cigarettes later he pulled up to the slip inside the submarine bunker. From behind the wheel he saw the black painted U-SS1 with its highly polished deaths head displayed prominently on the conning tower and cringed knowing that he had been the one to order its placement.

It seemed a good idea at the time, but then he had been drunk on Russian vodka. To correct this oversight, he'd have the men remove it. That was the least of his concerns at the moment. He needed time and didn't have any to spare. The war would likely be over in a few months so it was critical for him to initiate negotiations with Argentina before Germany surrendered.

This was necessary for several reasons, one he needed to have an intact government to make his mission legitimate and afford him diplomatic immunity. Without diplomatic immunity he would be considered pirate rendering any cooperation by Argentina diplomatically impossible. The entire plan was madness in the extreme but he had to try. Living his life as a fugitive, hiding in the Andes under an assumed name was not to be considered. His mind raced as he climbed down the ladder and walked to his cabin in the nose of the sub, where the torpedo room would have been on most submarines. As he entered the cabin through the canvas curtain, the doors being removed for noise and weight reduction, he placed his charts on the desk and flipped on the light that illuminated a full color chart of the Atlantic, Caribbean and Gulf of Mexico painted on is bulkhead.

It had been done in a classic style of 19th century navigational charts but with far more accuracy. The Atlantic was painted several shades of blue, lighter shades designating shallows or shoals and deep rich blue for greater depths like the Abyssal plains off the Virginia Capes with medium shades marking undersea mountains. The Eastern seaboard of the United States was marked in several shades of brown, tan, green and blue to depict topographical features like forested coastline, deltas, coastal mountain ranges and marshes.

Brass navigational calipers were fixed to the bulkhead and used to accurately track their route. His bunk was carved from oak and covered in the red and white-checkered wool blankets used by the Kreigsmarine. On top of this was his own personal quilt made of heavy canvas and wool stuffed with goose down. His desk was bolted directly to the bulkhead under the map so that he could work while marking their progress. It was to keep him busy while underway and out from underfoot of the crew.

He used his green pencil to mark their intended route and areas they needed to avoid. A red pencil would be used to mark their actual route and progress to help in timing their arrival on the west coast of Africa, where they were to wait for a storm to form.

Western Africa was the birthplace of hurricanes in the Atlantic. The equatorial sun would heat up the landmass creating updrafts that would draw moisture from the cold Atlantic and create the seeds of a storm. Trade winds would then fan the evaporation and the sun would heat up the water inside the dense cloud formation. As the trades whirled about drawing warm water into the atmosphere a storm would form and move along the equator, then up the convection current known as Gulf Stream which would then cause it to move up the east coast of the United States or into the Gulf of Mexico

The trouble lay in predicting when a storm would form and what path it would take. His concern was that weather had a bad habit of not cooperating. In Norway they knew with certainty when a storm would hit and roughly where because they had the weather station at Spitzbergen to give them hyper accurate weather reports in the northern Atlantic. When they reached the west coast of Africa it would be up to the shipboard barometer to tell them when a low pressure system was forming, but a low pressure system didn't guarantee weather. Their best chance lay in reaching Western Africa at the time of year when such storms were most likely to form and trust to luck.

Throwing his pencil down the General shook his head in disgust. Luck was something that Germany hadn't had much of lately. Ideally they could follow along behind a forming storm and use it to run interference for them by keeping ships blind to their presence and blimps grounded.

Blimps were especially dangerous to submarines because they could not be heard or tracked while the submarine was submerged. Too often a submarine learned of the presence of a blimp only as they were being attacked by it. So it was in their best interest to see that every advantage was taken, every precaution adhered to in order to give them the best chance to simply survive the Atlantic and using weather to keep blimps grounded was a sound tactic, if they were fortunate enough to catch one forming and if it moved fast enough to allow timely passage.

Taking a seat he stared intently at his wall chart and reached for the weather reports. They told him that a massive storm front was moving in from the north and would hit the channel in less than three days. He knew this already but he was looking for the slightest deviation in the expected path of the storm. Any changes in direction, speed and severity needed to be noted. They were cutting it close if they wanted to use the storm for cover through the channel. They would attempt to transit submerged if the storm was moving slowly enough. Otherwise they would surface and make a speed run through the channel keeping their fingers crossed as luck would have to be with them in that event.

Checking his watch it was less than two hours before they were to depart. He'd ordered Berger to get Beck and Prussien on board early because he simply didn't trust Berger to resist his lust for killing. Taking a deep breath he looked over at his bunk, it looked inviting. He would resist the temptation until they were at sea. He was not essential for the operation of the ship and so could afford to luxuriate once they were committed to the voyage.

The General leaned back and closed his eyes contemplating his fate. He held few illusions of what awaited him if he were captured. The carnage he had unleashed on Russia had guaranteed him a death sentence. Entire villages and towns were razed to the ground so severely that not even a brick, timber or blade of grass could be distinguished one from the other. As for the occupants of those villages they suffered the same fate as the brick, timber and grass. Nothing of their bodies remained to be identified as human...not one man, woman, child, dog or cat in any of the villages he passed over.

A hellish fury was his calling card and he had become the devil. It had been his intent to end the war with Russia himself, to destroy their ability and will to fight by being the most brutally horrific adversary they had ever known. But it hadn't been the Russian Army that beat them it had been what the Russians fondly referred to as 'General Winter'.

The severe Russian weather had been their saving grace since Catherine the Great. No invading army in three hundred years had been able to withstand a Russian winter much less fight in it. So to it was with Hitler's armies.

If it wasn't the cold, it was the mud from the thaw over which tanks, trucks and men could barely move. Only he, it seemed, had known what to expect if they didn't finish the Russians by early autumn. His thought had been to destroy every living thing in his path and then take Moscow. That may not have ended the war but it would have given them a place to fight from in the winter and would have eventually allowed them to force Stalin to surrender. However, he had been pulled from the fight just as the autumn weather was turning foul and just as he was about to make the final assault on Moscow, which he viewed as a mistake.

He could see Moscow and would have been there in a matter of days if not hours had he been allowed to continue his total war march. "Fools" he spat slamming his fist on the desk knowing that if he had been allowed to conduct the war as he knew it must the Russians would have been defeated again...and Moscow renamed Hitlergrad and Red Square renamed Hitler Platz.

Out of nowhere his rage exploded as he threw his cap at his bed in frustration and anger at having been removed from his command for doing what was necessary to win in the time they needed to. He had not been humane nothing about war was humane why not take it for what it is worth and do what must be done to end it quickly? Suddenly his anger ebbed and was replaced by profound sadness.

Twice in thirty years he was witness to Germanys defeat, each time victory was within reach and squandered. The war had been won in 1941. France had fallen and Britain was on its knees the entire continent of Europe under German control. It would have been easy to keep that control had Hitler simply waited. He could have then once Britain was secure negotiated a land deal with Russia from a position of strength. Once that was done it would have been a matter of time before they had acquired the Oil rich Baku region, Steppes and then the Black Sea Ports.

He let his imagination take him along the fantasy of what might have been had Hitler simply left well enough alone. Germany would have controlled an area far greater than that of the Roman Empire at its farthest expanse. What was and what could have been tortured him.

Fatigue began to set in as his bunk began calling to him more urgently. "Perhaps a short nap" he thought to himself as he considered giving in to the temptation of a nap in a warm bed. Just as he was moving to his bunk the speaker on the wall crackled. "*General Deitrich, Standartenfurhers Beck and Prussien have arrived on board*" the metallic voice of the topside watch announced.

He flipped the switch "See them to their quarters and have them report to me once we get underway. See to it I am not disturbed" he flipped the switch off, removed his tunic, placed it on the hook and crawled onto his bunk and fell almost immediately asleep.

Chapter 19
The End of Berger

TWO HOURS EARLIER Hans lay motionless on his bed after collapsing in fatigue and strain as Frederick paced back and forth angry at their situation. The idea of being guarded by thugs, most of whom should be in prison or hanging from a gallows was simply infuriating. There was also the voyage they were about to embark upon and the mission that only hours before was supposed to have saved Germany but which had since been revealed to be the ramblings of a madman. His guts burned with acid nausea a condemned man feels as he steps upon the gallows.

That feeling did not come from a fear of dying. He'd faced death often enough in the past to prove he wasn't afraid of death. Death was easy to face because the rules were simple, live or die, period. It was living that vexed Frederick, living in a world ruled by madmen and lunatics where sanity was killed and lunacy lauded as genius. If he somehow managed to survive the voyage, there was absolutely no way to achieve the goals the General had set for them. All he wanted to do now was survive the damned war and start his life over, if he could.

His eyes locked on the portrait of Hitler next to the mirror; strange how he had missed it before now. Then again Hitler had lost his luster with the German people when the first allied thousand-plane bomber force bombed a German city into oblivion. Now every major German city lay in ruin. Even Berlin was a wasteland of ruble and death. Hitler was no longer important to the people, surviving was.

Hitler was a genius in terms of inflaming the passions of a nation, especially a nation as down trodden as Germany had been after The Great War. At first it seemed he was truly a gifted genius at diplomacy, then came the 'night of the long knife' during which all of Hitler's political rivals were killed or disappeared never to be seen again.

His actions were justified by the progressive growth of Germany's economic and military power. Roads and factories were built or upgraded, new and more powerful automobiles rolled off production lines. The Autobahn was a technological/engineering feat of genius and would later inspire General Eisenhower who became president of the United States to build the American Freeway system, modeled after the Autobahn. Volkswagen or Peoples Car was an inspiration of Hitler's vision of Germanys' future. With such innovation coming from his leadership the 'rumors' of brutality were tolerated.

Frederick faced the prospect of being labeled a criminal for dedicating himself to an ideal that had seemed, at the time, the answer to Germany's problems. As brilliant as Hitler seemed early on he was, later, equally idiotic. Ordering entire armies to fight to the last man or abandoning them to the Russians simply because they were not able to carry out his insane orders while refusing to pull millions of men off the line to prevent them from being surrounded so they could be redirected at a more useful target and perhaps regain the initiative in Russia. Thankfully Frederick had been spared the horror of the winter war unlike many of his friends.

He had no wish to know of such things. He'd seen too many of his friends or what was left of them, return from Russia. Some with physical wounds so horrible that he wondered how they'd survived at all. Others came home wounded in ways bandages were no use. Ghostly, emotionally dead eyes met him when they first came off the train. Some seemed to wake from a trance while others seemed trapped in the horror they had lived, never to escape. Many committed suicide, some with a gun to the mouth while others took to the streets during air raids seeking out the bombs. For them death was easier than living with memories of what they had seen or had been forced to do in Russia. Such battle fatigue was not seen on the western front or in the deserts of North Africa, at least not among the troops he'd served with. There had been some certainly, but nothing that compared to the Eastern Front.

Stopping at the window he gazed onto the harbor, beyond the breakwater and out onto the open ocean. For most men it would have seemed like freedom but he felt as though he were looking upon his grave. An icy chill crept up his spine as dread surfaced forcing him to swallow to keep from vomiting. It was a feeling that no amount of whiskey or Schnapps could conquer. He was claustrophobic. It had been bad enough in tanks. But with a tank he could open a hatch and get out. In a submarine there would be no such escape and he wasn't sure if his nerves were up to it. The idea that he might die in a matter of hours didn't frighten him as much as how it was likely to happen.

What made it worse was that Germany had already won the war, once. It was effectively over in 1940-41 except for the peace treaties...

had Hitler not invaded Russia. Tactically Britain would have been out of it in a matter of months had Germany simply kept up their blockade. The United States would have been isolated and unable to mount an offensive in support of Britain, especially since it was, at the time, neutral. If anything there would have been a cold war between the two powers and Japan might never have attacked Pearl Harbor due to diplomatic pressure a victorious Germany could have put on the USA on Japans behalf.

Japan then could have secured China and its resources without fear of US intervention. Germany would have naturally acquired Britain's colonies of Canada, Hong Kong, Malaysia, India, Burma, Australia, New Zealand, South Africa and the British Indian Ocean Territories. Laying back Frederick let his mind ponder the possibilities of what could have been had Hitler simply waited. France had been theirs already. So eventually her colonies in Africa, Asia and South America would have been theirs also.

Lighting a cigarette he hooked his left hand behind his neck as visions of what might have been unfolded. In a matter of a few years Germany could have been the largest empire to exist since the beginning of recorded history. Taking an exceptionally long drag from one of his friends Lucky Strike he indulged a smile. Then he remembered Himmler and the legions of lunatics who followed him. Their tactics would have not been tolerated for long and Germany would have had a time keeping effective control of all that territory. "If only our leaders weren't out of their fucking minds," he thought.

Suddenly his heart lightened as he came to the realization that the world was better off without Nazi leadership. Sitting up he took another drag on his cigarette. "Germany will be great again. Germany had always been so…it was its leadership that had destroyed it, not the German people. This defeat was for the betterment of humanity. Had Hitler been smarter, less insane the war would have never taken place to begin with. Far better we lose like this than to have won under his leadership. The world is better now...Germany was better and would be great again, someday.

Looking over at his sleeping friend he decided to try and get some himself, suddenly at peace with the world. Laying back onto his pillow he gave his friend one last look before closing his eyes, smiled to himself as sleep took him.

As for Hans sheer exhaustion had taken over and nothing more. The mental anguish of recent weeks had worn on him. He had been prepared to leave Germany and take up residence in a Swiss Chalet and wait out the remainder of the war a wealthy man. One moment's bad judgment found him in Norway, captive and awaiting a journey on a mission so insane that it would be a miracle if he or anyone survived it. His skin was a mere shell covering a bundle of nerves that was set to explode. He had been sitting in the bathroom an hour earlier Luger in hand staring intently at it wanting desperately to die. His father's words kept ringing in his head "I want you to live, I want you to live." Over and over they repeated as if his father were inside his head desperate to keep his name alive.

Silent tears ran down his face as he stared at the device that could deliver him from his nightmare. His father's last words kept him from acting. For nearly an hour he willed himself to die but did not. When he emerged Frederick recognized the look in his friend's eye and resisted the urge to wrest the gun from his hand. Hans then sat on the bed, looked up, smiled at his friend and collapsed onto the pillow half feinting and half exhausted, falling immediately into a dreamless sleep his gun firmly in his grip. Only after his friend was asleep did Frederick pry the gun from his fingers and removed the clip. He then set the gun on the bed stand.

Outside Berger waited and watched. His presence outside their door was a deliberate, if figurative, poke in the eye. He knew they could not run there was no way for them to. His watching their every move might prove enough to push them over the edge and cause them to commit suicide. It was this type of treatment that had caused many of the others to take their own lives. Knowing the Gestapo was outside their door was often just enough to push them over that edge.

Berger took perverse pleasure from that knowledge and exploited it as often as he could. Checking his watch he smiled and nodded, another hour and he and two others would escort their charges to the submarines and see to it that they were on board and away... then...Berger smiled to himself as an insane rush of euphoria caused an erection. He had a plan to save Germany and to serve his Fuhrer.

Just then a messenger approached him. "Herr Berger, with the compliments of General Dietrich" then handed him an envelope. Tearing open the envelope he pulled the letter out. A sergeant in his squad lit his torch so that Berger could read the note.

Victor

There has been an urgent change of plan. Our window of opportunity has advanced by one hour. It is imperative that both Beck and Prussien be escorted to U-SS1 IMEDIATELY!!!

The advantage is tremendous we must act quickly.

Regards and best Wishes

General Dietrich

P.S. Remember that you must keep this absolutely secret otherwise our re-turn to power will be in jeopardy. It is imperative that you do what you must to ensure absolute secrecy.

Berger grimaced with disappointment at being denied the pleasure of sweating out Beck and Prussien. He crumpled the paper in his hand then shoved it into his pocket. Swallowing his disappointment he turned to look out over the harbor and saw the shadow of an S-80 Patrol Torpedo boat rumbling along the breakwater. Without tor-pedoes it had been reduced to a speedboat, forced to patrol the inner harbor for deserters. The entire German Navy had been reduced to ashes in port. None of its ships had been allowed the dignity of dy-ing in combat. They'd been bombed like sitting ducks in port unable to maneuver or fight back. Taking one last drag from his cigarette he let it fall to the ground and stomped it out. "Sergeant pick two men as escorts then dismiss the rest. Do not ask where we are going, or why. It is best you do not know."

Sergeant Schmitt came to attention and saluted Berger with crisp Nazi salute. "I understand, Captain." Schmitt knew of the two sub-marines in the pens waiting to depart, as did everyone on post. He also knew better than to share this with the Gestapo chief who was a raving lunatic, a violent and unpredictable raving lunatic. Schmitt picked two corporals who he regarded as trolls; two men who he knew to be Berger's spies who had informed on men who'd pilfered dried sausages from a Gestapo lock up whom Berger had himself shot. They worshipped Berger as only true fanatics could and would do his bidding without question, even if it were to put a bullet into their own brain, which was *exactly* what Schmitt was hoping.

Schmitt knew more than he was supposed to, as all sergeants did. He knew that a sniper had been ordered to take out Berger, if he did not kill himself. It stood to reason that if Berger were supposed to die, anyone with him or associated with him would also die. Hence his choosing of the two imbeciles Berger usually picked for 'special' duties. If they died it would be no big loss and certainly would make his life easier without those two weasels to worry about. "Good riddance you bastard, take your vermin with you". Sergeant Albert Schmitt smiled to himself knowing that Berger would no longer plague his men or those remaining on the garrison, not after tonight. The idea brought Schmitt a tremendous sense of satisfaction.

At that moment Frederick had just slipped off to sleep when a knock on the door woke him. "Yes?" he said sleepily.

Berger was tempted to scream Gestapo!! Only that would likely create a fuss he was in no mood to deal with. "General Dietrich has asked me to escort you to the submarine. You are departing earlier than scheduled." He said this as genially as if he were delivering room service to a honeymoon suite.

"Er yes, one moment please." The voice indicated a man who had just fallen into a deep sleep and had been awakened rather suddenly. Looking over at his companion Hans was sitting up pistol in hand pointing it at the door. "Easy Hans, he is here to escort us to the boat. Apparently we are leaving earlier than scheduled.

"Yes, I heard" he said dully. 'So' he thought 'we are actually going.' The thought was not cheerful. Looking over at his friend they smiled nervously and nodded. "Unto the breech" they said as one. Both men were busy brushing the wrinkles from their uniforms. "Where did you put my clip?" Hans asked noting the weight of his empty pistol.

Nodding his head toward the nightstand Frederick said "Over there. I didn't like the look in your eye when you came out of the bathroom".

Hans shook his head stepping over to the nightstand. "I didn't like how I was feeling. This whole mission is a nightmare we aren't likely to wake up from." He holstered his pistol and took one final look out the window speaking unconsciously "I rented a chalet in the Swiss Alps. Paid rent for a full year and even had my eye on a beautiful red SSK some Jew banker sold on his way to America. It was beautiful. I even spent a week in my chalet stocking it for the year. I have in my pantry 'real' coffee. I would have been there now in sitting by a fire counting the ways I could have spent my money."

Frederick shook his head. "The money is still there and you will get out of this Hans. The car might be gone but there will be others. Trust me."

Hans smiled sheepishly shaking his head not daring to believe it. Five minutes later they were riding in the back of a Kubelwagon watching the rainfall as they drove to the pen. Once inside they pulled up to the pier head and were assisted out of the car. Berger stood pistol in hand "This way gentlemen" he said.

Berger followed behind both officers his pistol pointed at their backs. The moment they had crossed the gangplank he lowered the gun saying "My duty to the General is fulfilled. Good luck on your mission. May you bring Glory to the Reich!" With that he called his men to attention. Berger took up station next to them. "Men, for the Glory and secrecy of the Reich we must die to keep this secret safe." With that the men both un-holstered their pistols, turned to face each other, put their gun barrels into the mouth of the other and pulled the triggers simultaneously. A haze of blood and brain coated Berger who apparently relished the gore as it sprayed over him. Berger smiled, came to attention and with his left hand put the gun to his head and saluted in the Nazi fashion then cried "Hiel Hitler!!!" and pulled the trigger spraying the contents of his skull over the pier. His body stood for a brief moment, tittering forwards and backwards before falling into the water and sinking to the bottom of the slipway.

Activity on the pier stopped momentarily to take in the spectacle. Most of the sailors merely shook their heads and went about their work. Apparently suicide was becoming a common occurrence because only that morning two senior officers, prominent Nazis both, had ritually killed each other in similar fashion and each fell into the slipway. Their bodies were left in the water because the morgue was overflowing with suicides. The crematorium in town was no longer accessible so there was no way to dispose of the bodies and there was no cemetery on base so the bodies were left where they'd fallen.

Two members of the security staff just pushed the bodies of Berger's two imbeciles into the water and hosed off the mess. In less than five minutes Berger and his two thugs ceased to exist. The only indication that they had ever existed was the red cloud of blood in the water. 20 yards away in a dark, empty office space Sergeant Schmitt clad in black mask, gloves and boots disassembled his Mauser sniper rifle placed it in its case then hid it in under the floor boards where he would come back and get it later.

Schmitt was actually Lt. Kurt Vessel of the Luftwaffe special duties squadron. A squadron formed by the Luftwaffe high command after secret negotiations with Eisenhower. Dedicated to Germany and its survival as a soverign nation, their mission was to dispatch those Nazis likely to form guerilla units thereby rendering Germany an untenable, hostile state in which growth and economic recovery was not possible. They wanted Germany back and decided to work with the Allies in secret to ensure that Germany remained an autonomous state once hostilities and the post war occupation were finished. None of them had illusions that an honorable surrender was possible under Nazi rule.

His job had been to finish Berger ensuring that he did not engage in a murderous orgy of killing German personnel when Germany surrendered. The fear had been that he would in a suicidal rage order the systematic killing of innocents. Schmitt or rather Vessel was to prevent that at all costs. In the end he had merely to witness Berger's own lunacy turn on itself. Not that he minded. The last thing he wanted was that sick bastards face lurking in his memories.

He took out his German/English dictionary and began thumbing through it looking for the word for 'Surrender'. He practiced the phrase "I surrender" in English all the way to the chapel where, for the first time in years, he prayed and gave thanks to God that he had survived the war.

Hans and Frederick looked at each other in numb disbelief. Frederick waved his right hand at the hose crew spraying the mess into the water "The legacy of the Third Reich. Blood and brains on a cold pier." Shaking his head, he simply presented his papers to the topside watch as bloody water ran over the edge of the pier. At least the menace of Berger would no longer plague the remaining personnel.

In fact that was the last suicide on the base because without Berger leading them the remaining Gestapo agents had no way of enforcing their authority. One by one they 'left' or disappeared leaving the military police in charge of security.

The topside watch announced to the officer of the deck that Standartenfurher Beck and Prussien had arrived. They then each heard the general give orders that they report to him once they are under way and to not disturb him until then. This suited them fine as each man was in desperate need of sleep. So fatigued were they that the prospect of dying on board the submarine no longer carried weight. It hadn't even come to their consciousness as each sought only the warmth of a bunk and a blanket. If death were to come they would likely sleep through it.

Chapter 20
The Captain:

HOURS BEFORE BERGER'S suicide deep in the bowels of the Bergen Submarine pens Kurt Heinz turned to his friend Captain Johan Krieg and relayed the news of the planned break out. "So, they intend to break out into the Atlantic then? I would like our chance better if we had sevens." The type 7 U-boats were the most successful blue water patrol submarine of the war and the preferred vessel of most experienced submarine captains. "Whose idea was it to make an Atlantic crossing in a cow?" he said shaking his head.

"I believe it was the cargo that dictated the need for a cow and there just aren't enough sevens left to carry what these two can" he said. Krieg nodded but his expression did not change. The three boats that got away had been sevens and were packing light with a skeleton crew. He knew the Cows were packing something heavy and would slow them down and they were already slow enough, empty.

"Kurt, I like the idea of painting a 'C' on the tower, it makes sense to pass ourselves off as captured submarines but why must we run through the channel? Not only are we entering into the most heavily defended waterway in the world, we will be under allied air cover until we reach Spain at which point we fall under Gibraltar blimp patrols. We won't be safe until we reach Africa. This idea of waiting for a storm to form and head west under its protection is fucking crazy. There is no guarantee a storm will form in the first place. Then the track it follows is not predictable especially if it makes it to the gulfstream, then it is a crap shoot of whether or not it moves up the eastern seaboard of the United States...or into the Gulf of Mexico where we may very well find ourselves under another set of blimp patrols out of the Bahamas, or Florida...and that is if we reach the western Atlantic unscathed and avoid the blimp patrols out of Bermuda.' Krieg was frustrated with the whole rotten mess and Kurt couldn't blame him. 'We are jumping from one rat trap to another while pinning our hopes on riding out a storm that may or may not form which is supposed to protect us from the blimps that we won't know are there until we are sucking on Atlantic seawater as it pours in on us."

Krieg looked down at the submarine he was to command and shoved his hands into the pockets of his Pea Coat. Without looking at his friend he continued "My sonar man was testing his set when the last attack occurred.' He paused for a long moment looking at his boat then continued. 'He heard no less than 100 separate explosions hit the hull of Vincent's boat. He put it on speaker for me. I heard our friend die Kurt. I heard his hull crack like an egg and the screams of his men as the Atlantic poured in on them. It was the most terrible thing I have ever heard" he said looking as if he'd seen a ghost. "He was my closest friend the closest thing to a family I had left. My family, friends and too many of my shipmates have all been consumed by this damned war...what else can they take from me Kurt, what else?"

Johan Krieg was no coward but he'd lost too many friends and family and the knowledge that he might join them in a similar fate was too great for his shattered nerves to bear. Without another word Krieg turned away, his fear threatening to spill out if he didn't move to hide it.

Fregattenkapitän Kurt Heinz watched his friend walk down the pier and salute the deck watch then climb down the hatch. He understood too well what his friend was feeling because he was feeling it as well. The idea of crossing the Atlantic in slow unarmed submarines was about as insane as walking barefoot across the north-pole, but then the war had been an insane mess from the beginning. The whole of Germany was a smoldering ruin of craters, shattered cities with the stench of death permeating the air. There wasn't a peak in the Alps high enough to escape the smell of rotting corpses littering Germany.

Vodka was the means by which Kurt kept his wits from shattering, numbing his nerves to the fact that he might very well be dead in a matter of hours. Like his friend Krieg he too had lost friends and relatives, but he had hope, if only a glimmer, to see his family again in Argentina. This thought and Vodka helped him cope, that and he knew what he was carrying in his hold, gold.

Heinz was pulled out of retirement in 1935 as the Kreigsmarine was rebuilding its U-boat fleet. A veteran of WWI he had served as XO of three submarines and once under the command of Karl Dönitz current commander in chief of the Kreigsmarine. It had been then Fregattenkapitän Donitz who'd convinced him to come out of retirement with the rank of Korvettenkapitän. Bi-passed several times for advancement he'd finally reached the rank of Fregattenkapitän but only after Donitz had interceded on his behalf.

Like many of his comrades he had no liking for the Nazis and the brutality that brought them to power. Too many of his friends and relatives had gone missing for merely speaking out against the 'all or nothing' mentality of the National Socialist Party who had taken power by killing the opposition and those who noticed.

Kurt Heinz was not at all disturbed that the world had done away with the Nazis. He saw the allied victory as the liberation of Germany rather than a defeat. This feeling was tempered with the realization that Germany would be divided in two with half of Germany going to the Soviet Union and the Western half to be divided among the Western Allies. Germany would be lucky if they were ever a sovereign nation again. He knew Germany would rise as an industrial power, but would they ever be allowed to govern themselves after the Nazis had stained their nation so horribly?

Germany in spite of minimal resources had out produced every other nation they had fought against. They had advanced technology to terrifying heights, produced the first fighter jet, the first intercontinental ballistic missile and even invented a synthetic fuel when Ploesti, their greatest oil resource, was destroyed. Germany had certainly proven its greatness to the world, except the world was not tolerant of the government that had exploited that greatness.

Shaking his head he was both relieved and saddened with the ending of the war. He wasn't sad for the war to be ending, he was sad at how it was ending. He would have preferred it if the German People had risen up against the Nazis thrown them all in prison then sued for peace handing the Nazi leaders over in a gesture of good faith to show that Germany was, like the rest of the world, an invaded land. The world would have then seen Germany for what it truly was and not for what the world thought of it now. Germany's two thousand-year heritage was stained forever from twelve years of

Nazi rule. But in the spring of 1945 Heinz had no idea of the economic miracle that Germany would undergo in the years immediately following the war. Germany would rise under the supervision of the allied powers to be the dominant industrial power in Europe within a decade of Nazi defeat.

However, in 1945, Kurt Heinz was contemplating taking up residence in Argentina where his father had a cattle ranch in the foothills of the Andes Mountains. His father had served in the Great War as a Naval Captain of a battle cruiser and had been badly injured in the Battle of Jutland when six British battleships sank his ship, Lutzow. Following the defeat of Germany in the Great War his father relocated to Argentina and took over operation of the family ranch.

They'd done quite well with contracts to supply the German and Argentine military with beef. Of course that was done through the Argentine Government. All they had to do was get the cattle to market and government representatives paid for the beef and then saw to its delivery. This voyage was a trip home. Once there he would resign his commission and take up ranching, and become a Gaucho. He had to get there first and this voyage was going to be long and dangerous. He would have to concentrate on surviving if he ever wanted to see the plains of Argentina again.

However, as he walked slowly back to his own boat, he wondered if he could ever get used to the winter and summer being reversed. He had always liked his Christmases in the winter. Singing 'silent night' in the middle of a South American summer would be something to get used to. Yet, getting used to a reversed season would be far easier for him than to move back to his home town wondering if Germany would ever again be what he hoped.

Bringing himself back to the moment he made his way to his command. Provisions needed loading and there had to be enough coffee on board to ensure that his crew didn't mutiny. He could run out of food before he could run out of coffee. Such a travesty was simply not to be tolerated. He'd steal it from the Gestapo if he had to. They weren't civilized enough to require that luxury, an opinion he wisely kept to himself, though it was an opinion shared by everyone but the Gestapo.

Later that afternoon he was sitting at this desk on board his submarine checking stores and sipping coffee thinking about the voyage ahead. Heinz had two submarines sunk out from under him in the last two years, the first off Scapa Flow when he attempted to attack the British Home fleets anchorage. Most of his crew had been captured and sent to a Canadian POW camp, but they had survived and would return home after the war.

He was the last man off the boat when a wave washed him overboard opposite his crew bashing his skull against the railing knocking him unconscious as his boat slipped under the waves. None of his crew saw him get off the boat and thought he'd gone down with the ship. He was washed ashore chilled to the bone on the northern Scottish Coast. His skull fractured the pain in his head was nauseating. Tying a belt around his skull reduced the pain and allowed him to function and avoid capture for two weeks while sleeping in barns and hay mounds while making his way to Aberdeen where he managed to steal a fishing-boat and headed straight for Norway.

The second sinking had been while in temporary command of the vessel he was transferring from an air-raid damaged dry dock to another in order to complete repairs. He had been nosing the boat, a Type 7, into the new dry dock when out of the corner of his eye he saw the aircraft diving out of the clouds. An RAF Mosquito fighter-bomber was in a shallow, fast dive its nose cannons firing tearing deck planking away as it zeroed in on him. Without thinking he hit the alarm bell, hit the intercom to tell the men below decks to get out. He watched as the hatches erupted with men who dove into the icy waters of Bergen Norway.

The planes cannon tore the submarine in half causing it to break apart and sink. Terrible as that seemed it was the saving grace for the remaining crew trapped inside allowing them to escape. The Mosquito then pulled out of its dive and dropped its bombs, which skipped over the water like stones landing inside the slipways of the submarine bunkers exploding harmlessly in empty slipways. Nobody had died in that attack though they had lost a submarine. That had been a year ago. The last air raid had been a nuisance raid doing almost no damage mostly because there wasn't anything left to damage. What ships could fit in the pens used them as protection from air-raids, mostly Schnell boats.

Heinz accepted this command only after he learned of their destination, which was an island off South America. He jumped at the chance to get home and avoid months or even years in a POW camp. If he knew for certain that he'd be taken to the United States he'd have surrendered in a minute. From there he could have become a US citizen and still been able to retain his Argentine Ranch. However, there was no certainty to be found at this stage of the war. So he opted for the next best thing which was a trip home where he knew he could, if needs be, disappear into the Argentine outback.

As he was about to pour himself another coffee his orderly brought him a message. It was from Dietrich. Groaning he expected an order to paint tulips on the conning tower or something to that effect.

Closing his eyes and taking a deep breath he prepared for the worst.

---Have acquired by chance a radar detection device---It was designed to give our submarines a way to detect surface scanning radar—having it delivered this afternoon and installed—with your permission.

"Finally good news from that lunatic" He thought. A radar detection device would be useful for their transit across the Atlantic. They would test its function as they transited the channel. Had this device been in service two years before the war might have ended differently? Not that he was in any way saddened by the Nazi defeat. They had been a nightmare for Germany even before the war, though he did long for the days of the Kaiser and Imperial Germany.

His longing for those days was tempered by the fact that the Kaiser was responsible for the atmosphere that caused the Allies to punish Germany, which in turn caused the Nazis to gain power. Shaking his head he wiped away the past. Only a fool dwells on things that cannot be changed, so he focused on the new ranch house and the barn he wanted to build in the hanging valley behind the home ranch to store winter grain for the cattle they wintered there. It proved a pleasant distraction.

Later that day a small device was installed in the sonar space. A small spoon shaped antenna was attached to the radio transmission/receiving mast. They would deploy the device at periscope depth without the periscope, which surface scanning radar was meant to detect. Nobody knew how sensitive the new scanning radar was. There was a chance that they could be detected by raising the antenna, but most agreed that there was little chance of that. He wasn't keen to being a guinea pig in any case not that he had a choice.

If they could avoid detection by steering clear of radar signals they could with luck transit the surface at night and speed their way across the Atlantic. However that was a concern for later. First they had to escape the harbor and the pickets outside. So far three had made it. He did not let his mind dwell on those who did not. The longer they delayed their departure the chance that the allies would get wise to their tactics increased. Then there was the channel transit. A submerged transit wasn't practical because the cows were so fat and slow that they'd have to surface to charge batteries half way through the channel. Running the Channel on the surface seemed an insane move. However, it was in the sheer madness of it where the logic lay because it wouldn't be expected.

The allies felt secure in the channel now that both sides were under their control. With such heavy traffic they were less likely to be looking for enemy vessels in their own shipping lanes. That and the storm they were planning to use for cover would keep aircraft grounded. MTBs, if they were spotted would be less likely to attack them with any effect and surface armament would be risky lest they hit their own ships, or so the logic ran. Reality could easily prove different he knew.

Heinz didn't waste time worrying about the SS. He would follow orders and leave when told to. His job was to dive and drive the boat and get them all to their destination alive. In fact Heinz was made aware of the two SS officers arrival when Berger delivered them. He knew this only because of the spectacle that followed when Berger and his two brutes blew their brains all over the coffee his crew had stolen from Berger's personal storage facility.

He'd been in his wardroom sipping a cup of Berger's coffee when the received the news. Looking up at his XO and shaking his head he said, "Well, Berger won't need the coffee we left for him. Send the Quartermaster and three men to take it all' he paused, 'Oh, and I saw six-dozen cases of Scotch whisky in there as well. Take it, all of it."

His XO smiled wryly. "I happened to see several cases of Napoleon Brandy when I was assisting the acquisition team. Perhaps we should liberate that as well?"

Heinz looked up surprised "Napoleon? By all means, take it. That lunatic certainly won't need it and I do not want something that fine wasted on the Gestapo. If you happen to see anything else of value take it as well. In fact take one of the big trucks and empty the fucking vaults and share it with the personnel, *after* you've loaded *our* stores first.

Two hours later *two* trucks with overloaded springs backed up to the pier. The crew took an hour to unload the stores raided from the Gestapo lockers. They hadn't limited their raid to Berger's personal locker, they smashed one truck through the door and took all of the stores seized or stolen by the Gestapo. A haul they shared with the remaining personnel.

Their haul included three full heads of beef, 50 cases of Bushmill's Irish Whiskey, 60 cases of Scotch and 14 kegs of beer and three tons of dried sausage links and various dried cheeses, wines, cigarettes and even a pallet full of British pound notes that mysteriously disappeared in transit to the bunker. The two submarines took on what they could fit aboard. The remaining goods were dispersed among the command personnel while a lookout was kept for the Gestapo.

Being that there were only six remaining agents they were no longer a worry. Had they been a threat their stores would have been left alone. In fact once the Gestapo realized their position they disappeared. Later reports indicated that they had a transport plane in a hangar on the far end of the field, fully fueled and loaded with enough cash to buy most of Spain. No further thought was given to them.

Chapter 21
Maneuvering stations!

"CAST OFF AFT, left full rudder, back slow." Lines were cast off the aft portion of the submarine. Slowly the stern of the submarine moved away from the pier. "All Stop, Rudder amidships!! Cast off bowlines, Right ten degrees rudder... back slow". The thump of the diesels echoed in the bunker as the submarine slowly backed out of the slipway. Both submarines emerged from the bunker in a seemingly synchronized effort and each pointed their bow toward the harbor entrance.

Once the bow was pointing toward the outlet Capitan Kurt Heinz wiped the sweat off this hands, even though it was near freezing with rain pouring down. "Ahead slow" His heart was beating mightily in his chest provoking fear that he might just die of a heart attack. Taking a deep, calming breath he began to concentrate on the matter at hand and not the gauntlet he was about to enter.

Panic and the rash decisions such emotions brought to the surface would certainly get himself and his crew killed, a fact not lost on him. So he concentrated on the fact that he was heading home...and that is what did it...instantly he was calm and focused. Nobody was about to deprive him of seeing his beloved Andes mountains and the hanging valley behind his boyhood home…the one he hoped one day to build his home and raise a family in. 'Yes' he thought 'I'm going home.'

As the submarine moved toward the harbor entrance he took a series of deep breaths to calm down as his new found focus became ever more-clear. "Prepare for diving, secure diesels." Automatically the thumping of the diesels wound down as a nearly imperceptible hum of electric motors took their place.

The usual diving sequence didn't occur. No bells or lookouts diving for the hatch. None of that was necessary. He didn't want to maneuver in the harbor on batteries because he didn't want to over extend them too early and use up the battery because they would need a full charge to get away unnoticed, but it was necessary to keep the noise down.

The whole process transferred power seamlessly. The boat maintained its speed until they came to the point where they pointed the boat straight out the entrance. Once in position they would dive. "Hard right rudder" and the stern moved hard left. When the bow was nearly in position "Rudder amidships, all stop" and the mass of the ship carried it so that lined up perfectly with the harbor entrance.

Kurt looked around him and took in the scenery. He'd miss Norway. "This is it gentlemen, go below". One by one each man reluctantly disappeared below decks. Captain Heinz had the distinct impression that they didn't want to. No man wants to consciously enter his own coffin. A sentiment he understood well but dared not dwell upon. "I'm going home" he muttered to himself and climbed down the ladder. Securing the hatch Captain Heinz headed to the con. Kurt took another calming breath before taking the microphone to address the men.

"Gentlemen, We are about to embark on a dangerous mission. We have lost comrades and friends to the wolves we are to sneak by. We've figured out a way to do it. Three ships before us have made it to their destination by doing what we are about to do. You were not told of this for fear of it leaking to the allies and in turn to the destroyers picketing our harbor. For this reason you have not been given the full details. We gave you some, you've also no doubt heard rumors, but we had to ensure none of you said anything to anyone about what we were doing or where we are going. Our destination will be revealed once we conclude the first leg, which is to sneak by our captors. This first leg will be the longest and most dangerous. We must not make any noise whatsoever. For this reason, our meals will be sandwiches and our coffee served in specially made canvas cups that have been rubber coated. Hopefully the rubber cups will not make the coffee taste funny" a murmur of laughter filled the boat in response.

"I will need you on your most professional and expert behavior. We must remain silent for nearly 24 hours before we are safe. It is of the utmost importance that we maintain absolute silence. We will be on a port and starboard watch rotation. Non-essential personnel will report to your bunks upon dive ship where you are to remain until your watch rotation is up. Given the tension of our situation, you may smoke in the hold or the con…if you must. Good luck to you all." He put the microphone up, looked around noting that all was in its place, sighed in resignation and nodded.

"Dive ship!" He said. As one the crew threw the valves open and a loud 'hissssss, hissssshhhh, hisshhhh filled the submarine. Each man held their breath as the ship slipped beneath the surface. "Ahead slow" the dial was turned and the submarine lurched forward. At barely three knots the submarine made almost no noise. Nets had been cut away entirely to make room for the larger submarines. At 20 meters they were at periscope depth but they didn't dare raise the mast for fear of attracting unwanted attention. The route and bearing was known as well as the perfect depth. They were to keep to three knots until they were a mile out then drop speed to maintain steerageway and maintain that speed until they were 20 miles out. But they had to clear the nets first and hopefully sneak by the wolves lurking over the horizon.

Taking a seat near the navigator Captain Heinz motioned for the runner. "Coffee, black" The runner, a boy of 17, moved swiftly past the watch officers and passed the crew waiting nervously by sonar. In a loud whisper the captain hissed "Sonar, I want you to report 'everything' especially if it is coming from the northwest. I don't care if it is seagull shit hitting the waves you report it." Sonar nodded acknowledgement of his Captains order and continued his scan of the ocean around them.

"Passing the nets sir" This was matched by an increased motion of the boat indicated increased wave activity. It seemed an eternity that they spent passing the nets. One scrape against a cable and the game was up. Heinz and Kreig had both agreed that if they heard the destroyers coming they'd surface and immediately return to port. If that were not possible they'd run the ships aground and abandon ship. Being unarmed cargo vessels that lumbered rather than sliced through the waves there would be no out-maneuvering or escaping a destroyer much less three of them.

In a meeting of both submarine crews prior to the SS contingent arriving on board it was collectively agreed on the course of action in the event they were attacked. No one wanted to die needlessly if it could be avoided. Of course this particular detail was not shared with the

SS personnel because everyone suspected they would insist on some insane foolishness such as dying for the Fuhrer. It was generally held that if 'they' wanted to die they could do so without their help or company. Mostly they just wanted to survive the war and rebuild Germany. It was one thing to die for a cause that was worthy but as it was their death would have been pointless and serve no purpose.

After a few long moments the sonar man took a deep breath and smiled slightly. "We cleared the nets 'sir'." Captain Heinz sipped his coffee not at all relaxed because their sister ship had yet to clear the nets and may yet scrape the cables and awaken the wolves waiting to pounce on them. He nodded acknowledgement closing his eyes mentally going through the boats operating systems in his head as a means of keeping calm. This boat had been relatively easy compared to the Type Sevens he'd commanded. They had weapons systems he had to become familiar with as well as all the engineering spaces.

The Tub as he had affectionately nicknamed his submarine had no such systems. Even the crane and loading mechanisms for weapons load and transfers had been removed to make room for their cargo. A cargo he was supposed to be ignorant of. The weight of which told him they carried gold ingots. He had also opened a crate late one night when the SS were in one of their 'meetings' conferring over god knows what. When he opened it he saw the gold glinting in the dim light and his excitement grew as thoughts of what he could do with the contents of just one box kept him entertained.

He could buy a new tractor for the Ranch, rebuild the house and barns and even expand the property to include the hanging valley where he had often gone camping in as a child. "Just one box he told himself and my life is set." He thought "Just one box." He kept repeating over and over in his mind, so the SS didn't overhear him.

His heart rate decreased significantly and his breathing slowed as he pondered the possibilities. He shook himself back into the moment "You've got to survive this voyage first." He thought and put his mind back on his current situation.

Heinz was one of the few submarine captains who could literally take his ships apart and do the work himself. His view was that a captain must know the ship better than his crew if he is to command them. He had also become a qualified naval gunner so that in the event he had to abandon ship he could still fight the ship as his crew escaped. His whole purpose was to be a captain worthy of his men's trust, a truly rare man, too rare.

His mind was racing through the inner workings of the diesels when the sonar man whispered "the second sub is clear of the nets sir…the destroyers are not moving in sir. I can hear their screw noise turning lowly. Based on repeat bearing rates they seem to be steaming in circles."

No scraping occurred and the ships slowed once they were a mile out. Sonar kept his vigil up for the next 12 hours eating sandwiches and drinking gallons of coffee. Thankfully his post was near the lavatory, which allowed him quick relief sessions. After 24 hours they slowly built speed up to three knots again listening intently to the distant screw noises of the patrolling destroyers that were still a danger.

72 hours after leaving port both submarines were cruising easily at 5 knots approaching the northern end of the English Channel. They were rocking heavily at 150 meters. Indicating that the storm had reached the mouth of the Channel as reports said it would. "Are we lined up with the channel through the mine field?" he asked the navigator.

Swallowing he nodded staring hard at his chart and said "Yes, Captain.' He looked at the captain after a moment's pause 'Sir, the motion of the storm may affect the motion of the mines anchored to the bottom. We may be forced against one or one against us. The best I can do at this point is to put us directly in the center and hope we have enough clearance." He moved in beside his navigator and looked at the chart. The channel through the minefield was surprisingly narrow. "How deep are they anchored?" he asked.

"Reports suggest that they are staggered from 20 to 30 meters with 20 meters between each mine to keep them from knocking together. We should be fine if we maintain a constant course down the center of this channel, on the surface. We cannot deviate so much as a meter if we are to navigate submerged and these vessels were not designed for precise navigation."

The navigator studied the chart for a few moments more "Sir, the way they were laid out seems to be meant to prevent submarine passage as well as larger, deep draft vessels like our battleships. A surface transit would be far less risky if we kept to the center of the channel" he said.

The captain called out "All Stop! Raise periscope." His screw noise stopping was the signal for the second sub to raise periscope. Through Morse code he signaled Captain Krieg. "Mine field. Staggered depths…submerged passage too dangerous, recommend a surface passage through mine field then dive once clear… thoughts?"

Almost immediately he received the message "Wait one". A pregnant pause followed as Krieg conferred with his XO and navigator. Just as Heinz was getting uneasy with the prolonged exposure of their masts the response came. "Agree, Nav suggests surface through mapped channel at medium speed then dive on clearing."

Heinz snapped a quick *'Agree'* in return then flipped up his handles as he cried "Down scope" Turning to his navigator "Give me the best possible course through the field". The navigator already had his course plotted and repeated it to his captain looking down at his Sonar man. "You need sleep, hit the bunk until we call for you. I want you alert for our run through the channel." Sonar knew not to question his captain and immediately gave his head set to another sailor with brief instructions of what to listen for letting him know that the storm on a surface run would render that station useless until they dove again.

Thirty minutes later Heinz spotted one of the SS officers emerging from his quarters bleary eyed from what had been a badly needed sleep. It was then he noted that he hadn't seen nor heard from the SS General since the voyage began. Beck made his way to the con and stood next to the captain wiping sleep from his eyes. It was apparent that he still needed sleep. The fact that his companion hadn't moved from his bunk other than to pee was testament to the strain they had been subjected to prior to the voyage.

"Coffee?" he asked of the still sleepy eyed Beck. The runner presented himself immediately to Beck's side.

Beck nodded and stifled a yawn and "Black, please". The runner was not used to SS officers saying 'please' and was off like a shot eager to please the unusually polite SS officer. In less than five minutes he came back carrying one of the black rubber coated canvas cups. Beck looked curiously at the cup and took a sip of his coffee. The coffee was good though he wasn't sure he liked the cup it came in.

Captain Heinz answered the question before he asked it "We took special precautions regarding noise discipline. We cannot afford to have a ceramic or metal cups making noise and giving us away." Beck nodded understanding. He would enjoy his coffee just fine in a rubberized canvas cup if it kept him alive. Glancing over at the navigation station he asked "Where are we?"

"We are passing through the mine field. We are riding the surface because we feel that it is a safer option. According to the divers mapping report, the minefield was meant to allow surface traffic while preventing submarines or any of our larger ships passage. If we follow the known cut through the mine field we should be relatively safe, unless a mine breaks loose and drifts into us."

Beck could have gone all day without hearing that. "How many mine fields are in the channel?" he asked looking a bit paler than the moment before.

"According to our latest reports they have cleared the channel entirely since they now have total control of it. With the exception of this section because we still hold Norway and Denmark. The channel through this field is about half a kilometer wide, so if we stay in the center we should be fine." Heinz said it more to comfort himself than anything, because he knew that the mines in this field were capable of blowing a battleship in half. He didn't want to think about what those mines would do to his submarine. "Starboard watch for surface stations!' he called out. "Once we are at the entrance of the channel surface ship and post lookouts. I will take the bridge." With that Heinz went to his locker and put on his surface gear.

Upon returning to the con he took the lookouts aside. "We are looking for mines as well as enemy vessels. The mines we should not see, if you see one call it out because that means it has broken free of its mooring chain. You all know what hitting a mine would mean to a submarine, yes?" They all nodded but said nothing. "Good. Once we surface I will take the bridge and you will follow, understood?" Again they all nodded.

Taking station under the ladder Heinz looked around and noted Beck leaning over the navigation station watching the navigator at work. He seemed calm on the surface but it was apparent by the beads of sweat on his temples that he was on edge and doing his best to hide the fact.

"Surface ship" he called out. Slowly the submarine began moving side to side and pitching harder and harder as it rose higher in the water. "Send the signalman to the bridge." Opening the hatch he climbed into the conning tower or what would have been the battle bridge on a fighting submarine. He broke the latch free and pushed the hatch open as water poured down on his head. The cold water was shocking and he gasped involuntarily as water found its way under his collar, even to the hardiest seagoing men the cold chill of Atlantic water rushing down the back of the neck was shocking.

Ice-cold salt water on his skin felt like hot razor blades running down his spine. It was a sensation he had felt often but something that nobody could ever get 'used to'. Pushing the hatch open he climbed onto the wooden deck grate and took his station. "I have the Con! He yelled into the communication tube. Immediately the lookouts took up station on the platform and hooked their safety lines to the ship. A quick scan of the horizon suggested they were alone. No other ships were visible other than the submarine 200 meters behind. The rumbling of the diesels soothed him. "Ahead 1/3rd" he called and they were off.

Entering the channel on the navigator's instructions they moved along the heading and made corrections as needed to maintain a centerline through the channel. Not a man on board dared breath or make a sound for fear that their breath alone could set off a mine. Beck had been wound too tight in the weeks prior to this voyage to get wound up now. He could not afford to let the tension surface again. That and he was simply too tired. In fact after thirty minutes of watching the crew sweating it out he decided to go back to bed. He figured that if the mine hit them they'd all be dead anyway, so he might as well be asleep when and if it happened. The gentle rolling of the submarine helped to rock him to sleep and was out almost the moment his head hit the pillow.

Heinz had no such luxury. He stood on the surface bridge watching the compass and keeping time on his watch to ensure that they made their turns on time. He and the navigator both were keeping their watches synchronized so that they would turn precisely when they needed to not before and not after. Luckily the storm was just getting bad. With luck they would be passed the field and dive before the full force of the storm reached them. Resisting the urge to accelerate he gripped the railing so tightly that he felt he might just leave an imprint of his hand in the brass rail.

Two hours later Heinz had his sonar man awakened to confirm that they were clear of the mines. Once that was done he ordered him to bed to be fresh for when they ran the Dover Straights. He would be needed to keep them clear of patrol vessels, especially in those tight and dangerous waterways. "Dive Ship" he called out after securing the surface bridge. "Take her down to 50 meters. Navigator you have the con through the channel. If I am needed I will be in my quarters.

The Storm blowing overhead had the effect they had hoped for by keeping the Allied fleet ignorant of their presence. Unfortunately the storm ate up their battery charge much faster than anticipated. By the time they reached Dover they would have no choice but to surface and run on diesels. 20 miles from Dover they were forced to surface. Both submarines made a high speed run through the Dover Straights hoping the storm would shield them from view. The weather was too rough to have anyone on the surface bridge so they navigated via periscope.

As they reached the Dover Straights Captain Heinz looked from Dover to Rue de Forte France and saw a lone soldier standing in the wind holding his binoculars up. He hoped the 'C' painted on the conning tower would fool him. "What did you do to get such shit duty?" he muttered to himself. Stifling a chuckle he turned the periscope back to the channel. "Fuel status" he called out to his engineer.

His engineering chief made a quick glance at the fuel gauge and tapped one what appeared to be stuck. "We have full tanks sir. Our using batteries through the channel saved us a great deal of fuel. I would still suggest topping off in Spain as planned just to be safe."

Heinz nodded "Very well. Maybe we can get some fresh fruit by trading some Napoleon." Nobody answered but everyone nodded in silent agreement. The worst was over; they had survived the channel without a scratch. Collectively the entire crew began to unwind and get ready for the long voyage across the Atlantic. If they had survived the channel the Atlantic would be nothing or so they told themselves.

*************** **Rue De Fort France** *************

The lookout

Corporal Lance Widget of the British second light armored infantry division was on extra duty for getting the daughter of a French General pregnant while on duty as her bodyguard. A post ostensibly meant to prevent that very thing from occurring. As it happened, the young lady was exceedingly beautiful and suffered from a condition politely referred to, in 19th Century terminology, as 'Chronic Hysteria'. In today's terminology is referred to as nymphomania. Such was her condition that she apparently required the services of a young man no less than six times a day. A service he was more than happy to accommodate for the first week. After which he began requesting reassignment.

After a week of solid use his male appendage had begun to swell from the constant friction making it difficult to walk and urinate. His duty was to last a month but was, thankfully, terminated when her mother walked in on them in the midst of a passionate exchange. Lance was standing holding Ingrid (the generals daughter) in mid-air connected to him at the hip with her legs wrapped tightly behind his buttocks howling in ecstasy and thrashing about in orgasmic bliss. The world stopped as Ingrid, who was happiest when being serviced, cheerfully announced "Mama I'm pregnant" a statement that so shocked Lance that he dropped Ingrid onto the coffee table over which she had been suspended, smashing it to bits. Ingrid laughed hysterically at the expression of shock on his face and said "Lance darling...you'll have to marry me now".

Lance simply zipped up his fly bid a civil fare well and walked directly to his barrack where his sergeant found him on his bunk chain smoking cigarettes where he was informed that he was being assigned to the General for 'special' duties until the situation could be diplomatically resolved. This meant that his life would be hell for the foreseeable future with a chaffed and swollen scrotum as a reminder. All Lance could do was inhale and exhale as he muttered a smoke filled "Fuck" under his breath.

Wind and rain pelted Lance as he stood on the point overlooking the channel. Due to the indelicate position in which he found himself and the need to make reparations for the sake of international diplomacy he was to marry Ingrid in the next week. Until then he was assigned extra duty in the most inhospitable places the French General could find. Just as he was wishing for a lightning strike to end his sentence Lance spotted a black dot in the middle of the Channel heading south.

Taking out his binoculars he noticed that it was a U-boat with a 'C' painted on its conning tower. Lance understood that to mean a captured enemy vessel, but he was ordered to note 'any' sightings in the log and so took this opportunity to record it. An hour later he spied a second submarine with another 'C' painted on its tower. Again he noted it in the log not thinking anything of it having seen German tanks painted exactly the same way to avoid being attacked by friendly fire. Not being in the navy he had no reason to believe that they would do things any different.

Six hours later his soon to be father-in-law came to retrieve him. Upon reporting the sightings the General seemed genuinely alarmed. "Are you sure they were Bosh?" he asked sharply.

Lance responded with a nod and replied "I know what Gerry boats look like, sir" he said trying not to sound disrespectful. He didn't need any more trouble than he had already.

"Get in quickly!! We must report this immediately. I told them you needed a radio out here. I told them!!" The General screamed as he raced his Citroen down the narrow roadway.

Lance was genuinely confused. "But they were captured. Isn't that what 'C' means when painted on a Conning tower?" he asked.

The General shook his head impatiently "No,no,no…a submarine is hard to capture. They would never be operating alone. It would be insane to operate an enemy submarine in the channel unless it was escorted by another surface vessel, and then it would usually be in tow. And I happen to know that the Free French and British Fleets have been ordered to remain in port due to the storm. The excessive motion of the wind and waves might drive a large ship off course and into an uncharted minefield. Ask yourself, why would anyone want to drive a submarine down the middle of the channel in weather like this? Those were two German Submarines making a break for open sea, likely full of fugitive Nazis heading to South America!!!" He screamed the last sentence to himself in French.

Still Lance was confused. "But we painted such markings on captured tanks, trucks and planes when we took possession of them in order to move them behind the lines to have 'our' regulation markings painted on them why not a submarine?"

The General took a deep breath, appreciating the question as valid, yet naïve. He spoke more calmly "A German submarine is different from our boats. Valves are in different places and the engineering is different, more complex so it takes a long time to evaluate and such an evaluation requires deconstruction. Such an undertaking is a peacetime endeavor. That often takes years due to the complexity of submarine construction, particularly German submarine construction. The Bosh do things extremely well, if complicated. But it wouldn't make sense for us to operate Bosh submarines without an escort. Why would we run an unfamiliar submarine in a storm like this when the fleet is in port? Not only this, but why operate a German boat in the Atlantic when every Allied destroyer and plane has been ordered to sink them on sight? That would be nothing short of suicide. No those were German U-boats breaking out into the Atlantic. The 'C' on the conning tower was obviously meant to do what it did with you, throw off suspicion, a clever tactic."

Lance nodded finally understanding the Generals concern. "When I was in North Africa I saw Gerry submarines patrolling off Tripoli and they seemed smaller than the two I saw today. These subs were Gerry subs but they were fatter. The ones I saw off Africa reminded me of sharks where these two appeared to be a floating cow. They didn't have deck guns either, neither one, not even machine guns."

The Generals brows furrowed "Unarmed submarines? And you say they were fatter?" Lance simply nodded but said nothing. "That's interesting. Still, it's not good to have two Bosh submarines heading to sea this late in the war. I'm fairly certain they are loaded with high ranking Nazis trying to escape the noose." He let out a chuckle "The Rats are abandoning ship."

They drove the rest of the way in silence and reported the sightings.

The General made it clear to the command staff his thoughts and insisted that a search be launched, believing that they were full of fugitive Nazis fleeing to Argentina. A search was launched but only after the weather cleared and by that time they were long gone somewhere out in the Atlantic.

Chapter 22
Archie's discovery

London 1945

AFTER HAVING BEEN called back from the field Archie was assigned the dubious task of going through the captured files of SS Officers. He was to catalog possible criminal charges that could be brought against them for war crimes. So he had to cross-reference their duty stations with reports by escaped POWs of criminal conduct where they could be positively identified. He had been relegated from field operative to a librarian. It wasn't the sort of job he relished but he didn't mind it either. It did allow him to rest and recover from the years of hard use he had been put to. It was pretty easy as each file had a photo of the officer in question. Archie would simply have the former POWs search the files until they found the man they recognized and have them write down everything they knew the accused did, preferably an eyewitness account. Hearsay couldn't be used in the courts. Like it or not the Nazis, deserving or otherwise, were going to get a fair trial and where applicable a noose or life long prison stay.

It was through one witness that he became acquainted with an officer by the name of Hans Beck.

Beck had saved him from getting shot by stating that he had commandeered the prisoner for labor duties. He then took the prisoner to his lines and released him. At the time the file had him at the rank of Major in command of a tank battalion that had been all but decimated the day the weather broke following the Battle of the Bulge. His name came up in a Gestapo file, suspecting Beck as being deeply involved in the black market. He was suspected of monetary exchanges for gold and silver, trade goods such as cigarettes, whiskey, wine and other food items stolen from SS supplies intended for the Fuhrer himself, a capital offense if they could prove it.

Archie dove deeper into his file and found Beck to have an outstanding service record. He had entered the SS in the middle of the phony war and participated in the 'Blitz' that took him to Paris and later to Dunkirk where he was forced to hold back his tanks instead of finishing off the British and French armies that were bottled up on the beach. By the time he had been released to attack the bulk of the British forces had been rescued as well as the French forces that had refused to surrender. His next campaign had been Russia and the Winter War where he'd fought with distinction before being sent back to Germany with severe frostbite following a near miss by a tank shell.

He'd been assigned another tank command in Italy where he once again fought with distinction in the mountain region of Monte Casino. He remained in Italy until the fall of 1944 when his battalion was reassigned to the Western Front in preparation for the Winter Offensive that was meant to divide the Allied armies down the middle and buy Germany enough time to build its jet fighter squadrons and tank battalions up to strength and then hopefully win the war.

Becks last known whereabouts was Foy Belgium where his tank battalion had been pushed back during the closing stages of the battle of the Bulge. An air raid caught his tanks in a tactical retreat where an estimated 60% of his force was killed or captured. Beck was not among the dead, wounded or captured so it was assumed that he escaped into Germany. After that no further notations on Beck could be found, just his basic statistics like hometown, family disposition and whether or not he had Jewish sympathies on his initial interview for induction into the SS.

As Archie tossed the file onto his MIA file a slip of paper fell to the floor. A slip of paper he' missed in his initial scan. It was a radio transmission from the Gestapo chief in Bergen Norway stating that Beck had turned up there in the company of a Standartenfurher Prussien and had been assigned to accompany Prussien and one General Dietrich to an undisclosed location and that any further investigation into Becks activities were to cease due to the sensitive nature of his mission. It was dated March 15, 1945 only two weeks earlier.

A mission? Germany didn't have the resources to launch a balloon. Never the less he decided it was worth reporting. He immediately phoned Colonel McKenzie with the news and was immediately summoned to fill him in on details.

Taking a seat Archie laid the radio transmission and Becks file on his COs desk. The radio transmission was what he was most interested in. "A mission, what could they possibly be attempting at this late date?" He stared hard at the document and read it over several times. "Accompanying? That suggests that they are going somewhere' he frowned 'but where would they be going?"

"Bergen is blockaded. No vessel has been allowed to leave that port for over a month. Every submarine that attempted a breakout was sunk." Again his brow furrowed. Reaching for a phone he called his secretary in.

Beth was a very well developed 22 year old Blonde with dangerous curves that caused men and certain women to look twice. "Beth, I need the reports of submarines and surface vessels sunk off Bergen Norway in the past two weeks. I also need the reports of known vessels still in port there and if there are any missing vessels that have not been accounted for in that time. I need it quickly, please" he said with an uncharacteristic charm that suggested that he 'knew' Beth a little better than most men should know their secretaries. She turned around slowly, looking at him curling her lips in coy smile meant for McKenzie eyes only which Archie noticed but pretended not to.

He already knew that McKenzie was sleeping with Beth because not long before, after a late night, he was awakened from his cot to a repetitive banging noise down the hall that made him believe that someone was rummaging through files and banging file cabinets shut in their search. Thinking it was a break in he took his .45 Colt from its holster and went to investigate. It took only a minute for him to put the gun down.

With a grin of cunning mischief he snuck down to McKenzie's office where he saw Beth naked below the waste with her military blouse open at the front exposing the most perfect set of tits Archie had ever seen. She was lying on her back on top of McKenzie's desk with her legs dangling in midair with McKenzie pounding away as she squealed in delight.

McKenzie was standing at the edge of his desk pounding his

secretary for all his life was worth. Archie noted with curiosity that McKenzie though naked below the waist still had his combat boots on. Instead of fixating on the fraternization rule that was being so flagrantly violated, he couldn't help but wonder how it was his boss got his pants off over his combat boots. He also noted that the boots were providing traction necessary to move his desk along the concrete floor, which now was banging against the steel file cabinets creating the noise that had awakened him. "So much for Beth being a lesbian" he thought as he walked back to his office leaving his commanding officer in peace to enjoy his piece.

As he lay back onto his cot again he grinned with admiration at his COs stamina and the fact that Beth was so vocal. He'd always enjoyed women who were expressive of their passions...and Beth was *very* expressive. Just as he was about to fall back to sleep Beth cried out in passion as she climaxed. McKenzie merely grunted...as the desk was once again shoved hard against the file cabinet. Beth's voice was soft in the distance as she laughed and they kissed in the after-glow of their mutual lust and apparent love. They were to wed on VE day with Archie as best man.

"Arch..what do you think about this? Where could they possibly go and what would they be doing?" McKenzie asked.

Archie hadn't had time to ponder that question in the time since he'd discovered the radio message. Looking at the world map behind McKenzie he used his knowledge of German U-boats and considered the question for a long moment. U-boats could reach the Atlantic coast of the United States he knew but there hadn't been any U-boats sighted there in a long time because so few of them were able to escape the ASW blimps, planes, ships that had very nearly decimated them.

He was looking for clear routes around the picket destroyers, blimps, submarines, aircraft carrier groups, patrol planes, mine sweepers and other ships now dedicated to the hunting of German U-boats now that the war was coming to a close. Nobody wanted a rogue sub sinking the ship carrying him home. Every sub discovered was killed with particular brutality…if they didn't surrender *immediately.*

Patrols were concentrated around the European ports where the Germans still had a presence. France was gone to them, Italy was gone and the med was particularly toxic to submarines. Germany still had a few ports open but they were so near the Russian advance that bombing raids from both sides had effectively neutralized them. All Norwegian ports were blockaded but that is where they still held seaports and a dangerous fleet. "No surface vessel could escape the patrols in the Atlantic," he said. Some submarines might reach South America, but only if they manage to break out and get to open sea and find a route where they can run on surface at night. Radar equipped blimps would be hard to avoid and outrun. But he knew that a skilled crew, if any were left, could find a way out.

The one clear route he could discern was a very long, route where the subs would have to navigate around Iceland and skirt the North American coastline to avoid radar detection. But taking that route would take them as far as the Florida Keys and maybe Cuba. A particularly bold captain might attempt a surface run through the English Channel now that it was packed with ships hoping to blend into the traffic, a night run. "Bugger me!!!" Archie said clapping his hand to his forehead.

"What?" McKenzie asked jolted from his own thoughts on the subject.

"Last week I heard a radio operator reporting an unconfirmed sighting of two U-boats, unusually large U-boats, transiting the surface off Dover. Unconfirmed only because nobody but one corporal on watch saw them and wasn't taken seriously."

He moved up to the map and pointed his finger in the middle of the channel. "The narrowest point in the Channel" he paused. The message wasn't sent urgent or reported immediately because the U-boats were flying a British Commissioning Ensign and had a large white 'C' painted in the conning tower. So he figured they were heading to Portsmouth either to be broken up or moth balled."

McKenzie stared at Archie for a long moment as the color left his face. Some French General alerted the Admiralty and was insistent that something be done immediately because he was convinced that they were German subs making a break for open sea. When nothing could be done about it he apparently took it to Churchill who, agreed with him, but said that the storm was too deadly to be putting any ships to sea."

McKenzie reached for his phone "Get me communications quickly" and hung up. There should be a confirmation on those sightings. If two subs were spotted in the channel heading south we need to confirm it," he said turning around to stare at the map. "Also...we need to check Portsmouth, Bristol and any port capable of taking two large submarines and breaking them down or moth balling them "Nothing has left Bergen in weeks" he said to himself more than to anyone else.

"That we know of..." Archie pointed out. "The Germans may have found a way around our pickets. Remember the channel dash when their cruisers and battleships ran up the Channel when they lost their French Atlantic ports? This may have been a similar maneuver. I want to see those reports Beth brings back".

McKenzie nodded "I'd be interested to know what they are up to. There is no way for them to win, not now; revenge?" He said looking hard into Archie's eyes, eyes that once again held the spark of purpose and excitement.

"Possible, but I don't think so. Its only two submarines, so far. What damage could two submarines do? They don't have enough submarines left to form a Wolf Pack and if they did our destroyers would be all over them. No, I think this is more likely a dash for freedom by senior Nazis or a desperate run to a neutral country so that they can begin peace negotiations while claiming sanctuary in a friendly, neutral nation like Spain or Portugal.

McKenzie tapped a finger on his blotter. "That might be it. They certainly haven't got the resources to mount a military operation and' he motioned for Archie to move in closer dropping his voice to a whisper. 'Himmler has been reaching out to Eisenhower to negotiate a separate peace. Word has it that he has offered to assassinate Hitler in exchange for a cease-fire and a return to pre-war borders once hostilities have ceased. Only thing is Ike is in no mood to accept surrender from Himmler now that we've been finding death camps all over Germany and Poland. Especially since Himmler's SS were apparently running them. He may be hunting for a neutral refuge to begin negotiations so that in the event talks go south he's on ship to South America.

Archie nodded understanding but then started to shake his head as the idea grew too complicated, too surreal. "Now that I think about it...wouldn't it be easier for them to fly from Germany into Spain? I mean they still hold parts of France…albeit a small bit…but enough to allow them to fly to Spain. Submarine travel is far too hazardous for Himmler to risk a run like that. He seems far too fond of himself to take such a risk knowing how easily we locate and sink their subs."

Just then Beth came in with several reports with aerial photographs. "Sir, I have a report here that says that nothing has been observed leaving Bergen in over three weeks. Yet two submarines that were housed in the pens there are now gone and they were reported as being larger than your standard Type-7, twice as large according to this report. Local, on the ground intelligence personnel, confirmed their absence two weeks ago. We received this report only two days ago. It wasn't marked urgent so it wasn't picked up and noted until today.' Beth paused and pulled out an additional sheet of paper "Sir, this was with the ground intelligence report." She handed him a photograph of a large submarine inside a pen with the crew fitting a British Ensign to the Jack staff and crew painting a large white 'C' on the conning tower.

McKenzie leaned in onto his desk. "Anything else?" he asked politely in spite of feeling like his gut had just been kicked. Beth picked up on his agitation and nodded quickly.

"Y'yes sir. This field report came in the same day after a diver. from one of the destroyers was sent to investigate the harbor. He noted that the net enclosing the main entrance to the harbor appeared to be intact, from the surface. The net buoys were weighted with cement to keep them low in the water, but the nets themselves had been cut away allowing every submarine in the harbor to escape submerged. A total of six known submarines are now at sea and have been for a minimum of two weeks that we are aware."

McKenzie sat down calmly and looked at Archie "Well, I think it is safe to assume that those two subs were from Bergen. Now...where are they going? Archie I'm assigning you that task. Focus on Beck and see what you can dig up. You are going back to Germany. Go to the last known location of Beck and see what you can pick up."

For the next week Archie was busy combing Becks file from early in the war up to his last known active duty command in Foy Belgium. He'd spent the bulk of his duty in Southern Germany early in the war where Beck had been placed in command of an ad hock patrol to search for a bomber crew seen parachuting from their stricken craft.

According to the patrol report in Becks file two of the crew had been recovered and the third had been found dead hanging from a tree with a broken neck. The location was 50km from Singen Germany. Shortly after this the Gestapo began paying attention to his activities as he had acquired an increase of cash availability while not having a significant increase in pay. It was noted here that he began smoking American Cigarettes 'Lucky Strike' being his preference. He was suspected of keeping a warehouse in the Alps within a 50km radius of Singen Germany, which they were unable to locate.

It happened to be Singen where he had been temporarily assigned following the destruction of his tank battalion in December of 44'. Throughout the many files Archie had perused Becks name came up repeatedly as a suspect in the disappearance of goods meant for most of the senior officers. He was suspected in the disappearance of a shipment of premium wine, beef and other goods meant to supply the Fuhrer bunker. As it was meant for the Fuhrer himself, personally the Gestapo escalated their investigation and locked in on Beck. Only Beck was way ahead of them and had disposed of the material mere hours after having acquired it. He was no fool. Stealing from the Fuhrer was an automatic death sentence. No trial just a firing squad, or a noose from a telegraph pole. On the other hand it proved extremely profitable having sold it to the American troops just prior to his vacating Foy.

When items from this shipment began showing up in the possession of American and British POWs the Gestapo were incensed. It was one thing to steal from the Fuhrer which was enough to get you shot already, but to sell the items to the Allies was base treachery at its worst. In March of 1945 an arrest warrant was issued for Beck. He was to be brought in for questioning, which was to involve significant brutality and execution by the most creative means possible regardless of evidence.

Archie read the last sentence several times causing a chill to run down his spine. Having interviewed quite a few SS already he had a good idea of what it could mean. He could be executed either by guillotine, face up so he could see the blade coming, burned alive in an oven, or hung by the neck with piano wire and left to choke to death. To Archie the Gestapo was the lowest form of human life ever conceived and was not to be taken lightly.

Archie began to admire Beck for his ingenuity and the brash manner in which he operated. He had always been one step ahead of the Gestapo whom Archie began to note were thorough, cunning and thuggishly incompetent, an unusual combination but one that was unique to the Gestapo as an institution. The bulk of the agents whose files he'd obtained were most often convicted criminals whom had been serving life sentences, murder being the least of their offenses in some cases, a cornucopia of psychopathic disorders and all in charge of state security.

As Archie rummaged through the captured files he found notes regarding looting of the SS Head Quarters in Singen. Apparently two Gestapo agents were killed in a firefight with two SS officers who were seen driving away in a Black Mercedes G4 staff car. One note suggested one of the Officers was Oberst Hans Beck. It had been the other unidentified officer who had shot both agents as they came running out of the building, apparently in pursuit if Beck.

The file suggested that the two agents had been sent in to take Beck into custody having spotted him entering the building. When he did not exit the building in the expected time frame they were sent in to get him. What they hadn't counted on was another officer aiding him in his escape. By the time they had realized what had happened Beck was in Norway, where the local Gestapo chief noted his arrival.

That firefight had taken place roughly a month earlier. Archie laid his notes on the floor like a huge mosaic as he began to put the pieces into place. Taking a seat on top of his desk Archie began mapping the movements of Oberst Hans Beck. First recorded action was in Singen Germany as an ad hock squad leader sent to search for downed RAF bomber crew, recovering two live prisoners and one body. It was also Singen where the Gestapo suspected he had a warehouse.

It was Singen where he had been last seen and was the center for what the Gestapo believed was his black market operation. That would be the first place Archie would visit. All the other places on the map were no longer accessible either due to ongoing combat operations or the Russians being obstinate in their control of their newly acquired possessions. In either case Singen was the last place Beck had been seen prior to his arrival in Norway.

Two days later Archie was driving a jeep through the remains of Singen Germany and toward the building that was formerly the SS Headquarters. Pulling up to the building he looked up the steps to the door way the doors long since taken for firewood. What remained was a concrete bomb-proof shell with chipped concrete from bomb blasts, strafing aircraft and blackened surfaces where smoke once bellowed from the windows.

A quick glance at his file he looked at two sheets of information that he'd received that morning. Becks driver Gunther Henchel had been found dead alongside a road fifty kilometers from the Swiss Border killed when a bomb dropped from a Mosquito bomber blew his car off the road. Evidence suggested that Beck had been in the car at the time of the blast but had obviously survived. Efforts to locate Becks remaining command found nothing. No reports of redeployment, reassignment not even among the POWs. His command seemed to have vaporized. However, about the same time as Becks confrontation with the Gestapo in Singen the Swiss reported finding 15 German Army trucks filled with German uniforms, guns and other weapons abandoned ten kilometers inside Switzerland. All of them parked neatly in a field with tire tracks of civilian automobiles leading away from where they'd parked heading into Switzerland.

The second page stated that an automobile had been found in Singen filled with cash less than two blocks from the SS HQ discovered by a British patrol. The amount of cash on board was no less than 20, million British pounds. Of course it was likely more as soldiers finding such cash will take some of it for themselves. The car was discovered on the north side of the building indicating that was the direction he'd come from. Pulling out the regional map he found several roads both paved and unpaved leading up to several civil air defense sites as well as sites used to house mobile radar units and AA batteries.

His eyes fell to an open field on the map that seemed to be an Alpine meadow. Remote and accessible, or appeared to be, but nothing to indicate that it was important to anyone; which was why he decided to drive up there and see for himself.

Using nothing but intuition and his training he discerned a path that was used by heavy vehicles on a regular basis but which had been carefully disguised. It was a roadway that skirted the tree line and just inside it. Archie followed the road careful not to move too fast or he'd miss it. Whoever used it made sure that they didn't use it too often. Archie figured that there was more than the one roadway to keep the grass high enough to keep it hidden from the air.

After an hour he stopped on the edge of a huge alpine meadow. The track he was following seemed to cut directly into a growth of trees. He didn't see how he could drive through it so he stopped and got out. Careful examination of the stand revealed that behind the trees was an old barn. So Archie looked around to see if there was anyone about. Seeing nobody, he climbed through a gap in the trees. A pathway was worn around the base of the barn from a great deal of use by the person or persons using the barn as a hideaway or warehouse, making use of it Archie explored the exterior looking for a way inside.

He found a doorway that had been used quite often by the appearance of the ground and the fact that it was the only area around the barn that was devoid of pine boughs and needles, that and the hinges were all new and freshly greased. Only after he opened the door did he realize the door was made of new wood but surfaced with old wood to keep up appearances of being an old door. Stepping inside the barn Archie was met with a barrage of odors ranging the pungent aroma of dried meat, an overpowering blast of French perfume that someone had spilled on a military issue wool blanket, which was hanging over what remained of a manger. Other smells included gasoline from a stock of Gerry Cans stacked neatly in the corner next to a BMW motorcycle with side car, next to that a brand new K-wagon, the German equivalent of a Jeep. The remaining stalls and lofts of the barn contained what could only be black markets goods, wine, cheese, meat, silk stockings, cigarettes, cigars and dozens of crates new woolen socks and several wooden kegs of beer.

Archie stood in awe of the range of goods that sat arrayed before him. "Well, Hans, you were quite the business man." Archie walked among the crates picking up a cigar along the way and a brand new Zippo lighter, with a new charge of lighter fluid and flints for good measure and shoved it into his pocket. He then proceeded to light the cigar. Wandering among the crates he noted a hollow sound under foot near the far end of the barn. He had discovering a trap door.

Pulling up the rug covering the hole and opened the door, a ladder went down. Next to the ladder was a light switch, which he flipped on and a room appeared before him. Lined up against the walls were crates of champagne, Napoleon Brandy and whiskey to suit every taste and craving. This was the place Hans kept the 'good' stuff. It was then he noticed the piles of cash stacked in bales the size of a standard sea chest. He counted 25 bales in all. There were clean 100 and 50-pound notes with a few fivers thrown in for good measure. Breaking open one bale he counted out 2, million pounds and he estimated that each bale had the same or similar. If that were the case he had at least 50 million pounds in cash ready for deposit, not counting the money that could be made selling what remained of

Beck's stock. Since he wasn't around to protest Archie felt no guilt in relieving him of his money.

There had been a time when his duty to Queen and Country would have driven him to turn the money over. However, his reality had changed. His dedication to catching fugitive Nazis had been harshly rebuked as foolhardy nonsense, to the point where his career had been threatened if he didn't quit pestering the brass about it. Apparently the reality of a pending guerilla war was not something the brass was ready to face, at least not while the war was still raging. His insistence that Odessa was a threat worth pursuing had tested his personal loyalty to a system too stupid to recognize the threat. And he was feeling less and less loyalty from the brass having over heard them speaking of 'retiring' he and McKenzie for being too persistent. They would realize that he and McKenzie were right, but only when it was too late to put a lid on it.

Odessa would run amok in Germany, murdering Allied soldiers and cooperative German citizens until the end of the trials in 1946 when their leaders would be convicted and hung. When it became clear that the allies meant business, Odessa began focusing on getting their members out of Germany. With the reality of a resurgent regime dashed those remaining in hiding had no desire to face the gallows and started fleeing to Argentina.

For what he had considered a betrayal of trust, he'd chosen to act for himself. Snatching a bundle of cash he decided to apply for a series of passes and a cross border order to allow him access to Switzerland to 'investigate' escaping Nazis. And with a truck he had borrowed took the bales of cash to his bank in Zurich. From that day on Archie had a grin on his face that no amount of latrine duty could erase, he was set for life.

Chapter 23
Explanations

Present Day

ARCHIE STOOD ON the running board of the G4 holding himself up breathing heavily, his bandages were leaking from his recent burst of energy otherwise he seemed well enough. "Hans, this is Rick, he is the gentleman who discovered our secret' pausing he looked at Rick with a grin 'How did you find it by the way?" Archie asked.

Rick blushed with embarrassment. "I went snooping around after you told me that the place was off limits. When I found the road I drove down it and came around the turn too fast crashing through the brush covering the tunnel. Once I calmed down I realized it was a man-made tunnel and then I could smell old machinery and oil, kind of like an old barn. So I drove into the tunnel and found the submarines."

Archie nodded looking over to the darkened side of the cavern then continued "Ok, so how did you find the road?" Rick then explained how it was he had tried to find a way up the mountain, earning him a grin from Archie who had told him not to bother with the mountain earlier that same day.

"Yes, I thought you were the contrary type. I knew that if I told you not to you'd go ahead and do it anyway, but I didn't expect you to find the roadway inland. You certainly are a curious bugger. Well to get back to why we were here…We've been keeping these old things in running order mostly because Hans here enjoys working on cars and I, well I caught the bug while helping him. This one', he padded the roof of the car he had driven down the tunnel. 'is my favorite. One of one G4 saloon hardtop specially constructed for the General who Hans came here with. This car was the very vehicle they arrived in Buenos Aires in when they attempted to convince the Argentine government to join the war on their behalf." Archie chuckled.

Hans at this point noticed that Archie wasn't well. "What happened to you? Why are you holding yourself like that?" He spoke walking up to his friend helping him to a seated position.

Archie attempted to play it off but the wince if pain gave it away. "Those two thugs I told you about? Well, they shot me rather the second one did, after he was killed. I don't know who did it but his gun went off as he fell backwards after someone put a bullet through his skull. I wasn't about to stay and see who saved me because I'd just shot the big one in the chest. I wasn't ready to explain myself to the police because eventually they'd be asking why they were look-ing for me and why it was I was packing a gun, etc. Gunshots and dead bodies tend to draw unwanted attention' he sighed weakly from the recent exertion. 'However, it would seem that whoever it was took care of the bodies so that the police were never called. It would appear that someone else is interested in keeping the authorities from interfering in our little game here' he said sighing as his energy faded. 'Hans, why don't you continue explaining what I started, you were here in1945." Archie smiled and leaned back against the cushy seat of the Mercedes.

Hans nodded and smiled gently at his old friend "Very well, I suppose you are right. The meeting Archie just spoke of didn't work out the way they'd planned, particularly the part where we were escorted from the capitol under armed guard. General Dietrich was under orders to convince the Argentine government to support his building a new Wehrmacht and Kriegsmarine fleet for Germany on their shores. This bullion was meant to both finance and bribe the Government of Argentina to side with us in this effort, in effect, to declare war on the United States.' Waving his hand to indicate the crates he continued. 'My mission was to disburse these funds to the appropriate banks and initiate the construction of a submarine fleet.' He shook his head smiling ruefully. 'I knew it was an impossible task given the time table." He paused taking a deep breath having become overly agitated in their recent exchange.

Hans then took a seat on one of the crates then continued when he'd recovered sufficiently "When we arrived to the island the war was nearly over. The General was frantic to get to Argentina while the German Reich was still intact. He needed an intact government to allow him diplomatic immunity in the event Argentina didn't cooperate, which of course they did not. I suspect, as did others that he knew it was folly to expect Argentina to enter the war on Germany's side. But he was under orders by the Fuhrer himself so he had no choice but to make the effort." Hans paused.

"I was here only because I was too greedy. I had already made plans to desert the Army and move to Switzerland when I chose to make one last trip to the barn where I had my money and goods hidden.'

He gestured to Archie. 'The very barn Archie later found and emptied." He said smiling and pointing a good-humored finger at Archie who laughed and piped up "And what was I supposed to do leave it? Likely someone else would have found it eventually."

Hans smiled at his long-time friend and continued "That misjudgment led to a series of unintended consequences that found me in Norway, trapped on an isolated base assigned to a mission so insane only a madman would believe possible; a mission to attack the United States from Argentina, through the Panama Canal and up through Mexico. This bullion was meant to fund the construction of a new army, navy and air force. Our shipment was the last one.

From here the General began cabling the embassy in Buenos Aires arranging a meeting with President Peron. Unfortunately, for the General news of liberated death camps in Poland and Germany arrived hours before his scheduled meeting with the President of Argentina. He made the mistake of parading our delegation through the streets openly displaying the Swastika.

Because news of the death camps had reached Argentina reaction to our presence was not what the General had come to expect. Our cars and trucks were pelted with fruit, rocks and even dog excrement not to mention howls of rage. I was in that car' he nodded toward the G4 'when we drove through the streets. When we arrived at the steps of the capitol there was no honor guard, no delegation to greet us. It was dead silent as we waited.

After a few minutes the General got out of the car and walked with his adjutant 'Frederick Prussien' a childhood friend of mine, up the steps and into the capitol building. I remained in the car. It wasn't five minutes before they were both being marched out of the building under armed guard; Argentine military vehicles then surrounded us.

Before we were to be escorted to the Embassy the commanding General of the Argentine police warned us to remain on the Embassy grounds for the duration of the war and that venturing beyond the grounds of the Embassy could prove dangerous to our personnel. He was polite but firm.

We were, in effect, being placed under house arrest.' He smiled looking down into his hands and the gun he held in them. 'I think it was because our escort troops were heavily-armed, each one a veteran of the 'Winter War'. I tend to think the Commanding General knew better than to risk an armed engagement in the streets of Buenos Aires."

Archie took over, after limping his way to the Kubelwagon and taking a seat, panting from both his recent exertion as well as from the pain of this wound. "Mckenzie was sent to Argentina after the war as a representative of the Allied governments to secure any intelligence that would assist them in prosecuting war criminals.

A Royal Marine detachment was sent in to secure the compound, immediately following the surrender of Germany to arrest any Nazi fugitives holed up there. They found the compound empty. Not a soul anywhere. After an extensive search of the grounds they discovered a large tunnel that led to a wharf roughly a mile away. The tunnel was large enough to handle trucks and obviously a car,' nodding toward the massive, gleaming Mercedes. 'We later learned that a large submarine was seen moored at the pier loading a car, spotted by a boy riding his bike making his early morning paper delivery.

Being only 12 he wasn't taken seriously until we discovered the disappearance of the entire legation six weeks later. The trucks and other non-essential items were left in the tunnel for us to find. The pier they used was isolated and too small for commercial vessels, but it happened to be perfect for a large submarine to tie up and remain obscured.

Hans smiled and piped up "We were in Buenos Aires only three days and left with what remained of the German Legation. We transferred them to a civilian vessel off Brazil, a Portuguese vessel that was owned by a German company. I understand that they made port in Spain three weeks later. The General was sullen and quiet but with a sense of deadly resolve that made me nervous, with good reason it would turn out. As the weeks went by and the end of the war drew nearer and nearer the General became manic. We were ordered to clean up the facility and make it presentable as if we were expecting guests."

"The Kreigsmarine crew was kept busy patrolling the island in their submarine. A month after Germany surrendered they were ordered to circle the island on the surface and then dive before re-entering the lagoon. I do not know what his purpose was. It was obvious that he wanted someone to see it, possibly to provoke an attack by Allied ships so that he could go out fighting. Since no one lived on the island at the time, who was supposed to see it? He didn't see fit to explain.

A few days later he began mothballing the base. Each submarine was Mothballed, sealed and coated with a mixture of oil and diesel to make sure they didn't' corrode. Each truck was parked and the gasoline drained. Oil was then poured into the engines to make sure they were properly stored and put on blocks their tires aired down and put in the back of each truck and covered with oil soaked canvas tarpaulins. When the base was secured an eerie calm settled on the General. He would spend all day in his quarters and all evening walking in the meadow inspecting the weapons cache." Rick nodded remembering the artillery shells and guns now rotting in the jungle.

Hans acknowledged him with a nod then continued, "In the months prior to our arrival weapons were shipped via Spanish merchant ships to the island."

Rick jerked his head up and said "I thought the base was secret? How come they didn't spill the secret?"

Hans smiled a dark, brooding smile that indicated a measure of deeply felt shame and embarrassment. "Our high command had the ships loaded with high explosives in the void spaces, hundreds of tons of it. So that when they were far enough out to sea it would be detonated. If they weren't killed in the blast they'd likely drown or' he paused 'sharks…" He didn't have to finish the sentence to make his meaning any more plain. "Three massive ships were blown to bits. I doubt there was enough left that could be called wreckage.' Shaking his head he said 'Nazi security measures were nothing if not thorough."

"Our mission was supposedly to take the Panama Canal and deny the Allies use of it while we moved our troops up the Mexican coast and attack the United States from Mexico after we convinced Argentina to enter the war on our side. Their involvement was supposed to give us time to build a new fleet, new tanks, planes and build an entirely new Army of Argentine Germans.' Hans laughed. 'What they failed to realize, the Nazis that is, was that a good many

Germans had moved to Argentina to get away from them. Argentine Germans did go to Germany to fight and did so enthusiastically but not 'that' many. Also the Argentine regime was 'sympathetic' to Germany, but sympathy and support are two very different things. Several high- ranking Nazis knew what awaited them if they were arrested and were the ones who convinced Hitler to fund a new front and exploited Argentina's sympathy. Only they knew that Argentina would not be drawn in so late in the war. This mission was devised to cover the escape of high ranking Nazis from Germany while lining their pockets." Hans sighed.

"It wasn't long before the General began to suspect that he'd been duped. His twilight inspections of the weapons cache were meant initially to catalog the arsenal before it was moved into the tunnel to be stored' Hans pointed roughly in the direction of the meadow 'all those weapons you saw in the meadow? None of them are functional; they never were. Those shells stacked in rows are dummy shells, hollow on the inside and inert. The guns meant to fire those shells were WWI relics that were seized by the French at the end of the first war and left to rot in a field. Not a single gun had so much as a firing pin and the barrels were so distorted that if they did manage to fire a shell, the gun would have exploded and killed everyone in a 50-foot radius. Clearly, that front was never intended to materialize. It was that discovery that put the General over the edge."

Hans stood up and groaned as his joints resisted movement. "Damn, I've never been able to sit for very long and not have my joints ache; not since Russia." The look on his face was serious; as if his war experience was ever present never giving him a moments' peace. "To continue,' he said stepping around the VW he paced back and forth to get his joints moving. 'He, the general, felt betrayed having been sent on a mission that was nothing more than an elaborate hoax. A hoax created for the purpose of robbing the Reich of its remaining wealth so that a few high ranking Nazis could enjoy their lives in hiding. His efforts were ultimately wasted on the greed of a misbegotten few, General Deitrich felt betrayed. His pride and honor could not take the betrayal and he withdrew emotionally.

The day we got word of Hitler's death the General withdrew further and disappeared into his rooms in the mansion for several days ordering all activity stopped. We had not been told it was a suicide. We were told that he had died fighting in the streets, a typically Nazi fairy tale. As a result the General felt ashamed at having failed his Fuhrer, ashamed at having not achieved the goal of creating an American Front and failing to prolong the war for his beloved Fuhrer.

We held a memorial service for the Fuhrer. He then again disappeared into his quarters this time for two weeks. When he emerged he was clean-shaven and dressed in his formal dress uniform, but with a queer look in his eye, a dangerously queer look but was otherwise his normal self. That is until he overheard one of the Kriegsmarine ratings suggest that we each take a truckload of gold and move to South America. To be honest most of us were thinking the same thing. It made sense. Why should it all go to waste?"

"However, that was the wrong thing to say particularly since the general had devised a new mission which was to avenge the Fuhrer by keeping the bullion and this base from those he saw as betrayers of the Fuhrers trust. The SS immediately arrested the entire Kriegsmarine crew chaining them to a barge, which was then floated out onto the lagoon. The General distrusted the remaining crew because one of the captains had gone to Argentina with the delegation and stayed. It would turn out that he had a family estate in the Argentine outback. This the general saw as another betrayal. Apparently the captain had taken several crates of bullion with him adding to the Generals anger and distrust."

While we were in Buenos Aires Captain Heinz took a legation Mercedes from the garage and used the tunnel to leave. He had left his resignation with the legation secretary before leaving. So legally he had not deserted but he knew that the General would have not allowed him to leave had he known. But with all the turmoil that followed our arrival the General did not notice him missing until after we had transferred the civilians to a transport off Brazil. It was that which I'm afraid caused the General to take the actions he took, which ultimately caused Frederick to pay with his life".

Rick excited by his having been rendered a multi-billionaire literally over night was almost too excited to pay attention but he was cognizant enough to realize the responsibility being thrust upon him. While Hans explained the history of why and how they got there the realization hit that the gold would have to be moved. But how do you move tons of bullion without the world finding out? It was a question he began to ponder. But the need to know why the crew had been killed so horribly surfaced drowning out all other thought. "Why did they drown the Crew?" he asked.

Hans shook his head and let a tear roll down his cheek, glancing over at the blackness of the water, roughly where the bodies of the crew now lay chained to the barge 40 feet below. "It was Fredrick and I who had been tasked with filming it. Believe me we tried everything we could to save them. Fredrick actually, once hearing of the generals plans pre-positioned re-breathers near the pier as well as a set of keys to the locks on the chains.

He had even managed to hide a couple of breathers on the crew telling them what he could of the Generals plans. So even after they'd been under water for a bit they were able to pass the breathers from one to the other to keep them alive long enough for Fredrick to save them. Sadly the re-breathers he gave the crew weren't all functioning properly. So when Fredrick finally did get to them only 8 of the original 25 crew were alive. He dove down to them the instant the last of the SS were below decks and went down to the bottom and unchained them. The remaining crew swam quietly to the pier and waited for the right moment to emerge.

I followed the SS crew on board making like I was going to follow them in the insanity. While Fredrick was saving the crew I was on board the submarine taking my place on my bunk in full dress uniform. Obviously I did not take the cyanide but I did take some bicarbonate of soda and made it look as if I had taken my cyanide capsule. I even made similar noises to those being made around me' Hans paled as he remembered that long ago day. 'I listened as 13 lunatics killed themselves in the name of the Fuhrer.

The General Started it by crying out "Hiel Hitler" followed by the crunch of his capsule which was followed by the choking, gagging noise one makes when dying of cyanide. One by one each man followed suit each taking turns. I happened to be the last one, but to keep up the pretense I still made like I had also done it just in case I wasn't the only one faking. As each man took his turn it was obvious that several others were having second thoughts. At least two went so far as to crunch the capsule but then spit it out. Most of the cyanide had emptied into their mouth, enough to do the job it just took longer for them to die. I could hear them trying to spit it out and fighting to stay alive. Fucking idiots' he muttered. 'Their deaths were especially difficult to listen to.

So when the fellow above me snapped his capsule I not only heard his gags I felt his death shudder and smelled the release of his bowels.' Hans shook his head as beads of sweat formed on his forehead. 'The movies don't do such a death justice. You do not get to experience the whole process. When a person dies all that is in their intestines and bladder is released. That is something few people consider when they commit suicide, the foul mess they leave behind.

The smell was beyond belief. After my bunk-mate expired I climbed out of my bunk and slowly began to inspect the remains. It was obvious in most cases that they were dead. I even checked their pulses. The smell was particularly bad as all 13 had shit themselves. What made it even worse for me was the fact that several of them were twitching violently and howling as their muscles made one last contraction in death squeezing air out of their lungs. It made it seem as though they were reanimating for a short bit."

Hans wiped his brow with a white, clean handkerchief. "It was that which caused me to take my service pistol and but a bullet into each of their skulls. To have a corpse make those noises and contract their muscles is unnerving. After that I got out of the submarine as fast as I could because the smell was becoming worse the longer I stayed. In fact I vomited the moment I got out into the fresh air. I then closed up the hatch and climbed down and went over to the pier where Fredrick was waiting with the 8 men he'd saved."

Taking the remaining K-wagon we piled in and headed to the tunnel. We were all in the need of fresh air and to be away from the madness that had just passed. We were half way out of the tunnel when we heard the large Mercedes roaring up behind us. There were three SS sergeants we had forgotten about. At first we believed them to be fanatics enforcing the Generals wishes.

Apparently they had been sane enough to know they could live the rest of their lives as extremely rich men and were in no mood to share. They came up behind us in that very car Archie arrived in,' he indicated the big Benz behind Rick. 'They came up behind us shooting killing four of the crew piled on the back eventually killing all of the remaining crew. Fredrick told me to bail out when we cleared the tunnel.

I did so thinking that he was going to as well. But he drew them off. They had to slow the big car to turn it so I was able to hop on the bumper. I saw Frederick ahead of us miss the turn and crash his K-wagon. He had been knocked unconscious in the crash. They marched up to him and killed him before I could stop them. They were laughing as they walked back to the car. I met them and emptied my machine pistol into each of them. Their bodies I dragged over to a pile of shells and left them to rot.

I buried Fredrick in the garden on the plateau and dumped the others in the lagoon with their shipmates.' Hans took a deep breath, letting a tear fall 'my friend died trying to save me. Burying him in a decent grave was the least I could do." Hans let out a sigh thinking of his old friend, and then continued. "I spent the next few weeks on the island living in the mansion and off the stores while I studied the charts and maps waiting out the stormy season. We had a fishing trawler that we used to drag the channel to keep it clear. I loaded it with fuel and provisions then I worked on the mechanicals and left the island for Argentina where I bought passage to Spain and made my way back to my Chalet in Switzerland, two months before my pre-paid rent was up. Of course I paid for another year and took my time recuperating from the war.

I had enough money in Switzerland and even more in the barn. As it turned out I had no need to go after it. The Swiss are very generous with their interest rates and I had accumulated a tidy sum above and beyond what I had already deposited. So for a few years I lived quietly in Switzerland. I met Sarah on one of my trips into Germany and she and I eventually married. Once I realized that Odessa was seeking me out, we moved to Portugal but eventually moved back to Switzerland when it seemed things had calmed down.

After 20 years of quiet marriage Odessa came to visit me at my home, where I learned of their plans to kill me and abscond with my cash. Supposedly for the cause, but I knew that was bullshit. They wanted to rob me, plain and simple. No more honor, no more cause…though they wanted to believe something like that. They were just a bunch of criminals seeking to be the international bullies they'd been before. Living to make war and to kill Jews or anyone they decided wasn't fit to live and breathe their air. They killed my wife and I killed them.

After that I moved to Miami but the Jewish population was pretty heavy and believing I was a wanted Nazi fugitive I located here, once I learned of a property. What better place to lie low than someplace they are not aware of, the base that nobody knew existed, a miniscule island in the western Atlantic? It was while here that I learned that someone had purchased the property containing the compound on the plateau. That meant that the same person owned the mountain and the lands surrounding it.

My first thought was that Odessa had found it and bought it. But when I sought out the title I learned of the preacher here. He bought the property and found the place grown over and barely habitable. I then moved here and started to attend church on Sundays.

He hadn't made it to the basement where, if he had, he would have found the horde and the submarines. I was the one who let him in on that. After that he and I cleared the overgrowth over several years. It took us a month just to get to where we could access the garden. We both knew that if the bullion was discovered Odessa and its many organizations would have found a way to access it. If not the world courts would have it tied up for decades. It would then go to waste. So we, he and I, appointed ourselves guardians of the bullion." Hans shook his head in disgust.

"I know first-hand what the Nazis were like. I was one. I saw the camps before they were filled. I knew what Hitler had in store for the masses he thought unworthy to live. If the Nazis ever got hold of this stockpile the world could very well see a resurgent Nazi regime. That is something I am not willing to tolerate again. I doubt the world would as well, still with that money they could make a good run at it and make life very difficult for millions."

Archie having rested long enough stepped in, "While it is true that I did not know of this horde and certainly not the vastness of it, I was aware that this was a secret base. At least I had suspected so' he laughed realizing that he sounded like a know it all 'but that is not to say that I figured this out on my own. There was a naval commander in WWI who put two and two together and sent a report into the Admiralty suggesting it. Britain didn't have the resources to mount a full-scale investigation into finding a base that may or may not exist, especially when other more plausible explanations were likely to arise. He was commended for his efforts and a communiqué was sent out to the fleet bound for those waters, but nothing ever came of it.

They were tasked with a secondary mission where if they happened to be in the region of one of the three suspected sites they were to identify any possible submarine base. He suspected that there may be a base either in Cuba, St. Vincent or the mangrove swamps in French Guyana. Nothing was spotted by any of the ships that happened upon these three sites. By the time the Admiralty had the ships to do a proper search the tide of war had turned badly against Germany. So even if they did find a base it was likely they would find it unsustainable because supply traffic had been virtually eliminated by the summer of 1918.

In the end the report was sealed and filed away and wasn't seen again until after the end of the Second world war when my boss, McKenzie stumbled onto it while cleaning out his desk after getting reassigned to the Pentagon. Our importance faded quickly with the end of the war. I was retired and he was sent stateside to keep him out of the hair of the senior staff more concerned with the economic stability of Europe than with locating and neutralizing potential threats. It was McKenzie who put me onto the island, but with post war turmoil I didn't locate this place until 25 years later. I wasn't surprised to find it overgrown. We are in the tropics and the jungle tends to grow fast in the wet hot environs of the world. Even man made islands like this one."

Archie then explained to Rick the history of the island. After nearly an hour the whole story had been laid at his feet and why the bullion must never be allowed to find its way into the hands of the world governments, especially since Odessa seemed to have been influencing a good many of them.

When Archie had finished his story and Hans filled in the details that Archie had missed. As a result Rick had a lot of information to process. Overwhelmed was the closest word he could have used to describe his feelings. Waves of stress induced nausea crashed over him as he realized his responsibility to see that all this bullion never fell into the wrong hands. From what Archie had experienced in getting shot it was apparent that Odessa or some off-shoot of that organization suspected that the bullion was here on the island. It was only a matter of time before someone figured out the full story and where the bullion was.

Archie and Hans had only to keep the secret hidden. Rick was now faced with the relocating the bullion to some other facility, but as he pondered this Archie piped up. "They may not figure out a thing. It has been only speculation so far. If we remain out of sight for a few days, even a few weeks it is entirely possible they may just go away".

Rick knew he was trying to bolster his confidence. They all knew that no matter what happened, even if they left, the bullion had to be moved. Odessa came too close this time…way too close. It was only a matter of time before they eventually discovered it. There was just too much of it to put onto the market without jolting the system and creating shockwaves and drawing the world's attention to him thereby getting him and his family killed. His newfound wealth was losing its luster.

Seeing his distress Archie patted him on the shoulder. "Son, we can still assist you with this for a while. We simply had nobody to leave this task to, and we both feel that you are the best one for the job. It simply takes a bit of guile. Now I've been pondering this very thing for decades and we already have devised a plan. So let's get you up to the mansion and see if we can get some hot food into you and we'll lay out what we have already figured out."

They all three rode up in the G4 to the plateau. That evening, if you were observant a light could be seen in the tallest room in the mansion, ever so slightly and only when the wind blew. In that room sat three men at a table eating sandwiches and drinking beer discussing plans to move the bullion. Rick was far more at ease than he'd been since learning of the bullions origins. The plan was ingenious and all he had to do was find a Lawyer to put it in motion. Laughing to himself Rick realized that he already knew one and his wife was banging him.

Chapter 24
At sea 1945

SIX HOURS AFTER breaking out of Bergen Norway Hans woke to the gentle roll of the ocean. He and Frederick had slept through the most harrowing portion of their journey where they submerged in the harbor and slowly made their way out to sea. It had been sheer exhaustion that allowed them to sleep through it, not necessarily bravado. Their bodies had simply shut down and ceased to function on all levels save for the most rudimentary needs to sustain life. The fact that they had been at sea for six hours created a sense of elation and tension release he had not felt in weeks.

Looking up he saw Frederick fast asleep. Had it not been for his chest rising and falling he might have thought him dead. Folded up next to his bunk was a pair of dungarees, canvas shoes and sweater. Changing into his new clothes Hans was pleased at how comfortable they were. Taking a deep relaxed breath he decided to get some coffee.

Passing aft of the con he went past the Officers mess and into the galley were he smelled coffee brewing. The crew was breathing easier but remained appropriately keyed up ready for action. They knew what lay ahead and that the odds were against them. For the moment they were safe and that was enough. Hans felt a sense of hope that somehow he might actually survive and somehow make his way back to his chalet stopping short of delusion. Too many dead lay on the bottom of the Atlantic to allow for more than cautious optimism…and even 'that' was a stretch.

Hans was beginning to understand why submarine sailors lived for the moment, because that is all they had…too often.

Taking a cup and pouring himself some coffee he was surprised to discover it was genuine coffee. In spite of the rubberized canvas cup it didn't taste bad. He preferred his coffee black, unsweetened and enjoyed two cups in the crews mess silently watching sailors play a game of spades on the table next to his. The calm peacefulness of these men playing an innocent game made him relax even further allowing him to indulge in thoughts of a post war life. Relaxing also allowed his fatigue to surface again reminding him of the price he had paid over the past several weeks. But the sound of the cards shuffling together and the gentle sound of a card being flopped down somehow soothed him and made him want to remain for the sound they made. Closing his eyes he focused on the conversation and the voices of men joking and talking of life after the war until fatigue took over and forced him to head back to his bunk.

On the way back to his bunk he noted the navigation chart and was pleased to discover that they had made significant progress in the six hours he'd been asleep. They were ten nautical miles beyond the nets and less than a mile off the Norwegian shoreline, well within reach of the destroyers patrolling the harbor entrance and far from being out of danger. Still they'd made it this far and were making their way to their designated rendezvous albeit slowly.

Their speed was barely over one knot just enough to maintain steerageway and maintain depth. At 12 nautical miles the plan was to
increase speed to five knots. Still a slow speed they would be far
enough away from the destroyers to hide their screw noise in the din
of shoreline currents and crashing surf. If sonar picked up anything
from the destroyers they would immediately drop to one knot and
keep to that speed until 20 miles out. Once in his bunk he collapsed
into an even deeper sleep now that hope had risen again.

Three days later Frederick stepped on his hand getting out of his
bunk waking him from his slumber. Sudden alarm rose in the pit
of his stomach as he realized that the sub was on the surface. Why
were they on the surface? Where they under attack? The fog from
his heavy sleep slowed his thinking.

Both Beck and Prussien made their way to the con where the crew
calmly navigated the ship. A speaker crackled as orders were given
to redirect course and speed from the captain on the surface bridge.
"Weather is too rough for a flank speed run so we will attempt a half
speed run and hope the storm keeps us hidden."

Once on their designated course the Captain came down and Beck
immediately asked him why they weren't submerged. The Captain
was handed a coffee and nodded. "Well, it appears that we didn't
factor in the weathers effect on the mine field. We also underestimated the undersea currents effect on their movement because a
mooring chain brushed against us as we attempted to follow the
channel as originally planned. It would seem the Allies have moored
their mines to longer chains so the motion of the waves will move
them further, rendering an attempt such as ours impossible or at the
very least unwise. It would seem our plan would have worked better if there were no storm, but then the whole purpose of using the

storm was to hide our noise. So, either we do as originally planned and ride the surface through the mine field or we attempt a suicidal run through a moving gauntlet of mines and die."

Beck looked at Prussien who appeared to be a bit paler than before. "So, are we in danger riding the surface like this? Aren't these mines designed to sink ships on the surface also?" he asked.

The Captain nodded sipping his coffee. "These mines we figure were placed here to prevent another channel dash from our Northern fleet and to prevent submarines from transiting submerged. Normally a submarine on the surface would be a sitting duck for land-based aircraft. We figure that the allies left them deep enough to damage large deep draft ships while leaving a functional depth for shallow or flat bottomed cargo vessels to transit the region unmolested while leaving them just deep enough for a surface transit by a submarine. Apparently they believe that a submarine would not want to ride the surface so near Scotland with the allies having complete air superiority up here. It would also seem that they had not made an allowance for an audacious move like this…during a storm.

The captain walked over to his chart and pointed. "We are here, in the center of this channel meant for larger ships to pass through. The channel was charted a month ago. Our divers didn't note longer chains then. But they did note the depth and precise motionless channel that would have allowed a submarine transit. As it is, on the surface we can transit this space in relative safety, but only on the surface. This is due to the fact that at the bottom of the channel are intermittent mines placed at random depths, guaranteeing that any submarine, attempting to pass through this channel will get hit. Like I mentioned earlier, they don't believe that a submarine would attempt a surface transit due to the proximity of the airfields in Scotland. However, with the RAF grounded we can safely transit this channel on the surface and perhaps even make the full length of the English Channel on the surface in relative safety. Not that I intend to be so foolish. I do not intend to risk any unnecessary exposure."

Beck stared down at the chart noting the wide channel they were now cruising through. "What about allied ships?" he asked. "Apparently the Allied navies are in port for the storm. We've been monitoring their radio chatter and it seems the entire allied fleet, patrol craft included are in port because this storm is too dangerous. They are apparently concerned that the motion of the waves may cause a stray shell to land on shore if they fire on a target. That is the concern they've expressed in so many words. The term they used was 'collateral damage' the captain said almost to himself. 'Anyway, it would seem that we have a clear shot through the channel if the radio traffic is accurate."

Prussien sat down and seemed to gain some of his color back. "Won't we be seen?" he asked.

The captain nodded. "No doubt we shall be spotted at some point, but that is why we painted those white 'C's on the conning towers and why we are monitoring their radio chatter. By the time someone realizes the ruse we should be beyond the channel and well on our way to Spain. If they do suspect something there isn't anything they can do until the storm passes. Their planes won't fly in this weather and if they did locating and attacking us would be impossible. The only place that poses a genuine threat of our being spotted is here' he pointed to the chart 'Rue des Forte France, the narrowest point in the channel. Again if we are spotted, there isn't anything that they can do until we are well away.

Nevertheless I intend to dive and go as far as batteries will take us then surface at the last possible moment to minimize the chance of being seen, as well as to save fuel." Hans and Frederick sighed in collective relief nodded at each other then headed to crews mess to have coffee as well as to be near the largest escape hatch…just in case.

⇒ ◉ ⇐

Two weeks later Archie was busy combing Becks file from early in the war up to his last known active duty command in Foy Belgium. He'd spent the bulk of his duty in South Western Germany early in the war where Beck had been placed in command of an ad-hock patrol to search for a bomber crew seen parachuting from their stricken craft.

According to the patrol report in Becks file two of the crew had been recovered and the third had been found dead hanging from a tree with a broken neck. The location was 50km from Singen Germany. Shortly after this the Gestapo began paying attention to his activities as he had acquired an increase of cash availability while not having a significant increase in pay. It was noted here that he began smoking American Cigarettes 'Lucky Strike' being his preference. He was suspected of keeping a warehouse in the Alps within a 50km radius of Singen Germany which they were unable to locate.

It happened to be Singen where he had been temporarily assigned while awaiting orders following the destruction of his tank battalion in December of 44'. Throughout the many files Archie had perused Becks name came up repeatedly as a suspect in the disappearance of goods meant for most of the senior officers. He was suspected in the disappearance of a shipment of premium wine, beef and other goods meant to supply the Fuhrer bunker. Being meant for the Fuhrer himself, personally the Gestapo escalated their investigation and locked in on Beck. Only Beck was way ahead of them and had disposed of the material mere hours after having acquired it.

He was no fool. Stealing from the Fuhrer was an automatic death sentence. No trial just a firing squad if you were lucky or a noose from a telegraph pole. On the other hand such items were extremely profitable having sold most of it to American troops just prior to his vacating Foy. The commanding officer took extreme pleasure from knowing that he was about to eat Hitler's personal beef and beer supply.

Upon delivering the contraband to the Americans Hans arranged to have his men met at the French Swiss border to surrender to the Americans, where he asked that they be taken to American or Canadian POW camps, guaranteeing the commanding officer that his men had never done anything against the Geneva convention nor taken part in any of the atrocities other SS were known for.

When items from this shipment began showing up in the possession of American and British POWs the Gestapo were incensed. It was one thing to steal from the Fuhrer, but to sell it to the Allies was base treachery at its worst. In March of 1945 an arrest warrant was issued for Beck. He was to be brought in for questioning, which was to involve significant brutality after which he was to be shot as a traitor confession or not.

Archie began to admire Beck for his ingenuity and the brash manner in which he operated. He had always been one step ahead of the Gestapo whom Archie began to note were as thorough as they were thuggishly incompetent. The bulk of Gestapo agents whose files he'd obtained were at one point convicted criminals themselves. Some of whom had been serving life sentences for murder, that being the least of their offenses.

As Archie rummaged through the captured files he found a few obscure notes regarding looting of the SS Head Quarters in Singen where two Gestapo agents were killed. Apparently in a firefight with two SS officers, seen driving away in a Black Mercedes G4 staff car. One notation suggested one of the Officers was identified as Oberst Hans Beck. It had been the other unidentified officer who had shot both agents as they came running out of the building apparently in pursuit of Beck.

The notation in the file suggested that the two agents had been sent in to take Beck into custody having spotted him entering the building. When he did not exit the building in the expected time frame they were sent in to get him. What they hadn't counted on was another officer aiding him in his escape. By the time they had realized what had happened Beck was on his way to Norway, where the local Gestapo chief noted his arrival but was unable to arrest him, per General Dietrich's orders. That firefight had taken place roughly a month earlier.

Archie put the pieces together on the floor like a huge mosaic as he mapped the movements of Oberst Hans Beck from the beginning of the war to the very end. Becks First recorded military action was as a squad leader sent to search for downed RAF bomber crew, recovering two live prisoners and one body in Dec 1939.

Assigned to a Tank battalion in Jan 1940 and was the third wave of tanks to drive the British and French forces into Dunkirk. He was reprimanded by his C.O. for requesting permission to finish off the

British on the beach. He was then stationed in France to be held in reserve. In 1941 he was assigned to the eastern front and took part in the initial assault on Russia where he fought with distinction but lost 80% of his troops in the spring when they were bogged down in mud and attacked by the Russian Air Force.

He was then re-assigned to a combat regiment as a replacement officer in Stalingrad where he was nearly killed by a Soviet tank shell in December of 1941. The regiment he' been attached to had been branded by the Soviets as the Demon Regiment stemming from an incident that drove fear into the hearts of the Soviet troops. So much so that when the German Army surrendered the regiment Beck had been attached to were not arrested but asked to leave Russia. The Russians had even escorted them to the edge of their lines to ensure that they left. Details of the incident in question are vague and likely exaggerated; something about a walking headless corpse. Archie dismissed the incident as Soviet exaggeration mainly due to a lack of Soviet cooperation. Beck was in a Berlin Hospital at the time of the surrender with severe frostbite.

In 1943 Beck was assigned to another tank battalion in Italy along the Gustof line where he bombarded the American and British positions. In October of 1944 Beck was ordered back to Germany in preparation for an offensive being planned for December 1944. He was ordered to surround and bombard Bastogne and was in the command vehicle when his Commanding Officer offered surrender terms to the garrison and received the reply 'Nuts' from the American General. At this the German General flew into a rage and was preparing an attack on Bastogne when the weather broke and an air-raid destroyed 60% of his force, decimating the remaining German Armor erasing any chance Germany had of ending the war in a position of strength. Beck took what remained of his Battalion to Foy Belgium from where he disappeared until resurfacing in Norway in March 1945.

His official record was straightforward and clear. The Gestapo files were anything but as they had nothing on him but suspicion and speculation. At no time did they have a clear tag on anything he'd been suspected of. They knew where he was, confirmed by his official record but otherwise they were chasing a ghost in Beck. Apparently in frustration at having been outsmarted time and time again they decided to arrest him, extract a confession then shoot him. But whenever Beck surfaced he'd evade their clutches either by luck or cunning infuriating them further.

In Bergen with the cooperation of an anti-Nazi Luftwaffe special-duties operative a report was sent through channels that Beck had been seen climbing down a hatch of a submarine; one of two Milchow submarines carrying an unknown cargo to a destination that only the Captains were allowed knowledge of as well as the route. The exact time of departure was not divulged, as the operatives did not wish to be party to getting his fellow Germans killed, they were anti-Nazi not anti-German. After that report Becks trail went cold.

Roughly a month later, in Buenos Aires a rather audacious Nazi delegation paraded itself down the main street and to the Capitol of Argentina. Intelligence suggested that the delegation was attempting to negotiate a treaty with Argentina, the object of that treaty was not clear. What took place was short and abrupt because the entire delegation was escorted from the Capitol building under armed guard minutes later to the German Legation and placed under what was in effect house arrest. Beck was suspected of being part of that delegation but it was never confirmed. Davis closed the file and made his report to McKenzie who, at the end of the war was sent to Argentina to arrest suspected Nazi fugitives believed to be holed-up in the Legation. When the allied forces crashed the gates, they found the compound empty and a tunnel leading to a Pier where it was reported that a sub was spotted weeks earlier.

Chapter 25
Horst's Problem

HORST STARED INTO his fireplace smoking a cigarette longing for the harsh bitterness of his wartime Russian cigarettes pondering what to do about Patrice and her recently acquired knowledge. Patrice had been hired to put the Operation on track with the modern underworld. Odessa had been a major underworld power due to their ability to instill fear in competitors. However, as membership died off their soldiers became less dedicated the competition lost their fear and Odessa lost influence. This necessitated a restructuring which is why Patrice had been brought in. She had done a masterful job in gaining access to most of the world's leaders and putting them in compromising positions from which they held leverage over them.

However, he had underestimated her. Somehow in her diligence she had discovered that the Operation was cover for Odessa. How she had figured that out was a concern because if she could figure it out Mossad could. That is, if they were still looking for them. However, Mossad was losing interest now that the important Nazis were mostly gone. Their focus was on matters closer to home like rocket attacks and suicide bombers from Hamas and Hezbollah, remnants of the PLO, which they, Odessa, had once funded for the purpose of exterminating Israel.

The few Nazis remaining at large were low-level prison guards and in their 80s and 90s and not worth the effort. Yet, for all the relief he felt at the lack of attention he was also insulted that he was no longer 'important' enough to pursue. He had considered it a matter of pride having been on their most wanted list. That he was no longer important enough for them to even bother with bruised his ego. Taking another long drag from his cigarette he considered the possibility that they thought he was dead. Few had reached the age of 103 and fewer still were able to enjoy the physical vitality he did much less the mental capacity to use it. If they thought he was dead, he could accept that. But if they thought he was no longer dangerous, that was something he could not accept.

That was a personal issue however and had no bearing on the matter at hand. Patrice Verga, his temporary right hand, his guide into the 21ths century, a woman of cunning genius had been dumb enough to let slip that she had discovered the Operations link to Odessa. Should he let her finish this current job then kill her or kill her and hope that her successor can finish what she had started?

He didn't want to kill her because she had been an incredibly important asset, but she knew too much, more than he was prepared to allow. He, Werner and two others knew about Odessa. Each of them devoted to world domination and a renewed Nazi Party. Patrice was too intelligent and too creative and far too moral to be allowed this knowledge. She knew enough to bury them and he was not prepared to risk all they'd achieved on one person's judgment, particularly a woman's judgment.

Somehow, Patrice had uncovered the Operations origins as a revamped and rejuvenated Odessa, an organization of former SS whose mission it was to protect its members from international prosecution.

It was also to someday renew National Socialism under a renewed Nazi Party. However, more pragmatic members decided that their influence was better served as a shadow government. Peddling their influence to susceptible and corrupt politicians who would do their bidding never knowing just who it was they were being controlled by. If a politician happened to develop morals they were threatened with blackmail, if that didn't work they were killed.

So far their 'flock' was under control and ignorant to their bene-factors identity. This was important because even the most morally dubious politician would not tolerate working for a Nazi. Miss Verga knew who they controlled and what the Operation had on them. With the knowledge she had, the entire operation could be derailed and their agenda destroyed if she chose to expose them.

Her uncovering their identity had unhinged his temper, which re-sulted in his threatening her life. Shaking his head he truly regret-ted his actions, but his dementia was getting worse, especially when angry or scared. Testosterone therapy had slowed down its progres-sion and allowed him to live a more vigorous lifestyle. He didn't even need Viagra anymore. In spite of his best efforts to prolong his vitality and lifespan, age had taken its toll.

During these episodes he could think clearly and have full control of his thoughts, but his physical reaction to emotions were beyond his capacity to reign in. He'd wanted to kill her, choke the life from her body as he pressed her against the wall. What had saved her was a wave of weakness that forced him to let her go. He made it to the chair before he fell to the floor in weakness. Thankfully, Patrice wasn't the killing sort. He sincerely did not wish to send Werner out on this task. But it was the only way to guarantee that she did not betray them. She should have known to keep her mouth shut. "Stupid girl" he muttered under his breath "Stupid, stupid girl".

Through the same diligence that caused her to learn of Odessa, Patrice had discovered the possible whereabouts of a long lost Nazi treasure horde. A horde Odessa had long sought after. A bullion repository so huge that his organizations grip on the world would be solidified and expanded, possibly even restoring the Nazi regime to power. But that was far too much to hope for.

A bitter smile broke onto this face as he flung his cigarette butt into the fire. He watched the flames consumed it. The Allied victor's, had written his former regime into the annals of evil empires. None of Germany's victories would be remembered neither would their technological achievements. Hadn't they built the first fighter jets of the war, didn't they have the best pilots and planes and tanks? Even the Russian MIG15 had been a Messerschmitt design with a working prototype already flying then stolen by the mongoloid Russian armies as they stormed the citadel of Berlin like so many cockroaches.

Shaking his head in disgust and mounting shame Horst drained the wine from his glass in one swallow then smashed the glass in the fireplace cursing viciously. "God damn it Werner!! We had the world by the balls." he made a fist as if grabbing an imaginary set of balls and made to crush them in his frustration. "We had the whole world at our feet and beaten!!! Now look at us, look at us, lurking in the shadows bribing politicians to do our bidding instead of dictating our will openly."

"We were beaten by that sniveling, manipulating Himmler. He used narcotics to manipulate Hitler. I witnessed it and when I took action to stop it I found myself out of the loop; muscled out of the inner circle because I was smart enough to see through his game. He manipulated Hitler to make asinine decisions that benefited his own personal goals, which I had discovered was to take over the Reich. Apparently Bormann was with him. He's the one I told about Himmler using narcotics to control Hitler and by extension Germany. In a few short days I was fired, by the very man I was trying to save."

Horst leaned forward and stared into the fire with his one eye reflecting it. The appearance was to bring to mind the devil himself with the fires of hell burning deep within his soul. For a long moment he stared unblinking into its light. Turning to Werner he motioned for him to pour him more wine.

As Werner approached him with the bottle and another glass he spoke quietly. "Werner you will soon have to retire Miss Verga. Recent events have presented that we cannot allow. She knows about Odessa. I don't know how she found out. You will have to learn that before you kill her. We cannot allow any loose ends, not now. Not when we are so close to finally achieving our Fuhrers vision.' Shaking his head he then continued 'sadly it will not be exactly what he had envisioned but we Werner, we are the ones ruling the world. We are ruling the entire planet through our network.' His excitement was surfacing triggering his dementia, 'I am now the Fuhrer of the world Werner...and you shall be my successor in our new and illustrious Fourth Reich." In his excitement Horst popped from his seat, came to attention and shouted at the top of his lungs "Hiel Hitler!!!

Werner stood with his hands behind his back at the edge of the firelight in the full dress uniform of a Standartenfurher in the Waffen SS. Werner seldom spoke because he found it tedious and unnecessary. But when his Fuhrer saluted Hitler he offered a sharp Nazi salute and joined in with enthusiasm not seen since the heady days of 1940 when the world trembled before Hitler's armies and cowered before his tanks.

Werner having joined in his support for Hitler he took up his post once again next to Horsts chair. Werner was a soldier, a Nazi soldier and a latter day disciple of Adolf Hitler and a true believer in National Socialism. He was also an escaped fugitive from prison for the criminally insane. Odessa gave him purpose and a focus for his demented ideas of world order. His new religion had become National Socialism as a devout member of the SS; albeit a self-appointed member. His genius was for silent killing and making it seem accidental, or health related. However, in the case of Miss Verga, a woman he lusted for and loathed he would gladly bloody his hands. Coming to attention Werner spoke "Mein Fuhrer, when should I dispatch Miss Verga?"

Horst took up his glass, the gleam of enthusiasm in his eye from his recent dementia driven mania. Sipping from his wine glass, he nodded acknowledgment. "I have not decided yet, but I want you ready on a moment's notice. I think that it would be best to let her finish this last task before we take that step. Dispatching her now I fear may set us back in locating the repository. If what she has told me is true, we will be able to bring about a more complete vision for our Fuhrer.

Governments run on money and with this bullion, if it is there on this island, we could buy every developed nation on the planet and literally take over the world, perhaps even bringing our Party back to prominence.' He waved his hand impatiently, 'I cannot get ahead of our reality. This may be nothing more than a wild goose chase, like the other times. Let's see how far she gets. If she succeeds and we have located it, you may dispatch her. If she fails to deliver…" he spread his hands as if to say 'Oh well'.

Werner came to attention "Yes, Mein Fuhrer, on your orders it shall be done."

Horst regaining his sense of self put the glass down and looked back into the fire. "In fairness to Patrice, being that she has been a good worker bee, I let her know that you would be the one I send to kill her, if ever she over stepped her place again. So it would be best, when I do send you, that you are not seen until you cannot miss."

"Yes, Mein Fuhrer." He replied.

"It's been a long day for me Werner. I think that I'll turn in now. Oh, and send in that new Spanish maid we hired a few days ago. She knows what is expected of her?" he asked.

"Yes, she has been informed of her 'extra' duties should they be requested of her" Werner replied as he pressed the button summoning her to his chambers.

Horst nodded "Good, Just have her waiting for me with her skirt up and bent over the bed. I just need a quick one tonight.' He smiled turning to leave through the open door then turned back suddenly and spoke 'Oh and Miss Verga will need some assistance in tying up loose ends on the island. Send two or three of our men to help her, killers, preferably the discrete sort. I want no complications to interfere with our plans, and dead bodies tend to complicate things by drawing unwanted attention. Patrice will know how to direct them. But when the time comes Werner, 'you' must be the one to see to

Miss Vergas…retirement. Oh, one more thing. As a favor to me, I do not want her to suffer. I expect you to curb your tendencies, am I clear?"

Snapping to attention Werner replied "Yes, Mein Fuhrer. I understand completely. Her retirement will be quick and painless, I promise." Werner hid his disappointment knowing that his Fuhrer had no tolerance for any such 'indulgence'. He also knew better than to challenge him on this matter. His want to hurt Patrice Verga was purely for the base pleasure of hearing her scream. That was less important than doing his Fuhrers bidding. With that Horst turned and left closing the door behind him. Werner remained standing until he heard his boss's footsteps down the hallway.

Once he no longer heard his footsteps Werner went about removing the empty glass and half empty wine bottle. As he went to leave he heard the delighted squeals of the new housemaid down the hall. He happened to know that his Fuhrer was hung like the proverbial horse because he'd over heard the other maids talking about it and comparing notes on their experiences. They knew the rules however, never were they to mention encounters, or reference them while attending to their regular duties.

He would initiate each encounter and they were to comply without question. His appetites weren't strange or deviant, at times he'd request they sit on his lap and things would progress from there. Most often though he'd have Werner send them up to his chamber and either lay on their backs, either naked, fully clothed or like tonight bent over the bed skirt hiked up and ready.

Horst liked women to make noise. He preferred vocal crying out to grunting and moaning. But he didn't mind the quiet ones so much that he'd stop fucking them. He just liked to hear them cry out in joy and ecstasy. As hard edged as he'd been in his youth Horst had never been a brutal man and wanted his women to enjoy themselves as much as he did; A rather incongruent match of character traits to be sure, but which seemed to work well enough in this case. Retiring to his chamber adjacent to his bosses apartments Werner reached for the phone.

Chapter 26
The Trio

THREE MEN SAT in an apartment in Miami Florida, paid for by the Operation, waiting for the phone to ring. They were to remain available and nearby while 'on call' to perform whatever 'duties' were required of them. In the organization they were known as the 'Trio', nobody knew their names or what they looked like, their specialty was disappearing. Whenever the 'Trio' was called in, whomever they were sent after disappeared without a trace so that not even DNA would remain after they had finished with them. They had originated as an Army unit in Afghanistan where their job was to locate and seize troublesome members of the Taliban, Al Qaeda or local tribal leaders stirring up trouble and make them disappear.

Their talents got the attention of the CIA who employed them as a wet team, used for extremely dirty jobs where 'official' involvement had to be avoided. They'd been used most heavily in the middle east where they'd honed their talents on the ready-made 'training' grounds of Iraq, Afghanistan, Syria with brief excursions into the Gaza Strip and west bank. They were a highly effective team until they discovered the high paying potential of the dark side. To them there was little difference one way or the other. They'd seen too many CIA, FBI and ATF agents abuse their authority and behave worse than many of the supposed criminals they'd been sent to dispatch.

The 'switch' flipped one day when they were 'hired' by an FBI agent who'd apparently gone rogue. Their target was a state department official investigating FBI corruption allegations, specifically allegations against the agent who hired them. A wrinkle they would discover too late.

After completing the hit they had been put on the FBIs most wanted list as a terrorist cell. The trouble for the FBI was the trio had been wise enough to black out their identities from their CIA training and offered up false credentials to the rogue FBI -agent. At no time had they allowed their faces to be seen, or voices heard. In revenge for his betrayal they sent the FBI the name of their rogue agent with audio recordings and photographic evidence of his criminal activities. He was immediately arrested and their names, fake though they were, stricken from the 'wanted list'.

Though cleared, they did have the blood of a state department official on their hands. That stigma would lead to their being disavowed as a CIA sanctioned team forcing them to seek alternative employment. They disappeared and became ghosts working for cartels and other criminal organizations bouncing from one employer to the next until they found permanent employment with a newly formed organization 'the Operation' which seemed to be well organized and well placed in terms of international presence not to mention well-funded.

Their contact was Patrice Verga, whom they had great respect for. She secured their employment in order to take care of a police officer who'd beaten up one of her girls in a drunken rage because she

wouldn't blow him until he took a shower, a requirement for all pa-
trons wanting any service. He had beaten her unconscious, broke her
jaw and slammed one of her hands in a door breaking it. Because
she was operating an illegal business and the fact that 'he' was a cop
calling the police wasn't an option. So Patrice looked to her underworld contacts to secure the services of the Trio to address the issue,
quietly, while sending a message. Her only requirement other than
to make him disappear was to let him know at the very last moment
who had ordered it and why, poetic.

The job was done so quietly and efficiently that nobody knew he was
missing for a week. His body was ever found and no signs of struggle
were noted at this home or any of the places he was known to frequent. In fact his home had been 'cleaned' so well by the Trio that no
finger prints could be found 'anywhere', not even his own. Having
noted the efficiency of the Trio Patrice negotiated permanent employment of their services as 'on call' to be ready whenever they may have
need of their service. So it was the night Werner called.

As usual the caller did all the talking. At no time did the Trio ever
speak. "You are to fly to St. Vincent to assist Miss Verga in locating
two men. You are to locate them and communicate that knowledge
to Miss Verga through your usual means. Upon arrival a disposable
phone will be waiting for you in a locker the key to which will be on
the plane with your instructions. Miss Verga will call you with further instruction when you arrive." Werner hung up the phone and
proceeded to arrange their flight.

'T' had answered the phone. "Ok, we're up. It's a hide and seek mission. We are to locate and follow someone for Miss Verga. We have
a charter flight out of Miami International." He said this as he hung
up the phone with Werner and shivered slightly. "It was that German

Security chief Werner who called. Man, I get the chills when I hear his voice. Something isn't right about that guy. He just seems off."

'J' looked up from where he sat playing 'Call of Duty'. "Yeah, I get the same icky feeling when he calls. Why call us to 'find' somebody?" he asked.

T' shrugged. "They must figure that we can find anybody. I would guess this guy has something they want. We get to work with Patrice again" he said looking directly at 'J'.

He looked up and smiled. "Ooooh what I would do to her, too bad she doesn't like men. Oh what a waste of fine ass" he said returning to his game "Shit., I forgot to pause it…some kid in Monterey got me..' he laughed suddenly 'ohhhh you did not just tea bag me…no…no…you did not just do that" he yelled into the microphone, before proceeding to re-spawn his character. "I'm coming. I hope you're ready." He said and got back into his game.

'M' was sitting in a recliner reading a book, when he looked up at 'J'. "You're just as bad, I've seen you do that. Hell, you did it to me last time we played."

'J' laughed "Well, that's because it's you. I mean who wouldn't tea bag you?"

'T' shook his head "We, leave here tomorrow at six a.m. I want to be on the plane by 7:30. If we get this job done quickly we'll be back by Friday afternoon." He said being ignored by both 'J' and 'M' who had just joined in the game. He looked at them both staring intently at the screen completely oblivious to his presence, shook his head and left to pack.

Chapter 27
Mounting Doubts

LATE AFTERNOON OF her first day on St. Vincent found Patrice lounging on the deck of her bungalow wrapped in a towel just out of the shower. Next to her lay the charter companies flight attendant Lisa also wrapped in a towel just out of the same shower. The fact that their shower had taken over an hour and used up an entire bottle of shampoo, it wasn't to conserve water.

During the flight, in spite of her hangover, Patrice had recovered sufficiently to notice the flight attendant Lisa, a college student taking a break from college to make some money to finish her degree in chemical engineering. One of her personal goals being to produce a non-carbon based bio-fuel. That however, was not what interested Patrice. On the contrary, Patrice was interested in Lisa, a farm girl from Boise Idaho with a body that a blind man would notice, barely 5'4" with waist length blonde hair and emerald green eyes. Patrice wasted no time getting to know her.

Well acquainted in the art of seduction, particularly the seduction of young women, Patrice soon had Lisa wrapped around her finger, literally. In fact the last hour and a half of the flight was spent with Lisa naked, lying on the couch wreathing in bliss as Patrice introduced her to the art of Lesbian sex, which extended to her hotel room, shower and now the deck of her bungalow on the bay.

While both Lisa and Patrice were sunning themselves a text message informed Patrice that the Trio had arrived on the island and were now using the disposable phone she'd left for them in the airport locker. Having already done her homework on the plane, prior to her seducing Lisa, she let them know roughly the location of each residence reminding them that all they were to do was locate, observe and inform her of their activities. She was careful to remind them to not be seen.

Acknowledging their instructions Patrice put her phone back on the table and looked over at Lisa who was relaxing in the warm afternoon sun. Only now her towel was open exposing her wonderfully taught body to Patrice as she looked up coyly in a non-verbal request that she was ready for more. Leaning over Patrice kissed the younger woman softly and whispered "I've ordered champagne and room service for us tonight. I hope you haven't got any place to be" she finished kissing her softly as a hand stroked her thigh working its way up her side and up where it gently cupped Lisa's left breast causing her to moan in anticipation of what the evening held in store.

"No I have until 9pm tomorrow" she said as she kissed Patrice back fully on the mouth.

Patrice broke their kiss and smiled at her "Actually, you aren't supposed to leave until I do. 9pm is my projected departure. The plane won't leave until I do' she paused to kiss Lisa long and hard 'besides I own the company you work for." She pressed her lips to Lisa's again. When the champagne arrived they placed the 'Do Not Disturb' sign on the door where it remained until noon the next day.

Patrice emerged the next day a little after noon dressed in a light, above the knee sundress that accented her curves nicely while wearing nothing underneath. She enjoyed the naughtiness of wearing next to nothing in public where the slightest breeze could easily expose her assets to the world. She had the body for it. The idea of being accidentally exposed in public thrilled her, knowing that few people would mind catching a glimpse of her Brazilian waxed charms. Lisa remained in bed asleep exhausted and content from their activity, which is where Patrice had asked her to remain until she got back from her morning excursion in a note left on the pillow.

The reason she had emerged was an envelope had been left for her at the front desk. In it were details of Beck's routine, which indicated that he lived on the island and wasn't' just there to retrieve gold. Something that concerned her, "Maybe the gold isn't here" she thought. That made her nervous knowing that her boss didn't take disappointment well, that and she was in effect on probation for her knowledge of Odessa and his control of it. Trying to keep her mind focused on the task at hand and not on getting killed she turned the page and found details on Archie Davis.

He also seemed to be living on the island in rather humble accommodations behind the church that now operated as a Maritime museum. The address of both the museum and residence were given. She hopped in a taxi cued up in front of the hotel and had the driver take her directly to the museum. Paying the taxi driver his fee and a tip she stepped onto the plaza and immediately saw the church. Initially it appeared to be a white stucco exterior with green mildew creeping up the sides. On closer inspection however, she realized that the structure itself was masonry in which coral was used as the brickwork.

The finish of the rough coating was whitewashed giving the exterior a stucco-like appearance. Otherwise it was a typical protestant church with a steeple complete with bell tower. The roof was made of red tiles like those found in the Virgin Islands. A styling cue from Dutch influence found throughout the Caribbean. It wasn't an unpleasant looking building but it seemed out of time with the newer commercial buildings around it. Clearly this was one of the oldest buildings on this island, though the island itself was less than 100 years old and manmade.

Walking around the perimeter of the church she found an 8' tall wooden fence that kept prying eyes from the courtyard between the church and the Vickers residence. A sign outside the gate found in the ally read "Vickers Residence-Do not disturb. Enter on invitation only or be fined $500.00 for trespassing. Thank You." Not exactly a warm welcome for a man of the cloth Patrice thought, but then Archie Davis she knew wasn't an officially ordained minister.

The fence itself was heavy and recently updated and clearly designed to keep someone from scaling it and getting over. An angled peak jutted out at 45' from the fence pointing out making getting over the wall more challenging. What she couldn't see was the barbed wire fencing that protruded inward to keep a persistent thief or nosey neighbor from wanting to go further. So far nobody had attempted the fence. If they had nobody had succeeded in getting over it. The residence itself was not visible except for the red tile roof, which matched the churches. She imagined that since the house was built at the same time as the church was also made of coral masonry. From what she saw it appeared a comfortable place, if not large.

Patrice sat on the park bench and continued reading the report. According to their observations a third man was seen entering the museum presumably as a tourist but was seen speaking to and leaving with Davis heading to his residence behind the church. The unidentified man was seen leaving two hours later from the side gate and followed to his jeep. Not being on the watch and follow list he was left alone; it was noted that his jeep was seen leaving town headed toward the island interior. She made a mental note to keep an eye out for the third fellow but did not believe him to be important.

Reading further the Trio had recognized two low-level 'Operation' thugs following Davis minutes after the third man left. Their photos were in the packet. She recognized them immediately. Dutch skinheads, dumb as dirt, brutal and without fear of consequences. She had used them once on a minor collection matter. After collecting the amount due they proceeded to beat the man to death along with his grandchildren, wife and daughter. The youngest killed was six months old.

When she took issue with their inexcusable brutality she had been rebuffed by Krupp. "Patrice, they were doing their job" he said. "The spectacle will send a message that late payments will not be tolerated. I doubt that we will have any further collections problems from here on." He then dismissed her leaving her feeling violated. Her loyalty to the Operation gone, not that she had a choice.

She had not been told that the operation had sent anyone else. Apparently her status in the Operation had taken a deeper hit than she realized. Not only that, but the skinheads brutality, knowing their methods, would likely draw in the Coast Guard and delay recovery efforts, if her theory of the bullion repository proved true. Finding that repository was the only thing that could possibly regain her status and save her life. However, down deep she realized that her days were numbered because she had been smarter than they were; a bunch of old male chauvinist Nazi bastards. Those remaining were so old that they were getting dementia, including her boss.

Being nearly 100, if she were to guess, he was not long for this world in spite of the gene and testosterone therapy. Therapy had slowed the progression of his dementia to some degree; it may have even extended his life span by a few years. Once dementia took hold it was simply a matter of time before the mind deteriorated beyond its ability to function and maintain life. He had perhaps two or three years of conscious function left before he deteriorated to a semi vegetative state. Until their last meeting she had expected to take over the reins of the Operation when he died. Now, she would be happy if they let her live but something in the back of her mind told her that she was hoping for too much.

Her best chance to buy herself time was to find the bullion. That required that Beck and Davis be left alone. With the skinheads there, they would not be. Chances were that they would try to beat the location out of them then kill them. The Coast Guard and ATF would have to investigate it as a possible cartel murder. If that happened the repository might be discovered, seized and forever put out of reach.

Placing the file in her purse she grabbed her phone and began texting the Trio leader.

Do you have eyes on skinheads? She asked.

'Yes, they appear to be ready to pounce on the old man. I don't like it' was the reply.

They must not get their hands on either of them. She replied.

'*Orders?*' was the reply.

Take them out quietly and dump the bodies in the ocean! she hit send, cleared all the texts and put the phone away. In case she was compromised and somehow arrested she didn't want these incriminating texts on her phone. She then instructed the Trio to do the same in the event things did go south on them.

Chapter 28
A Bitter End

1945

IN APRIL 1945 blimps were concentrated around the Panama Canal. With the end of the war approaching the brass were concerned about revenge attacks by submarines and secret weapons being used to destroy the Panama Canal. Theories being that the Nazis were prepared to assist the Japanese in any way they could to ensure Japanese victory and hopefully a negotiated reestablishment of their own government in return. No such threat ever existed but in the imaginations of the nearly victorious Allies seeking out possible threats to their hard won victory. As it was U-boats were no longer a threat and those they spotted were eager to surrender. Most often the crews were already in lifeboats with white flags raised and pulling away from their submarine to keep from getting bombed, strafed or torpedoed or all three at once.

Barely a week had passed since their arrival to St. Vincent after a harrowing journey past blimp patrols and destroyer pickets along the eastern seaboard of the United States. Once again they were heading to sea, this time to Argentina. Buenos Aires to be exact where they had confirmed a meeting with the president of Argentina so that General Dietrich could somehow persuade them to enter the war for Germany. It would be foolish for Argentina to enter the war, especially since the United States was on a War footing and fully equipped and ready to fight a war. Argentina was in no such state and if they were foolish enough to side with Germany in open warfare it would be a matter of weeks before Argentina fell.

The whole business had a bad smell to it. Nothing felt right about the rationale being used to justify the mission and the meeting. General Dietrich knew better than to say what he was thinking out loud. In all honesty his fear was near pathologic now. The voice inside his head was screaming "You are going to die!!" over and over so that he was barely able to keep his bladder control from fear of the gallows awaiting him if he were taken alive. Fear that he'd caused with his own brutality, brutality he once thought necessary to win. He knew that Germany had limited resources and that quick, decisive victories had to be vicious in order to shock the enemy and then take advantage of that shock.

All security measures were taken to ensure that they were not detected, especially with the French Government using American Blimps to patrol coastal waters off South America. The voyage would be less dangerous since most of the blimp activity was far to the north. Yet they chose to hug the coastline by night and hide in the mangrove swamps by day as added precaution against detection. The submarine was slow and drafted deep so they had few places deep enough to hide a boat that big.

In areas where the population was too dense or the water not quite deep enough, they would dive the boat and cruise submerged for as long as their batteries would hold out. Then if the batteries gave out too soon they'd set the boat on the bottom until dark then run on the surface charging batteries as they went. Still it was a dangerous voyage to undertake with little to gain for the exposure. Regardless of the outcome they were under orders to make the effort.

Kurt Heinz had come along as a translator being that he was fluent in Spanish, nobody had guessed or knew that he was a native of Argentina. The General wanted him to come along so Heinz agreed, eager to be home. This was a mission to persuade a neutral nation to enter a war that was already lost. Peron wasn't about to so something that stupid.

Kurt Heinz was not captain on this voyage he was along simply as a translator. However, he knew that Peron spoke German and English well enough that he was really not required, but was asked to come along for the sake of protocol. It was a perfect opportunity for him because his intention was to resign his commission at the Legation legally and officially. He would then take a legation car and drive to the Ranch 300 miles west. Kurt was careful not to share with anyone the location of his home in the outback. As far as anyone knew his home was Linz Germany. The General would have him shot or hung if he learned of his plans and thus he kept his plans quiet.

It took nearly a week before the submarine was tied up in Buenos Aires. The moonless night allowed them to off load the car and personnel in secret. Several legation cars were waiting to drive them down a tunnel that emptied into the legation parking structure allowing legation personnel to leave the embassy grounds unseen. It had become necessary in recent months with the news of the death camps surfacing. What the General did not know was to what extent the public of Argentina had turned against Germany, or rather the Nazis.

When the Ambassador to the legation informed the General of the general mood of the people regarding the Nazis he was dismissive and fully intent on displaying the Swastika as he paraded his delegation on his way to the capitol. Upon the delegations departure from the legation gate, Kurt Heinz quietly slipped away to the bathroom and remained hidden away until the delegation departed for their meeting with the President of Argentina.

His letter of resignation was on the legation secretary's desk with his bag packed. As the gates closed behind the last truck of the diplomatic mission, he stepped out the back door of the legation his lawful, discharge from active service in his valise and the keys to a new Mercedes sedan in his hands. He hadn't seen fit to announce the fact that he was leaving, he just did. In fact the car was packed and waiting.

The car had very few miles on the odometer less than 1000 miles when he put the key in the ignition. Taking the tunnel he headed to the pier head and emerged from the tunnel in broad daylight. At the submarine he enlisted the help of two ratings to off load two crates from the hold which were then placed in the trunk of his car on the pretense that the boxes were needed by the General. Saluting the men he then waited for them to return below decks before he left.

Turning the car onto the nearest street he made his way to the far side of Buenos Aires and out into the countryside. In less than an hour he was on one of the few paved roadways in Argentina. It was a minor copy of the Autobahn in Germany, a joint German-Argentine effort to promote an alliance between the two nations. Once on the roadway Kurt Heinz hit the accelerator to 100km/hr and made it home in less than 6 hours.

The early autumn of Argentina was beginning as the sun set behind the Andes. Pulling up to the gate to his family's ranch he stopped to take in the beauty. He was home. His father would be sitting down to dinner. The house was lit up and easily seen in the distance. Gunning the engine he drove along the winding drive attracting the attention of two of the older Gaucho's he soon recognized as boyhood friends. He drove up to the porch and got out as his father came stumbling out with his cane, having been informed that a car was coming. His father nearly fell over in shock to see his son walking up the steps. "Father I am home". His father wept in joy that his son was home safe. For Kurt the war was over.

Less than an hour after Kurt left for home the delegation returned under armed escort by Argentine military. The General got out of his car now bespattered with rock chips, dog excrement and all manner of fruit and vegetable residue having been pelted by the public for a nearly three mile journey to the Capitol and back.

Where upon his meeting with President Peron when he stated his hope to have Argentina engage the United States in open war in support of Germany, was met with a gruff rebuttal "General the News Reels are showing what Hitler has done to the Jewish people. The people of Argentina have not taken this lightly. Only today, reports of as many as six million Jews were gassed and burned in ovens have reached us. The Argentine people in shame of our close ties with Hitler's Germany have covered what few Jewish Temples we have in Argentina, in flowers in sympathy.

Joining Germany at this time in war will not be tolerated and would be suicidal. We have agreed to allow your comrades here out of our history with you. But as of today Nazis are not to parade themselves openly on the streets or declare their politics openly, anywhere." The president then turned his back on the general and returned to his offices leaving the military to escort them back to the legation.

The Warning from the General of police was plain enough. They were to hole up in the legation for the duration of the war. Weekly deliveries of supplies would be made to ensure they were not starved. But legation personnel were to remain on the legation grounds for their own safety. With that the General ordered an evacuation of the legation and prepared to take them all home.

When they'd transferred the legation personnel to the ship bound for Spain, General Dietrich noticed that Captain Heinz was no longer among them. His rage was extreme though he kept his outward appearance of calm authority on the surface. Hans noticed the glazed look in his eye as did several other men who were well acquainted with high ranking Nazis. It seemed that in order to become a Nazi one had to first lose their mind and become a raving lunatic. In the Generals case he seemed to fit that mold perfectly.

A chill descended on the island the moment the submarine arrived back to base. The general ordered the base cleaned up. It was already spotless but the crews were put to work cleaning up anyway. The general remained in the mansion sitting by the radio listening to James Joyce better known as Lord Haw Haw to the Allies and to Goebbels insanity in vain hope that some divine miracle would turn the tide of war back in their favor.

In desperation to hear the *truth* the General took to listening to the BBC and CBS radio broadcasts. For days he'd sit by the radio set and listen to the news as the Allies closed on Berlin. In late April it happened, Hitler was dead. Germany reported that he had died fighting his way out of the bunker. The BBC reported later that he had committed suicide and his body burned in a ditch outside the bunker alongside his longtime companion Eva Braun.

The Allies reports were more consistent and therefore he took them to be more accurate. German broadcasts were frantic, insane and panicked with calls for Germany to destroy itself so that nothing remained for the allies to occupy followed by the last broadcast of Lord Haw Haw who was drunk and clearly resigned to his fate.

The day that Germany surrendered Karl Donitz called for the submarines at sea to surface and surrender was the day that the General turned off the radio for the last time. His hope was gone. He hadn't shaved since arriving back from Argentina. His haggard face clearly showed signs of a defeated, hopeless man whose life was about to end. The manner of death had not been determined however. Rain beat against his windows as a storm passed over the island. But he did not see it, hear it or feel it. The general had gone into a near catatonic state where he remained for nearly a week, rising only to go to his bed where he slept for another week.

The day he emerged again the General was apparently back to his old self, a darker version as it would turn out. He had decided on a course of action and was about to make his decision known to this troops. He was going to commit suicide and they were going to die with him. It had not dawned on him that this course of action would 'not' be met with enthusiasm. Neither had it dawned on him that the men under 'his' command would want to dishonor themselves by taking any of the gold meant for Hitler's American Front.

Only as he approached the submarines where he planned to make this announcement he heard a young rating making plans to load several crates of gold onto one of the trawlers used for dredging the channel and head to Brazil. To his horror the men he was talking to were in ready agreement and were apparently already making plans to do the very same.

He had the entire Kriegsmarine complement immediately arrested and chained to a barge used to move heavy equipment around the facility. Hans heard what he'd planned and reported to Fredderick who instantly went about seeking out diving equipment to disperse among the men in the hopes of saving them. The General then took up station on the prow of the Black Submarine and began admonishing the crew for their treachery. "We must all die for the Fuhrer' he said, 'some of us against our will but we must die to protect this secret and the legacy of Adolf Hitler. One day this base will be discovered and our legacy will be that we and we alone stood with our beloved Fuhrer dying with him...for him" he openly wept stifling a sob as he nodded to one of his lieutenants who then disappeared below deck of the barge and opened a scuttle port.

The whistling of air rushing out of the hatch was deafening. One rating began tugging at his chains and screamed "I have children to care for you lunatic!! How will I care for them dead? You Nazis are a disease!!! It was you and your vile, wretched stupidity that cost Germany the war...this sort of insanity...you people destroyed Germany!!! My last breath General I shall spit at you...in death I leave you in a curse...and hope that hell awaits your murderous soul!!!!" With that the rest of the crew began fighting their chains. But all too soon the deed was done.

Fredderick however was already under water working on releasing them, even before the barge hit the bottom. Only, to his dismay the breathing devices weren't all working and one by one the men he was trying to save died, all but 8. They each remained under the water watching as the General ranted and raved. "Men, we must sacrifice our lives for Hitler. He has died and Germany has died with him. We SS mustn't survive the Fuhrer. He was our reason for being our leader our father. Follow me now… and let us join our beloved Fuhrer in Valhalla. Hiel Hitler!!" The salute was returned vigorously and with psychotic enthusiasm. Hans played along. His world had just turned surreal, again.

One by one the SS officers followed the General onto the submarine and took up station in the con where the General passed out cyanide, saluting each man as they each took their vile. The General then lead them into the berthing area forward and one by one they each ceremoniously and stoically entered their 'tomb'.

Hans noted that several others were apparently playing along but not quite in the 'mood' to participate, yet were too weak kneed to say no. How many of his colleagues had gone along with the rest simply because they were to 'weak' to say no? How many atrocities were committed by otherwise decent people because one of these, these… creatures of the abyss pushed them to? Now here they were…being forced to commit suicide for the Fuhrer with all this gold bullion for the taking, more than enough for each man to live out his life quite well and then some but which was going to go to waste for the sake of one psychopathic man's cowardice to face the world without his beloved Fuhrer.

Lying on his bunk he lay there with a vile of cyanide in his pocket waiting. Silence filled the submarine as each man took in his last moments on earth. In the distance the General in all his psychotic glory cried Hiel Hitler!!! followed by a barely audible 'crunch' of glass an act which was repeated one, by one by one…until the man above him crunched his vile. Following each crunch came the gurgling sound of men dying, two men likely the two he'd felt weren't 100% into this madness were foolish enough to crunch the vile but then tried to spit it out after the fact. "Not very brilliant apparently' Hans thought. 'If you were dumb enough to bite the damn thing you deserve to die.' he frowned listening to them all die 'Fucking lunatics'".

The choking gags of cyanide poisoned men filled the cramped spaces…then there was the unexpected side effect, the releasing of their bowels and bladders. The sound of which was nearly as disturbing as listening to them dying. Tossing the cyanide capsule into the sink he smashed it with a paper weight and then rinsed it down the drain glass and all. Covering his face with a kerchief he stepped out into the passage. Each man was twitching and emptying his bowels with each post mortem convulsion.

Moans and groans from air escaping lungs made for a horrific display as well as the oozy sounds and smells that were now growing more intense. Walking into the generals cabin Hans watched him twitch and roll as each muscle clinging to the last vestiges of life let go. The general ceased moving in a matter of minutes. Backing out and away Hans looked into each cabin and watched as each man twitched and moaned. One man sat up and screamed, rolled over… then fell down onto his face, as his limbs reached for anything it could grab onto. That was the last straw. Hans had nearly wet himself with that display. Covering his face with the kerchief he took his pistol and put a bullet into each of the men to ensure that they were dead.

Outside Fredderick tended to the men he'd saved and heard the muffled gun fire inside the sub. One shot followed by another every few seconds. 'Hans was making sure of them' he thought. 13 shots in all after which his friend climbed out of the hatch and closed it again. By the pallor of his friends complexion he could tell he was not well. This was made even more apparent when he fell to his knees and released his guts over the side of the submarine, retching violently until there was nothing left to bring up.

Once his friend was done he walked up behind him placing a hand on his shoulder "I don't know about you but I could use some air" he said. Standing together they both surveyed the scene around them. Nothing that met their eyes suggested the brutality that had just taken place. Both knew too well that what they had just witnessed would remain etched into their memories forever more. Hans spoke one word into the emptiness as his senses returned "Insanity" and he shook his head as if to wipe the vision of those dying men from his memory. A tug at his elbow urged him away from the scene and he took a seat in the K wagon numb from what he had just experienced. The rest of the men, equally numb and shivering climbed onto the K wagon as Freddy pulled away. There was no need to hurry as they drove up the ramp and into the long dark tunnel. No words were spoken as each man dealt with their recent brush with death.

Then without warning a roar of an engine echoed in the tunnel as the G4 sedan raced up the tunnel and bore down on them. Before they could figure out what was going on…machine pistols opened up on them killing 4 men almost instantly. They fell from the K wagon and were rolled over by the G4s massive tires. If they weren't dead when they hit the ground they were then. Freddy hit the gas and the K wagon lurched forward but not enough to pull away from the G4 now bumping their car knocking two more men down and who were also run over by the massive Mercedes.

Two more men fell to the gunfire…the loss of their mass allowed the Kwagon to pull away from the Mercedes. Once clear of the tunnel

Freddy said to Hans "Jump clear when we round the bend". Hans nodded thinking that his friend was going to do the same. "Take the gun and finish these assholes…" Freddy screamed over the engine. Once they rounded the bend Hans leaped behind a bush. Freddy did not jump but accelerated the K wagon just as the Mercedes came roaring out of the tunnel.

Freddy was a good ways ahead now and racing ahead of the G4 which had to slow to a near stop in order to make the turn. Hans then jumped onto the bumper and held tight as they hit the straight. Massive torque pulled the Mercedes along. Gun fire was sporadic as they couldn't get a shot. After crossing the meadow the G4 began to slow and then stop. The three men got out of the car and Hans leaped behind a bush and looked forward. Freddy was lying face down in the road and the K wagon was on its side. He had crashed. Apparently he had caught the wheel of the VW in a rut and with his speed to propel him along, launched the K wagon into a tree, spinning it so that it landed onto its side throwing Freddy from the driver's seat.

Hans saw his friend lying in the dirt apparently unconscious lying face down and spread eagle. The Mercedes pulled up to him and stopped. Three men, enlisted personnel, sergeants by their rank badges sauntered arrogantly to the prone figure in the dirt and stood around him laughing.

"Is he dead?" the shortest one asked.

"Not yet" the tallest one said as he stepped up putting the barrel of his gun to the back of Freddericks head and pulled the trigger. Hans brought his own gun to bear too late and emptied his clip into all three of the men standing around Freddy. They were dead before they had time to realize it. Checking the bodies of the three men to make sure they were dead and not faking it, he then checked out Freddy in vain hope that he was still alive. His hope was dashed when he saw the gaping hole in his friends head…its grizzly exit which took out his left eye. Hans was too numb to feel anything in that moment. He was in soldier mode, a survival technique most men adopt when faced with ever present death. But he could not deny the sense of loss of his friend, the one remaining vestige of his life before the war. He was now alone in the world, but he would not allow himself to feel it, not yet.

One by one he dragged the bodies of the three enlisted men to the tall grass next to a pile of shells and left them there. He wouldn't bother burying them…they could rot. Freddy he put into the back of the G4 and drove him up the mountain, numb and disbelieving. On top of the mountain Hans mechanically dug a grave for his friend. Had he not developed the ability to detach himself he would have, like many, gone mad with grief.

This time was different. The war was over and his one remaining childhood friend had just been killed… murdered. The feeling was altogether different and far too great to contain. His hands were shaking as he dug the grave but it was the digging that kept his growing grief at bay, if only for the moment. Once deep enough he put his friend in the grave wrapped in a canvas tarp then covered him up one shovel full of sand at a time. Hans stood over the Marker he'd made for his friends grave and considered his friend for a long, long moment as his nerves began to let go.

Falling to his knees he felt the same way he had when his family had been killed, only this was so much worse, he was now totally alone in the world. No more family remained his last best friend was lying at his feet. He broke down and sobbed like a child at the loss of his best friend, his family, Gunther and all the other men he had watched die.

That evening Hans entered his cabin on the plateau and collapsed onto the bed and slept for several days. Sleep had done wonders for his mental state allowing him to plan his return to Europe and hopefully the Chalet in the Swiss Alps. He still had 6 months' left on his prepaid rent and several kilos of coffee in his pantry and housemaids to hire. The idea of making his own plans for a change made the rest of his stay on the island much more livable in spite of what had happened there.

Three weeks later Hans sold the trawler in Brazil and bought passage to Spain on a Portuguese freighter. Since he was heading toward Europe and not away from it his ship was not stopped by Allied naval patrols and searched. The allies were searching for escaping war criminals attempting to flee justice. His heading toward Europe was and effective tactic against being sought. Though he had no reason to believe he was actually 'wanted', he wasn't about to test the theory by turning himself in.

An early autumn wind was blowing across the Alps as Hans Beck, former SS Standartenfurher and veteran of the Winter War pulled up to his Swiss chalet in a bright red Mercedes 540K, the very one he'd had his eyes on. The two housemaids he'd hired were waiting for him at the door scantily clad and smiling at their generous employer with a cup of freshly brewed, properly creamed and sugared coffee.

The war in Europe had been over for five months but his war was just ending. He'd had enough of war as soldiers who experienced it so often do. It is an understanding and wisdom that comes with having your soul ripped apart, a wound for which there is no balm, a wound from which there is no true healing. His being alive was a victory in itself and he was going to live his life to its fullest for those who had not survived, for his father, mother and brother. He would live for them. Entering the house a smile broke upon his face as the two housemaids Brauna and Anna were standing before the fire, naked and waiting. "I could get used to this" he thought and led them to the ladder and up to the loft where they spent the afternoon in blissful distraction.

Chapter 29
The home front

LAURIE WAS BUSY at her computer catching up on projects she'd let slide having caught up on her sex life with Greg over the past week. Torn between relief at having time to catch up on projects and missing Greg she struggled to concentrate on her work often finding herself staring out the window wondering when he would be back and wonder if her husband was up to something. A few days earlier her husband extended his vacation to take care of an old man who'd been mugged. Wasn't that what hospitals were for? Why all of a sudden is he such a humanitarian offering to care for a man he didn't know? To be honest the only reason it bothered her was that Greg wasn't there to keep her mind and body occupied.

When Rick left on vacation the kids spent the long weekend with Grandma, leaving her three solid days of one on one with Greg, her mother's estate attorney and economic advisor. They'd spent nearly every waking minute making love in every position imaginable. Greg loosened her inhibitions like no one else ever had. For several carefree days Laurie was as wild and energetic as she'd been in college, even more so. She was no longer ashamed to let everyone in earshot know what she was feeling, which surprised her when she first howled her uninhibited passions out her mother's bedroom window. What shocked her even more was that she didn't care if anyone heard her.

This particular change began the day she and Greg consummated their relationship in her mother's bed. She had never been with anyone who had unleashed her inhibitions so completely. The naughtiness of it was immensely satisfying, especially when they both became aggressive and forceful. Something she was learning to like, a lot.

At first his size had taken her by surprise, in a good way. Since then, every time they were alone and in the throes of passion she was expressive and vocal. In fact she'd never had such wonderful orgasms in her life, the result of years of suppressed sexual tension being released into a newly discovered and passionate universe.

Though she had initiated the affair discretely, as most affairs tend to begin, she had been caught in the act when she somehow dialed the home phone giving her husband an earful. Instead of getting upset he had suggested that she continue the affair if it made her happy. A reaction that left her perplexed, turned on and nervous. Most men would have flipped out and become an unreasonable wreck of human emotion. In fact since her affair began their relationship had warmed considerably. He even started acting like a friend. Strange how something that would normally tear a couple apart could be the very thing that brought them closer.

Still, it was early and her husband was moody and likely in shock at having discovered her affair. She refrained from asking to get this permission in writing, but the idea that she had been caught red handed then allowed to continue with it was something to ponder. Yet, she didn't know whether or not to consider herself lucky or totally screwed, both figuratively and literally. That thought brought a wry smile to her lips.

Before taking the plunge into a sexual affair she had put on a façade of a typical, American housewife, a moral, upstanding, conservative wife and mother. All of which she had been, until the financial stress and strain pushed her to the limit; forcing her to act out of self-preservation. She had resented Rick for his lack of enthusiasm and for giving up on himself and the world. To her he seemed not to tolerate the daily grind expected of a businessman. He seemed a naïve simpleton when it came to playing the game, with an overly simplified expectation that doing a good job for ones patients meant you should be paid...end of story. In a perfect world that might have been true, but the realities were that the insurance industry didn't have to play by the rules, and would often change them to suit their ends. Frustration and anger were typical side effects of the grind. There were times she expected him to become a homicidal maniac.

She played the game well and was able to navigate the system. Rick on the other hand found having to convince a person, who was clearly being paid to deny his claim, *why* he should be paid tedious. It was part of the game and Rick didn't want to play. He wasn't greedy, unethical or in any way morally challenged, he was a guy who wanted to help people. He never could understand why it was so hard to exist when trying to do the right thing, when the morally corrupt seemed to have everything handed to them. A petty sentiment but the truth behind it irked him to no end.

Anger and bitter resentment had altered her husband. He was no longer the fit, trim and happy sailor she had once known. No, he seemed beaten and unwilling to fight against the world that had trampled him. The day she decided to have an affair was the day she had pushed his most sensitive buttons to see if he would rise to it but he just looked at her with his defeated gaze. Only this time there was no spark of defiance left. It was a dull, flat 'I'm done' gaze that forced her hand. She saw in him a broken, defeated man she could no longer respect. That day she focused her amorous attention elsewhere, the very day she and Greg decided to get physically involved.

Sitting up she was angry with her husband for not getting upset with her. He could have at least shown some jealousy, why didn't he just get angry like he usually did? Had he given up on her as well? That thought didn't sit well, not even a little. To think that she was no longer important to him pissed her off while she was grateful for the freedom he had given her. Confusion wasn't quite the right word for what she was feeling but it was the closest thing she could use to describe what she felt.

Looking at her children, she wondered if he had given up on them to. No, if there was anything he did care about it was his kids. Which made her think he didn't want to upset them or embarrass her in front of them. So to keep the peace he decided to let things be. That final self-induced explanation was enough to calm her momentary anger at her husband while fueling her desire to keep seeing Greg.

Getting up Laurie decided to take a shower then see if she could get Greg on the phone. It had been barely 24 hours since they'd last been physically together and she wanted him again..bad. 'How long would he be gone?' She wondered. That thought got her thinking of trying her hand at phone sex. A new twist she thought closing the door to her room and locking it while dialing Greg's phone.

At that moment Greg was on a private charter jet heading for St.

Vincent. He was most certainly not impressed with his destination. It appeared to be an imitation of a Polynesian resort, a poorly executed imitation at that. He'd heard of it being used long ago as a drug transfer point that devolved into a pirate haven that devolved even further into a lawless colony of criminals that the Coast Guard had cleared out.

After the bad elements were gone locals turned to tourism for support and appeared to be doing well as a low cost resort that catered to blue collar union workers and their wives, a demographic that tended to be on the heavier side due to their Midwestern diets and beer consumption. Even the brochure had a picture of a hefty woman in a single piece suit, eating a corndog with her flab spilling out in places the suit couldn't keep tucked away. Shaking his head he put the brochure down, trying not to vomit, "Sweet Lord!!" he exclaimed.

ºSlamming his bourbon he ordered another and pulled out his brief case and read the letter the old man had sent while attempting to put a face to the voice on the phone. The old man was willing to pay a retainer of $50,000 dollars just to show up and his fee would depend on how much money was involved and the complications associated with moving it. Trouble was the Old man, at least he sounded old over the phone, had been tight lipped about the job he wanted done. All he knew at this point was that a sum of money needed to be quietly and discretely moved to be inherited by an undisclosed person, the name of whom would be discussed upon his arrival. Based on the $50,000 retainer a hefty sum awaited his talents.

Greg's talents as an attorney were that of asset protection and the transfer of assets to dummy accounts to keep the IRS and other government agencies out of his clients pocket. One of his most successful methods was to create a false inheritance where he would make it appear as if money had been kept in a secret account where the inheritance had been denied to the immediate relatives in accordance with the deceased wishes.

The less he said regarding the reasons for this denied inheritance the better. Imagination and speculation were always the best sources of plausible excuses, especially when none was given officially. Then through a series of clever computer maneuvers he could create the criteria necessary for his client to inherit a fortune from some distant, long dead relative.

However, it only worked if the client wasn't wanted by the FBI, DEA or ATF or by some other governmental law enforcement agency. Most of his clients wanted to avoid the attention of the IRS. High profile persons like Donald Trump or President Clinton or any such person who was obviously wealthy and well known who all of a sudden inherited a vast fortune from an ancient bloodline would automatically raise eyebrows. This particular ruse worked best if the person was not well known and certainly not a public figure prone to over the top displays like Trump or people who were just so well known that nothing in their life was private anymore. If any of his clients were celebrities, particularly well-known celebrities public scrutiny of the transactions and a careful, investigation of the records would show that the accounts were faked.

His ideal clients were private, reclusive types who would not make a spectacle of their new wealth and disappear quietly. Smart drug lords were his most frequent user of this particular service and they were most often eager to avoid any type of recognition. They were never heard of, seen or even wanted most of the time.

They tended to pull the strings through other more visible 'peons'. Usually peasants whose families they took hostage for the duration of whatever job they needed done. Particularly ruthless they knew how to keep their hands clean if not innocent. No less dangerous than the more visible 'ego' driven cartel members, they tended to live quietly in distant countries, far enough away to escape suspicion but close enough to deal with problems if needed, generally through a third party who would act on their behalf never knowing just who it was they were working for. Leaving them alive to be of use later and left with the warning that if they spoke to anyone, they would watch their family die before being killed themselves. This was how they kept from being noticed. Seldom did they ever have to carry out their threat.

The ones who made the news were idiots who made a public spectacle of their brutality, which got them noticed, getting noticed got them arrested. These were the drug lords who killed en masse, leaving 30, 40 or 50 bodies lying in the desert sun for the authorities to find in various forms of mutilation. Beheadings were most common and frequent because of the visual horror it created, often with the heads on a pike next to the body.

Sometimes bodies would be found with what is called a Columbian necktie where the victim's throat is cut and the tongue pulled through the hole to hang like a neck tie and left to be found in order for the spectacle to be noticed. These were persons with whom Greg would have no dealings.

If he knew who they were he didn't do business with them it was that simple. However, that did not mean that he could put his guard down. As mentioned before the smart drug lords tended to be extremely dangerous. If you screwed up you disappeared so that not even your body was found. So he kept the association with these types of individuals at arms-length and did not pry into their lives nor did he try to get to know them. If he could avoid it he never saw their faces, nor did they see his. He did what was required which was to create a false lineage, or a legend for them to inherit a large sum that he would then transport to a Swiss account transfer it to gold bearer bonds. Ship the bonds to a bank in the nation from which the inheritance was to originate, deposit the bonds in a safety deposit box in a high security bank that specialized in old accounts.

Greg Mitchell had no less than ten such banks with which he did business. Money came in and out of these vaults all the time. So he was able to establish through contacts a place where the funds could be transferred discretely if he needed to come up with an old account. Many of the oldest accounts in these banks where hundreds of years old. Many boxes were empty and the lineage of the persons who owned these boxes had long ago died off leaving the accounts untended for decades and decades. He would then take them over and pay the required maintenance fees and use them as his clients needed. It was easy enough to create an old account if one wasn't available.

It was from these old unused and defunct vaults that he would link to the new identity of his client. They would then be put in contact with the bank manager who would then verify their lineage that Greg had created for them. Sometimes all they needed was a key and a pass code to access the funds and fade away, but it was better in the long run for them to have a solid legacy to account for the origin of the funds, especially if they had no criminal record or dubious reputation to hide from.

In order to keep business solid Greg had rules that he operated by.

One of his rules was never to ask how the money came to be, the less he knew the better. Another rule was that he used only the name they wanted used in the inheritance. They would communicate to him only using that name and if ever they let slip their true identity their association was terminated, which he made clear from the beginning.

The smart ones never wanted their true identity known and took steps to prevent it. The ones who would 'accidentally' drop their name were the idiots who ended up on the most wanted lists and who tended to bring everybody down with them in a messy, media circus that they apparently thrived on, something Greg diligently avoided.

As an added measure his illicit clients would never know his true identity nor would they see his face. If they insisted on meeting face to face their association was over. He had learned early on that these insistent types were more often than not, the very clients he wished to avoid. Generally if they wanted to meet their 'banker' it was to show off their brutality as a means of intimidation and control.

It was because of those clients that he would communicate with them exclusively through an email on a server housed in Mexico and never in person. That was to ensure mutual safety so that if he decided to terminate their association he could just walk away without fear of retaliation. It also created a means of denying that he had any knowledge of such persons.

Any such association would destroy his legitimate cover business as an asset protection attorney in LA. Though lucrative, it wasn't nearly as lucrative as his dealings in illicit money handling, which of course he never paid taxes on, though he was paid in full on his legitimate business in LA. He endeavored to avoid being on the

IRS list when he could avoid it. Though he did pay his taxes late on occasion just for appearances, to make sure that he wasn't 'that' squeaky clean. To be too clean was to raise a red flag for the more astute members of the IRS fraud investigation teams.

In conducting business bank transfers were numbered and never named for obvious reasons. The created accounts of course required names, but that was a separate issue from conducting business. To avoid direct contact he had an account through which payments for his services were transferred.

Once the funds were present he would immediately transfer funds to a dummy account from where the money was cashed out in the form of an untraceable bearer bond. It would then be physically taken via private courier to a bank in Europe where it was deposited and again transferred to his personal numbered account.

Large sums were transferred in small amounts and spread over months to different accounts. He had three separate permanent accounts on different continents and hundreds of temporary, dummy accounts. Of course he had a Swiss account, a British account, which he kept small because the Brits were cooperative with the USA and one in Siberia where he kept the bulk of his private wealth. Nobody, not even the Russians paid attention to Siberia. As it was he held nearly 800,000.000 in the Siberian account and was creating another in Beijing from where he planned to transfer it to Australia where he would retire. With luck he'd steal Laurie away from her marriage and take her with him his reasoning being that money heals all wounds.

He'd fallen for Laurie the day they met. She was so beautiful. He remembered seeing her husband and wondering how he could have ever landed her much less keep her satisfied. Then he reminded himself that he was the one keeping her 'satisfied' at the moment, smiling with self-satisfaction.

He felt genuine love for her so he wasn't being a dirt bag, not to his mind at least. To him love erased all negatives. It was doubtful he would find many to agree with that sentiment, but he wasn't going to advertise the fact that he was in love with a married woman. Scandals were never good for business and he didn't want her to suffer any embarrassment if he could help it. "Fuck it" he said out loud and put up his brief case.

Leaning back in his seat he looked out the window he let his mind drift to Laurie and the day they'd met. The moment he laid eyes on her he had fallen in love, to be more accurate he fell in lust. She was smart and witty not to mention hot. They began talking about her mother's estate and meeting for lunch with her mother at first, later without her mother which led to things getting friendlier. Though she seemed content with flirtation initially he got the impression that she wanted to take it further but did not let it show.

He struggled to keep his attraction on that level until the day they had gone to her mother's house to take inventory of her estate prior to selling the house. She had dressed in a mini skirt, an extreme mini skirt, a loose blouse and a set of 'come-fuck-me' pumps that really set off her muscular legs. He had a hard time keeping his eyes off her when she bent over to pick up a box or something low. And she seemed to be deliberately pointing her ass right at him when she did so exposing the lacy thong underneath, the sight of which made walking difficult.

All morning he struggled to keep his eyes and hands off, particularly since her mother was present. It would have been rather awkward had he suddenly walked up to her daughter and grabbed a handful of ass. Ohhhhh but how he wanted to.

When her mother left the garage he decided to make his move. Laurie was preoccupied with making a list of the items they'd inventoried. Taking this chance to expand their flirtation to something more he walked over to her reached for a box immediately over the washer and pulled it down. He made it appear that he had accidentally brushed against her. Only he didn't pull away as he moved the box to the side.

Laurie gasped in surprise then pushed herself against him instead of moving away. Placing a hand on her waist seemed to be the signal because she turned to look into his eyes while pressing herself harder still against his groin. The fire in her eyes was not anger but unadulterated lust and passion. She turned to see if her mother was around then raised her skirt exposing her lovely ass cheeks to him and ground her bare cheeks hard against him. It was on! He could barely remember the brief interruption from her mother, after which she disappeared for a few hours.

Everything happened so fast after that his memory couldn't differentiate their first encounter from the many that followed that first day alone. His best and most clear memory was made that night on her mother's hide-a-bed when Laurie came to him. He was surprised to find Laurie so amorous with her mother just down the hall. It was that night he fell in love with her.

Laurie wore only a t-shirt when she came to him late that night. "We have to be quiet, be gentle with me ok?" she pleaded. With that he rolled her over onto her back, kissed her gently. She had to restrain herself from crying out when after twenty minutes of kissing she felt him pressing himself into her again. Whispering in a quavering voice she repeated "Put it in…put it in me"…she kissed him moaning into his mouth as he entered her again.

When he was fully engaged he rolled onto his back bringing her with him connected at the hip. Something came unhinged inside Laurie the moment she settled onto him. Laurie savaged him in silence struggling to keep her passions contained, longing desperately to cry out yet not daring to…not even with her mother's consent and knowledge. She didn't want her mother seeing her in the act regardless of her knowledge and understanding. Some things needed to remain 'private'.

For the next two hours they quietly made love with Laurie moaning in orgasm twice loving every moment she shared with him. Setting the alarm for 6am Laurie indulged herself by remaining in his arms until the sun came up after which she moved back into her own bed to keep up appearances.

What Greg did not know was that Laurie's mother knew everything and was encouraging Laurie to explore those feelings she had denied herself as a young wife and mother in the 1950 and 60's. It was her view that had she 'played' outside the marriage rather than adhere to socially acceptable behavior she may have not divorced her husband.

All she knew for certain was had she done what she wanted, she would have been much happier. How many times had the mailman come on to her, the plumber or salesman, all of whom had shown desire for her, pretending to be offended when in truth she was screaming to let them tear her clothes off and ravage her on the kitchen table.

Years of marriage to a man who'd lost is ability to satisfy her had worn down her 'moral' thought process giving her a hard outlook on life itself. Having wants and desires didn't make her less of a mother or wife; it made her human. But she had denied her human side in an effort to be what society had determined was appropriate. So on the outside she was the Betty Crocker of her generation, two kids, a husband a few cats; a picture perfect Currier and Ives print for the world to see and admire.

On the inside she felt thin and pale like the paper her life was printed on. Only that paper was no longer pristine or smudge free, but torn and wrinkled from years of trying to live as 'others' saw fit. She saw her daughter caught in that same trap she had been when it was clear her daughter was as passionate and full of life as she had been, even more so and to deny her desires was a sin far worse than indulging them.

So when she saw the sparks fly between Laurie and Greg the first day in his office she decided to make it easier for her daughter and hired him making sure they had plenty of time to do what they clearly wanted to.

Of her son in law she held no disdain or animosity. In fact she loved him as if he were her own son. Life had been harder on him than he would ever admit and her daughter, Laurie demanded much of him. His failings had worn on their marriage. His health had been going down- hill with each successive failure that met him. Each year he practiced his age seemed to accelerate.

It wasn't his ability or lack thereof that had been his nemesis; it was his willingness to accept insurance for the sake of his patients need. This compassion had led to many people taking advantage of him financially. It was these many disappointments that caused his health to fail and his ego to fade into an abysmal state of depression.

Laurie would not tolerate his depressed moods. In fact many of their fights had been due to his depression. So many times Laurie had come to her house seething with rage for the weakness in her husband for letting the world trample on him. She loved him as much as any truly devoted wife could, but she could not respect a man who let the world abuse him. So Laurie was torn between loving a man she couldn't respect and living her life.

When her daughter began showing her flirtatious side with Greg, she let it flourish saying nothing just in case her knowledge had an inhibitory effect. Lauries marriage had begun to wear on her daughter as much as her own marriage had, only Lauries personality was much more aggressive so the strain showed more readily. When she recognized the same misty-eyed longings from her daughter in the presence of her attorney she did what nobody had done for her, unlocked the door of self-awareness and closed the door on guilt and shame.

Chapter 30
On the plane

GREG STARED OUT the window his thoughts on Laurie, missing her terribly though he had seen her less than a day before. For almost six months they'd been dating. In that time Laurie had opened up. She was happier than she was when they first met and she was much less inhibited, much, much less he thought to himself with an inward grin.

He should have taken her on this trip. She was grown woman and wouldn't have to explain much to her husband. After all he was on a vacation by himself. Why couldn't she do the same? But she refused because her kids were in school. "Oh hell" he said to himself phoning his secretary.

"Lisa? Yes, I want you to book a two-way flight for one of my clients. For today if possible and arrange for a limo to pick her up. I'll text you her name and address when we hang up, okay? Text me back when you have it. I shouldn't be more than a few days, no more than a week. K- bye."

Five minutes later he received a text from his secretary confirming the information he'd sent. Ten minutes later she text the confirmation with departure and arrival times along with the limo confirmation, he smiled. "Perfect" he muttered to himself.

Laurie was just out of the shower drying her hair when the phone rang. "Hey babe" came Greg's voice. Before she could say a word he said "I've bought you a ticket to fly out so you can be with me. It should only be a few days, but I miss you and want you near me."

Laurie flushed "But, but…my kids?" she stuttered.
"I've sent with the ticket $1000.00 for your mother to entertain the kids this weekend. Your limousine will be there in an hour to pick you up. Oh, the island is a shit hole so don't' be too disappointed when you land and see a bunch of fat tourists ok? The brochure for this place is appalling."

Laurie flushed with excitement at the prospect of being with him. It didn't matter if they stayed indoors the whole time. Her mother showed up with a thousand dollars in an envelope with a curious look. They shared a significant look saying nothing as the kids were standing around surprised that their mom was suddenly leaving and grandma was coming to visit. Hugging each one goodbye, she tried not to run to the limousine waiting for her.

Six hours later her plane landed on St. Vincent. It seemed a pleasant enough place but that didn't matter as much as seeing Greg next to the tarmac in a Jeep wearing his khaki shorts and a white linen shirt sporting newly purchased sandals. Being fit and lean with a sense of style made her want him even more. Her husband had quit caring how he looked a long time ago. It was a lot easier being 'openly' sexual with a guy who looked the part of a sex god. The flight crew took her luggage and placed it in the Jeep while she threw her arms around Greg. The moisture and salt air made her skin tingle as she kissed him making her want to get naked.

Thirty minutes later they were in his bungalow in the shower covered in shampoo with Laurie's back pressed against the cold tile as Greg lowered her onto his waiting manhood. Soon they were connected at the hip as they each savored the warmth of the other. However, Lauries body began to react to her new found freedom of being able to enjoy sex with her lover…thousands of miles from where anyone knew her and her passion began to build…and build with an intensity she hadn't seen before then.

Meanwhile at that moment outside the bungalow Rick walked with Hans as they loaded bricks into Ricks Jeep. On their third trip Rick heard a woman crying out in orgasm and grinned. "Somebody is having fun" he said. But Rick did not think much of the fact that the voice seemed somehow familiar, like his wife…but that was impossible she was thousands of miles away.

Hans laughed softly. "Yes, apparently" he replied with a grin looking over at the open window from where the noise came.

When the crates were loaded they hopped in the Jeep and drove toward Archie's house. Hans drove, curious about the Jeepster's handling traits. He was seriously interested in buying the jeep from the hotel so that he could rebuild it. It was unique and he wanted to 'play with it' as he put it. He loved working on old cars, the older and more unique the better and a Jeepster Commando was a sufficiently unique vehicle to spark his interest.

He drove it checking the brakes and steering to see if they needed anything. "Ah, drum brakes they'll have to go' he said unconsciously as his whole person seemed to dial into the vehicle itself, like a true motor-head feeling for anything that needed 'the touch'. 'I've seen this jeep driving around for years and I was always curious to see how well it drove. I've never actually driven a jeep. I saw plenty of jeeps during the war but I never had a chance to drive one. This damned thing feels loose as a French tart" he said with a wry grin. Rick laughed out loud at the colorful metaphor having never heard it before. But his laugh was cut short when he saw Hans face darken as he brought the jeep to a sudden stop behind a bush and stared hard at a woman sitting on the park bench across from Archie's Museum.

She was beautiful with curves in all the right places wearing a sheer floral sundress that showed off her voluptuous curves underneath with a large brimmed hat to keep the sun off her face, neck and ample cleavage. A blonde pony-tail hung down the center of her back and brushed the tops of her nearly perfect assets. She was certainly easy to spot among the heavier tourists who dominated the plaza. Many of who had adopted Hawaiian Muu, Muu's to cover their ample bodies in order to keep cool and not get sunburned.

Rick watched her and pictured a lioness stalking prey. That image wasn't hard with the large people milling about the plaza. The jiggles of excessive mass did somehow remind him of hippos milling about on land. However it was the sharp dangerous look in her eyes that made his heart stop. Piercing ice blue eyes appeared to see through whoever she looked at. She would have you under her power in a minute. Her face was chiseled with high, soft cheekbones and a squared off chin that set off her full mouth. If he were to guess he'd have to say she was German or partly so and extremely fit if the shadow of her figure under the dress was any indication.

Hans stopped the jeep on the far side of the plaza. "That's the woman Archie saw the day he ran into trouble. She isn't very hard to spot in this crowd. It's clear she knows where Archie lives" As he said this she stood up and took a stroll around the church paying close attention to the fence. Her ear was to a cell phone listening. She's using one of those cheap throw away phones. That means she has an extra set of eyes somewhere. We have to change the meeting place."

With that Hans backed the jeep into an ally to watch her without being seen. Checking his watch he noted that they had two hours before they were scheduled to meet with the Attorney. That gave them time to change the meeting place and avoid trouble. "Call Archie and see if he can relocate the meeting place. I think it would be best if the attorney is not seen. If they are as connected as we think, then they'll be able to identify him and know what sort of Attorney he is. If they do they will figure out what we are doing and move in. With the amounts of money we are dealing with, they will stop at nothing to get their hands on it. That includes killing anyone who gets in the way." He paused staring at the woman as she returned to the bench confident that she couldn't see them.

Rick got on the phone with Archie who had been preparing for the meeting in his house. "Archie, the woman who you saw the other day, she's out front watching your place. I think we may have to change the venue for the meeting. Hans seems to believe that this group may be able to identify the attorney and figure out what we are up to. So we may want to keep him off their radar, if possible"

Archie frowned to himself but acknowledged their reasoning. "Perhaps that is best. I'd hoped that she'd have left by now. Apparently they know something or think they do. We're going to have to move fast. Give the phone to Hans." He handed the phone to Hans who took it and put it to his ear.

"Hans, meet me at the storm drain in ten minutes" he said.

Hans nodded "Yes, we'll be there, make sure you aren't followed" then handed the phone to Rick.

"Where is she now?" he asked as he moved to close the museum. Nobody was inside anyway so he closed the inner door and locked the outer doors, which were luckily already closed. He didn't want to draw any unwanted attention to his closing early. He then headed to his belfry to get a look at this woman to see if it was truly the same woman. He hoped that it was just a case of mistaken identity. The belfry door creaked loudly and he winced at the noise making a mental note to oil the hinges. He shook his head because it had been years since he'd been up there.

Peering through a loose slat in the belfry Archie had his phone to his ear while Rick told him where the woman was sitting. He recognized her instantly. It was the same woman. 'Damn' he muttered. There was something about her he recognized that went far deeper than her obvious physical beauty. Nothing one could describe with words but what is perceived with sense only old spies seem to develop, a sense that something is dangerous and should be left alone. It was that sense being awakened as he watched her. By the clothes she wore, she carried no firearms, no weapons, not that it mattered. With a simple phone call or a wave of her hand a bullet would come out of nowhere or knife find its way in your back before you realized you were dead.

She was talking to someone on her phone indicating that she was not alone, which made sense when he considered the fact that someone had killed the second skinhead. He was being watched and they had saved him, because they wanted to follow him to the bullion.

How they'd figured out his connection was a mystery. He'd only discovered it by dumb luck. Had a vague report from the WWI naval commander not found his way to his hands he would have never known where to look. It was equally dumb luck that the pirate colony that had once existed on the island hadn't discovered it or the compound on the mountain.

Archie decided that it was best that he utilize the storm drain to make his exit. Carefully he walked down the stairwell in the belfry and down the trap door that led to the basement under the church. It was what remained of the church archives, past member funerals and marriages and baptisms. Once in the basement he bolted the trap door in the event 'she' came looking.

On the far end of the basement was a grate that let water out in the event of a hurricane storm surge. At least once a year a hurricane flooded the basement, which is why they put in the storm drain that led out to the beach. There was heavy grate that covered the actual drain that provided security from curious rodents and mischievous teenagers looking for trouble.

It was hinged so that maintenance crews could be let down to clean out the flow way to ensure that when the next storm hit the water had a clear path out. He had the key to the lock so that he could let them down to do their job. It took him less than five minutes before he was closing and locking the grate. It had been cleaned earlier that year already so he could stroll easily down the dark tunnel and soon saw the proverbial light. Beyond which he could see Hans sitting behind the wheel of Rick's Jeep.

Chapter 31
Plan of Action

TWO HOURS LATER Greg showered off as Laurie slept. He left her a note telling her that he had a meeting that would keep him several hours and that he'd be back to take her to dinner. When he emerged from his bungalow, in the late afternoon a jeep with three men were waiting for him.

Archie got out of the passenger side of the jeep stiffly feeling the ache of his wound and greeting him with an extended hand. "Mr. Mitchell, our meeting plans have changed. Please hop in. There is a boat house not far from here and a boat that will take us to a place we can discuss our business in complete privacy."

Greg was pleased to finally be able to put a face to the voice on the phone. "Please, let's, I like privacy" he said. It wasn't until he stepped into the back of the jeep that he recognized the husband of the woman he was sleeping with. His heart instantly leaped into his throat. "Rick?" he said in utter surprise trying not sound guilty as his face flushed red and swallowed his heart nervously glancing over at the door of his hut.

Rick nodded and stifled a laugh knowing that Greg had no idea that he was already aware of his sleeping with his wife. He extended a hand and smiled broadly. "Hello, how was your trip?" It was all Rick could do to keep from asking about Laurie, because for all he knew or was supposed to know Greg hadn't seen her in months. Rick of course had no idea that his wife was less than 30 feet away sleeping in the bed she and Greg had recently shared. Archie on the other hand saw the nervous glance Greg gave both Rick and the hut in which he was staying and instantly put two and two together. His instincts told him more than logic could ever tell him. Somehow he knew Ricks wife was in the cabin and Rick had no idea. However, he kept his conclusions to himself, for the time being.

Hans pulled away and whipped the jeep around and drove to an old boathouse a mile out of town. Rick hopped out of the jeep and opened the garage door so that Hans could pull in and close the door behind them. He then flipped on the lights. The building they had driven into was built of solid concrete with no windows with forced air ventilation. If it weren't for the fan and forced air the humidity would have been horrendous. In the slipway sat a classic fully restored 40-foot long wooden Chris Craft commuter boat. Hans climbed on and assisted his friend Archie onto the boat, Rick and Greg followed suit.

On the stern sat a table and a few seats onto which Archie automatically took a seat, having not born the jolting harsh ride of the Jeep well. His wound was still too fresh to be bouncing around in a jeep. Greg then noticed this and asked. "What happened?"

Hans spoke up "We will answer all questions when we are in a more secure location. We need to make sure we are not heard, even by accident" He then started the twin Packard 12 cylinder engines and pushed the button to open the door. The old engines sounded beautiful as they burbled their deep notes into the water. Once clear of the slip, Hans hit the button again and the door closed tight. From the water the building was soon invisible. Had it not been for the wake he would not have been able to tell that a building was there at all. Nobody could see them slip away due to the location of the boathouse in relation to the main village. In a matter of minutes he nudged the throttles forward and 24 cylinders of two Packard V12 marine engines pushed the heavy wooden cruiser at a surprising clip of 40 knots.

Ten minutes later they slowed and approached the far end of the island and drove straight into what appeared a solid mass of mangrove trees and bushes growing directly out of the water. As they got closer Hans throttled back on the Port engine reversed the transmission and turned the rudder hard left and gunned the starboard engine driving the cruiser into a hidden canal twice as wide as the boat, but invisible to anyone who didn't know it was there.

The mangrove forest had been formed into a man-made tunnel that could not be seen from the air or from the surface. In fact several of the branches had been hung deliberately low over the entrance making it almost invisible. So when Hans drove the boat into the mass of growth Rick and Greg braced for an impact that never came. In a matter of minutes they were in complete darkness from the density of the growth covering the canal.

Archie saw the question in both Rick and Greg's eyes so he offered a brief explanation allowing Hans to focus on navigation. "This was originally meant as a seaway access to the cavern that would allow the use of the boats in the harbor for recreational purposes. If you can imagine being cooped up on an island for years on end, they needed some recreation to blow off steam.'

Greg having never heard of the origins of the island simply listened in silence.

Archie continued "The mangrove was planted to keep the sea swells from damaging the boats as they left the tunnel. They were finding that if they weren't careful the boats would hit the roof as they left if the waves weren't somehow controlled. Planting mangrove trees on the ledge and then shaping their roots as they grew and being in a wet, tropical environment they grew rather quickly. So within six months the mangrove had grown sufficiently to do the job intended. What they hadn't counted on was the fact that the mangrove would outpace their efforts to keep up with it. So they took the new growth and weaved it into the canopy you see here. It now runs about three hundred yards or so and is so dense that it is black as night 100 feet from the entrance.

This had the unintended consequence of attracting some unsavory inhabitants. Somehow, and do not ask me how this happened but we have acquired several South American green tree snakes. Highly poisonous and aggressive, they like to hang from the branches and drop onto the boat from time to time. So Hans has a light pointing up so that we can see them. We then shoot them with a paint ball gun until they drop in the water or climb back into the mangrove. They don't like the paint ball gun much. Apparently it hurts. They seem to have learned not to hang down when we come because they now climb back into the mangrove when they hear the engines. Still the younger ones try it once in a while. So, you might want to keep your hands inside the boat just in case."

He was looking at Greg when he said this because his hand was hanging outside the boat. Greg quickly pulled his hand back and moved to the seat next to Hans who was fully covered by the bridge canopy. Rick had unconsciously done the same having no want of a snake dropping onto his head, especially a poisonous snake.

Archie chuckled under his breath as he took a seat under the bridge canopy as well. A nervous silence came over both Greg and Rick as they passed under the dense canopy with eyes peeled for the bright green tree snakes. A chill rolled up Rick's spine giving him goose bumps in spite of the humidity that began to thicken as they moved deeper into the mangrove. Only the sound of the twin Packard engines could be heard as they all watched the canopy roll by.

Suddenly the canopy opened into a massive space. They had entered an external lagoon covered by a huge canopy of mesh netting and foliage. He felt fresh sea breezes and the sound of a distant seagull confirming they were still outside the main cavern.

Hans pointed the boat directly at a massive shadow in the middle of the lagoon. A ship sat at anchor hidden by the massive canopy above. Before he knew it they were tying the boat up to a floating platform above which hung the aluminum gangplank of a ship that was nearly 500 feet long.

After the boat was tied up they all climbed the gangplank and silently made their way to the main deck. Once on the main deck they followed Archie and Hans to the aft section and up another ladder that lead to the captain's cabin behind the main wheelhouse. Eyes having adjusted to the dim gray light Rick began to realize that they were on a freighter, an older renovated freighter, with a long prow with a bulbous protrusion just under the water line. The wheel house and crews quarters were housed in the superstructure mounted on the aft section of the ship leaving the forward sections open for more efficient load capacity. Barely half the size of newer ships she was sufficient for the purpose. It was also innocuous enough to go un-noticed in the busier sea-lanes and ports they would be traveling through.

At 500 feet she was big enough to carry the load and maneuver in the enclosed bay and moor stern first to the old salt mine pier head. "Victoria" was painted across her stern and on the bow. It had been formerly owned by a British shipping firm that had the habit of naming their ships after British Royalty having named this hull after Queen Victoria. Her blue hull was topped with a White superstructure and white trip around the gunwales. She was not an unattractive ship but neither was she one to stand out. Upon purchase from the breakers in Albania Archie had her refitted in an Irish yard with a new Diesel Electric drive in which the Diesels drove the generators that drove the electric motors that turned the screws, through reduction gears. The new system was designed to propel an 800 foot long ship at 20 knots. Upon trials they achieved an easily sustainable speed of 30 knots loaded with a faux cargo. Her range at 30 knots would be sufficient to cross the Atlantic 6 times before they needed to refuel. And they needed to cross it only once. Rick found his sense of adventure picking up liking the idea of taking a sea voyage. It was the kid inside him that he had never let die that fed his child like excitement. Only he didn't let it show, keeping his frowning 'serious' face present following the older men into the darkened cabin.

Hans turned on the lights in the Captain's cabin which was decorated richly with wood paneling, plush carpeting with a wood burning stove on the far side of the cabin on a pedestal of brick. The captains bunk was made of wood and built into the bulkhead with easy access to the wheel house in case of an emergency.

Hans and Archie both took a place at the table then invited Rick and Greg to take a seat. Hans motioned for Archie to begin the discussion. "Mr. Mitchell, our friend here, Rick said that you are an estate Attorney' to which Greg simply nodded. 'Good, we have need of your particular set of skills. Except, we need the skill set you reserve for your less savory clients." Rick turned to look at Archie and then back at Greg not knowing what he meant by that.

Greg swallowed and attempted to play dumb. As far as he was concerned this was a legitimate client. After all they had contacted him through his legitimate L.A. business. All other clients knew to contact him through the Mexico based email. His thoughts raced thinking that maybe he was being set up.

Shaking his head he began to deny any such business contacts but Archie stopped him cold. "My former job description Mr. Mitchell was with British Intelligence through which I was able to obtain contacts with MI6 and CIA which I have maintained in spite of being retired for well over 50 years. It helps to keep tabs on those you might have trouble with in retirement. I happen to know that you have a server in Mexico through which you do business with some very dangerous people. Of course the CIA does not know exactly who you are because you have done a masterful job at covering your tracks. I happen to know who you are because several years ago you created a new account for me, one that was to be used later, through that server. It was during that transaction that I had my CIA contact install tracking software on your server in Mexico. It took only one mistake on your part to let me know who you were. It was when you accessed the account on your laptop and neglected to close out your business email account. It was then I learned who you were." At this Greg went pale.

Archie smiled at his reaction "You needn't worry that we have sold you out. In fact I had my contact create an external firewall on that server to keep the FBI out. I do not want them following me any more than you do at this point. However, I knew I had to know everything about you if I were to trust you with this task. It was just happenstance that my friend here', he patted Rick on the shoulder, 'happened to have known you as well. I'd call that destiny wouldn't you?" Greg was too stunned to respond as sweat began forming on his brow and his stomach churned with the cold acidic fear one feels when he is truly caught.

Archie placed a hand on his wrist and spoke in his best and most comforting Preachers voice. "Mr. Mitchell. I didn't have that done for reasons of blackmail but rather as a matter of trust. Once we let you in on our secret, you will have us by the balls, so we in turn need to have a grip on yours. If you betray us you betray yourself it is that simple. What we are about to share with you requires your absolute silence because if what we tell you gets out we will likely all be killed and our bodies dumped into the ocean and that's if we are lucky. Do you see why I want your absolute cooperation and silence in this matter?"

Greg swallowed and nodded still wary of his predicament. "So what is this secret you are so desperate to keep? I have hidden billions of assets for a lot of people over the years. That is not so difficult, it is just a matter of knowing where to make it disappear and then reappear under a different name and origin. But only if you know how to keep it out of the 'official' channels."

Hans smiled, stood up and went to the liquor cabinet to retrieve a bottle of Scotch and four glasses. "I think we need to have a bit of a bracer before we begin our business" he said and poured each a glass of 12 year old single malt Scotch whiskey.

Archie then pulled out his old brief case, the one with SOE on the leather. "Rick several days ago found our secret, quite by accident according to him. He crashed his jeep into the tunnel leading to what Hans and I have attempted to keep hidden for the past several decades. A secret that if discovered would very well lead to a resurgent Nazi regime" he paused here looking directly at Greg who appeared visibly jolted.

"Nazis, you've got to be joking. They have to be all dead by now" he said shaking his head in disbelief.

Archie sipped his whiskey never taking his eyes off Greg then spoke softly "They are more of a criminal organization now, but they do wield a great deal of influence by means of blackmail and murder. If they got their hands on this 'secret' they could very easily subvert the world order and bend the world political powers to their will. That is obviously something that we are attempting to avoid by hiring your talents."

Hans piped up. "I was once in the Nazi party. In fact I was in the SS and one of the parties who brought this 'secret' to this island, which in WWII was a submarine base and was later to be used as a repository to finance an American invasion. I was supposed to disperse funds to build ships and help build a new South American Wehrmacht. Our General later learned that the weapons we'd been sent were scraped WWI guns and dummy shells that made for an impressive appearing shipment but were nothing more than paperweights in terms of warfare. Once our general figured it out he felt betrayed. In revenge he vowed to deny 'them' the prize."

Greg waved a hand to stop him. "You keep referring to this secret in vague terms but it is clear that it has a heavy monitory value. What is this repository?" he looked at Hans and back to Archie who in turn looked at each other and nodded.

Archie stood up, stiffly "Alright, let's show you because simply telling you won't be enough. There is a platform and stairs off the stern section of the ship." As one the group stood and made their way to the stern where, like Archie said was a platform apparently suspended in mid-air over the lagoon and attached to a set of steps that went up to a blacked out doorway that lead into the southwestern end of the cavern. A brow was set in place as a means to get onto the platform. Five minutes later they were inside the main cavern, which was pitch black. Lapping water echoed in the dark making it seem all the more vast. Once Hans closed the door behind them Archie pulled a heavy switch. Following a series of hum's, clicks and bangs the cavern lit up like midday.

Rick gasped at the sight having only seen parts of it from the headlight beams of the jeep and Kublewagon he'd driven into it. They were on a scaffold 200 feet above the main pier used by maintenance crews to change lights and access the cranes for loading stores and weapons. "Wow this place is massive" Rick said in astonishment.

The two submarines were much smaller looking from this distance and now that he could see the crates lined up along the pier he gasped in awe. "Holy Shit!! How many crates are in here?" he asked.

Archie directed them to an elevator. "Just what you see here is 3000 tones. What remains in the mountain vaults we have no earthly clue because we do not know how deep the vaults are. We do not have a close estimate of what it may be worth. But we can say at minimum, just what is on the pier is well over two-trillion current market value"

Greg paled and leaned heavily against the rail of the elevator. "T-T-Two trillion? D-dollars?" he barely got out.

Archie shook his head slowly and smiled. "No son, Pounds,' he paused gazing upon the base below 'That is based on what we have been able to calculate so far" he nodded indicating that he and Hans had been the ones to do the calculations. Then he turned to Greg. "Do you understand our need for secrecy now?"

All Greg could do was shake his head in dismay. "I-I've never had to make this much money appear out of nowhere. Such an amount has to have an origin that is at least plausible and easy for someone to comprehend. This' he gestured to the rows and rows of crates below them 'cannot be fabricated out of thin air!! There has to be some reasonable explanation of origin."

Archie smiled and put a hand on his shoulder. "Remember when I asked you to create an ancient estate title for me? The land is actually part of my families past. My ancestor Angus MacDaniels was bequeathed property on the Shetland Islands in the early 1700s from a relative rumored to have been a privateer. A pirate who only attacked the Spanish gold fleets, but who refused to spend the gold, believing money was the root of the world's evil. What gold he raided from the Spanish was kept hidden so not to temp the weak of spirit.

He never spent the gold he took and lived a life of devout poverty and chastity. Because of this the rumors of his being a privateer died out. Since the gold he was supposed to have looted never turned up the story was never taken seriously and considered little more than a child's bedtime story. This distant uncle apparently hated the Spanish and the Catholic religion so much that his life purpose was to deprive the Spanish of wealth and the world of temptation. Not an educated man he believed gold would dissolve in salt. Therefore he kept the gold he took in an abandoned salt mine under an estate left to him by his father, whom he detested as a Catholic.

I last visited the castle several years ago, the very same time I sought out your services. It is a fairly substantial estate on the Northern Shetland Coast, immediately above the salt mine. The residence is an old castle that has been converted into a walled estate with access to the mine hidden inside the castle dungeon, which serves as a nice wine cellar.

On the cliff side of the estate is a protected cove where ships once moored to take on loads of salt. That ship' he gestured outside the cavern 'will transport the cargo to this location where we will off load it and store it in the salt mines under the castle. There is more than enough room in the salt mine to hold the contents of this is-land. As I already have a lineage to the Shetland Island estate, all I need from you is to take a portion of this bullion and convert it to bearer bonds so that we have an inheritance for this lad to take possession of once he becomes caretaker of the family estate and fortune. This is to ensure that he has a mechanism to make use of the bullion. It would be a shame for all this wealth to go to waste." Archie said gesturing to the many crates along the pier.

All four men stood looking over the crates and the entrance to the tunnel, which gaped black and ominous in the distance. "Ok, so how are you going to load this onto the ship? Certainly you three aren't going to load this by yourselves are you?" Greg asked.

It was Hans who spoke this time. "Actually, the bullion was sup-posed to be loaded onto ships and taken to its final destination. This obviously never came to pass. They knew with the end of the war that a very few men would be available to move it and so it had to be made easy to load and off load with relatively few men.' he pointed up 'See those cranes? They were designed for the purpose of loading the crates onto the ship. There is a conveyer belt already in place that will roll the crates along a guided route onto the ship.

On board is a system of rails that are meant to guide each crate onto a hydraulic platform that will drop to make room for the next crate. When the last crate falls into place the next space in line will open up and the crates get stacked up again. It was designed to load from the centerline to evenly distribute the weight. It is also designed to offload the bullion by shooting out the bottom crate from each stack onto another conveyer that will off load it onto a pallet then will be rolled off the ship via fork lift, already on site. We figure that loading will take upwards of three to four days, given zero delays and malfunctions" Hans said.

Hans moved off the elevator and made sure everyone got off safely. "Follow me please" He led them toward the dark opening of the tunnel at the far end of the pier. Their footsteps echoed in the cavernous space as each lost themselves in their own thoughts. Rick was growing both nervous and excited at the prospect of becoming the wealthiest man on the planet. His recorded wealth would be far less than his actual wealth due to the need to keep a low profile. But the reality of his situation meant that he would be, literally, the wealthiest man on earth. In fact because of the transfer having already been completed he was at that moment richer than Bill Gates, Donald Trump and the Queen of Great Britain combined; a sobering and not unpleasant thought.

At the same moment Archie was relieved to be finally doing

something other than babysitting. Moving the bullion was long overdue. It should have been moved long since but circumstances hadn't warranted it. In truth he and Hans both had both become complacent, that was the only word for it. They had each taken for granted that nobody would find it, but as they got older and the island got busier and more populated, it was a matter of time before someone stumbled onto it, which is exactly how Rick discovered it.

At the same time a feeling of melancholy began to creep into his consciousness, a feeling that his life work and purpose would soon pass into the hands of a successor. It had to be done living forever was just not possible, no matter how hard he wished it. Then, just as they were approaching the pier head he realized that Rick needed help organizing to keep on top of developments for at least a few months if not a year or more. They all stopped and watched as Hans, stepped over to a box on the wall and flipped the lever.

Hans pulled the switch with a loud clunk and a series of hums and clicks filled the cavern. From underneath the stacks of bullion came a mechanical conveyor that moved into place level with the top row of crates. From behind the pile a hissing sound of a piston pushed the first row of crates onto the conveyor. As one each box moved toward the ship. The loading process had begun. Hans then said that they should get back to the ship. "We need to see that this first load gets loaded without incident. "We've run a few loads already to see if the mechanism works and so far we have had no serious setbacks. What few there were required little more than a nudge to correct".

The group of men silently reentered the lift and rode it to the top scaffold where they exited and walked single file down the narrow walkway and out to the platform that carried them to the ships fantail. From the rail they looked at the conveyor as it entered into the gaping stern hatch that led deep into the bowels of the ship. A steady stream of crates began to slowly make their way up the conveyor and one by one in six foot intervals the crates disappeared into the hatchway.

Rick followed Hans to the hold and watched as each crate found itself loaded into its designated space. The design was simple and efficient and appeared to be just crude enough to be easy to work on if necessary. Archie took Greg back to the cabin saying, "Greg, I have a computer system already set up per your requirements. I'd like you to look at it and see if it is sufficient, perhaps you could begin working your magic. We will see you gentlemen in a few minutes. We have sandwiches and coffee made" he said as he and Greg disappeared into the dark.

Hans nodded his approval and spoke to Rick who remained behind "We will stay on board tonight to supervise loading. Automation still requires supervision but the safeguards in place should shut it down if anything should jam up,' Hans looked nervously at Rick now that they were alone for the first time since he'd shot at him. 'I'd like to apologize for shooting at you the other day. I was afraid that Odessa had found me again." He sighed and seemed to shrink within himself. "I have been running from the world since the end of the war. I ran from my own country, your country, Archie's country, hiding out in places where I half expected to find myself either arrested or shot in the street. When Archie said that he was being followed I feared the worst, that maybe they'd found me again. I panicked, not that it excuses my shooting at you. The people who are chasing me aren't the sort you warn" he said placing a friendly hand on his shoulder. "Please do forgive me" he said

Rick accepted his apology and smiled. "I'm just glad you missed." He said laughing.

Hans grimaced and smiled back sheepishly. "Yes, I am glad for that. I have come to like you. Archie, I think, made a good choice in a successor." He sighed then turned to look out over the fantail and down at the long conveyor loading the crates onto the ship. "The mountain has a conveyor system built into the wall to help us roll the crates down. All we have to do is slide them into place, the rails should keep the boxes on the rollers so all we have to do is pace the load to make sure the boxes do not jam up against the loader. These are heavy boxes and Archie and I won't be able to lift them if they fall off the conveyor and I don't think you want to be lifting them' he paused, 'I went over the mechanicals of the system months ago and have made adjustments here and there lubing it as I went. It had occurred to us that the need to move it would come suddenly and we wanted to be ready in that event'. Patting the rail of the ship he continued. 'Your finding the base was that event. We truly never expected anyone to find it. I think we just got lazy to be honest."

For a long time they stood on the stern silent lost in their-own thoughts watching the crates disappear into the ship. Rick allowed himself some indulgent thoughts on how he'd spend the money dwelling mostly on cars and which one he'd buy first. As thoughts progressed, Rick discovered that his consciousness and wealth mentality had changed and his personal wants had modified. He no longer wanted to just 'own' a Ferrari he wanted an original, vintage Ferrari. To own a car not just for the sake of owning it but to experience a real honest to goodness Enzo built Ferrari. A car you had to drive and not one that drove for you. Then his mind drifted to a sailboat or rather a yacht. 112' long of wooden beauty, a boat that needed to be taken care of sailed and used.

He found himself wanting things for the experience they provided and not just the 'ownership'. The same went for his home. He didn't need a 'house' to display to the world; he wanted a home that he could live in, relax and spend his life in, leaving it to this kids and know that they would have a place to stay no matter how long they wanted to. Of course he would eventually want to get 'toys' but that was for a later time when he was better acquainted with his wealth.

Hans too had fallen into his own thoughts of Sarah. He had long ago grown weary of living without her. There had been no others. He had no desire for anyone but her. His friendship with Archie had helped him heal to some degree because he enjoyed his company. They had a bond that was found only among veterans of common experience. Even though they had fought on opposite sides of the same war, each man knew the other better than anyone. Had it not been for Archie he would have put a bullet into his mouth long ago. The aches and pains of war injuries, coupled with horrific experiences and a long broken heart were the most trying conditions in his life but he found life livable in the company of a comrade who could understand what he'd been through and not judge him.

However, the excitement of moving the bullion had awakened him to new purpose. He was a soldier trying to protect the world from another reign of Nazi horror. Having seen it firsthand he knew too well that man had not left that behavior behind. Hitler had been bad for the world, but Stalin was just as bad if not worse. Wars, atrocities and horror were the staple of the human condition. This bullion if discovered by those looking for it would bleed the world. If he could prevent the Nazis from getting their hands on this gold, he could die in peace. He felt the warmth of his Sarah's touch on his skin. She was there, waiting for him to join her. Unconsciously he put his hand on the spot he felt her touch and smiled letting peace and contentment fill his heart. She would wait by his side in spirit until the day he would join her forever.

Back in the ships cabin Archie and Greg sat at the table with Greg's face lit by the computer screen as he began to make the necessary preparations for the bullion to be transferred into cash. But his mind wasn't focused on the job at hand. He was frightened and less sure of his future security. Before today he was an anonymous soul in the criminal network. Now he was no longer anonymous but known to at least one other soul outside this group, the CIA operative who'd hacked him.

How discrete were they? Would they later locate and blackmail him? Had anyone else done what the old man had done? His concern must have registered on his face because Archie poured him a Scotch and placed it in his hand and said "Here son. Look… after our business is concluded you will have no need to work for anyone else ever again. And if I am any judge of character I'd say that you have a tidy sum put away in the event you needed to disappear. So I'd say that if you do your job for us you may retire. Besides, we did this to you 'years' ago. If anyone out there wanted to do something to you, or get to you they, I suspect, would have done it by now. Criminals I've known and dealt with tended to be impatient, hence the criminal conduct, easy, instant money etc."

Greg looked up at Archie angry "Ok, I understand your rationale, I understand your motivation, I really do. What concerns me is that CIA operative. How do I know they haven't sold me out to some drug kingpin? How do I know that I won't find some drug dealer in my home twenty years from now, seeking revenge because your man in the CIA needed retirement?"

He was pissed and the more he thought about it the more angry he got. His whole life had been carefully planned so that this very scenario would never take place, all of it undone by some James Bond has-been. In truth he was frightened by the fact that it had been done so easily. He looked back down at the computer screen then noticed the Scotch in his hand. He slammed it down in one gulp and Archie immediately poured him another.

Archie once again put on his preacher voice, "If it makes you feel any better that operative died three years ago in Afghanistan, killed by a road side bomb. So I don't think that you have much to worry about. As you can see I am old and already have more money than I could ever spend. And I will be dead soon anyway, in a couple years if I am lucky." Greg relaxed visibly at the news.

Greg then realized what the old man had just said. "Dying? You look like you could go another 20 years, easy. Hell, if I'm half as vital as you are at 50 I'll be doing good" he said.

Archie shook his head "No son, fact is I've got cancer, pancreatic cancer. I was supposed to die two years ago. It's a miracle I'm here now. It means to me that I am to finish this job, which is to keep this bullion out of the hands of those who would do evil with it. Turning it over to a governmental bureaucracy would almost certainly guarantee it fell into the wrong hands. I'm afraid that ineptitude is a common disease in government these days.

You may also be wondering why we included you in on the secret? Managing this kind of wealth is not for a single man. We, Hans and I, appointed ourselves guardians of this bullion because we both knew the types of men who wanted to get their hands on it. They are the kind of men who will stop at nothing, even murdering children simply to make an impression. Rick stumbled onto the secret by accident. But I'm a man who believes in destiny, which to me, in my simple way suggests God is at work. I used your services a few years ago, never again expecting to need them. Then Rick stumbles onto our find and in the course of our planning suggests your name, which of course I already knew." Archie stood up and stretched his legs groaning from the stiffness of his wound. "Destiny is at work here Son. You and I were brought together by a higher power, years ago for this very reason and purpose."

He paced around and continued to speak. "Hans is about my age, and won't be around forever either. This responsibility is for the two of you to shoulder when we are gone. It cannot be trusted to governments or anyone else…you two must be the only two ever to know if this. So you can't be divulging this secret to anyone. Rick won't be telling his wife about it and neither should you, even though you are sleeping with her."

Greg stood up in shock with the comment coming out of left field. Archie waved a hand to suggest he not speak "don't bother denying it Gregory'. Archie said in a stern fatherly voice, 'I was a British Intelligence agent, and a damned good one. I still have resources and ways of knowing things I probably shouldn't. So don't insult me by trying to deny what I know to be true. I also happen to know his wife is in your hut, sleeping off your recent activities. What you do in your private life is your own business, but it would be best that when you head to Europe you take her with you. Though I suspect Rick already knows about you two, I do not believe he is aware that she is here. And, with the dangerous people following us, it would be best that she be kept out of harm's way."

Greg shook his head not knowing what to say. All he could do was utter the word "How…?" Nothing else came out but a dry croak.

Archie laughed softly "Call it instinct, there isn't any other word that would fit for how it is I know. Also I saw the look on your face when we picked you up. The last person in the world you expected to see was Rick and there was a definite look of fear that came across your face when you saw him. That and I saw you look back nervously to your hut as he took your hand. Like I said instinct and some measure of past experience and training helped me figure it out. So, when you leave 'tonight', you will be taking her with you. We, Hans and I, will be making ourselves visible in our usual haunts to keep them off the scent. If we do what we normally do, they may never get wise to what we are doing, at least while the bullion is loading. Once it's gone it won't matter what they find because they will never know where it went or if it even existed if we play our cards right.

We are also concerned about you being seen. These are connected people with resources and if they get wind of your presence on this island it wouldn't take long for them to figure out we plan to move it. If that happens we are in trouble because the loading process will take several days, if we have no delays. So Rick and Hans will remain onboard tonight to supervise the initial loading and see that things move smoothly. Once you have done what you need to here, we will be heading back. We'll take my jeep. I want you to pack and get your stuff ready and I will drive you to the airport to ensure that you are safely away and unseen. You will be using a private charter jet."

Greg nodded but said nothing. There was nothing to say. The old man had read him like a book page by page. Sitting back down on the computer he chuckled to himself with a sense of growing admiration for the old man sitting across from him. "No wonder his generation won the war" he thought.

One hour later, Greg was dropped off at his hut. Archie pulled into the shadows to wait for him to pack. He was determined to see them off the island tonight. Inside the hut Laurie wearing only a towel met Greg and dropped it and threw herself into his arms and kissed him. Greg, who loved her more than anyone indulged in a kiss before breaking it off saying, "We have a change of plans. You and I are heading to Scotland. The job requirements have changed and we will be on a plane in less than 30 minutes. The plane we are taking has a bed so I believe we will be able to continue this on our flight. He looked lovingly into her eyes as her excitement showed on her face.

He then took her face into his hands and kissed her gently as his hands fell to her naked body wishing they could simply give in to lust. But he knew too well, that if they did they'd miss the plane. That and the old man waiting outside would no doubt interrupt their fun if they dawdled and the last thing he wanted was an old man barging in while they were fucking. "We need to get packing" he said.

"Ok,' she said 'Scotland?" He nodded but said nothing more while he threw his bags together. In less than ten minutes they were riding in Archie's Jeep racing down a back street on their way to the airport. Greg and Laurie held hands in the back seat.

She was excited about the spontaneous trip they were taking. 24 hours before she had been in her living room contemplating the state of her marriage. She loved both Rick and Greg each for different reasons. Greg was more fun than Rick had ever been. One side of her knew it was the excitement of a new relationship that drove her love for Greg. Rick she loved as the father of her children but she had long since lost interest in him sexually. Was it boredom, complacency? Her husband had let her have this fling and if that meant that she would be taken to exotic places on a moment's notice, so be it. She wouldn't complain, though a nagging guilt and uncertainty simmered under the surface.

The relationship with her husband had improved, mostly because he was letting her see Greg. A fresh new way of dealing with marriage for sure but there was doubt about where her marriage was going. She didn't think it was over, but she knew that it had changed and would likely continue to change. Still, the idea of loving two men confused her. She had for the longest time thought of herself as a good mother and wife. Now she was jetting off with her lover to Scotland. Was she still a good person? Her grip on Greg's hand tightened. "Am I a bad person for doing this?" She asked out loud.

Greg answered her by whispering into her ear. "I love you, what we have is a loving relationship that happens to be sexual. I don't think I could go on if I didn't have you here, by me. So if that means I have to share you... I will share you if that is what it takes to keep you." It wasn't really an answer to her question, but then she hadn't been seeking an answer either.

30 minutes later the corporate charter jet cruised smoothly through the night sky at 30,000 feet while on the queen size bed in the tail section Laurie knelt in front of Greg who stood on the mattress holding onto the overhead. They had shed their clothing the moment they'd reached a stable altitude and headed immediately to the bed and in full view of the stewardess who clearly had seen this sort of thing many times before and who had very often participated in the activities herself, fringe benefits of being a charter flight stewardess.

What doubts Laurie had expressed in the jeep were long gone. Because just as they had buckled up for take-off Rick, her husband text messaged her reiterating the fact that he loved her and that he wanted her to enjoy her time with Greg, when she saw him again. His encouragement of her affair helped to ease her guilt if only for the moment. An hour later the plane ran into turbulence while she was riding Greg grinding herself hard onto him causing her to cry out in bliss. This resulted in Greg calling the pilot to seek out turbulence or at least let them know when they were going to hit some. Laurie and Greg spent the majority of the flight making love with Laurie riding the turbulence when they found it. Six hours later they landed in Edinburgh Scotland, exhausted for reasons not travel related. Laurie's first ride in a British cab was spent sleeping. In a penthouse suite overlooking the North Sea they both dropped their luggage and dove between the sheets falling immediately to sleep in each other's arms too exhausted for anything else.

Chapter 32
On Edge

IT WAS NEAR dusk when Patrice not having seen Archie for several hours checked the museum doors only to find them locked. It was then that she began to get nervous. The fact that he was a former SOE agent suggested he wasn't to be taken lightly, in spite of his age. The Trio had reported that when the Dutch Skinheads ran into him he was holding his own and even took one of them out before their sniper gave an assist. But what made her nervous was the fact that Mr. Davis had been shot in the side when second skinhead fell. He couldn't tell how badly he'd been injured but given his age any wound was potentially life threatening.

He was one of two possible leads to the whereabouts of the lost bullion. The trio had lost track of Beck, a man who had eluded discovery for nearly 30 years. If he had gone to ground the chances of finding him were slim. Their best chance was Archie Davis and if he died she would have to go into hiding herself.

The skinheads had alerted their quarry to their presence so it would be harder to track them. Nobody heard what the skinheads said to him so it wasn't clear if they tipped their hand. Chances are they had, they weren't smart enough to be subtle. Patrice on the other hand was well versed in the art of interrogation. She found men especially easy, because 7 out of ten times all she had to do was get their pants off and her mouth working magic on their appendage before they were singing like canaries, especially if she held their orgasm hostage. The remaining 3 out of ten required she actually bed them before they spilled their secrets. No man could resist her charms and very few women. Actually Patrice couldn't remember anyone she had failed to coerce into her bed, as a sly, self-satisfied smile curled her lips.

Taking a seat on the park bench she couldn't risk missing Davis return or departure, if he was still inside or even alive. Patrice sat back and looked up sighing in exasperation and impatience. It was then she spied the slats in the belfry. One slat was askew and slightly out of place and it hadn't been askew that morning. Had Davis been watching her? Of course he had, she thought. After his run in with the skinheads he was going to be watching from the highest place in the square, his own belfry. It was so cliché that she hadn't considered it. Now, it was childishly obvious. Calling the Trio chief she shared her insight with him. As they were concluding their business the sniper who had holed up in a large tree, the only higher place than the church belfry, said that he saw Davis walking around inside his house, a positive ID, confirmed through his scope.

A wave of relief swept through her in the knowledge that she had not lost the one lead that might save her life. Now with her nervousness gone, she instructed the Trio chief to see if there were any alternative exits or entrances to the church compound. The Trio chief was way ahead of her and reported that a series of drainage tunnels had been added with in the past ten years to deal with the annual flooding associated with hurricanes and tidal surges, each with a maintenance access hatch/grate in the basements of the larger buildings. The main drainage duct dumped out onto a beach on the west side of the island. It was then decided that a man be placed at that duct to observe anybody coming and going. With that Patrice decided to take Lisa to dinner.

She hopped into an open taxi and headed to the hotel. On the way back she calculated her time frame understanding that it wouldn't be long before Werner realized the skinheads were dead. It had been two days already and he wouldn't have the patience to wait more than a week before he sent replacements, or came himself. That last thought frightened her, especially since she knew if he came it would be to kill her. Hopefully he would just send replacements. That she could handle because the men Werner usually sent were vicious and not overly bright, like the skinheads. She on the other hand worked with thoughtful intelligent people for the jobs she needed done. It was for this reason that she was off the grid and able to disappear if she needed to.

That had been her plan from the moment she realized the folly of remaining with the Operation, the day she found a bullet with her name and the words 'retirement plan' engraved on the casing sitting on her nightstand. She had simply wanted to make plans for retirement and chose to discuss it with her boss. At the time he seemed perfectly agreeable. Apparently he had a different idea of what 'retirement' meant. That same day she began making plans with her bankers to begin transferring funds to alternative bank accounts; Funneling the bulk of her assets to Switzerland in a series of transfers that would take three years to complete so that it would go unnoticed until she closed the accounts altogether and disappeared.

Looking out the window of the taxi Patrice began questioning the wisdom of completing this job. What would it benefit her? She had thought that by locating the bullion, she could somehow buy her life back. But the more she thought about it, the more absurd the idea became. It was clear that no matter what happened, if they found the bullion or not, Werner would be sent to kill her. The fact that the Trio had been given orders to call Werner in the event things did not turn out confirmed what she already knew deep in her heart. Luckily the Trio felt a tighter allegiance to her than to the Operation. At least with the Trio at her back, she held the upper hand.

Lisa was dressed and ready when she entered the room, stunning in a new kimono styled wrap around, mini skirt. Patrice heart skipped a beat falling totally for the woman standing before her. Taking a quick shower and getting dressed in an equally stunning sundress, they headed out to dinner and an evening of romance that would last until dawn.

Chapter 33
Werner's Dilemma

AT THE MOMENT Patrice was having dinner with Lisa, Werner sat in his apartment as an evening snow began to fall. Set up much the same as Der Fuhrers chambers it was much smaller but no less comfortable. In fact he preferred the smaller rooms especially on nights like this, where the fireplace could heat the whole space. Being raised in Austria he had never gotten used to June being a winter month, or having Christmas in summer but it was the reality he lived with and gladly to serve his Fuhrer. Only his mind was not on the snow outside, nor the upside down seasons; his mind was on the Dutchmen.

They had reported being on the trail of Davis and were about to make their move. That was three days ago, he had heard nothing since. The Trio reports were coming every six hours with nothing new to report, except that they had seen two large men following close behind Davis and asked if they needed to take action. He had told them not to do a thing and just keep watching and report back. That was the last he'd heard of the Dutchmen.

Neither team had seen anything of Beck. That meant that either Patrice had lied about the bullion, or Beck wasn't whom they thought.

Shaking his head he doubted it was anything more complicated than that, simple misidentification and an overly active imagination. He'd come to believe the bullion was a myth. How could a horde so massive escape the thoroughness of the SS for so long? Yes, the gold may have once existed, 70 years ago, but not in the amounts that she had suggested. The amount of gold bullion was clearly exaggerated, like an old fish story it had grown with each telling.

The men who were supposed to deliver it were never seen again. It was clear to him what had happened; they had absconded with it. He thought so, because that is what he would have done under the circumstances. Back then they could have gone just about anywhere they wished with that kind of money. The world was in chaos and if you wanted to disappear there was very little to stop you. No, those men had disappeared, moved to some distant land where they could live out their lives as wealthy barons.

Taking a sip of his beer Werner stared into the fire. He'd give them two more days before he sent is back up team. He wasn't about to waste resources on a wild goose chase, but because his Fuhrer had ordered a thorough search and the questioning of the man Davis, he was determined to see this project through on the extreme chance Patrice was right. With a sigh of impatience and mild contentment he leaned back and listened to the wind outside and the crackling of the logs in his fireplace, dreaming of the day when he would kill Patrice.

————)(◗)(————

It was close to midnight when the trios third man known only within the Operation as M took up station at the large drainage pipe on the west side of the island. He wasn't there five minutes before he noted two sets of tire tracks. One set of tracks appeared to drive up, stop and take off again, while the second set drove into the large drainage pipe, but had not come back out again. He laughed to himself. "Clever old man" he thought. Reporting what he found to his boss who in turn then reported it to Patrice.

At that moment however, Patrice was propped up against her headboard with Lisa's head between her legs. Placing a hand on Lisa head to indicate she should continue she answered the phone and listened to what the Trio team leader said. She replied "Have him wait there to confirm and do not call me until morning, unless it is life or death" she said, struggling to keep her voice even as Lisa, in a fit of mischief shoved three fingers deep inside Patrice causing her to cry out in passion. The phone fell from her hands causing Patrice to forget to hang up giving the trio chief quite an earful.

Patrice screamed in orgasm then returned the favor for Lisa who screamed in multiple orgasms as Patrice expertly administered her well-practiced talents on the younger woman. He listened to the goings on for ten minutes before Patrice noticed her phone was still active then speaking into the phone "I Hope you enjoyed that" she said icily and hung up. He knew better than to answer, hung up, smiled to himself then went to take a cold shower.

At that very moment Jay the trio sniper had an infrared sniper scope attachment set on a tripod and locked in on Patrice hut. The image he could see was an orange gray heat image of two women with one sitting up and another sprawled out and 'busy' between the legs of the other. The only thing he was missing was his laser microphone that would have allowed him audio. Of course he didn't tell his chief what he was doing because he'd have his nuts.

What he saw in that scope was better than porn and the action went on until dawn; his favorite part being when Patrice used the strap-on on Lisa. Lisa had taken position at the head of the bed on her knees and grasping the headboard. Patrice had put on the device and had crawled up behind her. The device, being cold and not holding body heat appeared gray in color but was otherwise clearly visible. Lisa had reached between her legs…grasped hold of the device and guided it to her waiting self. Patrice then took hold of Lisa's hips…and drove the device deep into Lisa whose head rocked back as the entire length disappeared into her in one slow, constant motion.

Initially the action was slow as Patrice ground the device into and out of Lisa in long slow strokes in what was a clearly pleasurable torture of the senses. But eventually Lisa was thrashing about in ecstasy at least that is what it appeared to be on camera…as Patrice then drove the device into Lisa fast and hard until both women were thrashing about in orgasm, or what he took to be an orgasm. Having no audio he couldn't tell for sure but then it certainly didn't seem in anyway painful…not from his perspective at least. In any case it was a pleasant distraction from the boredom of keeping watch.

This particular distraction occurred precisely at the moment Hans and Rick returned from the ship and entered Archie Davis house for final planning. The Jeepster was parked in an alley two blocks away under a bushy tree. They used the alley behind the sales huts to avoid being seen. Had Jay not been distracted, he would have seen them approach the gate, open it and enter the courtyard at 2 a.m.

Inside the house Hans and Rick sat across from Archie at his kitchen table with the lights off.

Archie dressed in a dark sweater and dark pants leaned in close to his friends. "They have a lookout in the tree across the square. I noticed him yesterday as I went about my business. At the moment he is distracted and watching something else apparently believing that I am asleep. So after this you two will go to the ship stay there. Looking at Rick he said. "I have already checked you out of your room and paid your bill. Your bags are here so when you leave take them because you are not coming back. Also I drove Mr. Mitchell to the airport last night and drove the Jeep into the culvert and up the maintenance ramp in the public garage. I eliminated that portion of the blue prints from the public record last year in anticipation of one day needing to be away unnoticed."

I'm hoping they notice the tracks. If they do they'll have no choice but to place a lookout there in anticipation of our driving out again. Whether they take the bait or not is a question I am not able to answer with any certainty. You two need to get the ship loaded, because once they realize we've gone to ground they will start combing the brush looking for us. If that happens it's only a matter of time before they locate the tunnel and the base, then we are in trouble. Once they realize the vast amount of bullion on deposit here, they will send every resource they have to gain possession of it. That includes killing us and dumping our bodies in the ocean for starters. That is, if we are lucky."

Archie sipped his tea then proceeded. "So by keeping to my normal routine for the next few days they might settle into watching me and perhaps get the notion that this was a wild goose chase and leave. Moving the bullion has to be done no matter what. Their being here is no coincidence and the lengths they are taking to keep tabs on us, is proof the bullion has to be moved. It simply cannot stay here" He said leaning back looking at his two companions' one after the other.

Rick nodded brow furrowing in thought "What happens if they send more like those goons who cornered you? You'll be down here alone and you might not get so lucky next time. I mean you got shot, a minor flesh wound granted, but a few inches to the right and you could have been killed."

Archie smiled at his young friend. "I see your point, but we have a second team out there apparently interested in keeping me around. So I am not exactly alone, though I cannot say that they are my friends. The reality is that we have to load that ship and make sure we get it out to sea before they are aware of it. Hans and I should have been loading it bit by bit over the years, but like I said earlier I think we just got complacent or lazy. Regardless, this has to be done; it cannot wait any longer. When it is secured in the salt mine and Mr. Mitchell has created your Legend we have to get rid of those weapons in the meadow". He looked at Hans who nodded acknowledgement. With that Archie pulled out an old cardboard tube and pulled out the original plans to the island, drawn by Johan Weiss of the Kaisers Imperial Navy.

"According to these plans, the lagoon where our ship sits was not the original lagoon. This whole base was supposed to house and maintain battleships and destroyers that were to be used as commerce raiders. That is why it is so massive because it was intended to house 3 Battleships and ten destroyers in the dome. It is clear that when submarines became operational that changed. It made better sense to deploy submarines from the base than to have massive ships waiting for the lagoon to drain so they could enter into the base. According to these notations in the log Weiss modified the lagoon to allow for multiple submarines to deploy and return at once. There appears to be a rail system under the water and a cradle car onto which the submarines would sit and use their screws to propel them into and out of the base completely submerged. So nobody would see the subs whether coming or going."

At this Rick looked up at Archie confused. "Ok, if they had this system in place why then were those submarines spotted so close to the island? If they were laden with gold wouldn't they have wanted to keep their approach hidden?"

At this Hans spoke up. "I think I can answer that. The captains of those submarines were not told of the rail system until they had gained sight of the island itself. According to what I witnessed the captain was handed an envelope only when we had reached the island, in which were instructions of how to enter the lagoon. Captain Heinz, who commanded the boat on which I arrived, became somewhat agitated with the General for not sharing this approach strategy sooner.

Apparently he believed that given their cargo, a stealth approach was best. The General simply said that he was ordered to pass the envelope to the captain only upon reaching the island. So that might explain the multiple sightings. It makes sense when you take into consideration that Hitler and Donitz were the only two senior members of the Reich to know of the island. Hitler likely was the one to require the last minute add-on, given that was his method of doing, particularly in the end, or so I am told.

Hitler was insane and prone to making blunders of epic proportions, which invariably cost us the war. Donitz would have, I believe ordered a more common sense approach so not to risk the crews. He was a good man that way. Does that help?" Rick nodded but said nothing turning his attention back to Archie who continued speaking while pointing to the chart.

"Apparently the second lagoon was dug out sometime in the 1930s after Hitler came to power and was made aware of the bases existence. The original lagoon was filled in at the end of the first-world-war to hide the evidence. The subs were sunk and then covered over to prevent their discovery to keep Germany from being punished even more severely. This base you see was the only one of its kind and a violation of international law. Germany paid a heavy price for its aggression as it was. Imagine the devastation they would have encountered had this islands existence come to light." All three men agreed that this was a plausible explanation for the bases non-discovery.

Archie continued "That meadow out there is the old maintenance lagoon where algae and other sea life were cleaned off the hull. If we were to pump tons of water into that basin and open the access gates to the sea we could sink the weapons, but that should happen only after the bullion is moved; First things first." He said. Then he got up and headed to the telescope to spy on the man in the tree. "Ok, whatever he's looking at has his attention, so I think you need to get out of here while he's distracted. Get loading started and keep it going until it's done.' He said ushering the two men out the door. At the gate Archie took out his binoculars to make sure it was clear. The man in the tree was certainly fixated on whatever it was he was watching. Instinctively Archie knew or at least suspected what he was watching and muttered "Bloody Pervert" under his breath. "Ok, now move along, quickly" as the gate opened quietly.

One of the many jobs that Archie had done that day was to oil the hinges of all the doors they were likely to use, most specially the door to his house and the gate which up to that morning had a horrendous squeak that would have alerted the distracted watchman to their activity. In a flash both Hans and Rick were in the alley and heading to the jeep. Hans drove to the secret cutout he and Archie created inside the scrub brush. The only access to it was from the beach near the boathouse. They cut it out of the bush to allow them to come and go from the mountain unnoticed. Over the years the canopy had become so dense no light could be seen inside it. It also masked the noise of the jeep sufficiently to keep them from being heard as they sped back to the mountain cavern.

Exactly 30 minutes later loading began, taking two hours to load the remaining crates on the pier. While that was happening, Hans and Rick both began to ready the roller conveyor that went up the spiral roadway. One by one the crates were moved onto the conveyor. Hydraulic brakes kept the crates from moving too quickly helping them to stay on the roller thereby making it to the loading conveyor. No hydraulic rams were available to push the crates onto the conveyor in the vaults but the loading ramp was moved so that the two men could easily push the crates onto the ramp letting gravity do the rest. Throughout the night each man set in motion the crates from their respective vaults. The loading was moving along more quickly than expected so that by dawn a full 1/4th of the shipment was on board and secure.

The conveyor system worked flawlessly giving them time to rest, which they each did on a military style cot set up outside whichever vault they were emptying. Napping one at a time so that one was awake and watching while the other rested. For the next two days they loaded the ship taking turns driving the K-wagon up and down the roadway to ensure that the crates would transition to the loading conveyor. Every hour one would board the ship and see if there were any issues within the ship itself. That usually fell to Rick because Hans, being near 90 years of age wasn't quite up to making that climb more than once or twice a day in spite of is apparent vigor.

By the end of the second day the rigors of keeping tabs on the loading process began to wear on them. They needed a third man to take up the slack. After two days someone had to stay on the ship to keep an eye on the loading rails inside, because every few hours at least one crate jammed up on a protruding rail bent when a crate that wasn't the correct dimension for the load rotated and jammed. It was easy to fix just a 3lbs sledge to the near corner of the crate and it was free. But the bent rail now created a space where other crates could jam up which they did with increasing frequency, necessitating that a person be stationed full time at the damaged rail. This fell to Rick who had to now spend more time on the ship and still assist Hans with emptying the vaults. Sleeping was no longer an option for either of them.

Early on the third day Archie drove onto the pier in something of a hurry with two passengers and a second vehicle following close behind. Instantly he recognized the woman from the bench. Her long blonde hair still in a ponytail and wearing the same sundress she had worn the day he and Hans spotted her watching the church. The second passenger was a young woman, naked save for the terry cloth robe she was wearing and a great black eye from what had to be a serious blow to the head. The older woman assisted her from the jeep and immediately hugged her. In the Land Cruiser behind them were three men, each armed with automatic weapons, who seemed to be watching over the two women.

Archie walked up to Hans who was clearly questioning the situation with Archie explaining it. Hans saw Rick and waved for him to come down, it seemed urgent so Rick wasted no time getting down. In less than a minute he was by their side and Archie began explaining what had happened.

Chapter 34
Playing Opossum

IMMEDIATELY AFTER HANS and Rick disappeared into the shadows Archie closed the gate and went back inside keeping the lights off. He wouldn't be able to sleep for a while, at least not until Hans called him letting him know they were safe. His wound was feeling much better but it had drained him. Still he couldn't afford to sleep just yet, though he needed it badly. How many times over the years had he gone without sleep? He smiled and tried to count the times he'd been forced to remain awake. He lost count at 50 or so and that was only the first year of the war. Yet, he wouldn't have changed a thing. His life had been one grand adventure after another and he had the luck to have survived where too many had not. "Oh the books I could write" he muttered to himself in his natural Welsh Brogue.

His falling back into his native tongue, forced to the surface memories of his home and the Welsh Countryside with its rural towns and farms. How long had it been since he'd been back' he wondered? 1950 had been his last visit when he'd returned to bury his father and sell the farm. His mother had been killed in the closing months of the war when a V2 Rocket detonated in the square, where she was having afternoon tea with her church group in a London tea house.

All they could find of his mother was a necklace, which was found on a lamppost a block away. Nearly 300 people died in the blast most of whom were incinerated leaving nothing but memories and ashes behind. Officially classified as 'Missing' nothing of her body was never found, at least not that could be identified. A memorial service was held for her with the necklace draped over the last photograph ever taken of her, no casket for there was nothing to bury and nothing to say goodbye to.

His father was crushed. He had loved her so deeply that when she died his smile died with her. In fact the only smile he remembered his father having in the end was the one he held lying in the casket. Archie remained in the family home for a week afterward making arrangements to sell the property and dispose of the family estate, such as it was. An only child he was responsible for the estate. So he hired an attorney to dispose of the property and had the proceeds donated to the Veterans fund after which he promptly left Wales never to return.

Now, as they were heading back to Britain to dispose of the bullion he might take the time to visit his home town, maybe even see the old place, if it was still there. He smiled sipping his tea 'Perhaps he'd buy it and live out his days there. A wave of soothing comfort made his decision for him. It was only right that he died in his hometown and be buried next to his family. With that he sipped his tea and looked into the scope to find the man in the tree focused once again on his house and looking around the courtyard. Tempted to wave back he resisted the urge and sipped his tea waiting for Hans to call. He didn't have to wait more than 30 minutes, before Hans called and announced the loading process had begun. With that he gave in to his need for sleep and went to bed.

Waking at 8am the next day he went about his normal routine having his morning tea, then sweeping the front step and opening the museum for business. He then had breakfast and remained about the compound for the remainder of the day, taking an occasional nap against the time when sleep would be elusive. Around noon, while settling into his first nap, the woman who'd been watching him strolled into the museum. She spent an hour or so inside lingering for extended periods around the back door. After she saw him lying on his hammock; apparently satisfied that he was not going anywhere, left the museum and took up station on the park bench, where she could see him leave, or so she thought. Archie smiled to himself, "That's right Lass, that's right, get nice and cozy, there's nothing for you here, nothing at all".

Late in the afternoon Archie decided to test his escape route to see how long it would take him to get to the public garage where his jeep was waiting, that and to see if his disappearance would go unnoticed. After closing the museum that afternoon he clicked the stopwatch and headed toward the church basement, unlocked the grate and quick marched to the grate in the garage. A total of five minutes elapsed before he could unlock and push up the grate. Taking advantage of the fact that he was alone, he walked to the back of the garage to see if he could drive out without being spotted.

Almost immediately adjacent to the back door was a jeep trail leading into the brush that he had planned to use. He had deliberately not used it to let it grow over to hide it from casual view. It was a trail you could see only if you knew it was there. The old spy in him had never truly retired, hence his current old age. On returning to his compound a total of fifteen minutes had lapsed and his watchers hadn't noticed his absence. So he determined that when the time came he could be away and clear without anyone being the wiser.

At that very moment in Bahia Blanca however, Werner Meyer was making a daily report to Horst Krupp reporting what information he'd received from Patrice on her efforts to locate and retrieve the bullion from the island. Interrupting him mid-sentence Krupp asked "What have you heard from the Dutchmen?"

Werner replied "I have not heard from the Dutchmen in nearly a week. Not since they reported that they were following the old man', he paused to look at his notes, 'Davis. I can only assume they are still tracking him to see if he leads them to whatever Miss Verga believes to be on the island."

At this he was cut off, "Have you attempted to get in touch with them?" Krupp said with obvious irritation in his voice.

"Yes, Mein Fuhrer, they have not responded" Werner said getting nervous, understanding moment by moment that he should have known something was up, when they did not return his messages.

Horst Krupp turned his head slowly toward his young contemporary "So, you haven't seen fit to find out if they are still alive? I know them and they never forget to check in, especially if they are on a job. I would, if I were you, send someone to find out what happened. If it has been a week, I'd say they are either dead or were arrested. If they were arrested we'd have heard something by now."

Werner took the icy demeanor of his boss as a warning that if his words were not followed to the letter, his life would be in the balance. "Yes Mein Fuhrer. It shall be done", he said sweat forming on his brow.

Horst then added "If the Dutchmen are dead, we have to assume that Patrice is somehow involved and will be attempting to go into hiding. With that end in mind I've had our section chief in Berlin watching her accounts and transactions. He tells me that she is slowly cashing out her holdings and transferring them to bearer bonds, which then find their way into Swiss bank accounts. She knows too much to be left alive. If she does go into hiding she could put The Operation in jeopardy with was she knows.' Looking back into the fire he continued with a sigh 'See to it that she is killed Werner. We can no longer trust her...I've been far too lenient for far too long. Oh...and if you miss and she gets away, contact the Berlin section, they may have an idea or two about where she plans to hole up....just in case. However, do not contact them unless you have no other choice. That section has the luxury of diplomatic immunity which we do not wish to compromise. They are the anchor to our existence in the event we run into trouble."

Turning his head back to the fire taking up his wine Krupp spoke as a bout of dementia took hold of his aging brain, bringing him, for the moment, into a state of absolute authority reminiscent of the days when Hitler took advice from him. "It is time that we get to the bottom of this island question. If our men were killed, or somehow interfered with, it is safe to assume that the bullion Miss Verga spoke of is there. You must go verify the find. Kill Patrice first, she is too smart for her own good and too moral. We don't need some Goody-goody woman denying our organization its rightful due. Do it quickly, Werner, your brutality is not to be indulged in this, is that clear?"

Werner came to attention and saluted his boss in a crisp Nazi salute "Yes, Mein Fuhrer, I shall follow your instructions to the letter. It will be a clean kill, I assure you."

At that very moment on St. Vincent Patrice woke with a start with Lisa wrapped tightly in her arms. She sensed that something was wrong, very wrong though she couldn't quite place the danger. Something had awakened her in warning of some pending danger. Somehow she knew that her employment with the Operation was finished.

Patrice smiled looking down at Lisa. Instantly she frowned realizing that she was falling for her, an unexpected but not necessarily un-pleasant and an all too dangerous feeling. Falling for Lisa would put her in danger, especially when Werner arrived as she knew he would. Far from fearing for her own safety she was more afraid for Lisa and she had no intention of letting Werner get his hands on her. That was something she would not tolerate. It was too late to dismiss her or to move her someplace safe, because she knew that Werner would, in his viciousness, seek Lisa out for his own twisted reasons. So the safest place for Lisa was by her side which at the same time put her in danger. "Shit" she muttered to herself.

Moving so to not wake the women in her arms, Patrice showered, dressed and left the hotel room. Immediately phoning 'T' the trio leader, "I need to talk to you.' She said before he could say a word 'What I have to say cannot be said over the phone and you are the 'only' person I can trust."

There was a long pause before 'T' responded "You know that we don't like revealing ourselves to clients. It's too dangerous. We've stayed alive by keeping invisible."

Patrice thought fast, understanding their position, but knowing that what she had to tell them could not be shared on the phone if by chance she was being monitored. "I respect that, but we have to talk and not over the phone."

'T' recognized her dilemma "Ok, You know the church? Inside is a confessional in the right corner as you walk in. It appears to be a left over from when the church was pulling double duty as a protestant and Catholic Church. I will meet you there. I will be in the Priests box, waiting for you."

Patrice sighed in relief. "Ok, I'll be there in ten minutes." With that she hailed a cab. Her mind raced with a sense of urgency that she could not explain. Somehow she knew her time was up and whether or not she succeeded or failed both her life and Lisa's were both now in danger. Both men they were following were aware of their presence and playing it cool, too cool given the gravity of the situation. Here was the old man, who'd been shot only a few days before, lying on a hammock like it was just any other day. If he wasn't going to move, there would be nothing to follow and if they couldn't follow him they'd have to search for the bullion separately and that could take time, time she did not have.

Then there was securing it and the inevitable visit from Werner. It was in her interest to abandon the bullion, because locating it would do her no good. She had more than enough money to last out her days in opulence. Locating the lost horde had been purely accidental. It was her locating it, through the old records of Odessa that had placed her in the precarious position she found herself.

Hopping into the first cab she found and took it to the square. Once there she quickly made her way to the church and marched up the steps and through the doors. Inside she stood in the doorway letting her eyes adjust and saw the confessional in the dark corner adjacent to the alcove. Stepping through the curtain she took a seat and was immediately greeted by the familiar voice of 'T'. So what is this urgent concern of yours?" he asked sounding both concerned and irritated.

"My life is in danger and so is the woman I'm with, Lisa and likely yours as well. In the course of doing my job I was tasked with a secondary mission of locating a specific person important to my employer. In my search, cursory as it was, I discovered that the island he was sighted on, this one, was a land fill built by a company out of Columbia "Cartegena Industrial Disposal" The owners photograph didn't appear to be that of a native Columbian but closer to European Spanish. The photo I had scanned and the computer search found that he was a serving line officer in the German Imperial Navy at the time. That got my curiosity up. What was a former SS Officer doing on an Island built by the Kaiser, coincidence? No. Then I discover, equally by accident, that the island itself is owned by a church, which in turn is owned by a single man, who happens to be a former SOE agent tasked with tracking down missing SS after the war." Pausing she let 'T' absorb the information before continuing on.

"The SS Officer was on the Odessa hit list for his black market activities during the war; They, Odessa, wanted to seize his money and execute him for not joining the guerilla war against the allies. In 1970 he was found living in Switzerland and his home raided. Six members of Odessa were killed after they had apparently killed his wife. After that he went underground disappeared and apparently moved here where he was spotted.

In the last months of the war he and several other SS officers including a General accompanied two shipments of bullion from Norway, to an undisclosed location in two submarines, I suspect to this island. A month and a half later, the General and one other officer are spotted in Buenos Aires walking up the capital building apparently with the intent of asking Argentina to join the war on the side of Germany or arranging for their government to set up shop in exile. Whatever the case, they were immediately escorted from the capitol under armed guard, and their entire delegation escorted to the German Legation where they were told to remain. At the end of the war the legation was found empty. Apparently the morning after being escorted from the capital the entire legation staff left with the General and Beck to a waiting submarine, confirmed by several witnesses. The legation personnel are reported disembarking from a Portuguese freighter in Huelva Spain three weeks later.

Beck, the General and the submarine disappear and aren't heard from again, until Beck shows up 1970 in Switzerland and now, if this is Beck. Given the history of this island and the fact that it was a German Naval base in WWI suggests the possibility that it was used as a base in WWII as well. Why would Beck come here of all places if he wasn't,' somehow, familiar with the island? It is highly unlikely that he would accidentally move to an island that just happens to have been built in secret by the Kaiser, as a submarine base." she added to emphasize her point.

'T' frowned taking in the fact that his employer, 'The Operation' was a front for Odessa, an organization he was familiar with and he was none too pleased about. "So your life is in danger?" he asked.

Patrice took a breath and continued "Werner, the man who hired you, has been tasked with killing me. My employer, an ancient German who insists on being called Der Fuhrer, let me know that I knew too much, that in my diligence I had overstepped the bounds of trust. He suggested that if I located the lost bullion I could redeem myself. Only the more I thought on it, the more I realized that finding it would only seal my fate. I would, once again, know too much. This request I'm making of you isn't for me because I can take care of myself. It's for Lisa that I'm asking. She is an innocent in all of this, and…and I'm afraid I've fallen in love with her.' She paused stifling a sob of desperation 'Sending her away isn't an option because all the people under me work for the Operation and if I am killed they will likely kill her as a precaution against her knowing too much. 'I suspect that Werner gave you follow up instructions to kill me when the job was done" she said.

'T' sighed "He didn't say it in so many words, but he suggested something along those lines. I was to let him know when the job was done and that he'd have further instructions. Given our line of work, it isn't hard to figure out what his intentions were. Something about him always gave me the creeps.' He paused, innately gauging Patrice tension. 'Miss Verga, of all the people we have worked for you are the only one who has ever shot straight with us. In our book that makes you one of us. Besides, 'J' has a thing for you. It's pretty bad' he said laughing softly. 'Also being that they are Nazis, I don't think we work for them anymore but if we suddenly up and quit reporting they'll get suspicious, if they aren't already. Werner likes daily reports and the Dutch clearly haven't been heard from. It won't be long before he sends someone else. I'll have 'M' sat-link to Werner's cell and monitor it. Maybe we can get a bead on who he'll send and when to expect them."

Patrice smiled, relieved that she had gained an ally. "Thank you" she said holding back a sob as an unexpected surge of emotion broke free. Taking a deep breath she gathered herself. "Since the Skinheads, alerted Mr. Davis to our presence, he and Beck have been playing it cool. It is clear they are onto us. That being the case watching them and following them will be a waste of time. I believe Werner intends to kill them when he gets what he wants and if he doesn't he'll kill them just the same."

'T' sat back thinking of his options. "We need to warn them. I wouldn't feel right just letting Beck and Davis alone to face Werner and whomever he sends. As sly as Beck and Davis might be, they're old men and guile only gets you so far, you've got to be quick as well. Davis is in his house right now. He knows we're out here watching him. In fact he's been watching you through the slat in the Belfry as you well know. So, I suggest that you approach him, carefully, and come clean and lay your cards on the table. If I am any judge of character he'll hear you. Don't expect him to trust you. I figure he's got you pegged as a player so he's going to be watching for it. Play it cool and tell the truth. Don't expect him to just roll over and tell you where this bullion is. He's no fool. But I think he'll know the truth when he hears it. Offer our assistance and tell him what is at stake and hold nothing back. Tell him everything, especially the part about your boss being an old Nazi that should open his eyes."

Patrice agreed to the plan and told 'T' to get 'M' to see if the phones were being monitored, and to scramble them even if he finds nothing. "Call me in an hour and I'll tell you if he's agreeable or not. Get 'M' on Werner's phone first. We need to keep on top of him. He won't be sending Cub Scouts that is for sure." With that Patrice said goodbye and left 'T' in the booth. Immediately walking to Archie's gate and rang the bell.

A few minutes later Archie Davis opened the gate and was instantly taken aback by the sight of the woman who had been watching him. "Good Morning Miss, may I help you?" He said in his most preacher-like voice.

Patrice made no pretenses nor did she waste any time. "Mr. Davis, My name is Patrice I have to talk to you. May I come in so we can speak privately?" Archie already on his guard stepped back and motioned for her to step through the gate and then closed it making sure that nobody was following. They then walked silently to this house with Patrice leading the way. Archie wasn't about to let her get behind him. Once inside he directed her to the table careful to keep the table between them and offered her a seat.

Without preamble or the usual pleasantries, Patrice sat down and began. "Mr. Davis, my life and yours are in danger, as well as that of Mr. Hans Beck'. She used Becks full name as a means of identifying the subject to be discussed without, actually saying it. 'I'm afraid that I am responsible for putting you in danger. My employer sent me here to follow you in hopes of locating a lost Nazi gold repository. I recently discovered he was a Nazi, or is if it comes to it. The organization I work for is nothing more than a front for Odessa, which I'm sure you are aware, was formed by members of the SS. We go by the name 'The Operation' now.

Several years ago I was tasked with locating Mr. Beck because he was one of the men who brought the gold to this island. We all thought he was dead until several weeks ago when one of our members recognized him while on vacation here. Being the only lead to surface in 30 years we had no choice but to follow it. Nobody expected anything to come of it, least of all me. During my research to see of if Beck was living on the island I happened across a photograph of the man responsible for its construction, Mr. Juan Dominguez of Cartagena Columbia, owner of Cartagena Industrial Disposal, who didn't appear to be Hispanic and was a bit too pale to have been raised in the tropics, at least at the time of the photograph. I ran a computer match on his photograph and found that he was an active duty line officer in the German Imperial Navy; Commander Johan Weiss, whose specialty was Naval base architecture and construction. I ran the match several times to ensure that we had a good match and it was a 98% match each time.

With the sighting of Beck and the fact that the island was built by a man matching the description of a serving naval officer in the Kaisers Navy the odds of coincidence were dropping fast. Then I looked into who owned the island and discovered you. A non-ordained minister who happens to be a retired SOE agent whose missions are blacked out or on a 100 year hold and who was later tasked with locating and interviewing members of the SS in the closing months of the war. Then there are your bank accounts 300,000,000 British Pounds Sterling in total. Not exactly the bank account of a military pensioner, even one with such a distinguished career, particularly after having been 'retired' with battle fatigue." She looked straight at him to emphasize the fact that she indeed knew more than he wanted her to.

"So with that information I reported to my employer that we may have found the lost bullion repository, at least a strong lead to it.' She sighed and took a breath reaching for a hot cup of tea that Archie had poured for her. 'Thank you' she said, and then continued on. 'However, in my zeal to impress him and advance my position in the organization I let slip, on purpose, my knowledge of 'the operation' being a cover for Odessa. This was my mistake, believing that I would be trusted with their secret."

Patrice sighed again and took a calming breath as the words she spoke registered. Slamming a fist on the table she hissed an oath "Idiot!!" Admonishing herself for being so childish and naïve.

Unable to hold back her tears they fell like rain as she fought back sobs of desperation. Archie however was not swayed, being far too experienced with such tactics. Yet, something told him the tears were genuine, but he retained a prudent distance, with his .45 pointed directly at her belly under the table, which had been in his waist band since his meeting with Hans and Rick.

Once she gained control again Patrice continued "That knowledge I'm afraid sealed my fate. In desperation and ignorance I believed that finding the bullion, would redeem me in their eyes and buy my life. Then my employer sent the Dutchmen, those men who attacked you and I knew then that they intended to kill me. Now you are in danger because they suspect you know where it is and will send more like the Dutchmen to beat it out of you. If they can't they'll get your bank account take it and then kill you."

Archie stopped her before she could go on. "Ok, so because someone saw a person who resembled this person named Beck...." He was stopped mid-sentence with a look of such intense anger that he pulled back the hammer of his .45 and steadied his aim at her belly.

"Don't insult me Mr. Davis' she hissed. 'I've done my homework. He lives on the western shore in a two bedroom bungalow and drives a 'yellow' 1973 Fiat Spider convertible. He has a heart condition that keeps him from over exerting himself due to the stress of living on the run and hiding from Odessa for the past 30 years!" she nearly shouted the last sentence, sobs of desperation choking her words. Shaking her head she sighed and let out a sob she couldn't contain.

"Ok, ok, I believe you. Understand, Patrice, please forgive me but I don't know you from Eve or Adam and you've already told me you work for an organization that makes the mafia look like cub scouts. So I'm not about to cut loose with what I know or whom I know. Please understand I have my caution and a healthy need for it as you well know. It is clear that you are upset. Being threatened with death will do that. So I'm assuming that you aren't just doing this out of the kindness of your heart, but to perhaps save your skin in the bargain?"

Patrice put her face in her hands and sobbed openly now. Again Archie was not swayed. But he played along so not to come off as a cold hearted bastard…just in case. "Now, now there' he said in his most soothing Welsh brogue. 'Just let me know what you need of me and I'll see if I can help."

Wiping her eyes with a tissue given to her by Archie she nodded. "It isn't just for me, but my team as well as the woman I love. She is an innocent in all of this and it would kill me if anything happened to her. Up until last night I was prepared to disappear and live my life with her in hiding but that is no life to share. Eventually she'd come to resent me and she'd have to stay because it wouldn't be safe for her away from me. What I'm afraid of is that she is already compromised so sending her away is not an option. As sick and twisted as these men are I work for they'd kill her just for the sport of it and to send a message to me. The men who approached you are typical of the men I work for, brutal Neolithic beasts with no regard for life whatsoever. If they get their hands on the bullion, they'll kill you, my team and Lisa. They would then take over the island killing anyone who got in the way."

Patrice sipped her tea looking out the window. "I'm sorry I brought this on you. I was simply trying to pad my position in the organization by impressing my boss. Looking back on it I should have known better. The leader of the 'wet team' I run suggested we team up. They have taken a liking to you; especially after our sniper watched you dispatch Olaf. He of course gave you the assist that took out the other idiot. Sadly he was unable to prevent you from getting shot. That caused us some distress with you being our only solid lead to the bullion. It was, I'm afraid, not out of concern for your well-being," she said with a soft laugh.

Archie sat back keeping his .45 pointed at her but released the hammer to the safety position having no desire to accidentally kill his guest. "Well, never the less, I do appreciate the effort, regardless of the motivation. I'm not the man I was, as much as my spirit might think otherwise. I have to consider your proposition and confer with my colleague. It would not be fair to him if I did not first speak to him given the circumstances."

Patrice nodded appreciating the situation she had just put Archie in. She wouldn't have trusted anyone either under the circumstances and to simply agree to her terms without first considering the options would be foolish. He had also not admitted to having the bullion or knowing of its whereabouts, but neither did he deny his knowledge. So she took that tack "It has been 70 years since the shipments were made. It is entirely possible that it disappeared and the amounts reported were exaggerated. The only problem with that is my boss 'knows' how much bullion was shipped because he was part of the Nazi high command and aware of all the details, except the location. It was because he knew of Becks association with the shipments that he had me seek him out. He doesn't know that I am aware of his high command status. Had I let 'that' slip, I wouldn't have been allowed to leave the compound alive, I'm certain."

That sparked Archie's interest. "What's his name?" he asked leaning forward.

"Krupp, Horst Krupp, A well placed aristocrat who found himself on the right hand of Hitler from the mid-1930s all the way until 1945 when, for some reason he was dismissed from Hitler's company…'

She was cut off by Archie who finished the sentence for her. "Injured in 1944 when a bomb exploded in Hitler's Wolf Lair in Prussia costing him his left eye. Who was pursued by the Gestapo for steal-ing Himmler's personal car and got away in a stolen Fiesler Stork Spotter plane in March of 1945 never to be heard from again. Later convicted in absentia of war crimes at Nuremburg he was sentenced to hang. The last note in his Gestapo file is from Himmler himself stating that he was to be shot immediately upon capture. It would appear that your boss was a man without a country." He said sipping his tea.

Patrice stared for a moment taking in what she had just learned. She had not known of his conviction at Nuremberg or that Himmler had ordered his execution nor did she know that the Gestapo had been pursuing him when he left Germany. "I never knew that about him' she said almost to herself. 'It would seem the snake turned on itself in the end, much like its doing now."

Falling into a deep, prolonged silence before realizing just what it was she had done working for them. "Oh my god, I spent the last ten years using my contacts and my talents of persuasion to advance their position and control of world leaders, heads of state. Entire governments have been compromised by my actions.' The last sen-tence she whispered as the shame of her actions came into full focus. 'What have I done?" her cup fell from her hands as the shock of it hit her. Her phone rang several times before she realized it and then answered it.

Before she could answer a highly distressed voice came over the phone "*Our friend Werner sent a team from South Africa known for massacres and genocide. They were used extensively in Sudan, Angola and were called in for technical help in Bosnia when the Serbs wanted to exterminate entire regions of Muslims. These guys are bad news. What's worse is that it took 'M' longer than usual to tap into Werner's signal.*

They're here, on the island already, looking for you with orders to kill you and Mr. Davis on sight and anyone associated with you. I expect that means us."

Patrice nearly dropped the phone in shock.

"Ok, get Lisa and meet us' she said then looked up at Archie. 'We're in trouble, a South African death squad has been sent to kill us and they are already here with orders to kill me, you and my team, is there anywhere we can go and meet safely?" she asked panic rising.

Archie got up and ran to his window. He saw a black Toyota Land cruiser pull up but saw nothing else. "Is this a trick?" he demanded but before she could answer the window shattered as a smoke grenade smashed through it. Instantly the canister burst into a thick cloud of smoke. Grabbing Patrice by the wrist while keeping his .45 in his hand dragged her to the bedroom opened the basement door and ran down to the basement, which his house shared with the church.

When the door closed behind them he wedged a 2x4 against the doorknob then raced with Patrice in tow. "Tell your friends to meet us in the public garage immediately with whatever vehicles you have. Be there in two minutes." She repeated the instructions and her instructions to get Lisa.

What Patrice couldn't know was that minutes before the grenade smashed the window two South Africans were kicking in the door of her hotel room hearing Lisa in the shower believing it to be Patrice. They smashed the door open and dragged Lisa naked to the bed. Upon discovering that she was not Patrice they kicked her in the ribs before they knocked her unconscious.

'J' and 'T' were on their way to retrieve Lisa even before they'd been told to arriving at the hotel just as a gun was being lowered to Lisa's head. The two South Africans were killed before they knew what hit them. 'J' shot them with his Colt 1911 modified to shoot .50 rounds. Each man took a bullet to the chest blowing a fist sized hole out their backs launching them into the air and throwing them against the wall. Both men were dead before they hit the far wall crumpling into a heap on the floor.

Lisa, unconscious, was carried to their Land Cruiser then headed straight to the garage. At that moment Patrice was following close behind Archie in near panic as gunshots above them riddled Archies home. Archie released her hand and reached for his key and opened the pad lock to the grate and lifted it. They climbed down the ladder and he locked the grate behind them. The gunfire faded as they raced down the drainage tunnel. "You need to keep up Lass, these men want you dead pretty badly". Patrice was too numb to answer and simply followed along.

As mentally prepared as she had been, or so she thought, that had been the first time anyone had actually shot at her. Physical manhandling went with her line of work and gunplay was common but never before had anyone actually shot at her. Her mind was disembodied looking down as she and Archie ran through the tunnel. "Shock, this is shock", she told herself and with that snapped out of it and was instantly back in her own body in control of herself and running behind Archie her fear replaced with a savage excitement followed by outrage and anger. "That sick old bastard!!!' She cried. 'He tried to kill me because I know too much about him. You son of a bitch!! That's right I know all about you!!! You just screwed with the wrong woman!!!" she cried into the tunnel. With that she had set herself a new resolve. There would be no running or hiding from them, 'they' would be running from her. She was going to turn their world upside down.

Archie felt the change overtake her. His sixth sense let him know that the dangerous part of this woman had just been awakened. He'd been correct in wanting no part of her fury as the hair on the back of his neck stood on end as his hand redoubled its grip on the .45. "Be sure you put that anger where it belongs Miss Verga. I knew better than to tackle you when I saw you watching me these past few days. You aren't a woman I'd care to have as an enemy".

The comment Archie made was viewed as a compliment by Patrice who squeezed his hand saying, "You aren't a man I'd care to have as an enemy either by what J has to say. He was quite impressed by the way you handled yourself against the Dutchmen. Those two were among the most dangerous men in Europe" she said.

"Well, for dangerous men they weren't all that bright" he said. She giggled liking Archie Davis more and more each moment, agreeing with him whole heartedly. "No, no they were not very bright".

In less than two minutes they reached the grate in the garage and lifted it up. Waiting for them were the Trio, armed to the teeth and watching from the shadows as a team of no less than six men fired into the compound with grenades and tear gas canisters exploding. Pausing only a moment Archie watched as the men shooting up his home, blew the gate and rushed in. "You follow me." he said to the Trio. With that he loaded Lisa and Patrice into his jeep started it backed out of his space, accelerating out the back door and down a dirt path crashing through the brush and onto the trail headed for the boathouse. From there they entered the hidden roadway along the beach. Both vehicles maintained a healthy 40 mph not wanting to make too much noise not knowing if they were being followed. Only when they reached the base of the mountain did Archie stop.

With the adrenaline flowing Archie hopped from his Jeep with the vigor of a much younger man and raced directly at the Trio and pointed to each one in turn. "You lot came here to follow me so that I'd lead you to something. The two men who braced me last week mentioned what they were after and were very clear of their intensions to kill me. I have absolutely no reason to trust you and don't think for a moment that because I let you follow me this far means I'll take you any further. So you had better come clean. I'm in no mood for any shenanigans' he said raising his .45 to chest height. 'Now, I may not get all of you, but at least one will come with me if you pull anything, if I get killed you come no further and you'll be two men short to face that lot back there." He indicated with a nod the men back in town where the staccato of gunfire increased to an alarming rate, mixed with several dull explosions.

The last sentence was directed at 'T', who stepped back, hands raised and sat on the bumper of the Land Cruiser. "Ok you've got a point Mr. Davis. We are known as the 'Trio' our names are secret so we go by T, M, J, while in the field' and indicated which letter referred to which team member. 'We are a former CIA wet team. Are you familiar with that term?' he asked. Archie nodded but said nothing. 'We were disavowed when we were hired by a crooked FBI agent to take out a member of the state department whom he had led us to believe was a drug king pin. Turns out he, the FBI agent, was the king pin and the individual we took out was investigating him. He then turned on us making us the dupe in his scheme.

What saved us was the fact that we were known only by our false identities of which we have several. His attempt to lay blame on us, back fired pretty badly when we released the evidence we had against him to the CIA chief. He is now in prison but because we were responsible for the death of a State Department official our credibility evaporated. They began using us for only the sleaziest jobs the CIA didn't want.

We then began to realize that the CIA was trafficking in heroin, cocaine and opium as well as prescription medications to fund their programs; or so they said. What we discovered was that most of that money was going straight into the pockets of senior operatives. They turned out to be as bad if not worse than some of the low life scum they'd been paying us to eliminate. Worse was that they were paying us government wages. When we said something they turned on us like the FBI agent had and targeted us for elimination. We now work for the highest bidder and have maintained our anonymity so that when we do retire we can do so without fear of unwanted guests raiding our homes in retirement." T took a breath and lowered his arms folding his hands in his lap to show he was not a threat to Archie.

"For several years we worked freelance for the South American Cartels. Work was sporadic but the money was excellent. We finally gained full time employment with the 'Operation' through miss Verga. She hired us exclusively and we worked only for her mostly because she had an ethical standard we admired, that and she never had us take care of anyone who wasn't in need of it. In fact we were doing better law enforcement work than the law enforcement agencies were.

Miss Verga paid us well and always shot straight with us. So we decided that she would be the only person we trusted in that organization. Werner the guy who sent us here, contacted us and told us that once we were done 'here' we were to call him for additional instructions. Given the line of work we are most often employed to do, it wasn't hard to figure out what and whom he was going to have us 'work on'. This knowledge was obtained while investigating the whereabouts of Mr. Beck, cost her position, authority and potentially her life. But 'M' has some information you might find interesting."

'M' took up position next to 'T' adopting the same non-threatening posture with hands folded in his lap to show that he was also no threat. "On our way here I was monitoring their coms. Apparently Werner is doubtful about their being any gold. He is of the mind that Miss Verga has fabricated the story in order to make good an escape and go into hiding. Because of her knowledge of Odessa and their contacts within world governments she now poses a serious liability to their objectives and continued influence on world events. According to what I've heard Werner has succeeded in convincing the 'old man' of his concerns regarding Miss Verga. Once they get her everyone she has ever spoken to, met or potentially shared information with is to be killed. Also, if by chance the stories are true and they find something, the entire island is to be exterminated." At this Archie lowered his gun and stared at 'M' in disbelief.

"Exterminated?" he asked feeling numb as his memories of Germany's death camps came flooding back. He'd not been present for their liberation. In fact he'd been to them months after the clean-up had taken place and the bodies long gone, but the horror they represented clung to him like a filth he could never cleanse himself of. The term 'extermination' for whatever reason struck him. 'What person seeks to exterminate other human beings?' he thought.

In all the years since the war he'd seen the world change for the better in more ways than one, but with all the good and positive changes he'd witnessed one truth remained constant, and that was human nature. With it brutality remained and horrific crimes perpetrated by human beings remained a constant reminder that we had a long way to go before we truly evolved. As these thoughts and memories stormed through his brain over whelming weakness over took him and he fell slowly to his knees automatically falling into a prayer for God to deliver his wisdom and protect the innocent.

After finishing his prayer he asked for assistance to get back up again. Shaken though he was he was fully capable of addressing the problem at hand. Calling Hans he informed him of the situation and asked that he be ready for additional company.

"We are taking a hidden road up the backside of mountain because if we drive up the front someone will likely see us. Once we are on top of the mountain you will have a view of the main roadway. Hopefully they haven't figured out the garage and the tunnel access. If they do they'll find the boathouse. Unless you know where our private road is and how to enter it nobody can find it. Hopefully they'll assume we took the main road. If they go too fast their tires will get punctured slowing them up some. If that happens they will try to slog it up the front. If they do that, you' he pointed at 'J' 'will have a clear shot and should be able to take them out before they know what hit them." With that he hopped back into his jeep and tore down the road like a madman.

Chapter 35

South Africans

CAPTAIN DEF THORSEN stared at the bodies of two black police officers sent to investigate the gunfire. Being keffers he felt no remorse at killing what he viewed as sub-humans. To him it was like viewing the carcass of a wild animal. To Def blacks or rather Keffers as he so often referred to such people were no more significant than the hyenas he had often run down in Africa. In fact he placed the hyena on a higher plane than he did Keffers.

When Apartide ended in South Africa he'd felt betrayed at having to share the world on equal terms with blacks. He had been part of the South African Police Force and was responsible for quelling unrest in the black population. This was done by being particularly brutal to anyone who protested and tried to awaken the passions of the otherwise passively subdued black majority. He had been good at his job, very good. So good in fact the black population in areas he was assigned never created so much as a whisper of trouble. His reputation had been enough to quell the black population just by his being present. His reputation was well deserved and earned however, which had been the point from the beginning. Burning the trouble makers alive had its benefits, particularly when you used the body as a torch to burn down the neighborhood. This was done no more than twice, but that had been enough to establish his reputation which had been paying dividends ever since.

When Nelson Mandela was elected president Def resigned is commission citing that he could not serve under a keffer. He then joined the South African Nazi Party a paramilitary group dedicated to countering the backlash of black retribution that spread over South Africa immediately following the end of national segregation or Apartide as it was known.

Never a full blown war, the conflict was primarily a series of bloody skirmishes between black militia and white militia with lots of casualties and collateral damage in the form of burned out farms and villages. In fact his team was so adept at exterminating villages they were hired by the Serbian government, unofficially, to train their men in the art of regional extermination for which they were handsomely paid. Word spread of their efficiency and consequently were hired out to factions in Sudan, specifically the Darfur, region where their services were used extensively. Africa was a very lucrative continent for their sort of business and is where they were operating when Werner summoned them to St. Vincent.

Recently they'd been hired by the Operation and used as a wet team to clean up situations that needed to go away. This job was a personal favor for his friend Werner who'd explained the situation as being one where the people he was to exterminate knew too much and could not be trusted with their secrets. However, he was told to keep the collateral damage to a minimum because Werner wanted the footprint to appear to be a cartel hit. It would be one among many such hits in the region and automatically draw in the Coast Guard who would do a cursory investigation, draw the obvious conclusion and leave. That would create an appropriate vacuum of activity for Werner to come in afterwards to do whatever it was he needed to.

Def watched from the square as his troops took care of business as they had done so often before. Not once had he been told that they had missed, until now. When his lieutenant saluted and reported that when they'd entered the residence the individuals targeted had somehow escaped the barrage of bullets. Def did not react. He didn't so much as blink when he heard the news. "You did send a squad to search the basement?" he asked totally nonplussed.

"Yes, captain. They are searching for possible exit points" At that moment his radio crackled with news. 'Targets not in basement no visible exits except into the church and nobody had come up from the basement. Searching for secondary exits now' and the radio went silent.

Archie having anticipated using this exit long before this, had created a pile of empty boxes tie wrapped together and then tie wrapped to the grate itself acting as a form of camouflage to fool anyone who might be following in the event of exactly what they encountered. All the South Africans could see were a bunch of old boxes piled up three high in the middle of the floor, not at all looking out of place therefore never considered twice. After a careful search of 10 minutes they reported that they had found no exits prompting Def to enter the basement himself to see what had happened. They couldn't have just vanished so they either had left, or were hidden. The question was where did they go or where were they hiding?

Upon entering the basement Def noted how neat and tidy it was and rather more open than he was used to seeing. The shelves were filled with the typical cleaning chemicals, towels and implements of maintenance usually found in such places. Boxes were scattered helter-skelter throughout the basement but not enough to provide a place to hide, except the pile of boxes conspicuously placed in the center of the room away from where one might usually find boxes. Directing two of his men to move the boxes they found that they were fixed and empty. Stepping away Def directed them to empty their magazines into the boxes. A hail of bullets shredded the cardboard. No screams or blood was forthcoming, the boxes were empty. They then ripped the remaining boxes up to discover the locked grate beneath.

Heavy caliber gunfire made short work of the lock and his men were soon in the drainage tunnel beneath the church. It wasn't long before they'd determined which direction they'd gone, but the camouflage had done its job giving Archie and Patrice time to get away. Def Thorsen was not in the least put off by this minor setback as he was not emotionally involved. To him this was a job and the setback was merely that, a setback and wasn't worth getting upset over. The only thing to upset Def in recent weeks was the fact that South Africa had been knocked out of the World Cup in the first round. Other than that, he had an even temperament and wasn't easily set off. You couldn't be emotional in this line of work and survive.

Sending his team after the targets he prepared his back up team to deal with the inevitable show down with the police now that they'd killed two. Police, even keffer police didn't respond well to their own being killed. But they weren't prepared for his teams level of expertise or firepower. Being that they had cleared the square already with their attack on the church compound police would be easily spotted the moment they arrived on the scene. However, when he stepped through the door of the church he was surprised to see that only his men were visible. No police, other than the two he'd shot, were visible. Shrugging it off he never the less told his team to be prepared and stepped into his custom built, blacked out FJ 40 Land Cruiser to await the report from his search team.

At that moment however, the team he'd sent through the storm drain reached the garage and were now looking for signs indicating which direction their quarry had taken. The team leader noted from the garage that the church compound and the strike team were in full view from deep inside the garage. It didn't take much to determine that they'd left out the back to avoid being spotted. Almost immediately they found the trail and were in pursuit.

Meanwhile Archie feeling surge of adrenaline showed little sign of his age, though he'd pay for it later when the adrenaline wore off. Such jolts of adrenaline had a draining effect on his aging body, but nothing a little rest and Ben-Gay wouldn't fix. That is what he kept telling himself as he drove the jeep up the mountain. Behind him Patrice held Lisa in her arms cradling her head against her bosom. Such sights were not alien to Archie as might have been expected. When Paris was liberated it wasn't long before Parisian nightlife was reinvigorated with sex shows and nudist clubs eagerly taking in American and British script from the troops. He'd stumbled onto a lesbian sex show more than once in his travels.

More recently, particularly in Europe it was not uncommon to see Lesbian couples out and about and even more recently gay male couples snogging in public. He'd been familiar with homosexuality and knew of it but it had never been something openly discussed or celebrated much less acted on in public, not in his day. It was something he paid little if any attention to because it had no bearing on his daily life. Still, it was something he wasn't prepared to reconcile as normal, but then it wasn't his place to judge.

Paying little attention to the distraction he put it out of his mind and drove. Though he did find himself envious of the young lady being smothered in the ample bosom in his rear view mirror, longing for a time when such pleasures were his for the asking knowing too well that his heart would likely not survive any such encounter. What he did have were memories, with that he smiled thinking of the many women he'd known. Following close behind was a black Land Cruiser with the Trio watching their back trail for signs of being pursued.

In a matter of a few minutes Archie reached the plateau and burst through the shrubbery they'd planted to help hide their mountain-top exit from observation. Hans had already opened the door to get a breeze flowing because the machinery having been in operation for several days was getting warm allowing Archie to drive directly into the garage and down the spiral roadway passed the crates as they rolled down the rail system and into the cavern where he met up with Hans.

As they entered the spiral roadway Archie saw Patrice react in realization that she had been correct about the base. The look on her face was a mixture of sadness, fury and frustration, the reasons for which were lost on Archie who had to concentrate on the road and not driving the jeep into the metal conveyor system as they entered the cavern. Slowing the jeep Archie braked to a halt at Hans Becks feet.

━━━━•((◉))•━━━━

Within minutes of first seeing Archie arrive Rick was walking along the pier and approaching Archie and Hans who were now conferring. When Archie saw him he waved him closer and whispered.

"We have a small problem. This is Miss Patrice Verga. You no doubt recognize her as the woman who has been following Hans and I' he said cheerfully then continued 'The people who sent her have turned on her. In fact they just tried to kill the two of us and may very well be on their way here as we speak".

Archie explained the whole business to Hans and Rick as quickly as he could. He then added "Rick, you need to take these men up to the mountain top compound so they can get their equipment operating and their sniper into position.' Grasping Rick forearm, he whispered 'Do not let them know anything about Mr. Mitchell or where we are taking the bullion. Do not share anything that is not immediately pertinent, is that clear? Circumstances are such that they are allies of convenience, more their convenience than ours. We simply cannot afford to trust them."

Rick nodded but said nothing. He'd been a trusting fool in his youth, a genuine sucker trusting his fellow man to be honest, finding out too late that he'd been once again blind-sided by a slick operator. That was no longer the case as his earlier brushes with seedy types had sobered him to the realities of life. As a result his coping mechanism was to isolate himself from others and to keep relationships at arms-length, women included due mostly to the frequency with which he was heartbroken. Again matters of trust were his main concern and he had long since lost trust of his fellow man, in the sense that he was always on his guard and expecting trouble.

As he was walking away from Archie, 'T' approached him with an extended hand. "We are with Miss Verga, you can call me 'T'. They shook hands and smiled. Rick instinctively liked him but remembered Archies stern warning about sharing too much. 'T' gestured to the two other men in the back of the Land Cruiser, the guy behind the wheel is 'M' and the guy with the gun is 'J'."

Rick stifled a laugh "TMJ? Seriously?" he asked as he headed to the K-Wagon.

'T' nodded saying "Its quirky I know but it keeps us anonymous and you'd be surprised how easy we can fit that into a sentence when we want to talk about 'stuff' we don't want others to know. It's a field title only. We have straight civilian lives back home. Kind of boring lives but it is necessary to keep our identity secret' he stopped as Rick got into the K-wagon. Looking around he took in everything and whistled in awe. 'Man! This place is huge. What do you know about it?" he asked.

Rick shrugged, instantly on guard. "Not much, you'd have to ask them about it. I'm just the hired help and they don't pay me to answer questions." Rick didn't want to sound rude but he didn't want 'T' thinking he was in the know either so he did what he did best and that was to play dumb. A talent he'd developed with marriage. It was, he thought, a married mans' secret weapon, feigned ignorance. Let'em think you're dumb as long as it gets you out of housework. Nodding over to the Cruiser, he said "Archie told me to show you how to get up to the plateau. 'T' got into the K-wagon and waved for 'M' to follow.

Gunning the K-wagon forward Rick headed for the tunnel. Since he and Hans had been on the mountain-top he'd been shown another way to the main compound by taking an immediate right as they left the basement garage facility and driving around a stand of over grown pine trees that had been groomed to create a covered roadway that emerged opposite the Main house between the garage and guest huts. Once on the plateau Rick gunned the engine and accelerated to the far side and into the front of the house. The land cruiser pulled up next to them.

'J' immediately hopped from the cruiser and stepped over to the edge with his binoculars to scan the landscape below. It wasn't a minute before he called for 'T'. "They are looking for us" he said to his boss. "It doesn't appear they are sure of our location."

At this 'T' shook his head. "No, they know we're up here. See the lead man? He's got his binoculars up and scanning for a way up. It's time we discourage them." He said. 'J', set up and put a hole in their radiators. But do it when they reach that clearing. That way they have to take cover under their vehicles so we can keep them pinned down. Take them out one by one 'J' he said.

It was at this point Rick pointed out the fact that the road he'd first discovered was adjacent to their position. "If they find that tunnel it's a straight shot to the base."

"Ok, you take 'M' back down the mountain and see what you can do to seal that tunnel." 'T' said indicating that 'M' needed to go with Rick. Without hesitating Rick and 'M' hopped into the K-wagon not sparing the engine racing down the roadway and back down interior road exiting onto the pier accelerating to the bridge and power braking into the turn so that it lined up perfectly with the bridge launching the k-wagon over the bridge and onto the opposite pier. At this Archie and Hans who'd been escorting Patrice and Lisa to the ship watched from the scaffold.

Archie looked at Hans, "You'd better go help them close the tunnel entrance and then seal it. Rick won't know about the sand trap we built." Hans nodded and left Patrice to support Lisa who was now shaking uncontrollably.

Having been pulled from the shower and beaten unconscious by two strange men had shaken her and made her wonder what she had gotten herself into. At the moment she was torn between loving Patrice and being repulsed by the fear of her. A fact that was not lost on Patrice who forced down a sob of heartbreak as the guilt of what happened to Lisa consumed her like a crushing wave.

They all walked up the gangplank and onto the stern of the ship or the 'poop deck' as it was sometimes called. Without warning Lisa grasped Patrice by the waist and let her head fall onto her shoulder "Why did those men attack me?" she asked.

Patrice wrapped an arm around Lisa's shoulders and rested her cheek on the top of her head. "Because they thought you were me. The man, who sent them after me, is very dangerous and believes that I know too much. I discovered, quite by accident, that they are Nazis. I made the mistake of revealing my knowledge in my last report. They responded by threatening me. This job was supposed to buy my life back. Apparently, he changed his mind and sent those men to take care of me. I promise, I will never let them hurt you again' she said sobbing uncontrollably, 'I am so sorry this happened to you, please forgive me…please' she felt her knees weaken as the sobs she'd been fighting down broke free. For the next few minutes Patrice shook with sobs. Lisa began supporting Patrice as much as Patrice was supporting her.

It was apparent to Lisa that her being attacked and beaten hurt Patrice far more deeply than any physical injury could. Patrice was the strongest, most sensual creature she had ever known. In the past week she had been brought to heights of passion and sensuality she had never imagined much less experienced. There, of course, had been some college experimentation. However, those experiences had never been passionate or sensual not when compared to being made love to by Patrice. Nobody had ever satisfied her so completely or exhausted her so thoroughly nor had anyone made her feel so completely like a woman than Patrice, but falling in love was a shock. Before this, what she thought was love was superficial, shallow pretend love with post-adolescent boys.

What she felt now was far more passionate and deep, which both elated and frightened her. At no time prior to this had she expected to fall in love with another woman. Now she couldn't imagine falling for anyone else. How would she explain this to her mother? What would her dad say? She thought as she let her emotions swirl as she reveled in the scent of Patrice perfume and the softness of her hair as it wrapped itself around her neck and fell down the front of her robe. The sensuality of that alone confused her. How could she love this feeling so and fear telling her family about it?

Her revere was interrupted by Patrice whispering to her, "I won't let them touch you again…ever. This is my promise to you. They made a mistake hurting you, honey *a very bad* mistake." Lisa was instantly aware of a power emanating from Patrice, an innate feeling that something deep within had awakened in Patrice something very, very dangerous. In that moment Lisa felt safe from harm but in no way alarmed by the power radiating from Patrice, if anything she felt safer than ever before.

A surge of affection for Patrice burst from her chest hugging her close turning to her and whispered, "I don't want you getting hurt. I know this is sudden…don't think I'm weak or silly, but I'm falling in love with you Patty and want you in ways I've never felt before, for anyone. I hope that doesn't sound foolish or stupid." She said as a tear rolled down her cheek.

Patrice heart leaped and whispered into Lisa's ear "I fell for you first" and they kissed passionately.

Archie hadn't heard their conversation but got the basic idea of it by the tone of their whispers and the obvious kissing. "The world has changed a lot since I was a young man" he thought with a sigh, directing them to the cabin next to his. "Miss Verga, once you get her settled, I need you to come see me in my cabin." He said pointing to his door.

Patrice nodded and said "I'll be right there" then disappeared into their cabin. 15 minutes later Patrice walked through the open door of Archie's cabin. "She is resting. What do you need?" she asked. Archie motioned for her to take a seat and poured each of them a Scotch Whiskey. Taking a seat he loosened his shoulder holster and removed his service .45 placing it on the table between them. "A 1911' Patrice noted out loud 'I'd have expected you to use a Browning or even a smaller caliber Walther" she said.

He nodded sipping his Scotch before answering. "I liked how it felt in my hand and when I needed to defend myself it did the job with one bullet most often. My original service revolver was an American made Browning, left over from the Great War, complete with lanyard and whistle, a standard Officers side arm in WWI. When I signed on to SOE the American Colonel who recruited me let me try the Colt .45 automatic and I took an instant liking to it and never took up the old Browning again, which seemed flimsy when compared to the Colt. Also the Browning was a .38 caliber police revolver more suited to law enforcement than combat. Loading a revolver in the heat of combat is a good way to get killed. As for my using a Walther, I never liked the feel of them. But this old 1911' he said grabbing it in his hand, 'feels substantial and if I ran out of bullets it was heavy enough to beat down my attacker in hand to hand."

Patrice never thought of such things. Then again if she had need of a firearm, she usually hired it done. In fact she had not once, held a gun in her own hand. But her curiosity was not such that she needed to see for herself. She was more than content with being curious. "What did you want to talk to me about?" she asked taking up her own whiskey, dipping a finger in and stirring it unconsciously then putting her finger in her mouth to taste it. The effect was to provide a sensual scene that Archie, had he been 30 years younger might have found alluring, but turned away and swallowed his whiskey in one swallow and poured another glass.

He then looked directly at Patrice who was smirking to herself at his reaction to her over teasing but listening quietly as Archie spoke, "Circumstances make it necessary for me to bring you up to speed on our situation here. It should be obvious to you that we are planning to move the bullion to a more secure location. The fact that you were able to find us after so many years is testament that we have delayed this move far too long. Before we knew it age had caught us, Hans and I, as did our complacency. We simply never expected to have to move it, to be honest. Then as life would have it extenuating circumstances forced us to face the fact that the bullion was no longer safe from discovery. I will not share those circumstances nor will I share the intended destination." He said in a tone he adopted when making a strong point.

"The purpose of our hiding it was to keep it out of the hands of the Nazis. It should be obvious to you why they should never get their hands on it. Even if they want it for reasons of greed, I'm not prepared to allow it, neither is Hans. Wealth of this magnitude in the hands of such men would be disastrous. We've spent the past 40 years keeping it hidden and out of their hands" he stopped to sip his whiskey giving Patrice time to inject her thoughts on the matter.

Pausing to find the words she responded "It was only my digging around and putting two and two together that led me here. The identification of Beck was purely accidental. Had it not been for my checking on the owner of Cartegena Industrial Disposal it is likely this find could have gone undiscovered." She said this sounding apologetic.

Archie nodded then added, "For a few years perhaps, but once Hans and I passed it would be a matter of time only before some large real estate firm acquired the land and discovered the base underneath. They no doubt would want to keep it quiet, but inevitably someone would leak it to the media. A civic-minded 'do-gooder' or maybe a disgruntled employee seeking revenge against his boss, or a simple-minded moralist would eventually divulge this horde to the world. No matter what happened or how, it would have been made public in a matter of weeks, which would tie the bullion up for decades. Not that it would matter because the minute Odessa learned of it, they would descend on this island, dispatch those watching over it with typical Nazi efficiency and disappear with enough bullion to rebuild their infrastructure and possibly bring them back to power in one form or another, which is something I cannot allow to happen, not while I am still able to prevent it."

Looking up at Archie she said, "You wanted me to come in here. Yet you haven't said one thing that I needed to actually hear, really.

You've already got things in motion and well in hand from the looks of it. The only reason I'm here is because my boss tried to kill me, you just happened to be with me when he tried. Had they been just a bit more careful I'd have been lying on slab in the morgue alongside Lisa. You wouldn't have ever known me as anything but an unlucky tourist. Now that I am here, what did you want to talk about...really?" She asked.

Archie nodded and put down his whiskey then looked her straight in the eye. "I am prepared to discuss sharing a portion of this wealth with you on condition of your silence. However, it will do you no good if your boss finds you and kills you or worse tortures you for information then kills you".

Patrice nodded her understanding with growing excitement not daring to believe what she was hearing as Archie continued on "That being said you need to throw them off the trail if possible. You might report that you found nothing here and that the persons you identified were not who you believed they were etc, etc. You get the idea" he said then slapped his knee and snickered "Tell your boss that the two men you thought were Hans and I are actually two old fruitcakes living like an old married couple' he howled in laughter as another idea came to him 'tell them the reason Hans or the man you thought was Hans was gone for a few days was because he was tied naked to a four poster bed in some sex slave bondage game." He laughed out loud as he imagined the look on the old Nazis face when he got a report that the two old, wrinkled men he thought were an old SS soldier and SOE agent were actually homosexuals who were still active and into bondage. He chuckled; thinking about it then fell into a bout of laughter so intense he had to support himself with the table to keep from falling off his chair.

Patrice joined in the laughter knowing the very reaction her employer would have in getting such news, a protracted coronary. Smiling in appreciation for the old man's sense of humor she added "News like that might just kill him" she said feeling a little better now that Archie had made her laugh. "I might send a report just like that. I'll say they made their money selling counterfeit Viagra out of Mexico to the senior citizens in Florida." At this Archie had tears of joy streaming down his face as he tried to keep himself upright.

Bringing him-self back into the moment forcing him-self back into a serious thinking mindset he continued his thought process whipping his eyes snorting one last chuckle. "Ok...back to business. You then report that you were attacked. Pretend you do not know who these men are or who sent them. He may not believe you. It might help if you threw in some hysterics. It is important for him to believe that you have fallen off the deep end emotionally. Feed his male chauvinistic ego. Make him believe you trust him to save you etc. That should at least slow him up a bit and give him pause in killing you."

Patrice smiled at the old man in genuine liking. '*He must have been something in his day*' she thought wondering just how much energy he must have had when he was a young man. "Why is it you never married?" she asked.

The question caught him off guard. "Ohh, well, I never found the right one I guess, at least not one that could tolerate my hunting Nazis. The women I knew had no patience for such things. I tried living with a woman, but the picket fences had splinters and rose bushes were prickly as was her demeanor when I didn't conform to the sedentary lifestyle she wanted me to live. One day, I caught her with the gardener. It was immediately apparent what was going on before I did more than opened the door. The war had pretty much numbed me to the triviality of infidelity. Compared to the emotional violence of war such intrigues were of little consequence, at least they were to me.

So I got a beer and went to investigate. She never noticed me standing in the doorway, mostly due to the fact that her face was buried in a pillow while he went to town on her from behind. He was working rather hard so I didn't interrupt them. Without another thought I went about my day as if it were any other. I was sitting in the living room reading a book when they came down stairs several hours later much to her surprise and shock.

The fact that I didn't get upset or angry made her madder than an old wet hen. She was the one playing hide the sausage with another man and she got mad at me? I never understood that' he said this shaking his head in dismay. 'We kept at it for a couple of years until one day she never came home. I later heard they got married and moved to Edinburgh and had three kids". Archie paused thinking of Skye wondering what their kids may have looked like had they had any.

He had sensed something was off the day she left him. Something he couldn't put his finger on, then. His mind was always on hunting lost fugitive Nazis for the CIA having been retired from SOE since renamed MI6. She had not been able to accept his being distant and caught up in things he could never tell her about. Skye had been a WAF during the war, an assistant assigned to him after he was put behind a desk in the last months of the war.

Their relationship didn't start until he asked her to accompany him to the wedding of Colonel McKenzie and Beth on VE day. It had been the euphoria of the war ending that likely sparked their romance. A

Scotswoman with a curvy body and straight blonde hair that she let grow once the war ended. She was lovely as anything he'd ever seen and immensely passionate, an insatiable lover and absolutely shameless, at least between the sheets. Otherwise she was a perfect lady.

He felt that she understood him and she had been patient with him for a long time, nearly seven years. But he had never let the war go or had it not let him go? He wasn't sure which. What he was sure of was the pain in his chest that never went away once he realized she was gone. He was going to ask her to marry him, even after she had cheated on him. He really wasn't all that bothered by her occasional lapses, such things were not as important to him as was her company. Something he came to learn but only after it was too late. He had always thought she'd be there waiting and give him children and be his companion in old age. A belief he held for years afterward in a vein hope that one-day she might again show up at his door.

That hope ended the day he saw her lying in her casket. Her children had invited him to her funeral by accident having found his address among the many in their mother address book. It was seeing her lifeless body in the casket that made him finally realize, at last, that she was the woman he loved, the woman who had saved him in the years following the war when he felt useless. He had taken her for granted…when he needed her most. That day his heart shattered as he fell to his knees by her casket begging her to forgive him as he sobbed openly by her casket, begging her to take him with her. Only at the gentle urging of Skye's daughter did he finally rise and take a seat with the other mourners. The ache in his heart never went away, ever. Her loss he carried with him like a wound and would be the reason he never let another woman into his life, to honor her, the woman he had learned to love…too late.

Coming back to the moment and the woman sitting across from him he smiled softly and said "Such things passed me by many, many years ago. Besides, I'm supposed to be an old fruit remember?" they laughed. Patrice saw the distant look in his eye and the building of a tear carefully concealed with a quick look away. Her heart went out to him realizing that he had lived his life alone never being quite free of the war that made him who he was and it, the war, had never let *him* go. In the reflection of his eyes she saw what could be her own future. In that realization she grasped his hand and squeezed it, hoping that she might, in that act, avoid a similar fate.

Leaning forward, Archie moved in close to her and said "If ever there was a woman I would have fallen for it would have been a woman like you." He patted her hand and smiled at her adding "I always liked dangerous women with nice tits." Patrice blushed and laughed out loud at the old mans atrocious complement.

With that she stood up and kissed his cheek. "Your offer is generous, very generous I'm ok with the pay out, but I can't speak for the Trio. You will have to discuss it with 'T' and the rest. I'm sure the 'fee' will be more than adequate to procure their services. She then left and returned to the cabin where Lisa lay sleeping. Archie watched her go and finished his whiskey in one swallow. Standing he headed for the fantail and down the scaffold to meet with T to discuss the proposal. If they were to get out of there alive he would need their cooperation if only to speed things along.

Chapter 36

Misgivings and Doubt

DEF THORSEN WAITED patiently in his FJ40 Land Cruiser as a scouting party searched the inland roadway. He had expected to be airborne and miles away already. There was no time to waste searching for people who now knew they were being hunted. They had apparently expected trouble considering the precautions they had taken. Prepared as they'd been it was now unlikely they'd be easy to round up and even less easy to kill. His misgivings mounted as the seconds turned to minutes. At the forefront of his mind was a tropical depression that his meteorologist brought to his attention before they landed. It was early in the hurricane season. It didn't appear to be a hurricane, though it could easily develop into one and he didn't' want to get stuck grounded. That and such a storm could easily damage the plane leaving them with no escape at all.

Local law enforcement was not equipped to face him but the Coast Guard would be and he was not about to face down a fully equipped and well trained military when he didn't have to. The fact that he was doing this as a favor to his friend Werner, didn't mean that he was going to take any unnecessary risks. Friend or not, prison was not an option. Werner wasn't 'that' good of a friend.

The job was supposed to be a kill and dispose action, leaving no bodies or bullet casings behind to allow forensic investigation that might lead law enforcement to his door. But the targets he was to eliminate were cleverer than he was led to believe and well prepared. These people apparently expected to be attacked otherwise they would not have had such an elaborate escape mechanism in place. According to his time schedule he should have been on the plane and in the air by now. It was while he contemplated his dilemma that the bodies of two of his men were found in the hotel where they were sent to kill the woman. Instead his men had been killed with a large caliber bullet that had nearly torn each man in half. The mangled remains of his men were lying in the back of a pickup truck as he examined the wounds. "Who did this?" he asked.

His lieutenant shook his head "We haven't a clue. They were each shot with a single bullet of .50 caliber, hollow point low velocity rounds, which is why the exit wounds are so massive. I'd say it was a Desert Eagle or a modified .45 Colt. From the angle of entry of each wound it would appear that they were, at the time of the attack, about to put a bullet into the brain of the woman. Whoever it was made sure that all means of identifying the target and themselves were removed from the room. It would appear that they were a professional team. They even erased the sign in log with the hotel."

Def thought for a moment "A cop on vacation?" he asked dismissing the idea before the last syllable passed his lips. Nobody carried guns on planes anymore, except air marshals and they didn't carry .50 caliber handguns. That and being government employees couldn't afford custom made firearms. "Alright then, put the men on their guard. Someone was aware of our coming and intercepted the target, assume they are professional and take no chances. Oh and lieutenant, if this takes more than 30 minutes we pull out. The weather report has a tropical depression heading for us, which would likely ground our plane and trap us here. If the locals have called in the Coast Guard we'll need to be away fast. They may even call in the French military being that we are 200 miles from Guyana. It would be a good idea for us to be away if and when they arrive."

Looking at his watch and then the approaching storm front Def immediately changed his mind. "Call in our scouts. We don't have time to search. If we get trapped here there will be no escaping. Call them back to the plane immediately. Take the bodies and put them on the plane and prepare them for a high level altitude sea burial.' Pausing a moment in thought then he continued. 'Take a few men and a truck and empty the bank of all available cash. We might as well make this run worth our trouble." His lieutenant saluted him and carried out his orders.

⸻⸺◖◗⸺⸻

On the plateau 'J' was preparing to fire on the lead jeep as they entered the clearing below. His high-powered scope was centered on the point he believed the distributor cap was under the hood and his finger was applying pressure. Taking a breath he held it and steadied his aim and just as he was about to let loose. 'T', who was looking through his binoculars said "Hold your fire. They appear to be turning around. Look at the last jeep in line."

Pulling back from the scope he looked down the barrel of his rifle. One by one the column of jeeps turned around and headed back up the road they'd just come down. "I wonder what that's about?" he said. "They have to know we are up here. It's the only logical place for us to be" he said.

'T' nodded "The trouble for them is, I think, time. They came in guns blazing. They had to know that shooting up the square like that would draw attention' he said scanning the far end of the island 'the plane his being prepped for take-off. They're bugging out."

'J' turned his scope to the airport and saw two jeeps drive into the back of the plane, which appeared to be a Soviet Era Russian transport, complete with Soviet style camo and Soviet military markings. "It's a Russian plane. Long range heavy transport" he said.

"Yup, I heard they took it from the Serbians when they did some work for them, just walked in one day like they owned the place, fueled it up and took off taking a few jeeps and trucks with them not to mention guns, ammo and other equipment. This is curious behavior on their part, come in like an invasion army then bug out less than an hour later?' Lowering his binoculars he scanned the horizon all the way around until he saw the approaching storm. 'That tropical depression is the reason I'll bet. They don't want to be caught on the ground and unable to escape if they run into trouble.' 'T' nodded to himself considering other options. 'That has to be it." He said handing the binoculars to 'J', "You keep an eye on them while I scout the house for a place for you to keep look out. I don't want you or the equipment getting wet." He then turned and walked to the door immediately went upstairs.

Less than five minutes later he discovered the glass room. It was situated perfectly except for the trees that were obviously a problem. That he would leave to 'J' to worry about. He knew how to prepare a tree cover situation without compromising his position. One other room offered a perfect view of the island and north face of the mountain, except that the window didn't open; again he would let 'J' worry about that.

Walking back down to where 'J' was intently watching the activity on the north end of the island. "Well,' 'J' said 'it would appear that they blew the bank. They took a truck and ten men, stormed the bank, blew the vault' he pointed at the pall of smoke coming from the east side of the town 'loaded the truck and drove it onto the plane. From what I could see, it was a lot of money." 'T' nodded but said nothing.

"They don't know about the gold. If they did they wouldn't have turned around so easily' 'J' said as he watched the big plane taxi to the end of the runway. Almost immediately they hit the throttle and the plane launched down the runway just as the local police drove onto the tarmac firing at the plane. In a surprisingly short sprint the heavy, soviet built aircraft lifted off. Taking a hard left the plane banked to the north and then to the right heading east across the Atlantic Ocean.

At that very moment at the tunnel entrance 'M' and Rick were pulling the doors to the tunnel closed just Hans pulled up in Archie's Jeep. "Once you get that door latched I need you to pull on that rope hanging over your heads' he sat in his jeep and watched as the two men yanked on the rope 'Pull it hard it's been a while since Archie and I put that thing together" he said smiling.

The two men grabbed hold of the rope and pulled hard. The rope gave way followed by a muffled hissing noise followed by a low rumbling 'thud' outside the door followed by an even louder, muffled hissing noise that didn't stop until the door they'd just closed began to creak from the pressure of what they recognized was sand pressing against it.

Looking at Hans he lit a cigarette smiling. "Archie and I thought that if one day we had to hole up in the mountain we wouldn't want to have too many entrances available. So we built that sand trap to close up the tunnel entrance. At the very least it would slow down the discovery of the tunnel and take a few hours of digging to clear it, at most it would prevent anyone from finding it. Archie sent me after you figuring that is what you wanted to do. In any event I believe it is wise to seal this entrance off anyway. We have no need of it for anything but ventilation and we have plenty of that. Also when we flood the meadow and drain it the activity will draw some unwanted attention by the locals and we don't want them to find our secret just yet."

'M' and Rick smiled at the old man then hopped into the K-wagon again, only this time 'M' asked if he could drive it back. "I've never driven a real 'Kubelwagon' before I'd like to see what it's like." Rick agreed and hopped in the passenger seat. They followed Hans back into the main cavern and back across the bridge where 'T' was waiting for them.

"They bugged out" 'T' said before anyone could say anything. They just turned around and headed back to their plane and took off. They robbed the bank before leaving, so the police are all lathered up down there." He said looking at each one in turn.

The fact that they left so quickly concerned Hans "Why?" he asked.

"I think it's due to a tropical storm heading this way. My guess is, and it is only a guess, that they planned on a quick in and out and were not prepared for an extended stay beyond a few hours. They had to know that going in hot like they did, with guns and grenades they had to attract attention. So when the targets eluded them they were forced to alter their schedule when the tropical depression turned toward the island that forced their hand. I imagine they didn't want to get caught on the island."

It was then that 'M' spoke up looking down at his watch. "Umm, they may have also been aware of the satellite window.' He looked up at 'T', part of my job is to ensure that what we do, when we do it is never seen by the satellites. There are geo-synchronous satellites that are in a permanent stationary orbit over areas like the middle-east where they can maneuver to look at hot spots immediately. Then there are the 'seekers' that orbit the earth several times a day, one orbit every four hours. There are several of these seekers orbiting all the time leaving a window of one hour where there is no coverage. That could also explain their rapid departure. The storm system may have played a role in accelerating their scheduled departure, though that could have been a mere coincidence, because according to my watch they have 20 minutes before the next satellite passes"

Hans sat back, "Spy Satellites? How does one get access to that schedule?"

'T' answered the question with one word "Money".

'M' spoke up, "'J' can hack their systems without them knowing he's doing it so we can get their intelligence without bribing anyone. Most others have to resort to bribing lower income programmers who are paid government wages to 'task' the satellites. These low level types are easily swayed with a 10, 15 or 20 thousand dollar bribe. They simply print out the schedule for that next week and mail it to some P.O. Box in BFE Where-ever. If they get paid like that every week or so, they can make a nice living giving out seemingly innocuous information to people whom they never know. Most of them really don't think that they are giving out anything 'harmful' and in most cases it isn't. But it is information that is useful to people who use these tidbits to commit crimes that they don't want the world do see or hear about, at least not while they are around."

Each man silently absorbed the information trying to figure out the best course of action. 'T' moved to sit in the passenger seat of the Jeep Hans had been driving. "Now that we are here and nobody else knows, I think it is prudent to stay put. I have 'J' monitoring their radio traffic. The local police are angry at losing two officers and the bank job has them scratching their heads because the two incidents, Archie's residence being destroyed and the bank are two separate crimes related only by the group who committed them. If Archie shows up now, they will likely detain him and start asking questions. If the Coast Guard gets involved the federal authorities will eventually be looking into this and may dig up information that would lead them here. As it is, they are bound to discover the compound and the base eventually."

Before he could say another word Hans spoke up looking worried "These satellites, these seekers you call them, we cannot afford to have the ship seen leaving the cove. If all of a sudden an unregistered ship shows up and is photographed by one of these seekers we could lose the entire shipment." He was right and everyone knew it. It's an older ship and will be easy to spot if the satellites are looking for it." He said.

However, Archie having tasked Patrice with monitoring the on-board loading process left the ship and had been approaching them as the conversation unfolded overhearing most of what had just been discussed. "I don't think we have much to worry about in regards to that' he said, 'I've already got the schedule for the 'seekers' as well as their routes, which I have mapped out." Archie was walking up to them showing no sign whatsoever that he had been shot. "If we follow the schedule we will leave the cove in the wee hours and be in the sea lanes by the time the satellite passes over us. But that is the least of our concerns at the moment. With that lot shooting up the town like they did and robbing the bank we will soon have the DEA, Coast Guard and likely the French Military keeping close watch on this place for the foreseeable future investigating what they can only assume was an attack by a cartel. If that happens we will be stuck. There will be no leaving the island and eventually they will find this base. The bullion will be lost.

Worse the remnants of Odessa will swoop down on this island like the vultures they are, fully armed and equipped to take out the troops assigned to guard over the find and take it. As you already know, Nazis with this kind of money is not something to be taken lightly.' He put his hand up as if to stop something, raised his finger looking at 'T' 'We are getting ahead of ourselves' he said 'If that lot left, as you said they have, it is likely they have destroyed the airport radar tower as well as disrupted the cable network linking this island to the main international cable running off shore. I'll bet they disrupted cell phone traffic as well."

'T' shook his head. We've been able to use our cell phones" he said.

Archie smiled we have a local tower network that allows us to use cell phones when the main system goes down. Have you tried calling off the island?" Before he finished the sentence 'T' was dialing 'Werner's number and there was no signal. Looking at Archie he smiled. "This would mean we have more time than we first thought." he said feeling elated.

Archie nodded but didn't look any less concerned. "It could buy us some time, yes. But more likely when the communication issue comes to light someone will send in either the Coast Guard or the Navy to investigate the situation. At best we have 48 hours before we have to leave, maybe even as little as 24." He looked at Hans with a questioning look. With the connection only years of friendship could create he knew immediately what Archie wanted to know, which was, 'how much time to finish the load?'

"We are down to the last few vaults. If we had more help loading them onto the conveyor we could have it done in 12 hours. We haven't touched the bullion on the submarines yet and it has to be manually unloaded. There is just no other way to unload them" he said waving a hand toward the two submarines. Then he paused, mouth open struck dumb by a thought then he slapped his head muttering to himself "Hans, Hans…you idiot. One submarines still has a crane on board used to load and unload cargo. We could use that to off load the bullion on the subs.

Archie nodded. "Does the crane work? If it does that saves us time and backbreaking labor. But we have to tackle that after we unload the vaults.' He paused looking at the loading conveyor. 'Is there any way of speeding up the process?" he asked.

Hans shook his head. "The conveyor is moving as fast as I am comfortable with, speeding up the load could set us back if something jams or breaks. We just need a few more hands loading the conveyor to ensure there are no gaps in the loading sequence." Archie nodded.

"Alright, I trust your judgment' he said looking over at 'T' 'If you are willing to assist us in loading you can have the contents of one of those subs as a fee." He said smiling. "I've already discussed it with Miss Verga. She is more than agreeable. We estimate each boat to have at least a billion or more of bullion" Both T and M were struck dumb by this news, but being aware of their precarious situation knew better than to get excited about it until they knew for sure the wealth was theirs and safe from being taken.

Without hesitating, 'T' asked "what exactly do you need us to do?" Archie then put them to work loading crates. Once they realized that the 'fee' for their service would be the contents of one of the two submarines, 32,000 bars of bullion they were on task and virtually tireless. The loading process went smoothly with almost no jammed boxes on board ship thanks to Hans being free to supervise loading.

Meanwhile outside, 'J' after learning of their 'fee' found himself motivated to ensure that nothing interfered with their getting off the island and pulled out his satellite communication antennae and dish. With luck he could shut down the satellite before it passed over or he could kill its orbit and dive it into the atmosphere. That would buy them a few hours especially if they left at night and covered the ship with dark canvas. By the time the next satellite came by they will have reached the commercial shipping lanes and just be one of the many other ships out there.

Less than five minutes later he had easily hacked the system and activated the thrusters of two satellites, forcing one down over the Atlantic and a second over the Indian ocean. By the time the first one reached them it would be in the atmosphere and burning up. They would however, be able to see it streaking across the sky as it pretended to be a meteor. The loss of two seeker satellites would give them an 8-hour window to disappear among the shipping traffic. If needs be he would drive them all into the atmosphere. However that would be viewed as an attack and open a can of worms if by chance his signal was tracked, which of course he knew it couldn't be due to his directing it through a series of satellites and towers on the opposite side of the planet. The signal would appear to come from a North Korean facility if they did succeed in tracing him. In that event the local computer system he was using via satellite would be fried to a crisp causing the North Koreans a massive headache but leave him and his equipment untouched.

"Damn I'm good" he said as he folded away his gear.

With that done he let himself think of his new wealth with which he could retire from criminal enterprise. Though they'd been 'free' to do as they chose as it was, they were no longer tied down to employment. In his elation he wondered if, now, finally he might be able to tell Patrice how he felt. He had loved her since he first saw her. She was a tigress, a woman who knew her mind, which is exactly why he loved her. Trouble was, 'J' was no lady's man and hadn't the faintest idea of how to let her know without coming off as an ass. Since she had never met him in the flesh chances were slim that he had much of a chance. He held few illusions, but he wasn't about to shy away from letting this woman know how he felt either. Doing nothing would accomplish nothing but jumping in too fast with a woman like that could back fire. He decided to bide his time and when the opportunity arose, he would approach her and politely let her know how he had grown to admire her and in looking after her found that he had fallen in love. He decided that a polite, face-to-face, private meeting would be the most appropriate way, with his keeping a respectful distance so that she was not in any way intimidated or made uncomfortable. However, that was something that could be done later, once they were off the island and safely out of reach of 'The Operation'.

Once his station was set up and his system wired for sound he began monitoring the military channels, local radio chatter, weather and cell phone traffic, which for the moment, was restricted to the intra-island system. All off island phone traffic was via satellite phone traffic of panicked tourists calling their relatives. Nobody called the authorities. This was due he figured to the fact that the radio transmission tower had been damaged by demolition teams for the purpose of isolating the island, as was the cable to the mainland.

The local CB radio chatter by the police suggested that they had killed two officers and one bank teller prior to leaving taking roughly 4 million dollars, a take hardly worth the trouble of flying over the Atlantic. They had come to kill Patrice and missed. With the approaching storm and the prospect of being trapped they hit the bank as a means of making the trip worth-while.

It was a sloppy mess to say the least and poorly planned, if it was planned at all. The wrinkle in their plans had been Archie. His being prepared caught them flat-footed and without time to finish the job. He smiled and laughed to himself making a mental note to sit down with Archie and pick his brain. It might do to have such precautions taken in their retirement in the event old enemies came calling. In the mean-time he had to report his findings to 'T' letting him know that the Coast Guard had not been called in yet and that he had splashed two satellites.

The nearest Cutter was still in port showing no signs of leaving according to latest satellite pass. If and when it did leave the Cutter was 24 hours away. The nearest CG C130 rescue plane was on patrol along the Gulf Coast six hours away looking for a missing surfer. If they were to leave their SAR mission they would likely have to land, refuel and then fly south. At best the Coast Guard was anywhere from 8 to 24 hour out if they were called in immediately. So far there were no indication that had happened.

His report to 'T' created a sense of relief overall, but did nothing to slow the process of removing the bullion. There was still a tight window in which they had to be away. Archie wanted to be away in 12 to 18 hours so that if anyone did show up within 24 hours they would be long gone and in the sea lanes. They also had to unload both submarines and load their contents onto the ship. Thanks to Hans remembering that the subs opened from the top and a crane could be used to hoist the crates out, the time he expected to take unloading was less than 40 minutes for each boat.

'T' and Patrice took inventory of their haul and were elated once they determined its actual market value of 2.5 billion Euro or 3 billion US. When the team was assembled and informed of this they didn't jump or yell for joy but sat down in numb disbelief. They would leave this island with 750 million each. Not a bad hall for a little hard labor and cooperation.

Chapter 37
Aberdeen Scotland

HAD IT BEEN anywhere else the rain would have been considered a torrential down pour, as it was Scotland it was nothing more than a mild spring rain. However, the occupants of the lemon yellow Austin Healy Frog Eye Sprite were thinking torrential down pour as the nimble little sprite bounced along and attempted to take flight with each gust of wind that caught it pushing it into oncoming traffic several times barely missing head on collisions with no less than two large trucks.

Laurie, never comfortable as a passenger to begin with, was sitting straight upright on the wrong side of the car with a death grip on her seat as she stared straight ahead watching the road through the opaque windscreen that didn't allow any real visibility even with the wipers going for all they were worth. Greg was supposed to meet with a bank official later that evening in final preparation of Rick's legend. No flights were available for the otherwise quick jaunt, due to the local custom of allowing pilots time to enjoy the seasonal weather, creating the need for Greg to rent a car.

In an effort to make it a romantic drive he rented from a classic auto rental/dealership and fell in love with the little Sprite. However, what love he might have felt initially had diminished somewhat with the bone jarring ride and the unfortunate tendency to go wherever the wind took it. Add to that a leak in the roof that each time a gust of wind hit Laurie's side of the car it threatened to rip the convertible top from the frame while dousing her with ice-cold rainwater. What should have been an easy three-hour trip had turned into a five-hour tension filled adventure. Neither would have called it a nightmare, but it had been anything but a relaxing drive through the Highlands.

The seaside cottage he had rented had a garage, which luckily had a doorway leading inside. "Well, at least you'll not get wet." he said trying not to laugh at the drenched spectacle looking back at him in disgust. Laurie was drenched there was no other word for it. Her hair was as if she had just come out of the shower, her coat was soaked as was the dress she wore. Having intended to play with Greg on their journey she had forgone wearing undergarments. Luckily the heater blew at the perfect angle to at least keep her warm if not dry.

Assisting her into the cottage they were pleased to find a fire already going and a pot of hot tea waiting for them. Having called ahead he had them draw a bath in the ancient cast iron bathtub for Laurie to immediately enjoy. While he unloaded the car of the luggage Laurie got into her bath.

Looking at his watch he sat on the side of the tub and stroked her cheek. "I was hoping to have more time with you when we got here, but the trip took longer than expected. I've got 30 minutes to make my meeting. It seldom takes more than an hour to finish up these last minute details. I should be back in time for dinner" he said kissing her warmly and left. She then sunk neck deep into the water and relaxed.

Greg was at the bank in less than ten minutes taking care of the necessary fees and access codes to inherit the accounts and the fortune therein or as in this case transfer the funds from the holding account. The meeting itself was merely a formality to ensure that the accounts were accessible and that no unforeseen legal barriers appeared. But he was never one to take anything for granted and made these trips with every legend he'd created to ensure that nothing ever got in the way of their inheritance. It was this bit of personalized service that allowed him to charge what he wanted and it was also good for his personal/professional reputation and was why he was in such high demand. As expected the meeting took less than an hour and he was soon on his way back to the cottage.

Entering the cottage all was quiet and the fire was blazing with all the lights out. Laurie, he correctly assumed had gone to bed exhausted. He didn't blame her because he felt the same way. The trip had been a bit unnerving. After a quick shower Greg put on his terry cloth robe, poured himself a Scotch whiskey from the bar and took a seat in front of the fire. After a few minutes of listening to the fire crackle and rain falling on the roof the door to the bedroom creaked and Laurie came out wearing a robe like his, wiping her eyes of sleep. "Sorry, hon, I fell asleep". He smiled but said nothing and patted the couch next to where he sat and she curled up next to him. It wasn't long before Laurie was asleep on his shoulder.

He was barely able to keep his own eyes open but needed to unwind and mentally prepare for his trip to the estate in the Shetlands. It was situated on the northern portion of the northern most Island of Unst, in a deep gash in the island itself that went north to south creating a loch, with a protected cove and pier just off the loch. He had hoped to fly there and back but the local weather made flight a hit or miss proposition forcing him to book on a ferry to the island.

On finishing his business with the bank he'd booked passage on a ferry leaving from Aberdeen, but he didn't have to leave for two days, which would take another two days to reach Unst with all the stops to off load and to take on passengers and cars.

His immediate dilemma was Laurie. He'd been with her for the better part of a week already and it would be another week at least if she came with him on this trip. Not that he minded her company that but there was the fact that her husband was supposed to inherit the estate he was to visit. She couldn't know about his dealings with her husband, at least not at the moment. It wasn't that he didn't trust her. But husbands and wives did divorce and such proceedings tended to get ugly and if his connection to her husband came to light in the heat of a divorce his life could easily find itself upside down and lose Laurie in the bargain.

As it happened she asked if she could go home because she missed her children. Arrangements were then made to send her home from Edinburgh non-stop to San Fransisco the day he was scheduled to take the ferry to Unst. The remaining two days were spent site seeing and making love. Once they made love inside an old Castle ruin. This was initiated when Laurie took Greg into a lonely alcove overlooking the loch, knelt down in front of him and took him to completion.

Later, after he had recovered, Laurie was bent over the ruin of an old wall and was taken from behind. Rain then forced them to drive back to the cottage where they continued their activities on the ancient four poster bed in front of a blazing fire. On the way to the airport Laurie took care of Greg in the back of the taxi a mere 15 minutes before her plane was air-borne. Greg then whispered "I love you Laurie. Know that." And she boarded the plane dazed, exhausted and immensely satisfied.

Greg watched her disappear down the jet way missing her the moment she was no longer in sight. However, he had a ferry to catch and a job to do. There wasn't any time to waste missing the woman he loved, knowing that they would be together again soon. The need to take a ferry and drive along rain soaked, windswept roads had thrown a wrench in his timing. What would have taken only a few days flying from one place to another now would take nearly a week. Necessity required that he visit the estate and take physical possession of it and prepare for the arrival of the new owner. As with the bank accounts his job was to make certain any legal entanglements were nixed with regard to properties and physical assets.

Two days later Greg drove the Sprite off the ferry and onto the island of Unst in the Shetland Islands. The drive was pleasant and uneventful unlike his trip from Edinburgh to Aberdeen. The Estate was high walled and heavily wooded with a mixture of oaks and pines. Archie had updated the estate and paid a grounds keeper to keep the trees at bay. From the looks of it they'd been there recently because the trees were all trimmed back and the gate painted.

Punching in the code for the security gate it opened immediately. Driving the estate was pleasant and lengthy taking a full ten minutes to navigate the winding road from the gate through the portcullis and into a massive castle courtyard that seemed to be as large as the grounds he'd just driven minus all the trees. The House itself was built of granite blocks aged by centuries of weather. Facing the house he saw to his left a massive, ancient turret that had been covered with a circular peaked roof. Immediately to the right of this tower was a long main house with a long picture window that ran the length of the upper story from the turret to the East wing of the house that turned to face forward creating an L shape opposite the turret.

Sitting behind the wheel of the Sprite Greg he took in the impressive structure and was immediately reminded of a popular kid's story about wizards. It seemed to him that someone had used this very place as inspiration for the book. Though obviously not as massive as the movie version the appearance of the old castle brought that to mind.

Pulling up to the massive front door he shut the engine off and got out. Taking an ancient skeleton key and turned it, but instead of unlocking the door itself it merely opened the black metal door revealing another keypad identical to the one at the front gate. Punching in the same code as the gate the door opened automatically without so much as a creak or groan, the silence of which Greg found unnerving as old doors are supposed to creak when they opened.

Entering the main hall he flipped on the lights. What greeted him was a massive dining hall with a shiny wooden floor and high vaulted ceiling, oak beams and several rather gauche chandeliers. Bright, gaudy Tartan draperies of Royal Stewart Tartan threatened to overwhelm but did not quite offend his senses. They hung from the rafters and archways separating the different rooms and passages off the main hall. The uniquely Scottish flavor and overall effect appealed to him, though he noted that it wouldn't make Better Homes and Garden. Though style and décor was not the intent he knew. The displays were meant as a declaration of their lineage and allegiance to the Crown of Scotland. Along the far wall over a massive, ancient fireplace was the flag of Scotland itself. The display of Tartan added a sense of style that matched the colorful, if violent, history of the Scots.

Surrounding the hall was a second level gallery containing alcoves with individual fireplaces with love seats arranged for individuals who wished to talk privately with Tartan draperies representing each Clan. With their crest mounted on the back wall of each alcove. It became clear to Greg that these were for 'private' discussions that he surmised involved adulterous liaisons the draperies were meant to keep private if not secret.

In each of these alcoves crossed swords, battle ensigns and ancient blunderbuss and muskets of many a bygone era were displayed prominently as were the family crests that emanated from this oldest of lines. From deep within his soul a deep appreciation for what this place represented began to glow. This building was the wellspring of the clans represented in these tartans. "How many rebellions were planned in these alcoves or at this table?" he thought. Scotland had been unruly a millennium before the Romans attempted, unsuccessfully, to subjugate its population. That effort resulted in Hadrian's Wall being constructed, to keep the Roman controlled portion of Britain safe from the wild men of the north.

However, such thoughts were far from his consciousness as he explored the old estate. It occurred to him that an ancient, remote castle situated on an even more ancient and remote cliff was the perfect place for the richest man in the world to rule over his empire. Though on paper Rick would merely be a billionaire, in reality he would be the most liquid asset wealthy man on the planet. Estimated value of the shipment to be deposited under these foundations was in excess of 3 or 4 trillion British Pounds, a conservative estimate since nobody had inventoried the bullion for well over seventy years. It was his guess that the estimated value was staggeringly low. It would be his job to take inventory and determine its true value once it was in permanent storage and safe from discovery.

Unknown to Rick Greg had a contract agreement with Archie, 100 million dollars to be paid over the next four years to assist Rick with managing his assets. However, if he in any way betrayed Rick or let it slip the nature of how it was he obtained his wealth, other than through inheritance, or let slip the existence of the bullion his name would be unceremoniously dumped onto the desk of every law enforcement officer involved with tracking down many of his clients. In short it was a guaranteed death sentence because such men were well connected and knew how to get 'certain' information via bribery and appropriately placed threats.

He, of course, had no intention of testing Archie's resolve because, the terms of their agreement were more than generous and he understood the need to make sure he didn't get too greedy. Not only had he no interest in putting his life at risk he did not want to harm the woman he loved in any way. If her husband's wealth became public knowledge particularly the source of that wealth the domino effect would naturally create problems he didn't need nor want. Worse, would be the inevitable loss of his relationship with Laurie and eventually his death at the hands of former clients. In short, Archie had him by the balls....again.

Indifference was the best way to describe his feelings for Rick. He neither liked nor disliked him. In fact he barely knew Rick except for what Laurie said about him. According to her he was a nice guy, depressed and angry for his lack of success and one of the nicest most generous men she knew and a loving father to their children. In short he was a standup guy who'd ran into a bad run of luck and personal challenges that resulted from not being paid for doing his job. "Money is not going to be a problem for him now" he said listening to his voice echo through the cathedral like chamber.

A long table filled the center chamber with candelabras placed at regular intervals with place settings for twenty people and very un-comfortable looking chairs. Exploring the castle took the better part of an hour just looking through doors and following passages. He counted no less than 20 different bed chambers and ten bathrooms, one Russian style steam bath, dry sauna, three office suites, countless sitting rooms one hidden stair behind a fireplace that went to anoth-er hidden room. It was a room he found interesting, a sex room with a bondage theme complete with antique stocks. In that moment he'd wished that Laurie was there. She might have enjoyed exploring this room. "Later" he said to himself smiling in the knowledge that Laurie would eventually learn of this room and invite him for a visit in the not too distant future.

Following Archie's instructions he located the access panel and stair-case 'carved out of the salt' to the mine below, via a bookshelf in the library on the basement floor of the turret, the former dungeon. A circular stairwell went down deep into the rock under the castle until it opened onto a wide, hard, polished salt floor. The chamber was immense easily twice the size of the base under the island mountain. The mine was a near perfect dome shape which also provided struc-tural strength with pillars of natural salt rock in key locations for added protection against collapse. Added to this was a crisscross of steel reinforced concrete beams adding considerable mass and sup-port to an already self-supporting structure.

The doors on the far side of the dome appeared tiny though they were large enough for a semi-truck and trailer to pass through with ease. Another task was to see if they would open. A five--minute walk brought him to the doors which he opened with a key provided by Archie into a control box and pulling a lever. Each door opened internally revealing a very sturdy albeit old pier head carved into the living rock of the islands mass. The pier lay in a protected cove just off a Loch that opened onto the Norwegian Sea which was frothy from the sea currents which the cove escaped. Walking out onto the pier he noted an impressively cold wind blowing off the sea with sprinkles of rain as another bit of local weather forced him back into the mine closing the doors after.

Once the doors were closed he made further observations of the space. On the far side was a chapel that had been carved out of the salt complete with pews and alters. Chandeliers hanging from the ceiling were made of hand carved salt crystals and linked together with leather. Stepping out into the main chamber again he saw the forklift adjacent to the door he'd come out of parked and ready for use once the ship arrived.

Various other rooms had been carved out of the salt rock. Some were storage rooms, long empty; others appeared to be a barracks where the workers slept in bunks carved into the salt. The general appearance was that of an ancient burial site similar to the catacombs under Rome and other ancient cities, but much lighter and less grim in appearance. It took Greg a full hour to explore and inspect the mine. He was impressed by the fact that it had appeared almost new, though the mine had last been dug nearly 500 years before. Hunger and an overwhelming need to sleep forced him to head back up to the castle. As he reached the stair he heard the moan of wind as it tried to force open the doors to the pier but they seemed to be holding up well.

Entering the main tower Greg went straight to the main entrance hall where he had first entered and took up Archie's instructions again. On the second floor opposite the front door he would find the butlers chambers complete with sitting room, fireplace and kitchen and of course bedroom and washroom with the cupboards fully stocked with everything his heart could desire. Expecting to find modest chambers he found them rather impressive with age black-ened oak paneling lining the entire quarters. It seemed a much more comfortable and up to date space than what he'd seen so far. After a quick, easy dinner of soup and a ham sandwich, Greg crawled be-tween sheets and under the thick woolen blanket and let the storm outside lull him to sleep where he dreamed of Laurie.

Chapter 38
The Escape

THERE WAS A reason none of the Milchow submarines survived the war. They were slow, cumbersome easy targets, especially while on the surface. The cargo hatches opened slowly and closed slowly, even when they worked properly and they couldn't dive while they were open. If they were ever caught on the surface with their hatches open it was all but guaranteed that they'd be sunk which they all were. It was one of the reasons the Germans quit building them in 1943. The two variants on the island were either special construction's built specifically to transport bullion to the island base or raised hulks from previous attacks.

If the latter had been true the crews would have likely refused to sail on them due to the superstitious belief that if the ship had already been sunk once Poseidon would want his prize back. The same held true with rechristening a ship. Bad luck usually followed a ship that had its name changed. Some sailors called them bastard ships and if it became known that they were sailing on one…mass desertions were not uncommon. Whatever their story was these ships had made it to their last destination unscathed and fully crewed. In spite of this they still suffered from the very same flaws that killed their sister ships during the war, slow hydraulics.

It was that on which Hans was working one week prior to Werner's arrival on the island. He was showing M, how to operate the manual hydraulic hatch valve that opened the cargo hatches of the Milchow when the main power plant was no longer operational. A redundant system the Germans built into the hydraulic systems in the event of failure of the main system. Under normal operation the doors would open in a matter of a minute or less. Manually however, the process took 5 to 10 minutes depending on the vigor of the crew. A stores load at sea was only viable if you had air superiority and were certain you were not going to get bombed, shelled or torpedoed. Even if the hydraulics worked perfectly the sub had to remain on the surface while the hatches closed before they could dive. It was in that space of time that most Milchows were sunk.

In the event an attacker missed the sub it took an eternity to dive and was limited to 240 meters. At 240 meters the hatches would groan and protest the water pressure giving their position away. At less than 200 meters the boat being so massive could be seen on a clear day. So tactically the Milchow was useless; they couldn't dive fast enough, go deep enough or be silent enough to evade an attack and their sheer size killed maneuverability.

However, that was not the problem, not now. At present Hans had an old hydraulic system that hadn't been used in nearly 70 years that needed to work 100% perfectly if they hoped to clear the subs of their precious cargo in time to vacate the island and get away clean. They had no idea when or if anyone would show up and nobody was willing to risk losing the bullion to anyone for any reason. Hans had it working in less than an hour and put the Trio to work opening the hatch, which took the three of them 30 minutes of taking turns because of leaks in the system that Hans couldn't find. The overhead crane was then employed to unload the bullion. Once they'd opened the hold they noticed the deck plate could be hoisted from its position using loading cables already attached to hard points, which served as hull reinforcement when the plate was lowered back into the hull. This made loading and unloading much more efficient. The Germans took the deck plate out, loaded the bullion onto it and used a crane to lower it back into place onboard. So Hans did the same in reverse.

It took less than 30 minutes to unload the first boat. The second boat was unloaded even faster because its hydraulic system was operating perfectly, thanks to a double dose of anti-corrosion spray layered on nearly every square inch of the ship 70 years before, the only mishap being a crate that fell from the net and into the hold of the first Milchow shattering the crate and spilling its contents all over the hold. The loose bricks were quickly retrieved and placed in another crate and loaded onto the Victoria, the damaged crate was left where it fell.

When Hans was satisfied that he was no longer needed to oversee loading, only then did he begin the startup of the Victoria's diesel. In a matter of minutes the massive engine fired up and one by one each system came on-line as Hans made sure they were functioning and properly lubricated. The whole process took two hours due to his double and triple checking the systems. They had a long journey ahead and he wanted to make sure that the ship would make it. He knew she would because he'd been preparing her for sea for several months 'just in case'. Victoria was one of the last multi-purpose ships to be built prior to dedicated one-use-only ships like super tankers and container ships. The Victoria had been well built but was out of date by the time she came off the ways.

In her day she could be fitted with tanks and be a tanker, or an ore carrier and even a container ship if the need arose. The trouble was that such ships were expensive to operate because the equipment, not being used had to be stored on shore, in the home port taking up valuable space. This meant that if they wanted to load a cargo of oil they had to rush home and reinstall the tanks and rush back to where the oil was. It was much more efficient to keep the ship in one configuration and set its load schedule accordingly. The unused equipment was either sold as scrap or installed onto another ship.

The Victoria was purchased in an expanded cargo configuration to carry extra heavy cargo, which was how Archie found her in the breakers yard in Malaysia. He then had her refitted with diesel-electric drive and maneuvering pods before mooring her in the island lagoon. Archie was able to hide her from view by dumping tons of dry ice into the ocean creating a fog that hid the ship as they maneuvered her into the hidden lagoon.

Once in position and anchored the mangrove covered clamshell doors were closed. As the years progressed the mangrove had to be cut to keep the doors operational. Luckily the Trio was equipped with mild explosives that would make quick work of the mangrove locking the doors shut. So that problem was quickly addressed and with surprisingly little noise.

Archie was tasked with monitoring the ships gauges on the bridge to make sure that all of the systems could be monitored from there. Being that they were going to undertake a voyage with less than a minimal crew they had to have a central monitoring station to keep an eye on everything. What better place than the bridge?

Luckily the diesel electric drive conversion from the original steam system simplified this endeavor necessitating only a few gauges be mounted on the panel from fuel, RPM, battery charge and a shipboard version of an amp meter, speedometer, compass, GPS navigation system and variable ballast to stabilize the ship at sea which with the load on board would not be needed. The weight of the bullion alone was more than adequate for that task.

Then there were the maneuvering pods. Massive bow and stern thrusters that retracted into the hull while underway and when needed were deployed so that a person could drive the forward pod from a bow cockpit and the second stern pod could be operated from the fantail. Each thruster was powerful enough to propel the ship along at ten knots independently so long as the generator was making enough electricity to drive them. Their placement at the bow and stern allowed the ship to be maneuvered to pier without a tug. Hans also saw to their condition before the loading process had been completed.

Archie gathered the Trio and Rick together and set about closing up the mountain top compound locking doors and turning down the lights. When Hans reported that the ship was ready for sea Archie decided it was time to open the sea valve and let the water saturated sand out of the old lagoon to sink the guns in the meadow.

It was deep enough that it would take weeks before anyone dove deep enough to notice what lay on the bottom. Being private property they would have to get Ricks permission to dive the lagoon being that he was the new owner of the island. As he was not to be found on the island they would have to look for him to get permission. Until then a barrier would be placed on the roadway with signs posted denying access to the property citing diving hazards and safety concerns. That was the task Archie assigned to the Trio which they had done in short order, returning to the mountain top compound after the job was completed.

Archie had already flooded the lagoon several days earlier by pumping sea water into the old lagoon which had become a meadow, the one Rick had found the day he discovered the base. As a result the center of the lagoon was already soggy and from the top of the mountain they could see the reflection of light on the water that had already pooled there. Several guns had already sunk into what was effectively quicksand. Once the old lagoon was saturated the external sea valve could be opened flushing the sand out to sea. That wouldn't be done until dusk so that the cloud of sandy water wouldn't be noticed right away. But the sand would fall away harmlessly into a deep crevasse.

They wanted to be away and far to sea by the time the flooding lagoon was noticed.

What Archie and Hans had expected was that the flooding lagoon would draw people to it. They hadn't counted on the mild panic that it would generate. Nobody dared venture near it for several weeks. There was no way for Hans or Archie to know this, so plans were made contingent on the reverse scenario.

Originally they had planned to leave while the lagoon filled with water and drained away the sand. Lisa had been the voice of conscience stating that it would be unsafe to just leave it because some kid might wander into the sandy bog and drown if they weren't there to make sure nothing happened. It was a valid concern in spite of the urgent need to be away. The solution was for Hans and 'T' to remain behind and take the Chris-Craft and meet the Victoria at sea after the danger had passed. Still, questions would eventually be raised and official inquiries made by investigating authorities, weeks later.

Questions were not the problem. The problem lay with the bullion, which could never be discovered. One reason was obvious, Odessa still wanted it, two Rick had no desire to lose his vast newfound wealth, nor did the Trio want to risk losing their 'fee', as it were. So the plan was to transport the bullion, secure it and have Archie and Hans disappear from view then for Rick to report his new discovery to the authorities, 'after' the bullion was secure and beyond their reach.

The Coast Guard was expected at any time. 'J' had been monitoring them and not so much as a whisper had been heard nor had any change in their routine been noted. This could change at any moment, they knew. News of the recent attack on the island had to reach the authorities at some point if it hadn't already. Then there was the flooding of the lagoon which would likely draw in EPA officials who would then report it to the Coast Guard. It was the unknown response time that concerned Hans and Archie the most. So far nobody had reacted or made any change to their normal routine. At least not that 'J' could determine. That did not mean that there wouldn't be one.

The lack of reaction was disconcerting, like waiting for the other foot to drop and not knowing where or how hard. Then there was the French military in Guyana only 200 miles south. In the event they were called they could be there in just a few hours. The Victoria had to be away and in the sea lanes when either the Coast Guard or French Military showed up or at the very least be far enough away to escape scrutiny.

The Victoria was up and operating on full systems with minor warming up issues that were expected, hence the early startup. The next item on the agenda was opening the harbor entrance, which the Trio had fixed with their explosive charges. The doors had to be opened in order to allow the ship to vacate the lagoon. Nobody wanted to find out too late that they couldn't leave because the doors wouldn't open. Hans disappeared into the mountain and from the control room opened the clamshell doors. After a brief yet agonizing period the doors began to open after a series of huge clicks and bangs echoed throughout the cavern. Being massive, concrete doors they were opened slowly to lessen the stress on the moving parts should they be weakened and compromised by corrosion.

As a result of his caution the opening of the doors took 15 minutes. It was an agonizing period as the noises and groans of the machinery worried Hans in that each bang sounded like a catastrophic failure, if sound alone was to be the determining factor. Yet nothing failed and the doors opened without incident in spite of all the noise. Not quite dusk the Victoria could not leave her long held anchorage until dark if they wished to leave undetected. Though there were no other ships in the vicinity, or satellites for several hours they needed the cover of dark to ensure a clean get away. Hans and T disembarked the ship from the stern and took up station on the plateau to keep watch over the flooding lagoon. As well as to keep watch for distant ships and local fishing boats that might get too close.

From the mountain top they watched as tall trees that had grown among the guns and faux shells began to fall into the lagoon. At first they'd sink into the sand then as the sand washed away the trees would pop up again once the sand released its grip on them. Once on the surface a prevailing breeze caught the branches, which acted like sails and drove the trees toward the northern edge creating an impenetrable barrier further ensuring that nobody got near the lagoon. Yet, they remained at their post until the sun set when Hans radioed Archie that all was clear. As the orange light faded to dark the prow of the Victoria emerged from the lagoon, lights off as her graceful lines emerged from the lagoon and disappeared into the vast dark of the Atlantic.

Chapter 39

Werner's Education

WEWELSBERG, RATHER THE Argentine version was complete in every way up to and including the funeral pyre in the center of the main hall, where venerated members of the 'SS' were to be burned and their ashes collected and placed in an urn. A macabre ritual left over from the days of Himmler when he and his ilk stalked the halls of the original castle of the same name in Germany 70 years earlier. However, none of Himmler's SS ever partook of this ritual. Most died in battle or in air raids, those who survived the war committed suicide, went into hiding or were arrested tried and hung. Himmler's twisted vision of a King Arthers Court of Elite SS died in firestorms that left every major German city a smoldering ruin.

Werner Meyer stood in the center of the circle and on top of the Nazi swastika inlayed into the floor of the pit as he had come to call it. His attire was the full dress uniform of a Standartenfurher of the RF/SS the ReichsFuhrer personal staff. Psychotic theatrics is all it was for it was he and Horst Krupp who currently made up the entire 'SS' contingent leading the Operation formerly known as Odessa. Everyone else was dead, dying or so far gone in dementia that it didn't matter if they were alive or dead.

Horst Krupp, suffering from dementia, was fading rapidly as it took hold of his aging brain. Testosterone therapy was keeping his body functioning nicely. In fact Meyer was rather envious of his Fuhrers physique at 103 years of age. However, it was painfully apparent that testosterone therapy had limited benefit on the brain. It seemed to accelerate the dementia while increasing the clarity with which it was expressed.

An example being Krupp's memories of the 'bunker' with Hitler in the planning stages of the war they had very nearly won. In his vigor he would stride about and call for his long dead aid 'Corporal Jergen' to relay a message to the Fuhrer that the supplies for the submarine pens were delayed due to the convoy being bombed by the RAF in the channel. He would also send messages to the Fuhrer advising him not to attack until the winter uniforms were delivered and the men properly equipped for a winter engagement in Russia.

Meyer, being present at the time of these episodes, became Jergen and prudently responded with the appropriate salute and acknowledgement expected of a low level aide. Of course there were the lucent moments when Krupp would remember his lapses into dementia and attempt to play it off as 'play acting'. Both were aware however, that he was fading into the netherworld of dementia from which he would one day never return. It would be a year maybe two before he was no longer able to run the operation effectively.

It was for this reason Meyer was in the funeral pit considering how he would burn his Fuhrer to ashes. It was not something he relished having worked in the prison crematorium where they burned the unclaimed bodies of inmates. There was no room left in the cemetery and the families of the deceased often had no money to bury them so they would incinerate the bodies and dump the ashes into the sea. His job had been operating the furnace which put him in a position to hear the sickening sizzles and pops as fluids were released and cooked of. Then there was the brain swelling which cracked the skulls open, coupled with the smell was enough to make him sick to his stomach. Prison furnaces tended to be cheap and therefore not sealed so he could smell the entire process from beginning to end. More than once he'd vomited from the stench.

As a result of this he had taken to embalming the dead by replacing their blood with Kerosene and letting them soak it up for a day before they would put them in the oven. Not only did the smells diminish considerably, it stopped decomposition in its tracks, particularly if you set the bodies in the chill box. The burning process was accelerated quite a lot as well making the process of cremation that much more efficient. So it was his decision to have the Fuhrer embalmed in this manner prior to the funeral, where he would be the lone attendee.

Just as he was stepping out of the pit his phone rang. Noticing that it was Def he answered it expecting to receive a report that Patrice was dead and her crew eliminated, not that they had escaped. Def had done as he was told and gone in guns blazing and took out the old man's house behind the church after they'd witnessed Miss Verga entering the building with Davis. The house was demolished and all exits blocked. He then explained about the drainage tunnel and their escape and the two dead men at the hands of an unknown. Meyer's face reddened as he asked "Why didn't you tear the island apart looking for them?"

The voice over the phone was in complete control of his emotions, as he'd always been and spoke as if teaching a class. "Because dear friend, we were 200 miles from a French Military Station. Our entrance was designed to get their attention, as you suggested. Making it appear to be a drug lord taking out a rival. It was meant to draw them in remember? The targets you sent us to kill were more prepared than we were expecting and I am not about to risk a prison sentence chasing a couple of people you have a problem with."

Meyer looked into the phone incredulous that his 'friend' would talk to him so flippantly, but refrained from letting his temper fly which took considerable effort on his part. Taking a calming breath he spoke evenly but icily. "Did you see anyone else besides the old man and Patrice?" he asked fighting to keep his temper down.

"I saw nobody but the old man and woman, the men I sent to get the woman's companion were killed by someone with a specialized firearm. They were cut in two with one shot each, private security it would seem to me' he said. 'In any case I lost men in what was supposed to be a quick in and out job. Again we didn't feel it was prudent to remain on island with a storm front approaching that could have grounded the plane trapping us if the authorities showed up. We had 12 men to take out two maybe three people. We were not equipped for anything more than that".

His friend had a point. Something had happened that neither had counted on. Had the Trio turned on him? That was the most reasonable explanation for a professional hit on two of Def's men.

There wasn't another team on the island, that he knew of. The reason for their being on the island was known only to him, his boss and the Dutchmen who were apparently dead, likely killed by the Trio who were still reporting in regularly and reporting nothing new. They hadn't even reported the attack on the compound, yet. Had he had lost control of them, did he ever have control? The idea didn't set well.

"Is there anything else you can tell me?" Meyer asked as rational thought reacquainted itself with his brain.

"Yes, we killed three people, two police and one bank teller when we blew the bank. We also blew up the radio tower and main cable to the mainland. So it is entirely possible that you may find either the Coast Guard or the French military waiting for you if you go there." Def said.

Meyer cared nothing for the reasons his friend blew a bank. What he was concerned about was Patrice escape. The sudden attack on the compound should have killed them both immediately. But both she and the old man escaped through an access tunnel. They had apparently been expecting something like this, but why? It then dawned on him that the bullion might not be a myth after all. But he dared not allow that idea to take form, there was simply no way for that to be true, not after all this time. Patrice had wanted to retire and she needed a plausible means of escaping the Operation and this was her means of escape. At least that is how he rationalized it. The idea that the island could be a lost secret base was just too fantastic to be plausible.

Then his friend added "We followed a group to the south end of the island. They apparently took refuge on the summit. My men reported that there appeared to be some sort of a compound on the very top but the approach was too risky if they had a sniper. That is what they reported after I called them back. They said it appeared to have been there a long time".

Meyer thanked his friend and hung up as the possibilities mounted. Could there be any truth to the story? Shaking his head "No', it can't be possible" he kept muttering. It was then he heard a scream at the far end of the castle coming from the Fuhrers apartments.

Running the length of the main hall he rushed into the chambers of his Fuhrer to find the Spanish chamber maid standing over him naked below the waste with Horst Krupp lying face up on the floor sporting the last erection he would ever have with his pants around his ankles with a permanent grin on his face. A non-dignified death to be sure, but a death most men wouldn't mind. I was then Meyer noted that the rumors were true, Krupp had been hung like a horse. That meant nothing to Meyer who realized, at last, he was Fuhrer and head of the Operation.

Horst Krupp was not cremated. Meyer saw no need of such an elaborate funeral, that and he was in no mood to shovel his ashes into an urn. Horst Krupp was buried in a neat and tidy grave in the local cemetery under the name of Werner Meyer in a strangely shaped casket that bulged in the middle.

One mourner attended. A tall, lean, broad shouldered man in a black trench coat. No music played, no trumpets blared, just a simple prayer from the Bible and a conventional salute. As dirt fell onto the casket Meyer smirked, turned and marched to his limousine and went directly to the castle.

Upon taking possession of the castle he quickly set the staff to updating the décor and removing the last vestiges Krupps long, neglected chambers. Once he was satisfied the staff knew their jobs and his wishes he retired to his own chambers and packed for a trip the St. Vincent to see for himself what was going on.

Since his friends attack on the island he'd lost contact with the Trio and Patrice. Complicating matters was the fact that Patrice Verga was aware, thanks to Krupps Chivalric stupidity, that if she ever saw him she was to run for her life. Complicating matters even further was the fact that there were no flights into or out of St. Vincent, due to the airport beacon being off line forcing him to make alternative arrangements to visit the island. The Operation owned several yacht chartering companies one of which was out of Guyana so he arranged to use a motor yacht that he would sail to the island.

However, due to the need to prepare it for sea it wouldn't be ready for nearly a week having just completed a cross Atlantic charter from the Mediterranean to winter in the Caribbean. The only other 'yacht' available was a 40' sloop that he didn't know how to sail and which had a top motoring speed of 15 knots. The next nearest charter firm was in Columbia but they were booked up through the winter and the distance was simply too far. So Werner resigned himself to wait out the week.

In the meantime however, he consolidated his control over the Operation. Since he'd effectively been in charge due to Krupp's long decline into dementia he didn't have much to do. He was already functioning as head of the Operation, and had been for nearly three years by the time Krupp sent Patrice on what he believed was a wild goose chase.

The yacht was a better solution for him anyway. He could butcher Patrice at sea and feed her piece by piece to the sharks as she watched her own body being fed to them. She'd done nothing to him other than be the most beautiful woman he'd ever fucked and the most satisfying. Yet it was for those exact reasons he hated her and he had to kill her in the most brutal manner possible. Feeding her bit by bit to the sharks was the perfect expression of his loathing of her.

He wanted her more than any other woman but due to his psychosis those 'wants' generated in him the antithesis of love. The more he was physically attracted to a woman the deeper his loathing became which was compounded by the act of fucking. Where most people felt the release of endorphins and the feeling of peace within with each orgasm, a chemical reaction within his psychopathic brain created anger and rage, which only compounded the more he exercised his desire. 20 women had paid the price for his 'desire' of them. The very reason he was sent to prison for the criminally insane. He had escaped by charming his psychiatrist to whom he was attracted and choked her to death as he fucked her then left the prison using her keys and ID ten years earlier.

One week later Werner docked the 60' foot fishing yacht up to the mooring buoy in St. Vincent harbor. All was quiet. His yacht was the only one present as his friend Def had caused the rest to leave rather suddenly. Taking the yachts Sea-Doo to the dock he tied it to the pier and walked to the rent a car center and rented a jeep. What had been a bustling tourist destination for fat Midwestern tourists was nearly deserted.

Only he didn't see the Coast Guard or anything that indicated the presence of any civil or military authority. The body count wasn't high enough apparently. Three dead was a minor issue when the usual body count in a cartel killing was 20 or 30 with most of them disfigured in some way. A bank robbery and an attack on a church compound with only three dead didn't measure up. As far as he could tell the locals were going on the best they could despite the recent violence. But the toll was apparent in that the streets and hotel were nearly deserted. From the reports he'd been receiving up to the day of his friend's attack he knew roughly where the two men lived. The preacher obviously lived in the compound, which was no longer habitable. The other man suspected of being a former SS officer lived on the western tip of the island in a small bungalow.

Having no reason to believe any of what Patrice had told Krupp he had no intention of wasting time searching for it. However, he knew thanks to Def that there was a compound on top of the mountain where Patrice and her team were known to have holed up prior to Def vacating the island. With that in mind Meyer quickly located the road south.

Thirty minutes and a flat tire later, Meyer pointed the jeep up the roadway leading up the mountain. His mind was in a rage of psychopathic desire to kill Patrice. In fact he had not considered the Trio once. Reaching the plateau he stopped the jeep to get his bearings. The immense compound was orderly, except for the overgrown bushes and trees. Scanning the compound looking for evidence of human habitation and finding none he rolled the jeep forward noting the neatness of the layout and the cabins along the southern edge of the plateau. They reminded him of a vacation lodge, but their being made of high density concrete also gave them a military purpose built appearance.

Pulling forward Werner drove slowly toward the mansion. He sensed that he was alone. A nauseating feeling in his gut told him that Patrice had somehow escaped. But he refused to let the idea form.

Her escaping would not be tolerated. But, the feeling in his gut persisted and worsened the closer he got to the mansion.

Nausea grew as beads of sweat formed on his brow and sweaty hands gripped the steering wheel tight as he let the jeep roll forward. Fighting the urge to vomit he looked down and noticed tire tracks in the gravel. Hope sprang forth and he jerked the wheel hard right and followed them to the opposite end of the plateau and through a stand of pine trees into which they disappeared.

He forced himself to drive slowly along the road along the back-side of the plateau. Entering a massive garden he saw a garage door closed tight with the tire tracks leading right up to it and under it. Pulling up to the door but it was locked from the inside. Luckily there was a door next to it which was unlocked. Meyer's excitement grew entering the dark basement garage. A strong smell of machine oil and ancient mildew forced him to fight down the urge to vomit having not yet quelled his earlier stress induced sickness. The silence he encountered however made his heart sink. No voices, no sound of any sort came from anywhere in the room. No indication that there was anyone about.

Opening the garage door to allow light in he noticed the garage door on the far corner open and leading into the mountain with a massive Mercedes sitting conspicuously on a platform designed for it to sit on.

On closer inspection the SS runes on the doors suggested that Patrice had been correct and that her stories to Krupp were not a ruse. With mounting comprehension his desire to dispatch Patrice was slowly replaced by the possibility that the gold she mentioned was real. Coupled with this was a growing sense of dread that he was too late. Still the idea of a gold hoard of that magnitude was too fantastic to comprehend in spite of what he was seeing first hand.

Getting into his jeep he drove it straight through the door and down the tunnel. Large open doors met him as he drove deeper and deeper into the mountain. Each one had a metal conveyor running from in-side to a larger conveyor running the length of the tunnel along each side. Each vault was empty with evidence of something very large having been in each one and recently removed. His dread mounted as one by one he checked each room, at least forty of them, all had been full and all were emptied. Entering the large cavernous space, the headlight beam was the only light available. Soon he could see in the headlights an old German Kubelwagon in good condition and appeared to have been recently operated.

Taking the torch from the glove box Meyer looked around and saw nothing of interest until the light hit something on the far side of the lagoon that made his heart stop. "No!" is all he could manage before choking down more vomit. Sitting squarely in the beam of his torch was a black submarine with SS runes on the side of the conning tower. In the shadow of that beam he saw what appeared to be a second submarine. The rumors were true.

Without a thought he jumped into the jeep and drove over the bridge braking to a halt immediately opposite the gray submarine. His mind in a frenzy of disbelief, rage and confusion he fell from the jeep and stumbled across the gangplank numb with disbelief and panic. Moving aft he got as far as the ladder, before he was forced to stop. The hold of the submarine was open. Stepping slowly to the edge he peered over the open hatch. On the deck was a smashed crate and on one of the planks was the word "Gold" branded into the wood. Falling to his knees in shock and dismay, he whispered "nooo….." Meyer's mind racked back and forth not daring to believe his eyes, hoping it was a bad dream. When he accepted his reality he screamed into the blackness "*That bitch*!!!!!"

Chapter 40
The Victoria

(Days Earlier)

SEVERAL DAYS BEFORE Werner discovered the base the Victoria lay at anchor in the lagoon with the glow of red light on the bridge to afford the crew instant night vision in the event of a casualty or emergency, at night. This was necessary in order for the crew to run outside and perform whatever immediate task was required without any delay. At sea, minor issues quickly become major issues if not addressed immediately. So red lighting was implemented to ensure immediate night vision of all mid-watch personnel or in this case maneuvering stations.

Rick was the only one of the entire group with any sort of 'ship driving' experience. Only the ships he drove were submarines, a task which was done strictly on the orders of the OOD or the Captain. Navigation was nothing he had done nor was he ever trained to do, just dive and drive...that was it. Luckily Archie had some navigation skills and already knew the course they needed to take to remain off the grid. Knowledge acquired via contacts with the CIA. It was Rick's job to drive the ship from its anchorage and through the now open gateway to sea. In effect he had, by default, become Captain.

Okay, Okay...his imagination was running wild and his ego was causing him to suffer a bit of self delusion. Take it easy, its fiction.

With that consciousness the realization that he was now responsible for those on board and for his family's future rose into his throat. If he fucked this up the wealth he now possessed and economic freedom he was to enjoy would be gone. But instead of creating a panic something inside him steeled for the task at hand. In years past this feeling had come over him many times, usually when danger was present. Something inside him thrived on danger, serious, real danger, where death was close at hand or the consequences equally severe. Those were the times he was the most powerful and most in control of his world. Something about those moments created in him a force no man could match. It was that force driving him now.

"Weigh anchor" he called out. Slowly the capstans took in the anchor chain slack and pulled up the anchors. Under his hands the ship seemed to come alive as the chains rattled and shook through the hull. One by one each anchor was hoisted into position and secured on the hull dripping with seawater and algae from their long stay under water. Once free of the bottom Rick felt the ship shudder and roll now that her anchors were no longer holding her still. To him she seemed eager to be at sea. Again the heady feeling of being captain took his consciousness as he called out, "Ahead Slow". A bell tolled as the screws bit into the water pushing the massive, heavy hull of the Victoria forward passed the open gates and out to open sea.

The passage through the gates was harrowing due to the fact that nobody knew for sure if the hull would clear the gateway now that she was loaded down with bullion. As a result everyone on board held their breath until the screws cleared and the ship was in the channel. If the truth were to be known the screws cleared the bottom of the channel by a mere six feet. Had but one ocean swell nosed the ship up at the wrong moment the screws would have dug into the sandy bottom possibly damaging the screws ending their voyage before it began.

Although the gate way was easily three times wider that the ship it felt to Rick as if he were threading a needle. On top of this was his concern that the current, if there was one might drive the ship's hull into the concrete barrier. His hands gripped the wheel as the nose of the ship moved forward. Archie was in the forward steering station operating the pod and keeping the bow from driving into the concrete wall. Nevertheless it was a strained few minutes as the massive ship slipped from its anchorage and out to sea. Once the fathometer read 100 feet beneath the keel, only then did Rick and Archie relax. With a hard left rudder Rick headed straight east at 5 knots to a designated spot where Hans and T would meet them in a few hours.

Their lights were kept off and the radar was turned on to ensure that they would remain clear of shipping traffic until they had everyone on board. Once they were over the horizon from St. Vincent they turned on the running lights and mast lights. They needed to run blacked out to remain out of sight of the island inhabitants. They didn't' dare remain blacked out for the journey as that would attract unwanted attention and draw the Coast Guard or other law-enforcement. It was while they waited for Hans and T to arrive that Rick became concerned that the ship was not registered, if that were the case they were inviting trouble, lights or not...that and he was not a registered sea captain.

Reaching for the radio he called Archie up from the forward steering cupola. In a few minutes Archie and Rick were sitting in the dim light of the bridge with Rick expressing his concern that if they were to sail the Victoria through the shipping lanes their being unregistered might invite trouble. In fact Rick felt kind of stupid for not having checked on this earlier.

Archie laughed softly and patted his shoulder "Take it easy son. The ship is registered as a charity vessel owned by the church and used for missionary work. My CIA contacts have created a false trail of embarkation points dating back a year in regions where security cameras are usually not working if they even bothered to put them in, areas only missionaries dare to tread. Our port of registry is San Jose Costa Rica and we've been in a repair facility for several months. A shipyard in Malaysia in fact, that just had its main computer system go down due to a nasty virus…destroying their records for the past year. Imagine that…" Archie grinned clearly pleased with himself. "So if you are concerned about anything or if we are hailed by the local authorities give me the radio and I'll spin them a yarn so thick it'll take them a month to unweave it." Again he grinned causing Rick to laugh out loud realizing that this worry was for naught.

"Alright then, if we are hailed by the Coast Guard you are the Captain. I'll just drive the boat and you spin the yarn" he said grinning back at Archie. Patrice then came in carrying two cups of coffee perfectly brewed and perfectly sweetened handing one each to Rick and Archie.

"Thank you Patrice' Archie said. 'If I were just a few minutes younger you, my lass would be in deep, deep trouble" Patrice smiled warmly and kissed him on the cheek handing Rick his coffee before formerly introducing herself.

"I'm Patrice, I'm sure that Archie has told you about how we met' she said. 'I'm very pleased to meet you. We're going to be onboard this ship for a while so we might as well get to know one another"

In an instant, Rick who was not normally shy couldn't speak. For the first time he saw to how perfectly beautiful she was and was instantly tongue tied and speechless. However a well-timed kiss on the cheek from Patrice untied it and he said "Ahhhh. Ahh I'm pleased to meet you" he said causing Archie to cackle like an old chicken recognizing the thunderclap attraction between them.

A thunderclap is an attraction where all reason is erased and re-placed by a purely emotional, animal drive. In this case the attrac-tion was mutual and explosive, the type that burns too hot and too quick and is not meant to last. Ohhhh but what a moment it is. In that moment, nothing else mattered. The attraction between Rick and Patrice was apparent and impossible to deny, something that Archie acknowledged with wry humor. "You two need to get a room" he said cackling as he walked to the captain's cabin leaving Patrice and Rick alone on the bridge so not to inhibit what he knew had to come.

Patrice attraction to Rick had come unexpectedly. She had seen Rick from afar and had not been impressed. But when he took the ships wheel and just 'did the job' without being asked and without formal training with no apparent fear or misgiving, simply drove the ship out of the anchorage. Something about that impressed her. Driving a massive ship through a small inlet didn't intimidate him. Most men would have found an excuse to let someone else drive, but he had simply taken up station at the helm and took command of the ship as if he were born to the role. That turned her on...a lot.

He wasn't the most handsome man she'd ever seen but that didn't matter. He was no pretty boy and he certainly didn't bother himself with fashion. This man had character. He had been dealt a harsh hand, but never cheated or shirked his way out of anything. He just bulled through whatever he faced and took what came. But as hard as he appeared to be, he was kind, the type of man who would enter a burning building to save a dog or a cat. Unlike Werner who would just let them die if not throw them into the fire. Suddenly she felt soiled for ever having let such a man touch her.

Rick was a much more attractive alternative. Something about his being real made her want him more than any other man she'd met. Something about him made her want to pleasure him, to release the stress he had experienced in life. "Was it pity?' she wondered. 'No' it wasn't pity. This man needed no pity. What he needed, if she were to guess accurately, was a good fuck and she knew exactly what to do about that. If she had a problem it was falling for Lisa. Being in love with her did not in any way erase her need for 'male' attention. But she didn't want to betray her new love, at least not before she had time to discuss this with her. Maybe they'd share him? Patrice smirked to herself, "That might be fun" she thought.

Patrice looked up at him and took in what she recognized as a genuine man. Not a false, piggish man who was trying to impress her but a man who knew his mind and embraced his frailties. It was his obvious imperfection and his acceptance of them that she found interesting. "You've driven a ship before, haven't you?" she asked moving closer to him.

He shook his head "No, not a surface ship. I drove subs...a long time ago. I'd just steer a course as I was ordered to and sit on my ass staring at a compass and depth gauge for six hours at a shot" he said as he stared out into the blackness through the screen.

"A submarine, you actually went underwater? How deep did you go?' she asked genuinely curious 'was it scary?"

Shaking his head he smiled "No, not as scary as you might think. Most of the time we were too tired to care about anything but getting to the rack" he said.

"Rack?" she asked

Rick smiled and chuckled. "Yeah, that's what we called our bunk, we usually had to share it with two others while at sea, it was called 'hot racking', because the 'rack' was warm from the previous occupant when you crawled in." This was met with a wrinkled nose as if to suggest that this was gross or disgusting causing Rick to clarify with "We showered before we got into the rack. If you didn't the crew would pull you from the rack and scrub you clean…with a Brillo pad."

Her eyes widened in disbelief and shock "No, you aren't serious. That is so awful. Those poor men" she said aghast.

"Awful? No…awful is sleeping in the stink of another man who hasn't bothered to wash…that's awful' he said as a matter of fact. 'The upside is that it usually happened only one time before the offending party got the message. On rare occasion it had to be done twice. The chronically stupid are rare, but they do pop up on occasion." This was met with a soft laugh that Rick found inticing. He looked at her taking in her beauty. "You are incredibly beautiful, but I'm sure you've heard that more often than you'd care to." He said looking away and through the screen into the night to hide his own forbidden attraction for her.

Looking at him she answered "I don't hear it as often as you might think. When I do it's usually from a man whose motivation is so painfully obvious the charm is lost. I can tell that you meant it, thank you' she moved in and kissed him on the cheek. 'I hope we can talk later, you and I, I'd love to get to know you better, if you wouldn't mind" she said with a smile that said more than words could.

Rick looked at her and nodded "Yeah, I'd like that, I really would". Patrice smiled looking deeply into his eyes and then without warning wrapped her arms around his neck and kissed him as deeply as she had ever kissed any man, or woman for that matter. Rick responded in kind and wrapped an arm around her waist and pulled her hard against his body. The fact that he was married did not seem to matter, not in that moment as his lust for this magnificently beautiful woman took over.

His free hand caressed and stroked her body and ass noting that she was not wearing anything under the thin fabric of her sun dress. Her tongue danced with his as they both lost themselves in the moment. Then as quickly as it started Patrice broke away and left the bridge through the same door as Archie had and closed it behind her. Rick couldn't take his eyes off her perfectly shaped ass as she walked away. The encounter forced him to adjust 'himself' after his brief encounter with Patrice so he could stand comfortably at the wheel, but the grin on his face remained.

It had been years since he'd felt such a surge of animal lust. He'd begun to think that he was getting too old for such things because his body simply wasn't responding anymore. Patrice had just proven otherwise. His heart beat savagely in his chest as he gathered his thoughts and tried to redirect his focus to the task at hand. Had she not broken off their kiss it was entirely plausible that he would have screwed her right there on the navigation station. He tested the console for strength to see if it was strong enough to hold the two of them just in case she came back. He decided that 'yes' it was strong enough, but she did not return that evening, at least not alone.

Her initiating the kiss left little doubt as to her intentions so he wasn't bothered with the usual confusion most men are left with. There was a genuine palpable attraction between them and it was clear that something physical would happen between them in the near future. It had been so long since he'd been with a woman who 'wanted' him he was uncertain if he could do the job properly. His hope was that he didn't disappoint her when the time did come. Smiling to himself his ego had been elevated by a woman who knew how. His wife could learn a thing or two from Patrice. Rick chuckled to himself as he thought of introducing Laurie to Patrice…that could prove interesting, very interesting and likely dangerous for him…but what a way to die.

Several hours earlier back on the island Hans and T both stood looking down from the plateau watching the lagoon fill with water. Trees and bushes that had once taken root in the meadow were now floating on the surface with several large trees jammed against the southern shore. Hans watched as the wind carried the debris to the southern shore as well as the current caused by the drainage. As the sand drained out of the bottom the incoming water began to rush through the lagoon with much more force than anticipated.

The force generated by the rush of water was enough dislodge one of three WWI German U-boats buried under the sand to break free of its sandy prison 50 feet below. The old boat seemed to come alive and rode the incoming current which hit the hull in a way that forced the hull to nose up. The effect of this was that all of the loose fittings inside the hull fell to the stern and forced the nose up even further. This caused the air pocked inside the hull to launch the ship toward the surface.

Minutes later the prow broke the surface and rode the current with its nose high out of the water due to the stern torpedo room now being filled with whatever had fallen into it when the ship first nosed up from the bottom. The hull was sitting at a 45 degree angle on the surface as it sliced through the water before lodging itself between two massive trees jammed against the shore.

Hans stared in stunned disbelief as he realized what was floating among the uprooted trees and shrubs. Of course he'd known long before this that the Kaiser had used the island as a base in WWI and those submarines based here had been sunk in the lagoon and buried. The fact that one of them was now exposed and sitting on the surface surprised him. The forces generated by the inrushing water had floated a 100 year old German submarine to the surface. But that wasn't his immediate concern. What did concern him was the fact that a portion of one of the submarines was now visible and if it were spotted from shore all their efforts to quietly escape the island could be compromised.

A WWI German U-boat on an island 200 miles off a French possession would raise a great many questions and draw the attention of international law enforcement as well as those nations still seeking reparations from Germany's plunder of the nations it had once conquered. Worse would be the danger of their being in the vicinity of the island at the time of the discovery. This would automatically warrant an inspection and the vast amount of bullion on board would be confiscated. Hans looked at it trying to find a way to cover it with bushes or something to hide it from view. Moving it was simply not in the cards, not now and certainly not with only two men and a jeep. It was then T moved up next to him looked down to see what Hans was looking at and gasped in surprise, "Holy Shit!! Is that what I think it is?" he asked.

Hans nodded and said quietly "Yes, it is. That is a WWI U-boat sent here by the Kaiser and later scuttled and buried to hide the evidence. If the Allies had learned of this island after the Armistice Germanys troubles would have been far more severe. It is likely Germany itself would have ceased to exist" he said his mind still figuring on a solution. "We've got to cover that prow. If anyone finds that boat now, before we've had a chance to secure the bullion we could lose it. The international reaction to this find could create a huge political windstorm and if our ship isn't far enough away, which it currently is not, we could easily find ourselves the center of a lot of attention."

But just as he was turning away a massive tree, popped to the surface its roots no longer weighed down by soil and sand and as if by divine providence came high out of the water and crashed down on top of the submarines prow covering it from view and dislodging it causing it to sink once again to the bottom. Hans couldn't believe what had just happened. One moment they were facing a potential catastrophe and the very next, a perfect solution addressed it without so much as his having to lift a finger. Dropping his head in relief he chuckled "Perhaps there is a god after all".

'T' then leaned against the wall stunned by the fact that he'd just seen a WWI German U boat breach the surface "A WWI U-boat buried in the meadow?" He asked still not sure of what to think of what he clearly saw.

Hans nodded "There are three' he said evenly. It is likely they pulled them out into the lagoon, scuttled them and then covered them in sand." Hans sighed as a sense of overwhelming regret and unexplainable sadness swelled within him. "Those ships were the sword of the German Navy, a noble fleet for the Fatherland. It is a complete and utter shame that they were treated like this."

"T" looked at Hans thoughtfully never having considered a 'ship' as anything but a machine. Then again he'd never been a sailor, then, neither had Hans. "You sound like an old sailor there Hans" he said with a laugh.

Hans smiled at him and said "You forget I did voyage on a submarine to get here. I had, by my circumstance, become a sailor, after a fashion. I stood watch, cleaned and maintained it and above all I learned to depend on that ship for survival, as did every other soul onboard. In that experience, brief though it was, I learned that a ship takes on a life of its own as each man gives of himself in maintaining it keeping it alive so that it in turn keeps them alive. So the ship, depends on the crew as much as the crew depends on the ship as a result the ship takes on a life of its' own. I can't explain it any better than that. It is something that one can understand 'only' if they have lived aboard ship for a time." Hans went silent and watched the swirling waters of the newly filled lagoon.

In time when the water level equalized the current would subside and the tides would then scrub the remaining sand from the bottom. If the trees weren't removed from the water they would, in time become water logged and sink creating a new habitat for fish to make the lagoon their home. Not to mention the guns and faux shells now sitting on the bottom. It would make for an interesting diving tour for someone he thought. Looking at his watch he figured that they'd have to remain on the island for another hour before it was safe to leave. In that time they had to secure the base to ensure that nobody found it by mere chance.

The entrance from the house on the plateau they could do nothing about. However, they could post no trespassing signs to discourage illegal entry and create a legal footing in the event that someone did break into the house. The only problem with that is if the persons' breaking and entering weren't law enforcement or military personnel legal ramifications were of little or no concern. Still, they had to do what they could to minimize the risk of accidental discovery.

As he watched from the mountaintop, Hans began to see the edge of the lagoon come into focus. The main body of which had been used to maneuver the subs into position in order to clean their hulls and do basic maintenance in the slipways hidden behind a mound of sand. Of course camouflage netting was likely used by the time war broke out due to the increased presence of military aircraft. Though it was very unlikely they'd have come out this far being that few planes in 1914 had the range or navigational capacity to fly long distances over water.

Also aircraft carriers weren't even a consideration until close to the end of the war, and were scoffed at as foolish because planes were not considered serious offensive naval weapons, most especially against heavily armored battleships Of course, time would see the aircraft become the most deadly threat a battleship would face, but not in WWI.

He had mixed feeling about the island both as a German soldier and as a man of peace. On one hand he was proud of his nations achievement in building the island when such ideas were not even thought of, much less achieved. While on the other hand he felt shame that such achievements were used for war and not the betterment of mankind. Trumping this was the frustration caused by his nation being destroyed twice by idiotic men who used Germany's technological genius for selfish purpose.

Before he could delve deeper into the past 'T' broke him of his revere. "We need to start closing up shop Hans' he said placing a hand on his shoulder. 'T' had recognized the conflict raging in the man before him mostly because he had similar conflicts as a former agent of the USA. What he had been asked to do for his country was frowned upon by most civilized nations. Yet, it was those very same civilized nations who behaved with a barbaric disregard for human life simply to maintain their civilized façade. For that reason, he found acting for a criminal organization easier than he expected as it was less hypocritical. As mentioned earlier, they had been a more functional law enforcement element as a criminal organization than they had as a government-sanctioned team. Even so, he had difficulties reconciling his 'criminal' reality with his legitimate, lawful past. Neither of which allowed him the luxury of a full-night's sleep.

Too often he'd lay awake at 3am with his guts churning with worry that his life pursuits were a waste of time; that his talents were being used for the wrong purpose. Yet, there was always someone who needed his particular service who was willing to pay for it. It was exactly 'that' which kept 'T' awake at night. Ironically as healthy as his bank accounts were, they did nothing to assuage the idea that his career path was a waste of time. Not only was he dissatisfied with his career he was genuinely confused by the fact that his legitimate past was more criminal in nature than his actual criminal occupation.

However, those concerns were merely academic, what bothered him most was his lack of family. In his line of work such a luxury was not to be considered. Not yet. He didn't want his kids to have a father who did *this* sort of thing for a living. He wanted to raise kids and be a proper father to them not a dad who might not come back one day because of what he did or worse get arrested and sent to prison. So his desire for a family life, a normal, boring, barbeque on Sunday afternoon with a hammock and beer, life was not to happen while he was engaged in this sort of occupation. But with the completion of this job, he began to see that hammock hanging in his back yard and he let the feeling blossom into a broad grin.

Both he and Hans locked the doors to the house and double-checked the sealed entrances to the base, including the entrance to the now empty anchorage. After which they drove to the roadblock and put up signs citing sink-hole dangers and falling trees hoping to scare curious persons away. One last touch was to pull a tree from the lagoon and place it onto the roadway itself guaranteeing that no vehicles could get passed it.

They then drove to the boathouse pulled the jeep into it and started up the Chris-Craft motor launch. It was an easy two-hour journey to their meeting with the Victoria. Where they were hoisted on board and the antique launch set onto its perch and tied down. Once the launch was secured both Hans and 'T' went up to the wheelhouse where the entire compliment waited for them.

Chapter 41
Inner Demons

(Hours Earlier)

"BENZ!!! MAINTAIN PERISCOPE depth dammit!!! What the fuck is the matter with you?!!" The captain bellowed into Rick's ear as he usually did when he was on the bridge. For whatever reason the Captain did not like Rick, not one bit and made it known whenever Rick was in his sight.

In front of Rick was a panel of gauges he needed to watch to maintain rudder angle, dive plain angle, depth, speed and course. His station was the helm. Six hours of boredom steering and diving the ship on the order of the Officer Of the Deck. It was his job to steer whatever course was ordered, dial in the speed that was ordered and dive the ship to whichever depth was ordered. Today they were supposed to collect flash traffic satellite updates to their mission and then go back to operating depth.

Today was different however, the ship was not responding. It would steer fine and come to depth fine but she would not maintain her depth no matter what he did. It was as if they were being pulled down by some invisible force. There was no flooding that they could find and there were no abnormalities in the mechanicals of the ship, but the ship would not maintain depth.

Once the satellite data was retrieved they dove to 150 and held depth for several hours until the ship began to nose up again and sink lower even though they were cruising at 20 knots. There was no reason for her not to be holding depth. Again a search was sent aft to locate where the water was coming from but no water was found in any of the spaces. No flooding was reported in any compartment, all compartments were dry.

"Ahead two thirds" the OOD ordered and the ship came under heel again and maintained depth of 150 feet without a problem for the next two hours. Then without warning the ship was suddenly forced down by the stern again, this time at a severe angle so the ship nosed up almost vertical, to the point that the air in the ballast tanks began to bubble out causing the ship to lose positive buoyancy. Then as if the stern had been released the stern came up to level again. Leaning against the periscope the OOD cried "Level the ship and blow forward ballast tanks and bring us up to periscope depth."

"Aye-aye sir" a shaky voice replied, but it was not his voice, though it came from his lips as Rick leveled the ship the rest of the crew scrambled find out what had just happened. The crew was a picture of professionalism and panic. No man, no matter how brave or bold wants to die inside a submarine in the Arctic Ocean…any ocean.

The captain came to the Con, glared hard at Rick then bellowed "What the fuck just happened? Did Benz fuck up?" Giving Rick a withering look, his hate palpable, he was hoping for an excuse to rip into Benz, his least favorite crew member. There was something about this sailor that made him want to break him. He wanted to destroy that self-assured attitude Benz carried himself with the ego Benz, in his opinion, did not deserve. Admittedly Benz had not done anything he could really nail him on, but he was convinced that he was a fuck up and was determined to prove it to his own satisfaction. In fact his hatred of this particular crewman was purely pathologic and had no basis in anything more than a series of events and incidents that he was certain Benz was guilty of, but could not prove which only made him hate Benz that much more.

The OOD reported to the captain "Sir this has nothing to do with Benz. He has done nothing. It's the ship, it won't hold depth. We were cruising when the stern was pulled down to the point where we nearly lost positive buoyancy. We are coming to periscope depth to affect repairs where necessary and to assess our situation at a safe depth." The Captain nodded his agreement to the OODs actions while stealing a moment to glare at Rick convinced this was somehow his fault, in spite of what the OOD had just told him.

Periscope depth was quiet and uneventful as they charged the emergency-blow tanks that had been depleted in the last failure. Two hours of calm was disrupted when the ship once again began to sink stern first. Again they rose to the surface only to be pulled by the stern into the depths. This time was different. The ship was not prepared to blow to the surface as the tanks were still half full and not near the pressure they needed to be at to overcome the crushing pressure of the ocean depths. Once again they set the screw to all ahead full and rose only to be pulled back again this time more urgently by whatever force was pulling them down. Again a search was launched for the flood, leak or whatever might be causing them to sink and again nothing was found that would explain what was happening.

When the captain ordered flank speed disaster struck. The ship began to shake violently as the screw seized causing the reduction gears to shatter under the force of the high pressure steam turning them. Then in a surreal turn of events the captain ordered an emergency blow but there was not enough air left to do the job and the ship then leveled and began to sink. Being that the screw was no longer serviceable and the reduction gears shattered there was no way to drive the ship to the surface. All pumps were employed to empty the main ballast tanks but it was just not fast enough to counter the effects of the increasing sea pressure.

Ricks heart began to beat impossibly fast with the knowledge that he was about to die. He would die as the ship's hull broke apart. The water would rush in compressing the air and what oil there was in the air would ignite in a process called dieseling and incinerate the crew before the water hit their bodies. "*This can't be happening*" he thought as his heart beat painfully in his chest.

The Captain then calmly ordered "Deploy the distress buoy. Send our position if possible and secure the watch." He then moved to his cabin and closed the door. One by one everyone on the bridge filed down to crews mess, each took a cup and got coffee. Several men pulled out cards and began playing 'Spades' with their shipmates which was made difficult by the stern tilt of the ship as it sank deeper and deeper.

Rick like the others got his coffee but instead of sitting at his usual table he took a seat at the Chiefs table right next to the digital depth gauge and watched as the numbers climbed, 700 feet, 800, 1000…1200…the bulkheads began to creak but the card players kept playing 'Bang!' Pop..pop..pop…1300…the hull started protesting the pressure with a low constant groan of stressed metal…1500

the noise coming from the bulkheads was constant now, creaking…
groaning in protest…1700…a long low moan came from deep in
the engine room. 'The digital gauge quit spinning at 2000 feet and
froze…then the bulkhead broke with an ungodly sound of ripping
metal followed by a loud BANG!'

Rick bolted upright in his bunk gasping in terror his body drenched
in sweat. Deep in his chest his heart beat mightily as if trying to
break containment. His throat croaked in a hoarse cry that didn't
quite make it out. As his mind came to itself again he panted as the
nightmare ebbed from his consciousness.

The mattress on which he had been sleeping was drenched with
pools of sweat where his body had been. His undershirt and boxers
were drenched with sweat. Panting in the dark Rick was still not
quite sure where he was or if he was safe because he was still, in his
mind, on the sinking submarine expecting death to come at any moment. Slowly his eyes adjusted to the dark cabin behind the bridge of
the Victoria and he began to realize that he had just had the nightmare again, the same one he'd had for the past twenty five years.

As he came to himself again a voice called out to him in a calm,
easy tone. "Just relax son, you are safe, you've just had a night-mare,
a pretty nasty one I'd say" came the soothing, preacher-like voice of
Archie Davis.

Looking around the dark cabin he saw Archie sitting in the chair
next to him and nodded at Archie as he finally came to grips with
reality. His heart was still racing as he spoke "I…I hope I didn't make
too much noise. Nobody has ever been around when I have had that
nightmare. I've been having this one at least once a month since I
signed off my boat." He said wearily.

Archie gave him an understanding look knowing all too well what Rick was feeling. It is an understanding only a veteran can have. A veteran who has faced death and come out the other end not knowing why or how he had survived where so many others had not. It is that question that often drives a veteran's emotional stress and the guilt of surviving when so many friends had not or were badly wounded.

Rick was suffering from PTSD that many veterans suffer from particularly those who had faced severe long term stresses associated with their service. Though different from combat related PTSD this came in the form of a subconscious fear that was inherent to submarine service, the fear of never surfacing again. The knowledge that one screw up, one mistake, one mechanical failure caused by a yard worker not fully engaged in his job could cause the ship to sink.

It was just such a failure that caused the sinking of the Thresher; a substandard bolt had been used to replace a hardened part to save time so the ship could be finished more quickly. A seemingly minor part, one of millions, which was not up to the task failing at depth initiating a cascade of events the crew could not overcome, resulting in the Thresher sinking off of Cape Cod in the 1963, in 8000 feet of water, with all hands. It was the Navy's worst loss of life in a peacetime incident.

Then there was the Scorpion, a Skipjack Class submarine had been lost under mysterious circumstances, speculation was wildly varied from the Soviets sinking it because it got too close to a top secret intelligence mission, to a runaway torpedo that was launched accidentally that armed and turned on the Scorpion sinking her. While the ship was found the location of the wreck was kept secret, feeding the speculation that it had been a Soviet intelligence operation that sank her and the powers that be were desperate to keep it under wraps, to avoid a war.

Sinking was not something he had worried about while serving on board the submarine. Dwelling on such things while on board a ship that deliberately sinks would be absurd and likely cause the person dwelling on such things to lose their mind; Hence the protracted psychological evaluation that each volunteer to the sub fleet undergoes prior to entering sub-school and of course during actual training.

Yet, every time they went to sea, a silent prayer was said by every man on board, from the Captain to the lowliest seaman, in remembrance of those two crews and subs, a reminder that what they were doing was not to be taken lightly at any time, in any weather, in peace time or war…ever. It wasn't until he was no longer going to sea on the submarine that the nightmare began, exactly one week after he had signed off the boat. It had been with him ever since.

That is how most PTSD episodes begin, once the stress of whatever it is you are facing is no longer present. It is then the subconscious releases what it has been keeping under wraps. While engaged in the heat of duty seldom does the stress of the moment take hold until after the fact hence the term Post Traumatic Stress Disorder. It is an age old problem for combat veterans since the dawn if civilized warfare, though warfare in any form is the antithesis of 'civilized'.

Once recognized as a condition it was named Shell Shock, Battle Fatigue, Combat Fatigue and more recently Post Traumatic Stress Disorder. No matter what it was called it is a condition caused by putting men in harm's way either directly or indirectly that causes the innate need for self-preservation to be suppressed in the performance of one's duty to God and country.

Getting out of bed Rick began to shiver from the wet clothes and cool sea air. Grabbing a pair of boxers and a new t-shirt Rick ran to the head and stripped off the wet clothes. He rinsed off in the shower, toweled off before putting on his clean dry t-shirt and underwear. Feeling more comfortable Rick then relayed to Archie the nature of the nightmare in detail.

Archie nodded his understanding "My night mares did much the same to me when I was still having them. Mine stopped about 20 some years ago. I guess whatever it was I was working through got resolved, it only took 50 some years' He chuckled, 'I've been a sound sleeper since. You need to get some rest, son. We are waiting for Hans and T to catch up to us and I think they will be a while yet. You might as well take advantage of it while you can and get some more rest. I'll come get you when they arrive."

Rick nodded and proceeded to change his sheets after flipping the mattress over being that it was fairly drenched. It was a quick evolution and being exhausted from the extreme emotional violence of the nightmare Rick fell instantly to sleep. Helping him to relax was the nearness of Archie who reminded him that he was safe and no longer in danger. Archie remained seated by the bed waiting for his young friend fall back to sleep.

It was obvious that Rick was a bundle of nerves. Archie had lived long enough and experienced enough to recognize the signs of shell shock or combat fatigue as it was called in his day. It was also painfully clear that his new friend had been living under a great deal of strain for far too long. The fact that he was now able to afford to take care of his family he hoped a lot of that stress would ease for him. Then Archie wondered if the strain his friend was living had anything to do with the fact that his wife was sleeping with another man.

RICHARD BEND

Archie was not sure if it was his place to butt into a situation he knew nothing about. He also did not wish to instigate a problem just as their venture was getting started. It was going to be complicated enough without adding infidelity into the mix. Granted his view of infidelity was atypical. Archie's wartime exploits and life experiences had numbed him to the trivialities of marital infidelity.

Granted the vast majority of people did not think of infidelity as trivial, but neither had they seen the horrors of war he had to give them scope. Compared to what he had seen other men do to each other, infidelity was a minor, inconsequential fact of human life. It didn't hurt anyone, unless you allowed it to. Yet it was that very 'triviality' that had started so many wars over millennia of time. How many people had died? How many families had been torn apart just so that one man could enjoy the physical charms of another man's wife? How many would yet have to die over such a trivial matter... even now?

Shaking his head Archie decided that it was best to leave it alone. Rick and Greg both needed to focus on the task at hand without any distractions. It would never do to have them trying to kill each other with Odessa on their heels. It was none of his business anyway. He looked over at Rick who was taking deep regular breaths indicating that he was finally sleeping soundly. He would need his rest, especially with the voyage ahead; they all would.

Once he was sure that his friend was asleep he got up and stepped onto the bridge to wait for Hans and T to show up. It would be a few hours yet. So he sat on the settee and watched the ship operate on auto pilot, a feature he'd had installed when the ship was refitted. He had thought it necessary to install an auto pilot to aid in navigating the ship if he and Hans had to make the journey alone. Such a feature would make the trip across the Atlantic at least possible with a minimal crew. It was there to free up the watch stander to address other duties, but not to take their place. With 8 people and an auto pilot the journey across the ocean would be less exhausting, no less dangerous, but less exhausting...relatively speaking. They would need everyone alert and ready for whatever was to come because the danger they faced would be ever present from this point forward.

Even though they had escaped the island and were now at sea, Archie had the feeling that danger was not far behind. The urgency he had felt on the island had eased but it was still there and would not go away fully until the bullion was secure, even then they would have to be cautious. As he sat in the red glow of the bridge light he let the sound of water shush and ripple along the hull as the Victoria rocked and swayed in the ocean swell. It was a sound he knew well. "How man times had he been put ashore in enemy territory from a ship?" He wondered.

He had been set ashore into enemy-occupied territory where air-drops were not possible from blacked out submarines, motor torpedo boats or MTBs, as they were otherwise known, and sometimes from small ships. They were nights very much like the one he was staring out into, a moonless, star lit night. A tingle of the old sensation of going into harm's way crept up his neck as the memories of those days replayed themselves inside his head. To Archie it was like meeting an old lover, a lover long missed and still inviting.

The war and his life following the war had been full of action, adventure and intrigue. He certainly had not suffered from boredom and as a result had not suffered the normal mid-life crisis most men encounter when life suddenly catches up to them. Neither had he settled down. The rich experiences of his life's pursuits had not included marriage or children. This had tempered his adventurous life with loneliness. It was emptiness he felt when he finally realized that the woman he loved and taken for granted would never again be his. It was a bitter realization that he had come to upon seeing his beloved Skye in her casket. The ache of knowing that he had lost her forever was a wound he could carry for the rest of his life.

It was at such times, when the shadows crept around him, that his most bitter memories plagued him. Glancing at his wrist watch, the same one he had used since his very first mission of the war, it read 3:00 a.m. Archie chuckled to himself wondering what it was about this hour that drew such thoughts to him. He knew he was not the only one to feel this way at this hour. He never understood why it was that at three in the morning, no matter where he was on the planet that his thoughts, his heartaches and bitterness came to the forefront of his thoughts. *"Why wasn't there an hour when those things that made you happy kept you awake?"* He wondered.

Skye, the woman he had once hoped to marry was usually front-and-center of his thoughts at this ungodly hour. Watching Rick in the throes of his nightmare reminded him of how she had sat up nights as he had once suffered through nightmares of his own. She had always seen to it that it was her voice he woke up to in order to bring him down from the heights of terror he had too often visited while in the depths of tortured sleep. Nightmares filled with screaming, dying men, men he had killed with his bare hands so that he felt their life leave their body. Worse still were the screams of the innocent men, women and children he could not save or those he had to let die to complete his missions for King and Country. Those screams and pleading voices were what tortured him the most.

He had awakened to her voice which soothed his fevered brain.

Thankfully he had never become dangerous in those times like so many others had. She was savvy enough to know not to touch him until he had awakened fully. Skye had been uniquely suited to his needs and he had fallen hopelessly in love with her. Only he was very poor at showing it. Archie had taken her for granted for too long which he had learned too late. Unconsciously he slapped the arm rest of the settee as the anger he held for himself panged his heart in blame. She had been the only woman to know how to bring him out of the war and center his thoughts on her...which she was doing even now, these many years later, beyond the grave.

May 8, 1945 VE Day

Archie stood as best man at the wedding of his CO and his secretary Beth. Skye had stood as maid of honor. The party that followed at the local pub had lasted well into the night when his CO took Beth to their honeymoon suite in the Savoy. London was aglow with euphoric bliss with the ending of the war. At midnight the last shots of the European war had been fired and a second wave of euphoria exploded upon the city. It was that second wave that had caused Skye to pull Archie close and kiss him. She had fallen in love with him having served as his confidential aide, pining over his picture while he was off on his missions in occupied Europe.

She was far too aware of his missions and the many close calls he'd had. He had been front and center of the war, in harm's way from the onset of hostilities and throughout the war up to the very end when the Allies were preparing for invasion. His last few missions were the most dangerous because the Germans were growing desperate which only fueled their savagery and they had been savage enough already. Skye had been attracted to him from the very moment she first laid eyes on him so falling in love was a natural next step. The knowledge that she loved him hit her quite suddenly on VE Day after her friend Beth had married Archie's CO. Something in the air made her take control of the situation once the bride and groom had retired to their honeymoon suite in the Savoy Hotel.

Skye had taken Archie by the wrist and dragged him to the nearest park where crowds had gathered to celebrate the wars end. It was no surprise to her to find couples in all manner of celebratory copulation. One woman was kneeling in front of an American soldier with his pants down around his ankles and her mouth working feverishly on his very willing and ready appendage.

Not ten feet away was another woman on her hands and knees with a British shoulder on his knees fucking her like there was no tomorrow and an American soldier in front of that same woman with his cock in her mouth while the Brit and Yank split a pint between them. Skye smiled to herself watching the spectacle thinking "*How bloody diplomatic*". Several other women were sitting on the laps of other soldiers on park benches while others still leaned against trees their legs wrapped around their respective soldier or sailor releasing years of untold strain with wanton abandon and lust.

Upon reaching the secluded grove of trees she pulled Archie through the split in the bushes. She was pleased to find it free of occupants because she wasn't keen on having company, not with what she had planned. Like so many she too was caught up in Victory Fever and had the sudden urge that needed to be addressed. Archie said not a word and just followed along as Skye lead him through the crowd. Skye turned to him and wrapped her arms around his neck and whispered "I'm glad we can finally be alone" and kissed him. One of her hands reached down and unzipped is pants and soon had Archie's cock in her hand which was quickly rising to the occasion. Having anticipated her being naughty already Skye had dispensed with her under garments save for the garter belt which was anything but regulation, her intention being to screw Archie's brains out at the earliest opportunity.

Breaking off the kiss she stared hard at Archie pleased that he was so quick to respond and dropped to her knees, locking eyes on Archie's then took him into her mouth.

Archie rocked his head back and moaned his approval "Oh my dear girl", which spurred her on to take the entire length of his shaft down her throat. It was quite clear that she was no novice to this activity not that Archie was complaining. On the contrary she took care of business taking his cock down her throat expertly over the course of the next 15 or 20 minutes bobbing back and forth on his shaft. When she sensed he was close she pulled off of him, stood, lifted a leg guiding his shaft into her burying his full length into her waiting, shaved and moist womanhood.

Moaning out in approval she nearly came from the girth of his divine, near perfect cock entering her. Once fully engaged she stared hard into Archie's eyes and in her most demure, polite, confidential assistant voice said "Now Mr. Davis would you please shag me?" Then planted a hard kiss onto his lips as Archie gently placed her onto her back on the grass under the tree and did as she requested under the stars of that first peace time evening sky.

There were few times when they were alone when he didn't have Skye naked and crying out in bliss. They had even used his office and desk top for purposes other than clerical duties which on one occasion caused one of the legs to break spilling them both onto the floor. He smiled to himself as that memory came into focus followed by the sharp pain of heart break having lost her to his own misguided focus.

"Ohh Skye...where did I go wrong?" he whispered into the night. A tear rolled down his cheek as he remembered the night their romance had ignited and he cursed himself for letting her get away. The pain in his chest was tempered with the knowledge that soon he would see her and express his regret at having never married her. Perhaps then, if she was willing he could spend eternity with her. There was no one he would rather spend the hereafter with than his Skye.

Chapter 42

Port and Starboard

ARCHIE GREETED BOTH Hans and T with a firm hand-shake. "How did it go, any complications?" Hans then went on to tell him of the near catastrophe of the U boat surfacing. Archie paled when he heard what had happened and relaxed when they reported the tree falling over the top of it. "Well, that at least buys us time." He said padding the sweat from his brow. Once Hans and T had made their report Archie had everyone take a seat as Rick steered the ship back into the shipping lanes, lights on and legal.

"Alright then,' he said getting his thoughts gathered, 'You all know the significance of what it is we are doing and the danger our cargo poses if it falls into the wrong hands. Sadly, we can't trust our governments to do the right thing as those we are hoping to avoid have compromised them. Even if our governments were not compromised I very seriously doubt that 'we' would enjoy the bounty of their generosity. Therefore it is in our collective interests to see to this task ourselves.'

He paused and turned to the map he had tacked up onto the rear bulkhead. 'Due to a tropical storm forming in the Eastern Atlantic we will be forced to skirt the storm front, our proposed route will take us into the commercial shipping lanes along the Eastern Seaboard of the United States staying far enough out to sea to avoid being noticed. We plan to circle north of Iceland through the Denmark Straights then come south to the Isle of Man. This is where our friends have requested they be put off'. He paused again with a grave look. 'Once that is done, we must never meet again. You must never learn the location of the bullion because that knowledge puts you and everyone else at risk. The people seeking it are simply too dangerous to take any chances with. We three' he indicated himself, Rick and Hans 'are to be the only ones to know where it will be hidden. In time Rick will be the only one here to know where it is." Archie deliberately did not mention Greg because there was no need.

Patrice interrupted Archie uncomfortable with what she felt was 'abandonment'. "Mr. Davis, I understand the need to keep the bullions location secret, which is why we asked to be put off on the Isle of Man, but I have just thrown in my lot with you for mutual protection against a common threat; a threat that won't go away because we separate and cease contact with each other. The fact that they know your identity puts you at risk so being separated in this case does not make any sense.

Because of your generosity and cooperation I have more than enough money, but what good is having all that money if I have to hide in a hole somewhere or limit my social calendar? We asked to be put off at the Isle of Man to protect the location of the bullion. We all understand the need for that but we are safer as a group than as separate individuals. Mr. Davis this isn't the war in which Queen and Country come first, this is an operation of mutual survival as well as world protection.

The Operation is well connected and if they establish a link to any one of us, the one they find is as good as dead. Not only dead but likely tortured brutally. I know, I've worked for these people for a long time and subtle niceties are not in their DNA. Not only would splitting up be a bad idea you would be throwing away a valuable asset in the Trio here. As of this job they have ceased employment with the Operation for the same reason I have, survival. With their talents and technical abilities we can stay one step ahead of the Operation. They are, for your information, former CIA. They were disavowed by the CIA because of a dirty FBI agent.' She paused looking hard into Archie's eyes. 'You cannot afford to allow an asset of this sort slip through your fingers. If you want the bullion kept safe you need to organize. What better asset than an elite CIA wet team and a person with my connections? We are wired into the underworld rather more thoroughly than you realize. The man who sent me, I just learned, died last week and the man who replaced him is dangerous and mentally unstable. At the moment he doesn't believe that the bullion exists. It is only a matter of time before he learns the truth. Once that happens he will launch a determined effort to locate this ship. He isn't stupid and once he puts two and two together, he will know we are at sea and he will be looking for us. The only question remaining is how long will it take before he figures that out?

The next question is how long after that before he locates this ship? If he finds you before you dispose of the bullion he will descend on you without mercy.' She paused taking a breath. 'Now, you are correct in keeping the bullion hidden from all but a few. It is only right that such knowledge be limited. I for one am satisfied with what I have. But you need our help to keep the wolves at bay. She sighed and grasped Lisa's hand for emotional support. 'You need us as much as we need you at the moment' she said letting out a sob of mild panic, 'please…we have to stick together…for mutual protection if nothing else."

Archie looked at Hans considering what she said. It was a logical argument. That the Operation would increase their efforts to locate them was certain. And she was correct about them figuring it out eventually. The question was 'when'. Hopefully they had covered their tracks sufficiently to avoid detection long enough to delay and possibly evade a search.

Again an unknown timetable plagued them. They had just evaded 'official' detection by leaving the island. The Coast Guard would be looking for criminal activity not necessarily a bullion repository even if they did find the base. Then, if they figured out that there had been gold in the base locating it would likely be hindered by bureau-cratic red tape and inept government employees who would prevent their detection long enough for them to get away.

The Operation on the other hand wouldn't suffer the same inepti-tude or procedural delays. Once they realized the bullion was real they would pull out the stops locating it. Now that they were at sea and moving, the possibility of being pursued needed to be con-sidered. It was for this reason they chose to sail in the commercial shipping lanes to hide in plain sight. If they looked like just another ship they might get away unnoticed. It was also more difficult to locate a specific ship, especially one among many.

What irked Archie wasn't that he was being challenged, but the fact that Patrice made sense. He was acting as if they were at war and he was waging it as if he had boundaries to hide behind. They didn't even have the law to protect them, not in this case. They were on their own and at the mercy of an adversary blind to ethical conduct, compassion and mercy. If the Operation tracked anyone of them down, those caught would be put through hell before they were killed and they would be killed, of that there was no doubt.

In that moment Archie gained an innate clarity of thought. His behavior to this point had been a reflex from long ago habits he'd developed 70 odd years before when the world was at war and men were expendable. He looked hard at Patrice who was struggling to keep her composure, then to Rick who was concentrating on the steering wheel and compass making sure the ship was going where he wanted it to. He didn't seem to have heard a thing but Archie knew differently, he had heard every word and was simply trying to stay out of it. Hans was sitting on the lounge staring off into his own thought process, obviously mulling over what Patrice had just said as well.

The Trio moved onto the lounge next to Hans as T sat on a Captain's chair in the far corner and lit a cigarette not saying a word but letting Patrice do her thing. She had struck a nerve in the old man because she had a point. Alone they were vulnerable whereas together they stood a decent chance. 'T' was well versed in knowing when to butt out and this was one of those times. He could see Archie's point as well. Where one wanted to keep the bullion safe, the other simply wanted to survive. Both objectives could be met without compromising either goal, but he would not say anything until it became necessary.

Archie smiled at her and patted her shoulder to comfort her. "You have a point Patrice. It was my intent to minimize the danger we faced by splitting up. However, letting you in on where we are depositing the cargo is too dangerous, not only to us as a group, but to the world at large as well' he paused to consider his thoughts then continued, 'Considering that we are only 8 people and Odessa comprises many thousands we must tread very carefully. Taking them on in an out and out fight is out of the question. So we will have to sit down and discuss how best to achieve our mutual protection. So after we settle into our voyage, we should all meet in my cabin to discuss it. First however, we must see to the operation of the ship so that we actually 'get' to where we are going' he paused taking a breath 'Ok, we need to set up watch sections.

We will need at least two people to man the bridge at all times and have a roving watch to make sure we don't have any unexpected surprises. 'J' I'm going to assign you that particular task as you seem to be well acquainted with security measures. Your job is to keep us safe. Is that alright with you?' Jay nodded but said nothing.

'Hans will be the engineering watch leader and will address your stations. Being that we are undermanned, we have to set up port and starboard watch sections, meaning, for those of you not familiar with that term, two sections. I think we need to do 4-hour watch section to allow for a minimum sleep requirement, so we will be 4 on and 4 off. Hans and I will be watch relief to fill in when we must. Just remember that we are not youngsters anymore and so won't be able to do full watches, only relief standing if you need it." Everyone nodded understanding and each person was assigned a watch station.

T was assigned to the wheelhouse with Lisa. Rick and Patrice were also assigned to the wheelhouse. 'J' was assigned as roving watch as well as engineering due to his specific skill set. 'M' took to his engineering duties as if it were second nature, which it turned out it was. He had been a PO2 Auxiliary man in the navy or what is often called an A-ganger when he served on an LST, a ship used to transport tanks. He had been doing exactly the same job on the ship as he had in the navy. Hans and Archie stood relief watches in all sections for an hour at a time, usually during day light hours. 'M' set up a bunk in his engineering space and treated his duty like a 24-hour on call job. During the day he'd see to the ships operation and sleep in the engineering space to be awakened if any alarms went off. Being that the ship was diesel electric there were few alarms that would be catastrophic in terms of mechanicals.

Part of 'J's added duties were to make sure the bilges were pumped. Bilges are seldom dry due to the condensation of the moisture in the air in the parts of the ship that are below the water line. Water intakes for the diesel operation sometimes leaked, oil spills and cleaning buckets are often emptied in the bilge, not to mention the occasional urination of a lazy watch stander. All manner of fluid can be found in the bilge and it is best that it be pumped off the ship for the health and safety of the crew not to mention the integrity of the ship. Hans, though not watch standing had a cabin immediately above the engineering spaces so that he could be on hand for any engineering problem. Archie, when he was in the mood, chose to assist 'J' in the security detail as an extra pair of eyes, mostly to keep from getting bored.

After two days watch standing was routine and the ship was humming along effortlessly as they entered the commercial sea-lanes off Florida falling behind six other ships heading for New York, Norfolk Virginia and Canada. It was then that Archie, Patrice and the Trio had their meeting where they decided the best way to maintain the integrity of the group while not compromising the safety of the bullion. First order of business was the disposition of the ship, which obviously could not be kept on site due to the fact that satellites were now used by the worlds' governments and a lone ship in a place where one hadn't been before would attract attention.

It was decided that the ship would be moored in Denmark because it was heavily traveled with several secure anchorages for seasonal research and commercial vessels. Their ship would be one among many and therefore go unnoticed and be close enough to be convenient if they should happen to need it again.

It had already been decided that Patrice and the Trio would be put off on the Isle of Man where Patrice had property. Its location was perfectly suited to their needs as Patrice had planned on escaping the Operations clutches by disappearing to her hilltop property using the Trio to cover her tracks. It was a huge stone manor house on a hill top over-looking the ocean. 100 acres of forested knolls and rolling pastures filled with grazing sheep and cattle. Wind was a constant reality, but one that Patrice found soothing. From this hill top estate she and the Trio would monitor the Operations communications via satellite thereby remaining on top of the situation.

After five days at sea Archie and Hans were getting edgy. Archie sensed that something wasn't right, though he couldn't put a finger on exactly 'what' that something was. One reason was that they were still on the wrong side of the pond and the Operation had a strong presence on the East Coast of the United States. The further north they went the more intense his feelings became. It was a feeling he'd often had during the war when danger was near. Trusting these feelings had kept him alive. Not once, had he ignored them which was why he was alive at 89 years old and not some name on a headstone or a pile of unidentified bones in a field in Europe.

It turned out that Hans was having the same feeling and was about to approach Archie with his concerns. Immediately they both knew something was not right if they were both having the same misgiving. Sharing it with Rick who was at the wheel along with the Trio who was having coffee between making their rounds, it was agreed that trusting the feelings of two old soldiers would be wise.

Archie was feeling as if they were 'heading' for trouble if they remained in view of other ships. He felt that it would be wise to turn east and head straight for Spain putting as much distance between them and the eyes and ears of the Operation as possible.

When they came abreast of the Norfolk Virginia Rick steered the Victoria into the commercial lane heading straight for Spain. Almost immediately Archie's 'itch' as he called it, eased but did not totally fade away. Such feelings never truly faded away once they surfaced which was why he had reached the age of 89 years.

Hans on the other hand saw an increase in his own personal apprehension, albeit for a very different reason. He had not been to Europe in over 30 years, the place where his ghosts were most active. He did not believe himself to be in any more danger but the fact was he had not seen his wives grave since he buried her. Her spirit was with him and his irrational fear was that he would somehow lose her connection to him if he visited her grave site.

Reinforcing this 'fear' was the fact that Odessa was now on the hunt for them or soon would be making visiting her grave impossible. So, he decided to put it off until they had secured the bullion and secured the ship. He would then employ the Trio to cover his eventual visit to his wives grave ensuring that it was safe to do so.

Their course took them straight east and in three days they were skirting the Azores where they turned north and headed straight for the Irish Sea and the Isle of Man.

Chapter 43
A Dangerous Mind

AFTER EMPTYING HIS guts over the edge of the dry dock
Werner leaned heavily against a wooden piling as he stared into the
empty hold of the Grey submarine. Where had they gone he wondered? The entire island was a huge repository with countless tons
of bullion…even more vast than the stories he'd heard and refused to
believe. His guts heaved again and more sick spilled into the black
of the ancient dry dock, splattering on the bottom. After a few minutes his nausea settled and with deliberate effort he stumbled to the
Jeep where he attempted to gather his thoughts.

He was still not fully able to comprehend the reality he was faced
with. The bullion was real, the vast amounts he couldn't begin to
comprehend, yet he was still in a state of mild disbelief denying that
it was even possible. How could it be? Before him sat hard physical
evidence that it did exist and had been there very recently. Rage and
confusion swirled in his mind as the urge to dispatch Patrice intensified while at the same time was displaced by the need to locate
the bullion. Taking in a deep breath he focused on the immediate
problem at hand, locating the bullion then retrieving it. Looking
around he decided to drive back across the bridge and see if he could
locate some lighting. He needed to investigate this space further

and hopefully find a clue to their final destination. Turning the Jeep toward the entrance from which he'd entered the cavern he spied the box and what he guessed would be the light switch.

Flipping the nearest switch the hums and clicks of the old lighting system switched on and little by little the cavern lit up. As the light filled the space he took in the vast emptiness then spying the elevator at the far end and headed for it. Stepping into it he flipped the lever causing it to move up. Once on top the lighting was sufficient to allow him a view of the door that led out to the lagoon where the Victoria had been anchored. Not quite noon the sunlight shone through the netting sufficiently to allow him a clear view of the entire lagoon and the platform and the stowed gangplank. A ship, they were on a ship!' he thought. Looking down he saw the conveyor which now jutted out into space where it once, obviously entered into a ship.

A mixture of both elation and dread filled his heart. He was elated at discovering how they were transporting it but his dread was in knowing that they had a vast ocean to hide in with countless destinations they could be headed to. Which direction did they go and how long had they been at sea? The need to do something surged through him as he whipped around and raced to the elevator. The nauseatingly slow lift couldn't move fast enough even if it moved at the rate gravity.

The instant it opened Werner jumped into the Jeep and tore up the ramp he'd come down and out the garage door, back up to the plateau where he skidded to a halt and started scanning the horizon for any sign of a ship. The sane portion of his brain knew he would find nothing while the fevered psychopathic portion hoped for anything that might indicate a direction in which to begin the search.

Off in the distance a lone ship, a freighter was followed by another ship of the same design with a tanker not far behind that one. All were traveling in a single file as if it were a highway or a designated route for ships. He would have his men monitor the shipping lanes, but what did the ship look like? There were hundreds, thousands of ships at sea and he couldn't raid them all. Then it occurred to him, 'The loading port!! I'll have them look for a ship with a door in the rear of the ship, the aft' he reminded himself. Taking a calming breath he had mild criteria for his men to follow which should narrow the search somewhat but what else would they be looking for? Reaching for his satellite phone he realized only then that he'd left it on the yacht which he could see from his perch "Shit!!!" he uttered. So close yet so far away.

One hour later he stowed the sea-doo on his mount not bothering to tie it down and ran to where he'd had his phone charging. He called the Miami contingent of the Operation and had them immediately searching for any ship moving along the coast with a door in the rear and see if they could locate a couple of old men, a woman, possibly two and a group of armed men. It was a start.

Miami

Two days later, Werner landed in Miami where he was met by the head of the Miami contingent of the Operation. Jose Hercsh, a Cuban, according to his paper work, but who was actually another Argentine German whose specialty was silent killing, messy silent killing. He was sent in usually to make an impression. He had a reputation for getting things done quickly which is why he was assigned to the Miami office.

THE LIMOUSINE PICKED up Werner at the hanger where Jose informed him of ten ships with the aft loading doors, but only one ship where a woman had been spotted strolling on deck. A photo of the woman, a distant photo, was given to Werner. Even from a distance he recognized Patrice and that sheer floral dress he liked her to wear when he frisked her. "Where is this ship?" he demanded.

Jose, looked at his file and said. "She was last seen heading north off South Carolina 24 hours ago. The route she was taking suggested that she intended to move along the eastern seaboard and possibly up to Canada. If it were heading to European waters they would have taken a southerly route near Bermuda. It might help to determine a destination if we knew the cargo" he suggested politely knowing that the man next to him was not as stable as his predecessor.

Werner looked at Jose, appraising him then nodded. "Very well, close the window so the driver cannot hear this' he said. The window shut and the intercom was immediately disabled by Werner, who distrusted everything and everyone. 'The ship has several thousand tons of bullion that belongs to the Third Reich" he said coolly as if the Reich still existed.

Jose's eyes widened "The lost horde actually exists?" he whispered? Werner was not aware that anyone else knew of the horde outside himself, Patrice and his now deceased boss Horst Krupp.

"How do you know of this?" he asked trying not to sound too shocked.

"Oh, the Dutchmen were saying something to that effect when they passed through here. I didn't take them seriously. I mean they aren't the brightest so why would I?" he said. Werner cursed under his breath. His boss had let it slip. With effort Werner kept his composure and swallowed the urge to vent his frustration at his now deceased boss for being such a loose lipped idiot. *"I should have killed you myself years ago you bastard"* he thought as he stared out the window of the limousine.

After a brief pause so that he could speak without screaming in rage and frustration, Werner continued. "I wasn't aware that he had said anything to anyone else. Obviously, this is something that needs to be kept as quiet as possible. If it gets out and the cargo of this ship is leaked we could lose it altogether. This bullion was allocated by Hitler to establish a South American Front from where we were to have attacked the United States through Mexico. For whatever reason the front never materialized and the people who had been in charge of that operation disappeared. It was assumed that they had absconded with the bullion, a natural assumption. It would now appear that they died in the service of Hitler' he paused for dramatic effect. 'They died to keep his secret safe."

An insane rush of pride surged through his body as he realized the importance of his mission. He was destined, obviously by God himself, to reestablish the Reich and restore the good name of Adolf Hitler. With murderous clarity his eyes sparkled and his pulse quickened. The effect was to make Jose lean away slightly so not to 'catch' whatever sickness this madman had flowing through his veins. With that bullion he would be Fuhrer of the world, or so his fevered brain told him.

Looking at Jose with what could only be construed as a maniacal glare he stated with a self-induced sense of importance "We must find that ship and take the bullion so that we may honor those who died keeping it safe. The world will see the rise of National Socialism once again and I shall be Fuhrer" he said. He had no way of knowing just how insane he sounded. Jose Hercsh began to realize that this was a mess he wanted no part of.

200 yards behind the Limousine an FBI van from the Organized Crime task Force was listening to and recording the conversation between who the FBI believed were two crime bosses. They were investigating what they believed to be the emergence of a new crime syndicate. The crew in the van stared at each other in shock as they realized that the Operation was a Nazi front, if this conversation was any indication. Agent Joshua Peel, the senior agent in charge of what he thought was an easy, pre-retirement cake walk sat back and exclaimed "Shit! Is this for real? You guys aren't playing some bullshit prank are you?" he demanded, desperately hoping they were.

At 55 he was slated for an early retirement because of government budget cuts. He wasn't looking forward to retirement because he loved his job. He wasn't the model agent seen on television where the lead man never smiles, the women are all hot, and the cases were the 'reason' they had for breathing. No, he had been a good agent and had solved a few crimes and arrested some bad guys and even shot a few. Retirement wasn't a worry for him economically because he had over the years accumulated a tidy sum of cash which sat off shore in various accounts.

He'd found truckloads of cash here and there when either gangs clashed or drug cartels got sloppy. If he was the first on scene the cash on scene disappeared and was never reported. If the cash on hand was too big to hide in his car he took what he could and reported the rest. On more than one occasion he'd been aware of a drug transfer and knew who was planning to double cross whom. He'd be waiting in the shadows when the deal went bad and help things along if needed. After all parties were out of commission he'd grab the cash and leave. One such event left him with a U-Haul truck loaded with no less than 400 million dollars which he just drove off with, stashing it in a temporary storage facility until he could move it.

He didn't consider himself a bad agent. The money wasn't stolen or taken from some retirement fund. It was all the result of criminals being stupid and killing each other off. He simply took it after there was nobody left to protest. He'd seen millions of dollars sitting in the evidence lockers all over the country, most of it would sit for decades doing nothing but take up space. In one case over ten million sat in a locker decades after the 'perp' died. So he took it upon himself to put the money he found to good use, his retirement.

But that was the last thing on his mind now. "National Socialism?' he was incredulous 'Isn't that what the Nazis called their government? Please, somebody confirm for me what I just heard so I know I'm not losing my mind'. The remaining team nodded apparently equally stunned but nobody could bring themselves to form the words. 'Son of a bitch' he hissed 'Nazis in Miami, Holy Shit!! Ok, ok...okay... and what about that ship? Did he say a ship filled with bullion? We need to contact the treasury and see if they can tell us anything about any lost bullion shipments or robberies we haven't heard of yet. If we are talking Nazi gold shipments we may have to go back 70 some years into the files to find an answer."

Once the shock wore off, an agent by the name of Aaron Smith stared hard at the printing transcripts locking onto the portion that suggested that 'Werner' intended to create resurgent National Socialist regime. Aaron Smith was an operative for Israeli intelligence or Mossad. To his fellow FBI agents he was a Lutheran raised in Corn Hole Iowa when in fact he'd been raised in Tel Aviv. He had been infiltrated into the FBI as a means of keeping tabs on them because so many of its operatives were anti-Semitic.

This new development however was a major concern. Being Israeli he had been well acquainted with the Holocaust and the price his people had paid. The Nazis were long gone, or so he had believed but according to this they had reorganized as the 'Operation'. The last thing he as an Israeli would tolerate was a renewed and power-ful National Socialist regime. The report to the Israeli Ambassador that evening would create an inferno of activity from Israel. Until then he had to sit quietly and do his job as dispassionately as he was able in order to get as much information as possible.

The silence on the speaker was broken by the continuation of the conversation in the Limousine. The voice on the speaker was Jose "Sir, if this bullion belonged to the Third Reich how is it these peo-ple have it and where are they taking it?" Meyer having never been a patient man forced himself to answer what he recognized as a valid question in spite of his urge to choke the questioner.

Picking up the photograph of the woman on deck he handed it to Jose. "See this woman? She is the one who discovered the hiding place of the bullion. My predecessor trusted her with locating a for-mer SS officer by the name of Beck who had been one of the men who had been assigned to disperse the funds for the attack on the USA. He turned up not long ago on an island where one of our members recognized him. We sent a team in to determine if it was indeed him or not. We sent in the Dutchmen to assist in this effort. Apparently he was the man Odessa had been seeking but there was a complication in that he had apparently partnered up with a former British SOE agent.

Together they were making sure that the bullion remained undiscovered. How they came together is a mystery but the fact is they managed somehow to enlist the aid of Miss Verga here' he gestured to the picture 'and her team we know as the 'Trio', A clever bunch and very capable of maintaining anonymity. Apparently they are more loyal to Patrice than they are to the 'Operation'.' He crumpled her photograph in irritation, having glossed over the fact that his effort to have them killed had been the catalyst for their desertion. 'Now we are to find this ship and take it. I don't have to tell you that the people on board are to be killed no exceptions. Is that clear?" Jose simply nodded.

Werner continued "The Brit apparently was a WWII operative tasked with finding our comrades and persecuting them. How he located the bullion is a question we are likely to find no answers to unless we get them directly from him and he doesn't seem to be the type to answer willingly. But the question is academic only, we 'need' to find the ship and get the bullion into our hands before these people spirit it away. We may never have an opportunity like this again if they reach wherever it is they are headed.' He paused and stared out the window again 'I wish I could say these people were stupid and predictable. I wish I could say this would be easy but finding these people and defeating them will be a bit of a challenge, unless we can sneak up on them and overwhelm them with firepower. They are only 8 people or less but we mustn't underestimate them."

Back in the FBI van agent Peel dialed the office to speak with his section chief to inform him of this new development. The news was met initially with disbelief "No, that is not what you heard, you must have been mistaken that isn't possible" came his chiefs reply. But when Josh played it back for his chief over the phone, twice, he was then asked to report back to the office immediately. A staff car was sent to retrieve him.

30 minutes later in his Chiefs office he played the entire recording back for his chief over and over again so that no detail was missed. "Shit, Nazis in the biggest Jewish community outside Israel, the real deal, not a bunch of rednecks in sheets drinking Pabst Blue Ribbon.' He stared hard at his most senior and trusted agent, 'This has to be kept quiet. If it gets out that we have genuine Nazis in Miami we could see the biggest riots Miami, hell Florida has ever experienced. We have probable cause with this recording. I think it would be wise to at least detain these people and question them to see what we get. Also, this ship he mentions, is he serious, Nazi bullion? By the sounds of it those people are in grave danger. I didn't get a name of the ship did you?"

Josh lit a cigarette and inhaled deep shaking his head to answer as he exhaled. "No, we are still listening in to see if we can get the name of the ship. We had the same thought because if the bullion is for real and this man means to create a new Nazi regime we would likely have to get hold of it before they did. If you think a riot in Miami would be bad imagine a worldwide riot. I think they call it war nowadays. If the Nazis started a government 'anywhere', the Israelis would nuke them into oblivion and I wouldn't blame them one bit. Not...one...tiny...bit."

Taking a healthy drag from his cigarette he continued "However, we have a bit more on the man named Werner. Apparently he is an escaped serial killer out of Germany. His MO is killing women he is attracted to. When he finds one attractive he has an overwhelming need to have sex with them. But instead of falling in love, he grows to hate them the more he has sex with them and eventually brutalizes them when his rage becomes too much to control, a genuine psychopath. He was in a German hospital for the criminally insane when he escaped by seducing his psychiatrist and killing her during their last session. Using her keys and automobile he disappeared. He was suspected of moving to Argentina where he began working for Odessa just prior to their dismantling and apparent reorganization as the Operation. Being a psychopath he apparently fit right in." Josh finished his cigarette and lit another immediately because he thought better while smoking.

"Chief, I think you are right about taking these people now. I can't see much good in letting them roam free, especially if this Werner character is the 'Operations' lead man. We can bring them in for questioning and 'discover his identity' while we question him and arrest him on an outstanding warrant. As for Jose we have enough on him for a death sentence, which means he's primed for a plea bargain. Throw the death penalty at him…he'll sing like a canary."

Just as he was taking a healthy drag of his cigarette the door to the office was thrown open. The chiefs personal secretary who was normally quiet and barely noticeable was in a frenzy to pass her boss the paper in her hand then left immediately looking nervous. The chief read the note as his eyes bulged in disbelief and clear agitation *"Fuck!!"* he exclaimed then tossed the note at Joshua.

Josh read the note and the cigarette fell from his lips as he stood up in shock and dismay "Son of a bitch!!"

The note read: *Lost Limousine briefly, reacquired limo parked in an alley with driver shot and Jose Hercsh dead with his throat cut. Werner is currently missing'*

"What happened?" he asked shaking in shock and disbelief. In less than a minute they had gone from planning the arrest of two of the most dangerous men in South Florida to losing them entirely. At least Jose wouldn't be killing anyone again. Nevertheless the new development held little consolation to having learned that full-fledged Nazis were at large on the planet and planning to reemerge as a political power. The resulting reaction would be nothing short of war.

20 minutes earlier Meyer sat back considering his options while Jose droned on about some local nonsense that meant nothing to the Operation or to its immediate concerns. As Meyer was about to ask Jose to shut up, out of the corner of his eye he noticed a silver disk that he recognized as a bug. It had slipped from its place under the head rest of one of the jump seats immediately in front of where he sat. At the same moment Jose was about to mention the name of the ship they were hunting. Meyer raised his hand to silence him and reached for the tiny disk.

Jose exclaimed "Where did that come from?" But before he knew it Meyer had slashed his throat nearly to the spine with a stiletto he kept up his sleeve. Blood shot out of his now severed arteries as Jose struggled to stem the flow of blood which he realized he wouldn't be able to do, but tried none the less. The driver having no clue about what had just happened was told by Meyer via intercom to pull over. The moment the car stopped the window, which was bullet proof was lowered and Meyer having pulled out his Walther PPK pressed it against the drivers skull and pulled the trigger. Gore exploded onto the windshield and the driver fell forward onto the wheel.

Meyer left the limousine with Jose still trying to stop the blood from escaping his body. His arms lost strength and fell to his sides as his vision began to fade. Just before he died a man he'd never seen before slammed the door open and began to help stop the blood flow. His eyes faded to black however, before he could do any good. Jose smiled at the man for his help but could not form the words 'thank you', before he died. Across the street in a taxi Werner watched as the white van pulled up behind the limousine he had just exited and smiled as the FBI agents rushed the limo with guns drawn.

Across town Joshua Peel stared at his boss who was in a fury; "Goddammit! Death was too easy for Hercsh. He might have struck a plea bargain but I would have been satisfied knowing that he would have been somebodies personal fuck toy in prison. Fucking Nazis in Miami!!' he screamed 'My dad would have loved this one" he said pinching the bridge of his nose as if to ward off the headache he knew was coming. Taking a calming breath the continued to speak as if to relieve the stress he was feeling. "He chased Nazis during and after the war well into the 50s. The Israelis used to pay him a bounty for each one he caught. Not officially of course, but he wasn't about to say no to a ten grand bounty, especially not while on a federal pay check, hell no. The bad ones he caught earned him 10K while most of the others were 5 or 6 grand each. When he helped nab Eichmann he was paid 20 grand." The chief then went silent.

Josh looked up at him. "Isn't your dad still alive?"

The chief nodded "Yeah, he lives alone on a canal about an hour from here. Loves to fish"

Josh nodded then said "Maybe we could ask him a few questions. He might have some insight being that he chased these people."

Chapter 44

Fog of War

RETIRED FBI FIELD agent Bud Richards hated fishing but sat on a dock with his fishing line dangling in the water on a daily basis because it was something to do. It was a hell of a lot better that watching 'The View', 'Dr. Phil' or the other mindless daytime programing he couldn't stand. At least fishing didn't cause him to scream at the television screen. Today however, he had a huge grin on his face. Phil his oldest son and current Miami FBI field office chief was on his way to visit and ask him some questions about a problem he had. "40 years retired and I'm still of some use to these young punks." He said with a good deal of satisfaction.

When Phil arrived with his partner Joshua he had coffee ready and waiting. Sitting at the table in his tiny kitchen Bud asked his son, "So what's this problem you have?" clearly eager to hear it.

Pulling the file out he handed it to his dad, Phil then turned to Joshua and said "Maybe you should fill him in since you heard this first hand."

Tapping his finger on the top edge of the transcript Joshua began "This is a conversation we recorded this morning between a local member of a new crime organization and his boss, a man named Werner Meyer and Jose Hersch the local. Can you read that and tell us what you make of it?" he asked.

Bud read and reread the transcript several times over to make sure he didn't miss anything. Clearly a habit he'd taught his son. As he read it a dark cloud descended on him. "This is bad, very, very bad." He said looking away letting what he had just read sink in. "I don't know either of the two men in this conversation but I believe I can shed some light on what they are talking about and whom, to some degree.' He paused as sweat surfaced on his brow. A clear indication that he was upset by what he'd just read. 'Back during the war I worked at times with an SOE agent by the name of Archie Davis, a nice guy and sharp as they came. He was one of the most active field agents the Brits had, spent most of his war service in country.' He laughed to himself 'That asshole never got hit during the whole fucking war. Got shot at all the damned time but never got hit, not once. I mean this guy was in the thick of it, he was no coward, I'll say that…but he had the damnedest luck of anyone I ever knew. I swear the guy was fucking bullet proof." He laughed at his memory of the man he'd just described.

"Before I get too deep into this, I have to explain that in the beginning SOE and OSS were tight as ticks and cooperated on everything. But close to the end of the war an interagency rivalry began, on the urging of our respective governments. You see, once our troops started finding gold and platinum bullion stashed here and there, cash hordes and what not, cooperation went south. Nobody wanted anyone else to know what they had absconded with.

Which is why what I'm about to tell you likely never got looked into more closely. I think they call it the 'fog of war'. Anyway, close to the end of the war, we, he and I, started hearing a lot about gold shipments only they weren't coming from banks or known repositories. No, the Germans were smelting it and shipping it straight from the mines. The bricks were being shipped before they were even cold. Once they were cool enough to be handled it was shipped, tons and tons of it. Where they were shipping it we never knew. We learned this from captured soldiers and workers who showed us a mine where this was going on. Once the vein ran out they took essential equipment and left. All we could figure was that it was going through France, Spain and Portugal and onto ships bound for some far off place. We heard bits and pieces of things like the ships being met at sea by a submarine where the bullion was transferred from the ship to the submarine which took it to where ever it was going, never heard exactly where. The shipments began in 43' and ended in 1945. We only knew this because some French General made a stink about two large subs he spotted in the Channel. He was upset because he thought maybe they were loaded with Nazis trying to escape.

I was Davis opposite number in the OSS. But since my boss would not allow me to cooperate openly with him I had to sneak about to get my job done. Since Davis had been in country he had access to all the captured files before anyone else did. He'd then take the files that meant something to him and leave 'me' to peruse the shit pile while he had the 'gold' so to speak. So when I had a question or twenty I went to him, quietly. But he wasn't looking for fugitive Nazis, he was looking for a specific one, Beck I think was his name' and it dawned on him 'The name being discussed in the transcript!!' He reached for the file again and read the name to make sure it was the same 'yup, here it is the guy Davis was looking for Beck. Mostly because his name came up frequently in the Gestapo files he had in his possession' he smiled. 'I knew of Beck from our own dealings with the black market. Beck got his hands on a shit load of our ciga-rettes and then sold them right back to us along with a ton of prime cut beef and, get this, Hitler's personal beer supply, good stuff to.

We did not feel any guilt in drinking every last drop. In fact our CO made it our 'duty' to do so. He said it was depriving the enemy of comfort and it was our sworn duty as Patriotic Americans to make sure that none of it made it into enemy hands." A smile curled his lips as his mind drifted back 70 odd years of that fond memory.

"Archie was interested in Beck only because he was somehow linked to those two subs in the Channel. I was never privy to exactly how he was connected. Archie was tight lipped about that one. So I did some snooping on occasion and once found a message from the Norway Gestapo chief about Beck being sent on some mission and that the Gestapo must not pursue him further.

They were supposed to go on some 'secret' mission for Hitler, obvi-ously the details were not broadcast. That was the last I heard of Beck during the war. Not long after that I was sent to Germany to interrogate prisoners and search for Nazis. It wasn't until after the war that I started hearing about Beck again.

Odessa was a growing concern for the Americans if not the remain-ing allies because they were all concentrating on rebuilding Europe. Since America had not been badly damaged by the war we could afford to focus on Odessa and their legions. Odessa seemed bent on locating Beck, but not until after 1950. Apparently they wanted the money he made on the black market during the war. By the lack of their mentioning his last mission it was fairly clear that Odessa had no idea he was connected to the bullion shipments, at least not then. On the other hand we were by 1948 hearing rumors of some 'South

American Front' materializing from Argentina, but that was coming from some of the more delusional or perhaps insane Nazis we found scattered over Europe. By 1955 it was clear that the spark had gone out of those we were catching because whatever 'front' they had been expecting never materialized.

Some, in desperation to make a 'deal' so they wouldn't be turned over to the Israelis, started sharing knowledge of bullion shipments to a secret base somewhere. Trouble is these men by the time we got our hands on them were so mentally disturbed by fear and living on the run they were not clear or concise about details. As a result nothing ever materialized in terms of an investigation. We had nothing to go on but the ramblings of petrified old Nazis who would say anything to keep their heads out of the noose.

The last I heard of Beck was a couple years after retirement when six known members of Odessa were killed on a farm in Switzerland, I think it was 1969 or 1970. Apparently they had been seeking Beck even then. He was living under his own name but as he wasn't wanted internationally the Swiss left him alone. Keeping his money in their banks may have been a key factor. By the late 1960s the Israelis were chasing the Nazis while the FBI concentrated on civil rights and Martin Luther King. We heard of it only because Mossad had been sharing its intel with us and the CIA in the hopes of mopping up the remaining Nazis. Of course by then chasing Nazis was not a major priority for the USA and the intel was sent to those of us who had chased Nazis as a courtesy and nothing more.

By the time I retired Odessa was almost finished as an organization. By the sounds of this transcript they reorganized as the 'Operation'. Oh!! One more thing this Krupp character was a big time associate of Hitler, came from some ship building family who built the

U-boats. He disappeared before the war ended and was rumored to be living in Argentina after 1950. He lived a reclusive life and was never seen in public. Mossad never got near him and he had enough pull with the locals to keep any official inquiries at bay. In time he just fell off the radar because he hadn't really done anything specific other than be Hitler's Logistics Officer, responsible for equipping soldiers in the field."

He sighed looking out the kitchen window at the canal he'd spent so many useless hours fishing on. This discussion brought that into sharp relief and a pang of regret with the knowledge that he was now just too damned old to be chasing Nazis. The prey he had once chased so efficiently was still at large and was apparently still a threat. The thought sickened him. Reaching for his son's wrist he looked hard into his eyes "Find that ship; that is your best chance at locating this group. Use the ship as bait if you have to, just get as many of those bastards as you can and interrogate the shit out of them.' He smiled in cunning and moved in to speak to both men quietly, though there was no real need to, 'If it were me, I'd take the photograph if this guy 'Werner' and share it with the Israelis. Let them know what this guy is up to and I'll bet you that within a week this outfit the Operation will cease to exist, period" he snapped his fingers to emphasize the point.

"We operated with relative impunity in my day. Nowadays you guys are restricted to procedure, which is all well and good, but this guy, even if you catch him, wanted or not, may get off on a technicality. Even if the bug is legal, since he was not mentioned in the court or-der it may not be admissible in court and therefore any actions taken against this guy could in some perversion of law be set free, guilty or not. You, hell, I can't afford to see the world erupt in war again…and that is what will happen if these guys establish any sort of influence anywhere, much less a government of their own.' He grabbed the transcript and the photo of Meyer, 'Let me show this to the Rabbi next door. He's a former Israeli General who fought in the Six Day War in 1967. This guy is Jewish Mafia and has connections all over the eastern seaboard, and he has more guns in his home than any red neck in Texas ever 'dreamed' of. So, if you let me do this, one you can save me from being bored out of my skull and two, you can get a network of eyes on the ground that aren't encumbered by procedural delays and bureaucratic bullshit. I'll be the go between, He'll keep me up on what he finds and I'll call you on your phone. That way you aren't stuck waiting for a court order or some such nonsense."

Joshua laughed out loud but not at the old man for being foolish, but for the fact that it was a pretty good idea considering that they needed to find this guy before his psychotic tendencies began leaving bodies behind him, which he reminded himself was already happening. "Chief, I think he has a point. If we can get hard fast intel on this guy's movements...we stand a better chance. And we can spend more time locating the ship' he looked at his watch. 'The ship was off South Carolina 24 hours ago which means it will to be off Virginia if it didn't change course. If that ship is spotted by the Operation before we get there the crew is dead and the bullion on board will be in their hands...which cannot be allowed to happen."

The Chief hadn't counted on his father throwing himself into the mix like this, but like it or not he had a point and to have the Jewish Mafia keeping tabs on things would be a quick solution to locating a known ghost. "Ok, but you are not to do more than use this phone, or leave this house until we are done with this. We cannot allow you to get hurt and this guy and those he runs with will not hesitate to hurt you. Sorry, pop, but you are 90. Just keep your gun close' he hesitated 'you can still shoot the thing right?" he asked.

The old man smiled broadly "I take it to the range every week and nobody can out shoot me, not yet."

Two hours later Phil and Josh were back in the office awaiting news. The crew was processing the scene and the bodies were in the local morgue undergoing the usual autopsy though the cause of death in both cases was more than obvious. Nevertheless it was a procedure that had to be done. Before they could do more than order a coffee Phil received a text message and photo. It was a clear picture of Werner in Charleston South Carolina with a large fishing yacht named 'Bubba's Bliss' in the background. In less than ten minutes they were in a chopper heading to the airport and on a charter jet heading for Charleston.

Chapter 45
Delayed Justice

RABBI WEISS SAT with his neighbor Bud Richards, a man with whom he'd sat often fishing on the dock behind their homes. At the moment he was unable to speak, a rare occurrence in the Weiss family. In his hand was a copy of an FBI transcript in which two Nazis were discussing the possibility of a renewed National Socialist regime and a photograph of the man who would see it happen. Rage is what he felt, only it wasn't the weak, mindless rage one feels when wronged or somehow injured by a petty injustice. Deep within his spirit the cries of the ancient dead wailed along with the cries of six million Jews killed by the Nazis; his father among the first to die at their hands.

The son of Rabbi Johan Weiss, murdered by a Nazi death squad in Berlin 1933, sat eyes hot with tears that wouldn't fall. A well-muscled man with the black full beard with streaks of gray giving him the appearance of a latter-day Moses, as the image of his father who he had found nailed to the door of a Berlin synagogue rushed through his memory. He'd been 5 years old that day, in fact he hadn't known it was his father hanging on that door until years later when his mother decided he was old enough to know the horrible truth. He knew his father had died, but he had been told he'd died when a car hit him in the street. A story told to a five year old boy to spare him, if possible, the horrible truth. His father's body had been taken back to Palestine and buried in a family plot, where young Johan Weiss Jr. grew up, away from war torn Europe.

In the years that followed he learned of how his people had suffered and saw waves of German Jews entering Palestine escaping Germany and its death camps. At the end of the war when the full scale of what happed became public knowledge, Israel was remade by a United Nations decree much to the annoyance of the Palestinian people. As a result Israel was a nation in a state of perpetual warfare with the Arab nations surrounding it. This reality forced the Israelis to become the single most efficient and well trained and disciplined military force in the world. During the six day war young Weiss had fought as a tank commander on the Golan Heights killing 20 Arab tanks. Johan had retired as a General in the Israeli Army, became a rabbi and immigrated to the USA.

Though people often believed he was part of the Jewish Mafia, he was not. He was part of an organization that was more efficient and even more dangerous. His group had done more to dispatch terror cells than any law enforcement agency. However, the manner in which this was accomplished was anything but legal. Disposing of a terrorist body in the Everglades was generally frowned upon by police but it was efficient.

The Everglades was and excellent place to dispose of bodies because the alligators tended to dispose of the remains efficiently. It was all in the name of a centuries old holy war that had been ongoing since Moses led his people from Egypt. A war that never made the news because the battle was conducted quietly, efficiently and with a permanence that ensured the danger posed never surfaced again. They called themselves the Brotherhood of Israel.

Looking up from the paper in his hand he smiled at his neighbor of 20 years and asked "Did his conversation happen this morning?' Bud nodded but said nothing as he had already told him what he needed to. 'What do you want me to do?" he asked smiling but knowing too well that his neighbor was a shrewd, albeit retired FBI agent and had to know more than he let on.

Bud smiled and drank his coffee "My son needs to know where this man is, where he is heading and if possible the identity of his entire organization on the eastern seaboard. If what is being said in that transcript is to be taken seriously we have to assume that Odessa never ceased to exist but morphed into something else.' Shaking his head in dismay and frustration he continued with a hopeful thought 'It could be also that this guy is just a delusional psychopath with visions of grandeur. However, since he arrived in a brand new and very expensive private jet and was met by one of the most deadly killers to exist, who I am told he killed less than two hours ago, we must assume that this man means business."

The tone he struck with the last sentence seemed to make all the difference. However, the Rabbi was no fool. Because the game he played was dangerous and by no means legal he had to breast his cards and feign ignorance. Shaking his head as if he might not be able to help he said "I'll make a call to friend who might know what to do. I cannot guarantee anything because I do not associate with such people, though, I admit, some of them may attend services at Temple." He looked up at his friend with a well-practiced look of confused patience that had he been speaking to anyone but a retired FBI agent might have suggested he was as innocent as a new born calf, but which only confirmed beyond any doubt that he was exactly what Bud had known he was, a kingpin of the Jewish Mafia or some off-shoot.

Bud restrained, with difficulty, a laugh at his neighbor's theatrics, thinking to himself '*Oh Rabbi…you are good*'. Slapping his thigh Bud moved to leave "Any help you could offer would be greatly appreciated.' Looking at his watch he headed toward the door 'I've got some laundry that won't wash itself. Just call me or come over if you hear anything ok?' he paused, hesitated then said as he opened the door 'Rabbi, these are people I used to chase for a living. No criminal element I ever encountered was as vile or more deserving of extermination. I saw what they did to your people first-hand during the war. If there is anything you can do to help find this man…you would be doing the world a great service." They both locked eyes on each other and shared a silent knowing. A knowing where each acknowledges the 'truth' that both knew better than to share openly.

Before Bud got half way across his yard Rabbi Weiss who had been watching him from the living room window, dialed his contact in the FBI to confirm the story. Knowing better than to trust the ramblings of an old man who might, possibly be suffering from age induced dementia, he wanted to make sure what he had been told was accurate before he acted.

Aaron Smith answered his cell at the crime scene where Jose Hercsh and his driver had been killed. He'd been finishing up processing evidence with the limousine being loaded onto a tow truck to be taken back to the garage/lab for further investigation. Once he realized who it was he immediately stepped away to be sure nobody heard what he said. "Yes?" he said. Listening carefully his face remained neutral and passive as Rabbi Weiss explained what had just been relayed to him. "Yes, yes that sounds about right.' He said 'I heard the same thing and that sounds very accurate.' He listened intently nodding then saying 'Yes, I think that would be best. I am unable to get away at the moment and any delay is, I believe, unwise, if it can be avoided' he paused to listen 'Yes, I agree. I'll be in touch as soon as I'm off duty." He then hung up the phone and sighed in relief. He wouldn't have to make a report to the ambassador because in less than ten minutes the entire 'Brotherhood of Israel' from Maine to Miami would be activated and in search for Werner Meyer.

The Mossad would six hours later begin searching for 'Operation' assets seeking to strip these assets from them using an old UN mandate citing that Nazi assets not known to be stolen would automatically belong to the nation of Israel. That 'rule' however did not always apply when they found assets which were clearly Nazi in origin but were otherwise legally held. In these instances legal claim to an asset was not as clear cut, so it was simply bi-passed and the assets taken, period. Often attributed to simple burglary where execution was rarely employed to avoid legal complications in the event Israeli involvement was discovered.

Such tactics had not been employed in decades, mostly because the Nazis were for the most part dead, those who weren't soon would be. Legality and procedure mattered little to Johan Weiss as he called his contacts in the brotherhood. What did matter was the total and permanent removal of National Socialism and its remnants once and for all. If that meant that 'he' and he alone were to spend the rest of his life hunting down and exterminating Nazis, so be it.

In minutes nearly two thousand members of the Brotherhood were on the move with a copy of Werner Meyers photograph and explicit instructions to locate and follow him. Provisional instructions were given to take him into custody for interrogation, but only if there were no witnesses.

In less than one hour Meyer was spotted in S. Carolina and a photograph taken. At no time was Meyer alone or in a position where he could be taken without it being noticed and reported to police. So a helicopter was called into service to follow the fishing boat Bubbas Bliss out to sea. Meanwhile, a photograph of the target was sent via private phone to Bud Richards who in turn sent it to his son with the name and location of the fishing boat.

Meanwhile the Victoria was running at a brisk 30 knots to put as much distance as possible between them and the east coast of the USA. The problem with running at thirty knots was that the ship was now loaded heavy with bullion so the electric motors were warming up. They couldn't do this speed for more than an hour without burning up. Perhaps if she were empty…but as they were laden with thousands of tons of bullion the weight being pushed by the screws tended to work the motors a bit harder than they were designed for.

Hans called the bridge after an hour and suggested rather urgently that they back off the speed to 20 knots. Rick had already pulled into line with three other ships headed to Spain. The convoy was traveling at 18 knots a good speed to cool down the engines. After 20 minutes Hans called and reported that he was pleased with the speed they were traveling and that the motors seemed to like this speed fine. Meanwhile on the bridge Rick appreciated the grace and simplicity of the ship he captained.

The Victoria was a beautiful ship with an 'antique' but not quite outdated feel. Her sleek hull sliced through the seas like a knife through butter and rolled with the seas gracefully. Her simplicity and ease of operation endeared Victoria to her crew. To Rich she had taken on a life of her own and seemed happy to be at sea again. To the Trio she was even more endearing as a possible base of operations for their new mission, the eradication of 'The Operation' from the world. Patrice had no such thoughts for the ship. She was far too busy taking care of Lisa and making love to her when she could to consider their voyage anything more than a working cruise.

To Hans and Archie the ship was a tool, nothing more. They each had too much on their minds to be concerned with a ship they had long since gotten used to. They felt vulnerable and ill at ease while the bullion was in transit. Too many things could still go wrong, far too many things.

The next morning Bubba's Bliss was running at a healthy 35 knots 50 miles south of Nags Head North Carolina. Her destination was Norfolk where Meyer planned to refuel and send out the helicopter to search for the Victoria. They should have gained on her by then and be within reach of her. Only 'J' was ahead of the Operation on that score. He had planted a false bread trail for them to follow. A computerized message from the Victoria was sent to a New York shipping yard where she was to refuel and repair the shipboard de-salinization plant.

The Operation having intercepted that communication headed straight to New York. 24 hours later another message was transmitted to the Victoria from the Ship Yard that their repair facility had just gone down because a truck had just driven into the ship yards power station. They directed her to Halifax Nova Scotia three days away with a message that they hoped she could make it that far now that their bilge pumps were failing. A fake message back to the yard suggested that they could just make it but may require assistance and a delivery of fresh water for the crew and some electric pumps to pump the water off.

These communications though false were intercepted by the

Operation each time and each time the teams were sent to the next point of contact. Bubbas Bliss pulled into Norfolk Virginia where Werner Meyer hopped on board his personal jet that was flown up to meet him. He then headed for Halifax Nova Scotia. With that message all communications were ceased from the Victoria. 'J' was now passively listening in on the Operation who he was pleased to report had concentrated their efforts on Halifax.

Was it luck, good timing or providence that caused the 'So'easter' to hit the east coast precisely at the time the Victoria turned east? It had hit exactly one day after the Victoria had turned toward Europe, forming north of Bermuda moving in a near perfect arch around the position of the Victoria, sparing her its wrath. Conveniently enough this storm was so massive that the system that fed it covered the entire north Atlantic in cloud cover obscuring the Victoria's passage from satellites the 'Operation' was known to have access to while limiting the ability of low flying aircraft to locate her.

Archie believed it to be an act of God. In spite of this belief God had not spared him from the cancer that had in recent days reminded him the 'he' was dying and would not be spared. Somehow his recent foray into his heady, youthful vigor had made the cancer that much more aggressive and had accelerated its progression whereas before it had been symptomatically dormant. The effect was to keep him awake, being that he couldn't sleep from the increasing pain while lying down, a fact that began to drain him of energy and focus.

12 hours out of the Azores Victoria vacated her position in the convoy and headed straight north for the Isle of Man. On the urging of Archie the speed was bumped up to 25 knots. Hans didn't like it much but didn't protest and just furrowed his brow. At this speed they'd be there in three days and it would be another two days before

they reached Unst. Archie had a feeling that they were going to be cutting this one a bit too close. The Operation was actively hunting them now, thankfully they had no idea where they were heading or where they were at the moment thanks to 'J'. Archie hadn't slept soundly in nearly a week and the effects were showing. Though he had not bitten anybody's head off it was clear he was on edge.

'T' noticed this and suggested he get some sleep. But the old man shook his head and stared out of the screen into the darkness which seemed to consume him. "No, I won't be sleeping until we get this cargo off loaded and this ship at anchor in Denmark. It's only a matter of time before they realize they've been played. Our best hope is this storm. They can't look for us because they simply do not know where to look and even if they did what could they do in this weather? We have to get this bullion secured and this ship out of sight" he said finally beating his fists on the wooden railing he was leaning against as a means of support. Fatigue was creeping up on him and he wouldn't be able to remain upright much longer. 'T' knowing to back off moved into the shadows and took a seat on the couch against the bulkhead.

The fatigue from both the lack of sleep and his advanced stage cancer was weakening him. The truth was that lying down hurt too much. The only way he was not in pain anymore was in standing. Even sitting was no good. He knew that if he made it a month he'd be lucky.

Looking up at the stars through the glass he smiled "You knew what you were doing all along…didn't you?' he said speaking to God. 'I wish I could rest, though" he said in a form of plea and prayer. "Please" he said "I need the rest".

Hans who had walked up behind his friend heard what he said and put a hand on his shoulder. "You look tired old friend. You should sleep." He said.

Archie nodded "Yes, I could use sleep. But I haven't been able to lie down without pain. I'm afraid the cancer has progressed. I can't even sit without pain anymore. Lying on my back is impossible. I haven't tried sleeping on my stomach though. Perhaps…that might work" and he ambled hopefully to bed.

Hans watched his old friend walk away. He was worried about him. Coupled with this worry was the knowledge that soon his one earth bound companion would be gone. Friends were something he'd had very few of in life. Those few he did have were lost in the war. His best friend Sarah was lost to him from a side effect of that same war…years…decades after it was over. Now he was to lose another friend, not to the war or some misbegotten left over but to a silent, unseen enemy no one had seen coming. Life would be lonely without his old enemy to keep him company.

Leaning against the railing he looked out into the black of night and into the reflection that showed his friends back as he stepped through the door to his cabin. "We were enemies once' he said to himself 'but you have proven to be the best friend I could have ever wanted." Out of nowhere his heart panged and a tear streaked down his aged cheek knowing how much he would miss him.

Patrice had been sitting on the bridge chair watching them. It was the first time she realized Archie had cancer. Strange how she felt a deep sense of loss in 'knowing' that this old man she had come to like, quite a lot, was dying. The pain in her heart was surprising. They'd known each other for such a short time but he was the closest she'd ever come to having a 'friend'. Lovers were plentiful, but friends...true friends were scarce...too scarce.

Two days had passed since Werner Meyer landed in Halifax. The storm itself had become much bigger and had engulfed the entire eastern Seaboard of the United States. Though it was currently stationary over New England, it had expanded to include the southern end of Canada. Both the Canadian and American Coast Guards were busy rescuing distressed boaters, fisherman and some commercial vessels which had been caught in the sudden storm. None of his teams could go out and search because no aircraft could fly in this weather. Even if they could get airborne searching wasn't possible with the entire north Atlantic covered in low lying cloud cover.

Standing in the window of the hotel Meyer stared intently out to sea. The Victoria was out in that storm, loaded with bullion, 'his' bullion, or so he thought it now that he was Fuhrer. Once again the heady, enthusiastic 'psychosis' surged forth as he imagined the power he would have with the bullion at his disposal. He could put the world in its place as Hitler had. Of course under the influence of his temporary psychosis, he conveniently forgot that the world had no tolerance for such things; the moment any such government presented itself, world governments, Israel in particular would have a thing or two to say.

Such things did not matter to Meyer at the moment. He was not concerned about such trivialities. He had billions at his disposal, hundreds of billions, hell he had more money to spend than most Governments, or so he thought. As he stood looking out the window dreaming of his 'Reich' the Operations assets were being documented and preparations made to seize them. From a tiny house in Tel Aviv under which sat a military bunker full of computer equipment.

Where no less than 20 separate stations 'hackers' were busy locating and preparing to seize funds in the accounts already located. But they could not act until all assets from the 'Operation' could be located.

Their intended goal was to financially break the Operation and the remnants of Odessa. No Nazi pig was going to have a cent to his name…not a solitary cent. And Israel would have its coffers spilling over with cash. However it could not be done until all the assets were located and 'latched' as they hackers called it. Latching was done when the accounts were opened by a hacker and 'latched' so that the account is under the hackers control and ready to be emptied, but is otherwise under normal function until the moment the hacker locks the account and empties it.

What made it better was that a virus was planted in each banks computer system, a virus that would fry the computer being used to transfer funds, leaving the surrounding systems intact. Computer systems through which this grab would take place would each be spiked with this virus and activated once the transfers were done. Being that most of them were individual lap tops, in empty hotel rooms using the systems WiFi to connect wirelessly to the bank would leave those who tracked the signal with nothing but a bread trail of smoldering computers from which nothing could be gleaned. One was in Glasgow Scotland, another was in Perth Amboy New Jersey, Key West Florida, Brownsville Texas, Monterey California and the last one, the one through which all the transfers would be divided into accounts and finally into Israel would sit in on a ship in the Mediterranean.

From the harbor in Halifax, on a fishing boat Rabbi Johan Weiss Jr. sat on the bridge monitoring the 'Operations' men who had taken up station around the hotel to protect their leader. Like Meyer he was awaiting the arrival of the Victoria with plans to board her first and 'prevent' the bullion from falling into the hands of 'Odessa'. He did not bother to reference them as the Operation because he knew who they really were and so referred to them thus.

He did this because it was necessary to keep his mindset focused on what he was doing. To refer to them as anything other than what they were was to excuse their existence or so he believed. Odessa was to be exterminated from human existence, not arrested, not sanctioned but permanently and irrevocably exterminated so that nothing of it remained to taint the weak minded who might admire such diseased thinking. The image of his father hanging on that door so long ago was his motivation; An image that had been imprinted on his mind as a young child and reinforced with the knowledge that the Nazi disease was still present, a cancer on humanity, cancer that needed to be cut out.

Rabbi Weiss was fatigued. He had not slept more than an hour at a time since he had read that transcript at his kitchen table nearly 5 days earlier. How he kept moving was by sheer force of will and a near constant surge of adrenaline that was taking its toll on is aged body. He was shaking and unable to think clearly. Once satisfied that his men had things under control only then did he consider sleep.

He was able to recognize the point at which is body would soon collapse. It was a feeling he remembered from the 1967 the Six Day war and many campaigns since. He had not slept at all during the entire war. When on the Golan Heights his tank was hit and his crew killed. But the tank still had a working turret and a full load of ammunition. He was soon surrounded by Syrian tanks as they drove by his tank thinking it was dead. He let them pass by him watching their soviet built tanks roll by his own now immobile tank. He said his prayers for the dead and for himself as he resigned his life to God. He would fight until he had no more ammunition or until they silenced his gun and killed him.

When the last tank passed he brought the gun to bear on the very last tank. Just as he was about to fire the regiment he had come with sat on the heights and opened fire. Raising his Israeli Flag from the turret he then buttoned up the tank reacquired his first target and fired. He was empowered by God or so it seemed as his fatigue faded as he loaded the ammunition, aimed the gun and fired and kept firing until his body simply did what his mind bid it to. All he remembered after the battle was sunlight coming from the open hatch of his tank and being carried from it. He did not remember the battle ending or when he finally faded into unconsciousness. He was nowhere near that state but he had no want to be. He would need his wits about him when this mission came to a head. The storm was a signal that he could rest and he did, the rocking of the boat soothed him and he was instantly asleep.

Chapter 46
Whirlwind

THE ISLE OF Man rose from the sea in the early morning haze. By midday the Victoria would be in position to put Patrice and the Trio off. By midafternoon they would be watching from the top most point of the island as the Victoria disappeared into the mist.

In the meantime Patrice was coming to terms with the fact that Archie was dying and found it hard to know how to feel. Friendship was not something she was well acquainted with. In her line of work friends were fleeting and usually kept at arms-length for mutual protection. It was the nature of her business. It was also the reason why she had not, before this trip, allowed herself to fall in love. Before now her relationships were superficial and purely physical which was why she had become involved with Meyer, a handsome well-built man with nothing beyond that to interest her, a safe bet. Patrice shook her head disgusted.

She and Archie had hit it off almost immediately. She had warmed to him at their first meeting while sitting at his table in his home… moments before the Operation tried to kill them both. Since then they'd had several long discussions about what the future held. To have gained such a good friend and then lose him was almost too much for her heart to take. Her heart felt it was being ripped from her chest each time she thought of it. As usual it was Archie, perceptible as always, who picked up on her conflict and pain and put her at ease. "It is the way of the world. I am sad at having made such a good friend and I am saddened by the fact that I will not be able to enjoy your company for as long as I would like' he then smiled his most contagious smile saying 'but had I met you a few years earlier you'd have been in trouble." He'd finish the sentence with a friendly pat on her thigh.

Then he looked her in the eye and got instantly serious grasping her hands with both of his "My journey is ending and yours is beginning a new chapter in what I hope will be a long and joyful life for you. Our meeting Patrice was, as I see it, destiny. Your life would have been fraught with danger and death had you not the courage to knock on my gate. The fact is you would have likely been dead already' the words shook her as she realized the truth of his words 'but you have been spared that end by being courageous. So, it is your courage that is to be tested and that will include facing life without me. But, if you think of me as your friend, even in death I will never be far away. You will always have me here' he pointed to her head 'and here' he pointed to her heart 'these two places shall have a bit of me in them for you to call upon in your time of need. A true friend never truly leaves once he has made an impact like that" he finished by kissing her cheek.

It was all she could do to not break down when he walked away as a tear rolled down her cheek. A smile crept to her lips as she realized that had they met in a different time and place she would have likely fallen deeply in love with Archie. But 70 years of living conspired against them. So she made a promise to herself to get to know him better and make the most of their time together by being the best friend she could be and to learn from his vast experience in order to honor him on his passing.

A knock on her door broke her thought process "Yes?" she called. The door opened and Rick walked through it, looking her straight in the eye. She was instantly alive in his presence and took his hand. "I am glad to see you' she said. Without saying a word Rick sat next to her and they kissed warmly 'Lisa and I have a surprise for you' she said 'close your eyes." A soft shushing noise filled the cabin as the door was opened, closed as a new scent of perfume permeated the space. "Ok you may open your eyes" Patrice announced. What met his eyes were two scantily clad women wearing garter belts and thigh high stockings…and sheer nighties and heels that went to the moon.

The grin that surfaced that day did not leave his face again for several weeks afterward. At once both women knelt before him as Patrice said "We both agree that you have been a bit 'stressed out' and need some relaxation. So we are going to take care of you, if you want us to' she smiled as she undid his jeans and Lisa peeled them off his body as she stared at the both of them in a daze. 30 minutes later Archie walked past Patrice cabin as Rick cried out "Oh God…Oh.. god, Please…please" followed by the soft laughs of two women. "Lucky young man" he chuckled.

In the past week Patrice and Rick had indulged in several such sessions with each other and Lisa. Rick had proven to be attentive and warm with regard to seeing to her and Lisa's needs before his own. It seemed to her that he took his own pleasure from theirs and reveled in their respective cries of bliss. A selfish lover he wasn't, though he did wear out rather quickly after being ravaged by two women. On the other hand when he recovered sufficiently he took care of business quite well, again putting his personal needs last and theirs first.

But that was a pleasant distraction from more pressing issues, such as disembarking the ship and driving up to her estate on the Isle of Man from where she and the Trio would begin dismantling the Operation. Considering the danger that they were all in at the moment all contingencies had to be allowed for. The Trio was monitoring radio, cable and satellite traffic known to be used by the Operation. All activity seemed to be limited to the Eastern Seaboard of the United States and Canada. The rouse 'J' had employed had apparently worked, but that did not mean that 'they' themselves weren't being played. To assume that they were safe was too dangerous. They had to be ready for anything, just in case.

At noon the cargo launch was lowered to the water where the cargo of gold was loaded and passengers disembarked and were soon pulling away from the Victoria and headed to the harbor entrance. The Victoria slowed to 5 knots to let them off then increased turns to 20 knots once they were clear and was soon moving at speed past Port Erin where Patrice, Lisa and the Trio were to make port. Patrice estate sat upon a hill top overlooking the western approaches' with the Castle of Peel in their view.

The house itself was a three story manner house built of granite blocks which barely showed their age of nearly 400 years. In fact the house was as sturdy as the day it was completed, a testament to the wisdom of using granite. Not to mention that building the foundation itself into the living rock from which the blocks had been hewn provided a nearly indestructible foundation which would easily last a millennium. As a result the house had the appearance of being part of the landscape with sections of the house itself apparently embedded into a rock outcropping. The fact was that the rock had been cut away to make room for the house.

On the Western end of the house was a turret built in the 1700s when the British army occupied the farm during one of the Scottish rebellions. Topping it off was a peaked circular roof which was enclosed in glass during WWI as a means of keeping the lookouts dry and alert while they looked for zeppelins and submarines operating off the approaches'. It had the appearance of being a light house with the glass enclosed turret encircled by a stone walkway where lookouts could stand and use their binoculars while being able to get out of the weather. Heat came from a cast iron potbellied stove that sat in the center of the turret, installed during WWII by the owner of the estate who had volunteered for the Home Guard and who didn't feel like being cold while on watch.

The effect was to give the house a melodramatic appearance, a castle from centuries past. Patrice later added a stone wall to surround the estate as well adding to its castle-like appearance. She had the wall topped with decorative wrought iron fencing with ominous spikes and protrusions that, while decorative, were uninviting to anyone wanting to scale the wall. Hidden from view on the inside of the wall was razor wire as an additional deterrent. More formidable security measures were hidden among the shrubbery at the base of the tower and on each side of the house, anti-missile turrets like those onboard naval warships for instance.

Radar control Gatling guns would fill the sky with thousands of rounds to create wall against incoming missiles. Though it was unlikely that missiles would be fired at her home the turrets would be adequate defense against someone using a helicopter to bypass her walls in the event they wouldn't take a hint. Additionally if anyone happened to get over the walls four other turrets fired shot gun shells loaded with buck shot at one thousand rounds a second. Enough to guarantee that whoever was foolish enough to enter uninvited wouldn't be missed requiring a fire hose and drainage pipe to clean up what was left.

Patrice had built herself a fortress to hole up in just in case the Operation came visiting. They would because she knew too much about them, enough to destroy their entire network. In threatening her they had made a fatal error lighting a fuse that would lead to their destruction. Had they left her well enough alone, she would have gladly left them alone. But when she had discovered the Operation was a Nazi front they had made a mistake by trying to kill her, a big mistake.

She had purchased the estate several years earlier secretly after finding a bullet with her name and 'Retirement Plan' engraved on the casing. The signal was more than clear; she was stuck in the Operation until they were done with her. So she played along while making plans to 'retire' on her own terms. Patrice had taken great pains to keep her assets private and out of the Operations view as one by one her once vast array of properties were sold and the cash from those sales transferred to corporate bearer bonds and shipped to Switzerland.

Recent events had accelerated her time table. Once it was clear that she could never go back to the Operation and remain safe she closed her bank accounts and transferred the funds to Switzerland. It no longer mattered if the Operation knew of her defection because they had already tried to kill her and Archie. The fact that Krupp had assigned Werner that specific task made it clear that she was finished with them and had been for some time. In a vain attempt to repair her standing in the Operation and save her life she had placed herself and those around her in grave danger, a situation that did not sit well with her new found conscience.

In fact in the predawn she had lain awake watching both Lisa and Rick sleep off their latest round of 'distraction', stroking Lisa's hair as she formulated her plan of action against the Operation. Her motivation being to keep those she loved and cared for safe from the danger she was responsible for placing them in. Needing time to think she showered off, dressed and went to the bridge where she had coffee while watching the ships prow slice through the cold waters of the Irish Sea.

The first order of business would be to put the Trio on point setting up defenses in the event the Operation found them. Second order of business would be to electronically seize as many assets of the Operation as she could while exposing their network to the world's law enforcement agencies, without putting herself at risk. The idea struck her like bolt of lightning. She could take the Operation funds over. All she needed was an account in which to stash the funds, several accounts would be needed because of the sheer volume of cash would have to keep moving for months to keep it hidden while she set up permanent accounts for them to settle in. What made it even better was that she had the account numbers in her little black book in the event she needed access to cash in her travels while working for the Operation. Even better was the fact she had the codes to access every single account, something that Meyer, she was certain, was not aware of…yet.

The idea brought a smile to her face, a very satisfied, excited smile. She could bring them down easier than she realized. The only reason they had control over governments is because they had money.

If she were to take it, she could step into the void left in their wake and become the most powerful woman on the planet. But did she want that? Such a move would require she travel to re-establish ties which would expose her to dangers she'd not faced as the seemingly unimportant go between, a roll she was well suited to. Then again she could create a shadow figure and still be the go between apparently working for someone else when in fact she would be the 'boss'. The idea had potential and with the Trio as back up…she could be bigger than the Italian Mafia and immensely more powerful.

'T' was at the wheel so she immediately shared her inspiration with him. After a brief discussion he agreed that taking the Operations funding and redirect their resources had merit. The possibilities were endless. But in reality it was more likely that once funding was gone and the leadership arrested, killed or whatever was to happen to them, splinter groups would attempt to take over the vacated markets. He also reminded her that she wouldn't have the backing of the Operations muscle either. She'd have nobody at her back. The thought rankled her knowing he was correct. She'd had an army to back her up when she made those deals. Now the majority of the muscle once backing her up was now hunting her. But 'T' said that taking their money was certainly something that bore looking into.

With that 'J' was summoned to the bridge and the idea laid out for him. He smiled confidently saying, "If I had the account numbers and access codes we could have that money in our hands within 48 hours. Four days if I had to hack the accounts.' He paused and looked hard at his boss. 'I need accounts to bounce them into. I can't just do this if I don't have someplace to put the money. At least 4 already existing accounts would be enough, preferably Swiss." 'T' nodded and looked at Patrice who was holding the booklet in her hands. He grinned "I'll set up my equipment once we get to your place and get to work" he said and then left.

8 hours later 'J' was setting up his equipment in the tower as Patrice, Lisa and 'T' watched as the Victoria disappeared into the fog of the Irish Sea. Letting out a sigh of both tension and relief Patrice looked over at 'J' and handed him the booklet "We're committed to our course of action gentlemen. We cannot afford half measures, not that we ever did, but it is imperative that we strip the Operation of its operating capitol. Without which they will fall apart and hopefully cease to exist. You each know what you have to do. I'll be in the house making coffee and sandwiches. I'll send some out to you ok?" she said looking at 'J' who nodded and smiled at her warmly...still not quite ready to express himself but content to be near her.

Chapter 47
Halifax Nova Scotia

SEVERE WEATHER HAD grounded all flights out of Halifax and along the Eastern Seaboard, severe enough to have the Coast Guard out rescuing crews from ships overwhelmed by the sudden storm. Meyer was a wreck nervous about losing the bullion to a storm. The Victoria was two days overdue according to their last transmission. Had they been sunk in the storm? A ship of that size heavily laden with thousands of tons of bullion would sink like a stone if somehow they were compromised. It appeared to be an old ship so she may have broken up in the storm.

The Victoria had not been heard from in nearly three days her last known position had been just north of Virginia. After that nothing had been heard from her again. According to the Coast Guard nothing had been seen of her in a 500 mile radius of her last reported position. The thought of having lost that much bullion nauseated him. Billions in Gold…possibly trillions were missing, 'his' gold or so he thought of it. When in such a mood he often became violent and irrational as well as physically ill.

Meyer was unnerved. Not so much by the missing bullion but in knowing that he was being watched. Minutes before he had seen a

Jewish Rabbi watching him through binoculars, at least he looked like a Rabbi. He had on the black clerical garb with the Yamika in place and the beard and curls associated with certain sects of the Jewish Religion with a military OD Green Army jacket. He looked like the military version of Moses complete with a black beard streaked with gray. For only an instant they had locked eyes on each other through the binoculars. When the Rabbi removed them Meyer looked into the coldest eyes he had ever seen. That was the first time Werner understood 'fear' for he was looking into the eyes of death, cold, merciless death.

The deck rolled under his feet as Rabbi Johan Weiss stared at the man he intended to kill. They looked at each other for only a moment but millennia of time passed between them in that moment. The earth had in and instant grown too small for the two of them, one would have to leave and it wasn't going to be the Rabbi...God Willing. Johan smiled at the fact that his being there seemed to frighten the Nazi bastard looking back at him. The idea warmed his heart like a soothing balm. "Yes, you...you godless, soulless bastard of Satan...you will die...and I will do it myself....I promise...I do so promise this."

In an instant Meyer was violently ill and ran to the bathroom where he wretched his guts indelicately into the toilet. Cold sweat covered his body...his body reacted to fear he had seldom experienced. His whole body shook as his nerves let go and he released his bladder and bowels into his pants...while he emptied his guts...out of pure, unrestrained fear. His mind was currently gone...he generated fear in others...it was how he coped with the world. That 'Fucking Jew!!" he cried as his guts erupted again. For twenty minutes his body released the fear he was feeling until there was nothing left, a fear induced seizure...and out of exhaustion his body came back to itself.

Lying next to the toilet Meyer was covered in urine, vomit and shit which filled his suit pants. In shame he looked around fearful that his men had seen this spectacle and began to gather himself. Tears streamed from his eyes…though he wasn't sad…he was afraid and ashamed for being so…so…cowardly. After stripping the clothes from his body he looked into the mirror and into his own frightened eyes and said through quivering lips "I am Fuhrer…I am Fuhrer…I must not be afraid!…I must not be afraid!"

Twenty minutes later he was showered and dressed. The clothes he had soiled were clean and drying in the shower, the shorts he'd been wearing he simply flushed down the toilet. With no evidence of his weakness left he stood before the mirror and reached for the phone. "Karl, there is a Jew Rabbi watching this room on a boat in the harbor. I need you to go investigate it. If you find a Rabbi on board, he'll look like Moses, kill him." He hung up the phone confident that he had taken care of the problem.

Later that afternoon Rabbi Weiss smiled in the knowledge that his prey had noticed him and was afraid. A cruel smirk curled his lips. Knowledge of being watched usually generated mistakes, so he prepared his men to capitalize on that mistake. "These men are Nazis. They will try to kill us because in their own twisted thinking we are inferior to them. You will kill them first…*without mercy*. They will likely attempt to board us in the night. We will let them come and be waiting for them. No part of the ship is to be left uncovered. Use silencers and make head shots, they will be low level soldiers working for other men and will know nothing of importance which is why they will be sent, so just kill them.

Once these men are dispatched we will use their boat and return the favor' he reached into his brief case and brought out a picture of

Werner Meyer 'This man is our target, he must be taken alive. We need what he knows so that Israel can begin seizing the assets of this organization. If we can accomplish that task we can do more to erase this, this…disgusting disease of humanity from the planet far more quickly than if we were to put a bullet to each of their heads." He smiled to his men who knew too well what that meant.

His men were not blood thirsty religious fanatics but true soldiers serving their God as a soldier would serve his nation. They were each professional veterans of an army that had been in the service of God 4000 years and had yet to be defeated. Before Rabbi Weiss could continue a runner came to him. "Sir, we have visitors!"

Taking his binoculars up he located the men approaching the ship and smiled "Well, it would seem we aren't going to have to wait gentlemen. Only we cannot dispatch them on deck in broad day light. We have to let them enter the ship and draw them down to the engine room. These men will be filled with confidence and arrogance so we must make them feel as confident and arrogant as possible by making them think we have lax security. When they are the most confident we will dispatch them like that" he said snapping his fingers.

In short order 20 Israeli soldiers took up station inside the ship securing all entrances and locking hatches so that their enemy had only one passage to follow. *If they were smart they'd figure it out and leave, if not they would die.* Rabbi hoped they just kept coming.

From the hotel Meyer watched from his window, this time inside his room and away from where the Rabbi could see him. He simply could not face those eyes again. Luckily his men had not witnessed his breakdown. Watching his men approach the Rabbis ship Meyer did not smile but rather grimaced as he ground his teeth together fighting down the urge to vomit again. His hands and body were shaking in residual fear that hadn't completely eased yet. Compounding the situation was the intense shame he felt at having been so completely consumed by fear of the old man.

The boat took ten minutes to navigate the harbor and to reach the ship on which the Rabbi was staying. When they reached the floating platform all six men walked up the gangplank and onto the ship. As one they moved with a fluid ease of a team long acquainted with working together.

Entering the thwart ships passageway they found the door agape with no sign of life. The point man was most senior as he had the most experience; his gut was telling him something wasn't right. Where there had been activity only minutes before there was no longer anyone, anywhere to be seen. His gut told him to abort the mission, which is a way of saying cut and run, only he knew that if he did that he'd be killed by the man who sent him. Werner was an unstable asshole who nobody dared to challenge due to his violent temper. "Fucking Asshole" he muttered to himself. Stepping into the passage way he was looking for a trap, it had to be…his guts were screaming to run…but he had his duty. "Goddamn Fucking Asshole" he muttered through chattering teeth. Nothing happened nobody was at their stations nobody was on watch.

Deeper into the ship they went following the passage way down, meeting nobody, hearing nothing but the ventilation fans blowing air through the ducts. The deeper they went the more nervous the lead scout became because he knew that he was about to die. Yet, in spite of this innate knowledge he went forward, urging his men forward, hoping for a locked door to bar their way so he had an excuse to turn around and get the hell out of there. The only open doors were the ones leading down into the bowels of the ship, a perfect trap. A trap he'd like to have set himself, only he was on the wrong end of this one. Still he went forward...still he went on...in the knowledge that he was going to find himself surrounded and likely killed, hopefully quickly.

Sweat trickled down his cheek, his heart beat painfully. The engine room "This is it" he told himself, 'This is where I will die. Perfect." Yet he opened the door and moved forward in the certain knowledge that death awaited, unable to run to save himself. The diesels were humming along smoothly turning the generators for the ships electrical systems. All seemed quiet. "Maybe they left the ship in fear of our coming" he thought hopefully. Looking up what hope he might have had ceased as above him on the engineering platform were 20 Israeli soldiers with their guns pointed at them.

The next thing he felt was a stinging sensation in his forehead. His next image was of his body lying on the deck plate...happy that he hadn't been killed...wondering what the red stuff was pouring over his eyes...happy to be alive...happy to not be dead...as his eyes went black. Looking down on the bodies of all six men was Rabbi Weiss. "Dump their bodies over the side after dark. Don't forget to weigh them down. The fish need to eat."

Back in the hotel minutes passed in which Meyer grew nervous and irritable not knowing what was going on. Just as he was about to lose control of his stress induced nausea again six men emerged from the ship in single file and piled onto the boat which soon was speeding toward the dock.

Meyer smiled, satisfied that the Rabbi was dead. He was safe. But just as he was putting his binoculars down his security chief Karl came in looking panicked, Karl was never panicked. "The men on the boat are not our men. One of our guys recognized two of them as Israeli soldiers he had a run in with in Jordan."

Meyer couldn't believe it. One minute he was safe from the fucking old Rabbi and the next he was in danger of being attacked by the Rabbis men. Dazed in disbelief the room began to spin as his mind distanced itself from his present reality "Our men were killed?" he heard himself ask. "All Six?" his lieutenant simply nodded. "We must go then…shouldn't we?" he said feeling not at all in control but acting the part splendidly…or so he thought.

"Sir, I believe they are Israeli soldiers! We have to get you out of here now!" With that Meyer remembered little except being rushed to a waiting car and piled over with men seeking to protect him from the Jew horde bearing down on them. They headed to the airport and to the hanger where he would remain on board the jet until cleared for takeoff with his men taking up station around the jet to protect him from the Israelis should they come calling.

Meanwhile onboard the launch which was only half way to the dock Joshua the team leader saw Werner Meyer being whisked away from the hotel by his body guards who pushed him into a car which then sped off. The remaining gunmen opened up on the approaching launch with a spray of poorly aimed gunfire. The highly skilled Israeli soldiers killed each one of them with perfectly placed head shots. Each man fell as one before the car carrying Werner Meyer had cleared the parking lot.

"Shit" is all the Lieutenant could bring himself to say before he had the launch return to the ship. "Turn around, we're blown. We won't be getting near him any time soon. Not now anyway" he said as the boat made a sweeping turn back to the ship. In the distance police sirens were blaring as the gun fire had undoubtedly made some people nervous. They would have to vacate the ship. Granted it wasn't theirs they had simply commandeered it. The owner likely had sheltered it in the harbor for the season. They would use the ships 'gig' to get away and their newly acquired launch as well.

On board Rabbi Weiss, from the bridge, saw his quarry escaping. Only he did not get upset or angry. No, he knew where Werner Meyer was going and he was stuck. Whereas, he, the Rabbi of the Brotherhood of Israel was not restricted or stuck in one place, not only this, but he had planted a new tracking device on Meyers plane. In the days previous his team had located his plane and planted a long range passive homing device on it, just in case he did get away.

The device was a gift from Mossad and was undetectable. Being passive it would activate only if it received a signal from the device tracking it, otherwise it was dormant. When a signal was detected an infrared beam of light pulsed in the direction of its activation signal, giving the device a general direction and distance to the target. All this was done in a fraction of a second and the device would go dormant once the tracking device had what it needed.

The device was used by Israel to track their enemies. If anyone got out of hand the device planted on the car or truck they were traveling in was targeted. This is how so many of Israel's enemies were killed in transit. Leveling an entire neighborhood was costly in both equipment and in political fallout. So it was much more effective to simply kill them in the car they were traveling in so that the innocent casualties, of which were always a few, were minimized. In war such tragedy is not avoidable when the enemy uses children to hide behind, knowing that if they die the children will die with them creating a problem for Israel, a twisted, sick form of martyrdom. Luckily, Meyer was not traveling with children so the collateral damage would be non-existent.

Trouble was the Rabbi didn't have any missiles so had to content himself with tracking Meyer and not destroying him utterly. Israel didn't release their secret weapons easily, even to soldiers of God. This did not bother him in the slightest. He smiled knowing that he would have the pleasure of doing battle with the enemies of God and killing them one by one...personally. To his mind there was no higher-calling nor was there any greater pleasure.

Meanwhile in the hanger Meyer, pale, sick and out of his mind, staggered to the jet and fell onto the couch drenched in fear induced sweat. Luckily he had not pissed himself and was able to fight off the urge to vomit.

Once he had a grip on himself his brain began to function again. "Miami' he blurted 'that is likely where they picked up the scent" he thought out loud. "Who was that fucking Rabbi?" he thought. He had not felt this hunted since he escaped prison. Back then he could rationalize being pursued. He knew what he'd done. He knew it was wrong but he felt no guilt or shame only elation and exuberance from the culmination of his violent, psychotic expressions. He could understand their hunting him then.

What he found disturbing was the fact that this old, gray bearded Jewish Holy man frightened him. Something in those eyes bore through his soul like a red hot dagger burning his insides with fear, fear he had not felt in this life-time. What he found strange was that his fear felt ancient. As if he'd felt that same fear in another time in another body, long, long ago.

Chapter 48

Worried Wife

UPON ARRIVING HOME from her weeklong with Greg Laurie was disturbed to discover her husband had not yet returned home. He had been gone just over a week when she left and she had been gone a week. The office couldn't stay closed like this and remain in business. The practice was their livelihood with no other income. Panic over took her as she began imagining her husband abandoning her and her children over the affair in which case he held all the cards.

Calling Rick first he had left his phone in the cabin so he didn't answer it causing her panic to increase exponentially. She began frantically looking through her husband's things, papers, phone calls, emails until she found the confirmation of his vacation plans. Though he had mentioned the name of the island he was going to she had not paid much attention to it, until now. St. Vincent was where she had met Greg. Horror replaced panic as the hotel was the same one she and Greg had stayed, in a bungalow...*immediately next door to the bungalow her husband had been staying in.*

That morning came streaming back in vivid clarity from the taxi ride to the door being nearly torn from the hinges as they fell through it impatient to be alone. Once the door closed Greg had pushed her hard against the wall kissed her savagely as he ripped her clothes off, shirt, skirt…both torn to shreds…as he tried to gain access to her body…Laurie tore her bra off…it was a quick release…but was ruined by the sheer force of her desire to be rid of it…leaving her thong…which he brutally removed…ripping the flimsy lace accoutrement from her body leaving her naked and panting against the hard wood paneling.

She barely remembered getting to the shower…or the water pouring over her head. What she remembered was the cold tile on her back…and his hard muscular body grinding her against it with his pelvis pressed hard against hers with every exquisite inch of his manhood buried deep in her intimate recesses. Three orgasms in the shower alone…with the rest a blur of passion on the bed as she faced the open window…riding Greg for all she was worth…grinding herself down onto him…as she tried desperately to get more of him into her as another orgasm…split the early afternoon heat with her passion. After two hours they both collapsed in a heap exhausted. Followed by the plane ride and a week in Scotland where she let go her inhibitions and unleashed her passion even more. That had been the most relaxing vacation she'd had in years. That is until she realized her husband had not come home.

In a moment of unexplained clarity she began to wonder what her husband was doing on the same island as Greg? One minute her husband is vacationing, the next he is extending is vacation to look after an old man who had been mugged. Greg was to meet an 'old man' about an urgent business matter, coincidence? The idea wouldn't gel. Her head spun as the idea that the two old men Rick and Greg had mentioned were one in the same. The odds were slim that the man she was having an affair with would be suddenly summoned to the very island her husband had been vacationing on, both of whom were dealing with an old man in urgent need of their respective services.

So she decided to make a phone call to Greg. She'd just ask point blank about her husband. Perhaps by her asking in an innocent tone he'd not have his defenses up and answer unconsciously. Being sneaky was not her style, she actually loathed the idea of having to stoop so low, but she was in desperate need of answers and men were generally stupid when it came to the women in their lives, especially women they wanted to keep fucking.

On the Victoria one day out of Unst having off loaded her cargo Greg Mitchell was at the wheel headed south along the east coast of Scotland. It was decided that it was best to have an extra hand at the wheel as the two elderly men on board were not quite up to watch standing. As easy and non- taxing as the voyage had been, it was still a bit much for two men approaching 90 and one with terminal cancer.

They were headed south due to the British Navy diverting all commercial shipping because several uncharted WWII mines had broken free of their mooring chains and were floating free in the shipping lanes. The Germans and British had laid thousands and thousands of mines in these waters early in the war, many of which escaped post war clean-up operations. As a result the salt water had corroded the chains…and mechanisms keeping them on the bottom releasing the mine which sometimes remained buoyant.

In some cases the explosive was so unstable that the mere act of breaching the surface was enough to set it off, sometimes with a rather impressive explosion…other times a mere fizzle and pop having been thoroughly soaked with salt water. While others still would float undetected for months possibly accounting for a fraction of the hundreds of people who go missing each year on the Atlantic. One such mine was capable of sinking a 40,000 ton ship, A 40' sloop rigged sail boat would utterly disintegrate in the blast if it happened across such a mine, casualties of a long ago war, casualties that kept mounting as the decades passed.

So they took the shipping lanes south and cut across from Edinburg to the Danish anchorage off Esbjerg, where the ship could lie at anchor among many other ships in relative obscurity.

Several days earlier Victoria was tied up along the pier on Unst with her stern to the cavern, luckily Rick had remembered his naval days well enough to tie the ship securely to the pier. It was an exercise in speed as he secured the stern first, then ran forward to secure the forward line; Greg being on the pier helped by looping the line over the cleat. Once the ship was secured the gangway was deployed. To the delight of Hans and Archie, Greg had discovered a roller conveyer in one of the many rooms carved out of the salt which he had taken the liberty of constructing with the aid of the fork lift. The off load went relatively smoothly and took just over two days to complete since the off load was mostly mechanized where the on load was a combination of both manual and mechanized.

In the meantime Rick was introduced to his new sprawling estate while Archie was escorted to his suite where he collapsed in sheer exhaustion, in spite of the pain. His body simply hadn't the energy to sustain consciousness much less muscular function. Mercifully he slept soundly for 24 hours. Hans also was also in need of rest and was shown his suite next to Archie and he too slept soundly, but for only 8 hours as he was not as lacking in sleep as Archie had been, nor as ill.

This left the off load to the two younger men which they started on as soon as Greg finished showing Rick around. Greg was nervous and Rick knew why. Greg was sleeping with his wife. Only Greg had no idea that Rick already knew and had consented to let the affair continue to ease the tensions between he and his wife.

However, since they would be working together for the foreseeable future they needed to trust each other. So when they had descended the stair into the mine Rick took the initiative. Stopping so that he could face Greg, Rick said "I've noticed that you've been nervous around me, like you are afraid of letting something slip. That being said, I already know about you and my wife.' He paused to make sure Greg heard him correctly. 'I've known about you two for a while. I was oblivious to it for a few months until one night Laurie's phone dialed the house letting me in on what was happening…with vivid clarity."

Greg paled but said nothing. Rick placed a hand on his shoulder. "I don't hold it against you. I let it go on because Laurie was happier and more pleasant to be around. Before you, she was bitter and cranky and getting worse and worse as my economic failures mounted. Honestly I expected my wife to take a lover, years ago. In fact I gave her permission a few years back to hopefully ease the growing tension between us."

Greg's color returned as did his breath once he realized he wasn't being 'confronted' but kept up his guard just in case, he was misreading the situation. "Permission?" he asked.

Rick nodded "Yeah. A few years ago we were struggling; in fact we still are in-so-far as the office is concerned. Reimbursements were inconsistent, often so paltry it barely allowed us to buy gas or groceries. That sort of economic struggle can wear on a marriage. When it began to affect our health, I decided to give Laurie a hall pass to take the pressure off. Only she didn't act on it until she met you. Then again she didn't realize that I was serious. This came out the day I confronted her. I told her then that it was ok to keep seeing you and that we should keep it between us, to not make you uncomfortable. Laurie was afraid that my knowing about you two would frighten you off.' He laughed slightly 'She wants to keep seeing you' he paused 'I think she may even be in love with you."

Greg wasn't sure how to feel about what he was hearing. He was in love with Laurie, very much so, and here was her husband telling him it was ok to keep seeing her and that she might even be in love with him. Hearing *that* come from her husband's mouth was surreal. One part of his brain wanted to belt Rick in the mouth for not placing Laurie on a pedestal while at same time feeling elated that he wasn't being asked to give her up.

Still, caution had to be exercised because the situation was delicate regardless of the cavalier attitude being expressed. Feelings change, particularly where wives and money are concerned and the guy standing before him had recently gone from being nearly broke to the single richest man on the planet in little under two weeks.

Adding to his conflict was the fact that he actually liked Rick. He was unusually direct in his communication with very little vagary to cloud his meaning. What he said is what he meant to say period and made no bones about sharing what was on his mind so long as it applied to the conversation. Otherwise, he didn't talk much. It was refreshing to find a person who said what they meant without any double talk to confuse the situation or muddy the waters. So it was now as he discussed the situation between himself and Laurie. He got the impression that Rick was indeed not jealous but somehow relieved at the affair and truly wanted it to continue on. Then Greg had lived his entire life around people who had alternative agendas and were adept at playing games while not seeming to, which is the tack he took as a means of defense.

Looking hard at Rick Greg took a breath and thought carefully of what he wanted to say. "I'm not sure what I can say to that. You say that your wife has discussed this with you. I know Laurie as a client. That much I will admit and nothing more. What you suspect is your business and it would be stupid of me to debate the matter not knowing what you have discussed with Laurie.

Rick nodded his understanding and smiled at Greg. He hadn't admitted a thing which he expected but neither did he deny anything. "*Slick*" he thought. "I understand. I didn't want to make you feel uncomfortable or anything like that. I just wanted to clear the air so that we could focus on the situation at hand and not have you feeling like you were walking on egg shells with me." He said.

Greg looked at Rick still not sure how to feel about discussing a situation that society over the centuries had demonized as an amoral sin; a situation that in classical times often had the suitor and husband facing each other in a duel to the death. What did not compute was Rick, in essence, saying "It's ok to have a relationship with my wife." The idea was incongruent to his way of thinking.

The idea of sleeping with Laurie with her husband in the know was mind boggling, unfamiliar and uncomfortable territory. Not that Greg made a habit of chasing married women either. The whole thing between he and Laurie was initially mutual attraction. Something neither had intended but something too powerful to ignore nor was his falling in love with her. That unintended consequence hit him like a lightning bolt about a month before their affair turned physical after which there was no turning back for him. But he was not about to discuss that wrinkle with the man *she* was married to.

They shook hands and agreed to discuss the matter later when Greg had made his phone call and was more prepared to discuss the situation. In the mean time they began the off load of the bullion. Loading had taken a lot longer because it was being moved into a confined space whereas the off load had what could only be un-limited space by comparison. There was no need to make sure each crate fit into its space like they had to on the ship. However, they knew that they had to inventory their cargo in order to ascertain its value and that required that they stack them in even rows for bet-ter record keeping. Something that Greg had already determined while on premises getting ready for their arrival. Even so he was amazed to discover just how much bullion was actually on board and ran out of room in the secondary cavern he had allocated for the bullion storage by noon the second day. They were then spilling the contents into the primary cavern taking up a considerable space there as well.

The offload went off as well as could be expected with minor hitch-es and some tension but not the sort that proved taxing or worth the bother of paying attention to. Rick hardly saw Hans and Archie as the two old men had remained for the most part in the Castle resting and getting ready for the second leg of the journey. A short jaunt by comparison, but one for which they had to be well rested in order to be of assistance.

Archie, after nearly 24 hours of hard sleep, woke feeling refreshed and was pleasantly surprised that the pain he'd been dealing with was less severe, for the time being anyway. While Rick and Greg off loaded the bullion he and Hans took to the nearest village to obtain some morphine. It was clear that he would need it. He had no want to go through a sleepless night again for want of Morphine.

Several days later they were on the Victoria heading south. Greg had not yet broached the subject of Rick's being privy to the affair he was having with Laurie, his wife. Doing so would raise questions he couldn't answer without compromising the group and their collective situation. As far as she knew he was doing a job for several clients in fact, one of them being her husband, something she could never know.

Little did he realize she had just pieced together the fact that she and Greg had just been on the same island as her husband, in the bungalow adjacent to his, where she had been less than shy in her expressions of bliss. The idea that her husband may have heard her in the throes of passion *again* was not as much a concern as the fact they were on the same island on some mysterious business venture. She elected to confront her husband about it, but he wouldn't answer his phone. After two days she decided to confront Greg having convinced herself that he must know where her missing husband was.

Greg's phone rang while he was at the wheel of the Victoria now cruising off the east coast of Scotland. It was Laurie yet he still didn't know how to breach the subject of whether or not her husband's story had any shred of truth. So he answered it hoping to have a nice, quick conversation with the woman he loved. "Hi" he said genuinely happy to have her on the line. Only the voice that met him wasn't the woman he'd said good bye to only a few days before.

"Where is my husband?' she asked her voice carrying a hint of panic 'where is he?" she asked with more force. Her voice was not the calm, sedate voice she had intended to use, but her full-on panic that met his ear.

Automatically he fell into his roll of feigned ignorance. "Hon, I'm not sure what you're asking. Why would I know where he is?" Rick entered the bridge that very moment and heard a familiar screech that had all too often pierced his eardrums. Only now his wife wasn't pissed at him, she was pissed at Greg. A satisfied grin broke out onto his face as for the first time since getting married he was listening to his wife rip someone else a new hole.

Meanwhile on the Coast of California Laurie was struggling for a place to put her emotions while trying desperately to contain the panic and rage fed by her innate knowledge that Greg somehow knew where her husband was. "Don't lie to me!!' she screeched 'He was on the island we were on in the hotel room next to ours!!! Immediately next door and probably heard us when we were together. Your being on that island wasn't a coincidence Greggory. Now tell me what is going on?!!!" The last sentence was an angry sob as she attempted to keep it together.

Rick had heard what Laurie was saying plain as day. By the lack of shock on his face Greg could tell that the words Rick told him a few days before were true. That fact alone didn't save him from dealing with the anger of the woman on the other end of the line. Greg looked at Rick and shrugged turning one of his palms up as if to ask "What do I do now?" Rick nodded and took up his phone and dialed his wife.

Laurie's phone began to beep with an incoming call and put Greg on hold. Recognizing her husband's call she was relieved, angry and scared having not heard from her husband in a few days and worried that the practice was not making money with him gone. "Where are you?" she asked trying not to sound alarmed.

Rick smiled before calmly saying "I'm on a ship off the east coast of Scotland, heading to Denmark."

The silence on the line was deafening. Only a few days before she and Greg had been in Scotland on business for a client. Now her husband was in Scotland, rather on a ship in Scottish waters. The puzzle she had put together linking her husband to Greg's recent activities were, to her mind, confirmed. She was furious and even more curious about why all of a sudden her husband was on a ship on the other side of the planet heading for *Denmark*.

Laurie struggled to keep her composure "Uhhhmmm…Whyyyyy are you over there and not here making a living?" The voice that came over the line was her pre-explosive, irrational rage voice indicating that if his answer wasn't the 'right' one heaven and earth would come crashing down on his skull which made Rick glad that he was on the opposite side of the planet. Her temper was not something that he enjoyed and often took pains to avoid, often making things worse.

Never liking his wife being angry he struggled to keep his nervousness under control. But the recent changes in his economic fortunes had changed his demeanor to one of confidence which easily canceled out his wives usually over-riding temper. "Remember that gentleman I was helping out? He had business in Europe to attend to and asked me to come along to assist him."

Laurie did not believe a word of it, not a single syllable. So being a cunning a woman she asked as casually as she could in spite of her pulsating rage "What is Greg Mitchell doing there?"

Rick smiled to himself trying not to laugh "Who?" he asked as coolly as he was able. That was it, her control snapped, she felt that she was being toyed with and you didn't toy with her when she was frightened, pissed and not in control…Oh no…not this woman.

Had he not been on the other side of the planet the look she gave the phone would have melted his soul. "Don't fucking toy with me Richard!!! Greg Mitchell was on the same island as you were, in the same hotel as you were and in the hut immediately next to yours I found out. I was there as well, for less than a day, but if you were around…you probably heard what we were doing." Greg heard the last sentence and looked up at Rick who was looking back at him, not in jealous anger but shock that his wife had been so near.

Rick smiled at Greg and waved his hand to not worry. He then walked out onto the bridge deck which was forward of the bridge itself so he could keep the rest of the conversation private. "Did you have fun?' he asked. 'Seriously hon, I haven't run into anyone here. I haven't spent much time in the bungalow especially since having to look after Archie. If you were here why did you not stop by?" he asked.

Her answer was blunt but truthful "I didn't stop by because I was busy fucking my boyfriend for one and I didn't know you were on the same island for another, until recently. Don't evade the question. What are you doing with Greg Mitchell and why aren't you back here in your practice earning a living?"

Rick was holding the phone away from his ear at this point because she was almost screaming into it when he replied "I'm not sure what I'm supposed to tell you. If I didn't see Greg I didn't see him. I mean you were on the island and I didn't bump into you because, according to you, you were busy with Greg. So it's likely just a coincidence." Once again *that* was 'not' the answer she wanted to hear.

"Coincidence?!! Coincidence?!!! I am not an idiot!!!' she screamed 'Tell me what is going on!!' she bellowed losing her composure as her anxiety grew. 'I left the island with Greg and we went to Scotland where he had some business to do for the client he met on the island. And now you are on a ship off of Scotland, soooo, I do not believe that your being on the same island as Greg and I and then Scotland days after I left is a *fucking **coincidence*!!!!!*"* Laurie seldom cursed but when she did it seldom ended well. Rich knew better than to push her further because she could go '*super bitch*' at any moment and if that happened…nobody would be getting laid…for a very, long time, neither he or Greg.

While on Unst just prior to their departing the island for Denmark he had taken the liberty of shipping a package to Laurie as a surprise, a surprise he didn't want to spill over the phone. Not with the Operation still seeking them out. But to keep her somewhat placated he decided to tell her to expect it. "I've sent you a package and according to my delivery notice you should be getting it sometime today. They didn't say what time they'd be there but the package would be delivered by the end of business today. When it comes I want you to call me before you open it." His giving her something to look forward to eased her anxiety somewhat. But her anger remained simmering under the surface. "Trust me, everything will be alright" he said when her silence became too much. "Hey, I've got to get going. Don't forget to call me when the package comes…and do not open it until after you call me." He said. She made a terse goodbye and hung up.

Laurie was still on the line with Greg so once she hung up with Rick she went on the offensive with Greg. "Ok, mister, tell me what this is all about. My husband is in Scotland, or at least on a ship off of Scotland, he was also on the island you brought me to in the same hotel and in the next bungalow over. He just tried to tell me that it is just a coincidence. Please do not insult me by repeating that same nonsense...please.' The last word was spoken in a dangerously 'sweet' tone that suggested that if she didn't get what she wanted he would be cut off. Greg loved what they had together...and most definitely did not want to lose it...for however long it might be.

Laurie continued her interrogation in her dangerously sweet and unnerving tone 'So...if you expect to get me into your bed again anytime soon...or if you want me to blow you...ever again...I want some answers...*What-is-going-on?*" she hissed out the last four words indicating to anyone who knew her that the foot was about to drop and drop hard. Rick who had just re-entered the bridge was waving his hands indicating that she knew nothing and to not spill anything.

Greg nodded "I wish you wouldn't get so upset. Yeah I think it's strange that your husband was in the same place as we were but the old man I am dealing with was alone when I met with him. What he did say is that he had an assistant helping him out but he never said anything about who or what his name was and he was never around. The old man I was dealing with had to travel to Scotland to tie up the loose ends of the business we had, but that is all I can say. I never saw anyone else but the old man when I was there." The lie fell from his lips in a tone that somehow satisfied Laurie's curiosity, if only for the moment. That and she wasn't really willing to give up fucking his magnificent cock, no matter how pissed she got. *"Hell*" she thought to herself, '*maybe I'll enjoy a nice grudge fuck.*"

Rick was helping an old man who'd been mugged and Greg was also assisting an old man with and estate transfer issue...and it was the old man who needed to be in Scotland. It is likely the old man was the common link...yet...the more she thought about it...the less she liked it...the less things made sense...and it struck her... why would Rick call right as she was ripping into Greg if somehow he knew she was about to make him spill the beans. "Son of a bitch" she hissed but not so that Greg could hear it. *'What the fuck is going on?'* she thought. It dawned on her that she would not get anywhere with them today. So she resigned herself to that fact and made pleasant small talk with Greg for the next few minutes before they had to hang up.

Laurie hated not knowing what was going on. Not knowing made her feel out of control and she was a person who needed to be in control of every aspect of her life. Yet the goings on around her, the trip to St. Vincent then the immediate overseas jaunt to Scotland pleasant though they were had been too sudden. Then her husband being in both places at nearly the same time...was far too convenient to be mere coincidence. Something was going on. Maybe the package her husband had sent her would explain it. It was something to at least occupy her mind...for the moment anyway.

She had been chilling a bottle of wine in the refrigerator and went to retrieve it. She wasn't happy about the situation, not one bit. What was worse was the fact she had no idea what was going on and worse still the practice had been closed for over two weeks. It would take them a month to recover from the lapse of income and they had been struggling as it was. They didn't need any more economic stress. In fact the breaking point had come and gone so often in recent years she couldn't tell one from the other as they all seemed to blur into one perpetual nightmare.

Then there was this latest episode, though it wasn't a nightmare, she didn't feel at all in control of the situation which was as bad as a nightmare for her. Yet another breaking point with yet another set of challenges they would have to surmount in order to survive and keep going. How much more of this could she take? How many times would she find herself or her husband in the hospital from some stress borne malady? It was this sort of stress that led her to pursue Greg and take him as a lover because she had come to understand that life with all its bullshit struggles...was to be lived in spite of it all.

Thankfully her husband was the understanding sort and had allowed her to keep seeing Greg. *'At least he isn't a selfish prick.'* She thought to herself as she swallowed the entire glass of wine.

Pouring another glass she settled into a chair and looked out the window at the clouds rolling by. She was frightened. What was going to happen to their children? Had her husband lost his mind? What were the two men in her life doing? Why the globe-trotting and why all of a sudden? Their economic situation was not near healthy enough to tolerate his being out of the office for more than a few days and here it was over two weeks and now he is on a ship heading for Denmark. Why Denmark? He had never expressed interest in going there, why now? Why was all of this happening?

Frustration with her husband's lapse of sanity and his ever present adolescence and willingness to not act his age had forced her to be the 'adult' in their relationship, to be the bitter pill he had to swallow. She didn't want to be the bitchy wife but neither did she want to have a child for a husband. Swallowing down her wine again... she imagined him with Alzheimer's and having to care for him as he descended into adolescence *'again'*. The thought did not set well as she poured more wine.

Half the bottle was now gone and it had been less than five minutes since opening it, but that did not prevent her from pouring another. Sitting down again she put the wine bottle near her seat so she wouldn't have to get up again resigning herself to consuming the whole thing, Why not?

Life and its constant struggle had nearly destroyed their lives. The only thing keeping them together was the fact that he was the bread winner. His income is what allowed them to survive otherwise she would have left him long ago. The truth of that bothered her a lot more than she expected it would. She had taken a lover out of self-preservation and profound contempt for her husband, contempt which had recently waned but was, at that moment, back in full force. "Goddamn selfish asshole!!!" she hissed.

The kids were still at school and would be for a few more hours. As a result the house felt empty and uninviting. This was the time she usually invited Greg over when he was in town or called him if he wasn't. Only she was pissed at him at the moment he and Rick both. Just as her emotions began to boil over with renewed frustration the doorbell rang. Remembering the package she put her wine down and attempted to stand up. Walking was interesting to say the least. She had not been a heavy drinker and so having consumed over half the bottle in less than 15 minutes made walking interesting if not graceful.

Concentrating on walking straight she made it to the door where she found a courier standing behind a dolly with a large fiberglass crate on it. Behind him were two armed guards whose backs were turned to her with their pistols drawn while they scanned the neighborhood menacingly. "Mam, I have a delivery for Laurie. I will need you to sign this please. I think it would be best if I put this down inside the house…it's pretty heavy." He said. Once inside Laurie signed the release and was then handed a key. After which all three men left. Looking out the door she saw the armored truck pull away followed by two black sedans each filled with heavily armed men. "What is this?" she wondered.

When the courier had put the crate down it made a loud 'thud' as it came to rest. It had to be 100lbs if she were to guess. She tried to move it so she could sit and open it…but it was simply too heavy.

So she knelt in front of it and used the key to unlock the crate. Once the bands were undone only then did she call her husband. He answered his phone immediately and she announced the package had arrived.

Rick then had her open the box. On the very top were four envelopes. One for each of the kids and one for her mother; in each were cashier's checks that paid their college tuition to any College they decided on and another check for her mother paying off the car and the house. In essence in those three envelopes was a cancelation of every debt they had and were going to have…paid in full. "Ok, when you open these envelopes…I need you to not to react, do not scream, do not make any statements over the phone about what you see. It is important…do you understand?" he asked.

Laurie was literally struck speechless by both the shock of the bulk of her stress being erased as well as a leg cramp from kneeling too quickly. "Ok…what do I do with this?' she said in a quavering voice. 'What is this?"

Rick responded. "Questions will have to wait. We are not on a secure line. Too many people can hear what we are saying. So, just enjoy it…and do not ask anything until I get home. Go put them someplace safe and come back, quickly.' Rick waited on the line for only a minute or less before she returned 'Ok, now I want you to open the bottom section. Do not scream…do not yell…do not ask any questions…and do not do a thing with what you see…not a thing…is that understood?"

Laurie was excited, nervous and irritated at the same time. Here she was being handed a blessing and she wasn't supposed to express her feelings…a very difficult thing for her. "Ok,' she said and Rick heard a shuffling noise and a harsh tearing of paper…followed by a gasp of surprise and a gag of her trying not to scream. "Uhmmm. Ahh…Oh shit…oh shit…oh shit….OHHH Shit!!" is all she could say.

"So do you realize why we cannot talk?" he asked.

"Uhh..yeah..Oh hell yeah…oh my god!" she said.

Rick smiled knowing that few things could ever truly shut his wife up. A bundle of cash in 20-50-100 dollar bills seemed to work well. "You need to find a place to put this…all of it…and not in the usual place for such a thing. Keep it in the house…someplace where we can access it…at all times. Be creative…but do not…do not…put this in the place you might usually put such a thing…is that clear?"

"Yes" is all she could manage before she fell into a fit of hysterical giggles.

"I'm glad you like it, but you cannot be blabbing about it to anyone even your mother…not yet anyway. Part of the reason for my going to Denmark is because of what is in that box. You are going to be very, very surprised when I get home. So I want you to relax and rest assured that everything is going to be just fine. Hey, I've got to go. Call me if you have to. Keep it safe...ok."

Laurie was numb with excitement but managed to answer "Ok... Yeah...Ok...sure. I need an explanation at some point' she said. 'But if what you are doing means more of this...I'll keep my questions until you get home." She said unusually sweetly.

"More? Babe...you have no idea. Okay...I gotta go...bye." And he hung up.

She was still too stunned by the pile of cash sitting in her living room to realize that he had hung up the phone. That and the fact that the wine she had taken prior to the delivery was now taking serious effect, where before she could walk, standing was now a problem. She couldn't stand without supporting herself and walking... well that wasn't' happening...not now...but that did not prevent her from emptying the bottle in celebration.

Once she could walk without falling she spent the afternoon locating places to hide the cash. She understood what he meant by not putting it in the usual place...he meant do not deposit it...the bank would want to know where this kind of money came from and so would the IRS...and she wasn't' that much of a goody-goody to worry about the IRS. More importantly, what stress she had been feeling up to that point was now gone. She had 4 million dollars in her hands sitting in a pile before her...physically in her possession. The smile that surfaced on her face did not diminish for well over a week and while she sat on the floor staring at the cash...she determined to give her husband the best blow job of his life when he came home. It was the least she could do to have 4 million dollars in her lap.

Chapter 49

Storm Brewing

WERNER MEYER HAVING recovered from his brush with the Rabbi had fallen into depression in the belief that the Victoria had been lost along with her load of bullion. With the reports of mechanical problems plaguing her he believed that the storm had somehow overwhelmed and sunk the ship. Only he wasn't as depressed at losing the bullion as much as he was at losing the opportunity to kill Patrice. He had been looking forward to making her suffer. But now that he had lost both the bullion and Patrice he was extremely depressed.

Not knowing where the ship had gone down or how deep the water was he was not sure if they'd ever find it or be able to recover the bullion if they did. He reconciled the situation in his own mind by remembering that the Operation hadn't 'needed' the bullion. It would have merely been a bonus and a way to accelerate their agenda, which was domination of the major world powers through blackmail and murder. As it was their agenda was in motion and gaining ground. So the bullion really wasn't necessary to that end. But to lose such a vast amount of bullion to something as inane as a storm was irritating, especially for Meyer who had nobody to blame so that they could feel his personal wrath. As it was the irritation just boiled under his skin driving his sanity ever closer to its barely tangible threshold?

Now he had to wait out the storm before he could return to Argentina. Trouble was the fire fight his men had engaged in with the Israelis, brief as it was, had woken up a hornets nest of Canadian police who were speeding about the highway back and forth between the hotel and town. Several ambulances had their sirens wailing to the hotel but none had their sirens going on the way back suggesting that the men who'd fallen in service to him were dead. He'd seen most of the men fall before he was pushed into his car and taken away.

As fast as they had taken up position and before they could fire more than a few rounds the Israelis had killed them. To have been killed by a Jewish horde like that was shameful in the extreme for a Nazi. How could he possibly honor those men having been so easily killed by a bunch of filthy Jews? He had conveniently wiped his memory of his own reaction to looking into the Rabbis eyes, eyes that filled him with such fear that he had been rendered a quivering, mindless wreck covered in vomit and shit.

After checking with the pilot to see if they could get airborne and being told that the winds were too heavy to even attempt a take-off Werner was resigned to watching television. Maybe the news would report that the Israelis had been apprehended or had died in a fire fight with the Canadian Police. It was a hope he didn't expect to have fulfilled. He knew far too well that the Israelis, as much as he despised and loathed them, were well equipped and well trained not to mention thoroughly dedicated soldiers. "Still' he thought 'they are only Jews". Again the Rabbi being 'only a Jew' conveniently escaped his thoughts.

Flipping through the channels he saw a BBC weather report based out of Edinburgh Scotland reporting on the storm over the western Atlantic and how it was expected to disrupt Scottish shipping and Ferry service for the better part of a week as it moved east. In the background was a ship cruising past the view of the camera but he didn't pay attention to it and flipped the channel to the Discovery channel where they were exploring the wreck of an ancient Greek barge, flipping the channel again he found the National Geographic documentary on Pompeii and flipped it back again to the BBC Weather service where he left it and listened while he poured himself a drink.

The report droned on about shipping schedules, ferry disruptions and the possible threat of unexploded war time mines dropped by the Germans and Allies during the war, thousands of which remained unaccounted for. *"It is entirely possible that with the severity of this storm uncharted mines from the war may break free of their mooring chains and anchors…and find themselves floating on the surface. At least one or two come to the surface each year in the stormy season. If you find one do not approach it and do not touch it…call the police…and remain at a distance of no less than 1000 meters where possible"* came the calm, knowing voice of the anchor woman.

Meyer was looking out the window of his plane into the black… listening…not listening, considering maybe going to bed. Pointing the remote at the television to turn it off, the camera did a close up of a ship passing behind the woman making the report. The ship was steaming in the background as the anchorwoman made some reference to the hazards of the storm on ships like this one. Curiosity drew his gaze to see what she was talking about and her voice was lost to him as he recognized the Victoria sailing along in slate gray seas off Scotland. It was a moment before he could react to what he was seeing.

"Son of a Bitch!!!!" he screamed nearly throwing the remote through the television screen. It was a pre-recorded clip used by the news stations to fill in their time slot. This one was at least a day old if not two. He remembered it being played several times that day but hadn't paid attention to it.

His security chief Karl came in to see what the matter was, as Meyer pointed white faced at the ship on the screen. "That fucking bitch played us...those messages they sent were fake...they had to be... throwing us of the trail. They were traveling across the Atlantic the whole time we were waiting for them here!!! Clever Patrice...but it isn't going to save you...not from me' he whispered. 'Call our affiliates in Europe and start combing the seas for that fucking ship!! Find them...find that ship...and take it...take the ship...get them on it now...and find out how much longer we are going to be stuck in this fucking airport!!!" His last sentence was screamed at Karl, red faced and veins bulging. He was on the verge of bursting a blood vessel as the red halo once again encircled his peripheral vision.

Six hours out of Esbjerg Denmark the Victoria sailed in calm seas. Yet the feeling on board her was anything but calm. For the past 12 hours they had been shadowed by a series of helicopters. One would leave and was replaced by another and another. The Operation had found them. That much was clear and they had no weapons on board to fight off an attack. Archie had filled the ballast tanks to full capacity to bring the ship low in the water to give the impression they were still heavily loaded. If the ship was riding high the Operation would know the bullion was no longer on board. As long as they believed the Victoria was still loaded heavy the Operation would likely bide their time and wait for them to drop anchor then pounce. Whether they pounced now or later...it made no difference. If they were attacked at all they were in deep trouble.

Archie was scratching his unshaven chin as he walked into the Captain's cabin where Rick and Hans sat at the table. "Well, the Danish port authority has told us that we may moor the ship in their long term anchorage...but we cannot enter it until tomorrow because the tide will be out when we get there this evening.' He looked hard at Rick and Hans 'if we ride out the evening it is entirely possible they will hit us. As we have no guns and even if we did... we are badly outnumbered. That being said I propose that we get in as close to the port entrance as possible...drop anchor and take the launch to shore and wait. Of course, I don't think it needs to be said, we leave the lights off. It would be foolish in the extreme for us to remain onboard. As much as I hate to abandon the ship...I believe it is our only real option." Hans and Rick both nodded agreement. It was foolish to remain onboard when the bullion was no longer there to guard. So it was agreed that they would drop anchor and go ashore for the night.

Reservations were made in a local hotel on the coast where they could see the ship from shore. Once they had dropped both stern and bow anchors they got into the launch and headed to shore lights off to ensure a clean getaway.

Around midnight from their hotel on shore Archie was in a morphine-induced sleep with Hans sitting with the lights out watching the Victoria ride at anchor. To him she didn't' seem as huge from that distance but her graceful lines were made even more so in the dim starlight. He had never seen her as more than just a ship, a machine but he had grown to appreciate her and thought she deserved better than to be left alone to face their enemy...undefended.

Rick was in the next room over with Greg both of them watching the ship. Everyone was keyed up and nervous that the clean get away they had hoped for had been lost. They knew that the Operation would be looking for them. The question was how badly were they compromised? How much did they know? These were the questions running through their minds as they watched the Victoria floating at anchor, vulnerable and alone.

Rick had grown fond of the ship. She was easy to operate and very forgiving. She had also been the place where he made some very interesting memories with Patrice and Lisa. He smiled to himself and thought *"I may never walk properly again"*. Not that he minded, he would most certainly have done it all again...and again. But his mind was on many different things that night. His families safety taking priority. Only he didn't dare phone anyone just in case they were being monitored. Though the bullion was now secure they were each concerned their lives were in danger, with good reason. Being in danger didn't make for a restful night's sleep.

Around 1a.m. a motor launch approached the stern and someone opened the hatch near the water line where they had disembarked. From a distance of two miles nobody could tell how many men were onboard. An hour went by...nothing...two hours...nothing...three hours later another launch pulled up alongside the Victoria and this time a bunch of armed men scrambled into the hatch. At least ten this time...certainly more than had boarded earlier. Minutes marched by like hours...nothing...then suddenly on the deck of the Victoria a long burst of machine gun fire ripped from the bridge deck to the bow...and in the distance the sound of gunfire met their ears, a sound like firecrackers being set off in a box, hundreds of them.

Who was shooting at whom? They all wondered. Silence followed... and a group of men crouched and ran toward the aft of the ship in a group...fired....ran forward and fired....until another long blast from a very powerful machine gun ripped through several of them... leaving the remaining few to run back and find cover. After that last burst...the remaining men from the second launch left in a hurry far fewer in number. In fact only two of the original 10 made it to the launch and they were badly wounded. Confused all three men watched from shore and wondered what had just happened.

Hans came into their room immediately after the second launch left. "Did you see what happened onboard ship?' he asked 'I'm not sure that it would be wise for us to return, at least not until that first bunch of men leave. We can't return that kind of fire power. We'd be sitting ducks." Everyone nodded agreement. Several hours remained before dawn and each man needed sleep so the rest of the evening was spent taking turns sleeping and keeping watch.

Just after dawn Hans came in smiling broadly. "It was Trio' he exclaimed 'They had been monitoring the Operation's radio traffic and learned that they planned to raid the ship and kill everyone on board. As a result they came early, and took up station and when the Operations men arrived onboard...they opened fire. Werner Meyer was not among them that they could see. He certainly isn't among the dead. So we aren't out of the woods, not yet" he said thoughtfully.

An hour later Hans, Archie, Greg and Rick, the latter two wearing masks against recognition as the ship was undoubtedly being watched, climbed onto the platform and entered the ship. Almost immediately the launch was hoisted on board and secured as well as the docking platform which was secured on the deck next to the launch. In the wheel house the Trio was on alert and more serious than Rick had ever seen them before. Each man was heavily armed with assault rifles and bristling with grenades, clips and multiple hand guns for close action. Rick greeted 'T' and the rest genuinely glad to see them. "So, what is going on? Are we still keeping the ship at the anchorage?" he asked.

'T' nodded then said "Yes, and they know the ship is empty now, so if they come back it will be to find out where the bullion is. That means you,' he pointed at Rick 'need to become invisible. We can't have your identity compromised. If they ID you it is only a matter of time before they locate your property rendering this whole exercise useless.' He paused and placed a hand on Ricks shoulder 'That means that once we get to the anchorage even before then you are going to have to get out of here." Looking hard at Greg he asked "Who are you?"

Archie answered "He's the estate attorney we hired to make using the bullion easier. Through his service we are now able to convert the bullion to cash as needed without having to explain where it came from, though' he sighed 'we do not plan to dump the lot onto the market as that would likely crash the markets."

'T' nodded accepting the explanation as given and turned to Greg saying 'Your job is done and like Rick if they ID you they'll start piecing together what has happened and start retracing events. None of us can afford to let that happen. So we have a plane waiting for you in Copenhagen.' Looking at Rick he said 'Take the wheel Captain and take us in."

Three hours later Rick and Greg were on a plane bound for San Francisco. Before the plane left the ground both men were fast asleep and would not wake until the plane touched down 14 hours later.

Chapter 50
Enough is Enough

IN A HANGER in Nova Scotia Werner Meyer flew into a fury after he received a report that 8 of the ten men he had sent to the Victoria were now dead. That, however, is not what angered him. The men who had survived reported that the hold of the Victoria was empty. Not a single crate of bullion remained onboard. Upon hearing that news he flew into a violent rage that burst the blood vessels in his eyes giving him a red eyed demonic appearance which coupled with the froth forming around his mouth gave him a less than sane appearance. Unconsciously his security chief placed his hand on the Luger in his holster while stepping back from the deranged spectacle standing before him.

Looking through blood red eyes at his security chief Meyer asked through gritted teeth "When will we be taking off?" His words were slurred as frothy sputum dribbled from his lips and chin staring fixedly at his security chief through blood red eyes. Had Meyer been sane in that moment he would have noticed the red halo around his vision, an indication that his blood pressure was so pathologically high he was likely blow a blood vessel and die. Something his security chief Karl was silently hoping for in that moment while keeping his hand on his gun, muscle keyed and ready to strike out if he was in anyway threatened.

Karl his Security Chief struggled to answer back. "M-mein Fuhrer", the tower has cleared us for take-off in two hours. We will be refueled and be first in line behind commercial traffic. The Canadian air traffic control is not allowed to let us leave before all commercial passenger traffic has cleared the tarmac."

This news did nothing to ease the growing rage that rushed through Meyer's fevered brain. Unconsciously Meyer let his stiletto slip slowly from his wrist sheath as he stalked toward his security chief who he wanted to kill for delivering such ill-timed news. *'Does he not realize what was at stake…does he not realize how important 'I' am to the world? I am the Fuhrer!!'* In an instant Meyer snapped out of his homicidal rage and was back in the realm of the sane or as close to sane as he was capable. "Very well, see to it that we are fueled and ready to go. Have the pilot fill out a flight plan for Denmark. Oh… find that fucking bitch, Patrice! She needs to die!!"

Karl flipped the safety on keeping his hands on his Luger backing away not wanting to turn his back, especially not on a man with a stiletto protruding from his sleeve. His mind was racing with serious doubts about his continued employment with the Operation. His boss had begun insisting he be referred to as 'Fuhrer' immediately upon the death of Krupp. Krupp had never made that request though everyone knew he'd been a Nazi a long, long time ago. This was a *job* nothing more and he was damn sure no fucking Nazi, *'Who the fuck does this asshole think he is?'* he thought to himself.

Karl knew that the Operation had once been Odessa. He had been around long enough to realize the old bastards back in Argentina were 'Nazis'. One would have to be an enormous dolt to not see it. A bunch of aging German men, obviously former military having moved to Argentina after the war and who never went back to Germany. Regardless of his misgivings he liked the money, but what he was being paid wasn't worth this, not by a long shot. With that in mind made the calls he'd been ordered to, his doubts filed away for future reference and pondering. Meanwhile he would transfer his money to an account on Grand Cayman then Switzerland and prepare to disappear.

The image of his employers blood red eyes, livid red complexion with foam dribbling from his mouth and the stiletto in the ready position was the end for Karl, though he had not made the 'conscious' decision to leave…yet. He began to realize that when things went south and he knew they would with this lunatic leading them, he was not going to go down with the ship. Besides he liked Patrice. She had been the only sane one of the bunch as far as he could tell, that and she was hot. He wasn't going to let Meyer touch her, not if he could help it.

Joshua Peel meanwhile found himself in Denmark overlooking the anchorage where the Victoria rode at anchor sitting high in the water her cargo of bullion, if it had ever existed, gone. Thanks to a laser microphone Werner Meyers recognition of the Victoria steaming off the East Coast of Scotland and the temper tantrum that followed allowed Agent Peel to hop a plane for Denmark the moment Werner escaped the hanger, where he arrived three hours after Rick and Greg were already halfway over the North Atlantic headed for home.

Day's earlier he had been monitoring the Operations communications in Canada in conjunction with the Royal Canadian Mounted Police. They had been watching developments in Halifax at a distance so not to interfere with the Operation. Both the Canadians and Americans wanted to gather as much intelligence as possible on the Operation and its infrastructure. It was a new problem that nobody had a bead on so they each opted to observe, learn and act only if they had no other choice.

However, Peel had a time convincing the Mounties to not charge in once they learned what and who the Operation actually was. Nazis in Canada was not something the Mounties were in the mood to tolerate. Not something one would expect from the Royal Canadian Mounted Police who were known for being polite. They are in reality among the toughest and most effective police forces in the world and not into taking crap from anyone. Peel smirked to himself wondering how it was a Mounty could beat the living piss out of someone and still be polite throughout the process. He had never felt the need to be polite as he had on more one occasion helped a dirt bag fall up a flight of stairs….or two, usually stomping and beating them until they finally gave him what he wanted. Shaking his head he just couldn't figure out how you could politely give someone a well-deserved beating. But he figured the Mounties could do it if it could be done at all.

Peel had been in Halifax waiting on the Victoria so that they could get their hands on the bullion before the Operation did, if it existed. According to the Treasury all known repositories were accounted for. As for war time bullion what was currently missing or unaccounted for was a fraction of what was reputed to be on the Victoria, but known to still be hidden in Europe, likely in some mine the Nazis had blown up at the end of the war. Many attempts at recovery had failed due to the fact that the blasts used to close up the mines had ensured that any attempt at gaining access to the gold inside would result in a catastrophic collapse.

According to official sources the amount of bullion reported to be on board the Victoria was impossible. Yet both American and Canadian authorities agreed that it bore looking into. Joshua knew that 'official' opinions had a habit of being less than accurate. Therefore anything thought to be impossible by the federal government was, to his mind, automatically plausible.

The Canadians were taking no chances knowing the US Government was usually full of shit, which is how the RCMP commander had put it to Joshua, politely of course, who readily agreed, unofficially and less politely. Both men liked each other instantly.

Both the Canadian and United States Governments primary concern was the bullion. If it existed they were to keep it off the international markets at all costs, even if it meant sinking the ship. Shaking his head agent Peel found it ironic that his government was more concerned with the bullion rather than the possibility that a Nazi organization was in functional control of no less than six NATO nations, two of which happened to be Great Britain and the United States.

That tidbit came from the Israelis who had been handed a treasure trove of files and business records reported to be owned and operated by the 'Operation' aka 'Odessa' as well as a list of compromised members of Congress and the parliaments of every NATO member under their control. The source was a woman who had strolled into the Israeli consulate in London and requested a meeting. She had been wearing a wide brimmed sun hat which covered her features and a black shapeless dress and gloves to keep her prints from being obtained. Anyone who knew her would have recognized Patrice immediately and those who didn't wouldn't know her from Eve.

Patrice was clearly aware of every camera in the consulate and knew exactly when to keep her hat covering her face and from what angle whenever she approached one. Within an hour of that meeting a flood of intel came into the FBI offices naming every single Congressman, Senator and Supreme Court Justice in the pocket of the Operation. That same flood of information hit MI6 with names of compromised members of Parliament and the Royal Court system. They had been given everything but the banking records which Israel was understandably keeping for their own use.

The shock wave was significant yet silent and went unnoticed by the general public as each compromised member of Congress and Parliament was quietly taken into custody and questioned. So quietly in fact that everyone was taken into custody so that nobody got wise to the fact. Such a thing hitting the news would jeopardize the very fabric of western democracy. So every precaution was taken to keep the arrest and questioning of prominent members of Congress quiet and as drama free as possible. Nobody saw anything but several congress men being escorted to a waiting limousine and driven away as though to a meeting, which of course it was.

Interestingly within 24 hours of their arrests their respective legislative bodies began functioning normally and actually began passing legislation they had been sitting on, in some cases for years. Once the compromised legislators were informed of who had been blackmailing them they each fell into a state of shock. Yet being politicians each had cut a deal that would keep them out of prison. The resulting deal they had struck was that they were to resign their seats and remain out of public life due to the extent and nature of their respective crimes, if they didn't wish to be prosecuted. They weren't allowed to run for any elected seat, not even the local school board...ever again. Many, upon release, quietly left the country for non-extradition treaty countries where each had extensive fortunes and vast estates on which to hide. The FBI let them leave and blocked their re-entry into the USA so that if they ever attempted to return they would be immediately arrested and sent, without trial, to prison for life. The unraveling of the Operation had begun.

Precipitating this was that two days earlier 'J' had accessed the entire Operation banking system and discovered exactly how much money they had in their bank accounts throughout the world. Six Trillion British Pounds Sterling was a lot of money especially if he expected to pipe it through the banking system, four accounts weren't nearly enough to keep things under the radar. Bouncing six trillion pounds through four accounts would get somebodies attention.

He could do it if he had enough bank accounts to pump the money through. He guessed he would need a minimum of 50 separate accounts to handle the volume and keep it unnoticed 100 accounts would be even better, if they were spread over several continents. The fact of the matter was he didn't have the time to set up 50 separate accounts much less 100. In the time it would take him to set things up the Operation could get wise and close the accounts. That they hadn't already was a monumental mistake, a mistake he didn't expect them to overlook for very much longer.

In his need to be expeditious he approached Patrice with his dilemma. She was lying in her sun room, a glass enclosed patio, a necessity in the British Isles, sunning herself in a knit bikini so tiny the fabric of which, if it could be called fabric, wouldn't have been enough to make a small doyly. In fact it might as well not been there at all for what it *didn't* cover.

Patrice was even more beautiful than he had imagined. Her legs were bent ever so slightly and her body was magnificently toned. Lying next to her was Lisa who hadn't bothered with a suit at all, equally stunning with her tight body glistening with suntan oil. Each woman had been waxed clean at a spa in town the previous day, a detail that did not go unnoticed by 'J'.

His mouth went dry as he entered the sun room and his eyes fell onto the women lying before him. Patrice smiled at him sweetly and smirked when his jaw fell open as the words he tried to form were lost in a croaking sound similar to a frog being stepped on.

"Yes, 'J' what is it?" Patrice asked trying not to laugh at the squeaky, croaking noise he'd just made. She twisted her pelvis deliberately toward him and let her thigh drop giving 'J' an eye full which only compounded his speech impediment. Their eyes met briefly and the fierceness of his love for her came flooding through. It was an exchange that only 'J' and Patrice shared. Lisa was nearly comatose from exhaustion having been ravaged by Patrice not two hours before. "Yes?" she repeated, swallowing hard in recognition of her own attraction to 'J', a man she had barely noticed before that very moment.

Focusing on the ledger in his hand he was able to regain the speech necessary to convey the message. "Er..uhm…we have a problem with the accounts.' He shook himself out of his daze, 'the amount of money the Operation has in these accounts is far too vast for us to hide in just 4 accounts. Even if we smoke the computer systems this amount of cash pumping through only 4 accounts will get some ones attention and with the Operation being as connected as you say… they'll know where the money is and get it back. What we need is an ally with the means to hide this kind of cash, for that we will have to share the proceeds with them' He paused eyes locked onto her long legs 'I'm not talking a crime syndicate or anything like that but a country. Israel could stash the cash in their system, hidden in their international markets. That and they would certainly have the motivation once they know what and who the Operation represents."

He was right she wasn't thinking in the right terms when she made the suggestion that they should take the Operations money. She was forgetting that they had many accounts throughout the world. Added up that made for a tidy sum, a sum that would be hard to hide in run of the mill bank accounts where 'regular' millionaires and billionaires kept their money. Most of the accounts had more than a few hundred million others a billion or two. "How much are we talking about?" she asked.

Flipping his note pad open he pulled up the total sum he had been asked to 'relocate' and showed it to Patrice. Her eyes grew wide "Six Trillion?' she whispered not wanting to wake Lisa who was now asleep. 'I had no idea it was so vast. I can see how that might be a bit of a challenge' she said smiling sweetly patting him on the forearm. 'I have a contact at the Israeli Consulate in London who I've been using to rid the organization of our more destructive elements. That is until I was made aware of my disposable status in the Operation. Now, I'll use this man to help bring them down. It's about time I retire anyway. If I give him what we have I believe he will work with us."

Two days later Joshua Peel in conjunction with the RCMP and the Israeli government decided to strike all at once. With the bulk of the tainted NATO leadership under arrest and no longer under Operation control they were concerned that the leadership of the Operation would disappear. What they had was very sketchy other than the bank accounts which the Israelis weren't negotiating with anyone over. As it was established this was a Nazi organization the Israelis cited a NATO policy that any known Nazi assets would automatically belong to the government of Israel, once identified. What the FBI had not been told was that 20% of the wealth seized was to go to an undisclosed account in Switzerland as compensation for the information leading to the capture and seizure of Nazi assets.

What Joshua knew and what he kept from the Canadian authorities was that he had an unofficial contact now tracking the jet which he learned was heading for Denmark. To throw the operation off, Britain was asked via the State Department to let them go about their normal flight plan as if the air traffic control was unaware of their fugitive status making them think they were safe, so they would act freely and lead them to more contacts. Only by the time the word had reached the British two jets had already been scrambled to intercept them, but were called back at the very last minute once the word had been passed through channels.

Meanwhile cruising at 20,000 feet Werner Meyer stared out the window at the clouds far below. He was nauseous again, not from motion sickness but from the stress caused by feeling out of control and not knowing what was going on. Too much had happened too quickly. It had all started with that fucking Rabbi and the promise of death lurking behind those cold eyes. That was when it had all started to come apart. Had he not panicked and sent out his men to kill the Rabbi...perhaps that was his mistake...the provocation. Had he just stood his ground and left the old bastard alone things may have been different...maybe.

"Too late for that now" he thought dismissively. *"What must I do to correct this?"* he asked himself over and over again. First order of business was killing Patrice. His pathologic want to kill her had

been replaced with the practical need to keep her quiet. There was simply too much at stake for him to indulge his personal desires. She had to be silenced. Somehow she was behind this or so he had convinced himself. Unconsciously he allowed the stiletto in his wrist sheath to spring in and out as he considered his options. The sound of it sliding out and clicking back in created a sort of metronome-like focus point soothing his psychosis while allowing the sane portion of his mind to work out solutions to his mounting difficulties.

All of their contacts in NATO had gone silent, or so he was informed. All of their most powerful allies in Congress and Parliament were no longer answering their calls. Nothing had been mentioned on the BBC or the American News channels. If anyone of that stature had been arrested it would have made the news. Had he 'known' what was going on he might know what to do. It was the information vacuum that caused him the most distress. Not knowing what the fuck was going on drove him to the brink. That and the knowledge that Patrice, the woman he loathed and lusted after was likely responsible for whatever was happening. Patrice had been the only person in the organization to know their identities because she had been their 'handler'. It was therefore reasoned that 'she' had turned their names over to the authorities to save herself.

To a sane, rational person it would make sense. Her life was under threat and she did what she had to in order to survive. However, Meyer was not sane and was nothing close to rational. As her 'Fuhrer' he had the *right* to kill her if she stepped out of line for the good of the organization. To defy his authority was treachery, base, foul treachery. He was Fuhrer after all...he was her leader and if he wanted her dead...well...she should accept it...willingly. This and many other delusional thoughts stormed through his mind filling him with inconsolable rage, rage that became more permanent by the hour.

The trouble was, as sharp as he might have been, once the psychosis took over he couldn't think of anything but what was vexing him and why. Reasoned thought was fleeting and when present not deeply rooted, to the point where the merest 'jolt' of emotional upset would see it uprooted and gone. It had been nearly 72 hours since his last fully rational thought. His brain had been consumed by rage over Patrice betrayal, the Rabbi who was clearly on his trail because of Patrice the FBI was on his trail because of Patrice and the Canadian Mounted Police were on his trail…again because of Patrice. The more he raged, the more he became convinced that Patrice had caused his troubles.

Being a psychopath Werner Meyer never once saw himself as the cause of his own trouble. It hadn't been his killing of Herche because *he* was an idiot who wouldn't shut up. He wasn't smart enough to figure out they had been bugged by the FBI. He had been killed because it was necessary. That had not been his fault. His killing the fueling crew had not been his fault either. That blame, he reasoned, rested on the FBI for having his cards declined. Their deaths were the result of the FBI interfering with his business or so he had reasoned. Nothing ever was Meyer's fault.

It was therefore the FBIs fault that he was forced to leave Halifax by cutting in front of commercial airliners and taking off out of order of their scheduled departure. And it was the FBIs fault that the RCMP crashed the gates and tried to cut them off and it was the FBI who had sent a helicopter to prevent their take off. Meyer's mind was awash with who was to blame for his misfortunes resulting in his making the decision to make a run for Denmark in order to locate the bullion.

It was no longer a question of using it to further their agenda it was now necessary to keep the Operation a float. Apparently all of their assets, bank accounts and properties had been seized in the USA and Britain. They still had no word from their European sections on their condition.

Internet connections were no longer available, blocked by the FBI. His phone was also disconnected so he couldn't even check on his own accounts. He had nearly ten billion on Grand Cayman. He was concerned that his personal wealth might also be gone. The fact he couldn't check on it drove him mad, which is what Joshua Peel had intended. So, all things considered, it was indeed the FBIs fault for Werner's current frame of mind.

What brought Meyer a measure of comfort was the fact that he had transferred his wealth from the Argentine account to Grand Cayman prior to this trip. Being a numbered account there was no way to track its origins since he had, like Patrice, taken precautions against a potential back lash against their organization. He had learned much from the Old Man who knew better than to keep his personal wealth in any named accounts or 'company' owned accounts. Being an illegal business there was always a risk of governments seizing funds. Therefore precautions were taken against losing personal wealth in the event of a government backed seizures, which is what he believed was happening now.

The fact that the RCMP and the FBI had attempted to apprehend him in Halifax was a clear signal that the Operation was now visible and on their radar. The Helicopter they nearly collided with was an FBI black hawk. The pilot he noted was blonde and had blue eyes and had absolutely no fear, but clearly had no wish to die. However the fact remained that the Operation was now being watched by the Americans and Canadians which meant that Britain was likely on the hunt for them as well. If he were confident they could re-fuel in Florida he would have headed home. But with recent developments and the fact that they could not pump and run from an American airport with the FBI on his tail, he felt it was best to head for Denmark. There he hoped to locate the bullion or Patrice who he figured knew where the bullion was.

What Meyer did not know was that the Operations wealth had not yet been touched. All the FBI had done was put a stop on their cards within their jurisdiction and limited communications to force a move. If they thought their money was gone they'd be forced to take action. It was Peel who had suggested it via a nudge from his boss who had been nudged by Rabbi Weiss through his father. "If they think their money is gone, they will get desperate. If they are desperate they will likely make mistakes, big mistakes."

The Operation did exactly what they expected them to and that was to panic. The death of the fueling crew was an unintended consequence. Otherwise the outcome was exactly what they intended. The Operation jet made a break for it once it was clear they were being monitored. The RCMP made a good show of trying to stop them and the helicopters near miss had been staged to create a sense of desperation while not actually trying to stop them.

Onboard a private jet following behind Meyer's plane Rabbi Weiss enjoyed a sense of irony and poetic justice while traveling in the Embassies Honda jet the former property of the Palestinian Government. Not only was it fuel efficient it was fast so he could keep up with Myers jet which wasn't nearly as quick nor as fuel efficient. Meyer's top speed was merely cruising speed for the newer more nimble Honda. As a result they found it easy to keep tabs on the Operations jet by remaining ten miles distant and 1000 feet above them. Where the skies were clearest they could look out the windscreen and see their quarry in the distance which to the naked eye appeared to be a black speck among the clouds. Once in a while the infrared tracker was activated to ensure that they still had a functional signal as well as to confirm that the speck out front was still the plane they needed to follow.

Immediately after the firefight in Halifax Rabbi Weiss had phoned the Israeli Embassy in Ottawa requesting a jet to follow Meyer the moment he left Halifax. The Israeli PM ordered the Embassy to organize transportation for the Rabbi and his men. As a result they were afforded the use of the confiscated jet. A prize seized during one of the many Gaza Strip incursions where they were seeking out rocket launch sites, one of which happened to be the airport where the Palestinian diplomats kept their planes and helicopters.

Being that the Palestinians were supporting the rocket launch sites striking Israel they felt no obligation to honor property rights, therefore 'confiscated' any aircraft that would be of use and flew them home. The Israeli Army burned the remaining aircraft before leveling every single building by turning the Airport into a makeshift training ground and impact range.

The Israelis designated the airport a 'temporary' training grounds for missile, bomb and machine gun practice for the Air Force as well as a temporary impact range for tank and artillery practice as well as a weapons 'disposal site' for all outdated weapons I.E. Rockets, artillery shells, bombs, cruise missiles and a host of experimental weapons that were just too expensive and too volatile to mass produce as well as all confiscated Palestinian weapons.

Once all ordinance had been expended the site was designated a tank practice zone to train tank crews to maneuver through, over and around obstacles. After a month of 'practice and training' what had once been a modern airport resembled the surface of the moon complete with craters and mountain ranges made of what used to be buildings. Topping it off was the odor of rotting corpses buried in the rubble. As a result rockets were never launched from 'official' Palestinian property again. The Israelis had a well-developed talent for making their point. It was a paradigm that Rabbi Weiss understood well and lived by and intended to exercise with regard to Werner Myer and Odessa, himself.

On board Meyers jet the Operations security chief Karl, was monitoring the radar noting the blip on the screen was keeping pace with them. There were several other planes on the radar but this one was making identical course changes to theirs. It was clear they were being followed. After Halifax it was to be expected.

Looking back at his boss he considered whether or not to tell him. There was nothing they could do about it at the moment and telling his boss was a dangerous proposition. The last time he'd simply told Meyer anything, 'Der Fuhrer', he mocked silently, had lost his composure and unsheathed his Stiletto with clear intent of using it on him for 'daring' to give him bad news.

The vision of his boss stalking toward him with blood red eyes, foaming at the mouth with stiletto threatening had been the last straw for Karl. How Meyer had risen to the head of the Operation was unclear. He was clearly unfit for leadership. He'd known of his previous employer though he'd never set eyes on him. However, the decisions that came from Krupp had been clear, concise and well thought out. Bad news was met with thoughtful consideration and a change in strategy or shift in focus, not so with Meyer.

His method of addressing an issue was to kill whoever was right in front of him when he got upset or was somehow thwarted. The latest example of his volatility being the killing of the fueling crew at the airport, which was going to back fire on them at some point, the question was when. Murder was not something you did 'just because you got pissed off.' As it was 'he' Karl was an accessory to murder in the first degree. Though Canada did not engage in the death penalty he was not keen on spending his life in a Canadian prison because his boss lost his temper. Enough was enough...he was threw with this whole fucking, idiotic mess, money or not. Money meant nothing in a prison cell.

Karl was not going to be around when the world came crashing down around Meyer. It would be a bloody mess when it did. Anyone associated with or in proximity to Meyer could get killed if not sent to prison. Karl was not looking directly at his boss but rather through the reflection on his computer screen. Meyers head was shaking side to side just enough to be visible as the stiletto clicked in and out of its sheath over and over again. Though Karl could not see his complexion on the grey screen he could see the changes of his pallor as he went from 'red' to green to white. After a time Meyer was once again frothing at the mouth. A clear indication that he was growing agitated by whatever it was going on inside that diseased brain.

Shaking his head in disgust Karl focused on finding Patrice. He had been tasked with finding her. Only he had no intention of betraying her to Meyer, nor had he ever. One she was too smart for him to simply track down and far too dangerous to confront directly. He had once believed she would succeed Krupp as head of the Operation. That had been generally accepted and to him it was not at all unpleasant because Patrice was unusually brilliant, cunning and vicious but only when she needed to be. She would have done well as the head of the Operation, which is what everyone had expected.

When this lunatic Meyer announced that he was in charge the jolt was palpable. But liking the money he was being paid he didn't say anything nor did anyone else. However, he did advise his closest friends in the Operation to follow his lead and move their money into 'other' accounts, just in case things went bad. As for Patrice she had apparently gone into hiding with the Trio, all of whom had been tagged for elimination. Not something usually done to senior members of the organization, particularly not someone of her seniority. Such 'housekeeping', as he termed it was reserved for low level thugs who'd over stepped or had somehow attracted the attention of authorities or had been turned.

From what he was able to gather from the vague nonsense Meyer spewed was that she had 'defected' somehow. Only she hadn't gone to the authorities he knew, but had somehow partnered up with her own team and three other men to keep the bullion safe from Meyer. Now that he had seen Meyer as the unhinged psychopath he was, he now understood and even agreed with Patrice actions, though he would never put such thoughts to words, especially not in present company.

Karl had no idea what Meyer hoped to accomplish in Denmark. The Victoria was anchored there no longer loaded with bullion that was clear. He also knew that the crew once manning her was long gone. Remaining with an empty vessel in a closed anchorage would be suicidal. That and if Patrice had joined them tracking the bullion from Denmark would be impossible, she was simply too smart for that. This trip, no matter how you sliced it was going to be a waste of time.

Also his own growing apprehension was brought to a head when he noticed on radar two jet fighters racing to their position as they approached British Airspace. Then suddenly, without warning, they broke-off and headed back home. Their clear intention was to intercept them based on their course and speed prior to breaking off. When they broke off at the last minute, it was clear, to Karl anyway, that they were being tracked. He chose *not* to bring this development to Meyer's attention because he would simply lose his composure again.

Taking a seat where he could watch both Meyer and the Radar screen Karl did some hard thinking. Being that they had barely escaped Canadian airspace with their skins and the fact the Canadian Air Force had not pursued them it was clear that they were being tracked. He was convinced they were heading into a trap, a trap he wasn't about to get caught in. Sharing his concerns with the pilot Rolf, a close friend, they both agreed that following their current flight plan was putting their heads in a noose.

Getting out the aviation map of Denmark, Karl pointed to a rural air strip. Nodding his approval and agreement Rolf silently made a course correction. The trouble was the lunatic in back he would very likely flip out once he realized what they were doing. Rolf then pointed to the oxygen mask and pointed to his nose indicating that Karl should put his on. Once securely fastened and the oxygen was turned on Rolf slowly depressurized the cabin so that Meyer who was already sleepy and nodding off was soon in an oxygen deprived, near comatose sleep.

When it was clear that Meyer was out Karl, carrying his oxygen supply went to the medical box and took out a syringe and injected Meyer with an extra heavy dose of Propophyl to ensure that he didn't wake up when they went below 10,000 feet where the oxygen level was enough to wake him again. They wanted him to remain out while they secured themselves a safe and permanent get away. The drug itself was illegal to possess being a surgical anesthetic and too powerful to use as a mere sleep agent. The Operation had taken to using it as a means of dispatching uncooperative politicians and rivals while onboard following a trip where either they were brought into the fold or not. Those who did not tended to end up with a needle in their arm followed by a long fall from ten thousand feet over the ocean. The lucky ones died of the overdose on the way down while the less fortunate awakened from their sleep while falling to their deaths.

With that in mind Karl dosed Meyer so that he might succumb to the drug. Not being a doctor he wasn't aware exactly how much of a dose was a fatal dose so he gave Meyer the entire syringe full and hoped that would be enough. Putting a bullet in his skull would have been a sure bet but he was concerned about a possible ricochet and puncturing the planes skin. Not being well acquainted with the possible effects he figured any hole in a plane at this altitude was not a good thing. So it was he chose the drug, old as it was…he hoped it was powerful enough to kill him…like putting a sick dog to sleep. Karl smiled inside his mask… 'This dog I won't miss or lose sleep over' he thought.

Once done Meyer was placed on his back on the couch and strapped in. Not a word was spoken as Karl took his seat and nodded to Rolf. Looking around to ensure that everyone was secure he whipped the plane hard left and dove into a cloud bank. At this Rabbi Weiss smirked thinking that they were attempting to evade pursuit. Only he knew the device would locate them easily again. So he activated the infra-red tracker tracking their flight path which indicated roughly where they were headed. He then instructed the pilot to maintain their current heading. This was meant to instill a false sense of security so they believed that they'd lost their tail or better yet had not been followed at all. He knew that if they suddenly changed course to follow they'd know for certain that they were being tracked. This way, he believed, they might calm down and let their guard down. However, he realized that this was too much to hope for. These men were making a break for it clearly aware of being pursued. The best he could hope for was to make them second guess their instincts and force them into making another mistake. So once their heading stabilizes Rabbi Weiss instructed his pilot to slow down and make a slow turn onto a plotted intercept course in twenty minutes.

Karl meanwhile made arrangements via satellite phone with the European sections of the Operation to have three SUVs waiting for them. He made it clear that they were not to be blacked out or in any way conspicuous. Just normal, innocuous, preferably beat up, most definitely not stolen, SUVs that were mechanically reliable so they could disappear into the Danish landscape unnoticed. Karl then proceeded to phone his closest friends warning them of the threat and for them to be on their guard. He however did not announce his plans to anyone, not even Rolf who he trusted more than anyone in the organization. Karl had arranged to have 20 million pounds stashed in each vehicle, the pretext being funds for a 'deal' going down and the rest for paying off police. The truth being he simply wanted to pad his retirement account. The idea had been to temp the others into absconding with the cash they would discover leaving him alone with his own plans to disappear.

The airfield they were headed for had once been a German Luftwaffe base which had been adapted for civilian use by the

Danish Government. Cost of operation and maintenance had forced its closure decades before. The only people using it now were drug smugglers and the odd Cessna pilot who ran out of gas. Being a defunct airport with no beacon or lights to guide them in they had to make it there before sun down in order to land safely. Once all his calls were made Karl focused once again on the radar screen noticing that the plane on their tail was keeping to its original course, but this did nothing to put him at ease. If anything it made him even more nervous, follow us across the Atlantic only to fake us out? "No' he murmured 'No…you aren't fooling me" he focused on the blip on the screen shaking his head.

"Rolf, our tail didn't follow, so either I was mistaken, which I seriously doubt, or we have a homing device on board", he said looking out the windscreen. Rolf turned to look at his friend and nodded but said nothing but his eyes asked *so what do we do?* to which Karl answered "We head dead north and make them think we are headed to Sweden or Norway. At the last possible moment we turn for the airport and land. Our transportation should be waiting for us in the hangar on the north end of the field. If the police show up they'll find sleeping beauty here' nodding toward the unconscious figure on the couch. 'We will then head to the nearest ferry to Sweden and then drive to Norway, where I plan to hop a plane to Spain. This lunatic has been leaving bodies behind him since he arrived in Miami. He killed Hercsh and his limo driver less than an hour after arriving in Miami. Since then, we've had a tail. Then there are the Israelis. I have no idea how or when we picked *them* up. The first I knew of them was in Halifax when 'asshole' here freaked out over seeing a Rabbi on a boat in the harbor. That led us to losing twelve good men and attracting the attention of Canadian Police, who apparently were already watching us along with the FBI, who we picked up after he killed Hercsh.' Karl balled his fist in frustration smashing his fist into the console 'All because of this idiot!!!"

"Careful there' Rolf said urgently 'you can't just smack the console like that you might accidentally kill the engines and this thing doesn't glide for shit" He smiled at his friend understanding the frustration he felt. Rolf being a lower level 'grunt' in the Operation he knew not to say too much and to ignore most everything he witnessed. He also noticed the shaking-up of the Operation since Meyer took over. His employment with the Operation terminated the instant Meyer had killed the fueling crew in Halifax. There was no reason to kill them when they had the petty cash to pay for fuel. Killing them had drawn in the RCMP and FBI forcing them to make a break for it. Now they had at least three major law enforcement agencies on them as well as the Israelis.

If Rolf knew anything useful it was that you didn't fuck with the Israelis, even a little. So he decided to move to the Baja Peninsula of Mexico where he had a nice vacation home on the beach. He'd always wanted to move there, now he could. A smile broke onto his face as he thought of the hot sand, cold beer and senoritas in string bikinis striding passed his bungalow, each ripe for the picking and oh so willing to share his beer, bed or wherever they decided to 'play'. Actually, now that he thought of it, his bed had never been used for anything but sleep. 'I will have to change that' he thought. Another smirk surfaced as he remembered the couch he broke in half the last time two hot senoritas had accepted his invitation to share his beer. 'I need to buy stronger couch' he thought to himself smiling as he started to hum a Jimmy Buffet tune into his mask.

Less than an hour later they touched down gently and then taxied into the hangar and inside where he turned off the lights and killed the engines. Karl, looked back at his former boss who remained unconscious with one arm dangling off the couch. It was his stiletto arm and he couldn't help but notice the blade slowly slide out of the sheath as he lie motionless. The sight of that stiletto blade sliding out of its sheath made him very uneasy. Something made him want to empty his gun into th figure on the couch and had been raising the gun to do so when the door opened. At this point he hesitated only a second…stared hard at what he hoped was a dead man and left the plane. Something deep inside told him he needed to be as far from that lunatic as he could possibly get.

When his eyes adjusted to the late afternoon darkness he saw three SUVs sitting parked at the far end of the hangar. A Mitsubishi trooper, an older one but solid, an older Mercedes van and a GMC Yukon, lifted and apparently hopped up. Choosing the GMC he tossed his duffle and case into the seat. He then located the bundles of cash in the back of his vehicle. A quick scan of one of the bundles suggested that he had at least twenty million pounds in his GMC. Each of the other cars would have a bundle. Hopefully they would all leave in separate vehicles.

Luckily everyone else hopped in one of the other two vehicles leaving him alone in the GMC. Sighing in relief Karl pulled up to where Rolf sat behind the wheel of the Mitsubishi Trooper counting a bundle of cash. "Put that down!" he yelled. "You can count it later! We have to be away from here now!" As he spoke police sirens blared in the distance, a lot of sirens indicating that the police were coming in force. Rolf heard them and tossed his cash away and nodded for Karl to lead on.

On the plane Meyer had been awakened by the jolt of the plane landing but had been unable to move, then passed out again as the plane taxied on the ground. When it came to a stop he had awakened but had been unable to think, focus or do much more than move his wrist which let the stiletto out of his sheath. Karl had been staring at him...why? Again he faded out as ...sirens echoed inside his brain...blue and red lights...flashed...distant...vague... Suddenly his brain clicked with a surge of adrenaline.

His brain fogged by drugs...he struggled to release the catches on the seats. When his fingers refused to cooperate he slashed the belts with his stiletto and ripped them off. Standing was difficult but the adrenaline helped. Making it to the door which was still open he threw himself down the steps landing hard on the concrete in a face plant. The drug he was on kept him from feeling the damage to his face. Not having time to figure out what had happened, not that he could have, Werner came to his feet realizing that the blue and red lights he was seeing were police.

He had to get away, but where? In the distance was a stand of trees...it seemed so far away but it was the only place for him to run. So in a stumbling run he ran ten feet and fell onto his face... got up and ran twenty feet...crashed again...he kept going until he made it to the grass where he crawled...and crawled reaching the trees just as the first police car reached the hangar. Unable to stand...he leaned against the tree and watched through a gap in the grass as no less than 20 police and military vehicles pulled up outside the hanger.

A speaker, strangely distant...said something...in Danish... English...and finally in German. "Werner Meyer, come out with your hands up...you will not be harmed... come out with your hands where we can see them."

Meyer managed a weak smile before falling into a drug induced state of semi-consciousness. Somewhere in his mind he remembered he had a gun, but where was it? Then he remembered…and found it… but his fingers wouldn't work and the gun wouldn't come loose of its holster. "Shit" he mumbled as his body went limp. He leaned against the tree his body tingling as if it were numb. His eyes remained opened and staring at the flashing lights which had the effect of hypnotizing him.

Darkness fell as the drug took him again. Waking some time later lying on his back he noted the stars blinking through the branches of the tree he was lying under.   took him a moment to remember where he was and another moment to remember that he had to be quiet but he wasn't quite able to grasp the reason why. Flashing lights reminded him.

In the distance flashing red and blue lights were far less numerous but enough to suggest a heavy police presence. Sitting up again he found he had more control and could see more clearly in spite of the drug. Standing was not an option even if he could and walking was even less of an option. Staring at the men buzzing around his plane he found that he was able to think more clearly. Little by little his brain became less fuzzy and began to realize that Karl and the crew had left him. Only he was too high to care. Yet, he was cognizant enough to recognize the danger he was in, so he fought the urge to laugh out loud.

He had run what he believed was a hundred meters to the trees. With the drug wearing off he began to realize that he had run less than 100 feet. He was so close to the action he could hear the conversation of the police chief and his supervisor discussing what they would do with the 50 million euros they found on the plane. It was clear that they had not shared this with anyone else due to the fact that they were whispering by the car they had both arrived in. That and the fact that they were each calling a Swiss Bank and discussing methods of deposit. It was more than clear they intended to keep it for themselves.

Meyer, had he been able to move could have easily dispatched them both and taken their car. What the two men didn't know was that what they found was merely a quarter of the cash on board. Money they had stashed in compartments in the event they needed to conduct business or bribe an official. But that is not what had Werner's attention now. He was working out how to get away. The drug was wearing off little by little and it seemed he was able to move with more control by the minute, if he concentrated. Stealing a police car was not the way. It would be too obvious and he would be too easily spotted once it was discovered missing. That and police have trackers on their cars so they wouldn't have to follow him to catch him they could just follow him via satellite and arrest him at his destination.

Remaining still was both risky and his safest option. It was risky in the fact that they could easily stumble onto his location while he was still too disoriented to fight back. It was also his safest option due to that moving through the grass would make noise and attract attention. So he remained where he was, listening to the two senior police officials make plans to abscond with his money.

Meanwhile, Karl had already pulled his GMC onto a ferry scheduled to depart at 6am the next day. He'd sent the other vehicles to the next ferry stop. It was imperative that they separate. Karl already suspected that they each had their own plans. But that was of little concern to him. He had already booked a flight from Sweden to Spain. Rolf had booked a flight to Portugal and the rest could fend for them-selves. Once secured in his cabin Karl took out the phone he'd stolen from his boss and started scanning the contacts list for the Trio and Patrice. He needed to warn them of Meyers plans to kill Patrice. Something he was certain they already knew but he wanted to fill them in on the developments and to give them a heads up. Once that was done he could, in clear conscience, re-tire from criminal enterprise. Once the phone call was done Karl chucked the phone into the North Sea.

Chapter 51
A Friendly Warning

TORRENTIAL RAIN POUNDED the roof and glass of the observation tower as Patrice stared at her phone not daring to believe what she was seeing. Werner Meyer was calling her. She was not concerned about being traced because her phone was untraceable. Still she hesitated to answer not quite sure she was up to hearing his voice. What attraction she'd had for the man was long gone. In place of it was a deep loathing and an even deeper shame for allowing such a vile man to ever touch her. That she had wanted him in any capacity disgusted her to the point of nausea.

If anything her attraction to Meyer had been shallow, base desire that was short lived and now, thankfully, out of her system. Yet the shame of that 'indulgence' lingered in the form of gut wrenching nausea as she debated whether or not to answer his call. Curiosity and the need to know what this man was up to forced her to 'suck it up' as 'T' would have termed it and answer, "Yes?" came an overly confident voice that did not belong to her but to some other person immune to the dread stirring in her heart. Bracing herself against the fear she felt Patrice prepared to hear the voice of the man who wanted her dead and who had actually contracted a crew to do it.

They had missed thanks to Archie's preparedness. Had it not been for Archie and his well-executed escape plan she, Lisa and likely her crew would have been lying alongside Archie, Hans and Rick on a slab in a morgue somewhere. Thanks to Archie she was alive as was everyone else. Yet, the fact remained she was about to converse with the man who tried kill her. What could he possibly want? The answer was obviously the gold but she didn't know where it was and even if she did telling him the location was an instant death sentence. Then again, not telling him would have the same result.

"Miss Verga? This is Karl, Meyer's security chief or rather former security chief, being that I have just abandoned Meyer to his fate at the hands of Danish police.' Patrice sighed in relief realizing that it was not Meyer on the phone, but one of the few people she actually liked inside the organization a man she knew only as Karl, a security specialist assigned to protect Meyer. But before she could respond he proceeded to speak urgently causing Patrice to focus and listen more closely. 'Look, I can't trust this phone safe and I haven't much time…I need you to listen' he paused to gather his thoughts. 'The FBI is on our tail and has been since we arrived in Florida, I think. We also have the fucking Israelis on our tail. Don't ask me when that happened, Meyer' he gasped in frustrated anger 'the asshole has been leaving bodies in his wake from Miami to Halifax. The man is out of control.' Patrice could hear the frustration in his voice but said nothing 'He put the word out on you. He believes you know where the bullion is and he means to find you and beat it out of you… then…I believe you already know this…but he means to kill you… slowly. As I said the man is out of control.' he paused 'I don't know if this means anything…coming from me…but I would rather he not hurt you…Patrice."

That Meyer meant to kill her was old news to Patrice and realizing that this was a 'friendly' warning from one of her former colleagues so she began to relax, but knew better than to let her guard down completely. She had herself used this very tactic to gain a mark's trust many times. That and showing a bit of cleavage with the occasional full service blowjob didn't hurt. Both had proved exceptionally powerful weapons in her business dealings. "Thank you Karl.' she said 'It means a lot to me that you would take the time to call me like this. I appreciate that, I really do.' She said 'Being that Meyer has already attempted to kill me, rather hired it done, of course they missed, but his intentions were more than clear."

Karl had been in the room when Meyer made that call. "Yeah…I was there. Believe me I wish I could have warned you sooner Patrice.' A gasp of frustrated anger exploded from speaker of Patrice phone 'Since he took power, he has insisted I address him as 'Fuhrer'. Can you believe that?!! I know the old guys back home are Nazis or were…but to play 'Nazis' with this fucking lunatic….' He paused to compose himself. Patrice could hear an audible sigh from his end 'The power has gone to his head and somehow he believes he is going to be the next Adolf Hitler' another pause and he continued 'The man is out of his fucking mind. I couldn't tell him anything without his drawing that goddamned stiletto and threatening me with it. My calling is to let you know what he is up to so you are put on your guard and to hopefully make amends for my part in this. We both would do well to fall off the grid until he is caught or killed.' again he paused 'I'm afraid the world isn't safe for either of us until he is dead" He said this last sentence as if coming to that conclusion himself.

Patrice heart jumped into her throat "I thought you said he was at the mercy of Danish Police" her voice was now quaking nervously.

"Yes, I left him tied up on the plane in the hanger and over dosed on some surgical anesthetic hopefully a lethal dose, but I do not believe for a moment that he will remain in custody for long; that is if he survives the drug and the police don't kill him. I was going to put a bullet in him myself only…only I didn't want to get that close to him again. I've never worked for anyone as out of control dangerous as this lunatic…ever. Believe me I've worked for some vile scum in the past but this guy, he takes the cake. So I took his phone because he has all our contacts in it and I'm calling the people I like and warning them to get out while they can. This whole thing is going to go south in a hurry…and I do not want to be anywhere near this guy when it does.

As for you I wanted to both give you a heads up and to apologize for the part I played in hurting you. We all thought you were to be the next Operation Chief and I for one think you would have done well. I'm sorry it didn't work out' he sighed then said 'so we've been talking long enough…I'm going to pitch this phone into the drink once I hang up. Good luck and watch your back. I'm going into hiding and it isn't likely we shall meet again. Have a good life, good bye." and the phone went dead.

Patrice stared into the phone not sure what to think of Karl's message. He could have just let it be but he had chosen to give her the heads up and let her know what Werner had planned for her. Old news of course, but to have Werner's security chief call to warn her indicated more than mere defection, it spoke of a monumental collapse of the Operation infrastructure from the top down suggesting that her visit to the Israeli consulate in London was bearing fruit.

What was more was that Karl had informed her that Meyer was currently tied up on an airplane on an airstrip in Northern Denmark and possibly overdosed on surgical anesthetic medication. But his arrest and possible death was too much to hope for. He was a psychopath and not stupid. "Funny' she thought 'how psychopaths are seldom stupid." As a result of this understanding Patrice wouldn't be counting her chickens until she knew Werner Meyer was truly dead, not arrested, not imprisoned, but dead; then and only then would she or anyone in her life be safe.

Patrice emotions were a mixture of relief and dread. Relief came in the knowledge that the end of the Operation was near. With that Meyer would have a more difficult time locating her, if he ever came looking. If he was alive, she knew he would keep coming and coming and coming, hence her dread. Werner Meyer was the most dangerous man she knew. If he somehow survived her life would be spent looking over her shoulder and that was not a live she wanted to live.

What damage she had done by placing The Operation in positions of influence and power among the NATO nations was now effectively undone, or soon would be. In that she took a measure of solace, that and the fact that she would be paid handsomely for her contribution to that end, a profitable cleansing of her conscience, "A nice fat profit" she said under her breath and smiled to herself. You could never have too much money.

Putting her phone on the table Patrice stared out into the tempest raging outside. Sheets of water cascaded down the glass obscuring her view of the frothy Irish Sea, a perfect mirror of her own internal storm. She loved nature's fury; something about it calmed her. Storms were frequent on the island. It was for this reason she chose to move to the Isle of Man and one of the reasons she chose a house on the top of a mountain where the winds blew constantly year round. The more savage the storm the more soothing it was for her. While torrential rain, wind and thunder combined to sooth her, it also energized her spirit.

Patrice had come out to the turret to watch the storm and think. She had not intended to bring her phone but had merely forgotten to leave it. However, not wanting to be disturbed again she picked it up and turned it off. She then tossed it unceremoniously onto the table before taking a seat on the couch from where she could watch the storm. Only her conversation with Karl lingered and drew her thoughts to Werner Meyer, the last person she wanted to think about but neither could she ignore him or the danger he represented.

Something deep within told her that he would find a way to escape, if only to come for her. There was no immediate threat, not yet. But if he survived and wasn't arrested he would locate her given time. As well as she might have covered her tracks there were ways of locating people who didn't want to be found, the very reason she had first hired the Trio. They specialized in locating those who did not wish to be found, then of course making them disappear permanently. She reminded herself to speak to 'T' about it when next they met. She would have them double check her efforts to remain 'hidden', and make corrections where necessary. Even then she realized that such action wouldn't be nearly enough to put Meyer off forever.

Even if the Operation ceased to exist Meyer was resourceful and would find ways of putting the elements of the Operation back together. Nazis she realized were vile, villainous scum but dedicated to their disgusting cause. Shaking her head she let shame fill her heart. They had paid her well and she had done a good job for them. Only to get betrayed when she discovered their true identity. The shame she felt came from her own willingness to ignore what she knew and had even planned to take over as head of the Operation. Granted she wouldn't have used her power and influence for anything but making money, the idea that she had positioned the Operation so that it could influence world policy sickened her, rather what they could have done with that influence sickened her, but she had done it so that when she took over the job would be that much more profitable...and only profitable. Yet she had been so childishly naïve about the whole affair that she felt stupid and incompetent. Hindsight has a way of making everything so irritatingly obvious that it seems foolish to not have seen it 'before' it all went to shit. This thought caused her to ball her hand into a fist and pound the back of the couch unconsciously in self admonition. Frustration mounted as did her shame and sense of guilt which seemed to pile one incident on the next feeding the storm of emotions raging inside her soul.

Though bringing them down was her way of making amends for her part in causing this problem, her recently developed conscience could not reconcile the fact that she had once been willing to keep working for them in spite of what she knew. Guilt twisted her guts into squirming knots so that she could no longer remain seated. Painful spasms jolted her followed by waves of nausea combined to force her out of her seat and begin pacing to ease the mounting discomfort. Guilt, shame and profound gut wrenching remorse tore at her so badly that she, after pacing for what seemed like hours, she fell to her knees next to the couch and sobbed bitterly into a pillow. Her soul was expelling all the shame she felt as well as the guilt, anger and overwhelming remorse for being so selfish and stupid.

Time stood still as Patrice grief erupted from her soul. What tears she had bottled up over the years came in a flood of regrets and mistakes. Mistakes she'd made that resulted in the deaths of innocent men, women and children, the youngest being six months old, all for the sake of a paycheck. She might have been able reconcile her actions had there been a component in which world peace were achieved or some other fairy tale scenario. No, she had acted for nothing more than a paycheck and the lives her mistakes had cost would never be justified. Her guilt ripped through her like a hot knife as the faces of the dead marched across her memory. So intense were the physical convulsions tearing at her insides she collapsed from the pain and blacked out.

From somewhere in the blackness of her unconscious she felt warm hands on her back and neck as a gentle voice called her name. At first she didn't recognize the voice. It seemed distant and far away. She couldn't tell if it was female or male just a foggy, distant voice... followed by soft kisses to her neck, ears and finally her lips. Slowly arms encircled her and held her in a cradling embrace as little by little she came to her senses. Coming to herself, Patrice found that she was still in the tower lying on the couch with Lisa embracing her back to front and stroking her hair. Lisa's eyes were filled with tears as she asked "Are you ok?" in a quaky voice when finally Patrice opened her eyes and her consciousness surfaced.

Attempting to lift her hand to grasp the one resting on her chest she found it immensely heavy. As heavy as her limbs felt her heart felt light as a feather with the stress she had been living under lifted. Subconscious doubts buried for the sake of doing the job where no longer weighing her down, her guilt lifted as once again Patrice discovered what living life could be like without the specter of death lurking behind each corner, alleyway or stop light. Apparently her speaking with Karl had unlocked that part of her subconscious. The portion that compartmentalized the guilt, shame and doubt, emotions not suited to operating an international crime syndicate. The damn had broken and all those feelings she had not wanted to face had come flooding out at once.

Her heavy limbs were not alarming to her. Somehow she knew that all she needed was rest. But she needed to let Lisa know she was ok and so made the effort to touch her hand and squeeze it, albeit weakly. The effort took most of the energy she had left and finally succeeded grasping Lisa's wrist. However words wouldn't form as she fell back to sleep in Lisa's embrace.

Waking the next day in the early morning she was now covered in a blanket with Lisa's arms still around her waist and shoulders. The storm was still in its full fury so she remained in Lisa's arms and listened as the rain drummed against the glass and the wind screamed its protest of having to whip around the tower. Distant rolls of thunder added their energy to the mix as well. They were the very sounds she had hoped to lose herself in. Now, however, her heart was light and airy, not constricted with fear, worry and anger. All those things she had buried while involved in criminal enterprise.

The realization that she would never have to engage in such behavior again served to lighten her heart even more. From then on she realized her actions...every single one of them...even her mistakes... would not result in the death of innocents. However, a new mission a new purpose had arisen in her, a righteous if not innocent purpose. To erase the corruption she had helped to foment in the world.

Granted she had not 'caused' the corruption she had, however, exploited it and manipulated it to her own ends. She knew who they were and how these people operated knowledge that would be used to address corruption and end it where she could. Patrice would avenge herself by taking on corruption...using her talents...and resources to make corruption costly to those who profited by it. It was lightning strike to her soul. All at once she had out of nowhere found an entirely new way of life, a life that would mean something in the end…a life to heal her soul and make the world a better place for good people to live. She smiled to herself as the idea formed in her mind and chuckled as she thought 'If you aren't a good person… life is going to suck' she smiled.

Patrice reveled in the raging storm outside as she unconsciously snuggled closer to Lisa whose arms encircled her a little more. Testing her one free arm she could move it freely again. With the emergence of her newfound purpose her energy had returned. Her heart was light and filled with contentment as she remembered one of Archie's pearls of wisdom "The Lord works in mysterious ways, darling. You may yet find a way to use those incredible talents you have to help people. Do not question your path…as long as you learn by it…and use the knowledge gained for good"

As she woke further she began to realize that she was nearly naked and the skirt she had been wearing prior to her collapse was now folded neatly on the chair next to the couch. What she had on… as far as she could tell was the blouse she had been wearing and her thong.

Looking around for the rest of her clothes she noted her lace brazier was among the items now hanging off the seat. Lisa had gone to some lengths in disrobing her. Sadly she had slept through it. 'I'd have enjoyed that' she thought. Smiling mischievously Patrice then unbuttoned several buttons on her blouse then moved Lisa's hand lying across her waist under the blouse and to her naked breast. It wasn't long before she felt a slight squeezing and gentle circular motion of Lisa's fingers over her nipple.

At first Lisa opened her fingers and slid Patrice nipple between them and slowly squeezed her fingers together sliding them over and around the hardening appendage. This was followed by a tender kiss to the back of her neck and kisses to her earlobe, down to her shoulder. Patrice responded by reaching her hand behind Lisa pulling her forward so that she could kiss her lips. Instantly their tongues were intertwined with Patrice sucking Lisa's tongue into her mouth like a tiny cock. This had the effect of driving Lisa wild and Patrice knew it. She loved Lisa so much that her newly found purpose and lightness of heart drove her to love this young woman even more intensely than she could have ever before imagined. Patrice 'wanted' her, she wanted this amazing young woman to love her…be with her…and do magical, naughty things to her…forever.

Never had she ever loved anyone so intensely. Yes she'd had incredible sex over the years…knew woman and men who could do amazing things to her body…but Lisa…as naïve as she had been…the day she seduced her on the plane…was a natural. It had been Lisa who had practically threw herself at Patrice even before she had made the first move.

Upon initiating her usual seduction, a touch here a touch there and a long stroking caress of the ass and thigh…Lisa had hiked up her skirt, which was already shorter than average…and straddled Patrice in her seat. Lisa then proceeded to unbutton her own blouse exposing the most beautiful set of breasts Patrice had ever seen, her bra and thong undies had been removed already, because Lisa had, upon seeing Patrice, decided she wanted her and took steps to ensure that she was completely accessible. From the moment Patrice tongue touched her breasts and her hands caressed her naked ass, Lisa knew that she was in for the ride of her life.

Falling in love was the last thing on her mind as Patrice literally tore her clothes from her body. Her uniform blouse was shredded by the aggressive lust to gain access to her body and her skirt was torn off, shredded in fact as Patrice ripped her skirt from her body. It was like living a dream as she was taken to the rear of the plane laid onto the leather settee where...for the first time in her life...she felt the experienced tongue of another woman drive her mad with pleasure 'never' before experienced. Fingers, tongue and an assortment of toys were used on her that first day. Next to Patrice...former lovers were left in the dust and utterly forgettable. Not only had she been turned upside down in the hands of an experienced lover...she had learned how to give pleasure...and had driven Patrice to heights of ecstasy she had seldom experienced. The fact she had a longer than average tongue didn't hurt and Patrice didn't seem to mind given that she had been brought to a screaming orgasm by its application. Their intensity had only increased since then.

However, on the Isle of Man as lightning and thunder crashed out-side...an inferno raged inside the tower with both women on fire. Lisa shifted herself to let Patrice fall onto her back so she could climb on top and straddle her like a horse, a favorite position for her when with a man. It was then Patrice noticed that Lisa had noth-ing on but her terry cloth robe now open in the front exposing her beautiful body to Patrice. "Oh baby, what a way to wake up" she whispered.

Lisa said nothing unbuttoning the rest of Patrice blouse and let it fall open. "I came to you last night' she swallowed 'and we found you on the couch crying but you weren't awake. Babe, it frightened me to see you like that" she said leaning in and stroking her face with one hand and cupping Patrice left breast with the other running her thumb over her sensitive nipple. Staring into each other's eyes they came together and gently kissed. Two naked bodies pressed together kissing passionately as thunder rolled across the grey morning sky.

On the opposite side of the tower 'J' lay on his bed wake watching the two women begin their morning love making session. Jay had been walking with Lisa when they found Patrice unconscious the night before and had spent the night on the couch opposite them at Lisa's request. He was now awakened by their conversation. Upon becoming fully aware of what was about to happen he was torn. Should he feign sleep and hope they didn't notice him or should he be noble and excuse himself and let them have at it?

Of course being a guy, he had a lascivious side, which he had already indulged to a degree using his infrared equipment, once on the island and several times in the house where he watched these same two women making love. Most often they were in the bedroom, sometimes in the shower, where the hot water usually distorted the image somewhat, but it wasn't enough to make him stop doing it. The best was in patio where their hot bodies contrasted perfectly against the cold air.

Neither of the women knew that he had been watching, as far as he knew...and it would be a cold day in hell before he ever admitted that fact to anyone. He liked his dick where it was and felt sure that if he ever let it slip that he had abused his technical expertise for the purpose of indulging his inner perv...Patrice would rip it from his body and feed it too him in pieces.

As it was he was supposed to be asleep and Lisa knew he was there. She had even suggested that he remain with them in case Patrice needed to be carried into the house. Had she forgotten he was there? Would they get upset if he got up and left or would they get upset because he didn't leave? 'J' had never been what would be called a ladies man and like many men found himself second and triple guessing his actions...a thousand times over in his head hoping and praying that the didn't somehow fuck it all up by being a clueless moron.

He spent the next half hour working out what to do while he watched two of the most beautiful women he had ever seen make love. By the looks of the beginnings of everything going on it was going to be getting seriously hot and heavy very soon. Oh and he wanted to stay and watch…but then he wanted to not die or lose his dick in the bargain. Closing his eyes…he decided to tough it out…and pretend to sleep and play it by ear.

Lisa had even asked for his assistance in undressing Patrice and then moving her to the couch. Lisa had done most of the disrobing. He had simply held Patrice up while she did so. Still he got quite an eyeful. Not only this but he was made painfully aware of Lisa's intentions by the fact that she had been carrying, quite in the open, a strap-on belt with the 'device' to be used in the inner pocket of her robe which she hadn't bothered to hide. He swallowed at the size of the thing wondering if he ever got busy with Patrice…if 'he' would be enough. He buried his thoughts in the ledger and swallowed and made as if he had not seen it.

Lisa knew what he had seen what she was carrying and smirked. She had deliberately not hidden what she was carrying because she wanted to see of Patrice would want to include 'J' in their playtime. Lisa, thought he was cute and hoped that Patrice wouldn't object to his 'watching', which she knew full well would lead to Patrice inviting him to join them, which she sincerely hoped she would because Lisa missed the warmth of a man. Though she loved Patrice and loved all the things she did to her…and was truly in love with her heart and soul… there was something that could never replace the warm, pulsing flesh of a man between her legs. So she allowed 'J' to see what she was carrying to tease him.

His stuttering speech and the sweat that was forming on his brow were indications that he had indeed seen the toy she meant to use on Patrice sticking out of her pocket. There was no doubt in her mind that he had over the past few weeks seen if not heard them in the throes of passion late at night. The fact that his room was across the hall from theirs made that a near certainty, that and the rooms were anything but sound proof. She was keen to let him watch as she seduced Patrice but that was all pushed aside when they both found Patrice laying half on and half off the couch sobbing not quite conscious and clearly in some form of emotional distress.

'J' had immediately recognized it as PTSD something that happens to a person who has been in combat for too long and has seen too much violence and death. War is the most stressful endeavor man has yet to invent and he like many had seen too much of it. Though not combat related Patrice was no less at risk for PTSD-like stresses due to the fact that if she slacked off her normal caution and restraint for a second she could easily find herself murdered in a field somewhere by the very people she did business with.

Being in survival mode for years on end and with the knowledge that death was the only way out takes a toll, no matter how tough you may pretend to be. As it was Lisa asked 'J' to stay, but not for the original purpose she had first intended. She was frightened and needed somebody there as back up. Seeing Patrice crying and unconscious frightened her and she did not want to be left alone with Patrice if something more serious happened. 'J' took a seat on an over-stuffed sofa across from where Patrice lay crying in Lisa's arms.

It had been 'J' who had covered the two women up late in the evening when the storm grew more intense and the wind robbed the cold stone turret of what little heat it had. He then threw a log into the stove but it did little to counter the cold because the coals had burned down too far. It would be nearly an hour before the stove threw off enough heat to counter the dropping temperatures outside but until then a blanket would suffice. Luckily there were enough to do the job.

As the gray dawn broke and the two women across from him began to stir he found himself in a quandary. Feign sleep and watch two of the hottest women in the western hemisphere fuck each other or be noble and leave them in privacy. Only the vision of Lisa burying her head between Patrice thighs…glued him to the spot as he stopped breathing. That and walking out now would be hard to do without embarrassing himself. You see, he was sporting an erection that would be hard to hide letting them both know that he had seen what was happening…and was aroused by it.

Whether he left now or later either way the women would know he was turned on. Few things are more embarrassing for man than to try to walk while sporting an erection while trying to be nonchalant in the presence of two very busy women. So he stayed as long as he dared and hope…that he could get away unnoticed.

Unlike women, men couldn't hide the fact they were aroused, especially if they were sporting a 'stiffy', an affliction that couldn't be explained away with a 'cool' breeze or be covered up with a shall. Men had to either wait it out…or visualize his 3rd grade teacher naked to make it fade away, which didn't really work all that well if your third grade teacher was hot. Then you had to resort to thinking of the nun-in high school whose method of 'correction' for sinful behavior was to smack an obvious erection hiding behind the jeans of an amorous male teenager with an oak yard stick. The trouble with that was 'J' had actually liked it, because it was the only attention he got from a woman.

However, when things had progressed to the point where he could not fake sleep even if he wanted to...as both women were now screeching so that not even a banshee could have out-paced their cries. It was during a lull in their activities that he got up as quietly as he could and started for the stair leading to the walkway connected to the house. He didn't want to seem too lecherous by intruding on their intimacy uninvited. But just as he reached the door Lisa spoke up. "'J' darling...you don't have to go...you can stay...we would love your company. Besides I need you to help me put this on." In her hand was the strap-on belt attached to which was the 'device' that he had spied inside her robe the night before. From that angle it didn't look all that imposing however, the situation was all the more awkward.

Rendered utterly speechless he stumbled, not necessarily walked, toward the two now fully naked women. Lisa tried not to laugh at the expression on his face as she turned her back to him and said "I really need you to make sure it's tight, because I'm going to use it on Patrice. It can't be loose...and I never get it tight enough to really give her a good fuck, you see she likes it hard and fast on occasion."

'J's jaw, had it not been attached, would have dropped clean off his face. Patrice struggled to keep her laughter contained from the look of utter bewilderment and shock he expressed and the 'matter of fact' tone Lisa had taken to describe what she was about to do with the strap-on. So she grabbed a pillow and moaned into it...or laughed so it sounded like a moan mostly to keep from embarrassing 'J'. He was sporting an erection that would have chipped the Rock of Gibraltar.

What made it worse…if 'worse' was a word for it…was the fact that while he was tightening the straps for Lisa…she bent forward…just enough to rub her ass against his arousal…more than once…while she looked right into his eyes. Then while she stared into his eyes she spoke to Patrice. "Honey…'J' seems to be in some distress. Do you think you could help him out?"

Patrice looked down at the tent now clearly visible to her gaze and said "Oh you poor dear…come here to me so we can have a better look at this problem." Once in reach she reached into the split in the front, hooked her fingers inside and tore his boxers open exposing his shaft, she then wrapped her hand around it and with the other took his hand looking into his eyes. Patrice once again recognized the passion 'J' had for her, or was it more? He was very handsome she thought and…he has such a nice cock. Looking at Lisa who was smiling at her "May I help him out honey…he is certainly in distress. We are definitely going to have to fix this, because I'm certain that we caused it" she said. Looking into his eyes she put her mouth over the end of his now painfully swollen member and slowly and expertly began to address his need.

Lisa who loved Patrice more than anything understood that she liked the attentions of men on occasion and had long since reconciled that fact. Knowing that Patrice would on occasion indulge herself, as she knew she would herself. Looking at 'J' Lisa said "I hope you won't mind sharing that with me…to" she said. As he did Patrice moaned her approval as Lisa now kneeling between her legs…raised her ankles to her shoulders then buried the full length of the strap-on into Patrice who moaned her pleasure around the appendage in her mouth.

'J' looked at the two of them in turn and said "I'll do whatever you want…I am your man' he said then looked at Patrice he said with even greater passion 'I'm yours as well…for as long as you want me… which' he paused to enjoy her mouth 'I hope is forever". Patrice, looked into his eyes and saw, not only passion and lust…but a deep and enduring love. Looking down at Lisa who was staring intently into her eyes she showed the same deeply intense love for her as she ground the device more deeply still. Tears clouded her vision as she let her emotions burst forth feeling lucky to be alive.

Outside nothing could be heard but the wind whipping around the turret and the rain pouring down save for the occasional cry of im-passioned bliss by Patrice who was to be the center of attention for the next few hours, a woman loved by two people. The end of the day would find them all in the Grand bedroom in the middle of the king sized bed with 'J' the center of attention and Lisa straddling him fully impaled on his manhood and Patrice riding his face kiss-ing Lisa, what he would call the love triangle. 'J' did himself proud by keeping up with both women's need far better than any other man could have. Yet, he did find himself having to rest while the ladies got busy without him from time to time, the sight of which got him going again and again.

The next morning 'J' woke with both women lying in the crook of each arm with each of them holding hands over him. Smiling to himself he smiled to himself and thought "So this is what heaven is like…I could get used to this" and pulled both of 'his' women to him, "This could get interesting" and fell back to sleep…content as never before.

Chapter 53
Home Coming

BOTH RICK AND Greg landed at San Francisco International airport just as the afternoon fog was rolling in. Not having checked any baggage and not having had anything to declare, except the $500,000 in X-ray proof compartments they passed through customs quickly. Greg wasn't far behind. Neither was in condition to drive. Rick had a four hour drive and Greg nearly eight. So they booked a room at the Airport Hilton to rest and take stock of their situation.

Neither man spoke as they headed to the room, not because of any enmity between them but of exhaustion. A lot had happened over the past several weeks and each man had a lot to think about but not the energy. All they could think about was the pillow on which to lay their heads…and rest. Only Rick, once his head hit the pillow, couldn't fall to sleep because of the storm of emotions, thoughts and doubts that flooded his consciousness in that instant.

Agitated and irritated and not having the energy to do anything but lay there he let the events of past weeks' storm through his mind. So much had happened in such a short time that everything seemed a blur one event into the next and so on.

He could not believe that he was now 'the' wealthiest man on the planet when only a few weeks before he was struggling to buy groceries and pay rent. However, his current wealth came with the burden of a deadly secret, a secret that would put his family in danger, *if* he weren't careful. Excited by his newfound wealth he was also frightened by it. It had dawned on him that he had to learn how to live quietly and keep his wealth from public view and resist the urge to spend it like a starving man would eat.

Such restraint was necessary not only to keep his family safe but to keep the vultures at bay. Such people tended to feed on those who have suddenly become wealthy, such as young NFL players and athletes who suddenly find themselves very wealthy and in need of management. Vultures prey on unsuspecting and innocent people stealing hundreds of millions from them in the form of 'fees' and small print traps that too often leave these same people working at Walmart and eating Top Ramen in their middle age, when they should be enjoying the fruits of their talents. Rick wasn't about to find himself caught in any such trap.

If he had learned anything in his dealings with people it was to keep his trust to a bare minimum. Knowledge he had acquired by being ignorant and far too trusting of a smiling face only to get robbed and cheated by those smiling, friendly faces. Experiences that left his ego bruised and himself far, far wiser, such that no con artist would get the bulge on him ever again.

Then there was Greg to assist in this effort. He was a lawyer after all, whose entire business was to help his clients avoid dubious and parasitic entanglements. Most often it was for the benefit of the client whose dubious past needed to be kept from the limelight of public scrutiny especially that of law enforcement. There was also the sharing of a deadly secret not to mention the love of the same woman…his wife. Both he and Greg were in love with her.

Greg had just recently learned of Laurie and Rick's arrangement to allow Laurie to keep seeing him. Strangely he 'Greg' was appalled at Rick's lack of jealously while being relieved at the same time. It was an issue he was struggling to make sense of. It was so much easier to sleep with another man's wife believing he was ignorant of the situation. How Rick had discovered the affair was explained on the flight home. The fact he had heard he and his wife in the act, over the phone was, to say the least, disconcerting. However, that knowledge, in no way, diminished his love for Laurie. What it did was make things complicated for him.

Rick on the other hand had long since accepted the affair as an adjunct to his marriage. Her taking a lover had in fact saved their marriage and made it more loving, if unconventional. Had he reacted as most men would have he would have put his family through a bitter divorce in which the kids would have been unwitting participants where hurt and confusion would have resulted. Then there would be the custody battles, a tug of war, which could last for years over who got the kids over which holiday and weekend, who got to take them on vacations and where, leaving their children scarred and unhappy.

Of course had he *not* learned of her affair and *not* accepted it he would *not* have taken the trip to St. Vincent and *not* met Archie or discover the base, the gold and the history behind it. In short had he not taken the very steps he had taken, unconventional though they were he would have remained in the same financial mess that had led his wife to take a lover. His life, which had been collapsing around him, would have continued to collapse and eventually lead to a physical collapse if not his death by heart attack or stroke. Had that happened it would have left his family destitute, a thought that added to the many other stresses he encountered, prior to all this happening.

Unconsciously he sighed and with it a strong release of tension followed but not enough to allow him to fall asleep. Archie was instantly front and center of his fatigue borne thoughts. Would he ever meet his benefactor again? How could he show his gratitude for changing his life? Yet, mere gratitude seemed inadequate for the massive change to his life's fortunes.

He had asked Archie this very question late one evening on the bridge of the Victoria on the approach to the Irish Sea. His answer was simple... "Just don't abuse it. Keep it from public view. Otherwise, use this wealth for the betterment of man and, not to make yourself look good. Charity and donations are best given anonymously. Ego is a toxic and poisonous motivation. One need only to look at Hitler as an example of such toxic egotism' he paused and put his hand on Ricks arm then continued 'You will be able to take care of your family now. Concentrate on them, live your life putting them first...and you my son...will be just fine."

That had been the last serious one on one talk he'd had with Archie. It was a good talk, short because Archie at the time was so tired from lack of sleep he was barely able to stand, but it was a good solid talk none the less. Hopefully it wouldn't be their last. He liked Archie and didn't want to see him die.

Han's on the other hand hadn't been nearly as talkative, no less pleasant but far more trigger happy, something he'd learned on their very first meeting via a near miss to his skull, when Han's had mistaken him for an Odessa operative and tried to kill him. However, they too had become friends and had some pleasant chatter, though fleeting as they had spent most of their one on one time monitoring the loading process of bullion onto the ship. The longest talk they'd had had been on the fantail of the Victoria as the loading process began in which Hans had expressed his regret for having shot at him and that he had come to like Rick quite well.

Those thoughts led to his thinking of the Trio during which Rick fell into a deep sleep only he didn't realize it for the dreams he had. Dreams in which a nameless foe was chasing him and bodies of his victims were everywhere he looked. Archie had been shot again... Patrice was panicked...but she decided to seduce him...then changed her mind...so Lisa seduced him...but she faded away into an angry version of Hans...the same Hans who had shot at him... only he didn't miss in the dream...which is where he woke...sitting bolt upright in the early morning hours drenched in a cold sweat.

Greg was out cold and snoring. Ricks bed sheets were drenched with sweat though the room was far from warm. It had been years since he'd had such dreams. Getting up he noted that there were puddles of sweat on the mattress and his bed clothes were literally soaking wet, as if he had just taken a bath in them. Looking at the clock on the counter it read 5:30am. They had gone to bed at 8pm the night before. Seldom had he ever slept so long, but the muscle aches he was experiencing suggested that his body had been working hard in his sleep.

Pulling out clean jeans and a sweat shirt, he rushed to the shower and rinsed the sweat from his body and placed his wet soaked clothes in a trash bag and put them in his duffle. As he got out of the shower Greg was talking on the phone. He recognized his wives voice on the other end though he couldn't make out what she was saying. It was only 6:00am an early hour for her. Her tone, however, didn't seem agitated or upset, so he didn't get worried. Greg was smiling and laughing while he talked to her and eventually disappeared into the bathroom to keep their conversation private. Eventually the shower came on and Greg climbed in. 20 minutes later he was walking out of the bathroom fully dressed, shaved and ready for whatever came.

Rick smirked at him and asked "So...how is my wife? She doesn't get up this early usually or did you call her?"

Greg smiled uncomfortably...shaking his head wondering how his world had become so surreal. The woman he loved was married. The man she was married to was his client, via contract with an old man who had him by the balls. He was joined at the hip with the two of them, one via contract and the other quite literally. "I called her,' he said as he splashed cologne on his face 'I told her I'd call her once I was stateside again. She doesn't know you're stateside, yet. So she asked if I could stop by on my way home.' He paused looking at Rick. 'I usually call on her when you are at work and the kids are at school." It was the first time he'd verbally admitted to Rick of the fact he was fucking his wife. Mostly he wanted to see how Rick would react to a direct admission.

Rick smiled, nodded "I figured. She told me before I left that you had come to the house a time or two. She didn't divulge what happened or where...'he paused curious about the where, if only to satisfy his curiosity 'but she suggested enough to make it interesting" he said.

Again Greg shook his head not knowing how to feel about this man's cavalier attitude about his wife sleeping with him, the *other* man. Once again the urge to pound Rick into the ground surged through him, for not putting his wife, the woman he loved on a pedestal. This was mixed with gratitude for that same attitude which allowed him to keep seeing the woman he had fallen in love with, Ricks wife. The incongruence of these conflicting emotions coupled with the early hour made him angry and it exploded from him as he beat a fist on the counter. "Why don't you love her?!!!" he hissed turning to face Rick who was now sitting on the bed looking out at the early morning fog of San Francisco.

Rick had sensed the anger surfacing in Greg moments before it exploded from him. Rick had seen it in his eyes ever since he had told Greg that he knew of their affair and was not bothered by it. As a result he wasn't surprised by the outburst. "I do love her, a great deal.' He said still looking out over the city. Not seeming to be vexed or nervous about his companion's anger. 'I didn't know how to feel at first. I was confused, angry and maybe even jealous though I will admit that quickly evaporated. Jealousy is too toxic for me to hold onto. It is an emotion that makes me sick and turns me into a thoughtless asshole.' he said 'Before I found out about you two, I did notice that she had been happier and more pleasant to be around. Of course I didn't think anything of it. When I learned of your affair, it dawned on me that she needed something I wasn't providing. That and I wasn't the nicest guy to live with either. Being broke didn't help the situation.' He said shaking his head not enjoying the taught sensation the memory created in his guts.

'Since she was happier and more pleasant to be around, I decided to let it be. When I booked this trip I let her know that she could invite you over while I was gone. That threw her for a loop. I then let her know what I knew and how I had come to know it. She, like you, didn't know what to make of it and got angry at my attitude regarding the matter, because, like you, she felt it was a sign that I didn't care about her anymore.

After we talked about it, I asked her if she would feel better if I forbade her from seeing you. She did not hesitate to answer me with an emphatic *no*. So, that being the case I asked of her to not hide it from me anymore and to keep it out of the kids view and to not run off with you. I'll ask the same of you, keep it quiet, don't hide it from me and don't let the kids see it."

Standing up he walked over to the dresser where Greg stood and leaned against it. "Greg, I love my wife, I really do. My letting her do this with you isn't a sign that I don't. On the contrary, she is very happy to have this freedom and is even more relaxed around me now that she doesn't have to hide it. In truth we are closer now than we have been in years. I love my wife enough to know that she needs this. I don't know how long you two will last, or if it will ever end. All I know is that Laurie is happier now than she has been a long time and I want it to stay that way.' Pausing one last time he looked directly at Greg 'I don't want my wife growing to resent me.' Smiling at Greg, 'You have no idea how much of a dick I can be sometimes… she needs a break from me once in a while."

Greg let a smile surface remembering those exact words coming from Laurie just days before their relationship turned physical. She had been near tears as they had coffee at a Starbucks across from his office. She had arrived to confirm his availability for the inventory of her mother's home. She grasped his hand while looking nervously around for anyone who might have recognized her then turned to him saying "My husband can be such a dick sometimes…I feel as though I need a break from 'him" she looked up at him and squeezed his hand as a tear rolled down her cheek. 'I think you know where 'we' are heading, you and I, I mean. I'm afraid of what I so desperately want from you, so if you are of the same mind as I am…I want you to help me take that step…with you. I want you to let me know' she paused…choking down a sob of fear as she forced herself to face the reality of her desire for a man other than her husband 'that…that…' she wiped another tear from her eye 'you want me as much as I want you. So if this is going to happen…please…I need to know how you feel about it."

His response had been equally emotional though he had to keep the desire in his heart from exploding in the crowded coffee shop. "I feel the same way…truly.' He leaned in and whispered into her ear because he didn't want to be overheard 'You cannot possibly know how badly I want you…we have to be careful. We can't afford to be 'walked in on' in the middle of things. Such things might be hard to explain.' He said smiling. Cupping her face with his hand he whispered 'but yes…I want you…I want you…we can talk about this at your mothers tomorrow, ok?" He said this just as her mother came striding into the shop taking a seat next to them. That next Saturday…they dove headlong into their affair and never looked back.

Nodding his acceptance of Rick's explanation he relaxed having a better understanding of their relationship dynamic. "Ok, what now? She is expecting me to come by today. It would be kind of awkward if, one we arrive home on the same day and you call her while, er.. um..while we… are…well…you understand…right?' he grimaced 'You know that she suspects something is up…and it would make it doubly so if we show up on the west coast on the same day. I mean she picked up on our being in Scotland at the same time, our show-ing up on the same day…same flight even, might tip the whole thing off."

Rick laughed a mischievous laugh, "It would be even more awk-ward of I walked in on you two…with her head banging against the headboard and howling like a banshee like she does with you.' He smirked at Greg who blushed at his remark 'yeah, she makes a lot of noise when she is with you, from what I've heard anyway."

Greg was at a loss for words but managed a weak smile. "Well, I'll never tell." He said joking, finally allowing a good natured smile fully break onto his face. Then his face got serious briefly "So, what should I do? I can make an excuse and make other plans...or can you delay your arrival for a few hours. She seemed eager to...um 'talk'" he said.

Of course Rick knew what he meant by 'talk'. Laurie was hot for him and wanted his attention. "You go on ahead. I have to go to San Jose anyway. I want to look at buying a new truck. That should take a few hours anyway. Will that leave you enough time?" he asked.

Greg blushed then nodded. Looking up at Rick Greg got serious and said "We have to tell her about this arrangement soon. I don't like hiding it from her. She's going to figure it out eventually and if we don't come clean about this whole thing and soon, she is going to have our nuts for lunch. I don't know about you but I like mine where they are."

Rick laughed knowing too well that what he said was true. "Yeah, you are right we do have to tell her. Like you said our arriving on the west coast on the same day is going to raise suspicions.' Looking at Greg he moved over to the bed and sat down sipping on his coffee, grimacing from the foulness of it. 'Gahh...I hate hotel coffee...I never could get it right' he complained, shrugged then continued 'When should we tell her?" he asked.

Stepping over to where the coffee was Greg poured a cup for himself and nearly gagged on the foul concoction. "Yeah…you're right… this stuff sucks…bad' but he continued to drink it all the same. He then shook his head in answer to Ricks question 'I think the sooner the better, honestly. If we wait too long, well, you know how she got the last time…It will be worse next time. That and she should be made aware of the dangers involved. We can't allow her to go off half-cocked and make waves thinking she is the dupe in some 'guy' scheme, which is where she is going to go with it if we *don't* come clean."

Nodding his acknowledgement Rick didn't' say anything while he gave the cup in his hand a disgusted look, stood up and dumped it into the sink. "Ok…If we are going to bring her up to speed on this I think we should both do it, together. I won't be able to answer some of the questions you will and you won't be able to answer the questions I can. But what do we tell her and what do we keep from her? The full truth will frighten her and not telling her will piss her off.' Rick paused and gave Greg a hard look 'The location of the bullion has to be kept from her. That knowledge is too dangerous. That said, do we tell her of it at all?"

Following Rick's lead Greg also dumped his coffee down the drain, shaking his head thinking of what to say. "Laurie isn't stupid. She'll eventually figure it out once she discovers your property in Scotland. That fact alone, if we don't tell her of it, will only inflame her and cause her to act rashly. So, I think we should tell her the whole story. Explain to her why she cannot know of the location 'yet'. Explaining to her who is looking for it and why it has to be kept hidden,' looking at Rick he continued 'If we don't tell her she'll figure it out anyway. If we tell her why it is best it be kept hidden…she, I think, will understand."

Rick had his doubts but acknowledge that not telling Laurie the whole story could prove costly in the long run. She had to be made aware of the dangers of letting it slip even to close friends and family. Gold, especially immense quantities of Gold can cause the best of men and women to behave badly. She had to be made aware of the fact that if she reported it to the authorities…even if she was doing it out of a sense of decency, that the act itself would be like telling the Nazis directly. "Ok,' Rick said at last, 'We should tell her today then. But we should probably wait until after you two have had your ummm…meeting" He said trying not to smirk.

Once again Greg didn't know whether to admire Rick or slap him. Then he sat down and thought about it. "You know I love her right?' he looked away not wanting to see Rick's face, at least not for this conversation 'I get jealous of you because you are the one she spends her time with. I envy that. I cherish her in ways you do not appear to. So it makes me angry that you are so…so crass about my being with her. I mean I'm the one sleeping with your wife and I am the one upset that 'you', her husband, aren't upset about it!!' he stood up agitated his anger rising. 'I mean I feel fucking psychotic about the whole thing. Part of me is grateful for your understanding while another part of me wants to rip your face off because you don't respect her."

Nodding his understanding Rick once again took a seat on the bed, where he had explained himself on this matter only moments before. "Greg, this is a life style change, only. I love my wife more now than I did when we were sniping and ripping each other apart for the most inane stupidity. We'd argue about nothing, slam doors because I gave her a 'look' she didn't like or I said something in just the wrong tone or the other way around, what I was wearing, how I was wearing it or where I was wearing it. We'd argue about which kid was a bigger pain and so on. Dude, before she met you we were on our way to a fast and ugly divorce and custody battles over which weekend the kids could come over, where we could take them on vacation and so on. So when I found out about the two of you, I was shocked as I said earlier, but I had to weigh the 'where and what for' of my actions and reactions. It was my choice to let it be, because she and I were getting along so much better since she began seeing you.' Looking directly at Greg he smiled pleasantly and continued 'Since I confronted her about this, our sex life has been more interesting and more satisfying. In short, we like each other now, because you make her happy in ways I couldn't."

Greg, once again, smiled and sighed as he once again seemed to understand Rick's situation. "So you've agreed to a semi open relationship?"

Rick nodded "Yes, you might say that. Granted she dove in before we had formerly agreed to it. I offered her a 'hall pass' years ago but she seemed reluctant and distrustful of my intentions so didn't take me up on it, thinking that I wanted her to give me one in return. However, as you well know, she decided to pursue an affair with you after our relationship had degraded to the point where her contempt for me was obvious and we were fighting all the time over nothing. That is until she started seeing you regularly. Since then we've been getting along fine.

So I want you to stop getting upset with me for 'not' honoring my wife. Before this she was terribly unhappy, she loved me, but she couldn't stand me, so I swallowed my pride and did what I thought was best for our marriage. Also, just so you know, I long ago let go of my social expectations because of what I witnessed as a kid in my church.

All the stuff that I wasn't supposed to do because it was a sin was being done by the people telling me I shouldn't do it. To give you an example, the preacher's wife was banging a local banker, the banker's wife was banging the preacher and that was just the tip of the iceberg. Seeing that first hand opened my eyes to the hypocrisy of society and the people who tell us what we can and cannot do.

Also every woman I dated cheated on me at some point. It is possible I just got used to the idea so that when my wife did it, I wasn't all that surprised or upset. Yes, I was hurt at first but that didn't last all that long once she and I talked about it. I mean this hasn't been going on for very long and I am, even now, still coming to grips with it. So, stop getting your dander up when I make a joke about it. I know you are fucking my wife and I know that she likes it. Part of my coming to terms with it is my dry humor. It helps me cope.

This kind of thing has been going since civilization began. Wars have been waged, murders committed, hangings, stoning…and violence aplenty because one man desired the attention of another man's woman. I took an unconventional step to save my marriage and to keep the peace so that my kids wouldn't have to go through the ugliness of a divorce. As a result my wife is much happier, I'm much happier and she actually takes care of me better…because you have been taking care of her.

In all honesty Greg it sounds like you are having a hard time accepting the situation because of your own social expectations. So, Yes, I am married to the woman you love and having an affair with. Now that I know about it and have consented to it, it is no longer an affair but an agreement. It isn't cheating as long as I am in agreement with the situation. You seem to be more comfortable with my being ignorant of it. It's almost as if you think cheating is ok so long as the husband is totally oblivious to the goings on.

Of course, society at large might have a thing or twenty to say about it either way, which is why we are keeping it 'private'. So, I actually want you to keep seeing her if only to keep her happy. Have you ever heard the saying 'A happy wife makes a happy life'?' Greg couldn't help but smirk, having heard that very thing many times growing up from his own father as Rick continued on 'I expect that you will keep treating her well and not ever allow her to come to harm while she is in your care." Rick paused to take a breath and to organize his thoughts.

"I do love my wife Greg and I want to grow old with her. If that means growing old with you in the picture, well, I'm ok with that. It's not like we can be separated from the bigger picture anyway. With this secret we share…and soon with my wife…it's going to be a long haul and we might as well get used to that idea right now."

Greg couldn't help but laugh as the tension and anger he'd been feeling for the past few weeks lifted from him like a massive weight that had been holding him down. "Ok…I'll have to come to terms with it as well, but if you don't mind I have a two and a half hour drive to make. So if you leave San Jose around 10am that should give us plenty of time' he looked at Rick to once again gauge his reaction and again he seemed perfectly fine with his making open comments about being with his wife. 'This is going to take some getting used to. But I think I can manage it since I really don't want to stop seeing Laurie." He stood facing Rick finally able to look at him without the urge to throttle him understanding at last what made this man tick.

Rick chuckled at him and reached out his hand resisting the urge to make a flippant comment not wanting to risk raising Greg's ire again. "Drive safe. I'll call just before I leave San Jose. It usually takes me an hour and fifteen minute to get home from there. Make it an hour and a half." Greg packed his duffle and left five minutes later far happier and less confused than he had been in recent weeks eager to see the woman he loved and strangely excited about not having to hide it from her husband anymore. An hour and a half later Greg pulled up to Laurie's house having confirmed that she was alone. He broke every speed law imaginable to make it to her in less than two hours, including ditching three police cruisers.

They had talked continuously on the phone for the last hour of his trip hanging up as he pulled into the drive. Stepping through the door he was met with Laurie wearing nothing more than a men's button down dress shirt, the same one she'd worn that day in her mother's garage. Her face was flushed with excitement, excitement she'd not felt since their first time together.

She looked up at him. "Greg...darling...I have to tell you something...I want you to know that I love you...and I want to be with you always...and because I love you...I want...no...need to tell you something. Only I don't want it to affect how you feel about me... and I'm...I'm... afraid of what you will think."

Moving in closer he stroked her face, grabbed her wrist and pulled her to him. Tears were flowing from her eyes as sobs erupted. "Babe... Don't worry about me...I love you and have loved you since the first day you came into my office. Besides, I think I know what you want to tell me." He said. Laurie's mouth slackened in nervous apprehension not sure what he did or didn't know. "Your husband knows about us, doesn't he?" She nodded 'yes' and swallowed nervously.

He kissed her gently to allay her fears breaking the kiss gently to say "I'm guessing he is okay with this arrangement?" Again she nodded. "Interesting, I've heard of these kinds of arrangements before, never thought I'd be part of one." And he kissed her again.

After they broke off the kiss Laurie asked "What clued you in?"

He smiled and pulled her to him in a long overdue hug saying "A few things, but I don't want to go into that right now, if you don't mind." Laurie smiled warmly and grabbed him by the wrist and took him to the bedroom where she closed and locked the door.

The next three hours were spent making love in every conceivable position. It was the first time they were together with all parties involved fully aware of their relationship and agreeable. As a result their passion was full and clear with no guilt or shame in having to hide it anymore. The feeling was entirely different, freer and less inhibited…far less inhibited, evidence of which could be found in the torn shower curtain and the broken kitchen chair now piled in the garage as firewood.

Exhausted they finally collapsed onto the bed after showering together behind a duct tape repaired shower curtain and fell to sleep. Sheer exhaustion made it so that when Rick called from San Jose Greg and Laurie both slept through it. It wasn't until he was approaching the off ramp that his call was finally answered. Greg's phone awakened them both. He answered…smiled…looked at Laurie lovingly "Oh wow, yeah sorry about that, I didn't' hear the phone. Very well…I'll see you in a few minutes."

Laurie sleepily smiled at the man she loved along with her husband…thinking she was the luckiest woman alive asked "Who was that?"

Greg rolled over next to her smiled, kissed her "That...oh ...that was your husband...he will be here in five or ten minutes. We have a great deal to tell you...and we decided it was necessary to fill you in on the situation." He said this as he rolled over on top of her... pinning her wrists to the mattress as his hardness came to her attention. "I couldn't tell you because of Attorney/Client privilege and since I'm your mothers Attorney and not yours...there was no technical conflict of interest...being that there was no official arrangement between you and I...I couldn't recuse myself and not give myself away."

Both her desire and anger flared as she heard these words. Anger at having been lied to and a hopeless desire for the man holding her down, but the instant his warmth touch her... the anger dissipated...she melted and made passionate love to him...missionary... because that was the quickest and most efficient way to get what she wanted...at that moment.

All other thoughts ebbed into a blissful haze. Adding to the intensity of the moment ...mere minutes before her husband was to walk through the door; open as their arrangement might be...she wasn't sure if her husband would appreciate finding her in his arms much less in the throes of physical passion with another man. Then again...he had caught her...once on the phone, a second time on the island...but never...had he actually seen her in the act...physically engaged and impaled. That could prove awkward. Never the less the thought of her husband catching her, seeing her with Greg, though nerve racking, was exciting and drove her to explode in orgasm mere minutes into their exchange.

Rick pulled up to the house just as Laurie exploded in orgasm. He smiled recognizing that sound having heard it rather often recently and made his way to the front door. He hit the doorbell instead of using his key, giving them time to get dressed and meet him at the door. He didn't want things to get any more awkward than they were about to get. Having Laurie freshly fucked and somewhat worn out…might be just the ticket to keeping her temper in check. He also reminded himself that the four million dollars he'd sent would likely have had a similar effect.

In less than two minutes Laurie answered the door fully dressed and looking surprisingly fresh in spite of her recent activities. Her eyes brightened and she threw herself into his arms and kissed him as lovingly and sensually as she had never done before. Then she whispered in his ear "Greg just told me that you two have something to tell me…I knew something was up…I knew it' she said with feigned anger. 'He's sitting at the kitchen table."

Taking him by the hand she led him to the kitchen where Greg sat drinking coffee and smiling like the cat that ate the canary. The two men smiled, Greg Sheepishly and Rick fighting to restrain the urge to make a joke that had that only morning provoked Greg to anger. "Good afternoon." He said. Greg nodded back and sipped at his coffee and nodded as he blushed red.

Laurie, in rarely bold fashion took a seat on Greg's lap while looking directly into her husband's eyes. She wanted to see if he was truly 'ok' with her being openly intimate with Greg in front of him. Rick didn't react in a negative fashion, not even a twinge of jealousy presented, so far so good. Greg, seeing this finally accepted their arrangement and relaxed which resulted in his arm encircling Laurie's waist as his 'manhood' began once again to harden. Perhaps they could have one more session before he left.

Feeling his arousal under her she smiled and pressed herself harder onto him but then moved to take a seat next to him. Rick once again didn't react or seem to care about the obvious display playing out in front of him. His wife was testing her boundaries to see if he would react. So he responded with "Just make sure the kids aren't around when you do that...ok?"

Laurie smiled and scooted nearer to Greg "Ok hon...we'll be careful."

Taking a seat across the table he poured himself a coffee and began. "As you have suspected, Greg and I, both being in Scotland and on St. Vincent was no coincidence. However, your being on St. Vincent was due to his inviting you there not knowing 'I' was involved in the business he was hired to transact.' Pausing he sipped his coffee and then continued 'That business is the reason I was able to send you that package.' Laurie nodded but did not say anything remembering the four million dollars sitting in her closet. 'What we are about to share with you is very, very dangerous. Not telling you would be even more so because we both know how strong willed you are. We are going to both tell you 'some' but not all, because this knowledge is far too dangerous and the people involved are ruthless and well connected."

Laurie whose hand was stroking Greg's thigh under the table was stunned "Dangerous, how?"

Rick pushed his coffee aside and told her the whole story, from his meeting Archie to his discovering the underground base and the submarines therein, Hans and this association to Archie and his connection to the island and last but not least the gold that had been stashed on the island and their journey to Scotland and later Denmark. He left out very little except where Greg was needed to fill in the blanks Rick could not have known the details to. In short she was informed of every detail except the final location of the bullion and the amount of money it comprised.

They both left out the fact that Rick was now, on paper the tenth richest man on the planet. His actual wealth was not mentioned due to the fact that they still hadn't calculated all of it. What they had calculated, a mere fraction of the total made him 'the' wealthiest man on earth. She didn't' need to know that…not yet.

However, they did mention the inheritance and the property in Scotland which was the reason for Greg's initial involvement. Rick decided to brush over his association with Patrice and the Trio more because they were an integral part of the situation leaving out non-essential details such as his threesomes with Patrice and Lisa, not to mention those stolen moments on the bridge when Patrice screwed him so hard he was unable to stand without assistance. Something deep inside told him 'not' to mention that tidbit…for the potential shit storm it offered.

When they had finished explaining Laurie was neither angry nor upset, if anything she was excited and appeared to understand the need to keep things quiet. Instead she saw her role in the grand scheme as being a caretaker of a dangerous secret with the responsibility to keep it so. The fact that it made her wealthy was a nice bonus for sure and made the information she'd been told easier to swallow.

She certainly didn't want to risk losing the wealth that she was still getting acquainted with. "So you just fell into this by accident?" she asked her husband in bemused wonderment. The circumstances were just too surreal to be mere coincidence. Rick met Archie on the island just because he was curious about the 'church' and struck up a conversation with him, the very same man who had hired Greg, the man she was having an affair with, *years* earlier to create a legend that Rick, her husband, was to inherit. The details were far too disjointed and disconnected to have been anything but destiny.

An irrational fear surfaced temporarily, a fear that this was all a dream and that she would soon wake up in the same shitty mess she had been in before meeting Greg. Had it not been for their having an affair and her husband finding out, none of this would have been possible, such is the hand of fate.

Looking at the two men in her life, two men who loved her, she wondered how she got so lucky. One man, her husband, understood her enough to allow her the indulgence of another man. The other man, the man sitting next to her also loved and understood her, satisfying her in ways no man ever had before. All of these revelations, her now wealthy husband, her wealthy boyfriend the fact that she was no longer financially destitute and the excitement of being a trustee of a dangerous secret combined to overwhelm her.

Unconsciously her hand lifted from Greg's thigh as her mind wrapped itself around the massive changes to their lives. So much had changed in the last few days not to mention the last few minutes having just learned the story behind it all. Daunted, overwhelmed whichever word best suited the situation was nothing close to how she was feeling in that moment. No longer would she be concerned with living 'beyond' their means, but living well within and under the radar of public scrutiny, a much more desirable situation to be sure but also something of a disappointment.

There would be no flashy mansions or stupidly expensive cars and parties with other 'wealthy' elites. If what she had just been told was to be considered, 'they', the three of them sitting at that table were 'the' elite of the elite if money was the sole consideration in that equation. A very, very brief sense of regret rose and then passed as she realized...she didn't really have any want to be rubbing elbows with some of the 'elites' she had come to know. Those few she did know rather had become acquainted with were, very often, pretentious assholes. Not at all concerned with substantive issues beyond the mundane gossip of who was being shunned that day...and who was fucking the pool boy. Knowledge she neither enjoyed nor wanted due to the images created of plastic surgery scarred women shamelessly flaunting their artificial tits in the face of some barely legal teenager.

Other wealthy souls she knew and actually did like weren't all that different from her-self or the people she considered friends. They, drove nice though not overly nice cars, some drove old Chevys or Fords. One such gentleman drove a rickety Plymouth Horizon but lived in a very nice house overlooking an exclusive golf club, which he owned. Not only did he drive a crappy old car...he dressed like a homeless man most of the time. But she did catch him being fashionable on rare occasion.

This thought brought her back to her husband who, even on his best day, wouldn't have qualified as GQ material. He would have gone out every day wearing his sweat pants...or worse pajama bottoms while scratching his balls, belching and farting in public without so much a concern for his appearance, something she had long ago given up any hope of ever changing.

Then she considered Greg who knew how to dress, took care of his body and knew modern grooming habits expected of men and appeared to apply them to his daily life. No two men could have been more different but neither could she consider living without the two of them in her life, not anymore. How much her life changed in the past few months, weeks, days and in the last few moments was far too great to fathom.

Only days before she was worried about buying groceries…now she was concerned about being too conspicuous in her spending of what was a very considerable fortune. This was a problem she would have to get used to, the challenge of having too much money. Then there was the unique situation she had with the two men in her life. Now totally open she didn't have to hide anything from either of them. She was in love with both and was able to express it, openly.

Then in a sudden moment of assertion as if coming to some realization, she composed herself sat up straight, looked at the two of them while taking their hands into hers and placing them on the table in front of her. She looked into each of their faces, serious and firm as tears welled up and rolled down her cheeks. "That being said' she paused 'I want it clear that I love you both. I want you both to be friends so that our lives together will be peaceful and loving. This situation we share is our link' she turned to Greg 'I love you so much I don't ever want to live without you and I want to grow old with you' she turned to Rick 'and you Richard. I want to grow old with you and we will grow old together. I don't want jealousy to come between us."

She took a breath as if to keep a surge of emotions in check then continued "I want to be open and honest with the two of you always in the understanding that this is a fully open and sexual relationship.' Her eyes hardened and she shook her head looking at Rick 'Also, just in case you two get any ideas…I will not be in any threesomes with you…is that clear? So don't ask.' The two men laughed looking at each other knowing that they had both had that that very idea in mind at some point.

Laurie then smiled and looked at Greg, then at Rick 'Now, if you are both in agreement, I want to finish what Greg and I had started before you came home.' She looked at Rick 'If you weren't aware, we were busy when you arrived and unfortunately Greg never got to… well…finish. I would like to take care of that detail. Do you have a problem with that dear?" she asked looking at Rick. He looked at his wife as she, for the first time, asked if she could take another man into their bed, while he was still in the house. His brain wasn't registering the full context of her meaning due mostly to the fact that he was still very tired from both jet lag and the highly emotional nature of his recent adventures.

It took a few seconds to get her 'meaning' in spite of her being clear on what she intended to do with Greg. Once her meaning dawned on him he started with the jolt and shook his head to indicate that he didn't have a problem with it and swallowed nervously. He had no problem with her doing this while he was elsewhere. He'd heard then both in the throes passion over the phone and another time outside the bungalow on St. Vincent though he had not realized it was his wife at the time. That was mostly because she rarely had made any such noise in the time he'd known her, with him anyway.

Her pointed question, directed at her husband had been a test to gauge his reaction. She knew very well that jealousy was a monster not easily contained. So she decided to test the waters by direct confrontation. Laurie was pleased to see her husband, though taken aback by the direct question, did not show any signs of jealousy or lingering doubt. "Good, you can either stay in the living room or you can go for a drive.' With a stern look and said 'you may not watch either."

They looked at each other and smiled. In her eyes was pure love for the man she married with an added heat that he loved to see burning in her soul. She was happy and that was enough for him. Sending Greg into the bedroom she stepped over to her husband wrapped her arms around his neck whispering "I love you Richard. Not many men would let their wives do something like this. I know it is because you love me and want me to be happy that you have allowed me this freedom. I'm so lucky to have you as my husband…I truly am.' She looked at him finally and recognized just how tired he was and said as a concerned wife 'Maybe you shouldn't be driving. Why don't you just take a nap on the couch here?' she padded the couch laying him down then covering her husband with a blanket. She kissed him and whispered into his ear 'I'll keep it quiet ok?" she said looking into his eyes…with the most honest love they had shared since they'd first met. She then disappeared into the room where Greg was waiting as Rick, fell instantly asleep.

Chapter 53

Revenge

WHILE RICK AND Greg were over the Atlantic and headed for home Rabbi Weiss was circling around the airport where Meyer's jet had landed. From high above the fray he could see the multiple lights of police and Danish military vehicles approaching his quarry. Bitter disappointment, anger and frustration all surfaced at once, followed by a mild sense of relief. With any luck the mad man he was chasing would resist arrest and get shot and that would be the end of that. Only he knew better. This man, the man he saw from the boat, was a coward. He would not make a stand against authorities, not this one. He would try to escape and hide then re-emerge someplace far away like the snake he was.

In the weeks he'd been pursuing this man a profile had emerged via FBI and Israeli intelligence. Both had concluded that he was smart, above the average insofar as IQ was concerned, with a decided lack of problem solving ability a fact that contradicted his functional intellect. His problem solving method was killing the person who created a problem for him or killing the messenger. His weapon of choice was a stiletto which he used slash throats or to pierce the heart. A method apparently adopted from a book he'd read about a German Spy in WWII, whose weapon of choice was a stiletto. This led profilers to determine that he lacked imagination or creativity and so copied the fictional character in his favorite book.

His psychological profile from prison indicated he had a neuro-chemical imbalance in which orgasmic release created homicidal tendencies directed at the women he was attracted to and physically engaged with culminating in a brutal murder of the woman, most often during sex. As far as the Rabbi was concerned this man was the devils' own, a demon from the pit of hell itself.

Reading the report in his lap over and over in the hope of glean-ing some further insight into the man he was chasing. The Rabbi couldn't help but feel that Meyers IQ was nothing more than book smarts and not necessarily functional. Functional Intellect requires that one have problem solving skills that do not require killing ev-eryone in arms reach.

He'd known too many people with genius IQs who lacked the most rudimentary social skills, skills necessary for basic social interactions like grocery shopping and buying new clothes and shoes or ask-ing directions. These people tended to be the type of 'genius' who worked the night shift at 7-Eleven or the night watchman at some department store where interpersonal interaction was kept to a bare minimum. Essentially people who preferred to go through life un-noticed, content to be in the shadows out of fear of their own shad-ow sneaking up on them. Meyer was somewhat socially functional, but could not manage basic challenges without resorting to violence.

The fact that the FBI placed is IQ at near genius where the Israelis were far less generous and placed him at just above normal intel-lect gave him pause. He had no liking of the FBI as those he had dealt with in the past were very often self-indulgent assholes with marginal IQs themselves and therefore not qualified, in his opinion, to determine the state of anyone else's intellect, but keen to whip out the badge and strut around as if they were God almighty. However, agent Peel seemed competent enough and decided to take the FBI assessment into consideration if only to be thorough in his own assessment of Werner Meyer.

Joshua Peel didn't strike the Rabbi as a typical FBI agent, that and he was surprisingly willing to let his men do what they needed to, provided they didn't make another conspicuous display as they had in Halifax. Dead bodies and machine gun fire on a hotel dock is hard to explain and tends to generate unnecessary complications in the form of news reporters speculating on 'terrorist attacks' or 'out of control gang violence' on the he evening news. These developments then manifest into visits by asshole politicians expressing their anal glands for the cameras in a show of theatric outrage to show the voter they have a handle on the situation when in reality they haven't a clue.

Shaking his head and murmured "American Politics" under his breath. Normally he wouldn't care whether or not his action caused anyone a problem, but he was the friend of his neighbor and seemed to be a decent sort of fellow. So he decided to make his best effort to make Peels job less complicated if possible, short of letting the man escape...or live.

Apparently the Israelis engagement of the Operations men on both the ship and on shore had complicated Peels efforts to observe and follow the Operation in order to ascertain the scope of their alleged influence on the US Congress, British Parliament and other NATO nations. Once bullets had flown Peels control of the situation ceased to exist forcing him to resort to damage control measures to keep his mission on point, if possible.

It had been difficult enough holding the RCMP back once they realized the people they were watching were Nazis albeit a latter day version. The Canadians weren't keen on letting such filth stain their land. When bullets began to fly that was it. Peel had to let them do what they needed to in order to protect the public from stray bullets by reducing collateral damage to a bare minimum and keeping it from public view where possible.

It was the State Departments speaking with Ottawa who in turn called the RCMP who were then ordered to stand down before things calmed down again. On his suggestion the RCMP, reluctantly, took up station just outside the airport where Werner Meyer was holed up in a hangar waiting for the weather to break in order to take off. However, when the fueling crew was killed, that was it. The RCMP rushed in again just as the jet broke containment. The FBI being better equipped had delayed the Canadians just enough to allow the jet to escape after which Peel was 'politely' asked to leave Canada, which he did, via Air-Force charter flight headed for Denmark carrying personnel to a NATO combined force exercise.

Upon his dismissal by a very angry, albeit polite RCMP Chief, Peel called Bud Richards and informed him that Meyer was now heading for Europe. Bud, in turn phoned the Rabbi who was waiting in a plane on a makeshift runway 30 miles north of Halifax. The beacon was turned on as they reached altitude and an intercept course was plotted. Reaching the desired altitude and having identified their quarry they settled in for the chase.

By the time they'd reached Danish Airspace the brotherhood sent teams to various points to lay in wait along the route Werner's plane was taking. All known aerodromes, municipal airports and any stretch of freeway that could accommodate anything like Werner's jet were covered. Thankfully Denmark wasn't over loaded with such places. All they had to do was hold tight and wait for them to make their final approach before they pounced.

The Rabbis men were already on the ground, waiting as the jet touched down. However, the arrival of the police complicated things. The fact they were more heavily armed than the police would have created a bit of a mess in the event of a confrontation. So they were ordered to pull back a few hundred meters and remain out of sight. This move happened to coincide with Werner's exit from the plane during which their backs were turned and he scrambled to the spot under the tree.

Had they known he was less than 50 meters from their position they could have easily snatched him from under the nose of Danish Police. However, luck was not with them, at the moment.

As it was Werner was suffering from a near overdose of a surgical an-esthetic, which hadn't taken full effect due to his pathologically high production of adrenaline countering much of the medications effect. Though conscious he was unable to walk or function in any capacity. He could think, but not clearly and what motor function he could manage, were, at best, uncoordinated. As the adrenaline eased the drug took more of an effect on him which would in turn cause him to panic causing another adrenaline spike giving him brief, erratic muscle control. In these moments Werner would ponder whether or not to steal the police car mere feet away.

This, he finally realized, was a bad idea recognizing the effect the drug was having on him. There was no other option for him but to wait out the drugs effect and hopefully then get away. Hours passed and the effect of the drug gradually began to wear off little by little. By the time the sun was rising again the bulk of police had gone home with only three policemen guarding the plane which had to be refueled and a pilot brought in to ferry it to the nearest police airfield.

Throughout the night he heard the two police officers making plans to refuel and ferry the plane out, so knew roughly when the fuel truck would arrive and when the pilot was scheduled to arrive which wouldn't be till noon. By 6am Werner could move his limbs with little difficulty and he felt as though he had all of his strength back. Only he wasn't sure if he was quite ready to take on three police troopers....yet. Scanning the hanger he found the Police Land Rover parked in the dark corner. All three of the officers currently on watch had arrived in it to relieve the previous watch right after the two officers who had his money stashed in their car left. Both men seemed giddy as they pulled away spraying gravel all over the spot where Meyer lay hidden.

At 7am he stood up to test his legs for strength and stability. He was apparently in full control of his muscles though slightly 'tipsy' as if he had a few too many beers. Remaining where he was not an option, he had little hope of getting away if more police showed up. Flying the plane was out because he didn't know how to fly it. However, he needed to get on board to get the money he had stashed there, the money they hadn't found yet. Trouble was the three police officers guarding the plane. Three he might handle if he did it quickly using a gun. He then decided that stealing the Land Rover parked next to his plane would be his best option.

Reaching for his gun in the shoulder holster he pulled the slide back and flipped off the safety. Then bold as the wind itself he simply walked at them carrying his gun in the open, something the officers hadn't noticed as he was walking at them as if about to ask them a question.

Turning one by one to face Meyer, none of them had recognized him because they were low enough in rank they had not been shown his photograph. They would never know what hit them because when the last one turned the first one saw the gun pulled out his own…and was shot dead with the other two following close behind. One shot each to the forehead. The shots had awakened the brotherhoods men to the goings on. By the time they were alert Werner Meyer was on board the plane and out of sight. The Brotherhood then fanned out to look for the gunman who they believed was in the grass. In the midst of searching the brush Meyer exited the plane with a silver brief case and headed for the black Land Rover parked next to the plane. Luckily for Meyer the keys were in the ignition.

As the engine started to life Werner looked up to find twenty heavily armed men emerging from the tall grass. "What the fuck is this?" he asked. Stunned he didn't move but focused in on their uniforms and almost immediately saw the Star of David on their shoulder patches. Instantly his mind went to the Rabbi. The men in Halifax had been wearing these same uniforms, "How?"…is all he could get out before his psychosis took over but not before he had pissed himself…again.

Throwing the car into gear he raced out onto the tarmac and gunned the engine aiming at a group of men who just happened to be in his way. They dove out of his way but not before they had opened fire. The car was peppered with bullets as glass flew everywhere but none of the bullets seemed to hit anything vital on the car or driver. Werner who was in a psychotic driven rage simply hunched over and punched the gas and kept driving. He didn't care if he hit anyone just so long as he got away.

Only he had no idea where he needed to go. He simply drove the Land Rover in the direction he had seen the police come from and hope there was a road that would allow him to escape. Just as he thought he was away and clear from his right peripheral vision he could see two tan 4x4 jeeps crashing through the grass attempting to head him off. An access road appeared on this left and he turned onto it hoping that it wasn't a dead end but then he had no other choice. Gunning the engine it roared as the dust and gravel pelted the under carriage and flecks of rock and broken glass poked his face now that his windscreen was gone.

The rear view mirror was filled with the two Israeli jeeps following close behind him. For a fleeting moment he considered braking hard…but thought better of it not wanting to risk damaging his car and being stuck to fight it out. As the end of the road approached he was losing hope of escaping when the road split and headed to the main road. Gunning the engine again he pulled forward and hoped that there wasn't any traffic coming because he wasn't about to stop.

There was no traffic at all luckily because had anyone been coming someone would have been killed. As it was the Land Rover came off the gravel road and onto the tarmac in a sliding turn that allowed the nimble Land Rover to pull away from it's pursuers. A loud thump hit the back of his car as he pulled away, believing it to be another bullet he did not pay much attention to it. What it was however was another tracking device being attached to his car after which the Israelis pulled back to regroup.

From high above the fray Rabbi Weiss saw the commotion and directed his troops from above. Had he just two more jeeps on site he could have blocked Meyers exit and trapped him. Being that they had not been expecting him to rise up out of the grass meters from where they were Meyer had inadvertently caught them flat, purely by accident. Some things you just cannot plan for and this was one of those moments when nothing had gone to plan, nothing. Only now they had another transmitter to attach and had his men get close enough to deploy it and back off. "If he thinks we are giving up he'll calm down and we can follow him. Go get the men and follow the signal we'll guide you in if necessary." With that they climbed to 10,000 feet and followed the signal on their map. Following close behind were the Brotherhood jeeps and trucks.

Once clear of the immediate danger or so he thought Meyer began to relax and take stock of his situation. The vehicle he was driving was shattered. How the engine was still running was a miracle if such a thing truly existed. Werner didn't believe in miracles so he attributed his getaway to his own tenacious Arian nature and driving skill. But the fact remained that he was driving a car that stood out. A vehicle with no glass and hundreds of bullet holes tends to draw attention and so he had to ditch the vehicle. Lucky for Werner they had not come upon him while he was still in the plane. He would have been trapped then and it would have been the end of him. The thought that he had just narrowly escaped the cold hands of death caused him to break into a sweat.

Having no idea where he was or how far the next town was he began to wonder why they had given up so easily. The past ten miles had been quiet except for the occasional plane overhead, a jet flying high and always entering his screen from the right and disappearing to the left. It then dawned on him, they hadn't stopped following him they were using a plane to track him. "How are they tracking me?" he wondered out loud. "How did they find me at the plane? How did they get so close to me...how on earth could the Israelis have tracked me......?" the last two words of his thought process shocked him like a lightning bolt. "Tracked me..." he said out loud.

Hitting the brakes he brought the Rover to a screeching halt, got out and looked over the car. Sure enough on the tail gate, the sound he had taken to be another bullet had been a tracking device being shot into his vehicle. The faint sound of a jet flying overhead drew his gaze upward. High above him was the telltale contrail of the jet that he had seen in his windscreen, circling his position "Clever... you fucking Jew...clever". Taking his pistol from the holster he shot the device and shattered it.

The beacon the Rabbi had been watching on his screen stopped blinking. "Damn!!" he spat. Reaching for the radio...he called for his men to close in. Only Meyer was once again in his car heading east. Ten miles later he found a town and pulled the destroyed Rover into a store parking lot just across from a Mercedes Benz dealership. Twenty minutes later Werner Meyer having bought a used, silver Mercedes Benz pulled out of the lot, having secured a GPS and a temporary phone. Ten minutes after that a desert tan Jeep with no markings drove passed the lot where he had parked the Land Rover.

Luckily the Rabbi had maintained a visual on Meyer and now knew he was driving a silver Mercedes. Only a rain storm blew in and allowed Werner Meyer to evade him. Frustrated anger seared the Rabbis brain as the storm clouds approached knowing that without the tracking device they would lose Werner Meyer unless a miracle occurred and miracles were for Gentiles. If he wanted a miracle...he would have to make one happen himself. However, knowing what his car looked like and discovering the new license plate registration they would, he knew, track him down again, the information he transmitted to Israeli Intelligence or the Mossad.

Six hours later after they had touched down and refueled the Rabbi was napping in the back of the plane. He was awakened by a gentle tap to his knee by a cautious pilot. "Rabbi…Rabbi…we have located Meyer. He is on a ferry heading to Britain. Mossad has also identified his phone signal so we can listen in on his conversations. They have suggested that if they listen in via satellite they can direct us to a point where we can intercept him. They said that our chasing him like a rat is getting us nowhere so we must get ahead of him and end this".

The Rabbi readily agreed. "Do they want us to get him in transit?' he asked still too tired to bother moving from his restful position. He was dreadfully tired and far too old for this sort of thing. But as a Rabbi…as an Israeli Soldier…it was his duty to God…to erase every last Nazi from the face of the earth… so God had commanded. 'Rockets can be set on the weakest cell phone signal. As long as he is using it…we can get him. We've killed Hezbollah leaders that way… many times"

The pilot shook his head to indicate his lack of knowledge to their wishes "They have not given that instruction yet Rabbi. We must also remember that he is not on Israeli soil and the British Government might have a problem with us launching rockets on British soil, regardless of our target. Tel Aviv has suggested we head to the Isle of Man. A recently acquired asset is under surveillance there' he paused to look at his notes 'Patrice Verga. They want us to go there and wait for instructions.' Turning to leave he stopped and turned back as if reminded of something important. 'Oh, sir… Mossad reports that they have seized all of the Operations bank accounts world-wide as of six hours ago. It would seem that Miss Verga was the person responsible for that. But I don't believe that Meyer knows that. Apparently he was sent to kill her by the previous head of the Operation, Krupp, Hitlers logistics officer prior to 1944 and who apparently took over operation of Odessa in 1950. It was Krupp who oversaw the transition of Odessa to the Operation after Mossad came down on Odessa after the Six day War. It would seem that Odessa was instrumental in fomenting that conflict as well as the conflicts previous to that. They saw the formation of Israel as their responsibility and therefore their duty to erase."

Rabbi no longer able to sleep from this latest news sat up slowly. Shaking his head in disbelief, anger with the ancient heartache of his long suffering people, sighed and silently prayed to God *"why must you test us...what is it you want of us...I do not understand...and if I do not understand...I being your servant...loyal and true to your teachings...how can the Jewish People...the Israelis...your people follow you willingly? Will there ever be peace...for us?"*

The pilot, Jaquim Efraham, had served with the Rabbi for many years...and understood his Rabbi was tired...aging and driven...he had always been so. From time to time the war they were fighting...a war that had been waged for 4000 years...took its toll. His Rabbi needed rest but he would never be able to rest...knowing that Odessa, now the Operation was still out there...in the world threatening his nation, his people, his God. "Sir, I can monitor the radio signal. We need you at your best when we find this bastard again. He must die...of this there is no doubt...but sir...if 'you' are to kill him...you must rest....please." Rabbi Weiss was too tired to argue with his young contemporary and desperately needed sleep. Nodding he smiled and laid himself back down and was out before Jaquim closed the door.

Meanwhile on a ferry heading for Dover Werner Meyer was fuming having been informed that the Operations assets were systematically being seized by the Israeli Government. They had established the Operation as Odessa and with it were using an old UN decree to lay claim and seize every available Operation asset.

The United Nations had awarded any Nazi assets to the Israeli Government once they had been identified as Nazi in origin and ownership. Topping it off was the call he received from his security chief in Argentina. He was told that the castle had been seized by Argentine troops acting on a United Nations resolution to take possession of the castle. He reported that they had been outmatched from the start with tanks and armored personnel carriers. In truth the gate guards once they saw the tanks approaching…guns aimed at them…threw down their guns…and stepped aside. This bit of news had been the last straw. His power, his organization…the one he had just taken over…was being dismantled bit by bit. Even before he could do anything with his new found power and wealth it was being taken from him.

Only this didn't create the psychotic rage that usually arose from such news. Rather it created an icy calm that allowed his brain to think rationally, a signal that he felt the danger of his situation and one which would not allow his 'lesser brain' to the surface. Ironically it was during such times when he was the most dangerous, not to those around him but to those on whom his mind was focused.

Staring out into the icy gray waters of the English Channel he considered calling his bank on Grand Cayman to ensure that his wealth was still intact, but then thought better of it remembering that his phone was a cheap throw away and not encrypted against detection. He didn't dare contact his bank…not until he could use the internet and make certain that his last form of refuge was safe, his immense wealth. With it he could remain at large and living as he chose for as long as he wanted. While rational and relatively sane he realized that he would have to curb his desire to kill women.

To indulge his inner demons would, he realized, draw unwanted attention. The result in the end would be that he would in time lose everything...even his own life. Smiling which had the effect of giving him a rather charming appearance that belied the sickness within, he resolved to indulge himself one last time...in the killing of Patrice Verga. He had been forced to put it off for far too long. If she was to be his last 'kill'...then it was to be his finest and most barbaric indulgence ever. She would die slowly and in pieces. He would enjoy himself to the fullest measure possible in making her death worth remembering.

Less than an hour after instructing his Berlin chief to locate Miss Vergas whereabouts he received a call and was given an address. This quick search was due mainly to Krupp having suspected her of making clandestine plans to disappear. Krupp having not underestimated Patrice had then instructed Meyer to put a tracer on her funds so see where she was sending money. When it began to vaporize beyond their efforts to follow Krupp put his Berlin chief on the scent. It had been long enough that Werner had actually forgotten that Krupp had done his homework in keeping tabs on Patrice.

According to his Berlin chief Patrice had purchased the Isle of Man estate several years before using an alias, but one that was linked to an account they had traced to Patrice. Meyer smiled and thought *"So, you weren't as clever as you thought...you fucking bitch...I've got you now".*

No longer able to receive or send emails viewing detailed plans of the grounds were not possible. On a whim he accessed the public computer in the ferry lounge area and typed her address into the Google Maps section of the computer. Being a public access computer, tempted though he was, he did not dare attempt to use his email account on the chance that they were being monitored, which of course he knew they were. Even if they weren't, the chance they were watching his accounts was too great to chance. That and if he were to access the account while on the ferry, where he had no place to run, they'd have him like a fish in a barrel. So he chose to look up Patrice address on Google maps to see if he could plan his approach.

However, Patrice was once again ahead of the game there. Though he knew where she was hiding she had paid the realtor to ensure that satellite imagining services kept her estate pixilated. The fact that he could not see her estate frustrated him and caused his lesser brain to surface for just the briefest moment "*That bitch*" he hissed under his breath. The idea that she had thwarted him, even in this miniscule way was enough to set him off. What kept him from losing composure was his conscious awareness of being in a room full of people where indulging his rage was likely to attract attention of the Transit Police who were stationed on the ferry. '*No…Werner… no…keep it together…she will be dead soon enough*' that last thought was enough to keep his rage in check, for the moment. In just a few hours he'd be on his way to the Isle of Man and there he would find and kill Patrice and thus he allowed his imagination to run as the ferry cut through the ice cold water of the channel.

Patrice place was a walled estate where she could live quietly and anonymously while she evaded the Operations clutches or so were her intensions. Krupp, upon learning of her desire to retire had her background searched for aliases in the event that she decided to 're-tire' without his permission. He then sent Meyer to place the bullet with her 'retirement' plan engraved in the casing on her bed stand.

Meyer then stood over her for the better part of twenty minutes watching her sleep. Not in adoration or in admiration but with ideas of taking her right then and there…making her take him into her mouth…forcing her to pleasure him…and then…when he was through…cut her throat and watch her bleed to death.

Only he had refrained knowing that had he taken the liberty of dispatching her 'before' he had been ordered to 'he' would have been killed. Krupp was a genteel remnant of Hitler's inner circle and was not blood thirsty nor was he tolerant of Meyer's personal issues with women. Under Krupp he, Meyer, was expected to curb his tendencies and not indulge his inner demon, as Krupp had so often termed it. However, that was no longer an issue now that Krupp was dead. He could now pursue and dispatch Patrice with as much brutality as he wished and nobody could do a thing to stop him. His only problem now was how he would get into her house without her knowing it, not that it would be a problem. He just didn't want her to know it until it was too late.

The few assets remaining in Operation hands were substantial. His Berlin section the principle hub of European operations, was still in full function and effectively isolated from the UN treaty. Some of his more prominent connections enjoyed full diplomatic immunity from prosecution as a result. It was his Berlin Section he had asked to locate Patrice and they had done so quickly. He then put them on the task of hiding their remaining assets and if possible getting the UN out of his Argentina property. Being that it was a near exact copy of the original Wewelsberg in Germany, Heinrich Himmler's own private HQ for the SS hierarchy he harbored few illusions that the UN would release it back to him. That realization came when he remembered that he was still a fugitive, a wanted man. Something he had forgotten while he was under the protection of the then powerful and influential Operation. Now that it was effectively diminished, if not totally defunct, he would have to be more careful and far less indulgent of his desires so long as he wished to remain a free man.

Hours earlier Joshua Peel arrived at the abandoned aerodrome with the Danish Police chief, a man who did not like playing at Taxi driver to the FBI. Derek Schulz, whose surname came from the German Soldier who got his grandmother pregnant during the war and later married her, did not dislike Americans but he didn't tolerate them very well. Tourists were bad enough with their arrogant assumption that 'everyone' should speak English and if you didn't understand what they were saying they said it more loudly. As if amplifying the volume of their voice was the answer to 'not speaking English', they were also getting grotesquely obese these days.

On the rare occasion that he'd meet a 'hot' American woman he found them incredibly boring in the sack. The whole country was so 'puritan' about sex that 'good sex to Americans meant howling at the top of your lungs while fucking missionary. He'd take a Scandinavian woman over an American woman any day because Scandinavian women know about long arctic nights…and have learned to pass the time creatively.

However, given the choice, Derick would have preferred fucking an American tourist to ferrying around the American FBI agents he was on occasion forced to work with. 'Arrogantly ignorant' was his favorite way of describing most American law enforcement officers he'd worked with. He especially disliked being 'placed' under them which he sometimes was due to jurisdiction and international treaty regulations governing specific types of cases such as international terrorism. This time however, he was pleasantly surprised to find agent Peel agreeably humble, smart and not that much of a prick. Peel hadn't spoken more than ten words since arriving in Denmark so hadn't placed his 'arrogantly ignorant' American foot into is big mouth...*yet*.

Peel simply had too much to think about. He wanted to get his hands on Meyer almost as badly as the Rabbi did. But where the Rabbi wanted to quietly eliminate Meyer in a lonely, swamp somewhere Peel needed to interrogate him to find out about the Operation and of course the bullion. He had already visited the Victoria in her anchorage several days before hoping to find a clue to where the bullion came from and where it might me now. The GPS hard drive on board the Victoria was gone so there was no way of discovering where the ship had gone or where it had off loaded its cargo. It had made no port and had not left any port that he was aware. It seemed to have come out of thin air. But he knew that it had been somewhere, hidden.

What he did know was that the Victoria was registered as a charity vessel and owned by a Presbyterian church based out of Costa Rica with the Victoria registered out of Singapore where it was apparently refitted with Diesel Electric drive and GPS along with a few other updated amenities. It had not sailed from Singapore, he knew because it hadn't been there in over a decade. So where had it been anchored and why hide it? The answer was simple the bullion had to be real, maybe not in the amounts that had been suggested by Meyer, but enough to warrant his pursuing it. Shaking his head he simply didn't know what to think.

The acting church pastor Archie Davis was at present a ghost meaning that his address was a PO Box in a building which had been replaced by a playground with his physical address being the Victoria now floating at anchor in Denmark, quite deserted. Being that he had been a British agent in the War and later worked for the CIA meant that he had resources that would keep him off the grid if he wanted. So he was forced to follow Werner Meyer in the hope of locating Davis, the bullion and some insight about the Operation and its current structure. He knew the Israelis had their bank accounts which they were preparing to seize. But he was also aware that once they did that the infrastructure of the Operation would be broken up into smaller bits…and that much harder to contain.

Organized crime according to Peel was tolerable if properly contained. It would seldom work against its own interests. He likened it to keeping a vicious dog behind a fence. So long as the dog was contained he could bark, pee and shit where he wanted so long as he didn't in any way break its containment. His philosophy was to keep the dog fenced in, well fed and content. Most of those he had contained didn't even realize it most of the time. But the Operation posed a more serious threat than your run of the mill crime syndicate.

According to the conversation he'd over heard that first day in Miami, following behind what he thought were two newly emerging crime King Pins was actually a Nazi front group positioning itself on the world stage in order to re-establish a new Nazi regime or so it was stated by Meyer, whom he'd since learned was a bit of a psychopath. They, the Nazis, had been chasing down a ship loaded with bullion or so Meyer had said which was to be used to fund their rise to power.

Having not seen the bullion himself and having no clear idea where this bullion was supposed to have come from, except for some lost Nazi horde, of which there was no record, Peel didn't know what to believe. The fact that there was no record of such a vast amount of gold gave him pause. Given the Nazis habit of keeping keen records on everything they did added an element of doubt for Peel. It made him wonder if there wasn't any bullion...what was on the ship? They certainly weren't taking a pleasure cruise, the bullet holes and blood stains on the ship's deck were indication enough that whatever had been on board somebody was willing to kill for it.

The why and wherefore of this whole job had him spinning. He had not so much as laid eyes on Meyer yet had chased him from Florida, to Virginia, Nova Scotia and now Denmark where it was reported that he had somehow escaped. Just as he was preparing to take him into custody and interrogate him he gets away. It was an aspect of the job that he both loved and hated. He loved the challenge of locating and capturing the bad guys, but the really bad ones seemed to get out of the tightest jams by being bold, aggressive and just plain fucking lucky.

It was situations like this that made Peel wonder why he hadn't turned into a raging boozer like so many of his colleagues had. He did drink and had on several occasions drowned his frustrations in alcohol...but when he had...the hangover was terrible. The memory of which prevented his diving head long into a bottle every time he ran into a situation like this one, where he saw the ambulance and the black van he correctly assumed was from the police morgue.

Pulling up to the hanger on a deserted airfield, reputed to have been a German built Luftwaffe base during the war he saw the jet in the hanger. Next to it were three bodies being photographed and chalked, three police officers by the looks of them. Peel went cold as he realized that Meyer had left more bodies in his wake, this time police officers. Cops do not like cop killers to see trial...where they too often get off light or get off entirely on some technicality. His job of both locating and questioning Meyer had just turned into a can of worms. He would be lucky to see Meyers body much less have the time to interrogate him.

As he was surveying the scene while he processed the shit storm he was about to walk into his phone rang. It was his boss "Josh? Dad just called. The Rabbi is on his way to the Isle of Man. A woman Meyer is looking for lives there. According to the Rabbi the Israeli Government is going to use her as bait. So if I were you I'd get my ass there quick. I'll have a charter waiting for you at the airport. Oh…Josh I've just heard that Meyer just killed three Police officers, is that true?" His boss was understandably worried because a cop killing would complicate things if not turn the search for Myer into an international fight over who got him first. Cops being murdered usually shifted the jurisdiction of who had authority over a case to the nation whose police officers were killed.

Josh looked at the three bodies out of his window "Yes…I'm look-ing at them now. I'll head to the airport now. Oh…sir…Could you please ask the Rabbi to not kill this man until after I get a chance to talk to him…please?"

"Ok, I'll do my best…but no promises…he isn't a sanctioned asset so we can't do much to stop him…but I'll ask. Oh…and don't tell the Danes…yet. We don't need to get any more fingers in this pie. Josh…you have no idea what a diplomatic shit storm this whole thing has become. 3 Congressmen have been arrested…and are making plea bargains to avoid prison…one Senator…from Texas… just swallowed a bullet at his home and get this…while wearing a Nazi (SS) uniform. This thing was a whole lot bigger than we first thought…and luckily…I think it has been neutralized. We are go-ing to have one big mess to clean up when you get back….a big fucking mess. Ok…get your ass to the airport and see what you can make happen."

Josh looked at his phone and paled. *Three Congressmen arrested and a Senator committed suicide while wearing a Nazi Uniform?* "How deep did this thing go?" he wondered. His heart fell into his stomach as he considered the possibilities. "A Senator?' he said out loud' a fucking Nazi?" By all appearances or by what he'd just been told the Operation had been well on its way to doing exactly what Meyer had suggested already. *How close had they come?* He felt instantly sick as he contemplated the possibilities. "Get me to the airport…quick!" he said. Derek having watched him the whole time knew something was up…something bad. However, he had other concerns to address and didn't need to involve himself in the dealings of the FBI…not if he could help it. Gunning the engine he pulled the car around and drove the ailing FBI agent to the airport.

Chapter 54

Full Circle

OUTSIDE CARMARTHEN WALES, just off the River Towy sat a property lost in time. It was a cottage set on a wooded knoll in its own picturesque haven. An isolated house but not so one would mind really because it was so beautiful and private. Where one might expect to find a picket fence lay a proper Welsh stone wall about a meter high and a meter thick with a gate made of oaken planks weathered, hardened and black as pitch.

Covering the fence on one end was an ancient rose bush which someone had trimmed back and sculpted to a perfectly round shape. The wall encircling the residence was covered in Ivy that had been trimmed back and kept neatly at bay but which was allowed to cover the west end of the house and was again trimmed back to make room for the bay window from which the front gate could be seen. Where old flower beds had once been were now patches of blackened earth as well as empty flower boxes under each window along the front. Around the house were pine trees which had been trimmed back to keep the boughs from touching the house and allowing squirrels a make a home of the thatched roof.

The cottage itself was made of stone blocks chiseled from granite each one being no less than 18 inches by 20 inches with the base of the house being wider than the top to allow wind to blow around it and rain to fall away from the house. An ancient technique used to build houses on windswept isles. At 200 years of age it was a fairly new house, for the British Isles. Being built of granite blocks it would easily last a millennium.

What had once been a thatched roof was now a synthetic copy of a thatched roof, one that would never need to be replaced because it would never rot or fall apart. A recent addition, one that Archie himself had insisted on as he was in no mood to deal with the frailties of a traditional thatched roof, neither did he want to do without the charm of one.

Archie stood in the doorway of his childhood home. Still very much a rural community the village was picturesque and mostly deserted. Most of the homes in this part of the country were now weekend escapes for business men and women from London, part time residents who lived there on weekends and holidays to reacquaint themselves with the human portion of their soul that living and working in London had stripped away.

The house was almost as he remembered it, almost because the house before him was too neat and too tidy. His father was not the sort to worry about leaving a wheel barrow in the yard or a broken shovel on the porch and the yard was never this green or neat, because his father kept sheep and it was the sheep who kept the yard green by leaving their droppings all over the place, so he didn't play in the yard much as a child.

Where the flower beds lay bare and ready for a gardeners attention had not been flower beds in his youth but weed patches the sheep wouldn't bother eating, nor would his father pull. That most often fell to his mother who was the gardener in the family. She was also the one the sheep would walk up to and graze in her pockets as she often had treats for them. It was also because of his mother that the sheep which were supposed be for mutton would never be eaten. Archie smiled as he remembered his mother and her flock of pet sheep.

A chuckle erupted from deep within as he remembered his father grousing about "All that perfectly good Mutton going to waste" though he knew his dad to have a favorite among the flock who was more like a dog that it was a sheep and would follow him around the yard nibbling on his pant leg when it wanted attention. After his mother's death in the war the sheep stayed with his father untouched until one by one they each died off. He couldn't bring himself to kill the flock his wife had loved so much.

Nearly 60 years had passed since he last stepped foot on this land. The flood of memories both cheered and saddened him. So much time had passed and yet it seemed as though he'd been here just yesterday when he'd enlisted into the Royal Marines. When he was with SOE he seldom made it home but when he did his mother would make him a whole apple, cherry or mincemeat pie depending on what ingredients she had available. They had a cherry tree as well as an apple tree from which many of her pies were made both of which were long gone. So he made a mental note to pick up both a cherry tree and an apple tree to plant in the yard. He might not live long enough to eat from them but one day somebody would enjoy the fruit of his labor, hopefully as much as he once had.

Stepping over the threshold of his old home he both laughed and cried at the flood of emotions that rushed through him. The floor was the same old planks he had once trodden as a child. He recognized marks he'd made by dropping a fork on the floor one Christmas when his aunt tried to hug him as he sat at the table. Deep gouges in the floor were still present though someone had long ago tried to sand them out, gouges from the table that sat in the window from the day it was moved in until it was removed after his father's death some 40 years later.

The bathroom off the living room was new. The outhouse they'd once had to use was somewhere in the trees and likely a pile of boards by now. Not that he would mind miss it. The cold winter nights he'd had to trapes out through the snow while in desperate need of the 'seat' was not something to be missed. If he had but to pee…the snow was more than sufficient. Depending on how cold it was outside…he would often open the door and do the business with his feet still in the house. If he'd ever been caught doing that… there was no telling what misery might have befallen him, more than likely it would have been a bruised and sore bottom. He smiled silently to himself looking through the very door he'd once done that very deed and was surprised to find it was the very same door.

Troubling him was the amount of time that had come and gone from when he'd last set foot in this house. Yet, it seemed only yesterday that he was playing by the fire as the rain fell outside and his mother hummed her favorite tune under her breath as she knitted sweaters or stockings for her family. A pleasant and soothing memory which he savored standing on the very spot he once played so long ago. With that thought Archie headed to the kitchen and made himself some tea and waited for the movers to bring his furniture home.

Over the next few days the furniture was moved it. All of it antique except for the new recliner he'd taken a liking to and the new television set which now sat exactly where the radio once sat. Where coal had once burned was an electric fire which kept the place warm and cozy on cooler days.

Archie requested that Hans move in with him and take the second bedroom. Hans also took over the garage where he planned a nice work shop for the cars he was hoping to work on. They had grown together over the years so that the idea of living apart was not to be considered. Each would have their own place and space as before but would be in close proximity to the other as they had been for the past 40 years. The arrangement brought a measure of comfort to the both of them as they no longer had the bullion to watch over.

As the days progressed each felt a wave of relief wash over them as day by day they got used to the idea of not having to watch every step they took or where they drove or when. However, having spent 40 years being cautious they would likely remain so. Also being that they were to remain in contact with the Trio and Patrice as a means of collective safety caution would be a necessity. That said, the ability to simply go anywhere they wanted without having to hide their movements was exceedingly freeing. Something they both looked forward to getting used to.

Yet, it had been less than a week since they'd departed the Victoria taking a ferry from Denmark to Britain. News of the Operations demise came to them from random BBC reports of some obscure politician being detained for questioning or some American senator from Texas committing suicide, omitting the fact that he had been wearing an SS Uniform, a detail he was made privy to by the Trio chief.

However, there was no landslide of political fallout to suggest that the dismantling of the Operation would have a lingering effect on world governments. Noting what he knew and by what he'd learned from Patrice he surmised that if every corrupt politician were arrested and sent to prison the world economies would collapse. As a result the taking down of the Operation or rather Odessa would not make the news except in snippets of obscure bits here and there.

Of course he had not expected any different. Corruption was a way of life for most career politicians, a world-wide pandemic, a disease so deeply entrenched in world politics that the world would suffer much too greatly if it were to be suddenly eradicated. No, such a change had to be done one corrupt politician at a time and even then the nature of their corruption whitewashed to save the world from anarchy. With that his mind turned to the last conversation he'd had with Patrice only a few nights before over the phone, her secure line. She had come to the conclusion that she could use her new found freedom and her underworld contacts to undermine corruption and clean up world politics. A worthy goal certainly but he knew far better than she that the corruption she had taken advantage of was far more deeply entrenched for any one person to clean up.

Chapter 55
Reckoning

PATRICE WOKE TO the doorbell ringing. At first she didn't recognize it because nobody had ever used it before, that and she had been in a deep sleep still recovering from her recent break down not to mention several very interesting days with both Lisa and 'J', who she was growing more and more fond of. The storm that had started several days before was still producing rain but the thunder was more distant. The rain made for a pleasant drone on the glass and roof which helped her to relax and sleep more soundly than she had in a long time.

The last thing she wanted was to get out of bed. Hoping they would just go away she tried to ignore them but as the ringing got more insistent with a harsh pounding on the front door mixed in she was forced to get out of bed, put on her robe and go see who it was. Looking at her clock it read 2A.M. That angered her believing that some inconsiderate drunkard had driven up to her house by mistake. At no time did she think she was in danger. Nobody knew where she was and the people she wished to avoid weren't about to use the doorbell. Then again she was sleepy and had not had her coffee… and wasn't about to, not at this hour.

"Who could be knocking on my door at this hour?" she mumbled. Just as she was about to open the door 'J' came up from behind and put a hand on her elbow holding a rather large gun in his other hand. Shaking his head he pulled her hand away from the door and quietly looked out the peep hole. An old man with a beard stood alone on the doorstep wearing the camouflage uniform of an Israeli soldier. What 'J' saw in the peep hole was the bad ass version of Moses complete with gray streaked beard and wild long hair.

Looking at Patrice he whispered "I didn't know Rambo was Jewish".

Patrice snorted trying not to break out in laughter at 'J's pun.

Standing to the side of the door he had Patrice do the same 'J' called out "Yes. Can I help you?"

The Rabbi stopped pressing the button to the door bell and spoke firmly but gently through the door. "I am looking for a woman by the name of Patrice Verga".

'J' pulled back the slide of his gun and took the safety off. "I think you may have the wrong house, is there something I can help you with?" he asked.

The Rabbi smiled as his assistant stepped up next to him and showed him a thermal image playing out behind the door then spoke gently through the door "I know you have a gun, I know it is cocked and ready. I also know that Miss Verga is standing to my right behind the stone support less than two meters from where I am standing. Had we wanted to harm you we could have done so many times by now. My name is Johan Weiss or more appropriately Rabbi Weiss. I represent the government of Israel. We've had Miss Verga under protective surveillance since she visited our Embassy in London several days ago. My Government feels that she is too valuable an asset to be left unprotected.

The Operation is being dismantled as we speak thanks to the information Miss Verga provided our intelligence staff in London. However, as a result of this, certain members of the Operation are now on the run and going into hiding, which is the reason we are waking you at this ungodly hour. Miss Verga and those with her are in very grave danger."

'J' was not prepared to quit the ruse just yet. Only a fool believes what he is told without first checking the facts. To buy time and think he asked "Ok, I'll bite. What is this danger?"

Sighing patiently and from fatigue the Rabbi stepped close to the door, pressed his face close and said "Werner Meyer has escaped our grasp. He is currently on a ferry headed to the eastern shore of this very island."

Patrice paled and slid to the floor stunned she as the icy grip of fear constricted her heart causing her mind to fade as she once again was forced to face her fears. She knew this day would come but she never expected it so soon. Looking at 'J' she steeled herself and said "We might as well hear what he has to say."

Rain fell in torrents as Werner Meyer pulled off the ferry at Douglas, Isle of Man. He'd booked a ferry to the Isle of Man the moment he had landed in Harwich then drove through the night until he reached Blackpool where he caught the ferry. It had been nearly two days since he'd last slept, but he was not tired. The prospect of killing Patrice energized him. Not only was he going to kill Patrice but he would have the bonus of killing everyone with her. A wicked smile surfaced as he watched the sheets of rain run down the windshield. He'd make her watch as he killed them one by one…slowly, painfully and then, he let out a soft chuckle, he'd kill her even more slowly.

He hated Patrice for reasons no sane man could understand. His attraction to Patrice was absolute for she was the most beautiful woman he'd ever known. Being that she was the most satisfying fuck he'd ever had…made him want her. But it was for these very reasons and the fact that he 'had' fucked her…that he hated her more than any other woman he could remember. Whenever Meyer would have physical relations with a woman with the end result being orgasmic release, the brain chemistry released was not that of love but of loathing and hatred for the person causing his pleasure and the more often he was pleasured the deeper the hatred went.

The only reason he had not killed her was because Horst Krupp his predecessor had forbidden it. Krupp did not tolerate Werner's tendencies and did what he could the curb them. Now that Krupp was dead…he was free to kill Patrice in any fashion he chose. The thought caused him to press the accelerator to the floor speeding his car toward Peel.

Meanwhile in an estate overlooking the city of Peel Patrice sat numb with fear at her kitchen table with 'J', Lisa and Rabbi Johan Weiss with 15 men patrolling her house securing any possible entrances that Werner Meyer might be inclined to use. "How did he find me?" she asked the Rabbi in a shaky voice that suggested a hint of panic. Werner Meyer was the only person Patrice truly feared, but only because of what Krupp had told her.

Rabbi Weiss looked at her with dangerous blue eyes. A man without fear nor mercy for those he hunted in the name of God. He looked at her for a long moment, neither approving nor disapproving but in a way that suggested that she could hide nothing from him and that he already knew a great deal more about her than she was prepared to know herself.

Shaking his head he took a breath and answered her question "Apparently, several years ago you made the mistake of suggesting that you wished to retire. Krupp, the man whom you confided these plans to had his Berlin section chief, a banker with the IMF banking cartel, monitor your accounts. Every transaction you've made in the past five years has been watched, every alias you used through these accounts is now known to the Operation or rather Odessa.

What my government has been able to determine is that Odessa knew when you purchased this place and what name you purchased it under because Krupp did not trust you to keep his secrets. I realize that you were trapped Patrice and that you didn't have much choice in this matter. However, the line of work you chose had its risks." He finished the sentence with a look a father would give a child who made a bad decision and got caught.

Tears fell in streams as her foolishness once again became apparent. Her desire to impress the old man, Krupp, to spill the knowledge that she knew the Operation was a front for Odessa and foolishly believing that she would be trusted to keep their vile secrets and remain alive now seemed utterly childish. Her foolishness had put her crew, Lisa and all those she had come to love in danger. "So what do we do about it now? I've already assisted in the dismantling of the Operation, as you already know. What else can I do to protect my friends?" she asked genuinely concerned for the lives of those around her and not at all concerned about herself.

Rabbi Weiss sipped the coffee he'd been served and considered the question before answering. Looking into Patrice eyes he spoke softly but firmly "I do not believe you have much to fear from the remnants of the Operation itself. Israel has stripped them of their assets and those politicians they had been blackmailing are being questioned as we speak. From what I've been told so far they are cooperating and making plea bargains. It would appear that your government and that of Britain are not prepared for this development to become public. The political fallout could be devastating if the scope of corruption were exposed, the prevailing fear being loss of power and control…that is to say…money. If you wish to protect your friends from your former associates the answer is both simple and complicated.

First Werner Meyer needs to die, that goes without saying. He is simply too dangerous to allow to live, even in prison. Second, Israel has asked me to procure your services and talents when and if we may need them.' he paused to put a hand up against Patrice protestations, if any had been forthcoming. 'You are the only person we know of who has inside knowledge of their inner workings. Yes, you have given us the knowledge to bring them down. However, we may need assistance from time to time to iron out a wrinkle or two should any surface.' he smiled and sipped his coffee 'I seriously doubt we'd need your services beyond answering questions that come up. The long and short of it is this' he paused looking into her eyes 'You work for Israel now and will be on our payroll for the foreseeable future."

Patrice had expected something like this. The information she had passed to the Israelis was invaluable in terms of underworld contacts that could help to undermine the arming and support of Israel's enemies. If Israel could intercept and interrupt arms shipments, monetary exchanges for those arms shipments and possibly kill the terrorists who were procuring those arms they could enhance their already formidable external security.

Patrice knew that once the Israelis realized who it was she had been working for they would want to keep tabs on her. Only she hadn't realized what that would entail. Apparently that meant she would be watched and monitored by a private army of soldiers who would be her protective guardians in the event a threat surfaced. Not necessarily an unpleasant thought, but it was disconcerting in the understanding that she would be under surveillance making her feel like a caged animal.

Picking up on this 'concern' the Rabbi placed a hand on her wrist as she pondered her new reality. "You needn't worry about our interfering with your life Miss Verga. We are simply protecting an asset in the event that we may need some information from you. I doubt seriously that we will be asking anything more of you than information. We will not be asking you to intercede directly. However, if that does happen for any reason, we will be nearby, you may trust in that."

His reassurance that she would not likely be used as an active participant in any of their operations eased her apprehension but not the fear she currently felt as the threat of Werner Meyer seemed to amplify in the time she had been listening to the Rabbi. It was as though she could feel his approach. The idea that he was coming to kill her was unnerving. What was worse was the fact that had these men not showed up to protect her from him there was no telling what might have happened.

Again the Rabbi who was well skilled in reading emotions picked up on her distress and spoke to her as he might a member of his Synagogue. "Patrice, you must relax. We are here now and there are only a very few places he can approach from. All of them are in the open. Joaquim my security chief is impressed by the fact that you have three Vulcans in your shrubs. That they shoot shot gun shells is interesting and potentially messy' he said with a chuckle. 'He also tells me that you have a drain grate and a high pressure wash system to address the mess.' Again he chuckled in admiration for the woman sitting across from him. 'It would seem you were preparing for trouble should it come calling."

Patrice took in what he said, realizing that she would not have to face Werner alone, if at all. That is if the Rabbi had anything to say about it and she smiled.

Around dusk later that same day Patrice was nervous but no longer afraid, if that makes any kind of sense. The knowledge that Werner was on his way to kill her certainly didn't put her at ease by any stretch of the imagination. However, since she had 15 heavily armed Israeli soldiers stationed throughout her house, she had no reason to be afraid. In her nervousness she decided to visit her upstairs patio. A glass encased sun room where she could sit and both watch and listen to the rain as it droned against the glass. It was her hope that the sound of the storm outside would calm her nerves. However, as she was walking along northern hallway heading to her sun room something made her look down. What she saw made her heart stop and her knees weaken with fear so intense she couldn't breathe or move. Along the roadway at the bottom of the hill a Mercedes Benz was parked in the scenic overlook. Standing next to it was the unmistakable figure of Werner Meyer looking up at her with binoculars.

It took all of her will power to remain standing and not faint. She had the presence of mind to pretend not to have seen him. Slowly turning away from the window she slowly walked back toward the stair and down to the living room where Rabbi Weiss was sitting in front of the fire and speaking to one of his men who appeared to be making a report. Patrice moved as if through a fog and walked up to the Rabbi. Her heart was beating dangerously fast and her pallor was alarming. Rabbi knew what she had seen, because the young soldier walking away had just reported to him that Werner Meyer was casing the house at that very moment.

Noting the state of shock Patrice was in he immediately stood and grabbed her to keep her from falling down and set her on the couch. "You needn't tell me, I know he's here. My men spotted him on the road north of here looking for a way in.' he smiled at her and patted her cheek. 'My sniper is watching him now. Because he is in such a public place we cannot allow him take the shot. Otherwise... he'd be dead already. We are under orders to retain a 'ghost' stance. Officially we are not 'here'. As friendly as Israeli-British relations are...they tend to frown on our dispatching an enemy of Israel on British soil. However, if we happen to be 'hired' as personal security by a British resident...and said enemy is dispatched after breaking and entering...onto private property while brandishing a gun..." he shrugged and spread his hands as if to say 'oh well'.

Patrice, still in shock wasn't keen on letting Werner in her home but knew well enough what the Rabbi said was true. "Ok' she said with her voice quaking. 'What do you need me to do?"

Later than evening Patrice was an emotional wreck though you wouldn't know it to look at her. From the outside she was the cold professional she had been while working for the Operation. On the inside she was mush. As the Rabbi suggested she was sitting on her couch so that whoever came to the door would see her from the window. The Rabbi suspected, as did his security chief, that Meyer would just walk up to the door and ring the bell...then when she didn't open it he would shoot the lock and kick it in.

The plan was for Meyer to see her then have her run down the hallway leading out to the court yard where the sniper would dispatch him from the tower, only Patrice had another idea about that. It was simple enough but it couldn't seem obvious either. She had to lock the doors behind her and make it seem that she was in a panic for her life. For Patrice it wouldn't be an act so she had no doubt her flight would seem genuine enough.

Hours passed as they waited. Midnight came and went still Werner did not show. 12:30 came with nothing but the chime of a clock from somewhere in the house. However, at a quarter to one in the morning there came the unmistakable sound of a hard revving engine roaring over the hill which then skidded to a hard stop at the front step of her door. Werner was frothing at the mouth as the red halo of psychosis reddened his vision. The proverbial seeing red so often equated to being angry or afraid.

Only he was not afraid or angry...he was in a psychopathic kill zone, a state of euphoria created by the thought of finally being able to exercise his hatred for Patrice. She had evaded him for far too long... and now...now was the moment of his victory over that fucking bitch.

Stepping from his car he didn't bother to shut the door. His mind was focused on one thing...killing Patrice. The hatred he held for her was worse that all the women before her. She had evaded him, made him look stupid…betrayed his authority…stolen his gold… destroyed his empire. She was the reason he had no home to go back to. All of these things and more were what he had focused on all day as he scouted the house for a way up. To his dismay he had no way of getting to her other than through the front door. So his sneaking up the hill would be a waste of time. He had opted for the bold aggressive approach to make her run in fear so he could at least enjoy the chase before he finally cut her to ribbons. Nobody else mattered, he had even forgotten about the others living in the house. His mind was bent on killing Patrice, no…*destroying* her.

'J' and Lisa were locked in the control room overlooking the courtyard, which was the safest room in the house. Nothing but a tank shell could penetrate the armor built into that room. So it was where Lisa and 'J' sat in the dark waiting to let Patrice in when she came running. They would then quietly lock the door behind her and let the Rabbi have his fun.

Patrice having heard the car coming deviated from the plan by leaving her seat on the couch prematurely and stood next to the fireplace her body shaking like a leaf. No doorbell rang no knock on the door came only the sharp Pop-pop-pop-pop of a heavy caliber gun being fired at the door. The sound of the slugs ripping through the door and then thudding into the paneled wall opposite made her jump inside her skin as she stood there staring, desperate to run but holding her ground, waiting for the right moment. Werner stood at the door long enough to see Patrice standing there…frightened… as he let a smile surface. "I have you now Patrice" he said only loud enough for himself to hear. But as he was about to kick the door in he heard rapid foot falls behind him and the unmistakable sound of a .45 automatic being cocked.

"You've gone far enough there lad' came the voice of Archie Davis who was brandishing his service .45 which was pointing right at Werner's chest. 'You've done enough to her you bastard." But Werner barely noticed the old man running toward him. His quarry was getting away so ignoring the old man he turned to kick the door in and started to run after Patrice. But as he turned Archie cut loose and emptied the clip at him hitting Werner in the shoulder which did nothing to slow him down. Werner's pathological psychosis was at its peak expression dulling his senses to all else but what his mind was focused on.

"Damn it!" Archie spat marching steadily after his quarry reloading the .45 as he followed after Meyer. He could have sworn he'd hit him. "How could I have missed that bugger?" he asked himself.

He hadn't missed him. Meyer under the full blown rage of psychosis did not feel the bullet pass through him. Werner Meyer was in such a state of mindless rage that his body was incapable of registering any sort of pain. Adrenaline coursed through his veins at such levels that his blood pressure and heart rate had they been monitored were pathologic and potentially lethal, yet he was determined and focused on getting Patrice no matter what his personal cost. Not that he was aware of any such cost, he simply wanted to kill Patrice and make her death as painful as possible.

The faint sound of doors slamming deep inside the house drew him to the hallway down which Patrice had run. He saw through the doors enough to know that she was closing the doors behind her to slow him down. Adrenaline fed his rage allowing him to smash through each door as if they were paper. None of them came close to slowing him down.

His quarry was in his sights…he was not going to be denied his prize. Each door splintered as he crashed through them, the pain of the impact was nothing compared to his desire to kill Patrice. His psychosis was in full bloom and amplified by a vicious blood lust that only the most deranged psychopaths can experience.

Just as he broke through the last door Meyer could see the heel of Patrice shoe disappear around the corner. Pursuing her at a dead run he saw an open door leading to the courtyard and ran through it his gun at the ready. Once through the door he stopped to locate Patrice or at least the direction she' had gone. The faint sound of surf crashing mixed with the wind whistling over the walls met his ears, but there was no Patrice. She had to be there behind some doorway or hiding in a bush. She had nowhere to run, at least nowhere he couldn't find her. An evil grin surfaced as he went on the hunt for Patrice…his blood lust drowning out any other thought.

He searched the bushes and found several weird cylinders that he took to be some sort of gardening device. It was after this that he saw the drainage ditch a concrete half culvert buried in the ground with a series of large drain pipes entering into it, and a grate covering the concrete culvert. He had no idea why anyone would need such an extensive drainage system because it didn't rain 'that' much even in Britain. The grate itself was heavy duty but had a weave pattern of rebar that would allow large billiard ball sized objects pass through it and that was built into the wall itself. It appeared to be a bit of over kill, for a drainage system.

It was then that he heard a door open with a creak that suggested the door needed oiling…decades ago. Taking it as a sign that Patrice was trying to get away…he rushed toward the noise at a dead run around several bushes brandishing his gun before looking up he stopped suddenly as shock and fear surged through him. He was confused by what he saw, it wasn't possible how....? He choked out a low moan in the form of one solitary word as denial and reality tore at his guts. "Noooo!!" he choked.

Before him stood Rabbi Johan Weiss machine gun at the ready in full Israeli combat uniform with his Star of David prominently displayed and his grey streaked beard blowing gently in the breeze. Werner's limbs went cold as the shock he felt took hold as his head shook side to side in denial. "Y-y-you can't be here...you couldn't have tracked me...not hear...it-it is not possible."

"Yes...Werner, it is very possible, you made it so. I came here...for you...as a servant of my God and protector of my people. My job is and has always been to seek out the enemies of Israel and to kill them so that their stain will not spoil this world or vex my people... ever again. And you Werner Meyer...are a very nasty stain" he said, his voice cold as an arctic wind.

Meyer shrank back stepping back into the courtyard shaking his head in disbelief. "I saw you in Halifax...how, where did you come from...*why are you following me?*" shrieked the voice of a man facing his death...but who had not quite grasped the fact that he was about to die.

Smiling coldly the Rabbi leveled his gun at Meyer to ensure he had his full attention. "You invited me Meyer. Your plans to raise the stain of National Socialism from the grave were not viewed as acceptable by my government. I read what you said from a transcript the FBI let me read. When Israel got wind of your plans...they sent me. It was my plan to kill you myself. Only I have seen the terror you caused in the eyes of a woman I know. You frightened her...because she knew what you planned to do to her friends and again to her. So I think that she should decide your fate. In the corner of his eye Werner Meyer saw a middle aged man standing in the door, a man wearing a beige trench coat and a well-worn hat that was decades out of style yet somehow suited the wearer. He had the look of a man who was not easily surprised and had seen too much in his life to be easily frightened. This man simply stood in the doorway staring at him in curious amazement with a .45 automatic in one hand and a pair of hand cuffs in the other.

Agent Joshua Peel was laying eyes on Werner Meyer for the first time. He saw immediately that there was no point in arresting this man. What he saw was an animal, a rabid and inhumane beast, in need of being put down. The froth around his mouth and blood red eyes served to confirm that any questions he had for this man were not as important as removing this man from existence. And so he put the hand cuffs away, but prudently kept his gun pointed at the deranged spectacle before him.

Archie Davis was panting as he shuffled in close behind Joshua Peel where he watched the proceedings from the shadows content that his gun was no longer needed. Seeing the door next to him he knocked and was let in. Patrice embraced him and kissed his forehead as tears of gratitude welled up, thankful that she had such a good friend as he, a truly gallant gentleman…as her friend.

"Thank you for coming to my rescue Archie. It means a lot to me. It really does" she said stifling a sob of gratitude. However, her job was not yet complete as she pulled away from Archie and flipped on a switch. The light went on in the control room where the sprinkler systems were operated from as well as the control panel for the Vulcan machine guns. Werner saw Patrice mere feet from him…

lovely as ever and in need of killing. Without thinking he raised the gun in his hand and shot at the glass where the bullets from his gun created round opaque blossoms as so often happens with bullet proof glass.

Patrice didn't even flinch…but smiled at him, through the clear portion of the glass that had not absorbed his bullets. This simple act, smiling, infuriated him so badly that the foam began to form and the red halo came back to the surface. "You fucking Bitch!!!" he cried. In response to this Joshua Peel raised his gun just in case Meyer decided to turn his gun on him or anyone else.

The Rabbi simply smiled and leaned against a pole which was a retired London gas street lamp that had been transplanted and used for exterior lighting around the manner in the years following the Great War. At the base of this particular lamp was the year of its casting and subsequent installation which was 1880, the height of Queen Victoria's reign, the high water mark of the British Empire. He simply raised his assault rifle, leveling it at Werner just in case. He knew Patrice was safe enough besides he wanted to see this man squirm before he was dispatched and hoped that Patrice would allow him the honor. Who did it didn't matter so long as it got done… period.

Grasping the microphone on the control panel Patrice Verga flipped the switch and spoke in her most professional tone. "Werner, you should have left well enough alone. These two men are here for you Werner. 'One man is here to kill you' and she indicated the Rabbi, 'the other is here to arrest you. The choice is yours." With that both the Rabbi and the agent disappeared and their respective doors closed behind them.

A psychotic grin surfaced as the stiletto came slowly out of its sheath. "I choose to be arrested' he paused 'if they dare."

Patrice smiled back at him and considered the situation for a moment. The look in his eye was deadly and cocky. Meyer believed that he had avoided a death sentence and as a result his psychotic demeanor surfaced in full bloom again. She could see relief set in his eyes, yet he was not yet ready to surrender either. He was playing for time, looking for a way out. Only he was stuck and she knew it. For a full minute she stared at him, looking into his eyes. Danger lurked behind this man's eyes, only she was no longer afraid. This was because in that moment she knew what she had to do. Werner would have to die if she and her friends were to live without fear. Smiling her most charming, dangerous smile Patrice shook her head. "No...I don't think so" she said and flipped a switch. Suddenly the heavy sprinkler system came on dowsing him in a deluge of ice cold sea water.

He laughed "What, are you going to drown me?"

Patrice shook her head and said in a definitive and final tone "No". What she did next was flip the switch on a box behind her. A hum of something spinning up met Werner's ears, another object was spinning up behind him and one more machine began spinning up deep in the shrubbery with a red blinking light that caught his eye. A laser was pointed at his chest...another at his back...and one last laser on a hip. His psychosis was in full rage mode as panic rose in his throat and he moved to get away from the lasers...but they followed him wherever he went. The more he ran the more angry he got the more angry he got the more red he saw...the more red he saw the more he needed to kill....Patrice.

He finally lunged at her in a purely psychotic rage intent on breaking through the glass, which his bullets had not penetrated but he was stopped short by a noise he recognized as an automated gun being loaded. The sound he heard was a 'chunk-click' followed by the electric whine of a motor spinning up the barrel of a mini gun, then a second 'chunk-click' and another whine and yet one more 'chunk-click...whrrrrrrr'.

Listening to the whining of what he finally recognized were mini-guns spinning up. It was then he knew what was about to happen and his heart leaped into his throat and his eyes went wild with rage that she, that fucking bitch had outsmarted him AGAIN which was something he could not, would not tolerate as he raised the gun to the window and emptied the clip into it screaming in rage and hatred as his brain finally and irrevocably succumbed to his psychosis as foam dribbled from his lips and chin and blood vessels burst in his eye so severely that blood now ran down his cheeks. Sanity let go as he shook his head side to side staring at Patrice focusing on her alone still not believing that she had the upper hand. He let the stiletto out of its sheath and raised it threateningly and hissed "I'm going to get you...and slice you to ribbons you cunt!!"

Threatening her did not have the reaction he'd hoped. The very last thing Werner Meyer saw in this life was Patrice glaring at him in hatred as she pushed a big red button in front of her. He for the briefest moment realized his mistake, again too late as he cried "NOOOOOOOOO!!!!!" his hand reaching out to her in desperation. Werner never heard the buuuurrrrpppp sound the guns made nor did he see the bright flash of light erupting from the barrels as thousands and thousands of shot gun shells hit him at once, obliterating his body into what bomb disposal personnel call 'A Pink mist'. What mass there was of Werner Meyer attracted the sensors directing every barrel of each Vulcan to concentrate on the largest mass until there was nothing left to detect and then shut down with a 'whirrrrrrrr' and a sizzling hiss as the water droplets fell onto hot barrels before the barrels retracted and the doors closed with a nearly silent 'click.'

In less than ten seconds what remained of Werner Meyer ran down the drain with the water. The only part of his body not vaporized was the heel of his left shoe that got stuck in the grate which the Rabbis men disposed of so that any evidence of Meyer ceased to exist except for what the fish could find and his gun which was a mangled bit of metal no longer recognizable as a gun but as a useless piece of scrap, was also disposed of.

Archie Davis had been chasing after Meyer when he ran into Agent Peel who had been in the bathroom as Meyer shot through the door. He'd arrived in the midafternoon just as Patrice was heading to the upper patio. Archie was winded having run, or what could be called running down a hill after Werner Meyer. He had moved pretty well for a 90 year old man but had been spent by the time he reached the living room where he bumped into Agent Peel who then took over the chase. Archie then followed at a much slower pace no less determined to offer assistance if it was needed.

Patrice just stared out into the courtyard at the pink stream as it faded to nothing in a matter of seconds. It then dawned on her that she, herself, had just killed a man. A deed she'd *had* done numerous times. This time she had deliberately pulled the trigger, or rather pushed the button that ended a man's life. There was no elation no pride in what she had done for killing a man is not something one should be proud of. What she felt was relief. She had killed not to be vengeful, hateful or otherwise malicious. She had killed a threat to her family and friends. She had done what she thought necessary to save them from danger she had caused.

As she turned off the pumps for the sprinkler system a clap of thunder shook the building just as a deluge of rain came crashing down. It came down so hard it seemed to roar. The sound relaxed her and allowed her to once again feel her exhaustion. Surrounded by her friends, she smiled at the fact that she actually had friends, she hugged Lisa close. "I need some rest. I hope it isn't rude of me but I need to get some sleep." She smiled and walked arm in arm with Lisa down the hall which was now littered with broken doors, up to their bedroom where she slept until noon the next day.

Epilogue

Archie Davis died one year later in his home, his last month of life spent in a drug induced coma. He died somewhere in the night as Patrice held his hand. He did not die alone or unloved. Patrice had seen to that. It was the least she could do for a friend. He was buried with full military honors in his home town where his official record during the war was read for his neighbors to hear. Archie Davis was remembered as a true hero and is never without flowers on his grave to this day, left by those who recognized him as one of their nation's unsung heroes.

Hans Beck died exactly one week following Archie's funeral after having made a visit to his attorney leaving special instructions for the attorney to execute in three years following his death. He then went to see the grave of his wife Sarah where he died. Hans was found sprawled upon her grave smiling and griping the edge of her head stone as if trying to hug it. The smile on his face suggested that he died content and happy. He is buried next to his beloved wife Sarah. It has been reported that an ancient Mercedes with a happily married couple can be seen from time to time speeding down the autobahn going outrageously fast before disappearing into a fog bank.

Lisa graduated from college and successfully developed synthetic fuel and sold the formula to a major oil company for a huge profit of nearly $50,000,000.00. The fuel never got made and the formula is now locked away in a vault. Lisa was forced to sign a contract forbidding her from ever attempt any such endeavor again. She moved in with Patrice and 'J' and now lives quietly on the Isle of Man. She had three boys by 'J', Patrice is known as 'Auntie P'.

Rick moved his office to a better location and upgraded all of his equipment with state of the art digital x-ray and therapy equipment. He also purchased an MRI machine and began doing research on Migraines. As a result he discovered how to successfully address migraines in 98% of his migraine patients. His practice flourished like never before as did his marriage to Laurie which remained open and loving with Greg now a permanent fixture in their lives. The kids never caught on.

Greg retired from criminal enterprise and took Laurie on annual trips to Europe, eventually bringing her to the castle on Unst where he introduced her to the secret room behind the fireplace where Laurie learned the joys of bondage…quite a lot.

Joshua Peel retired. He bought an island in the Bahama's where he took up snorkeling, deep sea fishing, sailing and needle point, which he found relaxing especially with the surf crashing on his private beach.

Bud Richards took up yoga and senior Ti Chi to keep his joints limber. He was hired as fire arms instructor at his local firing range and is now teaching gun safety and giving shooting lessons for the local police force. He is also known to assist the Rabbi on occasion for 'charity' work. Nobody can out shoot him yet.

Rabbi Weiss continues to this day to hunt the remnants of Odessa, but still manages to conduct services every Sabbath and on occasion sits on the dock fishing where he talks with his old friend and neighbor who restored his sense of purpose and faith.

'T' moved to Mystic Connecticut and married Wall Street executive who gave him two children and coach's soccer and little league baseball. He spends his Sundays on his hammock drinking beer and listening to the trees rustle in the breeze and his kids playing with their Great Dane who his daughter named 'Ed.'

M now lives on board the Victoria with boyfriend Eric whom he met while vacationing in Italy.

They have three cats and make clothes for cats which they sell on Amazon.

Lightning Source UK Ltd.
Milton Keynes UK
UKHW041133260520
363801UK00004B/370